THE SHADOW SOUL
BOOK ONE, THE TRAILOKYA TRILOGY

by K. Williams

BROKEN WIZARD PUBLISHING

Copyright 2015 Kelly L. Williams

Cover Design by Scott Deyett
Edited by Cecile Jagodzinski and Kara Storti
Previously published by Booktrope Publishing as
The Shadow Soul, The Trailokya Series, Book One, 2015

ISBN 13: 978-1533107619
ISBN-10: 1533107610

Library of Congress Control Number: 2015902263

"If you want to find the secrets of the universe, think in terms of energy, frequency and vibration."

—Nikola Tesla

"Whoever fights monsters should see to it that in the process he does not become a monster. And when you look long into an abyss, the abyss also looks into you."

—Friedrich Nietzsche, *Beyond Good and Evil*

Descent

Guts seethe in resistance,
Tired of your absurdity,
Wondering what exactly
Made me so unworthy.

Thousands of allegations,
Pointed a denouncing claw.
All but my twisted up soul,
Blame my human skepticism.

Thoughts revise old words,
Once meant for loving help,
Sensing the hidden truth,
Shadows and raging fire.

Lost between light and dark,
Clutch firm your sacred hope,
Just so players can watch,
You squirm in anguish.

Pain reaches the pinnacle.
The dark subdues the struggle.
Speculating your forged love,
Vengeance slicing me to the bone.

Grins on contented grim faces,
Remind me of radiance and vision.
Innards coil in final rebellion,
Against my willful descent.

Through lies and temptation,
I strove to make it all true,
But shoved into my destiny,
This empty shell filled with fire.

Bleak darkness falls over my lids.
No reprieve from the burning,
To feel release is to cave to rage.
Liberation is my black descent.

Map of Zion

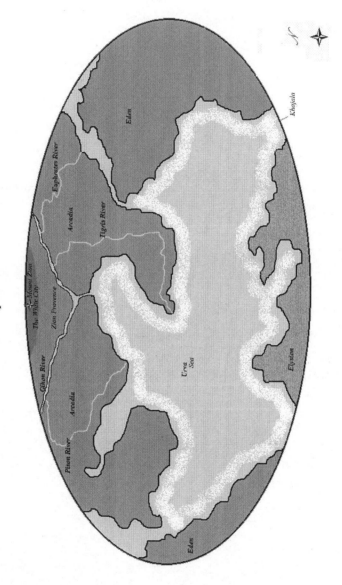

Map of Jahannam

Lucifer's Prison

Tophet

River Styx

The Frozen River Cocytus

Abaddon

Erebus

Khajala

Cocytus

River Acheron

Pit of Acheron

Sheol

Tartarus

Acheron

Demdamiel

Old Man of Crete

Asfodel Fields

The River Lethe

Gehenna

Erebus

Abaddon

River Phlegethon

Tophet

PROLOGUE

THE VEIL, HIDING WHAT IS BEYOND perceived reality, is the border of space and time, called the khajala. It is this veil which keeps life blind to the reality of its universe, until such a time the knowing takes hold…

At the dawn of existence, the universe was of thought and singular, a place named Nirvana. Nirvana was a world of technology beyond comprehension, where thought commanded reality, and was populated by beings unbound by flesh, atman of immense ascendancy called the Jñanasattva. Over the distance of years, thought became increasingly formed and the beings of Nirvana created two further planes, each infinitely vast and separate from the next, in which they could experience and play out their ideas. Time lengthened further and these new planes, the Astral and Avernus universes, which provided an unbounded existence in new resonances, were found wanting.

Adonai, King of Zion, and a Jñanasattva of Nirvana, ordered the creation of what he called Trailokya, a trinity among three further territories: Jahannam, Samsara and Zion. Trailokya would serve as home for the curious children of Nirvana, and each would be the life force living at the core of new beings called sattva, or the body kind. Jahannam was an echo of Zion, a dark mirror image, a grave and prison, while Samsara provided innumerable worlds floating in a sea of untapped potential. Grateful to their ruler for the gift that brought them such freedom, the first children of Nirvana populated Zion, and called one another duta. The duta were an ascending race that never died but instead re-formed themselves as their energies changed. Their favored form was that of a hairless primate, strong and tall, graced with elegant wings and the speed and potency of light. For them, Zion was made a boundless globe of land and sea beneath a blue sky, always stretching and growing into infinity, basking in the glow of a golden sun and awed by a silver moon and her stars. If ever they wished, they could return to the world that created them, as they were bound by no requirement or position.

Upon the center point of that sphere, the king made a mountain and on the mountain he made his citadel, the White City of Zion. A link between Zion and Nirvana was kept in the form of the Perpetual Light, a column of pure white light that blazed into the beyond and instilled sattva, atman, and their world with all that would ever be desired. Here, sattva lived in peace, where they slowly forgot the home they left behind, yet forever yearned for. Though their atman grew, their ascendancy was slow. It took many incarnations, and through this process some stagnated, others decayed in their appetites, and the remainder returned beyond the vale back home.

The peace lasted until the formation of sattva that the duta called souls. Souls were atman of lower resonance that never came to fruition in Nirvana, and required the spaces of Trailokya in which to grow. Their growth was slowest of all. By the resonance of their atman, such creatures were better suited to more physical teaching. Thus, they were given the spaces of Samsara, beyond the barrier realm of the Avernus and the mental plane of the Astral. From the port of Zion, they would interface with biological appliances on ether lines; this activity meant to heighten their resonance until they evolved into duta. The highest in resonance among these small sparks dominated their worlds, creating civilizations that echoed the home world. Among these souls were humans, a race that resembled the duta, but were small and wingless. There were taller human-like races, like the pale Aghartians and dark Cetians. There were the twin races of Grails: the Zeta being the taller and the Grey being the smaller. The bull-headed Hyadeans and the horse-bodied Orions. The half-snake Nagas, the half-goat Ikyls, and the half-fish Vetehinen. There were Oreiades almost identical to humans but for their dazzling large eyes and curious elemental-based variations. The giant Els, with their black orbs and massive muscular forms. The arborous race of Boarwellum. The scaly Drago. The fiery, crimson-skinned Jinn and their counterbeing, the water-dwelling Naiades. Last, the avian race of Aurai. Each of these crossed the khajala and filled their new worlds, and were followed closely by other souls, the flora and fauna that would live among them and under their protection.

Alas, many of the first race were insulted by the presentation of such a grandiose gift to those whom they considered unworthy clay. The desire or even need to take form, whether plant, animal, or thing, was to be despised and ranked as lowly. To such minds, souls were simply well-shaped pets, brought to existence to amuse the higher forms. Adding insult to their argument, they declared them perpetual children, as they required guardians and teachers from their betters. Because of this, they could not be granted self-governance or the promise to become duta like those who naturally resonated thus. However, those who stood with the king's decision regarded all atman equally valuable. To them, these atman were the expression of Seraphim, either realized or in the process of becoming realized. Seraphim was the highest resonance any atman could attain before returning to Nirvana. It was because of this they deserved the respect and love of duta.

All beings struggled for balance, but opposing factions spurned peace, and used their differences to forge a great divergence. War raged between the citizens of Zion and much blood was shed throughout the three realms. The clash was called The Conflict of Hosts, and it saw the people of Zion split apart, families broken, and lines ended. Both duta and souls were held to account for this bloodletting. Thus the lands of Jahannam were filled with those convicted of crimes of murder and rape against the souls. These acts were an insistence of the souls' subordination and inadequacy. The worst among these criminals were the duta who used the souls under their charge, as they were given the task of watching over them in Samsara during the beginning days. These offending duta were sealed off from the others beneath a thick mantle of stone. In the dark, broken echo of Zion, cut off from the Perpetual Light and forced to exist in a realm that resonated far below that of Zion, the atman starved and became twisted cruel monsters, shadows of their former glory. They came to be known as danava.

The Conflict carried with it a further price. The beings who fought on the side of the king had been too willing to shed the blood of their kin despite the light of their atman, and were now deemed greatly flawed and incomplete. Duta and souls alike were required to undergo lengthy evolutions, each succession a rising, to ensure the purity of their atman before they could ever hope to return to Nirvana. The process was overseen by a court of councilors. These judges would weigh every action and determine the course of the atman they steered. Those bent toward the dark would fall into the abyss of Jahannam, some eventually to rise, others to self-destruct. For those whose atman found no restoration and proved too dangerous to others, the Jñanasattva created the final realm of eternal and utter destruction. This dark place was called Oblivion.

An increasingly complicated system built up around the new practice, cloistering the king and his advisors away from those they loved. They were protected by endless levels of councils all tasked with the guidance of each and every atman in existence, whom they now coldly termed assigns. There were the armies who protected the gates of each world, which were virtually closed off to any other beings than duta. To inspire the places and cultures of Zion, the muses cared for new atman and watched over those choosing to incarnate into the other realms. With any system came the troubles of bureaucracy and the defense of their way.

Eons passed. Wars were waged. History became lore. Some believed that The Conflict never ended and that it rages to this day. Regardless of history becoming fable, the danava had broken free of their prison, finding a way to open the seal and activate doorways to continue their struggle for control of Samsara and its people, a path to conquer and return to Zion. With control of the souls as soldiers and bartering chips, danava believed they were guaranteed their goal. The failure to realize that their defiance caused the decay of their atman and blinded them to the ultimate price: complete and utter destruction in Oblivion. Their pride brought them as far as the Avernus...

* * *

Gediel, a watcher, knelt behind a layer of thick brush just in view of a wide glade. A spring pool occupied the north end, deep and wide, sprung from nothing in particular and was out of place and, oddly, a perfect circle. Ages had worn the hard surfaces that appeared more fitting to a cliff face or seaside. The smooth lines of the rock consisted of a vertical projection and a broad, smooth stone floor, like an irregular clamshell. The forest framed the area with a natural canopy missing from the crumbling arch. The water at the edge of the pool would be pleasantly tepid in the late afternoon sun. The glade and its strange pool reminded him of places in Elysion, the furtherst continent circling the inner half of the southern hemisphere of Zion, and where he lived outside the tight confines of society. The glade was the most beautiful in all of Eden. His appraisal may have been biased, for the location was also the bower of an erela Gediel favored above all others. No Naiades or Oreiades female could compare in charm to her.

Gediel at that moment was fraught with trepidation, as the bower of this erela, the glade was considered by her a sacred place that none should trespass upon. Though they were friends and he came there to deliver a special gift, he hoped his black garments, the uniform of his order, would sufficiently hide him from her detection. Recalling the shining circlet of silver on his crown, his golden, wolf-like mane, and the silver of his wings, which would stand out against the earthy browns of the forest, his breath turned anxious. What if she could see him? A single glint from whichever conspicuous attribute, and he would be in grave danger. He tensed and considered burying the mark of his svargaduta, or svarg, resonance inside his jacket or put his back to a tree to conceal his appendages. Yet he was afraid to do either, for so rare was he that there was no confusing him with any other engel in Zion.

The water of the spring moved around her sleek form as she swam, unaware of the watcher. He caught a glimpse of her crimson head bobbing above the stone ring. Something squirmed and whimpered at Gediel's side, reminding him of why he'd dared to come there in the first place. He scooped up the white fur ball and smiled. Argus, a wolf soul, was just weaned and already endeavoring to roam away to his own pack. His iron-blue eyes sparked mischievously. Gediel snorted, a quick, light sound that startled the puppy. Argus's ears pricked and he anxiously grumbled. Regaining his confidence, he licked Gediel's hand. He was perfect for the job. Argus was the most handsome, loyal, and brave pup ever to grace his packs, at least since his sire, Chiron. The seventh born in the alpha litter, he would bring great luck to his companions once his eyes were gold and his legs were long.

"Argus," Gediel whispered. "This is where you'll make your new home."

Gediel lay back on his stomach and showed the pup the view through the tangled brush. Argus stared intently for a brief moment, squirming to get back on his own feet. He had befriended some young Naiades who lived in the stream near their den, and the sloshing of the water made him think of them. Gediel gave him a hard stare and the pup relaxed. He set him in the grass and the pup cocked his head. Gediel pushed back a lock of his own shaggy hair. He wanted to see the wolf clearly and remember the moment perfectly. Leaving this particular soul would be difficult, but it was worth every pang to be sure his friend was safe and her order well equipped for battle.

"You see the duta? She's an erela—a—a girl, like your Naiades friends." Gediel pointed to the ring of stone. "But she needs you."

Argus offered Gediel his paw. He sniffed his hand, and gave a lick to the sharp markings embedded in his skin. For some reason, all the pups thought the marks would come clean, but they were there to stay. Each was earned in hard battle or was the brand of his clan.

"Please listen, Argus. This is important."

Argus set his paw down and sat up at attention. His new eyes stared hard at the svarg speaking to him, soaking in each word with obvious under-standing. Argus was intriguingly smart and simultaneously juvenile. Gediel sighed, reminded of the pup's sire. He would most definitely be the alpha needed to lead a pack under Maiel's command. A wish that somehow he could keep him despite the future would not change things. Argus was hers, deep within his resonance.

"You see her, just there." He pointed. "Her name is Maiel. She's a member of the Order of the Moon. A milite, who serves General Mikhael. She's just a draco now, but will soon be an evocati."

The puppy whimpered as if surprised by his friend's knowledge. His attention slipped to the black metal badge pinned to the left breast of Gediel's jacket. The circle was Gediel's legion order insignia, called a penannular. The interesting piece of technology marked his membership to the Order of Fenrir. It was his rank and miraculously housed the armor that shielded him from the dark. The opposing triangles, one red and one yellow, also housed a small atman that powered the nanotechnology that made it work. It was yet too small to do more.

"That's right. That means you'll be in the legions, Argus."

Argus growled, practicing his ferociousness. He lowered the front of his body and lifted his haunches. He looked as serious as a young pup could, which was far from intense. A wagging tail warned that mischief came next.

"I thought you would like that."

Gediel paused. His pale gaze misted over. He wiped his face, then retrieved a small cobalt and silver disk from his pocket. The penannular fixed on Argus, and the silver articulated about his neck, sealing him. Dread crept up his spine as he granted the wolf his first suit of armor. Rubbing the marks that ran up the sides of his neck, he hoped he did the right thing by being so secretive. The guardians of Walhall, Zion's armory, had found the request quite strange, but had granted his wish. It was time Maiel received her companion and Gediel was the most promising trainer and watcher in all of Zion, so they did not question his method. This would be the first that Draco Maiel heard of her new assignment.

Argus was meant for a great journey at the side of a great officio. Gediel saw at least that much of the future the first time he looked into Argus's eyes. He scowled, petting the pup for the last time. Maiel's future also grew clouded when peered at too deeply. A svarg such as he shouldn't have trouble with such basic premonitions. The unwritten promised a great trial. Yet only Gediel sensed the danger in such revelations. Even Chiron thought him too protective.

Shaking his shaggy head, Gediel dismissed his worries as mere excuses to hold onto Argus, if not the whole litter. He was sure to regret letting any of them go. Yet, it was not his decision to make, for it was Argus who felt the tug of his destiny and it drew him further from the pack each day since he could walk. Each member of his litter would experience the same. They were souls and had free will.

"Maiel will be good to you," Gediel told him. He hesitated, cleared his voice and continued, "She's a good leader. Keep your pack close to hers and treat them as your own. She'll always have your back and you hers. She's going to need a good friend someday. Someone who can be there no matter the cost."

Argus listened to his friend's assurances, understanding them all but only caring a little. He sat, lolling to the side. Suddenly he barked. The quick, sharp sound startled Gediel, causing him to shake and then stare, dumbfounded. Waking back to the moment, Gediel grasped Argus to his side and pressed tight to the ground.

Maiel stopped swimming and wiped the water from her face. The vivid blue light of her eyes flashed as they scanned the tree line. The bend of each red wing framed her head, spreading in preparation for a leap. Instead, she lifted herself on the rock ring of her pool and peered in their direction. Her eyes failed to discern their hiding spot, but she still hunted. Her precision would find the source of the noise. An angry look flattened her beautiful mouth, as she suspected a spying Ikyls had violated her sanctuary.

"Just lovely, Argus," Gediel hissed. "This isn't how I wanted to introduce you. She was just supposed to find you after I'd gone. She'll never take you as a gift from me."

Argus whimpered apologetically, wrapping his paws around his head.

"It's too late for sorry now," Gediel whispered to him, stammering as Maiel rose from the water, not wearing a thread.

The rumors about her bathing were true. The water drained from her naked curves and his mouth went dry. Her very long and very wet hair covered her breasts, but the rest of her sleek sattva, marked by delicate clan symbols, a knot-work girdle about her hips and across her lower back, were quite visible to his eyes, which were helplessly drawn to where they had no business going. She turned to the side, calling her blade to her. Between her shoulders, where her wings connected to flesh, another working of the knots rested, spreading across her back and down her spine. Coming back around, she flung her wet hair back over her shoulders. In the center of her chest was a marking like a medallion, the seal of her heart, the place her ketu's symbol would appear upon their bonding. He cast his eyes to the ground, too late to excuse himself or spare her dignity. He swallowed his guilt, his breath bursting hard into the dirt. Shaking, he shoved Argus into the brush. Maiel stalked in their direction. If she caught him, he was sure not to escape the glade unscathed. Only Adonai knew what she would be capable of then.

Gediel lay frozen, warring between the strange desire of being caught and retreating into the woods where she could not catch him. He had left his feelings hidden too long, paralyzed by doubt. Three weeks ago, he had built up all the courage he could muster and watched it dashed to bits by her dolt of an akha. Would she ever wear his symbol? The girl had a tendency to exact reprisals for crass foolishness. Did he dare try again? She likely regarded his attentions as silly. Rumors of her having hunted a man in Samsara, after he dared to look at her naked, were common chatter among their orders. More likely it was an atrin, a male danava, who'd crossed her path while she guarded one of her assigns. The danava tried to mate with humans and whatever other soul they could put their defiling hands on, by force, will, or manipulation, even after all these centuries since the Conflict. At least it was rumored so, but her nakedness showed how true some rumors could be.

Argus growled from his position inside the brush. His attention was on the naked erela who carefully approached. His puffy tail wagged mischievously, as he prepared to charge at her. Gediel quickly found his feet and without another glance back, he darted into the misty forest to a safe distance. A gray trail shimmered behind him, fading from view like smoke in the wind. Sliding, the quick movement from here to there preferred by duta, which could only be described as a slide, saved him from a very embarrassing explanation. As a form of travel beyond running or walking, there was only one form faster. Simply concentrating on a place or person, the traveler could choose to slide along the space, and watch the world go by as if he or she stood on a fast train.

On the opposite side of a thick tree, the svarg found refuge. Gediel was sure the erela pursued him, so he held his sattva in a stiff line against the bark, listening for her footfalls. Poor luck, he found himself in a nest of Boarwellum. They chuckled to themselves and watched him with great curiosity. His mind raced as he sought escape. If they continued, she would find him for certain. Nothing he faced in any mission to Erebus or Abaddon, not even Tartarus, was as frightening as being found spying on Maiel, let alone when she was naked. In his mind, he saw her take the form of a brown panther, as she did in battle. He shut his eyes, imagining the laughter of the tree souls.

Certainty faded with the high, playful yips and barks of his Argus. The echoes indicated he was far into the wood. Gediel waited for the delicate pad of wide paws on leaves, which would tell him the hunt had begun. A cautious peek around the Boarwellum's trunk put him at ease. The brush he had crouched behind moments ago was a distant ring of green. He had travelled much farther than he estimated. Argus tried to keep up with him, but was only twenty yards from the clearing. He stared worriedly into the woods, trying to find Gediel and the way home. He whimpered, looking frightened and lost.

"Go back," Gediel hissed to himself, baring his teeth and hoping the pup could hear him.

To Gediel's surprise, the trees lowered their branches and prevented Argus from retreat. They also provided a screen for Maiel's nakedness. She pressed through the ring of bushes, her wings spread wide. Indeed, she was ready to fight whatever or whoever dared to be there, like the goddess Diana humans mistook her for. Her sapphire-topped gladius glinted in her hand, glowing along the silver blade. Gediel pulled back behind the tree soul and knocked his forehead against the bark, condemning himself for sneaking around her bower.

"A puppy," he heard her say. "What are you doing here alone, little one?"

Maiel knelt to pick up Argus. She turned him over and gasped.

"A wolf." She sounded puzzled. Her eyes looked about, seeking the pitarau, or the master. "Where is your amba, little one? Who left you here?"

Argus barked at her and wagged his tail. Good. He liked her.

Maiel touched the penannular and scanned the wood. She knew the meaning, but a frown said she felt bad for the young soul.

"I am sure you're very hungry. When was it you last saw her?"

Gediel shut his eyes, hoping Argus would not betray him and reveal his presence. Instead, Argus stared at Maiel with cheerful, loving eyes. He panted and wagged his tail, forgetting his former master. He was in love, and Gediel couldn't blame him.

Maiel laughed. "All right then. Keep your secrets. I'll get you some dinner and then we'll look for her."

Maiel stood, cuddling the puppy close to her. The image warmed Gediel's heart and his cares melted away. Argus licked her face and she laughed again. She disappeared through the brush, hair winding into a braided bun at the back of her head, taking the pup with her. Gediel's job was done. He exhaled his relief against the Boarwellum and it rumbled with a laugh. Now he just needed to escape the wood before they gave up his position to the erela.

"Maiel!" Gediel heard someone call.

At first, Gediel thought the trees betrayed him, but then Joel, Maiel's exceptionally gifted but highly irritating twin akha, sauntered across the smooth stones at the back of the pool. His penannular was fixed to the shoulder of his white tunic uniform. Joel had gained the rank of captain in a unit of Mikhael's legion a century ago. He gained his promotions quickly in the Sun Order. Maiel was even more gifted and would soon be granted the same rank, as her evocati moved into the position of captain, a promotion sure to be brief as he too moved quickly through the ranks.

Joel stood taller than his khata by more than a head and his hue was the tone of the sun. He was broader and bolder of personality. Their eyes matched, as well as the marks of their family clan, though he was marked with the memories of the many battles he waged. Head to toe, draped in gold when wearing his armor, he was the Apollo to his khata's Diana, complete with golden wings. She was shy and he was daring. If he was the sun, she was the moon.

Gediel dashed to a nearer tree to see better. Maiel set Argus on the ground and dashed for one of the trees overhanging her pool, her search momentarily suspended. Her wings spread wide and she leapt to a high branch to hide her sattva from their eyes. She crouched against the trunk, wrapping her wings and hair about her, as Joel laughed. Gediel's eyes widened as a human entered the space and went to Joel's side. The man wore the same Sun Order uniform, and even claimed a sun-shaped penannular. Being a member of the legions was reserved for the best among sattva and didn't denote permission to enter any space and abuse the people they found there.

Gediel's eyes narrowed while he gnashed his teeth at the betrayal. His wolfish wings rose defensively. Something about this human stunk. Joel's audacity was expected. The engel found a great many inappropriate things humorous, especially when they were at the expense of his siblings. Maiel was an unwed girl, a virgin. She prided herself on that status, now that she focused on the glory of a warrior's life, instead of being groomed as a mere wife or a simple alder for the councils like her pitarau. There was truth to the rumors surrounding her because she let no one of any race leer at her naked flesh without dire cost. Tempering his anger, Gediel kept rooted to his tree. He was unable to run to her rescue because such a rash action would ruin his successful placement of the pup and reveal his presence where it was not desired. To quell his chivalry, he promised to respond if she called for help. Yet there she crouched, like a cornered kitten, trying to conceal her vulnerable sattva in abject humiliation. Gediel's eyes flashed with silver ice. What became of the lioness he feared? Why did she not transfigure and fight for her dignity? Unable to satisfy his sensibilities, he maneuvered closer until he stood behind the crumbling stone arch.

"Maiel!" Joel called again. He grinned up at her, still amused at finding her so helpless. "Come down. My friend Dominic has come to supper. Show more hospitality than that, khata," he said.

"Akha," Maiel called back. Her wings tightened around her. She swallowed and added, "Accept my regrets, but I'm in no condition to entertain your friends, unless you mean to call me to a licentious end."

Joel laughed at her tremulous response.

"It's I who have regrets, dear girl," Dominic spoke, wearing a rather wry grin. He straightened his handsome features, and eloquently continued, "I wouldn't have allowed my friend to lead me here, had I known in what condition we'd find the great warrior, his khata."

"Pretty words. What is it they call you?" Maiel asked rhetorically, climbing farther behind the tree. Pink blossoms stained her cheeks. "Dominic, yes, I know you—and you should know that no one places an eye on my flesh without a taste of my sword. You'd best leave," she continued, as the fire inside her returned.

Dominic stared, rendered speechless by her beauty and unhindered by her warning. Joel placed a hand on Dominic's shoulder to jar him out of the spell she cast. The human was absolutely mesmerized. Gediel well understood the reaction, for he had been its victim for some time.

"That she does mean." Joel grinned and then urged him away. "Come to the house—and meet our pitarau. This is no time to tell her. Likely her friend Zaajah's waiting to ambush us from behind this broken cave. I don't wish to wrestle two devil cats, though the dark tigress is a treasure to hold. You're welcome to tangle with the other if you want to stay. It's your right."

"Tell me what?" Maiel called down from the tree, peering further round the trunk that hid her.

Joel peered over his shoulder. He shook his head ruefully.

"Speak, or you will see a devil cat. I'll tell Zaajah what you've said. Be mindful of your words or the dark tigress will hear them."

"Your betrothal, khata. Adonai has decided it's time you become a wife and stop wandering the wastes without aim," Joel answered, casting his eyes back on her. His aspect revealed some regret. His eyes shifted to Dominic. "Come. You don't want to wait out this storm."

"A wife?" Maiel questioned. The horror was plain on her features. She examined the bark for the answer to her dilemma, mumbling, "What horror is this? Why didn't he come himself to deliver such news? At least send my captain."

Gediel bared his teeth at the sun soldiers as they turned away. The human wasn't just some friend Joel brought along for amusement. Maiel's akha commanded a mixed regiment of souls and duta. Those souls granted the special station of defender of Zion were believed to be exceptional, often trained in the ways of duta. The twins had a knack for soul work, and were often selected for guardianship, despite their indispensable leadership in their respective orders.

Their words battered Gediel's mind, but the chaos settled to display a disturbing truth. Maiel's ketu was made. Joel's words from but a moment ago repeated. Was there any engel among them that could make a decent husband for such an erela? Gediel's eyes swept the forest, deciphering the answer from the endless stream of knowledge at his watcher fingertips. He swallowed, hoping he was the one for her, but fragile hope wilted. Not only had Joel's words flagrantly mocked this hope, but the mate they intended for Maiel also came to parade. For what other reason would the human dare to come here and view an erela without a shred of clothing on her finely sculpted limbs? Though ketu were always a matter for celebration, and all friends were invited to enjoy a feast with the family, Gediel doubted Joel would bring a mere sergeant to partake in such celebrations. Attendance at such an event was an honor inside his inner circle. Joel might be after a little amusement from the association, but that was wishful thinking.

Gediel's gaze returned to Maiel. Her sattva trembled with the echo of her sobs. His gut clenched. Tears blurred his eyes. Pressed against the stone, he looked to the brilliant mosaic of green and blue created by the crisscross of tree limbs. Such a ketu made no sense. Matching one such as her to so unworthy a mate was beyond profane. Not to mention that his friendship with the draco should have allowed him foreknowledge of the announcement. Gediel pulsed with panic, fearing he had lost his ability. If he was in love with this erela then he was a Grigori, an oath-breaker destined to burn until he saw sense again. That could explain the blockage of information. His mouth flattened in a hard line. Such thoughts, especially the emotions around them, must be locked deep inside. With a hand pressed to the center of his chest, he strangled the storm inside him.

Intending to find out the truth, Gediel quickly slid from the wood. A pang shot through his chest. He paused, clamping a hand over the pain. Sucking in his breath, he growled a curse. It was not possible to feel this way. He drew up straight, scowling darkly at the trees. A Boarwellum stared back, astounded by what he saw in Gediel. His hoary eyebrows fell over his great eyes. Gediel frowned at the tree, not liking the acknowledgement. He wondered if the soul knew of a certain lineage. He stalked off, refusing to be the subject of such unwanted examination.

Once the truth was known, Gediel could worry about his ill-placed attachment. Until then, nothing was certain. His glower softened to concern, and he sensed in his core that his suspicions were on track. The wisest action to take in that event would be to exile himself in order to save his atman from falling. To spare himself the sight of her was the only way. He looked over his shoulder one last time, and then disappeared in an arc of light.

* * *

Maiel sucked in a shuddering breath as she wept into her hands. The news her twin had brought must have simply been wrong. She trembled at the awful lie. Her chest tightened and twinges of grief crumpled her sattva. She sat on the branch, wondering how this could come to pass. She only knew it felt like damnation. Was Adonai so cruel, or had she done something to deserve his wrath? Swiping the hot tears from her eyes, she refused to blubber like a baby over such news. Warriors did not cry. They obeyed with honor. Besides, Joel always played jokes, and this was one for the record.

Adonai did not make ketot. Ketot were made by the atman that gave them their sattva and life force. This fact warned of a lie. Her gut twisted as the sky darkened with the setting sun like a poisonous shroud, warning of lies and what would come of them. Surely her heart would break apart if this match was accepted. Ketot were joyous occasions but this one would be more akin to a Samsaran funeral or an execution. Nothing ever shook her so wholly, not even the gargantuan monsters that populated the reaches of Tartarus, or the princes of Jahannam.

Maiel wondered what Joel intended by the presence of his friend. Her dear akha was delicately informing her, in his subtle manner, that this Dominic was no mere guest at the party. The human had been part of Joel's unit for a very long time, and worked toward a well-hoped rising. He was a sergeant, a rank below her draco, and they had nothing at all in common. They had never been introduced, as they were both quite busy with their own lives, but she knew of his friendship with her akha and recognized his face from infrequent passing. She admittedly knew a bit more than that. Dominic was an ambitious man, if not manifestly arrogant. He was as tall as most duta and claimed the golden features that stereotyped him as a sun soldier. They also seemed to mark him for unwarranted partiality. Many of the unmatched women favored him. He would have been better suited to one of them, not to an erela far beyond his resonance. In fact, no erela batted a lash in his direction. Maiel sniffed at her lie. Well, not none. A few. Perhaps, more than a few. Her stomach twisted with disgust. He was handsome, but that was far too little on which to base a ketu.

Maiel rolled her eyes at her inner dialogue. Dominic's appearance meant he was trouble. She imagined him vainly prancing in the practice yards for any and all who would watch. Then there was the matter of his audacity at coming there with her in the nude, despite the rumors of what happened to any who dared gaze upon her naked body. A good look at her ugly side and a solid slap with its paws would fix him. Maiel sniffed.

Thoughts turned to blame. The alders, who counseled all beings along their paths were at the root of her problem; a section of them favored humans above all others, and hoped to advance them, even unnaturally. They had taken King Adonai's orders to respect the humans as an order to lavish them with all they desired. Dominic's placement in her akha's regiment was no happenstance. All things taken together showed that Zion's leaders favored this man greatly and had connived to plant him in her way, that she was some trophy to be gained in his quest for betterment.

From the corner of her eye, a wisp of gray coiled through the distant wood. When Maiel turned her gaze in the apparition's direction, it had gone. She stared into the forest, trying to see if the sattva, or apparition, would show again. Was that a Naiades or, perhaps, an Oreiades come to use the pool?

Maiel suddenly remembered a ball of white fur.

"The puppy," she gasped and climbed down the tree.

The pup stood on his hind legs between the roots of her tree, attempting to scale the trunk and reach her. He looked absurdly determined. She picked him up and returned to the shade of the stones. Her garments lay discarded on the flat surface, just behind one of the benches. She set the pup down and then wrapped herself in the creamy muslin fabric. The pup swatted at the material and tried to wrestle it from her while she wound it around her body. As she tucked the last bit about her waist, the pup chewed her hem to shreds.

"Oh, no. This day can't get worse," Maiel said, clipping a round penannular onto the shoulder of her wrappings. The shield-shaped object was rimmed in silver with a field of cobalt that held a silver half moon.

Maiel scooped up the puppy and held him before her. The hem of her shroud knitted back together.

"I realize you're very hungry, but that is no reason to eat my clothes. I will need them. As you can see, the engels are terrible and will make mince of me without them," Maiel said.

The puppy whimpered.

"No, not really—" Maiel smiled. She eyed his handsome countenance, melting for him. "What do they call you? What shall I call you?" she pondered aloud.

Argus. The word floated around her mind, as he communicated. Sattva not of the dominant races used thought to convey meaning.

"Argus it is then." She smiled, quite used to his method of communication. He panted happily, and she smiled wider, saying, "Let's get you some dinner."

Tucking the puppy under her arm, Maiel followed after her twin and his guest. It was time to face her destiny like the milite she was, Adonai willing. She darted back, drawing her sandals from under the bench.

Tramping down the narrow path on bare feet, Maiel emerged on the crest of a flower-strewn hillside. A pair of phoenixes swooped and wheeled between land and sky. Squirrels scurried in the high grass, playing with a serval that discovered their field. Maiel cradled the puppy on one hip. Her sandals dangled from the other hand. In the distance between tall cypresses, the roof of a grand marble villa gleamed in the sun. The porticos and gardens, the fountains and pools, were overwhelmed by guests. She gritted her teeth. Everyone she knew was there. She thought to run for refuge from their congratulations. If only she had remained at the Moon barracks in Arcadia instead of visiting home.

"You look as cheery as a rattle snake," a voice called from the cypress row to her left.

Maiel's eldest akha, Zacharius, stood there, dressed in the black robes of his alder trade. Of the two akha, it was this one she most resembled. Though the same height as Joel, Zach was of slimmer build and paler color. His hair was crimson like hers. He wore his with the sides tied back behind his ears. The locks were a constant nuisance when he stooped over paperwork, but he refused to cut them. His gravely reserved demeanor mirrored her own at the moment. Usually, she was the more playful one of the siblings.

Zach stepped from the line of trees, regarding her stonily.

"Akha," Maiel acknowledged him. She clutched the puppy close.

"What is this?"

"It is a puppy. And he is named Argus," Maiel said irritably.

"Argus?" her akha said. "It looks like a wolf, not the keeper of the Greeks' underworld."

"Zacharius," Maiel sighed. "I have no patience for your humor right now."

"Ketu is not a death sentence, khata," Zach said, taking the puppy from her.

Zach lifted Argus before his face and studied him closely. The sleeve of his robe fell back, revealing his pale hands. A second black sleeve clung tight to his wrist, but the weavings of clan marks snuck out from underneath and traveled up the back of his right hand. They matched the knot-work his khata bore.

"You approve of binding a man with an erela? I have heard you say otherwise."

"King Adonai would not bind you with just any mate."

"Still, not having any choice," Maiel muttered. "I feel like a Grigori."

"You would question King Adonai, or just the alders?" Zach lowered Argus into the crook of his arm. When he saw how serious she was, he added, "They took mates who were not theirs. They were adulterers and rapists. You hardly count as either."

"In anything other than this, I would question neither."

"You thought perhaps Zaajah would be your ketu?"

Maiel gave a dry, derisive laugh. She was very close to the other erela. They had grown together. There was indeed love between them, but not the same as the engels wished to believe. Still, Zaajah would make a far more reasonable mate than ketu with a human. She was in her resonance. They must have understood that danger. They risked her welfare by placing her in bonds with a human. Did they not even consider someone among her other friends?

"No not Zaajah," Maiel said. "We are just khata."

"Perhaps the likely deliverer of this package?" Zach teased, holding up the white wolf pup.

Maiel paled.

"Most certainly not." She blushed.

"A svarg watcher is as bad as a human, I see. Peace in your heart." Zach smiled, eyeing her profile knowingly. He decided not to press her about Gediel. "You're not being led idly. Though I don't exactly see the good of it, your alders do. Think of it—" He paused, seeing something cross her eyes. He grimaced and continued, "Think of it as a mission."

Zach again lifted the puppy to eye level. The small ball of white fur tried to lick his face, but found his enthusiasm met with a stony response. Maiel longingly watched her new friend in the hands of her akha. The wolf was well trained and content with them. She wavered between finding his amba and keeping him. He would make a strong soldier and perhaps even a brilliant leader. The pup panted, eyeing her in return. Her affection was won. She frowned, wanting to keep him and fearing that a guardian would soon be by to collect him. The worst would happen if Gediel showed now.

"He has lost his way. I was just going to feed him and then look for his amba," Maiel explained.

"He's weaned," Zach murmured.

Zach handed the puppy back to her, indicating the penannular he wore. She stared at it as if it would burn her.

"I think he or Fenrir means you to be his dam, now. Not that you won't be too busy with your own litter soon." He looked to her with a tiny curl at the corner of his mouth, his finger wiggling the penannular on Argus's collar.

"Not amusing. They wish me to bed and bear children for a human. This is most dreadful," Maiel said.

The symbol about the wolf's neck was forgotten for the moment. Zach cheerlessly petted the puppy's head.

"You an amba, isn't amusing in the least, dear khata."

"That is not what I meant," Maiel said.

"Come!" Zach clapped his hands. "You'll be late for your own party. You know how amba and Matula are. At least you'll have Zaajah to comfort you. Who knows, perhaps the king will give her to you in Dominic's stead, when he sees you so miserable."

"Would that he could. I'd accept any other mate but this."

Zach turned and made his way toward the garden of gathered revelers. Maiel threw her sandals at his red wings, but they fell to the ground powerless, stopped by an invisible barrier. She stared after him, clutching the puppy to her chest like a shield. Argus's little belly vibrated with a growl. Then a bark puffed from his small muzzle.

"What is it?" Maiel asked, bouncing him on her hip like a fussy infant.

Someone behind her cleared his throat. Maiel turned round. She had been so lost in her thoughts that she had not heard him approach.

"I apologize for earlier," he said.

Maiel's eyes met Dominic's. He tried to smile at her, but she only glared, silent as a stone, now wholly resembling the elder akha. The light of her eyes flared white and he appeared discouraged for the moment by the threat of being unmade by balefire. He gathered up her sandals and offered them to her.

"Did you ask for this?" she blurted, tears standing in her eyes. She snatched her sandals from his hands. "I know you are favored by powerful alders."

"I wouldn't. An honorable man doesn't ask for such things. It is as much a surprise to me as it is to you," Dominic answered, appearing hurt by her words.

Maiel cast her gaze away before she cried in front of him. She faced her amba's garden and scowled, pouring all her angst into vigorously patting the puppy's bottom. The family put out the food and lit the torches. How could they celebrate this miserable thing? Her akha had not even had ketot yet. There was more to this than met the eye. She was the last of her siblings to settle on her path and was still considered a youngling in the eyes of her alders. She had only just gained status as a draco a few decades ago. Her martial practice should have been the focus of her near future, not starting a family. A ketu at this time should have been dismissed as outlandish.

"Here," Dominic said, taking Argus from her. "Where did you find this fur ball?"

Dominic looked at the puppy in his arms, cradling him carefully. He tried to pet his muzzle but got his small finger locked in a set of sharp jaws. Maiel spluttered, attempting not to laugh. The man was an oaf.

"Hungry boy." Dominic grinned.

Argus barked at him and whipped his tail. Both of them appeared very proud of themselves.

"I was going to feed him when Zach stopped me." Maiel sniffed, wanting to take Argus back, but afraid to touch the man holding him.

"Is there anything I can get you?" Dominic asked, sensing her apprehension.

"Away from here," Maiel whispered. Her shoulders tightened and her frown deepened.

Dominic tucked Argus under his arm and took hold of her hand. The rough calluses of sword work pressed against her flawless palm. He gently urged her along, but she could feel the restrained strength in his arm. It stirred odd feelings inside her core and the aching agony ebbed.

"That I can do."

Maiel gawked, then avoided his gaze as he led her back toward her pool. Buzzing ripples of energy waved through her sattva. He urged her onto the stone bench and placed the puppy in her lap. Wandering to the edge of the water, he waited. The man watched the wind blow the tall grass of the field. Maiel felt her energy surge again. She scrutinized him from head to toe while his back was turned. She tried to imagine how his atman was the other half of hers. There was no way they were hewn from the same crystal. His energy was so different. Lore said her kind was born of molten mineral. His kind were of moist clay, and had to undergo many trials to earn wings and literally re-form themselves in the process. What was it that the king had noticed between them?

Dominic's presence was not upsetting, but neither was it comforting. She recalled each encounter or passing they had. Never did she pay him deference. The brief moments only stood out as suspect in light of where they stood. She barely remembered his name and knew no member of his clan. Oddly, she had yet to cleave him with her blade, or prickle him full of arrows. That was a start, though it could be blamed on the lack of weaponry within her immediate reach.

Squinting at the back of his head, Maiel wondered why she did not remember his energy. If they were of the same material it should have been familiar. There was no memory, no vague suspicion. He was as foreign to her as the new class of children in the Ordo Prioria.

"Did they tell you anything?" Maiel asked, feeling lost, as though she slogged through the fog of the astrals.

Maiel watched him slowly turn back to her, regretting she spoke. It was hard to keep her eyes on him. He wore the uniform tunic of her akha's regiment. The gold breastplate and other pieces of armor were put away inside the sun penannular on his breast. His clean-shaven face was much handsomer than she first thought. He scrubbed a hand through his yellow hair and smiled crookedly. His skin appeared unmarked and his eyes held no light, like most of his race. They reminded her of green jade. All they had in common was the nearness of their age and a similar pursuit of labor. And, of course, her akha.

"No—not really," he lied.

"Tell me," Maiel begged, setting Argus at her feet.

Argus skittered toward the edge of the pool. Maiel jumped up to pull him back and found herself very close to the man she had been hoping to keep a distance from.

"Please tell me what they told you," she said, incapable of breaking with his gaze.

Dominic shrugged. A smile curled his mouth. He bit his lip and explored her eyes too deeply. When she cocked her head to the side and silently pleaded, he grinned and shook his head.

"Am I that atrocious?"

"Atrocious?" Maiel repeated, scowling. "But, you must understand that I am—"

"You are a duta and I am a man, and never the twain shall meet. Mating apes and doves is an abomination. I have heard it before, but I did not think the sister of my best friend thought those things."

"If it is destined by Adonai, then it shall be. I was going to say that I am caught off guard by this."

"And you're never caught off guard?"

"Never," Maiel replied, distracted by Argus, who crawled from the pool with a small fish in his mouth. He shook his fur dry.

"You must be slipping, erela," Dominic said.

"Between the two of you, I have never had such a day," Maiel murmured, watching the puppy eat the fish.

"It's the best supper for him. You don't want him to grow up soft if he's to be a war dog." Dominic smiled. He then led her back to the bench. "The shades won't go easy on him, a puppy or not," he continued.

"I suppose they wouldn't," Maiel said, watching Argus chew.

Cocking her head to the side, the young erela thought of the Order of Fenrir, which was responsible for the training of such races. Mostly she thought of one of their leaders. Gediel was a close friend of hers, often joining her unit at their parties or hanging about for no reason. His alpha pack had a litter a small time ago and were promised to be the best yet. Argus resembled the alpha male of that particular group, one who kept with great loyalty at the wolf leader's side. She smiled softly, thinking of the engel's unique appearance. His lustrous silver eyes distracted her away from the moment.

Maiel sighed and closed her eyes. The gray apparition in the wood might explain the presence of the wolf pup. Her heart raced imagining the svarg spying on her at the pool. She hoped he hadn't heard the terrible news, but judging by the figure's quick retreat, he probably had. Maiel's gut twisted. With a few steps further into the woods, she could have avoided her akha and Dominic, and instead given her forward friend a solid beating. But more so, she could have prevented this coming to pass.

"What is it?"

"Nothing," Maiel lied, eyes popping open with a lustrous blue glow.

Dominic frowned at her lie. She raised a brow, meeting that expression defiantly. A mate was not one you could hide things from, even if you'd just met him. She frowned back. It looked like he was her mate. But, then, why did she think of another?

"We have plenty of time to understand each other," Dominic said, sitting at her side.

The man's gaze surveyed the grotto, then returned to her. While he was distracted, Maiel noticed a line of jagged marks that peeped above his uniform collar. Her eyes snapped to his as his face came around. He raised a brow at her this time and scratched the back of his neck, self-conscious at the scrutiny and their proximity.

"There is no need to reach the wedding bed tonight," he said.

Maiel looked stricken. Her ivory features turned ghost-white and then a brilliant red. Her eyes flashed silver lightning.

"No need," Dominic repeated, holding his hands up in surrender.

Maiel's eyes narrowed and he laughed.

"Your brother said you could be prickly," Dominic said.

"You're brave," Maiel growled.

"You wanted to know what I know?" he asked, giving his slanted grin. She nodded. "Then don't run me through with your blade quite yet."

"I suggest you speak quickly," Maiel said, snatching a small knife from his belt.

"I can't tell you," Dominic said, gently pushing it aside. He wore a mischievous look. "I have to show you."

Maiel marveled at the bold proposition. He was the bravest to dare such a trick. He must know she could summon her squad to her aid and be done with this ludicrous match in a few short moments. Yet she didn't. She sat there, waiting for what he would do next, like some smitten adolescent.

"Here," he said, noticing the perfect tilt of her head.

Dominic awkwardly leaned his face closer to hers, submissively holding his hands up. He slowly closed in, testing each inch. She watched in shock. Her mouth opened to speak, but her voice failed her in the face of such brazen behavior. His lips touched hers, lightly, and he pulled back to judge her mood. Maiel couldn't have moved if she wanted to run or strike. His crooked grin returned. Then his mouth was on hers and he closed her in his embrace. Her eyes fluttered closed as his resonance intimately mingled with hers. Everything became a tornado of sensation. Their mouths labored to express what they could not with words. Argus growled and yipped, just as her senses numbed to everything but the world that danced inside her mind. The kiss grew urgent, as if he had just come home after a long tour in Samsara. As if she had always known him and wanted him.

When the kiss broke, Argus was tugging at the laces of Dominic's sandals. Already the pup played guardian. Maiel snatched him up before Dominic reacted to the nuisance. He seemed little bothered by it, holding his gaze on her. She stroked Argus's ears, uncomfortable under the appraisal.

"Will you be my ketu?" Dominic asked.

Maiel had no answer for him. Her mind was too scattered to make such a decision. He reached to scratch Argus's ears and was immediately snapped at. His hand jolted back and Maiel laughed. He was as handsome as they said, but not quite as arrogant as he let on. Rather, Dominic Newlyn was a clumsy fool. This man needed a great deal of help if he meant to rise. That duty was her specialty. The fear left her and she faced the ketu with growing ardor.

"I am your ketu."

CHAPTER 1

1960, England

MAIEL OVERLOOKED THE ROOFTOPS of London, from her roost on edge of the Great Ormond Street Hospital. In the distance, the crosses of a Union Flag thrashed in the breeze. Big Ben's clock tower jutted its great face into the skyline. Deepening dread filled Maiel's thoughts. Streams of light disappeared into the milky firmament, a dazzling show that might have comforted the ones left behind if they could see it. If they only knew that their loved ones had merely disconnected from this world and were quite safe back home in Zion.

The erela had matured into a fine leader in the Moon Order. The five piercings in each ear were strung witiuh silver hoops, each marking the destruction of a Lord of Jahannam and two marked with cobalt to denote barons. Upon her form, cobalt armor declared her order, similar to the style of the ancient Greeks and Romans centuries gone from Earth and the Samsara Universe. The penannular normally on her shoulder was embedded into the breastplate, an empty, narrow ring of silver over her heart. When at rest, the device would be a silver circlet around a cobalt center boasting a small full moon. Her crimson wings lay folded on her back, partially concealing a round shield of the same hue and design as the penannular. Silver gauntlets and greaves piped with blue adorned her limbs, ending in claws that could shred the toughest shade's hide. The blade running the length of each greave nearly completed the destructive combinations in her armor. Her flame tresses sprung from the crest of her spine-crowned helmet in a thick braid that parted into several others. Each rope formed a crushing barbed whip. At her side hung her trusted gladius, the same blade given to her by the guards of the Armory of Walhall, keepers of the arsenal of Zion, upon her placement in the order when she was just a skinny youngling. A quiver of arrows and a bow peeped from behind the shield. Still, these were not the only weapons she carried. A multitude of unseen arms could be pulled at will, like her handy curved dagger in the holster at her knee, the tip of a silver hilt the only hint of its presence.

Maiel set her sandaled foot on the edge of the roof and stepped up to gain a better vantage of that section of the city. Her fingers flexed the articulated armor. The skin of her upper arm showed the tail of a dragon, its head hidden beneath the armor where it reached to her wrist. The marking prickled with electricity. There was nothing to dread, for the cause was not present in Samsara, but she felt the warning all the same and was glad for every blade.

Caer Wydion, what the humans called the Milky Way, and her Earth changed a great deal since she first traveled there, preferring it to the other worlds of Samsara. The humans used this training ground as intended, but sometimes they abused the privilege to their detriment, struggling to dominate a place between three-twined worlds where they could at last be the supreme race. This struggle was not unique to their species. They reminded her of the shades of the Jahannam. Other souls who shared their plane, hidden galaxies apart from one another, made the same claims. Every so often lights of promise sprung up among them all. This day, she was there to guard one of those atman.

Maiel's solemn gaze lowered to the street. Cars slid up and down the narrow artery stories below. The cloak of her penannular prevented the humans from spotting her perched far above, observing them with a clinical eye. Her kind watched and guarded. They were always watching, waiting for the shadows of the enemy to show. If she wanted, the veil of the penannular would release. However, eons of experience and the warnings, that were like tiny sharp electric pulses along the surface of her skin, suggested discretion.

Maiel's assign lay below, through several floors, ready to disconnect from a bio-interface appliance, or bio-vessel, which made her time in Samsara possible. When the divide occurred, Maiel would guide the girl to Zion where the energy converged back to full consciousness in her real home. That process required all of Maiel's attention. This wasn't the time to have a lark and go hunting.

The smell of sulfur tingled in Maiel's nose. She scowled at the city, trying to detect the direction it came from. A deep frown turned the corners of her mouth down, making her resemble the common expression of her eldest akha. The hospital was rank with the dregs of Jahannam, mostly shades and imps, stealing treasures for the princes of Abaddon to curry their favor. The oath breakers filled the city in great numbers, darkening the paths of those trying to rise, and fanning the flames of war between Zion and Jahannam by disobeying the demarcations. That flirting had caused the other races in Samsara to crack down hard. Some succeeded in destroying their inroads. Some still struggled to do so. The struggling posed a dangerous threat to all of Samsara and thus alliances were made and greater threats yet unseen built up in yet unknown places.

Stepping back down, Maiel faced a dark-hued erela who waited in silence behind her. The second guardian was also a captain, but of the Order of Horus. Upon her figure she wore a breastplate of gold scales with a winged scarab over her heart. A golden falcon helmet covered her neatly arranged braids. A pair of sable wings shifted on her back. Clear black eyes pondered Maiel, as she waited for direction.

"I smell a mudeater," Maiel told her.

The darker erela's eyes glinted eagerly. A flash of white teeth revealed her disgust. Maiel nodded with a mix of the same emotions. She glanced over her shoulder. A gloomy, distracted expression drew her features down. Her energy pattern flickered.

"I'll keep the way open," the dusky erela said, raising her hand to produce an ethereal seal. "I still don't know why they didn't involve the outposts. This would be easy as pie and the package certain to be delivered."

"You know how they are, Zaajah," Maiel sighed.

"The fewer the better," Zaajah said wryly.

Blue light formed in the air at Zaajah's fingertips, concentric circles marked by ancient script. In the center, a diamond and concave-sided square merged, surrounded by more circles. Lastly, a crisscross set of parallel lines intersected. Zaajah touched the center and opened the door back to Zion. A tiny glimpse of the orange sunset over a vast city of impossible heights lay beyond the rift in space.

"It's time, Zaajah," Maiel said, her blue eyes glistening.

Maiel held her gaze on London.

"Oh, Lena," Maiel murmured. Shaking off the gloom, she focused on the moment and her task again. She pinned Zaajah with her eyes. "This will be quick, so should they try—"

"Let them try," Zaajah replied.

"We'll be at her window." Maiel smiled, setting a hand on her friend's shoulder.

Maiel stepped forward, disappearing from view and leaving Zaajah alone on the roof. A blue-silver streak, like that of the seal, raced along the rooftop to the stairwell door and was gone. Zaajah refocused on her vigil.

Maiel walked the dim corridor unseen by all except for the other duta and miscreant shadowalkers. Unlike the average soul, she saw the guardians upholding their duties of watching and protecting their assigns. Some offered a nod. Some simply stared. Continuing on, Maiel's expression hardened. Friendly faces encouraged chatter. She didn't need to be delayed by a chatty guardian. Her pace quickened to be certain.

The passage took her near a small chapel and the figures of the frieze above the entrance seemed to watch her, seemed to rise out of the marble. The smell of sulfur thickened in the wards, making it hard to breathe. At the end of the hall, a boy crouched against the wall. He chattered to the barrier, running a hand across it, spilling the story of his life. There was no guardian near him and she didn't expect to find one. Maiel drew a deep breath. The boy was a lost one, the gray—souls who refused to realize the story of their life ended long ago. He looked tired and disheveled, ripe for the taking by a clever shade. So fixed in a trance of lies was the gray that the shades would have no difficulty in trying to tempt him, but likely would succeed, his only hope then being a unit of duta dispatched to retrieve him from Jahannam later. Maiel understood his prison well. It would be so simple to reach out and touch his fragile shoulder, and carry him off home, if only he could see that she was really there. Stubborn belief in the life they lost kept them bound and unable to rise past the Avernus. His mind created a strange reality to augment the emptiness and answer the confusion at never growing older and how the shadows bit into his flesh. Thus, a prison fortified its walls.

Reluctantly leaving the child to his whispers, Maiel followed the corridor to the right. A squad might be able to dislodge him, and the suggestion would go in her report. However, right then, there was someone whom she could not ignore. Dashing past the open door of a dim room, Maiel caught a glimpse of a shadowalker. She halted and took several slow steps back. A dark cloud hovered over the bed of a young patient. The curious brown ether was what her kind called smokers. A nurse checked her pulse with great dismay. In the corner of the ceiling, a youngling was trapped in web-like bonds. Maiel grimaced at the guardian, drew her bow and aimed.

"Smoky," Maiel called out to the shade.

The wispy figure ignored Maiel, as it crouched over the child, drooling and licking its lips as it waited for the final moment. A string of light stretched from the child's mouth to that of the shade. The human's heart beat much too slowly. Maiel's eyes flicked to the shade and back. The kid didn't have much time. If the shade drew much more energy, the bio-vessel would die and she would be returned before her time, or stolen to Jahannam.

"I'm talking to you, shit-eater."

The figure stopped feeding, turning its blank face to look at the duta addressing it. A macabre mash of scars adorned the head. The blank face opened where a mouth should have been. Sparks of lightning flashed in the cloud, followed by a long, snake-like tongue. It sniffed the air through tiny slits and hissed.

"I'll count to three. Give you a head start."

The shade opened its mouth, every wisp of smoke making up its sattva tightening, and bellowed a terrible howl. Maiel loosed her arrow. It landed its mark at the back of the smoker's throat and pressed through. She grimaced as it slumped and dripped black blood all over the bed and floor. She entered the room and freed the young guardian with her dagger. The nurse now checked her patient's blood pressure, unaware of the battle surrounding her, though her clothes were splattered by smoker blood.

"My apologies, Captain," the young duta said once he regained his breath. "First time?"

The small guardian nodded.

"Aren't they training younglings anymore? Or does the council want to sacrifice you to the danava? Maybe they think we have too many and can just send more?" Maiel snapped.

"My alders declared me ready," the youngling replied, shamefaced.

"Your alders know nothing of what is required here," Maiel said. "I'll have a personal talk with them to make sure that they do. Now—get back to your assign. Vigilance at all times. A companion from your order will be sent to help you, as they should have done in the first place, despite the council."

"Yes, Captain."

The youngling pulled the corpse of the imp from the bed and laid it on the cold floor. It was too kind a gesture for a shadow, but the child didn't need to pass with a shade hovering on the edge of death, longing to restore its body with stolen energy. It rattled and grasped for the guardian's skinny limbs. The youngling struck with his blade. The nurse sighed with relief, stroked the child's forehead, and exited. The smoker faded in a mist across the floor.

Maiel stepped out of the room, moody from the delay. Distraction could upset the mission. She bit her lip before she mumbled another word against the alders. Dissension could upset her comfortable position.

The smell of sulfur clung to the corridors, growing distinct as she closed in on Lena's weak energy. Any moment her assign would pass and Maiel must be there to transport her across the Avernus. The halls crawled with scores of beings from all of Trailokya, increasing the threat to her success. It would be difficult to find a clear track.

Passing an office, Maiel glanced through the door. A doctor chatted into a phone and leafed through a girly magazine, his feet on his desk, half-listening to his wife on the other end. Behind the doctor, a swarthy duta wrestled back a shade who sought to usurp guardianship. Under other circumstances, she would have been happy to lend a hand. Walking on, she knew she couldn't without failing dearest Lena.

Maiel at last reached her assign's room. It was slightly larger than the others and empty except for the lonely bald girl asleep on the farthest bed. The guardians of Lena's pitarau stood outside, grown wasted by constant vigilance as the threats had grown constant. The smell of sulfur thickened in the dim square of the room. Maiel looked to every shadow, but did not see the intruder. She pushed open the curtains to let in the light. The soldier was there, lurking or cloaked from view, unsure he wanted to test the guardians' strengths. Warily, Maiel made her way to the bed and sat. The girl's amba and janya were asleep, one on the bed and the other in a chair near the door. The girl's guardian went missing a few days ago. The occurrence was a bad sign, but explained why they had pulled a captain to the duty. Her experience and strength were a reassurance to the council.

Taking up Lena's hand, Maiel let the girl know she was there. She sat on the edge of the bed. Lena's black eyes opened slightly. Only those from outside of Samsara could see the amber glow that ringed them. Maiel smiled and stroked the cinnamon skin of her naked crown. She frowned, remembering the thick tresses that reached her waist, the envy of all and pride of her pitarau. Now they were replaced by scars.

"Mai," the girl breathed.

"Shh, they cannot see me and you don't want to frighten them. Sleep. I will stay right here," Maiel said.

The pitarau stirred from slumber at the sound of their daughter's voice. The pair were weak enough to be on death's door alongside their daughter. Maiel's heart sunk, remembering what it felt like to watch her child die, and unable to do a thing about it.

"Lena," her amba called.

Lena fell back into her drugged slumber. Tearfully, her amba approached the bed and took up the frail hand. Tears stood in the woman's black eyes. Maiel held her breath, leaning back. Sometimes the living saw those who walked between. They had to be in a perfect state of mind for it. She watched Lena's amba worry over the vessel of her dying child. Any overbearing emotion could trigger sight.

"Morning," a woman's voice said from the door.

A nurse entered, accompanied by her very tall and thin guardian. The woman wore a red sweater and a dark scowl, discouraging the hope the pitarau may have still had. The guardian remained at the door, acknowledging Maiel and her cohorts with a slow, respectful nod. The nurse went to the bed and ran through the motions: checked Lena's vitals, the intravenous drip, and felt Lena's head. Everyone knew the girl was nearly gone. They just liked to pretend a miracle would happen so they could hold off their anguish.

Sheets of paper rustled together. Maiel's attention went to another person entering the already crowded room. A doctor, flanked by more nurses and unseen guardians, sauntered in reading the chart. He looked up briefly. His glance shifted over the pitarau and back to the girl. He seemed rather clinical, but it was a shell Maiel easily saw through, like an egg held up to light revealing the embryo. The doctor hated this process nearly as much as the pitarau, and he had seen it too often. His only child was frail, and one was in the ground. To protect himself, he locked his emotions beneath a brittle but jagged surface. Maiel looked back to her assign and stroked her forehead. She knew just what the doctor felt, but at least she also knew that Lena was not gone forever. She was simply returning to her original state.

"It won't be long, little one," Maiel said. The connection inside of the ravaged bio-vessel thinned. The link would wink out for several beats as the signal detached and then all would be done. "No more pain. No more injections. You'll have your pretty black hair and you can play all day outside like you used to. I'll even take you to see the dogs and you can come play with my children. Perhaps we can even color in books again. I miss that."

The doctor asked the pitarau to leave the room and they quietly complied. Maiel listened to his voice murmur the distressing news. There was no chance she would improve and he believed her time was at an end. Lena's amba wilted. She sobbed, gasping for breath between prayers spoken in her native Hindi. Her husband stood at her side, stoically listening like a proud British soldier. The doctor gave them a moment for their suffering. Then, he turned and left them to his staff.

Surrounded by their weakened guardians, Lena's janya stared. She supposed he had seen suffering when he served in foreign lands, yet it hardly compared to what he saw right then. A trickle of tears spilled from his eyes. He didn't look at his wife. He probably didn't even hear her cry. But he wasn't staring at nothing. He was looking at his future, one without his only child.

The doctor's guardian stared at Maiel from the door during her quiet observations.

"Where's Gamael?" she asked.

The guardian was a Fire Order and quite abrupt.

"He disappeared a few days ago. A member of my unit is looking for him now," Maiel said.

"Do you need help?"

Maiel shook her head, wearing an intense gaze. The council insisted on as few guardians as possible. Otherwise the hospital would be surrounded by those marked by a triangle-framed eye.

The guardian nodded and made an awkward exit. Maiel returned part of her attention to the pitarau. She wondered if there had been any advance in discovering the lost guardian. The pair would need his added protection and guidance in the coming days, to be sure they continued on their proper paths. Gamael's position wasn't just that of watching their daughter.

Lena's amba, bereft of strength, crouched on the floor. Her miserable sobs carried through the halls. Maiel's gaze lowered to the small hand on the white blanket. It was easy enough to understand what they faced, having experienced similar loss when helping her husband during his many incarnations, but her current view precluded real understanding. Maiel learned a great deal about the human heart, not to mention the frail interface that anchored them in that world. Despite her empathy, reason somehow made their outpouring futile, like a toddler tantrum.

Maiel drew a deep breath. She held Lena's hand for some time, completely focused on the shape and texture of the fingers. They felt cold, when they were once so warm. The bio-vessel clung just on the precipice. Each time it wavered, the smell of sulfur grew rank. Maiel didn't have to turn to see the shade behind her, emerging from a gate like a black tornado. They sent Mort. She would have recognized his stench among a dozen of his kind. He was the slipperiest serpent they had; a fallen naga, who rose to chief of the Bhogin, one of many kinds that came every day from their putrid Jahannam to steal souls. Sadly, these wretched beings were more common than humans, as rampant progeny formed through the millennia. They too found ways to interface with Samsara; after all, it had been their expertise before the Conflict.

"Mort," Maiel said. She set Lena's hand down and waited.

"Pious rat," Mort sneered back. He drew close, hissing over her shoulder.

Maiel sighed, unimpressed by his bravado. Chiefs ranked well below her prowess. She faced him as he coiled to the other side of the bed. The line of Lena's life feebly fluttered. Maiel needed to keep close and make sure none of the other shades claimed the child.

"Where's Gamael?"

"I ate him," he replied, smacking his strange jaws. "His frail meat was just an appetizer for the big meal." His voice rumbled like a distant storm.

Maiel watched him lick the opening of his mouth. She was not intimidated by his performance. He simply annoyed her by being needlessly disgusting and arrogant.

"Stay away from my assign. She's not for you. I have ways of making you suffer terribly if you insist on trying," Maiel warned, grasping the hilt of her sword.

"She's no more than a bite. I had something else in mind to fill my belly," Mort taunted, chortling. His scaly tail rolled and swung.

"Mind? Really? You'll taste your words and no more," Maiel said, brandishing her sword.

"I'll taste this delicious pain, too," Mort rasped.

Mort sucked in a great draught of air, reveling in the anguish of the pitarau. Their guardians moved to help her, but Maiel motioned them back. It was what the enemy wanted: their backs turned on their assigns so they could steal from them. Maiel's eyes narrowed and she neared the creature. He cocked his head to the side and watched her. He drew another deep breath through his nose, smelling her. He hissed in disgust.

"You'll fail, duta. I'll have her. I'll enjoy her."

"You won't get through me," Maiel said, edging him away from the bed.

"Arrogant slave. Like your arrogant master. You can't do this alone and those whelps are done for," Mort growled.

The Bhogin backed away, trying to near the bed from the other side.

Maiel smirked. "I'm not alone, snake. And, you're the slave who follows nothing but promises without payment."

"Brazen puppy," Mort snarled.

"Woof," Maiel said.

A low growl rolled through the room. Maiel grinned with blue fire in her eyes. Argus sauntered to her side, his gleaming white fur on end. He lowered his muzzle and the penannular collar opened. The plates of his armor quickly covered his sattva.

"Speaking of brazen puppies."

"I'll break you both. Then give you to Morgentus for a whore," Mort growled.

The Bhogin snarled and crouched in the corner beside the door. In a flash of smoke, Maiel found herself on the defensive. The limbs came fast, darting back and forth to strike and claw her. Feet kicked. She deflected the blows with proficient efforts and the grace of her armor. They had met before and usually he gave up soon after this began, a spoilsport who was full of hot air. He was lucky she did not fancy pursuing him any of those times, but his luck had just run out. Mentioning his commander fanned her hatred and guaranteed her focus. Morgentus would be the next ring on her ear and this would be the last time she'd let his dog get away.

Argus danced between her and the bed, avoiding contact with the chief and making sure the guardians stood at post. Their interference would hardly help. Distracting them all, Lena choked, then coughed. The girl's line winked out a moment. With a well-placed sandal, Maiel sent Mort reeling back and he fell against the wall. Dashing back to the bed, she checked on the child. Mort's presence finished the process. He had drawn off her last energies. When Maiel first returned to her assign, Lena already had little enough strength to stay in Samsara longer than the morning.

Lena's amba returned to the room and, despite many tears, tried to revive her daughter. Her husband went to her, begging her to let go, the agony turning him red and making his blood vessels strain against the skin. Relief could not be found. Their battle was lost. Maiel's resonance anxiously pulsed, blaming herself for getting distracted by the serpent.

"It's all over. Let her go. Let her rest," the janya said.

"It's not over! I won't let her go—how dare you tell me to let her go—my baby," the amba snapped, choking on tears with her last words.

Their guardians looked to Maiel, unsure of what action to take. She gestured them to stand down. The serpent fed from the distress, swelled and grew stronger, yet he retreated to a corner. He disappeared in the shadows once more. She told the guardians to focus their wilted strengths on their assigns, to ease the pain and deny the danava's feeding. The distraction of the child's passing and the need to return order tore Maiel's attention in twain and she wasn't prepared for his abrupt return. Mort whipped his tail into her back. She fell to the floor, losing her grip on her sword. The metal clattered across the tiles. Mort lunged, but Maiel jerked belly-up and struck him in the gut with her clawed gauntlets. A chilling howl escaped him as he stumbled back.

"You haven't learned yet," Maiel said

"It's you who hasn't learned, youngling," Mort rasped, holding his middle. He looked at the black blood pouring from his wounds and over Maiel. A hissing laugh escaped his throat as it burned her skin. She refused to admit the pain. "I'll eat you all by nightfall. Then I'll taste your children for dessert—half breeds make sweetest meats. I'll finish your cursed clan starting with your ape ketu."

Maiel focused on the task, though the blood was like acid to her skin. Mort was fooling himself if he thought he could fare better against her akha. The hilt of her sword slid into her outstretched hand and she raised it to his snubbed snout. Despite the mocking expression twisting her features, something inside trembled. Mort snapped the last ounce of her coolness.

The alarm on Lena's monitor pierced the thick atmosphere. Everything stood still for several moments before the room erupted in human screams.

Lena's mother called for help, but the help she sought was beyond the abilities of hospital staff. Her daughter was dead long before the monitor registered the passing. Mort drew in the suffering with avid delight. Maiel pushed hard with her feet, sending the Bhogin slithering into the corner where he could nurse his cuts. She went to her assign, knowing the presence of so many held the enemy at bay.

"Lena! Lena!" the amba cried, as her husband dragged her back.

Hot tears filled Maiel's white fire eyes. The pitarau crumpled on chairs outside the door, ushered out by the staff who rushed to assist. The humans who had given Lena life held each other close, quaking with anger and despair, confused and refusing to release her even though they knew there was no holding on. Outside the room, surrounded by their keepers, they were safe. Lena's janya wept against his woman's shoulder, losing the last tether of control to disguise his manly hurt. Maiel's sorrow turned to anger. Lena died on her watch and her failure had hurt them beyond repair.

"Argus," Maiel said, going back to Mort and gesturing to the body of the girl.

The shade drew in threads of succor from every pain-ridden emotion in the room. Lena fluttered in and out of focus, lying peacefully on her back, just a breadth apart from her dead vessel as the living tried to drag her back from the brink. Snapping to, she sat up with a scream. Argus leapt onto the bed and the girl stilled into repose. His great head lowered, keeping watch of the threat, daring Mort to dislodge him. His bright, keen eyes promised death to the chief.

"You failed, Adonai's slave. I'm not the last. Others will come. They'll take her and feed from her bones," Mort crowed.

"You've won nothing. I should have ended you a long time ago," Maiel said.

The white fire of her eyes filled her insides until a wild-white glow emanated from her skin. Rage wound around Maiel's core and melted everything inside until she was pure fury. She embraced the forbidden, forgoing protocol to avenge her assign. Filled with bale, blue light glowed from her eyes and mouth, until she stood as a pillar of fire that blinded the Bhogin. He raised his thick arms before his face to protect it from her brilliance. His flesh smoked and bubbled like sweets left on the burner. The resonance of perpetual light, which beamed into the White City for all time, reflected from her atman, was certain death to the shadow. She drove her sword deep into Mort's middle, then yanked it free, pushing the wounded sattva back with the flat of her sandal. Mort collapsed, unable to hold up his perverted torso. Maiel swung her gladius and sent his head rolling.

Maiel released the heightened resonance and the light faded as she returned to her placid form. A black circle in a ring of silver appeared, resembling a polished ebony medallion: the Seal of Oblivion and the king's permission to destroy. The putrid carcass dissipated beneath it into black puddles that receded to nothingness. A gray fog hung above the floor, lingering as though the mudeater would return. The seal faded and Maiel went to Argus, who still guarded her assign. He sniffed then sneezed.

"Rancid," his thoughts said to hers.

"Good job," Maiel said and gave his ears a scratch. He licked her hand, nuzzling it affectionately.

Argus hopped from the bed as Maiel sat. The hospital staff had gone from the room. Their efforts to revive Lena were, of course, in vain. The other guardians hung their heads in dread and sadness. The girl's pitarau wept, praying to any god to grant their request of restoring their daughter. However, Lena had an appointment to keep and plans to fulfill. This was what souls agreed to do in Samsara, though they didn't recall it during an incarnation. Maiel wished she could make them understand, so it might not hurt as much, but her task wasn't to comfort the confused. It was to guard a youngling bound for home.

Reaching for Lena, Maiel offered a small smile. The reedy resonance thrummed once more, undetectable to any instruments upon which humans relied. It would be sometime before they realized that technology, and gladly so. They were not advanced enough to understand the workings beyond Samsara while incarnated. In the meantime, she could ease their anguish by taking the girl through the way gates and lessen the pull of her resonance on theirs.

Lena's hand clasped hers.

"I'm sorry," Maiel whispered to the girl, while fighting back tears. Running her finger across the girl's temple, she watched the stilled features.

In her thoughts, Maiel cursed the council for insisting on sending her there with only Zaajah. They needed help if they meant to get this soul back unscathed. The guardians in place had been too weakened to make much difference. The alders' faith in her was flattering, but she had failed, by allowing the shadowalker to feed while she toyed with it, and to choose to leave the others out of it despite needing their help even if she judged it negligible. They were sure to punish her, if not demand a lofty penance, such as a demotion in rank. The shame of it burned her essence.

"Mai," a small voice called from nowhere.

"I'm here. Focus on me," Maiel replied.

The girl's image shifted as the sattva awoke from the shell. Maiel wrapped the girl in her arms, happy to have her released from the misery of her illness. Lena was theirs once more, strongly clinging to her guardian's armor. Stroking the girl's long black hair, Maiel clung tightly back, quietly remonstrating herself for losing focus. She shut her eyes, thanking fate for siding with her. This was too great a risk for too great a prize. They never should have allowed this atman to travel in such a manner.

Maiel picked Lena up, gestured to the other guardians and then carried the girl to the windows. Lena wore the silver gown of incarnation and looked well despite her ordeal. Maiel stroked the girl's hair again, assuring she had a good hold of her. Then she lifted her hand to the air and a circle with a leafy tree and intricate roots appeared. Maiel touched the knots in the trunk, the leaves, and root coils in a sequence that made the apparition glow brighter until the image widened to a door. Maiel, followed by her trusty companion, entered what appeared to be a mirror of the hospital. She set the girl standing on the bed. Here they could acclimate in peace.

"You're much taller than I thought," Lena said, eliciting a tearful chuckle from her guardian. She was so tiny in her arms. Just seven human years old by last count. "Did you bring the doggy?" Lena asked, forgetting everything of her short journey, except for her new friends.

"Yes, I did." Maiel smiled.

Argus placed his paws on the bed. He gave Lena a good sniff. She giggled at the tickle of his whiskers against her feet. He smiled up at her and she knelt down to pat his great head.

"Are you ready?" Maiel asked after they rested a moment.

Lena looked unsure, crouched on the bed with her knees drawn up. She then cast her black eyes around the room. No one was there, just Maiel and her dog, as they rested inside the dreamy paths of the Astrals. The hospital was eerily quiet, as if the world had stopped. Returning her sparkling gaze to the armored duta, she nodded.

"Okay," Maiel whispered.

Where the windows once were, a forest path led into a sunny wood. The birdsong was inviting. Colorful flowers bobbed in a warm breeze. Peace whispered through the trees.

Maiel helped Lena from the bed and led her along the path. Their steps brought them to a door. Lena eyed it, wondering at its meaning. Maiel crouched beside her and the girl leaned in, unmoving despite Maiel's encouragement. It was the door home, but Lena was still floundering between her life on earth and her true self. Maiel took the girl in her arms and the surety of her guardian's protection loosened her jaw. Lena chattered in her ear, a million questions falling from her lips at once. Maiel tried to keep up, answering them as simply as possible.

The door stood in the path apart from any other structure, gothic in style and thus intimidating by its enormity. Maiel took hold of the door ring and electric blue flickered in the seams until the Seal of Zion appeared. She pressed the middle, then a sequence of squares with the tip of one finger. The light grew intense, a brilliance that became an open archway to another place. Lena was silenced for the moment and they passed onto a platform overlooking a great and dense city. Arcadia.

The final descent of the sun streaked crisscross in the sky. Duta and birds played in the air. Flaming gold blanketed the horizon. The gate to Samsara and the Avernus closed, leaving Maiel and her assign under an arch erected on the top of a tall stone pillar, which looked like the ruins of a destroyed church. Another step and they would fall or fly.

Argus brushed against Maiel's leg, reminding her of the present business. The council would seek an answer for what had happened between her and Mort. There was nothing to do but face them, as she promised the youngling. Before they lectured her on her conduct, she would make it known that their disregard of her and the other guardians was equal to dissent. Something was wrong somewhere and their lofty seats would not keep her from figuring it out. They had either sent her into a trap or she had betrayed everything she held dear. Her skin still stung to remind her.

Sending atman directly into Samsara was harming their world, just like the days before the Conflict. The millennia of missions proved to be extremely dangerous at best, while the council ignored that proof. Many were lost, and resulted in sattva wandering the wastes and worlds with no purpose. Still more were stolen to the prisons of Jahannam. Yet the majority of incarnations were now done in this manner and had been so for as long as she served the legions. The attempt to better train the guardians was made in vain, as was the effort to keep Samsara safe.

"Are you ready to bring her to Otzar?" A familiar voice spoke from alongside the arch.

Zaajah lounged there, previously unnoticed. Maiel stared over the close, dingy structures of the city. Spires and roofs stood in the clouds, sharp and ridged, all aged and weathered. Humans flew their airships, dirigibles and engines. A gothic nirvana. The narrow streets between were like threads sewing the world together. The humans buzzed around in land vehicles too. For them, blinking was imperfect and difficult, sliding even worse. Blinking was the less flamboyant of the two forms, but the fastest. The traveler again thought of their destination and suddenly they were there. Souls trusted their hands to build them buggies or to simply walk on their trusty legs. Her eyes searched for an answer to her quandary, a little more enigmatic than the combustion engine. She needed more time to sort out a plan. The alders would not make it easy for her to wield her accusations to any effect. They could be manipulative and decide that making her look a fool was a minimal price for preserving their reputations.

"Is something the matter?" Zaajah asked. "Look at you. You're burned. Damn serpents. I told you we needed a watcher's help," she continued, taking Maiel's wrist and lending her energy to heal the Moon Captain.

"I'm tired," Lena said, enamored with the erela's beauty.

Maiel held the little girl's gaze a moment. The molten amber glowed intensely. How could she tell Lena she'd failed her? That she was tired because Mort had fed on her, undoing years of improved strength? That she'd cost Lena her rising? She supposed the greater goal was simply bringing her back.

Maiel smiled through her concern. "You'll get to rest very soon."

Placing Lena on her feet, Maiel urged the girl toward her friend. Zaajah regarded the move skeptically.

"Would you mind, Captain?" Maiel asked, distracted.

Zaajah took the girl's hand reluctantly. Younglings were not her thing.

"Hi," the girl said, staring up at the darker captain.

"Hi," Zaajah replied, not knowing what else to say.

The Horus-helmed guardian gave her friend a dismayed look.

"I think Mort drained me. Take her to Otzar for safekeeping until I can present her to the council," Maiel lied.

Zaajah's mouth flattened. She knew it was a lie or she knew the voyage into Otzar was going to be the truly draining part of the whole mission. She'd just given a good portion of her strength to fix the burns and Maiel should have felt fine. Before she could protest, Maiel turned away and stepped from the platform, gone instantly.

CHAPTER 2

ON HER WAY HOME, Maiel's battle with Mort replayed in a loop, intensifying her guilt. The blur of the sunset-hued city faded to watery tones. A quick pause and then the hills of Eden surrounded her. Maiel soon walked the edge of her garden. The cobalt armor ran like recoiling mercury into the penannular. The layers of pale yellow gown extended to her ankles. The device slipped to her shoulder, holding the garment in place, and returning to the shape of a small silver moon in a field of cobalt. Her hair, now freed from the helmet and braids, hung in long, soft curls. Her sour mood sharpened her ethereal features. Her presence in the White City would only allow the alders to corner her before she had her temper battened down. They would sense her weakness and use it.

Maiel moved slowly along the stepping-stone path, seemingly indifferent like a feline, but deliberate nonetheless. The tall ginger structure, reminiscent of a gothic home, towered at the center of the garden. It had been built to Dominic's design once she carried their first child. Now the house was a reliquary of their lives and a refuge from their mortal incarnations. The shadow it cast currently darkened that edge of the garden. The windows looked down on her, shining like polished sheets of hematite and reflecting the azure sky and tree line. The house stood as it always had, as did the garden, but something was changed. She felt it deeply. She eyed her surroundings, trying to pinpoint exactly what, but failed, and dismissed the sensation as residual energy from Mort. Energy affected Zion in odd ways, especially unpredictable forces in emotions.

The front door swung inward. From the dark interior of the house poured several children with small wings raised up on their backs and shouting with joy. They hurried down the steps, red and gold hair gleaming as their heads caught the sun peeking around the house. Their faces beamed enough to return the orb's favor. Maiel's heart leapt, revived by the cheery greeting. Five children in total danced around her, vying for her attention. She smiled at them, though the pain was still in her eyes, shame at her lack of discipline.

"Practicing again?" Maiel asked, gathering them all in a warm embrace.

The children quietly murmured or nodded in answer, accepting her affection. She was the center of Zion to them. They leaned against her until they all crumpled to the ground in a giggling pile of limbs. Maiel lay for a moment with them in the cool grass. The ground drew away the anger and shame. She was left with a knot in her stomach, a mix of remorse and affection, regret and love. The eldest—Ian—lay on her shoulder. His golden head received a quick kiss. Then she kissed another golden head—Samuel, her fourth child—on her other shoulder.

"You didn't give your janya trouble today, Ian—I hope," Maiel said sternly.

"No," the eldest replied.

"That's good. We both hate lectures."

Maiel lay in view of the warm sky, feeling cold. Her twin daughters, small copies of their amba, jumped up and danced about the yard. Their revelry overturned a mouse nest and the girls set to fixing their mistake, while being awed by the tiny pink young of the doe. Samuel and Ian joined them. Maiel sighed, sitting up to watch. The children had few cares but what their pitarau brought to them. The youngest remained, holding himself on her legs to keep her still. Little Michael squealed, tossing his golden curls and grinning wildly. He was as bold and brave as his namesake, her commander, General Mikhael. She gave the name to honor his faith in and favor of her. The others took to calling him Mikey.

"Half devil, the lot of you! Let's go inside. I've missed you." Maiel laughed and snatched up the toddler.

While she placed Mikey on her hip, Samuel raced over. He grabbed her free hand, always desperate to be acknowledged. The girls skipped around the peach roses and dark green shrubs, singing a rhyme. Maiel drew a deep breath and felt that she might forget what had happened by evening. Her children's joy lifted her spirits like nothing else. It was possible to fix the small bit of damage done. After all, Lena was secure, and all she needed was a rest and a quest or two to fix the damage.

"Daddy's been painting, but he had Chaiel and Amaiel watch the babies while you were gone," Ian told on his janya, as they made their way back to the porch.

"You and Sam didn't help either, I'd wager." Maiel smirked.

"Girl's work." Ian grimaced and turned away.

"Why is it always girl's work?" Maiel sighed to no one in particular.

Ian laughed and played. Maiel sighed again. She squeezed Samuel's hand and looked to her romping daughters. She waited for the usual response of indignation. They held their tongues, but only because they had not heard him. Lifting her fourth by his arm, she looked at his smiling face.

"Don't you be like your akha," she said and set him back down. To the girls, she asked, "And how were the little ones, my darling girls?"

"Good," Chaiel replied, running a circle around her.

"I don't think they'll ever be ready to help daddy," Ian said, pulling a toy sword from a bush and bouncing the blade on the toe of his shoe.

"Perhaps not," Maiel said. "But that would be a good thing, because your janya will rise very soon. That will make you man of the house for a time."

Maiel heard her words and felt the hollowness in them. They were said too often. Hurrying the children up the steps and through the front door, she remained a moment on the porch. The shadow in the garden darkened, like the future she foresaw. A deep breath relaxed her shaken ego. Everything would be fine again in a few passings of the sun and moon. Rest would return her strength and good sense.

Argus's pack converged from the woods, conferring with their leader on the mission. They acknowledged their captain with their solemn wolfish salutes, a paw set forward with a shallow bow, and passed to their dens outside the rear garden. Turning on her heel, Maiel entered the house. The children were already scattered through the rooms, pattering along stairs and halls, shouting and carrying on. They would play at being children at odd times during the next few cycles, as they prepared for the next incarnation. She treasured these times; they brought back memories of when they were truly small. She shut the door and Argus nosed through his hinged panel.

The telltale click of nails on the wood floor roused her attention to the hall between the foyer and the kitchen at the back of the house. A long-bodied, black wolf looked at her from a pair of startling gold eyes. It was Shee, Argus's mate. Shee was wild born in the far fields of Elysion. Argus had discovered her in their random travels. The she wolf was a wanderer in the wild lands who'd stolen her best friend's heart. Shee's large belly hung low with her first litter of pups, due any minute. By all appearances, the pack was about to double. Maiel gave Shee's head a solid stroke, understanding too well how the soon-to-be mother felt right then, and moved toward the stairs to the second floor. The black wolf stole her heart too, for she was a noble soul and patient teacher. Shee followed her, leaning on Maiel's legs affectionately.

The house fell mute, except for the small voices whispering in other rooms. The serenity was a good sign that her husband worked alone in his studio. Dominic's guardian, Evocati Luthias, often came to visit, altering the energy of the dwelling like bass drums in an orchestra. The young and rough-hewn legiona made it difficult for her to be candid in the household. She liked him well enough, but there were limits to the things she shared with anyone outside her immediate family.

Maiel and Shee reached the second floor, where they found Argus lying in the hall on guard duty of the nursery. Metiel and Muriel were fast asleep in their cribs. The alpha leader reported to position, expecting his mate to need him. He sniffed his hello to her, ready to go wherever either female needed him. His devotion warmed Maiel.

"Make sure the children do not disturb us," Maiel said to him.

Maiel peeked into the nursery. She could make out the golden autumn heads of the boy and girl where they lay in their cribs. They'd come to her keeping after Dominic's last incarnation and her brief absence. They would remain small for far longer than their human counterparts, but it was still too short a time for the one who enjoyed them so. She crossed inside, desiring a touch to know they were in fact there, or to know she was in fact there. In the middle of the room was a soft, round cushion and blankets for the expectant amba of the house. Shee usually slept in the nursery, making it her job to protect Maiel's youngest.

"I have much to say and don't wish them to overhear," Maiel whispered to herself, smoothing the blankets and touching their foreheads.

The twins were completely down, suckling in their sleep. Argus locked eyes on her, his butt drooping to the floor. He gave a soft woof and ducked his shaggy head. Shee drew up to his side, giving his muzzle a quick lick and then lay down with some effort. Maiel stepped past them. She remembered a time when she felt that way about Dominic. She told herself it would be that way again soon, but she only felt dread. Her refuge had become a gilded cage where she was tied down with a mother's drudgery and no relief.

"Pray thee, be too busy to hear me," Maiel whispered to herself.

In the middle of the hall, a set of stairs rose to the third floor. The steps went around until they stopped at the opening of a broad, cross-shaped space with large windows peering out over the landscapes and skyscapes. Maiel entered her husband's lair. The air was full of the odor of paint, lacquer, and dust. Worked canvases hung on the bare plaster walls and supports to dry. Tools hung from exposed beams overhead. She looked up to the point of the turret roof, where two small box windows peered into the azure above. Work tables were cluttered with brushes and bottles, cups and palettes, blank and half-worked canvases.

Dominic came through an arch near the far south window. A staircase beyond the tiny bathroom led into their bedroom below. He dried a brush with a clean rag. A frown darkened his matured features, framed by a dark-gold goatee. Instead of his old uniform, he wore a paint-smeared black T-shirt and drab green pants. Paintbrushes and palette knives stuck out of the pockets along his leg like barbs. A sadly stained rag hung from his back pocket, forgotten in his haste. His golden head was hidden beneath a backward flat cap. It was his usual state of dress when he was lost in the throes of his art, a trade he had taken up soon after their ketu. He wanted to be with his young family and not work from long distances. He eyed her a moment, halting mid step, then flashed a smile. He was alone.

"How's Lena, angel?"

"Fine," Maiel answered, reluctant to speak yet. He gave her a sidelong glance and she added, "I had Zaajah take her to Otzar."

"I had no doubt you'd cross her safely. You didn't need the Samsaran Order to help."

But she did. How could he not tell that by looking at her faded state?

Maiel stared at a painting hung above the work table. It was she, lying beside her pool, a hand in the water and her filmy gown barely wrapped about her. She had not posed for the piece. He had the picture of her lying like that imprinted in his mind after their first night together—something neither would soon forget. Her stomach twisted, knowing it was his favorite work. She sighed as he returned to his latest creation. It would have been easier if he stopped what he did and decided to make love to her instead. She gathered he understood that by the wry grin on his lips. Maiel ran her hand over a work table, preferring to stay on the other side of the room if he meant to make a joke of her. She felt strangely awkward there, as if she were an intruder. A memory flashed in her mind that turned her cheeks crimson. She rolled her eyes, picked up a cup of red paint and swirled it with a brush from a blue cup. It was aggravating at times how he still had an effect on her after all these years and children. The memory of that night by the pool persisted, making her even more prickly. It was ridiculously sentimental.

"Why would I be too busy for you, Doll Face?" he suddenly asked, watching her from the corner of his eye.

That look was like razors to her skin. It went too deep, too quick. The thoughts in her mind were no memory, but a suggestion placed by Dominic's increasingly skillful mind. She set the cup down, feeling the hair on her arms stand up with anticipation.

"Your growing abilities are trying, to say the least," Maiel said, standing on the other side of the easel, with her arms folded to hide the goose bumps.. "I thought perhaps Luthias might be here."

"You'll still love me in the morning." He smiled, running his brush down the canvas with slow purpose. "And Luthias is at the council halls finalizing some details for our next trip. It may help you relax."

Dominic's eyes flashed. He was changing, despite his outlook to the contrary. She stared at him a moment and decided not to mention it. Retreating to the windows, she looked out over the forest that stretched forever. She knew he would take ahold of her in another moment, and as much as she welcomed him, at the same time she wanted to drive him away.

"What happened?" Dominic asked, setting his brush down and wiping his hands on the rag from his pocket.

Maiel rubbed her arm and watched an Aeris Order with blue plumage fly across the sky. She didn't respond. Her failure with Lena had grown too painful a shame and she wanted to bury it. Now would be the best time for him to do as he wished. She didn't want to talk about it. The need to think of anything else but her shame and guilt took over. She could feel him near her before his arms closed around her and he placed a kiss on her neck.

"Nothing to worry over," Maiel replied weakly. "Just bruised pride."

"Your brothers stopped by just after Argus returned," Dominic said, holding her tightly. "They thought you'd be home by then. You just missed them. They waited for you as long as they could," he added, when she kept silent.

The world disappeared beneath her feet for a moment. Her sattva pulsed anxiously. Stammering, Maiel spun around and freed herself from his no longer comforting embrace.

"What did they want?" she asked with a troubled look.

"They said the alders wanted to see you on some important matter. Your mother sent them," Dominic answered. His face was marked with confusion.

"The alders," Maiel repeated.

"It seemed important."

"Did they say anything else?"

Dominic pursed his lips and shook his head. Her obvious concern for the visit gave her away. He was suspicious now. Alders often called on her before and after an assignment, but this was different. She lost her temper, risked Lena in the process and threatened to abuse them for their treatment of a poorly trained youngling. They had dealt with her strong words before, but she'd never claimed their tactics breached the law.

"Tell me what happened, Doll Face," Dominic said, sensing the tatters.

"What happened is what should be expected from spending centuries incarnating into decadent flesh with no realization of the goal. What happened is that I'm overcome with emotions and forgot my place. I questioned their authority. I lost my focus, and in vile anger I nearly let the shadowalkers drag Lena to Jahannam," Maiel said, her mood intensifying.

Dominic stared at her, taking in each blast. He crossed his arms, trying his best not to be angry at her accusations. The fire in his eyes lit up again. Indeed, he was changing, but he refused to acknowledge it or embrace it and she grew weary. Regardless, he believed her demeanor was wrong, if not shockingly bigoted.

"It is your right and even your duty to say what you observe," Dominic finally said. He measured his tones carefully, but his control slipped and his anger showed. "But don't you dare say I'm not trying, or that humans are diseased because of the path they must take. Would you shame Luthias and declare his efforts lazy? Call him diseased?"

"Over two thousand years," Maiel breathed.

"You were born a duta; don't judge souls. Your brother doesn't."

"It's my place to judge you. I'm your wife—your helpmate," Maiel snapped back, blinded by anger. "Your guardian has nothing to do with your choices and I wouldn't think to mark him with the shame that belongs with you. I may have been born a duta, but I too had to learn what that meant."

"How dare you," Dominic growled.

"How dare you."

Maiel's eyes narrowed with anger. They stared each other down, both refusing to relent. Her blue eyes turned the shade of the moon, the shade before she became a four legged menace.

"This is stupid. You don't truly feel this way. What's wrong? Is it because they didn't give you the watcher you asked for? You didn't need them. They're dangerous besides, and you shouldn't be so keen to work with them. They're the reason so many fell," Dominic snapped.

Dominic took her arm. He saw the marks of the burns. They'd heal in a few passings of the sun and moon, but he gathered she was poisoned by serpent blood until then. His gaze returned to hers, and his suspicions grew.

"Perhaps we should have allowed you to go in directly. At this point, you'd have burned down and I'd be done with you," Maiel replied.

Dominic gestured, waving her accusations away. He knew she had a close friend who was a watcher, whose history was questioned because of his familial relations and work. He was a good engel and she didn't like others talking about him. Dominic leaned on his work table, turning his back to her. This wasn't the first time they'd fought about who she was friends with. He'd all but isolated her, quite concerned by her connections.

Maiel gripped her fists at her side. Her rage only grew. She wanted to pound her fists against him until he broke. Her head filled with accusations and blame. The whole process should have been resolved long ago, yet he kept delaying. He enjoyed living in mortal flesh too much, and he was in no rush to shed it. Tears stung her eyes as she felt her energy flicker. Dominic had torn her, not Mort. The shade merely had pulled on the brittle strings still holding her together. Turning his back was unforgivable.

"Put this right," Maiel choked on her agony.

Dominic snorted at the request. With a fist on his hip, he shook his head. He wouldn't look at her.

"You can put this right. Just focus on what you're trying to accomplish and we can move past this. I'll heal then," Maiel said.

"Angel," he breathed, half turning. His mouth opened as he struggled with his words. He always struggled with his words. Then he said, "I do as I'm instructed by the alders. The ones who send me to Samsara. Not my choice. If it were, I would have my wings by now. Luthias does the best he can, but his hands are tied. He can't just fill my head with every drop of information. They would cast him out! He just graduated from the title of youngling. It would be devastating for him."

"You're being sent back because you refuse to take control, not because Luthias won't cheat for you. Not because of the company I keep. The fact that this even comes up makes me wonder about you."

"I've watched you die a hundred times—murdered, aged, sick." Dominic turned. He looked ashen and tears glistened in his eyes. "You think I want more of that?"

"And I, you," Maiel said. Her eyes faded to their brilliant sapphire tones. "It's I who suffers, because I remember it all like it happened minutes ago. Don't you see that? Can't you tell that I'm being torn to shreds by this? Are you so concerned with advancement that you care nothing for those you use to get it? What of your friend Luthias? Isn't he precious to you?"

"I won't fight with you; you're just tired. You're better than this," Dominic said, rubbing his face with both hands.

Dominic returned to his easel and picked up a brush. His hand didn't tremble. It was steady as she'd once imagined his love for her. Her heart twisted within her breast. A tear slid from her eye and she stood watching him, waiting for him to say anything.

Several tense moments passed before Maiel gave up hope of him doing what he should: fighting for her. Fighting for his family. She took the stairs to their bedroom. Sleep was needed before she said another thing and irreparably hurt him and herself. There were other ways to go about such a discussion, but she was too fatigued to think them through. Of that, he was wholly right. Maiel felt sick at having slammed him with anger and racist thoughts.

Opening the door at the bottom of the steps, she traversed the short hall and entered their room. She examined her sattva for nails, the rough spikes shadowwalkers used to anchor a burning in an atman they targeted. Mort may have stung her before he died. There was no wound aside from the burns. She doubted his acid blood had made her lash out.

No one wanted Dominic to fail, least of all himself. That was why he entered Samsara through Otzar. In such an interface, the dark effects of his experiences were lessened. However, the same effects on a duta were quite different, and she found herself suffering. Like her mind, the house was full of niches and alcoves, every space filled with a memory that made her ache. Drawing the heavy curtains, she made the room as dark as possible and then crawled into bed. She pulled the covers to her chin, trying to insulate herself against her reflections. Every thought was tender and she forced her eyes closed to ease the pain. A sigh escaped her and then the flood broke. Curling into a ball, she wept in frustration. She missed the barracks and her fellow soldiers, where a night of revelry in the lunatic's pit would dissipate her misery.

Dominic's soft caress woke Maiel from a black slumber. She dreamt nothing and remembered nothing except for inconsolable tears before unconsciousness. He pulled her close, rolling her over for a kiss. Maiel felt weak, too weak to deny him or respond. She was still half asleep and wanted to continue her rest, so tattered from her mission. Her mission. She lost herself in his lovemaking until they were both satisfied. Lying there, drowsy with passion, she felt how routine it was. Suddenly, the events of the day clamored for more attention. It severed the sweetness of his touch like a heavy ax and left only the painful tenderness. He pulled her close, attempting another round.

"Enough," Maiel murmured.

"It's the best thing for it." He smiled, insisting with another kiss.

"I need to rest. I spent too much energy on this mission," Maiel said, pushing him back.

"Trust me, Doll Face," he said, pulling her under him.

"I said—"

Maiel let him kiss her. She was in no state to fight him and her sattva now responded to the attention, as if made to. As he persisted, she thought of their argument and her guilt squashed her protests. She tried to put it out of her mind, and wrapped her wings around him. She pulled him closer and returned his kiss with equal energy. The doubts in her mind vied heartily for her attention, until she was forced to imagine them in another place and time, a trick that was becoming commonplace to find any arousal.

Exhausted, Maiel slipped back to the mattress. Her wings folded miserably and she looked at him, lying there satisfied. A frown spread across her face.

"This isn't going to fix anything," Maiel said.

"Mai," he breathed.

Dominic's hand stroked the curve of her side. He eyed her, concerned, the desire still apparent on his features so that he reminded her of an ikyl. Sex wasn't going to dissolve her worries or reverse her actions.

"You think the answer to every disagreement between us is to shut me up with—"

Dominic stopped Maiel's words with a thumb over her lips. He eyed her with warning. She wanted to clamp her teeth down on the finger, but she only scowled. He took his hand away and dared another kiss. The embrace whipped the flames of her tender emotions. She hated him when he ignored her feelings like this. She pushed him away and rose from the bed. Her wings sagged miserably.

"Come here," he said, angered.

"No," Maiel said, looking back quickly.

Dominic meant to have his way. Not a single well-formed muscle on his sattva could have changed her mind right then. She lifted her chin and turned her back, quickly moving toward the bathroom door. Making love after everything that had happened made her feel so grimy.

"I'm going to take a bath."

"Then I'll come too," he said, jumping up from the covers and following after her.

"I want to be alone," Maiel said.

"You can't hide from me every time you're mad—we have problems. And you can't just hide from the alders, either," he said, as she disappeared behind the door, locking it shut.

Maiel stood with her eyes closed, trying not to explode again.

"Maiel—I've been your husband for too long for you to be so shy," he added more affectionately.

Maiel sat on the edge of the tub and hugged herself. Shy? She was hardly shy. She just didn't wish to lie there hurting with someone who couldn't care less.

The room was appointed with everything a human soul required. Things. Belongings. She had grown accustomed to their use. That idea oppressed her. There was a time when all she needed was Argus and the pool. She shut her eyes and thought of the moonlight over the glade, Argus lying in the grass nearby as Shee lay with him. Her skin being cooled in a soft breeze that played with her hair. She could feel the breeze along her curves, like Dominic's hand when they were newly bound, trembling and unsure. The water was decadently consoling as it slipped round her hand, back and forth, back and forth.

Maiel opened her eyes and found herself in the place of her dream. Blinking was better than sliding, as it did not leave a strong trail, and in this case, she did not want to be followed.

Lifting her head from the stone, Maiel saw a naiades female watching from the waterline. They didn't speak, but she recognized the young soul as one who came there often at night to relish the waters. Maiel understood and allowed it. In fact, there were several naiades younglings that took a shine to this place and to her. Their forms were a wonder, much like the element they favored.

Maiel's attention went past the girl to where Shee and Argus lay in the grass of the field, twined comfortably with one another beneath the moonlight. It was time for her to birth her litter and her discomfort grew. The hardwood floors of the house pained her joints and swollen belly, even with cushions. A small curl in Shee's lips warmed Maiel's heart. Shee was comfortable in the soft high grass with her mate beneath her muzzle. They were perfectly matched and never showed a shred of doubt.

Guilt swept through Maiel. After three millennia of devotion, she was asking the same questions as on the day of their ketu. She thought the years gave them an unwavering bond despite her doubts. So unwavering that Dominic would know where she went, regardless of how she travelled. There was only one place she ran to find solace and it wasn't in the safety of her order. He'd open the door, hoping to find her in the tub where he could master her, but instead would find her gone. If she didn't sink into his embrace, she ran to the pool. She rubbed her arms and decided to walk the glade instead of taking a swim. She didn't need to help him by being caught vulnerable. She was too weak to fight him, especially if he was bold enough to follow. He was usually patient, but since the last incarnation, his temper was closer to the surface and his demands more fervent. The thought made her wonder which one of them had changed and how.

*   *   *

Dominic listened outside the bathroom door. It was deathly silent on the other side. Trying the knob, he found it still locked. Closing his eyes, he concentrated. He had seen others unlock doors by their thoughts alone. His children could do it, but it was impossible for him. Gritting his teeth, he tried again. It opened and his eyes popped open with it. An emerald glow twin-kled inside his iris, pulsing before the color returned to normal. He smiled to congratulate himself. Perhaps his wife was right. He just needed to focus.

"Mai? Doll Face," he called.

The bath was empty and so was the room. He bared his teeth, half amused and half angry. She would rather run from him than face what had hap-pened. Understanding his bride after all this time was still quite the chore. He chalked it up to being of such different races. Stepping into the room, he tried to think of where she had gone to avoid him. Her words repeated in his mind. Dominic caught his reflection in the mirror. The pool. His eyes flashed and he lost his thought. Leaning close to the mirror he looked for the strange light to flash again. His eyes stared back at themselves, two plain, jade stones. He was about to poke fun at his foolishness when they flashed again. The light pulsed inside his irises, in a ring of heat, similar in appear-ance to his wife's eyes. Then the glow faded, leaving a stinging sensation.

"She's right. About time," he muttered, rubbing his eyes.

Gathering himself, Dominic focused on his wife, who ran from him to lick her wounds alone in the woods. He should be with her. The light in his irises would surely lighten her mood. It meant that it was time. It had to be. If she was so upset about his efforts, this would wipe that all away. They could cancel their incarnation and work on themselves.

Dominic raced out the front door. Shadows on the edge of the garden shifted like a line of people. He drew up short. Two figures moved toward him: Zach and his old commander. Joel wore a bright grin, but his elder brother was straight-faced. Dominic guarded his thoughts. He couldn't let them know she had run. She'd never forgive him if these two invaded her refuge to confront her. The only thing worse would be allowing her mother and aunt out there. He prayed they hadn't come too, and proceeded to search the garden.

"Akha." Joel grinned, clapping Dominic's shoulder with his large hand. It was often hard to realize this tree-sized Apollo was the twin of the fine creature he called his wife.

"Where is our khata?" Zach said, jumping to the point.

Dominic stammered a little and rubbed his neck.

"Resting," he replied.

Zach frowned at him, even deeper than usual. Joel laughed and clapped Dominic's back, setting him off balance.

"Shouldn't you be at home with Cora?" Dominic asked the younger of the two.

"She's busy preparing her assign for his next incarnation. Where were you off to?"

"She—Shee isn't in the house. I was checking to see if they had gone off. With the puppies due, I want to be sure they're safe."

"Thoughtful." Joel smiled at the lie.

"The council wishes to meet with my khata immediately. They've been waiting long and are irritable. Lord Ganesha will be most displeased," Zach informed him.

"Yes. You said the last time," Dominic said, raising his brow. A beat passed and then he asked, "Why didn't they involve the union? Or the outposts? Do you know? She was pretty angry about that."

"No need for them," Joel answered.

Dominic nodded, not convinced after Maiel had showed up so drained. Another hand couldn't have hurt to make sure the kid got back all right.

"Wake her," Zach insisted.

"I don't dare, not with how she showed up," Dominic said, crossing his arms. He stood tall, trying to match their height and breadth.

Zach crossed his arms and glared down his nose at him, bewildered by his display.

"You may think it's all right to wake that wildcat, but I know better."

"I'll go. She loves me best anyway," Joel said, stepping toward the house.

"Joel, don't. Let me," Dominic called him back.

Joel raised his eyebrow at this. Dominic knew he wasn't fooling either of them. He eyed the brothers a moment, then turned and went back into the house.

"Where's my daughter?"

Dominic stopped just inside the door, startled by the sudden and robustly spoken question. He faced a dark-clad alder, many years older than he, female, tall and slender. She wore the full black robes of her vocation and kept her silver mane beneath something like an orthodox priest's habit. In her arms, she held his youngest children, a set of twins who resembled their parents. It seemed that twins ran in the family. This was his second set. He looked them over and then tried to smile at the matriarch.

"Mother," Dominic said, winding past her. "I was just going to wake her."

"She's not in bed," his mother-in-law informed him. "Where's she resting?"

"Well, she's in my studio," Dominic lied.

"Here," she said, passing the children off to their uncles, who blocked his retreat.

Joel received his niece with cheer, immediately cooing at her and making her bubble with laughter. Zach received his nephew with reluctance, holding the boy before him and examining him like a scientist peering at a cross section of some organ. The boy regarded him in the same way.

"It's good practice for the both of you," Alexandrael told them, patting Zach's arm in attempt to ease his discomfort.

"Why in all of heaven would she sleep in that dusty old room?" A new voice called down from the top of the stairs.

"Aunt Magiel." Dominic half-cursed the name as he spoke it under his breath.

Dominic rolled his eyes shut and rested his head in his hand. His wife's moody aunt was the twin to her mother. They called her matula, duta for aunt, he learned. He rarely used their terms, quite settled on human language. Besides, it was a sign of familiarity and affection that he simply didn't feel for them. Magiel was an expert at goading him, trying his patience more times than he cared to admit. If it weren't for the love of her niece he would have given her a piece of his mind and suffered what might come of it, just to see the shock on her pale, curdled face.

"Because she finds comfort among my things," Dominic replied. She cradled his first born, as Ian played at being a kid again. All of them tramped around at the ripe age of six human years. Far too big to be coddled so, and most likely in desperate need of sleep. "Must you get them up?"

"Why not? They should be witness."

"Witness to what?"

"To the alders' decision," Aunt piped, as if it were obvious.

"Decision? What decision?" he asked, but they sternly stared at him in silence. "She isn't here," Dominic added, turning from them.

Dominic went into the dark, front room, seeking space away from his in-laws.

"Why in Jahannam not? Zaajah said she went home," Joel said, quite forcefully.

Joel was the only one of them actually welcome in his home. Dominic glared at him, not feeling so at that moment. He sunk onto the sofa.

"I wish I could tell you," Dominic said.

"What did you do?" the aunt demanded, setting her grandnephew back on his feet. She charged into the dim sitting room. "Did those shadow creatures lure her away again? Were you and your guardian drinking all day? I've never seen so much alcohol fill the gizzard of an engel as that one. You'd think you'd float away," she said, assessing him like a snob.

"I didn't evolve to her liking yet," Dominic said bitterly, beating them to it. "Not to your liking either, as you won't forgive me one incident."

Dominic didn't have to see their faces to know that his mother-in-law raised her eyebrow, or that her sister looked satisfied. Zach stood there, stoic as always, and Joel's brows furrowed, torn between Dominic and Maiel. Joel was the only one, other than his sister, who treated humans as equals. Well, that was until tonight. Dominic sighed. He sank more deeply into the couch.

"I didn't mean that. We had a fight and I'm still angry," Dominic said, expressing the apology he wanted to hear from his wife.

"We forgave you long ago. And none of us blame you for your guardian's vices," Joel said. "Forgive us if we worry over her, but it's not something to take idly when one of our ranks goes into the Pit of Acheron from a Samsaran incarnation."

"None of my doing," Dominic said, though they believed it was. He stammered on, "The alders laid out that plan. Your sister chose to stray from it."

"You weren't meant to die like that. My khata was beside herself to find a way to make something right that couldn't be righted. It was the demons that forced her hand. Not you and not her. What else was she to do under such torment?"

"We could've protected her until it was time," Dominic insisted coldly.

"She was going to be lobotomized—that man would have continued to rape her," Joel said, confused that Dominic would suggest she remain in such a place.

Joel pulled the cord of the lamp on the table next to him. He eyed Dominic a moment, then sat opposite him, using the table as a stool. He passed the infant girl back to her father. Dominic quickly found himself confessing, unable to hold the truth back from those who loved her as much as he did. It was something in his daughter's eyes.

He told them everything Maiel had said, from blaming him for his laziness to pointing her finger at the council for denying her the help of the outposts. He waited for their finger pointing. The room was quiet for some time. His eyes slowly glided to the stairs. His eldest sat with legs dangling between the spindles. White-knuckled fists held tight to the banister over his head. He stared at his father with glowing green eyes in the shadows of the staircase. His son was scowling at him, a look Dominic realized he needed to get used to as the boy matured. Still, it was the first finger pointed at him and not from whom he expected. His eyes slipped to the floor. Ian had always been his cheerleader. He was a typical teenager now, and perhaps too old to believe in him anymore.

Zach relinquished Metiel to his father. Dominic cradled the infants, looking at their peaceful faces. Their small wings poked out, barely big enough to even be called wings, except that they had feathers and they used them to their advantage. He remembered when his first was born and he saw the naked appendages on his back. He thought something was wrong, so unfamiliar with his wife's kind at that age. His only experiences were with the adults, who neatly folded their wings on their back like the folds of a cloak. It looked so natural you'd forget they were there. Maiel had been so amused by his reaction. Exhausted from giving birth, she fell asleep laughing to herself. He softly smiled, watching the twins fight to hold their eyes open. They held onto each other tightly.

"Are you all right?" his mother-in-law asked.

Alex did, in fact, care, if only for her daughter's sake. Dominic shook his head and realized he was smiling like a fool while tears slid down his cheeks. He was not. He'd failed his ketu and himself. Her words weren't about his race. They were about him. No matter how hard he tried, it felt as though he had made no progress. Every time he was thrust into a life, he had no recollection of his purpose and floundered in the ecstasy of every sensation. It was like he had been drugged, as if the alders purposely dulled his wits to make a mockery of him. He stopped fighting or wondering why they dangled destiny before him when they never meant to follow through. Their ketu, the whole thing, probably offended them so deeply they couldn't help themselves. He knew how Zach and their aunt felt. He guessed the others merely tolerated him as the incidental father of the ardhodita children.

"Crying?" Joel scoffed. "Did she pull your hair and break your dolly? Did she forbid you to go out and play with your little friend?"

Dominic glared at him, but Joel only smiled back. Dominic wondered how the smart-mouthed twin's wife could stand him.

"Wipe your face and go get your wife," Joel said. "She's not that prickly that you can't get your hands around her. There are about seven reasons I can point out to prove that."

"Yes. Fetch her back here, like a good lad," Aunt Magiel nosed in.

Dominic bit his tongue before he sarcastically asked for a cookie or if he should show her the new trick he'd learned. He passed his children to Joel and got to his feet. Zach watched him closely, assessing each move to find something new with which to accuse him. Dominic wished the engel would speak and let him have it. Despite preferring his silence to his brother's sarcasm, he hated wondering what jagged quip Zach would toss at him next.

"Dominic," his mother-in-law said as he stepped out of the room. She stood by the archway and he faced her. She put a hand on his shoulder, and continued, "I often forget Maiel's human qualities. It's good to have you about. After all, it was your voice that broke the prison. You truly are a wonder. You'll make a remarkable duta someday. I just hope you'll rethink becoming Joel's milite again. It'd prove a waste of your talent. You should be a muse and inspire others, spread beauty. You do truly remarkable work with your painting—the newest is quite something."

Alex smiled and patted his arm. Dominic eyed her, suspicious of all her words. She leapt from the subject of Maiel's sojourn in Jahannam to his paintings as if discussing tea cakes. He gave her a nod, but her step back and doubtful expression told him his features betrayed his heart.

Dominic left them and escaped through a back door in the kitchen. He crossed the garden out into a field beyond the hedge and disappeared on a worn path that wound into the wood. With any luck, the way would not be blocked by the endless khajala. Maiel was an expert at confounding him in more ways than one.

CHAPTER 3

PACING THE BANK OF A PLATINUM RIVER, a man crossly muttered to himself from a pair of pale, thin lips. He wore black from head to foot, with what appeared to be a leather cape draping down his back and clasped over his clavicle like the knuckles of two fingers. His pale skin was the hue of a fresh cadaver and his eyes pallid azure. His jet hair, perfectly coifed, framed a mature yet ageless face, both handsome and cruel. Much like his appearance, his presence in the strange land, which was so imposing and desolate, seemed contradictory in the sense that this did not seem a habitable place.

The atmosphere around him was heavy and warm, carrying the smell of burning decay on gusty winds. A low ceiling of purple clouds eclipsed the rock barrier that sealed him inside Jahannam, but the radiance of early evening reached through the distance from some indiscernible source. The flat plain pushed toward a sandstorm cloud. Red dust and scattered rock wended east and west into a bleak horizon. Black to the east and fire to the west. Lightning flashed above and behind. The only structures were a worn wood dock jutting into the water and a boulder shack upon which rested a pointed scrap-wood roof. A gothic lantern swung from one of the brittle piers.

The silver river this man wandered marked the border of the wasteland Sheol and as far as his kind could go without being harassed by lightwalkers. The man toed the water lapping the shore. It foamed angrily against his boot. He rubbed his palms together and then scanned the far bank. A mist shrouded the other side from view and the land beyond—the Asfodel Fields—was wreathed in black shadow. Beyond that lay the Avernus, a barrier that kept out the light and the prying eyes of King Adonai, he who cast their race into the shadows, a place that would eat their very being.

Poking from the shadows was the sterling head of a weeping giant, coined the Old Man by some, it was the guardian Yahweh, ever watchful over the dark dominion. The old seraph had encased himself inside of the statue, which was submerged to its elbows in a wide body of water. The rest of the seraph's prison lay cloaked in the spray of some liquid pouring from the hand-covered eyes. The effect elongated the statue's hair and robes. He recalled an era when the tears trickled and the rivers threatened to dry up. Many starved, for the liquid was suffering and thus life to Jahannam. Now great suffering poured in from Samsara, thanks to the many gates they'd forged to encourage the flow. Yahweh never fought them. Instead, his tears fed the acrid lands and broad, swollen rivers in his world. The danava would not starve again with such abundance pouring in from their gatekeeper. More than likely the seraph's atman had spent its last centuries ago and was a useless lump sealed inside. That or Yahweh had taken sides with Jahannam.

Whatever the man upon the shore waited to see remained hidden from him in the khajala barrier across the water. He grew impatient for the first signs of his expected delivery. The water lapped the shore more vigorously, suggesting that moment had at last come. He stopped muttering to himself and watched the ripples. Something indeed moved on the water.

"Lethe bring me news," he said.

A ghostly high-bowed skiff slipped from the khajala. The gleaming stem of the ominous vessel branched from the water like the elegant scroll of a violin. A crust of mineral circled the sides at the waterline. When the vessel drew closer, the structure was revealed to be composed of the twined bodies of souls in varying states of death. Their putrefying skins were dry and stretched tight on their bones despite the water. The forms writhed to break free, but were lost in the crippling stupor that enslaved them. The stem was also a corpse lashed into a gruesome figurehead, no doubt with an equally gruesome history. The ship's captain, Kharon, was an esthete collector of souls.

The ship came to rest at the dock, securing itself by automated rope moorings. Only two passengers stood on the low deck. Kharon, who guided the vessel, perched on a stunted aft deck, making three. The dark-haired man lifted his chin and pursed his lips. He scanned the boat's length again, striding along the dock. He had expected at least one other passenger. His fists worked, as he imagined throttling his soldiers for their failure.

"Lord Morgentus," the broader of the two men said, inclining his bald head.

Morgentus folded his hands and waited. The passenger who'd spoken to him hesitated, then crossed his bare arms over his great chest and frowned.

He was a fallen El, named Grag, whose form resembled a gigantic man from the age of barbarians. He had been an insidious creature, enjoying the feel of blood on his hands as much as subduing young females who made the mistake of crossing his path. His talents suited the sort of work Morgentus needed done, and helped him escape the chasm of torment long enough to promote him to the rank of knight. Such work as Grag's deserved to be rewarded a bit, but doing so had made him lazy.

The second soldier was Segrius, a chief among his serpent kind. He hailed from the fallen Dragos, easily led to darkness by his morbid obsessions. Serpents were similar to Bhogins, but had no recognizable faces. They just had a flat skull with sharp-toothed mouths and slits for a nose. Their sattva was covered in greasy skin the color of swamp mud. They were aptly named mudeaters. They had an uncanny awareness of their surroundings despite their blindness.

"Grag, Segrius—where is Mort?" Morgentus nodded to each.

Grag thought a moment, as if he were in fact capable of thought. Beside him, the reedy Segrius flexed his fists, clicking the long claws of his demented fingers. He clattered his stained teeth together and hissed. Morgentus should have sent him alone for this job, with a pair of his atrin. He would not stand on the banks of the Lethe empty-handed. The Bhogin was the worst choice he could have made.

"He dint survive the mission," Grag finally answered, in his stunted tongue. He noted Morgentus's dismay and rattled out, "The red duta slew him."

"Maiel," Morgentus breathed the name, both delighted and irritated.

As Morgentus considered the forms making up the boat, he reflected on the information. He didn't think taking the precious Gamael would have whipped up the red erela so powerfully. A grin surfaced on his face and he ran his hand over the brow of a young human female who formed part of the vessel. She rolled her face away, as if overcome with loathing. Then her skin softened to the same hue as his, changed from the red-black of her rotting flesh. She felt frozen to his burning hands, not quite fallen and not a gray.

"She'll kill more of our ranks so long as she looks for the guardian and watches the mortal. Let him go before she brings more to search."

"Of course she will. Because you're slovenly in your duties. Do you not have one good thing to tell me? Must I do this myself, like I had to when he threatened to steal her from me?" Morgentus said, distracted by the woman.

Placing his morbid black stare on his minions, Morgentus emphasized his meaning. Grag stared down his crooked nose, quite sure any response would be unwelcome.

"And what is it that I should tell Prince Belial?" Morgentus pressed, when the beasts kept quiet. "We let a guardian go because my men were afraid of a little erela?"

The threat of Belial's reprisal reminded Grag of his place, which was nowhere unless his baron ordered one. Kharon chuckled in delight, but didn't dare to otherwise involve himself. As the second Prince of the waterways, and weakest of their atrin, he held a precarious position. Morgentus's lips curled at the corners while he ran his gloved hand over the face of the woman again. Kharon would not raise a finger to prevent him from taking the burning soul. On the precipice of becoming a Jiangshi, she retained her human qualities and had the right measurements. Her aspect paled in comparison to the one who owned his affections. Despite his touch rousing her flesh to living form, a tint of color and fullness appeared that would not change. She wouldn't be enough, but she would tide him over. Her eyes opened; they were hazy, sightless orbs. Careful not to rend the restored flesh, he drew her from the other corpses that occupied the ferryman's boat.

"I've grown tired of waiting, but not all is lost. I have a new toy to keep me occupied until you find me what I asked for. Perhaps she can ease your worry about the old engel by eating his atman, since you cannot bring yourselves to touch him," Morgentus said, taking a long look at the treasure he'd found.

Kharon was miserable that he'd stolen the girl, but he dared not move to challenge the baron. He feared reprisal from his Acherite counterpart and the loss of all his souls. It was better to seek another girl from the sea to fill the vacancy. There were always more.

The frail limbs of the woman barely supported her. She crouched on the dock, shivering despite the heat, and scanned her surroundings with blind eyes. Morgentus pulled her onto her feet and walked her back to the dusty shore. She stumbled along on bare feet, staring past his shoulder into the bleak clouds. Her long chestnut hair hung past her waist in strings. The only article of clothing she wore was a tattered and stained smock. She was soiled and would need bathing. Morgentus gave the garment a tug, freeing her from it. Instinctively, she attempted to cover her bony frame by crossing her thin arms. He left her standing on the dusty bank of the Lethe, blind, weak, and naked, to circle her for a better view. Throwing the garment to the ground, he smiled appreciatively. The wasted shape had promise and he imagined that in life she was far more lush than this and would be so again.

"Yes, you'll do just fine," Morgentus said, cupping the back of her head with his hand.

Morgentus drew a long black nail from inside his sleeve and inserted it into the gristle of her neck. The metal barb would ensure she remained his and that his intentions for her were fulfilled. His prisoner would never suspect such a creature of malice and she'd wend her way into his prison easily.

The woman blinked, the fog of her eyes clearing to a crystalline hazel. Warmth filled her pale cheeks and lips, and her sattva thickened.

"What do they call you?" Morgentus asked, eyeing his handiwork. The girl looked at him, but gave no answer. She appeared confused, awakened from her nightmare to find herself not at home or anywhere familiar. "Yes, of course. The Lethe," he said warmly, smiling.

Morgentus rubbed his chin and returned to his soldiers. Sighting them on the dock, his expression hardened.

"Find me a better reason than Gamael to drag her down here," Morgentus ordered, his tone quite harsh. The blue and white of his eyes turned black with shadowy power. His minions tensed, making him angrier. "So help me, if you fail me again, I'll bring you to Cocytus myself," he added with great rage.

The leather cloak shifted on his back. It was no cloak he wore, but the featherless wings of his kind.

"We won't fail you, my baron," the mudeater said.

"You best not," Morgentus warned, turning away from them. A bitter taste filled his mouth as he sensed their betrayal. "I can find others to do your job. There are millions," he threatened.

Stalking back to the naked girl, he paused to study her flesh again. His mood shifted to a different kind of fire and his black eyes sparkled with heat. The wide hazel orbs peered back; she seemed as innocent as a child. That innocence would be stolen from her quickly. To feed on a duta was a great evil that sealed the fate of the offending atman, and he was going to give her her fill of those he kept locked in his dungeons. He clamped his hands on her shoulders and sniffed her filthy hair. The little marditavya already burned. Oh, what horrors this one must have committed.

"Where am I?" she asked him.

Morgentus smiled at her again. His hands slipped down her shoulders and he stepped around to look in her face.

"Sheol, my lady," he said, taking up her hand and kissing it.

Tears filled her eyes. She sought to speak but was silenced, as she looked over the wide empty plain that stretched east and west—a desolate tract of red dust. The nail in her throat worked to yoke her and she swallowed her words.

"Your corpse has long since rotted, but take heart that there is so much more than black death to welcome you here. I have saved you from wallowing in your misery as the ferryman's hostage. To thank me, you will do exactly as I ask," he informed her, veiling the threat of his very presence behind his grin. "I will call you Cursia," he whispered to her.

"Am I bound for the ovens of Gehenna?" she stammered. Her frightened eyes scanned the dusty plain.

"Not yet, poor Cursia. Not yet." Morgentus grinned.

Morgentus held her hand and walked backward, urging her toward the red desert, enjoying her nakedness.

"I did nothing wrong. I did nothing. I did—I can't remember," she tearfully insisted.

"Oh, you were terrible," he assured her, delighted by her terror, though he knew nothing of her sordid tale.

With her form restored, all that remained was to refurbish her mind. He clasped her head tight in both hands. He read the folds of her memory and they told the tale he found. Instead of sharing that tale, he twisted the memories just a touch to suit his desire.

"You betrayed those who loved you by lying with another. For this you were punished and you sought to punish your lover for being caught, insisting you were raped. He went to the gallows protesting innocence. He never raped you, did he? And when you bore a bastard you killed the infant to appease the wrath of your husband. You set up the one you loved and killed his son to hide your shame. The shame of a whore. Well, now you are my whore."

Morgentus drew her close and looked down at her with grave warning. Cursia shook her head and choked on her protests. Yes, she was going to do quite nicely in helping to complete his plans.

"You lied for power and you destroyed innocence," Morgentus said, holding her to his strong frame. Cursia struggled to be free, but the expression on his face as it shifted to reveal the pollution beneath, stilled her with its vileness. "Oh, dear heart, tears won't save you from your fate. When you suffocated the innocent babe, you won your sentence. This isn't Zion. This is no realm of forgiveness. This is the house of retribution. We shall have ours of you. You'll do as I order—to the letter, or you can go back to Kharon's raft."

Cursia collapsed at his feet weeping. Either choice was doom and torment. Morgentus released her, annoyed by her easy reaction to his intimidations. He sighed, fixing the gloves on his fingers. Yet Cursia was still useful to him. He would feed on her misery to begin with. While he drew the energy spent from her pain to take back what precious energy he had given, Morgentus pondered a devious plan that would ensure his success regardless of the bumbling fools he'd sent back to Samsara to find the key. The female he truly desired was weakened and the time for her to fall had come.

With an eased mood, Morgentus faced the desert. He thought of leaving Cursia there to harden her hate in the wasteland. Once full of spite, she would be ready to fulfill her tasks. The torment that would be unleashed upon her made him smile. A soul could spend years rambling the rim of this land, a ready victim for any soldier or imp that came by, and there would be many. He needed her ready much sooner than that and the Pits of Acheron, his lair, was the best place to ensure that swiftness. The recesses of shadow there held the deepest iniquity, beings so malevolent they would feed upon the flesh of their own kin and even themselves. Pain was their pleasure and suffering a nectar that made them strong. Besides, he would not have to trap her from the wilds and show her the path to Gamael's door. She would find it quickly if left to her own devices in the maze. The less she stank of Jahannam, the more easily she would tempt the wizened elder.

From the swirling dust in the distance, a pair of riders approached. Armored by the plate of Prince Belial's house and lofting thorny pikes in their hands, they approached quickly. These messengers had likely come to take him to the commander, not pick a fight they would surely lose. The thunderous hooves of the grotesque mounts pounded the dirt of Sheol in a circle around him. The riders came to a stop and stared down at him from crimson eyes. Their twisted features were the stuff of ancient nightmares. In their features he saw the picture of what had happened to the children of those who went against their king and refused his laws. The Nephilim ranked as knights in the prince's armies, Belial's misbegotten children and reminders of his exile and constant torment. Their livery was red, to recall the blood they shared, and their eyes the tone of fire as they burned for-ever within. Without the grace of his Jñanasattva light, their existence was now mangled, enfeebled, and scattered. This alone was enough to keep the hatred burning between this world and the place of their origin, but it also proved they could exist without their king. Adonai's weakness, his curse and torture of their young, demanded he be deposed.

One of the nephilim lowered his pike and pointed the tip at Morgentus. The baron followed it, unimpressed.

"Belial seeks an audience at his keep," the rider said.

It was not a request. Morgentus gave him a stiff bow.

"Be so kind as to take my baggage to the pit," he said, indicating the female.

The hollow eyes of the guards went to the female. They frowned hard, disgusted by the sight of the woman. Her kind was why they were deformed.

"Be sure none touch it, or I'll skin him and teach him what it means to damage a danava's possession."

Morgentus stepped toward the far curtain of dust and disappeared, leaving the woman at the mercy of the riders. Her screams chased him, but he was certain they would leave the insufferable harlot at his doorstep none the worse for wear. However, the pit that preceded his labyrinthine sanctuary would be another matter. He waved his hand, not looking back. Fire flashed on the girl's forehead, taking the form of his seal. Smoke rose from her singed flesh and she cried out in agony. He smiled to himself, tucking his hands behind his back and taking his time to comply with the orders. Whatever Belial wished of him best not take long. Otherwise, he might miss the fun his imps would have with his new toy. The worst his minions would do is give her a scare or scar. At least until he returned. Then he would see how far he would let them go. Above all, he didn't want to miss Gamael pouring himself into saving the woman, who he had no doubt would make him think of his assign and what she could become without his guardianship.

Strides broadening, Morgentus disappeared inside a black tornado. Within seconds, he reemerged from the smoke on the border of Belial's Acherite city. Crawling the walls of the cavernous stretch, the shadows who served him filled the black stone houses with their filth. A broken wall stood along the border, an old gate marking the path. A cold light, like the full moon in winter, shone down from the black ceiling with no perceptible source, proof of cracks in the seal of their prison. Morgentus navigated the dry, gray landscape, his eye always on the towering castle deep inside the stone city's heart. That was where Belial concealed himself. The old structure was a menace over its city, ready to topple from a broken foundation and its impossible weight. However, the tower remained strong, regardless, just like its master.

A sea of souls wandered past him and through the open gates, lost souls digging themselves deeper into despair's clutches. Each numbered food or fodder for the shades and shadows urging them on. The marditavya grew restless, picking one or two off the line and dragging them into the confines of a dwelling.

Not wishing to keep his prince waiting, Morgentus decided to transport himself once more. It would be much faster than entering the city along with the throng of cattle. He took a step forward, raising his wings, and disappeared in a swirl of dust. Now without the ability to blink like his ancestors, Morgentus could only slide, in a similar but broken mimicry of the light-walkers. Morgentus mourned the lost form of transport. He could no longer move as fast, nor was he able to reach as extreme a distance in one step. At least Adonai had not cursed them with walking like the Samsaran souls, who were completely reliant on artificial transportation or their inadequate legs. Thus, in a smoking cloud, he reemerged deep within the city. The dust swirl billowed away from him like boiling smoke as he took several steps forward and repeated his effort until he came to the tower wall. There, his leather wings settled on his back. He stared up at the impossible structure, gathering his strength in fear of the prince who might be prepared to chastise him for his minions' failure.

Morgentus peered at the dark windows and doors of the decaying buildings pressed to the wall. The wall barred the city from encroaching on the prince's fortress, leaving him with a wide moat of dust that spanned more than two city blocks. Dust and random fragments stretched to either side, disappearing into an obscure nothingness. Though it appeared empty, Morgentus was aware of the fate that awaited any reprobate who ventured there. Not even the fallen Boarwellum, who they called the Bachlachs, set root there.

Stepping through the arch, the baron entered the ring that circled the fortress. Before him, a worn path led to a twisted black iron gate. The way was guarded by pike-bearing giants in crusty armor and chainmail. At their feet skulked wraiths on chains. The giants were atrin of the riders who summoned him, members of a multitude that Belial fathered in Samsara before the Conflict. Their lot was to be despised and loved by their fathers, used and retained for the day of reckoning with Zion.

Slowly taking the dusty path, Morgentus approached under their horrid watch. He lifted his arms in submission to the guards. Their thick hands searched his garments for weapons. He smirked at the futility, but it was that or wrestle with them to get through the gate. Belial would not be in a good mood if he was late.

When the guards completed their fumbling search, they took several ungainly steps back to their posts. The rusted gate opened with a whine. It was a long walk to the prince's chambers. Morgentus nodded to the nephilim and left behind his footprints in the thick dust. Eyes peered from the recesses of the halls and rooms. Daeva slipped past, threatening with rattling throat slits. He paused, eyeing the hall that looked more like a medieval haunted house than the residence of one so great. The chamber he sought was too far a walk, with too many twists, stairs, and obstacles. Daeva drew closer. He disappeared in a swirl of smoke.

"You've kept me waiting, Morgentus," a voice rumbled from the shadows as he reappeared inside a narrow but high-ceilinged chamber.

Morgentus widened his pale eyes, hoping to appear docile before the prince. Belial sat on a throne of bronzed bones, raised upon a dais of black marble. His great legs were all that were visible in the darkness. The room was lit by a single shaft of light coming from a window high on the wall. The chandelier did not burn, but was covered in the melted wax of centuries of burnt candles. The tapestry and heraldry on the walls were tatters of their former glory. Belial's favorite son, Ezrodial, along with his jiangshi, lounged aside the throne. His dolls, a gaggle of young asuri and atrin from the Aghartian strain, draped their bodies over the furniture and fixtures, some in repose and others in the midst of coupling. The dolls watched him close in on their master, a flash of hatred in their eyes. The Aghartians were an easily corruptible and decadent people, much like the nobility Belial controlled throughout Earth's paltry forest of Europe. It galled them that they had failed to conquer either world.

"I was delayed by my filthy, fumbling servants," Morgentus spat, thinking of the despicable dolls of his master.

"They would not fumble if their master were not so weak himself," Belial returned.

"Indeed, my liege. Indeed," Morgentus said, tucking his hands behind his back and going to his master's foot. He knelt before the dais and bowed his head. Regardless of his contempt for them, the presence of the concubines made it difficult to focus. Morgentus continued, with one eye on their displays of ecstasy. "Mort has failed and paid with his existence. Adonai's pet took him, along with another of our dark atrin."

"You profess to be capable of subduing this erela. Yet you haven't been able to prove it," Belial said, waving his claw to dismiss his rabble.

"She was mine, not so long ago, trapped in a cage of her own creation, one she ceded to my control. If her contemptible husband hadn't rescued her, she would yet be ours. It's where she truly wanted to be. Where she knows she belongs," Morgentus said.

If Belial knew of the sattva Morgentus marked for his bidding, would he be so quick to judge him? The barbs he planted would work their dark influence. The marked would be theirs in time.

"Does she?" Belial questioned.

"Her love for him is what blinds her from her destiny, but she will fall, and so will he," Morgentus answered, knowing a secret he wouldn't share.

"I think you misplace where her love is."

Belial shifted forward on his throne. The figure of a rat skittered along the wall; imps took many forms to fool those with whom they lived. The mass of concubines now watched them from the western antechamber and its shadows. Belial's great horned head leaned over Morgentus. The prince breathed his hot breath down his baron's neck, and gripped the arms of the throne tightly.

"Don't mistake that or you will fail," Belial growled.

"Understood, my liege. We can't attack the king directly. He is yet too powerful. We must weaken him first and show the others, our lost kin, the way and the truth," Morgentus said, suggesting the crux of his plan.

"What of this human the erela is mated with? You insist he is destined to fall? Is this a weakness we may exploit?" Belial asked, sitting back. He crossed his legs.

Morgentus tried not to notice the foot of his master, deformed to an animal claw during his fall from grace. Adonai had been most unkind in his punishments. Morgentus swallowed and focused on the floor. Adonai left the likes of Morgentus merely singed by his disappointment.

"He's favored by the light as much as she. Their ketu makes him unlikely to fall from grace. That is why they stole her from her true mate. I'm that true mate and because of my fall, I left a vacancy for the king to abuse."

"All the more tender it will be if we succeed. The beloved captain of his highness's general. I have so long desired to deal a blow to that inflated ego they named Mikhael. The soul will provide us a means to do that whether or not you succeed in gaining the erela to our side. There are deeper secrets your pandering ass can't fathom. Secrets that make Mikhael burn." Belial grinned, with a flash of sharp yellow teeth. His eyes blazed like fire.

"It's something I've contemplated—but what to do with him after our success? The female will be mine and he'll feel betrayed. He may work against us."

"Curse him to your labyrinth so he may watch you enjoy his bride. A jiangshi is no threat in any form to danava, though I have great doubt in your ability to bring down either. Your assumption that she belongs to you is merely the wishful thinking of a lustful heart. I care not, either way. If you gain her, you may have her. Revenge will be had regardless. But fail to gain both, you'll suffer for damaging my plans," Belial said.

Morgentus knelt in the dark, silent for some time, as he thought over the orders from his prince. He had the prince's backing in his efforts. The erela would belong to him. His stomach tightened and desire took over his thoughts. Blood flooded his eyes.

Belial rose to his feet and stepped from his throne. He paced the room, then stood behind Morgentus. Morgentus felt the hot eyes burning his back. He blinked, regaining his concentration. Sniffing the air, he tried to determine the prince's mood.

"She's the vulnerability in their defenses. A tremor shakes the border of their world—barely perceptible, like a thread whipping in the wind. I stand corrected, Baron. Your men have struck a blow, though you think they failed you. That blow has left a crack that will widen if pressed."

"Then I shall press it," Morgentus told him. He was certain it was more than just his efforts that had caused the crack.

"Turn the human and I believe you will. After all, he is only human. His desire and ambition make him weak. Promise him—everything, what Adonai promised him. Give him a kingdom on Earth with his bride as his infernal queen."

"My prince, but you just promised her to me," Morgentus wailed, eyes blackening with rage.

"Tell him! It matters little if we give it. This is about making the thread pull and undoing the whole stitch. I care very little about your cruel lust for the lightwalker. You'll grow tired of her in time, as you have with your Sabereh. Our focus is rending open the gates and taking back Zion. I won't risk that for some pathetic erela," Belial raged, picking up the querulous Morgentus and pulling him close to his face.

Morgentus had overstepped.

"Yes, my prince," Morgentus said, struggling to speak.

Another silence fell. Belial's gaze narrowed as the color returned to each orb. He looked into his baron's mind, digging deeply to know if his orders were to be carried out. Lust was a terrible malady when it wasn't kept in check. Many of their soldiers had been sent to Oblivion, destroyed by it. He needed to temper his desire with that knowledge. They bided their time in Jahannam until they found a way back. That was the only goal.

"Fail me again, and I'll strip your powers and send you to Lucifer to spend out your eternity," Belial warned.

Belial set him down roughly and Morgentus lost his footing. Quickly picking himself up, he found he was alone in the chamber. He brushed himself off, covered in the dust of Acheron, a dust that clung to everything and made it rot. The dust of the Conflict.

Abruptly, a heavy door to the room burst open and a cloud in the shape of a great angry face swept in. Its sharp-toothed mouth opened as it soared toward him.

"Go!" the voice of Belial roared.

The cloud fell in a cascade of dust, covering him once more in the filth of the cave. The silence passed and the dolls whispered their siren calls. Morgentus scowled. The prince was exceptionally irritable that day. He would be sure to pass on the sentiment to Grag and Segrius the next time he saw them. Lifting his wings, he quickly took his leave before Belial returned or his whores set their claws into him. The dust that covered him swirled then settled back to the floor upon his retreat.

* * *

The halls of the White City spread like a web beneath towering vaulted ceilings and gothic halls, each a twin of the last. A brilliant light lit the distance, cascading through small windows carved near the very top of the polished white walls, and through the cathedral-like windows below them. The light cleansed and the light revived everything in its path. Zion, the seat of king Adonai, the house of the High Council and the home of those closest to the light, was forever united by him to the realm of Nirvana.

Zaajah felt a little out of place among the higher duta, despite being near a centaur soul and his Ikyls companion. There were other souls present too, known better to various worlds around Samsara, and far more out of place than duta, such as the Grails, who haunted human nightmares since their recent interference in Earth affairs. Others, more human-like, such as the Oriades who shared a planet called Satyr with the Ikyl, the hairless and brown-skinned Cetians, and the bluish-tinged Aghartians were more difficult to discern. Lena stared eagerly after a Naga warrior that slithered past them, his four arms gesticulating as he conversed with the giant El female. The El was pale of skin and dark of eye, and nearly as hairless as the Cetian. The girls' wonderment did not wane. A water element, Naiades, escorted a Vetehinen to the council chambers. The Vetehinen were water-loving beings with fish tails, but on land their scales dried into legs. The bull-headed Hyadeans, the fiery Jinn, and the avian Aurai all paraded among the citizens. A gasp then escaped the child as a Boarwellum female waved her branches and grinned, for she was just as delighted. A spiny Drago spat out his long forked tongue in their direction and went back to his conversation with a duta alder, uninterested in a Horus warrior or a human.

"What is that?" Lena whispered.

"Drago," Zaajah quietly answered.

"He looks like a dragon," Lena said, a little frightened.

"He looks like a Drago. Now, c'mon. There's nothing to be afraid of here," Zaajah said, a little embarrassed.

A few of Zaajah's rank and race also presented themselves to the polished halls. Governing alders and their staff wandered here, either lost in thought or in their own conversation. They created an atmosphere that was forbidding. Mixed among them were the keepers of this fort, Dominions and their colleagues the Virtues. Both were strange beings. The Dominions wore brown robes and boasted elongated bald heads; their only hair was their white brows and the beards of the males. Their counterparts, the Virtues, were even stranger, duta only in shape. Their wings were ethereal wisps of energy. They took the form of seemingly sexless bodies of pure energy, lit with currents of alternating hues, like something one might see beneath the very deepest waters of Earth. To watch over all this, Zion enjoyed the protection of the Guardians of Light, who were called Powers. The eyes of the heavily armored Powers, silver guardians of light, and the multitude of others peered after Lena as she made her way among them. The Powers kept close watch over everyone from behind the red lenses of their strange helms. Their articulated armor and double set of white wings gave them a startling appearance, which was backed by a flawless reputation for following truth and order. She stared at their insect-like heads and long, claw-like hands and feet, and began to question her merits. It was all but determined a legiona would grow into a power as he or she rose. Some said the change was far greater than they let on.

Because of the presence of so many higher duta who enjoyed a close union with the light, the Soul Keepers Well, or Otzar, and even Guf to others, was kept in the heart of Zion. It resided beneath the perpetual light, which cast its radiance deep inside the cavern. Some declared that Zion had been built around it when the king first made his home here, with the help and hands of the Seraphim, the first children of Zion. Regardless, it was the safest place. It was also the reason for the child attached to Zaajah's hand. Though she actively avoided trips this deep into the citadel, Maiel had asked her to deliver the girl to her protectors. She would do anything her dearest friend asked. Besides, denying the request might make her fear obvious to her friends, and that would be most detrimental to her reputation.

Zaajah held her chin high, determined to complete her promise, even if Lena might have been just as well at Maiel's side while the captain recovered. At least there, she'd have other children to play with and Zaajah could return to the practice fields with her younglings, instead of being assessed by the probing eyes of light guardians.

Zaajah's black eyes slipped over the top of the girl's head. Lena skittered along beside her, humming a bizarre little tune. Her small mouth opened now and again, emitting what she guessed was singing. Zaajah didn't know what to do with so young a child, so she didn't speak. Her only experience had been long ago with Maiel's progeny. She grimaced, thinking of the twins. A little practice would do her good. Maiel was sure to call on her at some point to help with them. She felt her gut twist at the idea. The last time made her wish for a family of her own, and exposed feelings to someone she'd rather not bring closer. Thankfully, a bond had not transpired between them, as the engel understood her reluctance to acknowledge such disconcerting things. However, it would only be a matter of time before ketu was settled between them.

"You're afraid," Lena suddenly blurted. She stared ahead into the reaches of the tall corridor.

"Pardon?"

Zaajah wasn't sure she'd heard the girl accuse such a mighty warrior of such a lowly human emotion. Was she not proving just the opposite? She puffed up her chest and looked very serious. Lena looked at her and smiled a little. Zaajah swallowed, uncomfortable with her wise gaze.

"Not of them. Do you love him?" Lena said.

"Of who? What?" Zaajah stammered. She came to a halt. "Is there something on your mind, human child?" she asked, towering over the girl like an Amazon.

"You don't like it here. It's too stuffy. You like the outer ring of the city best, where you can still see the trees. You're a lot like Mai. That's why you love her," Lena said, on point.

"You mentioned him?"

"Oh, that," Lena said. She looked suddenly uncomfortable. She continued in a raspy whisper, "I'd rather not say here. They might make you marry him. You call them engels, right? If they hear us and if you're afraid of him that is no good. Ibajah is the engel's name. Yes?"

Zaajah's eyes widened at the statement. She lost her voice during the conversation, which suddenly seemed to overwhelm the atmosphere. Lena was special, and her ability to discern Zaajah's thoughts was proof. Lena's eyes glowed up at hers. The light was robust and she could see that it was most definitely time for this small soul to rise. No doubt her human sattva even boasted wing buds.

Opening her mouth to speak, Zaajah quickly bit her lip. The approach of a black-clad svarg, prevented another utterance. It was Primus Gediel, the Wolf Leader of Fenrir. He rarely made an appearance in Zion, although the rest of his immediate family made frequent appearances there since the Conflict of Hosts. It was an old wound of great embarrassment to them, having a patriarch among the fallen. Still, he had proven himself solidly and shouldn't hang his wolfish head in shame or hide from the rest of their kind. Maybe he just liked to be alone. Whatever it was that kept him apart, he was a brilliant watcher when not being a brooding dog trainer. Zaajah stared at him, hoping he hadn't overheard the girl. Her eyes lingered on the silver circlet marking his crown and status.

"Wasn't Maiel supposed to bring her?" Gediel asked, narrowing his pale eyes.

"Wow," Lena breathed, staring up at him.

Gediel was indeed a striking figure among the lightwalkers. His chunky-shag locks of dark gold resembled the coats of the animals with which he spent much of his time. He also had a pair of great, gray wings. His pale eyes were still bright and clear: a rare blue tone that could instantly become the hue of the wolf. His smooth, fair skin was just as young as the day they met and his well-carved features made him a favorite of all the unmatched females. They particularly remarked on his odd coloration for a younger lightwalker, unique to a few of his age and race. It was a sign of great aptitude and wisdom. Zaajah always thought he was a little too boyish, even when he decided to let his facial hair grow in around his mouth.

The main issue was his link with the dark prince, after whom he was named. More specifically, Gediel claimed a progenitor, what her kind called Jyoti, who was not merely the reason most thought him so withdrawn, but destined to burn down. The women wanted to tame his wildness while toying with the idea of darkness without ever having to cross the khajala. It drew them like flowers to sunshine. Up close, he was certainly handsome, but he was just a gentle, well-mannered engel. It was a shame that Adonai hadn't blessed a union between him and Maiel. Though she was just a youngling back then and he already a young svarg, there could be no better ketu than one made between the moon order and Fenrir. They had been friends and it made greater sense than pairing her with a strange human. A svargaduta wouldn't have diminished the light of her atman, even if his jyoti was an oath breaker.

Zaajah hadn't seen Gediel in quite some time. The watcher was either gone on a reconnaissance mission or in the wild lands of Elysion raising his packs for the armies among the wildest of souls. He lived alone and worked alone—another reason the females flocked around him. There were no others to tempt him away from her should he flatter them with his attentions.

"Mai is home. Shee is due any moment with the new litter," Zaajah replied.

Gediel smiled. He was the reason Maiel had the pack at her hip. It hadn't taken long after Argus's arrival to figure that out. Despite her protests, she wasn't able to locate him and bring the pup back. Come to think of it, Gediel was all but completely absent since the wolf showed up and Maiel's hand was passed to Dominic. Zaajah's eyes narrowed, wondering about that intriguing detail. No. That was impossible. She and their friends had already exhaustively gone over that possibility. But, then, what if he was responsible for Shee, and not just Argus?

"Can you tell me why they told us no watchers? It would have been a great help getting this one across, but Maxiel had it in his head more than two guardians would have brought all of Jahannam onto us," Zaajah said, shaking herself out of her gossipy, meandering thoughts.

Gediel shrugged and shook his head.

"If I can be of any assistance, have her call on me directly," Gediel said.

"If you can be found," Zaajah said.

Gediel opened his mouth to respond to Zaajah's remark, but was immediately cut off by Lena.

"You're the dog man? Mai said I could come see you and play with the dogs," Lena said, beaming excitedly.

Gediel crouched in front of the girl so he could see her better. He stood very tall, like most of his kind, who commonly reached above seven feet in height. He smiled at her pretty cinnamon-colored face. Zaajah couldn't help but be warmed by their moment. It was quite adorable.

"I am. Some call me Wolf Leader because I raise the packs who serve in the Legions. I teach them to chew the malefic limbs of the dark dwellers, so they can't hurt little girls like you," he told her. He gave her a bright smile. "But you may call me Gediel." He shook her hand.

As she held his hand, Lena studied his digits, poking from the black, fingerless gloves, and refused to let him go. Lena very much liked dogs, and this was a kindred being, very much like them.

"Did you raise Mai's puppy?" Lena asked, pulling at the loose buckles of his leather coat.

"Argus? No. Maiel raised him on her own. Taught him everything he knows."

Lena stroked his wing and then touched his svarg crown, not daunted by the one duta in all of Zion who could intimidate even the king.

"Does Argus really go into the bad place with her?" She touched the shoulder where his penannular should have been. She made a circle with her finger and traced two opposed triangles.

"Primus," she whispered his rank.

Gediel looked slightly sad. Lena pulled at his boot buckles. She was a rather uninhibited and curious child. Too curious perhaps.

"He has gone to that place. Yes."

"Because you're soldiers."

"Yes."

Zaajah watched the exchange and saw that she should take Lena on to her destination before she asked any more questions, like the one in her own mind. She would be mortified if the child asked him something as personal and painful as that. And by the direction of the conversation, it was getting close. She was sniffing out Maiel around the corners of his thoughts.

Taking the girl's hand from his sword hilt, Zaajah cleared her throat.

"We should be going. The soul keepers are expecting us," Zaajah interrupted, sensing his discomfort.

"I look forward to your visit, Lena," he told the girl with a sweet smile.

Lena grinned back, chewing her nails and giggling. Even she was affected by his presence. Zaajah rolled her eyes and shook her head. Someone needed to match this young svarg before he had all of Zion in a stir.

Gediel rose to his full height, towering over Zaajah by more than a head. He shifted his doublet back into place. He gave a sharp nod and suddenly looked stressed. Zaajah turned Lena from him before she asked him what he had just sensed.

"Tell Maiel that I'm here if she needs me," Gediel said to her back, sounding more distressed.

Zaajah hesitated, looking over her shoulder at him. A shadow flickered on his face. He turned without another word and made his way down the opposite corridor, disappearing in the crowd. Zaajah's breath stopped; whatever affected him had touched her too.

"He loves her," Lena said.

Zaajah's mouth became a flat line.

"We all love her," Zaajah said, guiding her along again.

"Not like he does."

The words bit Zaajah's core. It wasn't possible. Maiel had a ketu, and had been so for a long time to a man she desperately loved. The friendship between her and Gediel had waned ages ago and love was never possible between them. Besides, the hearts of svargaduta were true. They didn't lust like silly souls. Zaajah chewed her tongue, thinking of Gediel's jyoti. Her khata was no Grigori, either. The sooner she placed the child with her caretakers the better. The shadow that afflicted Gediel now afflicted her. Some change had come to Zion, a grave and uneasy change. The vision and the girl's words were a warning.

CHAPTER 4

DOMINIC DIPPED HIS FINGERS through the glassy surface of the pool, dragging them in figure eights. It was always the perfect temperature for swimming. Yet the stones around the rim were dry. There was no sign of his wife's presence. She must have gone elsewhere to sulk and avoid her alders. Suddenly a spray of water struck his face. He straightened from his crouch, drying himself with his shirt. The naiades giggled and disappeared below the surface. She was lucky, because he would have torn her from the pool and duly taught her better manners.

Trying to temper his mood, Dominic looked across the moonlit meadow. A flash of white appeared in the tall grass near the southern tree line. A flock of ground-burrowing owls batted their wings and took to other places in reaction to the wolf. Hands on his hips, Dominic frowned. If he moved quickly, he might catch them. Then again, he might catch a lioness's wrath, or the mighty jaws of her companion. Wisdom suggested he call on his guardian for help, though Luthias would be long in getting there, and he was a pushover for Maiel. He would take her side like a smitten swain. In his eyes, she could do no wrong. He wasn't sure he wanted to listen to the fun the guardian would have at his expense.

Dominic walked through the tall grass, holding the leaping white wolf in his sight. A cool breeze came over the trees and dipped into the meadow, sending a shudder through the clearing like an ocean wave. As he drew closer, he saw the top of Maiel's crimson head as she knelt over something. He closed the distance between them. There, the gentle whines of a wolf reached his ears.

Shee lay in the grass, while Maiel gently arranged some dark bundles along her belly. His wife stroked her companion's side and whispered encouragingly.

"That's a good amba, Shee. Just rest, they'll come when they're ready," Maiel said.

"The puppies are coming?" Dominic said, announcing his presence.

"I'm sorry I left like that. Just sometimes it's better to be left alone, before you say something you'll regret," Maiel said, after a moment.

"I should be the one apologizing," Dominic said. Her expression didn't alter. He added, "I shouldn't have pushed."

Shee whined and licked her hindquarters. Another puppy was on its way.

"How many?" Dominic asked as Maiel moved to help her friend birth the next pup.

"Five, so far," Maiel answered. She wouldn't look at him. "You didn't bring Luthias?"

"No. He would only help you."

The puppies lay on the shredded skirt of her gown. Maiel's bare knees rested on the thick grass. His wife was always selfless like that, using whatever it took to comfort another, regardless of the discomfort to her. She would say: it will mend; and mend it would. She bore no thought to how or why or even when. She just knew that all things would mend if she gave her time and love to another. His lips curled in a smile. Still, she could be stubborn. After all, she still expected him to mend.

"Your family is back at the house," Dominic said.

"It was only a matter of time," Maiel quietly replied.

Shee whined and turned to cleaning her new children. Maiel petted her and whispered encouragingly. She seemed rather calm or was wholly focused on helping the little mother. That was also much like her, very soft for the females and their young ones. He guessed that was only natural, being a mother herself and so dearly loyal. Yet it was something that had begun well before he was her suitor or their first child was born.

"There you go," Maiel said.

Shee struggled for a moment and then Maiel came away with a handful of wet fur. She set the pup with the others. A few strokes and assurances later, Maiel turned her intense gaze on him. The ring of shimmering cobalt pierced his heart.

"Did they say what they wanted?" she asked.

"Same as I told you before," Dominic replied, feeling stripped bare.

"And if I go to the alders?"

"They only said they've grown impatient."

Maiel stared at him and lost her confidence once more. Dominic tried to smile but the attempt faltered. He'd only once seen her afraid: after an incarnation that seemed to be rife with interference from the dark dwellers,

Maiel cut the thread that linked her to the mortal form by the strike of her own hand. The act was so abhorrent to her being that she created a prison and cast herself into the Pit of Acheron to pay for what she felt was a grievous sin. Unfortunately for all of them, Acheron was the home of a deranged shadowalker, the Baron Morgentus. The demon had instantly grown smitten with her and endeavored to keep her. Her move to submit herself to his punishment made him believe that she belonged to him. The prison was strong and it would have served Morgentus's plan well, yet Maiel's love and loyalty to the light was stronger. She escaped the clutches of her would-be jailer and returned home. Maiel hadn't been the same since. He'd mishandled their agreement. He knew she believed that, too. Regardless, they would return to Samsara to continue his path, endangering them both to prove he was worthy of rising.

Dominic was sure everyone blamed him for what had happened, though they pretended otherwise. They celebrated him as a hero, claiming his voice alone had called her back to them. Perhaps it had. He told himself it had, with the pride of a Roman pugilist. He soon realized that the timbre of his voice was nothing compared to the seed of light kept within her heart. She would have dug herself out without him. That was a notion he'd gotten familiar with, so was the notion that he'd stained her very being. She struggled because of him. He couldn't help but wonder if he was needed at all. It was his actions that had brought her to the act of surrender. Had he listened and waited until he was called up by the draft board, their plans would have played out correctly. Instead, he ignored his better judgment and satisfied the desires of the man he pretended to be, altering his whole path and those of many others. His children suffered as well, in too many ways to consider.

"Well, there seems nothing for it."

"Maybe it's just about the coming incarnation," Dominic said.

Maiel's eyes narrowed.

"Because it's always about you."

"It's not always about me. You'll be going with me and have plans of your own," Dominic said, trying to keep the argument contained.

Maiel returned her attention to Shee, who struggled to deliver another puppy. In a few moments, seven puppies lay along her belly. Shee carefully cleaned them and Maiel stroked her back. Dominic could tell by her expression that the conversation should not continue. However, he had come to fetch her back home and let her family convince her to go to the alders. Eventually, she would have to and he saw no sense in delaying matters.

"Doll Face, I'm sorry," he said.

"For?"

"Making it appear that I'm only concerned with myself. I'm sorry for that."

"Dominic," Maiel breathed. "We have children to think of now. Ian has grown restless with his position, rejected by the legions. Sam has watched these many years and it has made him melancholy. It's time you move forward, if rising is what you intend. You need to focus for their sake."

"I have focused. You just think this should be easy for me. I'm not you. I'm human," Dominic replied, with a sharp edge.

"I only expect what you're capable of," Maiel replied.

"Maybe you're wrong," Dominic countered.

Maiel glared at him over her nose. To call a captain of Mikhael's legion wrong was a serious misstep. They were never wrong. He wished they could be, even if just once. That was what gnawed so deeply. They knew what he was actually capable of, and they set him up for failure each time. They wanted to prove Adonai wrong, a very brave thing to do, but it would end in their shame and exile. He wondered what the alders were up to, to risk such possibilities. Did they see Maiel as a casualty of war? One they could spare in preventing humans and duta from mixing? Or was Maiel right and he was just playing at evolving into something greater? Sometimes he was a victim of his own pride and arrogance, yet he wasn't unwilling to admit to himself when he was the cause of his own failures. He opened his mouth and hesitated before he said something else he would regret.

"I'm sorry—I didn't mean that."

"You meant it. You wouldn't have said it."

Maiel walked back toward her pool. Argus took her place, eyeing him with shining gold eyes. A low rumble told Dominic he'd best move on.

"You don't have to protect her from me," Dominic told him, unsure of which female he guarded.

Argus stared. Dominic got to his feet and followed after his wife. He hoped she went home of her own accord to deal with the matter. He called to her but she didn't slow. Her long, bare limbs strode through the tall grass; she was determined to reach the house quickly. Then, suddenly, she turned on her sandals. Her cobalt eyes had transformed to pale gold, like the moon. He stopped and put his hands up to slow her temper. This was going exactly where he didn't want it to go.

"It's not meant to be easy! If it were easy then anyone would be what we are. You were given a chance to achieve the impossible because they believed you could do it. They gave you a guardian who has done it. King Adonai is never specious and neither are the alders. What you're doing— that is misleading. You think it amusing to make us run through hoops for you, to slave and strain while you sit idly by? Do you think wings will just be handed to you, like some ornamentation for a costume ball? Is that all you think we are? Ornaments, perhaps badges of valor? Strutting peacocks? At least you have the strutting down," she blasted.

Maiel stood close to him, staring angrily into his eyes. She stepped back, sighing in frustration, as if she had no idea where the anger came from. The pause let her gather her thoughts or will to express more. Her shoulders slumped and she rubbed her hands along her arms, refusing to look at him.

"I failed Adonai. That's what they want me for. They're concerned I've turned. They should be concerned. I am," Maiel said.

"You didn't fail, Angel. Lena is safe. She's in Otzar," Dominic said.

"You weren't there. You don't know what happened," Maiel said.

Silently gazing into his eyes, Maiel disappeared within herself. The agony reflected in her mien stabbed at his heart. Suddenly, she drew a deep breath, and at last continued.

"Mort distracted me so easily. I was so full of anger. I allowed evil to take me over and I struck him down with no other desire than hate and want. There's no desire I've felt so strongly as I did today."

Dominic smiled. "I can think of a few."

"Does it always come around to that for you, Dominic? You have no idea what this means, do you?" Maiel stared into his eyes. He lowered them from her examination. "You understand nothing but your own desire. You've no empathy. That's why you fail," she added.

Dominic couldn't look away. He was stricken by her words. Her gaze extended past his shoulder, seeing something that silenced her. When her attention was his again, her eyes filled with accusation. The grass shifted in the meadow behind him, though not by the stroke of wind. He looked over his shoulder and saw two figures headed their way. Joel and Zach had decided to join them. None of them had an ounce of faith in him.

"Khata, are you hurt? What's been keeping you?" Joel called.

Joel and his brother quickly drew closer. Dominic clamped his hands on Maiel's arms. He could feel the strain in her muscles as she prepared to run.

"Run with me. We'll figure this out," Dominic said.

"You brought them here?" she accused.

Her flesh burned like ice.

"No. I wouldn't. You know I wouldn't. I came to apologize—to help you, Doll Face. Run with me and I will help you."

"Zaajah brought Lena to the soul keepers," Maiel quickly blurted to the others. Zach looked down his nose at her and she hesitated. "What more could they want of me?"

"The alders are interested in your exchange with Mort. They think there's a plot to invade Zion," Zach finally revealed.

The alarm in Maiel's features was clear and Dominic was sure any moment she would run. Panic rose inside him. He held on just the same. It was his fault, he heard his heart tell him. He would need to make this right, starting then. She slipped like water underneath his hands, but he was still able to hold onto her.

"And I'll attest you need not fear our interview," the matriarch said, her voice heard before she was seen.

Alexandrael swept into view from nowhere. Her sister walked at her side. The pair clasped their hands at their waists and waited. Dominic looked back to his wife. Her eyes were on the dark, distant meadow.

"Are there no doors on my home, no sanctuaries left that you won't intrude upon?"

Maiel tore herself free of Dominic's grip and took a step back. Her brothers eyed her warily. In their haste to corner her and end this chase, the women closed in.

"If you've any pity, leave me in peace. There's no forgiveness for me and there'll be none for you when this has played out," Maiel growled.

Joel grimaced, clamping a hand on his chest. His color paled and he stumbled back. Alex closed in on her daughter, while Zach tried to help Joel to his feet. If Alex placed one hand on her, Maiel would find herself in the halls of Zion before she could say another word. Dominic reached his hand out to her, offering another way out.

"Angel—we can fix this," he said, imploring with his soft, jade eyes.

Maiel bared her teeth. Her broad ruby wings spread wide. Alex halted in shock.

"It's your fault," she growled.

"Give me a chance to fix this," Dominic begged.

"I've given you countless chances," she snapped.

Maiel's form shifted, an ability unique to members of the legion who also held the attributes of future virtues. Her skin grew fur and her wings disappeared inside her back. Her moon-colored eyes peered from the face of a sandy-colored panther. The sentiment expressed in them was no kinder than when they were blue and framed by duta features. She opened her mouth to give a warning call. Her anger was at its apex.

"Mai," Joel called from where he knelt in the grass. "Don't do this," he begged.

Being twins, Joel and Maiel often felt the emotions of the other, especially when they were so intense. Joel's form wavered between the golden duta and the mountain cat. Zach let him go, unable to help.

Dominic took a step forward to end the debacle before it manifested a true tragedy. He offered his hand to his transformed wife, but she stepped backward. Her legs tensed and Dominic knew he had only a few moments to try and stop her. He wrestled with his thoughts and breathed.

"Stay with me," he murmured. "I need you. Think of the children."

Maiel's eyes narrowed, incensed that he used her words. She lowered on her front legs. Her delicate long-fingered hands had become wide, thick paws, capable of tearing skin like paper.

"I'm sorry," Dominic begged, his eyes filling with tears.

The changes since her imprisonment made all of them wonder if she had really left Acheron. Dominic trembled at the idea of her still trapped there, even if only in her mind. It was no place for the erela he loved and his actions had put her there. She was right, but she needed to let him try to fix it.

Maiel bared her great fangs and a horrible sound reverberated from deep inside her throat. Zacharius stepped back, not wishing to be mauled by either sibling. The twins glared at each other with gold eyes and hissed threateningly. Dominic bravely stepped between them. Springing off her haunches, Maiel threw the full weight of her altered sattva against her husband. Dominic toppled to the ground, pinned there as she stood on him. Her eyes stared into his and she gave another call, clearly threatening the others if they came near. After exchanging a few swipes with Joel, she was gone. Her shadowy form leapt across the meadow, disappearing inside the tree line.

"Well," Aunt Magiel said, gasping, deeply affronted by the display.

Dominic rolled onto his stomach to watch the retreat. A flash of white abruptly blocked his view. Argus stood there, the hair on his back standing straight up. He growled low at those watching his mistress disappear into the dark.

"Easy, Argus," Zach said, stepping toward the wolf. "We'll let her be. Go to your mate and care for your pups now."

Argus didn't back away. He didn't appreciate the condescension. He sat on his haunches and watched them intently. Wolves were not dumb souls. On hands and knees, Dominic tried to regain the guardian's trust. Argus jumped up on all four paws and made sure he wouldn't pursue. Dominic slowly stood up, and offered a hand in peace.

"No need to worry, Argus. She's safely away," Dominic said.

Joel gathered himself, shaking his head. Taking in a deep breath, he drew up to his full height and usual form. Zach swung a hand and roughly patted his back. Joel eyed him disapprovingly as he regained his focus.

"That went well," Joel breathed.

Zach raised an eyebrow at his brother's assessment. Dominic grew weary of their intrusion. She would've had her words with him and they could've moved forward. They were always so impatient when it came to their own needs, and it took eons for them to take care of another's. They dawdled and waffled on his status, preparing him in the smallest of increments, as if he were a toddler in need of kid gloves. They seemed to forget that one of their own was in the middle of that. It was no wonder Maiel had lost faith in their way, suffering in the crossfire, as the battle waged between the two sides. Their arrogance in believing they were untouchable in Zion, tucked within the circles of hallowed marble, made them blind to any possible defeat. They chose vocations far from the fields of war, in the grand bureaucracy, never paying the price of their declarations. What did they know of the dark and its tactics? Perhaps they simply didn't care and the whole thing was a game of chess to amuse them. After all, the danava could never penetrate the Avernus; the resonance of their atman barred the way. So, to them, any real threat was barred from Zion.

Dominic shook his head and bitterly told them, "She needs time to heal her heart. You shouldn't have come. The council and Ganesha be damned."

"Those are bold words, coming from a man," Maiel's aunt said.

Alex stepped forward, stilling her sister from further utterance with a soft touch of her hand.

"Yes," Alex said, going to his side. She held her chin high and studied his face a moment. "I often forget my daughter's growing human qualities. It's good to have you to remind us from time to time. We should have waited," she repeated herself from earlier.

"Human qualities. Bah!" Magiel snorted. She turned away from them. "It's a waste of my niece's talent to bandy about with humans. I don't care their reason," she added to no one in particular.

"Check your pride, Matula. You forget he's standing right here," Zach reminded her.

Joel gave a derisive flash of his brilliant smile at his aunt's remark. Dominic grit his teeth, refusing to prove her right in some comment to defend himself. Besides, Zach had said enough. Though he often felt the elder brother cared little for the ketu, he surprised him from time to time by defending him. He reminded himself to make no mistake though, it was for his sister's sake that he did so. He was as bigoted as the rest.

"Ever since her first encounter with you, she's lost all clarity. It was the same when they mistook the child for a god. She panicked, thinking Adonai would be angry that the humans—with help from those blasted shadow-alkers no doubt—spread tales of her deeds as some goddess. It was good, either way, that she hunted down that little atrin, the pervert who disguised himself as a hind to rape unwary girls. The gall some of those dark dwellers have," Magiel said, pursuing her course.

"Joel wasn't much more comfortable being thought of as a god either."

"Actually," Joel said, smiling.

"My khata's love for this man has made her strong. The alders mean to raise her, I'm sure. It's most likely a promotion in the legion, in the very least. It'd be delightful to see her wear a crown, but that's yet far off. At one time you all thought Joel would far outshine Maiel. Now, she surpasses him in becoming a commander under Mikhael's wing. A crown is far off, but not that far off," Zach reminded his aunt.

"From where have you heard this? She's only just celebrated her 5,460th birthday. She's too young yet. It's too soon. What of the children? You think that Dominic can possibly raise them on his own?" Alex said doubtfully.

Dominic rubbed the back of his head, gesturing in frustration; he was invisible as they discussed his wife and their family. He felt a scream building in his core, but he stuffed the rage back down and drew a deep breath to stamp it out. Sometimes, he wished he'd refused the path they insisted he take, as if there were no other choice in his evolution. One way or another, they would have bound them together. That was the fate of bound souls. They sought their echo and couldn't be parted long by other distractions. If only he had insisted on waiting to marry, but then, he never understood that it wasn't a given that he would rise. At present, he labored under the promise, or rather, languished. He was angry because she was right.

"Maiel's left Zion. I can't feel her," Joel said, clearly anxious.

Dominic's gaze narrowed on him. He resented the bond of the twins. It should've been he who'd felt her going. The muscles of his jaw tightened. The matriarchs considered him, just then remembering his presence. They also knew how strange it was that he hadn't announced this development first, that he never declared knowing her feelings as more than an assumption.

"We should bring her back, before Morgentus catches wind of this. He's been waiting for a chance such as this. It'd not shock me to find he's orchestrated the whole thing. Lascivious mudeater!" Joel spoke again.

"Maybe we should ask the Samsaran watchers," Dominic suggested.

"Dear me, no! We best keep this quiet. We don't want to bring shame to our clan," Magiel said.

"There's no shame in expressing emotion or doubt. She's the better for having feelings. Her empathy, at the very least, will vastly improve duta-soul relations. Something you all seem to need a lesson or two in," Dominic countered.

"You've the audacity—" Magiel replied, showing quite a bit of emotion.

"Now's not the time. We should inform the general of this. Perhaps he will retrieve her," Joel said, coming to his rescue.

"I still say we ask the Illuminati, what if the union gets wind of this?" Dominic mumbled to himself and was ignored.

"He'll be in Zion at this hour," Alex said.

"Then to Zion we go," Joel said.

Alex hesitated at the idea. Her sister appeared mildly annoyed, but ultimately she would do whatever the majority decided. Dominic agreed with the brothers, so that gave them the weight they needed. Zach and Joel were wise for their age, but youth gave them a rashness that quickly brought them to the right decision. Too many years of wisdom often led to too many deliberations. Their mother and aunt suffered from this slow progress. They should have replaced the alders with younger members before they found themselves losing another generation to the sulfur pits. In the least, they could temper the boards with youth.

Dominic gasped for air as they came to a sudden stop at the doors of Zion. Sliding might soon become his preferred method of travel, but until then he still needed to get used to its suddenness. It was a hard-won ability for humans that few mastered, as it took a great deal of focus and energy. Without these, the wits could be addled permanently. Dominic shook his head, to counter the spinning, wishing they'd blinked there instead. Joel smiled at him and he realized that there was no pity available, even from friends. Rather, the captain enjoyed ribbing the humans in his assign, like an annoying older brother.

Zach passed ahead of them with the slightest of smiles curling the corner of his usually serious mouth. That was where Joel got it from. Zach had a wicked humor, even if he rarely exercised it before others. Zach perfected his art, likely on Joel, who now took out his childhood angst on others.

"Hurry—this way. The general resides in the upper levels. It will take time to get there." Alex gestured to the group to follow along behind her to the hall.

"We should have gone after her ourselves. I could have gone alone," Dominic said.

"Earth is no place for a soul without flesh to house it, a plan to focus it, and a guardian to guide it. You would be dragged away by a shadowalker before you found her," Magiel said.

"Aunt, I didn't know you cared." Dominic smiled.

Magiel lifted her chin and peered ahead, clamping her lips tightly closed. The insult was felt, but he wasn't sure to what degree.

"Please, no arguing, you'll bring unnecessary attention to us," Alex hissed, worriedly taking note of the Powers who noted them.

The family traversed the endless ways of Zion, struggling to keep their pet human in pace. The ceilings towered beyond sight and light as bright as a sunlit cloud blinded the rest of the expanse. It was never dark inside the lower halls of the citadel, and its light allowed the dwellers of the house to bask in the invigorating glow. As the path continued, the halls narrowed and the vaulting lowered. They passed through a silver gate and entered a hall with a cobalt ceiling dotted by ornamental stars. Lanterns provided extra light from the glow of weakly formed atman. The hall narrowed again and the frescos that covered the walls and the marble reliefs and statuary seemed to observe their every step. Doors made niches ominous, barriers to the unknown apartments of high-ascended duta. More gates framed the meandering passage.

Dominic's worry faded with each step; his strength was returning. His eyes cleared and his thoughts untangled. This was the strangest sensation he had ever known, and he wanted more of it. Unfortunately for him, once Mikhael was apprised of Maiel's defection, he'd be back at home, useless, waiting for others to take care of the problem instead of helping on the front line. He blinked the thought away before the others said something. Maiel said he thought too much of himself and here he did so again, just when she needed him most. She was right about him, more than he was capable of admitting.

Alex led them to the silver doors at the end of the east passage. The light poured in so white it blurred and stung Dominic's vision. Once his eyes adjusted, he saw two principalities in heavy plate, like white chess pieces, guarding the entrance. Dominic's mouth went dry. They didn't move when Alex knocked on the surface to announce their presence. The statuesque duta barely breathed, despite their senses telling them of the urgent matter which brought them to the door. Dominic's eyes swept their reed-thin frames. The guards seemed to emit a silver glow. Solid ebony eyes peered forward, looking at nothing in particular. In one hand, each held a pole arm of ivory and each wore the armor of the general. Dominic tried not to stare, but he rarely saw their kind. Maiel's janya, Gragrafel, ranked among them. Their resonance often kept them tied to the halls of Zion or in the field. In fact, Dominic only recalled seeing the patriarch when the ketu took place and when each of the children were born. Gragrafel stared at him in the same manner and Dominic returned that stare, astounded. Dominic was sure the duta wasn't pleased that his only daughter was bound to a human.

The door to the apartment slowly opened.

"The soul remains here," one of the guards said.

They meant Dominic. His kind was often referred to in that dismissive manner, but not quite in such a trivializing tone. Joel and Zach looked at him, then at each other. They gave a nod to the guards and Dominic felt as though they had both stabbed him in the gut. Alex lingered, as the others moved to the rooms beyond. Dominic expected as much, after all, it was his wife they came there to discuss. Despite him being the only one who understood what had happened, this was how they responded. They never thought he could explain it better than they. He was too simple, too inexperienced, to be a voice of reason. Essentially, he was not evolved.

"I'm Captain Maiel's husband," he informed the guards. They looked vacantly upon him. "I have to speak with Mikhael. She's why we're here. I'm the only one who can make him understand."

"The soul remains here," the guards repeated.

"My name is Dominic. I was a draco of the Sun Order."

"It's regulation," Joel said, returning to him.

"Screw regulation. Maiel needs help. None of you can tell the general her state of mind better than me," Dominic blasted.

"Now he professes to know our minds," Magiel drawled.

"I said her mind. I'd hardly pretend to know such a dark recess as what you call a mind," Dominic growled at her.

"This isn't the place for this," Alex pleaded, standing between them.

Magiel's eyes lit up. She shut her opened mouth when her sister faced her.

"Can you not be lax this once?" Alex begged the guards.

The statues eyed her.

"Well, after all, I'm the wife of Gragrafel and I serve the High Council. Mikhael is her superior and this soul is the captain's husband. For light's sake, he'll be raised soon and serve in the legions once more!" Alexandrael told them.

Their cold eyes shifted toward Dominic. He clamped his jaw shut and stared back. Their racism shocked him in the face of that for which they claimed to stand. Both rage and desperation boiled over and he moved to give them his fists for emphasis. Joel held him back.

"What in Zion goes on out here?" A voice boomed from the doors.

A very tall engel of broad shoulders and thick arms appeared. He stood on two legs that were like sailing masts, fists on his hips. He wore armor in the fashion of the guards, but it seemed more like his skin than dress. A shaggy tousle of golden curls rested on a thin silver circlet. His face was framed in a bronze, close-cropped beard, and the wings on his back were like the feathers of a great peacock's tail. His surly expression shifted over each of them.

"Alex," he said, going to her. "What are you doing here at this hour? Where is my captain? I hear the council still waits. Ganesha is asking me questions I can't answer."

"That is why we're here, Mikhael," Dominic interrupted.

Mikhael set his eyes on Dominic. He squinted, not knowing him. The consideration wasn't accusatory, but it wasn't warm either.

"General," Dominic said, correcting himself and inclining his head.

Mikhael nodded back, still not knowing him.

"I told you no more visitors, souls or otherwise, but I didn't bar my friends," Mikhael told the guardians of his door. He smiled back to them. "They're so literal. I apologize. Where is your wife, son of Newlyn?"

Dominic grimaced. He was blunt and farseeing.

"She's gone to Earth," Joel told him.

"For what? The assignment is over."

"She's run. She's run in fear that you plan to punish her for submitting to her anger," Dominic said, since the others refused.

"Anger? What nonsense is this?" Mikhael rumbled. When none of them replied, he continued, "Mepheus, bring me Gragrafel. I fear this may be worse than our friends let on."

The guard named Mepheus moved to do his commander's bidding. Mikhael halted him, grabbing hold of his forearm.

"Fetch me Primus Gediel from Voil and Uriel. We'll need the watcher's services. You may find him at Fenrir or Elysion," Mikhael whispered. He half smiled, looking back down the halls. "Perhaps in the city," he added.

* * *

Gediel's pale gaze followed alder Alexandrael as she led her family along the east corridor. By their expressions, something went wrong between the time he met with Zaajah and the early risen moon. He felt a ripple in the air that evening, as if a dark storm came over the horizon. Maiel's absence from among them made the clues all the more worrying. The packs had murmured all morning about a new set of puppies due to arrive that night. He hoped that was all that kept her away, just as Zaajah professed. Despite assurances to the contrary, he couldn't be convinced. Such darkness meant great difficulty arrived on their doorstep. Yet it wasn't without a pending sunrise. It held the whispers of hidden truths and healing.

Deciding to follow the family, Gediel eavesdropped to satisfy the curiosity their presence gave him. Information of any kind would be useful. Pricking his ears, he caught Dominic's voice. It was filled with emotion, which wasn't necessarily unusual for humans, who lacked expression control. Considering the circumstances, it troubled Gediel until a tremor ran through his core. When Dominic exploded, it was obvious that he was desperate. Then Gediel sensed something like poison, a jagged tear ripping through his energy. What the soul said gave a small clue to what had transpired, but the poison coursing through him revealed a larger issue. He wasn't rising. The faint embers of a burning were well underway.

Gediel slipped beyond the arched entrance of an adjoining corridor and pressed his back to the marble wall. He only haunted Zion in the hopes of seeing Maiel again when she delivered Lena to the keepers. He hoped, if he stayed for the soul's rising, that he would catch her then. It had been forever since they spoke, but recently something pushed him to renew the friendship. If she ran to the Samsara, then he was too late. Gediel scowled at the hall. Why would she risk herself needlessly in that place? What had they driven her to do?

While Gediel's thoughts sought answers to the many questions, Gediel's gaze slipped to the floor. The polished marble reflected his image, a hazy and shadowed version. He saw the silver glow in his eyes, as he instinctively sought her presence. Calming himself, he drew a deep breath and then pushed off the wall. In the Samsara, she was beyond his immediate reach and he would be detected by the others if he continued. He ran back to the gate and crashed through. Zaajah would know what was wrong, if anyone did. She was as close to her as her children. But, he needed to reach her before Mepheus got to him.

Impatient to learn what he could, Gediel slid to the practice yards inside the Order of Horus, Zaajah's home on the outskirts of Arcadia. Arcadia was the province circling the citadel and mountain of Zion, an area incomprehensibly vast and wide. The border was created by the Urva Ocean on three sides and the Gihon River between it and Zion. With all that said, it took some time to reach his destination. Architecture shifted in styles, the territory identified with each order that built there. As he entered Zaajah's space, sandstone carvings and hieroglyphics marked the architecture. Brilliant blues and reds stained the stones, accented with gold. He crossed through the open entrance and found himself among a number of armored legionae. Their skin hues ranged from pale white to soft red; some had deep black tones with wings of many other shades. Unlike the masses of the Samsara, they weren't segregated by the tones their skins manifested. Still, with silver wings and black armor, Gediel attracted much attention.

The Order of Horus, along with its related orders, had been so remarkable that they and their similar units inspired the souls who remembered them to contrive a society on Earth that reflected the assembly. Unfortunately, the souls poisoned that image with hate and blood, twisted it in the rented minds of their bio-vessels and by the shadows that whispered in their deafened ears. The relics of that inspiration were lost in the sands of an Earth desert thousands of years ago, leaving clues of their real home.

"Wolf Leader—Primus," a member of the legion spoke, easily recognizing him and quickly correcting his salutation. He stepped toward Gediel smiling, and his great sable wings rose in respect. He tucked a gold helm under his arm and offered his brown hand. "What brings us this honor from Fenrir?"

"I've come to speak with Captain Zaajah," Gediel replied.

"She's on the sword field, this way," the milite said, pointing with the helm in his hand.

The soldier led Gediel along a sandstone arcade to a sandy courtyard of palms. In the torch light, two figures circled each other on the sparring square. The milite noticed his hesitation and indicated the way with a reassuring smile. It wasn't that he didn't want to interrupt them. He'd just rather not embarrass her.

"I didn't know you were a friend of Captain Zaajah," he said to Gediel.

"Zaajah's been a friend since she was a youngling. We've parted paths for a time, but it appears those paths are about to cross once more."

"If we can be of any assistance, Primus, I'd be happy to help," he told Gediel, sensing the focus of their guest.

Watchers had the dubious reputation of being dangerous, yet trustworthy to those they served, a contradiction that caused many to confess everything with terrified apprehension brought on by a desperation to save themselves.

"I'll call on you." Gediel nodded.

The stones led to a set of stairs, which then led to the sword ring. It was a large, square stretch of stone overlooking the skyline of orders, with Zion in the far distance. Monkeys slept in the trees; a mother squawked at Gediel for disturbing their rest. Torches burned in the four corners. A worn circle of red marked the center. Gediel waited for Zaajah to notice him and his escort. At this time, she was intent on her opponent, a rather large officio with a two-handed crescent blade. They circled each other, Zaajah keeping her shield between them. She clutched a spear in her other hand, swiftly raising it to strike a blow. She was met with a fast block and was nearly swept off her feet by a swing of the engel's leg. Her dark wings flapped and she saved herself the fall, striking with her foot in return. The pad of her sandal clapped on the engel's wrist. He lost his grip on his blade and she brought down her shield to disarm him completely. In a blur, she struck several blows, ending the match, with her opponent subdued beneath her, a knee in his back and the spear pole tight against his throat. She flashed a grin and laughed. Kissing the top of his black head, she released him.

"Captain—Evocati Ibajah," Gediel's escort called. He grinned delightedly over what he saw.

"Strike that grin, milite, why do you disturb us?" Zaajah said, before her gaze caught sight of their guest. Her angry features softened. "Gediel—what brings you to our nest?"

"I have questions about a friend of ours," Gediel said, stepping toward her.

"Ibajah, take the draco for spear training. Make sure he's not smiling when you finish," Zaajah said without taking her eyes off her guest.

"Yes, Captain," Ibajah replied, bowing his head and then rushed to do her bidding.

A very young erela dashed onto the square and took the weapons away. Her yellow wings were still growing out and she looked barely of age to be in one of the regiments, but that explained her menial duty. Younglings started low and worked their way up the ranks very slowly. They needed to grow strong, able to hold the weapons they looked after, before they could use them in battle. She looked to him, her face melting into that of a chee-tah. She hissed and then struggled to hurry away. Gediel watched her go, amused by both her outburst and lack of strength. Zaajah shook her head. As the spoiled daughter of a high official, the girl was giving her more trouble by being rude to her ranking officios.

"You've come to ask me about Maiel? Who sent you?" Zaajah commanded his attention.

"I sent myself. I overheard her husband and the others talking in the halls of Zion. They said she went back to Earth. I want to know what you know of this. Since you lied to me earlier," Gediel explained.

"I didn't lie to you. I don't know anything more than I shared and you shouldn't be asking, watcher, unless there's a trial to be convened," Zaajah said frankly, growing more suspicious of his motives.

"You want me to believe that?"

"It's the truth."

"I'm not one of your commanders, Zaajah. I work outside of Uriel's ranks and you know I don't report often, even to Voil. I swear to you, Horus won't hear what you have to say. If Maiel has run to Samsara, I need to know why. It's not safe. Samsara is vast and wasting time could be dangerous. Can I trust she went to Earth?" Gediel said.

Zaajah frowned. Her attention slipped to the space behind his head. To give him what he wanted was a betrayal of her friend's trust.

"If you know anything, it would only help to share it with me," Gediel pushed.

Zaajah's almond eyes swept back to his. She held his gaze for several tense moments. They reported to the same legion general. There was no doubt he was just completing orders. If he wasn't, she could not bear to think of the consequences.

"How did you really find out? Did Luthias tell you?"

"I overheard. I swear." Gediel placed his hand on his breast.

"You're sure she's gone? Have you spoken with Bade or Callidora?"

Gediel nodded and then shook his head. A watcher kept his questions few and went to the source least likely to betray the mission.

Zaajah moved toward the edge of the sparring square, where several falcons roosted, asleep beneath leather caps. He followed, not giving up. Her gaze cast over the city; she was still reluctant to speak what was in her thoughts. The struggle crossed her features as she pushed her chin down. Zaajah shut her eyes. He couldn't track her on his own without opening a door that wouldn't close. Worse, a certain prince stood to gain ground from this event, something that should have raised alarm for the captain. Going to the falcons, Zaajah cooed one awake and brought it to perch on her elegant hand. Whispering to her feathered friend, Zaajah thought further on Gediel's request, weighing the consequences.

"You're right," Zaajah breathed. "She's gone. I feel just a twinkling."

"Where is she?"

"I can't be sure," Zaajah answered, staring into nothing. "Wait. Maybe—I think she's returned to Lena's home."

Zaajah was angry with him for making her share that information.

"Why would she return?" he asked.

"I can't share with you what I don't know. If you want the answer, you'll need to ask her yourself. Perhaps Dominic's guardian will know. Perhaps Cal."

Zaajah eyed him. A question was on the tip of her tongue, but she feared digging too deeply.

"Do you know why they wouldn't involve the outposts in Lena's extraction?"

Gediel's scowl deepened. She knew something, but refused to share it with him. He shook his head at her question. Lena's importance should have had Illuminati extraction as part of the mission. The council played a dangerous game with Maiel, sending her alone.

"Captain!"

The voice stopped their conversation. They watched Ibajah return with a most unexpected companion. Mikhael's guard Mepheus stepped up to the platform in two strides. His glowing skin cast a cool light, contrasting with the warmth of the torches.

"I am Mepheus. Mikhael has sent me to summon you to Zion, Primus," Mepheus said, staring hard at Gediel.

Gediel's gaze switched between them. How had this principality discovered his location? He'd left no trace. Guarding his unease, he gave a quick nod. To Zaajah, he offered a glance that said their interview wasn't over. The erela crossed her arms and stared back. Accompanying Mepheus, he left to do as bid. In the least, Mikhael would have answers and it looked like he was bringing him in to assist. For Maiel, the clock wound down and he wasn't about to waste her time by arguing with Zaajah or the principality over who had more right to recover the captain.

CHAPTER 5

DOMINIC OBSERVED THE ODD surroundings from one of several chaises set inside the circular antechamber of Mikhael's home. A pair of griffins lay before the inner apartment doors, snuggled together, their fierce natures less threatening as they dozed. His wife's family settled on the other furniture that was scattered along one portion of the arc. They hadn't spoken a word since they passed the gate. There was little else inside the space for their comfort or distraction. It was marble, end to end, with metal fixtures, a style hard and cold and entirely Mikhael. On the far edge of the circle, directly across from the door they'd entered, was a second set of silver doors leading to the general's home. Glistening candelabra stood in the deep alcoves, each framed by a pair of pillars. A chandelier hung above their heads, scattering the light as it spilled down from the open dome beyond with its dangling crystals. The room was made of the same white marble as the rest of Zion, but the center of the floor was blue marble outlined in a ring of silver. Dominic stared at the sterile space, reminded of his wife's shield. His eyes traced and retraced the circle. The room felt vast and lonely, very much the reflection of his inner emotions and regrets. He leaned back and stared at the sky-toned scallops of the dome, the white trim, and the sparkling light.

The door they entered through opened again, stirring the griffins and making them complain. Gragrafel led the way and the griffins backed down. The principality was an intimidating figure despite his lack of armor and weapons, like a storybook rendition of Zeus: curled white hair, rolled white beard, and the required white robes. His expression was hard as stone while his penetrating black gaze swept over his family, lingering most disapprovingly on the soul. Behind the patriarch entered a ghost from the past. Though expected, Dominic's anger leapt up at Gediel's actual appearance. The circlet of rank glinted, mocking Dominic's want of position. Even Gediel, with his horrible past, was capable of rising. The primus's past friendship with Maiel was not something Dominic took lightly. He'd known for a long time that the svarg gave Argus to Maiel. That wolf was a gift she prized above all others. They were friends for most of his wife's youngling days, but Gediel all but disappeared into his duty sometime around Dominic's appearance in her life. It was rumored that if Dominic hadn't gotten mixed up in the business of the duta, Gediel would have been Maiel's ketu. Gediel's fame was known throughout Zion, especially with the unwed females, all of whom hoped to capture his attention. Unfortunately, Gediel never settled down, probably afraid to produce progeny like his grandsire, certain he was bent on the path of the same or worse crimes.

Dominic cupped his head in his hands. His adolescent jealousies wouldn't help Maiel. After all, Gediel had stayed away all these years and Maiel rarely mentioned him. It was hardly her fault that she cared so much for Argus. The watcher and his wife had parted ways and there was no longer an attachment there. Dominic told himself Gediel was present because of his reputation as a scout, but that suggested Luthias should have been included. No one thought to call the guardian. His anger raged and his suspicion deepened.

Dominic's most dangerous suspicion was that other rumors surrounding the primus weren't just stories, and that the watcher was bitten by the shadow whose name he bore. He tried his best to disguise his thoughts, as he felt the pinch and twist in his features, before one of the duta decided to prod him. To help, he turned to thinking of Maiel's commander and second-in-command. They weren't asked to attend the meeting either, nor was Captain Zaajah, her incarnation's guardian, best friend, and compatriot on the mission. With their absence, Luthias being overlooked didn't seem quite so odd. However, it returned him to the petty jealousies. The alders may have reached out to the primus to guide Maiel out of a downward spiral, suggesting Dominic was deemed incapable and that his rival was being neatly positioned to steal his wife.

"General Mikhael," Gragrafel said. "You summoned me."

"Indeed, Alder Gragrafel," Mikhael said, with a voice steeped in reverence.

Mikhael clamped his hand on Gragrafel's forearm and the gesture was returned.

"It's regrettable to have to meet under such circumstances," the general added.

"There are no regrets, only experiences from which to learn." The patriarch smiled.

Gediel wandered to an alcove and leaned on a pillar missed by all but the human. The griffins drew to him, rubbing their heads on his knees. He seemed uneasy there. It was no wonder, for he was dressed in black from head to foot like some chieftain of Jahannam. His clothes looked similar to the hellspawn who'd tortured his wife. Dominic watched him from under a lowered brow, careful not to be caught staring, as the primus studied each of them. That was his specialty: observation and analysis. He served the sect that caused the issues in Samsara and split the duta in twain. Dominic disliked him more for his seedy vocation.

Gediel folded his arms and frowned, near to turning his gaze on Dominic. Instead, Mikhael urged Gragrafel toward Alex and blocked the view. The general didn't acknowledge the primus either. Instead he addressed the reason for their summons. Dominic frowned deeply, an expression that grew increasingly severe with every word spoken. His heart awaited their accusations and his guilt stabbed his gut. While they wasted their time in conference, they left Maiel to the whims of the dark forces able to access Samsara. Was she safe or had the baron taken her? The threat of the baron quickly pushed out the Wolf Leader. In Jahannam, it was feasible to keep her for eons.

"The danava make another move on our gates. They think to cut their losses by attacking the assigns of our guardians and preventing the rise of targeted souls and duta in the process. If they can break our ranks—then no one stands between us and Adonai. This makes the direct links very vulnerable. That was the reason for taking Gamael and then targeting Maiel." Mikhael paused, letting the severity of their situation sink in. "It's true the king can handle the worst they offer, but that means destroying everything he and the Jñanasattva worked for. They would have to start from nothing again. We don't want that."

"We failed to consider Maiel as a target and that her attachment to Lena or her other assigns could be manipulated to push her over to them," Alex said.

"Indeed this isn't her failure," Magiel added, putting the blame squarely on the council who gave her assignments.

Dominic's face twisted. To him, blame lay elsewhere, though the council certainly didn't help matters. The missions and incarnations distracted from the real culprit, when it should have boldly pointed to Dominic After all, it was the very incarnations to assist him which provided the means for Maiel to decline. Cycles in Samsara had a way of wearing out an atman, and made emotions uncontrollable imps in the mind. Those imps were the inlets of shadows.

"No."

The word hung there, resonating through the marble and silencing the others. Eyes shifted to him and he thought he would be able to explain the interjection. He lowered his gaze and swallowed. A dry bitterness filled his mouth and burned his throat. For Maiel's sake, he needed to say this.

"I'm to blame. Both my pride and failure prolonged the process—for too long. She never should have submitted herself to it. It was always my path, not hers, and I was too stupid to recognize it and make her stop," he insisted.

Gediel raised his chin. His mouth made a hard line and his eyes narrowed. That scowl agreed with every word Dominic spoke. Dominic returned the gaze, sensing the same resentment that he felt, aimed at him from the Watcher's end as well.

The silence of the others spoke volumes; there was universal agreement. He imagined Magiel's features twisted up to rival the self-proclaimed king of Jahannam. From the corner of his eye, he saw Alex touch her sister's arm. The silence lengthened and Gediel quietly snickered to himself, returning Dominic's attention to that section of the circle. His eyes bored through the Watcher, but Gediel was hardly threatened.

Magiel walked a very fine line that some saw as opposing Adonai's designs and should have seen her exiled to Jahannam. The only thing that saved her was her love of her niece's children, respect to her duty, and fair treatment of the souls she dealt directly with. She wasn't warm and fuzzy with those souls, but she'd proved more than once that she would sacrifice herself to save them. The majority of duta behaved so. Sometimes, Dominic hoped it was just a defense mechanism, a way to protect herself from what she saw as the inevitable failure he faced. Other times, he saw the erela's desire to watch over her niece not just as a protective reaction toward his influence, but as real hatred of what he was. Her hardness was intended to keep him in line and remind him that someone always watched. She believed he was dangerous and certain to consume Maiel.

"That too would be our fault," Magiel said, offhandedly defending him. Better than nothing.

Gediel folded his arms, still considering him. The spy picked his mind, stepping through his memories like a ghost. After milite service and his long years of traveling between the worlds, he at least learned how to shut them out. Dominic snapped up a barrier, shoving the primus out of his mind. Gediel raised a brow.

"Oh, Dominic. We blame the dark dweller responsible for this trickery, our blindness to her needs, but not you," Alex said, surprisingly reassuring.

Gragrafel patiently waited for them to press forward on the issue, unconcerned that they wasted time pointing fingers while his daughter gallivanted through Samsara. Only the king knew what planet, as she faced untold dangers. He was reminded quickly of her imprisonment.

"It's Morgentus again—isn't it?" Dominic asked.

"No doubt," Joel seconded.

"If that's the case, we have greater worries. Morgentus is owned by the Acherite Prince, Belial. No doubt he holds the dog's leash." Mikhael almost grinned. His eyes sparkled with a strange anticipatory joy.

"Belial? But—he'll break her."

Dominic paled.

"Not bloody likely—he believes he can turn her, and then he'll have weakened me. He needs her to fall, convinced her absence will cripple the legion. He's right that Callidora isn't yet ready to lead them. He forgets Maiel is only one captain in one Order. There are three other legions behind mine, filled with hundreds of Orders. He needs a better plan," Mikhael said, wryly smiling.

Hubris was a pesky matter that brought down mountains. The idea was ludicrous, but exactly what the danava would try. There must be some other attachment they suspected through which the result would be devastating. It was no secret that the other races, thriving in Samsara, had turned a violent eye to Earth. They thought to stem the tide of shadowalkers entering that world through the opened gates by destroying the planet. Relentless, the danava strove to break the barriers and the duta strove to protect humanity's gift. The greatest effort by the shades had been wrought against Earth, beginning over a millennium ago. They had hoped to conquer it and then use the spoils to take the rest of Samsara, employing a great legion of sattva to do their bidding, and that bidding was to tear down Zion. Other worlds stood in line to fall, but none so threatening as the campaign against Earth. A few stood bold against the fall, like a Samsaran legion led by the remaining Samsara watchers. Outposts of the legion called Illuminati were dotted across Earth as well, each bound to the United Watcher Orders of Samsara, a faction that oversaw soul interests in that middle realm. It always seemed to lead back to the watchers, whether they were a union beyond the khajala or shadowy outliers in the distances of Elysion.

Dominic imagined Maiel serving the princes, defying her very nature, let alone friends and family. More than regret, panic or anger would be required to make her fall. Yet the pit of his stomach still turned over with disgust. The existence of the princes proved that she could be undone. If they succeeded, Maiel would make a terrifying enemy. Dominic trembled at the realization he had done nothing but help them. Guilt mixed with fear and made a cocktail that burned his throat.

"Forgive my doubt, General, but I find it very easy for you to say so. Adonai created you to fight the princes, not my wife," Dominic said.

Mikhael stifled a laugh. Dominic didn't see what was amusing in his words. The schools all taught the prophecy that Mikhael would face the princes in battle on the final days of Trailokya. At his side, the other generals would strike deciding blows. When Samsara ceased, it would obliterate the shadows and they and all their kind would be gone from existence forever, crushed in Oblivion. His wife wasn't among the names in the legend.

Alexandrael touched Dominic's shoulder. Her black eyes sparkled as he stared in wonder at how well she crept up without him knowing. She pitied him. At least that benign expression she wore intimated pity.

"Adonai made my daughter to battle the danava, as every duta is made. The lore you speak of is an exaggerated bedtime story. I believe Zacharius is right in saying that this is a test of Maiel's will. In fact, it may be a test of yours; your chance to prove yourself. First, we must consult with the council, for our intrusion may not be allowed," Alex said. The silence returned and Alex was compelled to add, "If I'm wrong, then we must have faith Maiel will return to her senses and to us."

"My only care is that the United Watchers will view this as a major breach and enough cause to decimate Earth," Mikhael said.

Dominic drew a deep breath, casting his eyes to the sapphire floor. Pressure built inside and around him. He swallowed, trying to digest Alex's words. This was his last chance to prove them all wrong and earn his place. What did that mean? If they watched him, how he went about reclaiming his wife mattered. He shouldn't consider the consequences for whatever actions he took to get her back, but he couldn't keep from worrying about how he would be perceived. Regardless of anything else, he must bring her home. None of them factored into the matter; they were just a means to an end: regaining his wife and preserving his favorite planet. Was that right or wrong? A tickle in his throat made his eyes water.

"In the meantime, we should gather our forces," Gragrafel said. He paused for them to wake from their thoughts. "Find Zaajah. She's the clearest head among you and will be the most help with my daughter. Her Order is one of the oldest and most tested. They're also the least likely to mind going against council orders—you best tell your wife you won't be home for some time," he instructed his younger son.

Joel nodded. Gediel bid his farewell to the griffins, encouraging them back to their posts at Mikhael's door. He then stepped toward the others. They seemed to have settled their plans without the need of him. Dominic fought the smirk of delight forming on his lips. He didn't want to be caught reveling in the primus's exclusion of him. Allowing Gediel to see him would only exacerbate the problem.

Gediel was about to excuse himself when Alex doled out more instructions that caused the primus to pause from his retreat.

"Magiel, we must keep the council apprised of everything and see that they provide what's required if they grant a rescue. Can you serve us as messenger?" Alex addressed her sister.

Magiel inclined her head, agreeing to the task. The job suited her well. She was utterly domineering and unafraid of speaking her mind, both qualities required for working in the councils.

"Zacharius, go prepare the children for an extended stay. They'll be safest with their jyoti behind these walls while we deal with this matter."

Gragrafel circled behind Gediel and placed his hand on the younger duta's shoulder. He stood beside the Watcher, waiting for his wife to finish speaking. His gesture was an effort meant to hold the Watcher there until Alex noticed him again, before Gediel escaped without an assignment. The gesture was also one Gragrafel never wasted on his son-in-law. The snub made Dominic's sattva pulse, like when his bio-vessel's blood pressure heightened, and his dry throat burned.

"Oh—Gediel," Alex noticed him. She smiled apologetically. "Can you go with my son and bring Argus back with the children? Your commanders don't have need of you right this instance, I hope?"

A protest rose from Dominic, but words failed him. The intense emotions raging through him were converging. Not to be asked to prepare his children or the wolves, when it was his home, was the final pebble to break the back of his carefully constructed calm. His children could use an explanation before their pitr whisked them away in the night. The watcher, most of all, had no business near the house or children. Sweeping his gaze over them, he saw that the move was carefully calculated, perhaps by conniving alders intent on destroying a ketu they despised.

"Of course. General Uriel won't miss me, but Voil may have a concern. I'll speak with him," Gediel replied, casting a quick glance at Dominic. "Should someone pay a visit to her Order? I'm sure Bade and Cal will both be awaiting word."

Gragrafel nodded. "Someone should."

"Argus won't come," Dominic said, finally able to speak.

"Why wouldn't he? Argus is familiar with Gediel," Alex said.

"Shee just birthed the litter," Dominic said, contemptuously.

"Maiel will need both of them," Joel said.

"I have females that will care for the newborns while their pitarau are away. You need not worry. Argus and Shee will both return with me."

"If anything happens to those puppies," Dominic warned.

"Maiel and you can rest assured, nothing will happen to the litter. We're not on Earth. They'll find my packs very welcoming."

Dominic held Gediel's stalwart gaze for several intense moments.

"Mikhael, do try to track down Evocati Luthias. I hate to see Dominic without his guide at this time," Alex added, maneuvering the group's attention away from the tension.

Mikhael nodded.

"I'll speak with Gabriel about his service."

Dominic relaxed a little. With Luthias at his side, he'd bring her back by dawn. Then the councils and her family would know his worth.

"Good. I go now to inform Ganesha and the High Council of this disaster." Gragrafel smiled, patting Gediel's shoulder. "Alex, Dominic, with me. The rest of you, work quickly. The council may already know and have made a decision. If we're already at work, they might grant us the right to continue."

Dominic nodded, unconvinced his presence before the High Council was necessary, but suspected his absence from the search was key to whatever they really planned. The Council would decide without the consideration of attachments and emotions, just as Gragrafel said. Dragging business like this to Metatron's table imperiled the mission. Metatron enjoyed great privilege with his crucial duties. The seraph was second to Adonai and kept company with the king. Because of this, the supreme councilor's empathy might be lacking, after so many generations of rigid control and because of the disturbingly wide view he held. Zion rarely saw their leader, though his presence was constantly among them, casting light on their days. Dominic couldn't imagine Metatron stooping to help with their trivial adversity.

The idea of being near the leaders of their world was more than Dominic could bear. Each member could decide to make his life hell on a whim. They should have just torn through Avernus and snatched her back. Even reaching out to the outposts was less likely to cause such a stir. Maiel was just letting off a bit of steam and would be of no real trouble. It seemed to him rather dramatic to roll out some extensive plan to capture her.

Gragrafel led the way from the general's apartments and Dominic's eyes met Gediel's again. The Wolf Leader smirked, having prodded his way past Dominic's mind barrier. Dominic returned the expression with a flat stare. He slammed the Watcher out of his thoughts once more and pursued his in-laws to the higher halls.

*   *   *

Joel passed through the gates of Horus. The practice yards were quiet and the torches burned, lighting the desolate space. The members of the regiment he sought would be resting or in meditation, some even recharging from over-spending their energies. Due to the late hour, Zaajah was likely to be in her company's library studying for Maiel's coming incarnation. Several volumes laid out the history of Earth as experienced by members of the Order, and their perusal had become something of an obsession with her. Since she undertook the duty of guardianship over her closest friend, she believed the research could help, even though she was forbidden from directly interfering. Zaajah would allow no other duta to watch over his khata.

Instead of finding Zaajah in the usual spaces, Joel discovered the captain in the small sword yard at the back of her company's barracks. She stared over the city, lost in thought, with her favorite falcon asleep on her bronze shoulder. Joel followed her gaze to an obelisk that stood at the center of a black pool, next to which torches, braziers, and lamps burned an orange light. She wasn't really thinking of the obelisk, or her barracks, not even the pyramids of the commanders. Zaajah's helmet rested at her feet, atop her discarded blade. She wore her simple linen tunic, fixed at the waist with a gold girdle. Her braids hung loose over her shoulders, instead of tied back. She'd intended to go to bed, but strayed from the idea to stand in the night where she thought she could figure out the answer. Joel went to her and waited for a word.

"It seems so strange—you coming here without her," Zaajah murmured, contemplating the permanence of such an arrangement.

Tears swam in her dark eyes.

"I thought surely she was next to rise. This is terrible. Cal isn't ready to accept the post," Zaajah continued.

"Zaajah—it's terrible what happened, but that doesn't mean she's lost." Joel smiled reassuringly.

"Lena requires more training—the keepers told me when I brought her to Otzar," Zaajah said, facing him. Her hand absently stroked the scarab in the center of her chest. "I should have known. Maiel doesn't overreact. What did Mikhael say? Did they rescind her command?"

Joel shook his head and laughed. Zaajah's large dark eyes held a poignant pain that made him feel uncertain. Everyone seemed to have their doubts and that darkened his sunny disposition. Joel placed his hand on her shoulder and tried to cheer her with another of his smiles. Zaajah drew a worried breath, not eased in the least, and turned back to her view of Arcadia. The sun had just about finished setting, leaving the sky indigo and orchid. Towers and rooftops made a strange seascape dotted by motorized marine life.

"I feel her changing," Zaajah spoke again, placing the bird back on his perch and hooding him.

"We knew the dangers of her incarnating. Yet Mikhael keeps faith in his captain. This may be a final push before Dominic's granted a rising," Joel finally answered her question.

"Has anyone called Luthias to see his perspective on this? What of Bade? He knows his captain well. Shouldn't someone consult with him?"

"Mikhael goes to Gabriel now. Gediel will deal with the Moon Order."

"Cal will be most unwelcoming to him."

Joel crossed his arms and stared at the intricate design of his bracers. He didn't want to think about his khata in Samsara alone or that the danava had possibly outsmarted them. There were other duta on Earth, but none powerful enough or near enough to help their lost khata. All the shadows would be on watch, waiting for a chance to strike at her. She was a mighty fighter, but against a mob of the mudeaters, she would lose. Then they would drag her to the labyrinth and imprison her in the dark again. Morgentus would torture her and they would be unable to heal those wounds. He hoped Zaajah was wrong and the others wouldn't risk Maiel's fate over petty differences.

"How could Mort convince her she'd failed the soul?" Joel wondered aloud. There was no answer to be had from Zaajah. "There must be more to this than we're seeing."

"That is what I'm thinking, especially when the outposts didn't involve themselves in the girl's transition. It must be the last test. There's no other explanation for making us go alone. The final journey won't be easy," Zaajah said, pressing her hand against her stomach.

"She makes it as easy or difficult as she sees fit," Joel said.

"Our Maiel will be very hard on him." Zaajah smiled through her sadness.

"She wouldn't be our Maiel any other way," Joel said.

Zaajah quietly smiled and organized her thoughts. The perpetual light inspired, raining from the atmosphere onto the tip of Mount Zion. The glow spilled over the citadel and island. The light penetrated every crevice, a silver glow between the tall towers and buildings, causing strange, long shadows. The moon called down to them; it missed her guardian.

"Where is Dominic?" Zaajah asked, noticing Joel's gaze.

"He went with my pitarau to speak before the council. I'm to bring you to Zion as we prepare to retrieve my khata."

"They foresee a battle? The Order of Horus is at your disposal," Zaajah said.

Zaajah activated her penannular, and took up her sword and helm.

"Let's hope it doesn't come to that." Joel grimaced.

"I must brief Ibajah before we go," Zaajah said, turning away.

"How is the old engel?" Joel grinned.

"Come see him for yourself if you must know," Zaajah replied.

"You're as bad as Maiel." Joel followed her from the raised platform. "I remember her being as excited about her ketu."

"What do you mean?" Zaajah asked, pretending not to know.

"Zaajah—everyone knows how you feel about each other," Joel said.

"Everyone should mind their own business."

"They're just happy for you."

"Happy to be nosing about another's business." Zaajah gave him a side-long look. They stepped along the arcade, falling into silence. "I won't be bound to another before my duty to Maiel is completed. She needs me and my time is spent filling that need."

"Well," Joel said, sighing, "she's already married. You're wasting your time."

Zaajah swatted him with the back of her hand. "Why must you boys always say such things? If it were true, none of this would have happened. That's certain."

"Because it gets a delightful rise from you ladies," Joel admitted, tucking his hands behind his back. "And you won't put your hands on me any other way."

Zaajah smiled and her eyes brightened. These khata were bonded by stronger stuff than family.

"Infuriating beast. Do I need to have a talk with Corabael?" Zaajah mumbled.

"I can love you as well," Joel replied. She shook her head, but he persisted. "Is there no hope for me and you anymore? I'm sure Cora can accept a khata ketu."

Zaajah clucked her tongue and refused to answer. She led him into the hall. He heard the soft murmur of conversations. A few younglings sat beside the door, waiting for instructions. A cheetah lazed before the fire, rolling her tail up and down. A sparkling gold Horus penannular hung about her neck on a thick gold collar. The warmth of sleeping hounds surrounded her. Braziers burned, casting a soft orange glow through the stone expanse. He followed the mistress of the order toward the end and to a much brighter room. There they found Ibajah and several others.

"Captain Joel! It's been too long," Ibajah said, welcoming him.

"How are you, Evocati?" Joel asked.

"Well. Very well." Ibajah's eyes almost went to his captain.

Joel grinned, glad to have the distraction from the tragedy that befell them. He waited for Zaajah to explain the situation to her second-in-command. She then excused herself to fetch something from her apartments. Once she had gone, Joel turned the conversation to lighter topics.

"Congratulations," Joel said to Ibajah.

The officio was confused by his words.

"The ketu," Joel clarified.

Ibajah laughed deep in his throat. His eyes sparkled with the light of stars.

"Not yet, my friend. She won't have it while her khata is in transition," Ibajah said.

"You've let my khata stop you?"

"I don't dare fight that firebrand for Zaajah's attention. Coming between them is the deadliest thing an engel can do, no matter how desirable that image may be."

"Mind yourself. You speak of my khata."

"Mind yourself. You speak of my captain."

The engels postured but quickly fell to laughter.

The smile on Joel's face faded as memories of his friendship with Dominic rattled about his mind. They'd been close once, too. He thought he knew him, at least knew his strengths and weaknesses, and what it would take to adorn his back with wings or cast him into Sheol until the end. What he didn't know was why Dominic was so reluctant to achieve his highest potential, and why he was so willing to risk his wife in the effort. Perhaps it should've been he that played guardian and not Luthias. He knew him better than anyone, even that engel.

"You shouldn't worry," Ibajah told him, clapping a large, strong hand on his shoulder. "She'll return, stronger than ever."

"Sometimes my view's clouded by my vantage," Joel said. "I'm not assured this'll be overcome."

Zaajah returned to the men at this moment.

"Make no mistake," Zaajah said. "I'll hunt her down and bring her back myself, even if she's become Lucifer's whore. They know not who they're meddling with."

"See," Ibajah said grinning, "the deadliest thing an engel could do."

"Let's hope so." Joel grimaced.

"Stay safe," Ibajah told her. "Bring your khata back to us."

Zaajah stared into his eyes, placing her hand on his cheek. She then laid a soft kiss at the corner of his mouth. Joel turned aside out of respect. When she walked away, his eyes followed her, but he felt no relief from the awkwardness. These two were as bound as any pairing—just no one had told them yet.

"Keep up the practices. When I return, I'll test them all," Zaajah called back over her shoulder.

"As you wish, Captain," Ibajah replied.

Joel smiled at him. The engel looked worried by his commander's leaving. Joel clapped his hand against Ibajah's shoulder, then followed Zaajah from the room.

CHAPTER 6

MAIEL WANDERED THE STAIRCASE between the floors of Lena's Earth house. The dim glow of street lamps cast through the windows provided the only light with which to see. Maiel looked around, allowing her eyes to adjust to the dark. Now was the perfect time to renew her effort to undo Mort's poison and return home vindicated. The human pitarau slept, so their thoughts were quieter. She tried to locate her assign and redirected her searching mind. The rest of the family were in bed.

Inside these walls, Maiel sought refuge and amends. To start, she gathered her tattered emotions and planned a way to heal the wounds her rashness had incurred without reaching out to the watchers. Her flight from her family weighed heavily on her shoulders, distractingly so. The quiet of Lena's home once made it easy to piece together scattered ideas. At least few would follow her there. At worst, the Illuminati could break down the door at any moment to return her and take over the mission.

Having a vague idea of what needed to be done, Maiel reached to the minds of the pitarau. Four days had passed in their life. Their thoughts were deeply focused on the overwhelming pain of their loss. Maiel sighed. Past the living room, she caught sight of the guardians in much needed meditation. They attempted to heal the wound left by Lena's death and their spent energies in protecting their assigns during the transition, but it would take much time.

Decorated with framed photographs, the hall to the kitchen showed the humans in happier times. Lena's laughing face peered back at her. A tear slid from Maiel's eye and she pressed her fingertips to the glass covering the photo.

Only a few short months had passed since Maiel came to fill the shoes of the lost guardian and she'd forged a nominal bond with the two who remained. A thread of emotions whipped loose at the memories. No one thought of Gamael in the crossfire. His disappearance coincided with Lena's illness, a time when he would be vulnerable, weakened by the droves of opportunist imps to beat back. Yet no one mentioned a thing about him. Had they honestly abandoned Gamael to the shadows?

Staring into the darkness, Maiel recalled the day she'd tried to figure that out. The alders in charge of Lena's incarnation and the alders in charge of administering orders to the assign guardian had strangely summoned her from the Moon Order. She'd answered them promptly and received orders to replace Gamael. She heard their voices ringing in her ears and even saw the black marble room in which they disseminated little information.

"Gamael has been abducted by shadowwalkers," Alder Maxiel said, with a pale, grizzled face.

Because Maxiel was also Dominic's alder, she felt very familiar with him. He regarded her with a pair of eyes that seemed completely unmoved by the information. They weren't black like many of the elder alders; by her assessment they seemed more human. A dark brown, perhaps. That was significant, because it might mean he was unworthy of his post. However, pigmentations in duta could stray from the norm, like they did with her onetime friend, Gediel. If Maxiel sat there, then Ganesha had determined him worthy. She wasn't of a rank to question him. Maiel did her best not to think too much on it, though she cared for other personal reasons. His pale, balding head was a sign of his advanced resonance.

"You'll need to replace the guardian during the soul's transition back to Zion. When it has crossed the barrier free of physical form, you'll bring it to Otzar to be raised. It is necessary for the soul to be without physical form in order for it to cross the khajala. This task is very important, Captain. Don't allow the dark dwellers to gain this one. It's the next soul to be raised and will serve as a youngling in your regiment, once graduated from the Ordo Priori. That should be incentive to keep the transition smooth."

It. He'd referred to Lena as an object. Maiel had received the orders with no outward display of emotion. Inside, she had been excited to return to her duties as a guardian. Her last assign had been centuries ago. Her command filled the space her ketu didn't claim. Preparing and drilling others for such duty, along with fighting dark dwellers that crossed the khajala to wage war, had become her main occupation. Her light endangered souls if assigned to them for too long, but her strength was a great threat to the shades who dared to cross her. She expected to face a heavy number of them due to the soul's status. She thought she'd enjoy the assignment, though it would keep her from her family for a year or more. The assignment also happened just when she and Dominic had gotten refocused on his rising. Sending the cursed back to the pits was a pleasure for all duta, if they were not allowed to send them to Oblivion. Dominic understood, as a former milite, and would be happy to wait. Besides, she had the opportunity to lessen the number of shadows who could harry them when they incarnated. However, Maxiel calling a human child "it" left a bad taste in her mouth.

"May I call for assistance as needed, honorable Maxiel? Perhaps the outpost can send aid," she asked.

"You may call in one. It's our fear that too many of you will only serve to provide a beacon to your location and incite a full-scale battle between the worlds. Not to mention that the energy might heal her. It's her time to pass and there is a time requirement. The Illuminati and their union will only prolong matters with their extensive bureaucracy."

"I request captain Zaajah's assistance, then," Maiel said. They noted it in their documents. Maiel eyed, them asking, "Is there any other reason they're so hungry for this soul?"

Maiel was puzzled by the refusal to involve the outpost. Illuminati specialized in extraction and regulation in Samsara.

"There is, but we're not allowed to divulge the information to you at this time," replied a female alder who served the soul. She had a funny smile on her lips. She was younger than the others and more apt to show emotion. "Not having the information won't affect your duties. Are you sure you don't wish the aid of your leader instead, Evocati Callidora?"

Maiel gave a nod. She thought for a moment, trying to puzzle out the answer without their help. By the look of Lena's alder, a grand reward was in store for her guardian. Yet that same revealing expression also stopped further inquiry. She wasn't to look too deeply into the matter.

"Leader Callidora will command the regiment. She's in need of such practice," Maiel replied.

The room fell silent. Maiel returned to her thoughts.

"A unit shall be dispatched to retrieve Gamael while you're gone," Maxiel said. "Should you get any information regarding him, please send it via Captain Zaajah. You're not to leave your assign at any time."

"That's most wise," Maiel agreed. "The quicker you retrieve Gamael, the better. Leaving him there for too long is a dangerous thing. I speak from experience."

The head alder eyed her a moment. Something in that gaze spoke of doubt and anguish. He knew of what she spoke. It was an event that was still fresh in the minds of the alders and she had to prove herself again because of it. The judges deemed her worthy, but the other duta were still deciding.

"I shall retrieve Captain Zaajah and report to duty immediately," Maiel said, clasping the sapphire hilt of her gladius and bowing snappily. "May we use the three strikes rule on these cursed enemies?"

"The guardians of the pitarau are sharing duty while she's without. Make your preparations quick. They are spread thin," Maxiel said.

"Of course, Alder Maxiel," Maiel said, with a smile that was much like her eldest akha's.

"Three strikes, Captain. This is an act of war. We shall send word to your commander of the assignment. You must leave right away," Maxiel added.

Maiel gave a satisfied grin. She would definitely enjoy this assignment and its narrow odds.

A light flicked on in the upstairs hall. Maiel returned from her memories, as Lena's father loped down the steps in a T-shirt and flannel pants. His hair was messed, but no sleep had come to him. He lay tossing and turning, unable to quiet the bio-vessel processor. Dark circles marked his eyes and the wrinkles of his face had deepened by at least ten years.

Maiel wiped a tear from her eye and stepped back as he passed. Her wing brushed a picture on the wall and offset it. The erela held her breath as the man righted the frame, thinking that he was the one who'd bumped it. He lingered a moment, staring into the smiling eyes of his daughter. His face pinched and turned varying shades of red. Tears filled his eyes, but he blinked them away and continued toward the kitchen. His military training had taught him to suppress his emotions.

Maiel released her breath and followed. Light from the refrigerator brightened the dark kitchen as he pulled it open. He vacantly stared at the containers on the shelves. Relatives came during the day with crocks and casseroles so they wouldn't have to cook. They barely touched a bite at any meal, filled with both guilt and resentment at living. His guardian appeared and wrapped a wing and arm around his shoulder. The comfort would be felt, but the pain squelched that comfort's true scope.

Maiel heard the quiet mourning of Lena's amba who was upstairs in her daughter's room, desperately seeking some connection with the lost soul. Maiel looked up to the ceiling, feeling pulled in too many directions. Over the course of days since Lena left them, another rift grew. The couple barely spoke and, if they did, the conversation ebbed quickly and then they would wander to other parts of the house. She thought the flat was too small for them to avoid each other, but they both wanted to stay apart, so stay apart they did. The guardians were at a loss of how to bring the pair together. It wasn't written they should be parted by the loss. However, the course of their plot changed with each moment, undoing all their plans to create a new path. It was all the guardians could do to try and keep things in the correct direction. They were most thankful when Maiel arrived to offer her energy to the mending.

Maiel blinked into the bedroom. Lena's amba wasn't there. It appeared that neither of them had even tried to sleep in their bed. Maiel went to the hall and from there discovered the woman in Lena's room. Her guardian kept vigil at the foot of the bed on the trunk that once served her father, but was painted orchid and white to fit the room. Maiel passed the guest bedroom to join them and saw the tousled blankets. The couple slept in separate rooms. Maiel hesitated, supposing such was to be expected while they healed and there was nothing to really worry about. She and Dominic once experienced a similar instance.

Inside Lena's room, Maiel planned a way to bring them back together. Mort's poison had to be removed before it caused deeper suffering. Once the humans were healed and the guardians felt they had a handle on the path again, she would go home and mend matters with Dominic, no matter how angry he was for her running away.

Maiel brushed a hand over the woman's hair. It was black like Lena's. In fact, Lena entirely took her beauty from her amba. The couple met while the man served the British imperialists in India. The romance was a fairy tale, despite the British occupation, and was an unlikely pairing: romantic like Maiel's match with Dominic. The thought made Maiel smile a little and the pain of her guilt briefly lessened. The effect was great, for the woman's pain also eased. Light and warmth filled Maiel's core. Now was the time to accomplish healing, while she had an opening. Time to replace Mort's persistent sting with the warmth of love and cleanse it away with her light. This fairy tale wasn't over.

"He loves you. There will be a day when this doesn't hurt so much and you'll look for him. Keep him close so he can be there," Maiel whispered in the woman's native tongue.

The woman brushed away what she thought was a stray hair, but was really the breath of her guardian whispering in her ear.

Maiel stood back and let the glow of the woman's atman be her focus. She spread her arms and closed her eyes. The whispering light spread through her, lifting her off the floor. Her form filled with a soft glow and her wings spread wide. They just needed a little reminder of what they felt for one another. Once a seed was planted, it would anchor them back on their path.

The door to Lena's room opened. The man sought his wife.

"There you are. I was going to see if you wanted a bite to eat," he said.

"I'm not hungry," the woman said.

"Come to bed then," he said, after a pause.

"I just want to be here right now."

"We've got time for that later," he said, going to her. He sat on the edge of the narrow mattress and took hold of his wife's hand. He smiled at her and said, "Come to bed. You need to rest from this."

"I see her in my dreams. There is no rest."

"Then you see she still lives," he said, kissing her hand.

The man laid a kiss on his wife's cheek. The expression seemed to rouse the woman from her despair. She gave a small smile and touched his shoulder and cheek. He smiled at her in return.

"You're right," she said, picking herself up.

Maiel weaved the light from her core through them and through the room, erasing the stink and decay of the shadowwalkers. By morning, they would be healed enough to continue on their path.

The man picked up his wife. The smallest of laughs escaped the woman's lips.

"What are you doing?" she asked.

"Taking you to bed," the man replied.

"No. Not yet. This just isn't right. Not yet," she said.

The man set her on her feet. An annoyed expression crossed his features as the pain returned, pushing back at Maiel's energy. Mort's poison fought her, but it wasn't strong enough to battle three guardians. The others joined her, sensing the dark. Maiel pushed harder, weaving the light brighter, bordering the balefire that burned away the wicked serpent feeding on them.

"It won't ever be right, love," the man said softly. "But, I won't lose you too. I love you and you're the only thing that'll make this hurt less."

The woman placed her hand over her husband's heart without realizing she sought his atman and the energy that filled her with joy. Their eyes peered deeply into each other's. The soft glow of her light filled the couple, but new threads worked within that glow—the light of their bond and love. The man kissed his wife, then picked her up. Without another word, he carried her to their bedroom. The door closed behind them.

Maiel regained her footing and entered the hall, the light slowly fading from her form. The woman's guardian inclined her head in admiration.

"You know what to do—a boy. They don't need a replacement," Maiel said.

The second guardian passed behind her. An approving smile curled his lips and he stepped through the wall of the bedroom. The other followed and Maiel took her position at the top of the steps, in case they needed her. By morning, the humans had to be back on their path. They were running out of time. In three more sunrises an altered path would be set and her failure would be set in stone.

The dawn brought drizzling rain, as though Zion cried for the losses of Earth. Maiel watched the light brighten through the frosted glass panes of the entry door. There was a little park on the opposite corner up the street. She drew a deep breath, and sensed her work from the night before had given them an enormous edge in the battle. They could spare her a few moments after this success and she could use a bit of fresh air to clear her thoughts for the next step. The bare ground and open sky would restore her.

Maiel trudged down the stairs and out the front door. On the stoop, she turned her gaze to either side of the street. Several humans were up and living their lives. A car passed down the street. A man walked his little dog. The soul barked at her, dismayed by her presence. Next door, another human climbed into his car with a thermos of coffee, on his way to an unfulfilling job. His guardian waved to Maiel and she raised a hand in return. The dog continued to bark and his human hushed him with an order to stop his nonsense. It was early and the dog would wake the village. However, the terrier didn't comply as terriers were wont to do, forcing his human to scoop him up and rush off to the park before angry neighbors came outdoors. Maiel smiled softly as his guardian and the four-legged youngling that protected the dog followed after them. The poor terrier must have been beside himself at seeing her. She stood almost two feet taller than most humans and had great big red wings. Souls were unused to duta, even in Zion.

Crossing the patch of garden, Maiel decided that she too, would take a stroll in the park. Distant hissing and curses warned of shadows lingering in the recesses, defiling the dharma of those they reached. Her long stride took her to the corner, across the street and then away from them. Maiel kept her pace slow, not wishing to pester the poor terrier. When he reached the wrought iron entrance and passed through, she lingered until they moved farther along. Once out of sight, Maiel made her way onto the lawn. The wide space was peaceful, open to the light and air. She drank in the muted light and the energy of the soil.

Glimmers of lost souls wandered between the trees. Duta were among them, trying to convince the wayward to go home. One duta beat back a cheeky imp come to cast astray whatever sattva it could. Maiel watched them for some time. Then the guardians suddenly looked worried, as if something far darker than imps drew near. She was about to ask when she smelled him. The odor was stronger than usual, indicating danava. The duta clamped onto the souls and disappeared to safer spaces where they could hide the souls for a time. Their retreat confirmed the presence of danava. The sky darkened and the little dog barked with all his strength. Thunder rumbled.

Maiel stepped backward to retreat through a gate. It would be best to get back to the flat and keep watch with the other guardians. The danava likely came there for trouble and Maiel wagered it was a response to her efforts last night. Turning toward the gate, she hurried along, but was promptly stopped by a familiar voice.

"Going so soon?"

Maiel faced the source, the raven-haired baron she never thought to see again. She instantly wished for her friends, but they couldn't reach or hear her. Dread and disgust twined into a rope that tied her mouth shut. Not one danava in the vast prison of Jahannam frightened her save for this one, not even Lucifer. Morgentus smiled at her. The lascivious spark in his pale eye turned her stomach. He revolted the rain as well, which first bubbled angrily on his shoulders then reversed its path, refusing to fall on a shade.

"I hoped we'd have some time together. I have missed you, Maiel," he said, ambling closer.

Maiel's feet rooted to the ground. Since she'd imprisoned herself in his labyrinth, his presence paralyzed her, as if a piece of him wound through her atman and chained her to the Pits of Acheron. Her akha told her how he'd struggled to convince her to stay. He was smitten with lust. She feared some of his words had left an impression. An image of him in a doctor's coat flashed in her memory. He'd once cut a fine figure, before his betrayal revealed the ugliness of his true self. He was clever and used truth to work a strong poison in her head. Maiel would have rather stayed in that awful life than make herself available to the baron, but she was never to know of the peril that faced her. It was a good thing they'd rescued her when they did.

"Is that any way to greet an old friend?" Morgentus asked, too close.

"I won't greet you with more than my sword point. What do you want, incorrigible shade?" Maiel snapped, raising her weapon.

Morgentus laughed, a low gravely rasp that died in his throat. The sickening stench of him made Maiel frown. Her eyes focused on the man and the dog as they exited through another opening in the fence in the distance behind Morgentus's shoulder. The baron circled her and she followed, turning her back in the direction she had been headed. Rain fell from the platinum sky, intensifying steadily. She listened to the unfortunate drops hiss on his coat. Rain didn't touch her, for the resonance of her being created a shell of protection.

"That was interesting work you did last night," Morgentus commented. He grinned at her reaction and continued, "Is it customary for your kind to encourage fornication? I thought your beloved creator hated such things. Then again, he did mate you with an ape. Such a waste of your—"

"Clip your tongue, Grigori. My husband is none of your concern and neither is our bedroom. Spill your venom elsewhere," Maiel said.

Morgentus circled her again, meaning to confuse her sense of direction.
She didn't follow him, using her other senses to keep in control.

"Isn't it?" Morgentus said over her shoulder. He laughed under his putrid
breath. "I'm just—jealous. I mean if an ape can have you, why not one of
us? They're filthy, really. Lesser beings. At least we once stood as the same
kind, erela."

"You were never one of my kind," Maiel replied, stepping back to face
him. She drew a dagger from her belt.

"True. I was a power much better than a simple duta," Morgentus said,
coming back around.

Maiel snapped her wrist, threatening to cut him.

"Easy, my little kitten." Morgentus eyed the blade. His eyes darkened, flicked
back to hers, and returned to their icy pallor. "Put away your claws. I haven't
come here to fight with you. I've only come to show you how futile your work
is. You're wasting your energy while your family falls apart. Shouldn't you be
at home, raising your ardhodita and that—husband of yours?"

"We'll see, Morgentus. The seed is planted and the path anchored. Mort
failed and he won't return to complete his assignment. I made sure of that,"
Maiel replied.

"I know you did. A lovely job, too, I might add. Such fire struck him down.
I wasn't sure it would stick, so unrighteous a blow was used." Morgentus
smiled. "No wonder you're so red," Morgentus added, in a desirous tone.

"Shut it, you!" an angry voice called from the lane.

"I've nothing to say to you," Maiel said through gritted teeth, ignoring
the shouting.

"I think you do. The union were alerted last night by that little trick you ran."

Maiel stared, clearly dismayed. Morgentus laughed and nodded to the
street. Motorcycles with black riders turned the corner. She cursed.

Lena's janya was the man who'd shouted, moments before the baron
dropped the news on her. Morgentus raised his brows and rubbed his
stained hands together, knowing that it bothered her. He was quite pleased
with himself. He was responsible for what had transpired while she took
a stroll in a park, ignoring her duty. He even managed to time it with the
worst possible witnesses.

"If you wanted to see a proper coupling, erela, all you had to do was ask,"
Morgentus said, with a thinly-veiled threat.

Maiel grimaced with revulsion, but she didn't strike. If she stayed and
fought, she would do so until someone came to assist or he dragged her off,

victorious. She swatted him with her sword, choosing to get back to protect the humans from his meddling with their guardian's aid. The watchers were the least of her worries, and their arrival might offer the help she needed to stop this nonsense immediately.

Maiel rushed out of the park. She listened to his mocking chuckle behind her. He so enjoyed her futile maneuver. As she made it further up the street, Maiel saw the man exit the house. The bikes were slowly rolling by. Judging by the twist of the man's features, they'd been fighting again. He threw a jacket on his shoulders and fumbled with his keys. The woman followed onto the stoop in her bathrobe, spewing a diatribe of Hindi amid tears. He responded with angry shouts, flinging his bag in the trunk of his car and getting into the driver's seat.

"It's of no use," Morgentus said, a step behind.

Maiel ignored the danava and continued to the assigns. The bikes halted and she knew they spotted her and the beast trailing her. They'd make of it what they would. She never should have left the house. Once more, the shades were able to wreck her work due to negligence. Shades and imps peered from the houses they soiled, attracted to the raised voices and the presence of a master. There wasn't much time before they converged and irreparable damage was done. The only thing holding them back was the riders and her.

"I'm leaving and that's final. I've had enough of being blamed," the man growled at his wife.

Maiel drew up short on the driveway, shocked that her prediction of their recovery was so wrong. Morgentus's words played in her mind. Their time together was not fornication. She meant to help them ground their bonds through an expression of their affection.

The riders closed in, parking their bikes a few houses down so as not to bring attention to themselves. One removed his helmet, a tall man with warm-toned skin and long black hair. He reminded Maiel of the American tribes, but the markings he bore said he was once duta. Her eyes went to the other, a pale man, reed thin with an austere and sunken expression. Morgentus spoke, his harsh voice snapping her back to the present. He wasn't intimidated by the proximity of the watchers.

Maiel stretched her senses toward the assigns, ignoring his continuing taunts. He meant to stop her by convincing her she'd done his work for him. She distrusted the reality of this too convenient of a clash, awfully well-timed.. Her senses quickly disappointed her. This was no illusion. Her eyes searched for the guardians, but they were gone. They were most likely detained by Morgentus's slaves in the house. Her mind stretched toward the woman and there she found a glimmer within the shroud of the sattva, not her atman. Maiel pushed past it, refusing to alert her enemies to the tiny hope she'd given the humans. They could still win this battle as long as it wasn't taken over.

"Human suffering is nectar. Taste it, erela," Morgentus whispered in her ear.

Maiel rounded on him, blade in hand and he jumped back, nearly suffering a cut. She boasted an earring in each ear for his akha. The piercings should have served as a warning to him. They must have, for his eyes quickly went black and he hissed angrily.

"You've single-handedly caused more pain than we could cause on Earth in a week—and it's only been three human days. Why do you deny what you are?"

"Four weeks and don't count yourself the victor quite yet, Grigori," Maiel warned.

"Four. Your dear Adonai must be so proud. You tore the fabric of that child, prevented her from rising, then broke sacred bonds, satisfied your blood lust on my soldier and caused a written path to unravel. And to round things out—encouraged some raw copulation."

The man's car peeled down the road. The woman called out to him, collapsing to her knees. Maiel grit her teeth. Morgentus undid all her efforts. He'd caused this, not she. Anger hummed through her, building the fire she'd felt when Mort threatened her assign. Lightning flashed and thunder rumbled in the sky. Hate wouldn't take over this time. Only focus could undo this. Tying down her emotions, she quieted her mind and thought of how to scare Morgentus off.

"I couldn't have done better myself. You're fast becoming one of the greatest shadowwalkers ever to exist," Morgentus continued to taunt.

Morgentus stepped toward her. The veins beneath his skin pulsed black, like his eyes. He was ready to strike. She backed away. He smiled, rubbing his hands together, thinking of what it would be like to lay them on her skin. Her eyes locked on the strange pointed nails and stained, cadaverous fingertips. Maiel lifted the blade between them, to remind him that he'd get a nasty cut if he tried to put his filthy claws on her. Her eyes faded to moon gold and her features took on a distinctly feline aspect.

"Lucifer has taken notice, my flame-haired girl." Morgentus smiled.

"I'm surprised he's noticed anything but his own reflection in the ice," Maiel countered.

"One such as yourself can bring the attention of every prince in Jahannam," Morgentus told her. He took a deep breath as if smelling the air. "You're changing. The anger takes root. I'll miss your sweet perfume once you become baroness, but that is worth the gains," Morgentus continued, grinning to reveal his bloody tongue.

Maiel froze, control slipping from her hands. His brand of truth wasn't far from reality. The distant weeping of the woman throbbed in her ears. She wished she could just remain silent and go inside, out of the rain and to her guardians. The presence of the watchers threatened Morgentus's minions; the watchers would shield her. Maiel could do nothing for her, for she was forced to shield her own being from the danava.

"You've learned nothing from our first encounter? They'll come for me, and they won't be forgiving," Maiel said, finding her voice.

"Why can't you just enjoy the moment, Maiel. You'll be one of us, sooner than you think."

"Not ever," Maiel replied.

The watchers closed in.

Maiel focused on a place far from there. The image of an incarnation a century ago took shape in her mind and she focused on it with what strength she could spare. Her form vibrated, then faded into a narrow white light. A devious curl twisted her lips moments before she dematerialized and the energy caused Morgentus to step back. He bared his teeth and growled.

"You'll fail. I will find you again!" he called, as she disappeared.

In the distance, through the vault of thought, Maiel still saw the woman soaked by the rain. She at last retreated inside, safe from the baron. Morgentus cursed his failure, only interested in subduing Maiel. The woman was just a pawn. He sneered and called his minions to him. In a furious smoke cloud, he dragged his toxic corpse elsewhere before the watchers could dispatch him. The humans were safe.

The shadow's retreat cleared the rain. Birds sang in the trees and the sky brightened to a nursery blue. Maiel was no fool. Morgentus would try again, no matter how fast the planet rebounded from his touch. Maiel released her connection to Lena's family to focus the last of her energy on a haven. Until she figured out how to fight this enemy, she needed a safe place to rest and hide. Morgentus had drawn much energy.

* * *

Zacharius and Gediel arrived at Maiel's home in Eden as ordered. They found the first child on the porch steps, backlit by the porch light and foregrounded by a neat little garden that suffered in kind with its mistress. The youngling looked rather glum, despite the laughter of his khata emanating from the open door. His wings, slighter than those of a duta, lifted with his awareness. Ian stood to block their entrance with a scrawny sattva. In the plain clothes of an ardhodita, he looked very much like Dominic, and unfortunately behaved like him too. The half-engel was just about the equivalent of twenty human years, but was nearly two thousand. Zach neared him, offering a consoling twist of his lips. Ian seemed little enthused by his pitr's version of affection and kept his position. They each knew the boy could not keep that position if it came to blows.

"A rather long face for such a bright soul," Zach said.

"Where is my amba?"

Zach exchanged glances with the watcher he brought.

"I'll see to Argus." Gediel excused himself before he was made to explain. He barely knew the boy and it would sound better coming from his pitr, alone.

Zach sat on the steps, urging his nephew to join him in an effort to show he wouldn't trespass without permission. Ian slumped, elbows on knees and head in hands. Zach assumed a similar position, instead clasping his hands before him. He respectfully waited for the boy to speak. In truth, Zach had nothing to say and often found silence was the better option. It little mattered what Ian would say. This young version of Dominic was as hotheaded as his janya, and had already decided what to make of the situation.

"Is that Gediel? What's a watcher want with Argus? Is Fenrir taking him back? They can't do that," Ian said, panicked.

"Argus is needed by your amba. Relax, nephew," Zach said, placing a hand on his arm to keep him still.

"He's not back there. He's in the glade. He won't know how to find him without me." The boy watched where Gediel went around the house to the back garden.

He moved to follow the Watcher, but Zach pulled Ian back.

"He knows where to find him," Zach quietly told him.

"You still haven't answered my first question," his nephew said.

"Because you already know the answer. My saying it won't help you."

"And my janya?"

"Your janya is in Zion, Ian. You already know that too."

"They should let me go get her. I'd bring her back and this would be over. He just let her go. Let her fend for herself, like he always does."

Zach's intimidating stare should have silenced him, but his nephew was half Maiel, and just as bold.

"My janya is selfish. Don't give me such a look. We all know it's true. Ask Luthias. He would tell you," Ian snapped.

"You shouldn't speak ill of your janya," Zach said, emotionless.

"I shouldn't but it's all I can say when it's true. I wish I didn't bear his name."

"Strong words for a youngling."

"And if he were your janya?"

"He's not."

"Well, you're the lucky one."

Zach gave him another stoic but corrective glance. This time the meaning was clear.

Ian looked to the dark sky and the twinkling stars. A netted balloon carried a wooden ship through the air with the aid of a propeller they couldn't hear at that distance. He was angry; it showed his human side. Zach turned his gaze upward as well.

Argus would be reluctant to go anywhere with a stranger, even a Fenrir. Gediel was no stranger to the wolves of their world, but he and Argus hadn't been a part of each other's lives since the day he delivered him to Maiel. They revered Gediel, for he was one of the very few two-legged creatures to truly understand them. He only hoped that would sway the soul to comply. It was very likely Argus would run off to find Maiel on his own and they'd be out to rescue the pack and their khata.

"Ian, your janya loves you very much," Zach said. He believed it to be true, recalling the look on Dominic's face when he first held his son. That moment created the first spark to light his eyes since marrying Maiel. "He's only human," Zach added, sounding hopeful.

"And so he'll remain. He's no intention of changing. He likes things the way they are," Ian said.

"Then there'd be no point to his hard work all these centuries to gain the wings with which you were born. It's very easy to judge him from your perspective—born a step ahead," Zach responded.

"I am only half, Pitr—an ardhodita. You forget. I'll need to rise, become a youngling again. Rejected by the legions, I understand his issues very well."

"Yes, well, your rising is guaranteed, unlike your janya's path, and likely more quickly. The legions don't reject you out of a lack in your ability. They're simply not your path yet."

"What does that mean?"

Zach looked at him frankly. He knew what it meant. After everything, it was still Dominic's choice if he would rise or not. The man had supposedly made that choice a long time ago. Now they would see if he could fulfill it. His son's lack of faith for his father's resolve came from anger, like the rest of them. In addition, his son's inability to join the legion was based on the fact the youngling refused to accept his path. He, too, was like his father. Poor child.

Gediel returned, carrying the majority of the puppies as best he could in his limited grasp. Their pitarau helped, each held one by the scruff. Shee placed her babe on the grass and barked at Ian, then sat. She blinked, tired from her draining night. These pups were her first litter and her sattva was not used to the draining experience. Shee's bark carried a reminder that Ian wasn't alone in his trials and he certainly wasn't the only one to suffer. Ian snorted and gave a smile.

"You're right," Ian said to her. He got to his feet. "Why don't you come inside, while I find something to carry them in? I'll let my khata know to get the others ready."

Gediel looked to Zach, a bit surprised by the boy's response to the wolf-bitch. Maiel must have let her play nursemaid when she wasn't at home, for Shee was the only other mother figure around since moving to the remote stretches of Eden. The wolf was a wise choice, as her kind made dutiful dams. The boy's obedience was proof of it. Shee was the perfect babysitter for the brood of coarse ardhodita.

"She's trained them better than I'd ever hoped," Gediel said, a bit wistful.

"Argus, actually. His duty is to train his pack," Zach said.

"Impressive." Gediel blinked.

"Well, she did train him," Zach admitted.

Such ability was known only in his Order, but then the Moon Order was quite twined with his. It shouldn't surprise him.

Zach approached Gediel and took two of the tiny bundles from his arms. He scowled as they whimpered and nuzzled against him. He had never seen the like in his long existence and wasn't sure what to make of them. They were stubby nosed and black, with wrinkled ears and tightly closed eyes. He supposed they might be what some called cute.

"They won't bite. Not yet anyway. We should get Shee inside. She's had about enough for one night," Gediel told him.

Gediel stepped around him and Shee quickly picked up her pup and followed. Argus approached Zach where the duta stood studying his children. The alpha whined. Zach looked down at the white wolf and raised an eyebrow. Argus stared expectantly.

"They're rather fine, aren't they?" Zach said, flattering the new janya.

Argus's ears pricked up and his head cocked to the side. He whined again, then put his pup down. The wolf hoisted his head into the air and howled a long, mournful call. The sound was answered by other, distant howls. Satisfied with the result, Argus picked up his pup and trotted proudly into the house. Zach looked around as the tree line came to life with the sound of snapping branches and crunching leaves. He watched several four-legged apparitions converge on the yard. It was the rest of the pack. Zach turned from them and went inside, studying the littlest members of the pack he still held. The others shuffled in around him, stomping up stairs and through all the rooms on the first level, familiar with the human den and seeking the masters.

Just before Zach entered the house, the ground shook as in a quake. He scowled at the night, stepping back onto the porch. Between the trees, giant elk trampled and leapt, spurred on by orion shepherds. The moonlight lit their track. A majestic and rare sight. Their leader paused at the garden and watched Zach suspiciously.

"Pitr Zacharius!" the distinct voices of the first twins called to him.

Zach passed through the door, forgetting the Orions. Chaiel and Amaiel jumped down to him. They also ceased to play children, and adopted their usual appearance instead. They were growing younglings, all arms and legs and batting eyelashes. In exuberant greeting, they wrapped their long arms about his waist. Their pretty little faces, mirrors of their amba, brightened and their blue eyes shone as they caught sight of the puppies in his hands. They were the first muses in the family in a long time. Each a ball of energy; they craved experience.

"Shee's puppies!" Chaiel exclaimed, snatching one of them in her arms.

"Oh, they're darling!" Amaiel said, snatching the other.

"Congratulations, Shee!" the girls said to her, bringing her bundles back to her safe keeping.

The twins forgot their favorite pitr in the foyer, gathering around the alpha and her babies. Gediel fed Shee some small biscuits from a pouch on his belt and whispered to the girls. Zach folded his arms and waited. He didn't see their elder akha anywhere. Footsteps on the stairs brought his attention around and he thought for sure he would see Ian. Instead, Samuel joined them. The boy's aspect warned of trouble. Also resembling his janya, this child was more a mix of his pitarau than Ian could ever hope. He was just entering the last youngling stage and was rather morose most of the time, if not combative. He liked to paint, like his father, but had not found a purpose.

"I want to find her," Samuel said.

His nephew was combative that night. The boy's blue eyes flashed and dimmed as he wavered between emotions.

"It's too dangerous." Zach folded his arms.

"She's my amba," Samuel insisted.

"She was my khata first. Now pack your things. You too, Chai—Ama. You're all going to your ampa and jyoti's to stay until your pitarau come home. Now, help each other get ready."

"Why can't we stay here?" Chai asked. "We're old enough to care for our-selves and the twins."

"Though imps are unlikely to breed in Eden, it's still possible on the edge of Elysion, and you live far too close to be certain. You may ask Gediel the truth of that. Besides, the moment we turn our backs, the lot of you would be in Samsara hunting for your amba. We can't risk you putting yourselves in danger like that. Who would care for the little ones while mudeaters chew your sattvas off?" Zach answered.

"She needs us more," Samuel insisted again, unafraid of shades.

"She needs you to stay with your jyoti and watch your little akha and khata. You don't get to spend much time with him. It'll be nice for all of you."

Zach stared him down. Samuel tried to be insolent a moment longer, but he soon turned up the stairs and did as his pitr asked. He wasn't about to challenge both a watcher and an alder. The girls passed him, also taking the stairs to their rooms, heads hung low.

"That went much better than I thought," Gediel said, when they could only hear the younglings tramping about the upper floors.

Zach eyed him. He paced the foyer and awaited his nieces' and nephews' return. Argus approached, leaving his pack and new puppies with his mate and the watcher. He licked his mouth and sat, drumming his feet on the floor to gain the attention of his captain's akha. Zach tried to ignore him, but the wolf's insistent voice filled his head.

"I'm sure she'll be fine," Zach said to him, irritable.

Argus looked stern. He wasn't so convinced by the tone. Zach returned the look and received a gentle low growl. He folded his hands behind his back and refused to say a word in response to Argus's worries. Still, it was unsettling to see both his nephews so doubtful and the wolf so concerned. He wondered what had occurred in the house. Of what should he be aware? The stairs beckoned him and Zach decided that answers might reside in rooms normally closed to him.

"Where are you going?" Gediel asked, as Zach gripped the rail to take the first step.

Zach cast a sidelong glance and then continued on his way. At the top of the landing he faced the west hall. There, he saw the girls gathering the things needed for the youngest members of the clan. The infants flitted around them, cooing and giggling. The rooms here belonged to the younger, while the east hall was for the older siblings. He cast his eyes in the latter direction, seeing two of the doors tightly closed. He sensed the boys still within the walls of the house. They sulked, as he expected. Zach slowly turned back, noticing the south-facing hall that led to his khata's room. It was dark; almost ominous. He continued to the stairs that led to the attic and Dominic's studio.

The staircase was lit to the first turn of its steps. In the darkness above, Zach noticed the same ominous shadow as in the south hall. Such darkness felt stranger than just an absence of light; some energy remained to pollute it. There was enough angst in that house to make a full imp that would test the will of the unwary. He flipped the drape of his robe back, revealing a sword at his hip. It was a slender blade, slightly curved, with a fluid grip. It was a weapon that was preferred by the alders—each carried one. Duta were never foolish enough to believe a threat was barred from emerging in their world. Bad energy built even in Zion. These anomalies never lingered, their resonance too heavy to allow them. The presence of such entities suggested untrained minds or the warning of a burning. The blade Zach drew was just the thing to deal with it. He stepped up to the next landing.

A light blinked on above. An iron lantern.

"Afraid of the dark, pitr?" Ian asked.

The boy watched from the hall. Zach gave him a small smirk.

"Imp," he told him, showing his drawn blade.

"It'll go in the morning when the sun rises," Ian said, dismissing it.

"I'm going to have a look around your janya's studio. I'll take care of it while I'm up there," Zach said.

"Do you need help?"

"Get your things together. I'll be down to take you to Zion in a moment. Don't hang about."

Zach continued up the stairs. The studio beyond was still in shadow. He crested the landing, and a form dashed behind a stack of blank canvases in the east alcove, spattering black the whole way. Ignoring the nuisance for the moment, Zach crossed between work tables to an easel set before the arch of glass that overlooked the night forest dotted by bubbles of light and iridescent movement. A discarded palette lay on the end of one of the tables, the paint dried in streaks and blobs. Zach was surprised Dominic had left his things in such disarray.

A can of black oil paint had spilled over the table and floor. Finger and toe prints stained the floorboards. The canvas on the easel was half-worked. He approached it and saw that the shadow had been leaving its mark there, too. The image was scored with black smears. With a soft sigh, Zach waved his hand in front of the painting. The black ran from the bottom of the easel as if water had just been poured over it. The rest of the painting remained intact. Zach paused, struck dumb by what he saw there. Flipping his sword behind him, he impaled the lingering shadow who was sneaking up on him. The energy crackled like a firework and popped on the sharp edge of his blade. The smell of a doused match wafted through the air. His eyes remained on the canvas and his normally stoic expression filled with concern. Was this the same painting his amba had seen earlier? It was far from stunning, depicting a rather ominous outcome for his khata. A marditavya bent over a faceless, red erela, rending her atman from her torn abdomen.

Zach returned downstairs to find the younglings gathered in the foyer with the pack. Gediel sat on the arm of the sofa, his arms crossed. The watcher's aspect was dark; his scowl unlike any other. Zach nodded to him.

"We blink. No detours, straight to your jyoti or you answer to me," Zach told the younglings with a point of his finger.

"Yes, Pitr Zacharius," they whispered, dejected by his expectation that they would betray his trust.

"I'll see if I can arrange for some training while you wait. It'll do you good to have the distraction, and I'm sure your Matula Corabael will check in on you. I'll see she brings the cookies you like," Zach said.

None of the younglings appeared excited about anything he said.

Gediel gave him a questioning glance. School wasn't something younglings looked forward to. However, their pitr had something much more interesting in mind, something reserved for those in evolution well beyond their own. They would need it. Zach revealed nothing though, casting his eyes over his nieces and nephews as a last warning not to test him.

"Ready, then?"

They stared back without an answer. Then they were gone and the house grew dark and still and without inhabitants to brighten its interiors.

CHAPTER 7

DOMINIC PRESSED HIS BACK to a cold marble wall. Vibration emanated from the rock and he lost himself in the peculiar sensation while he waited. Gragrafel had disappeared around the far curve of the lengthy corridor quite some time ago. The bend appeared a mile away. He stared into it, thinking. He hadn't raised a sword since trading in his legion kit for a paintbrush and fatherhood. A delicate curl turned the corner of his mouth with nostalgia. He'd never regretted the choice, happy to work at home and be his wife's rock while she made Trailokya safer for his and all kinds. He was proud of her and proud of being a part of her. This was the problem: When would it be his turn to achieve? He'd showed his paintings in the White City and through Arcadia, starting over two incarnations ago, but the work never gained the admiration it deserved or the success that was comparable to his service in the legions. His talent was no more impressive than grass growing; it was simply expected of him as a budding muse.

Pocketing his hands, Dominic stared at the floor. He saw the edge of Alex's robe as it hovered just above the marble slab. Perhaps he still hadn't chosen the right path. Perhaps he was blocked from advancing because he couldn't decide where he belonged. All around him, the others knew where they fit in, but he was never so sure. If he returned to service in the legions, it might be seen as competing with his bride. He longed for his own accolades and to be free from comparison to the exceptional Maiel. Perhaps he needed to stop rethinking things, but he couldn't help but wonder about what Alex had said to him back at the house. A muse might be just what he was cut out for. In a way, a muse's work was quite similar to that of a soldier. Their resonance filled others with inspiration, and their work could be likened to the strength of a blade. He imagined himself inspiring others, filling them with the will to achieve wondrous things. That ability alone was greater than any skill known in Zion. It was kith and kin to Adonai's talents.

"When we are summoned in—you'll see things rarely afforded your kind. Please remain calm and stay focused on the task. This interview is my daughter's only hope. If Adonai senses a change in her—" Alex said, cutting herself off. She watched the hall before them and touched her forehead as she fought with her emotions.

"Adonai will see the truth and send us to retrieve her." Dominic filled in the right words for her, grateful to see his wife's family felt something.

Because he was a mere human, Dominic couldn't sense Alex's heartache and needed to see it acted out to discern it. Despite their differences, he still empathized with that part of his family. All duta struggled to understand souls, like why humans struggled with decisions that were so clear to them. And those very questions could be applied to each incarnation of duta up to their king. Thus, their differences united them in the goal of attaining ascendance. He worried what the council would say, so far removed from a struggle they were likely to find wasteful.

"Yes, but Metatron little understands or sympathizes with emotion and that's all we have to explain our situation," Alex said, looking to him.

"If we're doomed, what is the point of dragging me before them?" Dominic asked.

"Adonai will hear you from the chamber, that's the point. It's him we really implore," Alex replied.

Alex turned back to her thoughts, waiting for Gragrafel to return. She clasped her hands together at her waist, squeezing the fingers tight. Dominic smirked. They could be just as manipulative as those they'd cast away millennia ago. He started to wonder if any of this really mattered against the tableau of time. They ran their world under a tight bureaucracy of string-pulling alders. An unseen king reigned over them all, his power even more influential because his intentions were supposedly those of a loving father. Hard work never really amounted to a thing. Plans were orchestrated behind doors and set into motion with or without the agreement of the one expected to carry them out. For instance, punishing Ian's lack of faith in his own path by denying him service in the legions. Furthermore, Alex didn't just happen to mention muses. She covertly directed him the way the council wanted. He rubbed the back of his neck. He wished they would stop the show of individual sovereignty and be honest that there was no real choice in what a soul, or any atman, did.

Dominic felt Alex's stare. She scowled, barely disguising her hurt. The alder said nothing, and quit her examination of his eyes to turn her gaze back to the hall. She'd likely heard his thoughts by digging into his mind without permission. Dominic grit his teeth hard. He forgot that he always needed to be on guard. Though they had no right to violate his mind, they should realize that his thoughts, raw like his heart, didn't indicate wickedness or the beginning of something that should concern or even disappoint them. Nor could Alex blame him if he came to this conclusion after his experiences. If souls were allowed to grow without constant monitoring of all thought, or extensive deliberations over nuances in an effort to guarantee a preferred end, then perhaps events like this wouldn't happen. The alders should know after centuries of unfailing service that he belonged in Zion and deserved to rise. If his actions weren't enough, the ketu should never have been established between him and Maiel. He desired her the moment he first saw her, but that was neither here nor there. Bonds weren't made on such simplistic terms. He recalled the day his council told him of the ketu and the moment her brother dropped the news on her. It was a dream come true for him, but something still seemed odd about it. It seemed far more arranged than any ketu he knew. Some part of him still blocked what they called the knowing. Their ketu was just one more example to cite in his long line of stunted abilities. Was it possible that they'd also meddled with his form? Bonds were discovered by mates, not announced by their alders to them. Yet she was his and he'd never doubted the bond. When he first made love to her, he could hardly believe it was happening. Like everything else, perhaps he just came to his accolades differently. How else could he succeed when he was so monitored? He envisioned himself as the council's puppet, given only the understanding needed to remain at Maiel's side so long as it suited the story they wove.

"Ah, there he is," Alex said, stepping toward her husband.

Dominic pushed off the wall and followed her. A giant svarg was with him, wild-haired and dressed in armor that looked like carved bone. Gragrafel and this giant whispered to each other, but Dominic could make out none of it at that distance. Then he saw the penannular bearing the triangle-framed eye. The svarg was from the outposts. He swallowed hard, worried that Maiel was to be hunted like a shade. The distance closed in moments and the strain in Gragrafel's withered features became terribly clear. The patriarch's black eyes tried to console Dominic, but the human burned with rage. The Watcher left them without warning, bid to some immediate duty.

"I fear they might strip her wings before we've a chance to beg time from them—as you humans would say. I just want you to be prepared for the worst," Gragrafel informed them.

"What did they say? Will they speak with him?"

"Of course," Gragrafel said, as if nothing else were possible. He calmed and touched his wife's face in apology. Her mood eased and he said, "They're waiting now. Not a moment too soon, either. Ganesha is with them. General Barachiel just reported that they've pinpointed her location in England. A pair of their operatives were en route when he left."

Dominic looked at them questioningly. He wondered exactly what the father referred to, still feeling stung by the mother's prying. Had something happened to his wife? Why did they fight to stall him? Alex and Gragrafel watched him expectantly.

"What should I say?"

"Tell them what happened and everything you know. Tell the truth," Gragrafel replied, placing a hand on his shoulder for the first time.

Dominic stared in disbelief, tucked under the principality's arm. The gesture's significance wasn't lost on him. He'd hoped to fall into his good graces at some point; this approval he both longed for and loathed. But the moment wasn't filled with the fanfare he'd imagined: just a simple gesture that when denied became a coveted treasure, and once owned became an absurd bit of sentiment.

Gragrafel led him along the hall. The old engel's arm dropped from his shoulder and he walked beside him, seemingly lost in thought. Dominic wondered what else they'd said. The engel looked quite bothered. After the time that passed, he knew the council spoke more than just a few exchanges about a soul coming to beg for help. While his wife strayed further and further from help, they bothered to interrogate her father. Dominic hung his head. The concept of time was too human a construct. If they could be taught the delicate intricacies of the idea of time, then they wouldn't be so slow to act, and many more might be saved from the sulfur fields. He would be more than happy to assist. A smile brightened his features. That might just make his humanness less detestable. He could be a hero. The smile turned into a sneer.

After the bend of the hall, the passage came to an end before a pair of opalescent doors similar to those that separated Mikhael's rooms from the rest of Zion. Unlike those barriers, these were carved and polished from a single slab of snowy agate, like none he had ever seen. His eyes widened. They were more like palace gates from a dream than doors.

The carved panels folded inward and Gragrafel urged them on. Dominic slowly entered the next chamber—a plain white room. The doors closed and he suddenly felt quite underdressed for the occasion, in his paint-smeared shirt and pants. Duta had a trick to change clothes at will. If only his penannular was still with him and not relinquished back to the armory. The handy little device was greatly missed.

The trio stood in the plain white room. There were no benches or chaises, no braziers or chandeliers, just emptiness flowing with light. Most unusual, there was no other door and no passage. Alexandrael paced the border, the sound of her shoes echoing off what he presumed were walls and a ceiling. Dominic turned in a circle, trying to get his bearings. The room had no corners and the only edge was made by an alcove in which the pearl doors stood. In fact, the room appeared to have no definition but the door they entered through. The architecture was smooth as glass, as if the space were hollowed out of stone and painstakingly polished.

Alex paused, meeting her husband's stare with her own. The couple were displeased with waiting again. On that they could all agree.

While Dominic continued to study the odd room, the doors behind him opened again. The duta stepped toward them, nearly leaving him behind. He rushed to catch up, wondering if their interview had been denied. The question fumbled on his lips as he passed through the door into an antechamber and yet another room. He was struck dumb, trying to comprehend the space.

Alex and Gragrafel approached what resembled the balustrade of an old palace balcony. Two statues framed the opening, one rendered like a sphinx—or cherub—and the other a multi-faced throne. Beyond them hung a raspberry-streaked sky twinkling with stars and a few clouds. They must have been at the mountain's peak, where the tower stood above all of Zion and the perpetual light beamed into forever. Dominic had no words. He stepped into the circle, taking note of the sculpted walls and vaulted ceiling. A small, navy blue door, smattered with silver stars, swung back. From it, a dark-skinned engel in brown robes joined them. Behind him arrived the elusive Lord Councilor Ganesha. The Lord's great elephantine head turned toward them, and Dominic wagered he saw through their facades. His trunk twirled in dismay. A double set of arms hung tensely at his sides. Metatron had chosen to embody his svarg sattva for this meeting. On his head he wore a narrow cap of silver that came to a point in the center of his forehead. His black eyes scanned Dominic.

"Your offspring betrayed us, Gragrafel. She follows her own orders and risks several souls in the process. This doesn't bode well for your line," the brown-robed engel said.

Gragrafel hadn't met with the grand council yet. He'd seen those who controlled access to them. Dominic frowned, disappointed he had lied.

"Mighty Metatron." Gragrafel stepped toward him.

The statues beside the balustrade came to life. Dominic's tongue stuck to the roof of his mouth, rendering him speechless. They were not statues, but the ancient duta themselves, the eldest of their kind. His lips became further sealed by Lord Ganesha passing but a pace from him, standing several feet taller and considerably wider than he. The councilor's eyes searched him again, but the councilor didn't speak. He chose to sit upon an ivory pedestal and wait.

"Please heed my words before you cast final judgment. I brought this soul to speak on my daughter's behalf. We know it's your right to cast her out—and we all know the gravity of the situation, which may warrant such extreme actions. But this soul is here to ensure that such actions won't be necessary," Gragrafel said.

A single seraph floated into view beyond the narrow pillars and balustrade. Dominic stepped back, startled by the apparition's face. Its head was adorned with a helm of gold, and six radiant wings camouflaged the sattva. Their eyes were upon him, pinning him to the spot like a hunted deer. The cherub lifted its three pairs of wings, arched its back, then rose from the pedestal to turn and view Dominic better. The councilor scowled from a man-like mien, tail whipping irritably. On the other pedestal from the throne, a similarly human face watched him. It turned into the mien of an eagle, then changed to that of a bull, and then a lion. Each watched him expectantly. Each offered a different perspective. Dominic froze, attempting to process the sight and subsequently forgetting for what he came. Panic fanned the flame in his throat.

"You'll heed my words as well, before you dare cast judgment," a voice boomed through the room. "What mean you by involving Illuminati to trap my captain? She's no rogue, you overzealous politicians."

Mikhael swept past him, blustering. He bent to one knee before the High Council and crossed his arm over his chest, fist on his left shoulder—a gesture of respect among the legion guards. The supreme alders were unmoved by his arrival. If Mikhael met with such a reception, then hope was foolish.

Dominic reeled. They were sure to question him and he was uncertain he could withstand an interrogation. He practiced the words in his head. He need only speak them to be done with this. Yet his mind continued to track back to the watcher and Mikhael's words, stirring a panic inside him that glued his mouth shut.

"Give him a moment. The boy hasn't ever been in the presence of such high resonance. He's but a soul and needs to comprehend. You must recall when I was a lad and stared open-mouthed at each of you. Oh, how doubtful you were of me," Mikhael explained.

Dominic's blood boiled. He was tired of how duta dismissed souls as weak, confused children. He had spent more than four millennia in their world, served in the legion for centuries, and spent all of that time combined in and out of the White Citadel. If he were anywhere else, he would prove his strength and character. However, a contest with the general wouldn't return his wife, but neither would speaking about souls' inability to comprehend higher forms. Despite himself, Dominic aimed for the high road and bit his tongue.

Mikhael went to Dominic's side with a friendly smile. His great hand clamped on Dominic's arm, dragging him forward to the towering triplets. Dominic nodded to the high council, sliding the backward flat-cap from his golden head. Sparring with these surly hulks would not be much of a contest, he decided. They made him feel pathetic. His heart sank.

"Thank you for seeing me, wisest of all alders," Dominic said.

Metatron shifted on his feet. The councilor's restlessness and intense demeanor put Dominic on edge. Mikhael gave Dominic's back a sharp pat that nearly shoved him off his feet. He forgot his speech as though the blow had struck the words from him.

"Let's be introduced properly," Mikhael said. He boisterously added, "This is Dominic, Maiel's ketu and retired draco of the Sun Order. The soul my captain helped for the last three thousand Earth years."

Mikhael stepped behind Dominic and scowled at the supreme alders. They weren't the only ones to have Adonai's ear. His presence dared them to defy the king's wishes. He'd march through the door to the ruler's chambers and have a good word with the king about that.

"This grizzly-looking fellow is Metatron. The Voice, some call him, because he carries orders from up above to the rest of us. This well-profiled chap is Corpheus the Throne. The sour kitty cat is our own Denius, a cherub of exemplary character. Don't let him frighten you; he's merely bored. And the odd-looking number outside the window is Lemitus, a seraph and what Metatron usually looks like when he's not playing at being a man. They're decidedly undecided creatures. Lastly, I am sure you're familiar with the gentle Ganesha," Mikhael continued.

The council peevishly waited for Mikhael to complete his introductions, which they received humorlessly.

"I'm most pleased to meet you," Dominic said, brave enough to now step closer, but not enough to speak to why he was there.

"Speak your piece," Metatron demanded.

"I've come to beg a stay of punishment," Dominic blurted.

"On what grounds?" Corpheus asked, shifting faces.

"It's my fault she ran and I can explain how."

"If I may, great Corpheus. I'd like to respond to the question, as a fellow alder," Alex interrupted.

"The question is for Dominic," Metatron said to her.

The whirling ring drew closer, turning the full breadth of her circle toward them. Lemitus's wingspan kept her from entering the room, but her face cast a comforting look upon them.

"Allow Alder Alexandrael to speak," Lemitus said.

"Grand gesture, Seraph Lemitus." Alex bent her head toward the ring of feathers. Continuing, she explained the situation. "As you know—Belial makes a bid for my daughter's loyalty. He's using the baron of the pit, Morgentus, to manipulate her, as he did when she was imprisoned in his labyrinth. Adonai knows to what lengths they'll go to accomplish this. My daughter has gone to such lengths on behalf of Zion. We simply want to bring her home and see her reconciled with her family, where she can heal properly from the wounds they inflicted."

"The same gentle words were said of Belial before the Conflict. I believed him loyal, but we saw him led astray by Lucifer," Metatron said, sneering.

Dominic stepped forward, defiant against the accusation of the supreme alder. A large hand clamped down on his shoulder. Mikhael thought he could hold him, but no one could stay his rebuke. His wife wasn't danava. She was loyal to the king and this whole thing was due to their negligence. They would answer for their words even if they struck him down right there.

"Belial no longer helps souls gain their wings. He was cast out for averting them instead. And so he continues, hindering us from our course and casting deceitful snares in our path. No danava would try to correct that," Dominic reminded them.

Metatron raised an eyebrow at this insolence. A deep silence stifled those in the room. They were shocked he'd dared to speak so openly. Before the matter escalated into a confrontation he couldn't hope to win, Dominic capitulated, eyes cast to the floor. He swallowed, humiliated. Mikhael gave him an encouraging pat and wink. Then the general's golden brow quickly darkened. The svarg turned that mien on the grim alders.

Denius rose, displaying the fullness of his lion form from the pedestal where he made his seat. The human-like face was intent on Dominic, with a deep reaching gaze, swimming with the light of galaxies. After a too lengthy moment, the features of the cherub relaxed and he switched his attention to Metatron.

"The human speaks from his heart. I sense the purity of his intention."

Denius dropped his chin and then his head tilted aside as if he heard something. Lord Ganesha rose from his pedestal.

"Adonai Elohim has announced his arrival," Denius spoke again.

Dominic looked to his companions, fearful of what would come next. This was what they sought, but Dominic was yet unprepared. He stammered, desperate to have a moment to talk it over. The atmosphere in the chamber shifted and he knew the king was upon them. The dry burning of his throat became an inferno, then suddenly all was peace and he only knew awe.

The light of the alders faded and Lemitus disappeared from view altogether. The room seemed to darken and the sky became midnight. A white sphere of light like a tiny star appeared beyond the balustrade. It grew in size, coming to hover between the pedestals. Dominic shielded his eyes from the piercing radiance. It grew taller and wider until the form of an old man stood before them. Though aged, he wasn't feeble. White robes hung from his broad shoulders. He gripped a tall shepherd's crook in one of his thick hands. Long white hair and a long white beard cascaded around his solemn face. Tucking the thumb of his free hand into his sash, he smiled at Dominic. The king's piercing eyes intensified. Dotted with the dust of stars, they seemed more like windows on the night sky. His features softened with fatherly care.

"Denius, what's so grave that I'm summoned here to frighten this poor man to death? Oh, Lord Ganesha. What a surprise!"

The silent councilor bowed graciously to the king.

"Great Adonai Elohim, we beg your pardon. The soul came to request a stay of judgment on behalf of a duta, Captain Maiel of the Moon Order. This is her husband, Dominic, son of Newlyn. The family and General Mikhael have come as witnesses and assert her innocence," Denius replied.

"Oh." Adonai shifted the staff between his hands. "Step forward, son of Newlyn. I've heard of you before. Your words carry the truth you wish to make of them. You really mean to claim that your wife's endeavor is your fault?" Adonai called to him.

Dominic opened his mouth to speak but found his voice gone. The others stepped back, bowing their heads in reverence to the leader, abandoning him to look foolish. King Adonai placed a hand on Dominic's shoulder and the dumbness cleared.

"Forgive me if I act improperly, my lord. I'm without my guardian's council," Dominic rasped.

Adonai offered a tentative smile.

"No need for such concern. You don't always need to lean on a guardian. You've expressed yourself rather well thus far," he reassured Dominic. Indicating his form, he added, "And I rather like how you see me."

Dominic looked him over, confused as to the appearance and bearing of the great leader, but then King Adonai wasn't bound by rules of physical form and human expectation.

"Thank you, your highness. My wife—if I may."

"Yes, I remember your ketu well. How are the children? Your wife bore a set of twins recently—a boy and a girl, if I'm not mistaken—Muriel and Metiel, yes?"

"Uh, highness, yes—yes we did," Dominic replied. His brows skewed.

"Happy tidings indeed, my lord." Alex stepped to Dominic, taking tight hold of his arm. "Why we've come, you see, my daughter is in danger of turning herself over to Belial."

"Falsehood!" Adonai bellowed, upset by her impertinence. He waved his arm to dismiss the nonsense. "Maiel is as pure as her general. She may have run, but she's not fallen. A pretty punishment she'll win from Commander Bade, too, when she returns. I've dispatched Barachiel's team to fetch her to me."

"Even purity may show a blemish from time to time," Dominic said, frowning at the comparison.

"Indeed it does," Adonai rasped, staring through him. "I've only said she hasn't fallen yet. When ships cross Samsara, we'll know the gravity of what has been done," the king continued.

It was little wonder that Dominic's rise eluded him, with a king so undecided and expectations set too high. Now he threatened them with action from the Samsara union. His intentions were maddening enigmas. Adonai regarded him questioningly; he was a master of reading the minds of the children of Zion, yet he left no indication of doing so. Dominic's throat dried as he struggled to coherently form his thoughts into a response. Alex detected his struggle and swooped in to rescue him. Dominic fell behind, clutching at his throat, tears filling his eyes and he was sure he would fall victim to a fit of choking. When Alex stepped between them, the burning ceased. Dominic cleared his throat, stepping toward the anterior wall. Mikhael looked to him with disapproval, so he turned from him, but Ganesha also watched. Dominic kept his distance, hoping his conduct would be read as concern for his bride.

"Despite your belief in her, Maiel went to Earth to seek refuge from Zion and all those who love her. We only wish to see her set back on her true path after the fight she had securing the youngling Lena. Until she is back with us, Prince Belial will hunt her as one of the chosen in his plan to weaken our defenses. He must be thwarted, my liege, whether you feel threatened or not. It is only a matter of time before they are able to trap Maiel as they plan, for she is exposed and unprotected in the wilderness. By my calculations, the longer she strays from the light, her fall is guaranteed. She may take form as we speak. Our gates are threatened. The union will destroy Earth to protect themselves in the name of your crown."

Adonai looked troubled. He muttered about ships again. His mouth compressed into a frown and his eyes darkened. He grasped the shepherd's crook with both hands, as if to strike or to hold up his suddenly weakened sattva.

"My light shines even there. My law still rules them," he assured them.

"Not so brightly these days. Belial and the other princes have spread their forces throughout Samsara since they broke the seal of their prison. More incarnate and mix with souls in flesh, spreading their sickness and despoiling ways. The Grigori are vast and so are their offspring. Earth has suffered greatly in this change as the humans struggle to evolve. Their vulnerability makes them ideal prey," Alex informed him.

"Don't speak to me as if I don't know what passes in my world. Your short-sightedness is what is in question, councilor. Do not be so proud. You fail to realize the fallen children can still be turned back to the light," the king said, with great emotion.

"My humble apologies, my lord."

"Mine, as well. I should not have lost my temper with you—especially at this time, but please remember that the fallen are also my children. Now you know what pain I feel at their wandering from my light," Adonai said.

Alex hung her head.

Drumming a finger on his lips, Adonai's mind wandered. He paced the floor and then stared into the stardust beyond the balustrade. Ganesha pressed the palms of both sets of hands together, rubbed them, then shut his eyes as he fell into meditation. The king absently caressed the polished railing. When Ganesha returned from his mental foray, the king turned back to Dominic, and the latter realized that despite their silence, they had been consulting one another.

"You must go—find her," the king said.

"Find her? I can't track her. It'll be too late by the time—"

"You'll bring her home or Earth will become a battleground. Are you willing to sacrifice others because you're afraid?" Adonai cut him off without raising the volume of his voice.

Dominic stopped talking. The fire in his throat raged. Adonai turned his back. His orders had been given and he was finished talking. The king filled with light.

"What of my children?" Dominic choked on the desert in his mouth.

Adonai turned his head, but didn't look upon them.

"What of the children? You waste precious time, Dominic. What will the children do without their amba? What will you do without the planet I gave you?"

Dominic shook his head, not sure he should answer.

"I will call off Barachiel. You have but days to accomplish the task. Then the Watchers come."

Having given his final word on the matter, Adonai exited the way he came. The fire in Dominic's throat dissipated with the king's leaving, and in its wake left frustration. Alex and Mikhael traded uncomfortable glances, attempting to conceal their feelings from him. They failed. Their expressions showed doubt, probably in him. Rightly so. How could the king expect him to track her? He couldn't even sense her whereabouts, even if she was in the next room. They must send Joel or even Zaajah. It was just another chance to watch him fail, a chance that would cost their lives. Seethe as he might, the conversation had ended. The supreme alders returned to their meditations. Metatron indicated a silent dismissal, folding his hands in front of him. When they didn't retreat, he was forced to speak.

"The king granted your desires. If that is all—you may take your leave of the council chambers to do as he commands."

"We thank you for your temperance in our moment of need. As we progress in the mission, my khata will carry messages between our councils. I ask that you communicate with us through her," Alex said, inclining her head.

Metatron looked to the Lord Councilor and the elephantine head inclined to him.

"So be it. Alder Magiel will be expected," Metatron replied.

Dominic sneered, readying a response to Metatron's discontent. The seraph too easily minimized the trials of the lesser beings, and needed to be reminded that he wasn't without faults. This was proof: his former partner sat in the frozen prison of Cocytus. Metatron and his council acted as if Maiel had already signed her name in blood and surrendered to the prince, although until this incident, her loyalty had remained unquestionable and her service exemplary. Their attitude was inexplicable. The High Council should've been falling over themselves to get her back.

"Come along, Dominic. We must prepare you quickly if we hope to succeed," Alex said, intending to stop him from speaking.

"Wait—I will need Luthias," he demanded of Mikhael.

Mikhael glowered, surprised by the human's temper.

"The evocati is on his way to Walhall with your arms keeper," Mikhael gruffly replied.

Dominic rethought his tone and allowed Alex to lead him away. Mikhael's brow darkened ominously. Dominic moved slowly, still thinking of speaking his mind. What could they possibly do if he challenged their authority and demanded an answer?

"Gragrafel," Metatron said, calling the principality back.

Dominic listened over his shoulder, still guided to the door by his mother-in-law.

"This'd better work. We can't lose her now," he said, with a hardened gaze.

Gragrafel nodded, swallowing the misery of a father. He took Mikhael's arm as a crutch and together they joined the retreat from the council chamber.

CHAPTER 8

Saint-Chely-du-Tarn, France

MAIEL BREATHED IN THE COOL AIR and watched the gloaming creep in. Water flowed far below one of the bridge's arches where she sat, as she dangled her feet and leaned against the stones. An old tunnel spilled runoff into the Tarn River with a sound once deafening to her ears. The wind on her skin and through her hair smelled of earth and the road. The last time she was there, it was without her acute senses. Colors were more saturated and sounds more perceptible. Scents overwhelmed and the feel of the rock against her body was coarser than she ever recalled. Birds sang from roosts in the masonry. Cars sped overhead and the soft whispers of human conversations persisted beneath it all. Her memory flooded with cherished moments from a lifetime long ago. Among it all, the shadow persisted.

Maiel wrapped her arms about her waist. She felt cold and sleepy. With wings sagging, she tried to focus on regaining her energy. The water should have helped. It didn't, however. Tears filled her eyes and her thoughts wandered to home. Would she ever see her husband and children again? She missed her friends and family, even their meddling. She should've asked the watchers for help, or accepted Dominic's offer before she ran. The council might have granted a unit to put things right. Her interference only helped the shadowalkers to cast their evil webs, but with more forces, she would need no more than a day to put things as they were intended. Callidora could assist her and Primus Bade would be more than happy to dispatch the units needed. She just needed to ask, though she hated to admit she could not do this alone.

A glimmer twinkled over the eastern horizon. Her thoughts wandered to another place where the sun had already set. Turning her face in that direction, the point of light disappeared behind her closed lids. Such a strong presence whispered of hope. Someone powerful, of her kind, was closer than the border of Astral. She pressed her mind toward the glimmer. The closer she drew, the more of a mystery it became. The light belonged to an earthbound human atman. She sighed and returned to her vigil, resting her head against the stone. A human could offer no protection.

"Thinking of jumping?" A voice filled the arch.

In one swift and fluid motion, Maiel faced the intruder and pointed her blade at him in warning. Her wings curled threateningly around her shoulders, ready to carry her to safety. He stood at the other end of the opening, eyeing her like a prize horse. His rage had ebbed, but he was no less threatening. In an instant, his shadowy strength could fell her like a dead tree. He chuckled to himself, amused at his own jest and unaffected by the potential threat she posed. He adjusted his gloves, flexing his fists. They were an improvement over the putrid flesh they hid, although composed of the hind of a marditavya that dared step out of line.

"It'd make things faster. But you already know that."

"Fast? You'll know the meaning when I make short work of you, just like your useless atrins," Maiel warned.

"I'm sure you'd like to believe that, but we both know you won't. You need me. I have information."

"Ha!" Maiel bellowed. "I can gather my own intelligence. I'm no young-ling, baron. There's nothing in all of Trailokya that you can offer me which I can't obtain alone."

"Mere paltry things—a husband and family, not true succor. The anger of your want fills you—it blots out Adonai's light. You feel Belial's lure already. He can promise you great things. No more responsibility for those who fail you—no putting yourself and yours last, no saving the little apes from their fate. No guilt for condemning your children to be ardhodita."

Morgentus settled his hands at his sides and looked her over. He was disappointed his words did not affect her.

"I can help you survive this. Those recidia you summoned can't offer the same," he said.

So Morgentus thought she'd called the Illuminati. Too bad she hadn't. They would have arrived in time to help her take him down.

Maiel stepped back until her heel teetered on the edge of the arch. He would persist until she struck him down, if she could strike him down. His strength was more than she wanted to deal with on her own. The battle out of Acheron was still fresh in her memory. Her wing twitched, as she remembered how his henchman wrenched it when she'd tried to slide from reach. If he got close enough, she would be paralyzed by the pernicious hold he kept on her.

"You know nothing, shadowalker," Maiel replied, baring her teeth in a snarl.

"Oh, but I do. You're angry because they mated you with an ape. It disgusts you." Morgentus drew closer. He gave a smirking grin and continued with mock sympathy, "What's more is they gave you one who can't even manage a simple evolution in three millennia. A buffoon. Why should you care about these sattva? They use you up, and are fat on what your efforts win them. They do nothing for themselves. You can't spare the time to train your soldiers, and have left them vulnerable to their enemies. Come with me. Let Belial reward you."

Maiel looked to the water running beneath them. It was a long drop. The water moved swifter than it appeared, and was shallower than a safe jump required. Her eyes went back to her adversary. Another step and he would feed on her energy, rendering her helpless. He'd drag her to the Pit of Acheron and his labyrinthine prison. She wasn't going back there without a fight.

"Belial will mate you with one of his nobles more suitable to your station," Morgentus persisted, taking another step closer.

"You?"

Morgentus nodded with a purse of his lips. "Perhaps—would you like that?"

Maiel said nothing, carefully watching him posture. A bad taste filled her mouth. A slow, broad grin revealed his yellow teeth and turned her stomach. Somehow, the baron had wheedled a promise from his overlord that he thought bound her to him—if he could manage to bring her to Jahannam. Princes rarely kept their promises and, most likely, Belial had something more hellish in mind.

"They're not coming to rescue you, Maiel. They believe you betrayed Zion. You can sense the truth of that. Do you detect a single glimmer? You're alone—except for me," Morgentus said, losing his temper. He held out his hand, now within striking distance. "I can make the transition very easy. You need a friend. Let me be that friend." His tone shifted to what he thought sounded kinder, but it just made him sound even more sinister.

Maiel eyed the extended appendage. A corner of her mouth curled and she snorted. He stood in the middle of the arch just outside the range from which he could draw her energy. He feared a trick as much as she, and he was right, because she was waiting for him to step close enough to push him from the bridge.

"Must you subject me to your loathsome appetites? Fitting you were cast out, Grigori—oath breaker," Maiel said, sneering.

Maiel lowered her weapon, keeping her eye on Morgentus. He was quite pleased with the move, but he didn't understand the reason. His mind was too full of his plans to pay attention. He thought she'd surrendered.

"Grigori? Is that not you, nephilim dhatri?" Morgentus's eyes flashed with desirous fire.

"I yield you this battle, shadowalker. The next time, I'll have your head for a trophy," Maiel growled, choosing to ignore the accusation that her children were the same as his.

Morgentus stepped toward her and his smile turned to a lecherous grin. Panic pulsed like prickling electric inside her. Leaping backward, Maiel somersaulted off the bridge. He lunged, but she planted her foot firmly against his throat as she went. Morgentus stumbled backward, trying to catch himself, but the force threw him on his back. She was free to escape. Her crimson wings opened wide. Righting herself under the arch, she flew east toward the growing darkness and toward the only hope left.

Morgentus regained his feet and watched her go. He was quite displeased. She'd expected more taunts, but words were weak. They could not harm her. Or had they? She thought of her children and for a moment she saw no difference between her and the danava.

Maiel focused on the atman she'd discovered, a stream of light sliding into the horizon. She must reach safety before Morgentus calculated her trajectory and brought friends to assist him in her capture. He wouldn't make the mistake of facing her alone again. Furthermore, the aid of the watchers was out of the question. Their duty was to hunt the fallen and either cast them into Jahannam or force them into service with the outposts.

* * *

Joel converged on the largest gothic edifice at the base of Mount Zion, with Zaajah close behind. The granite stones of Walhall, dark gold in hue, sparkled in the light of the coming dawn. They were carved and arranged millennia ago by the first of their kind, some of whom had fallen in the Conflict of Hosts. The structure served as an inspiration for numerous likenesses in Samsara, in the form of citadels both secular and devotional. Copies even existed in the circles of the shadow world. Sliding to a sudden stop, the pair continued forward at a rapid walk, only to find that Zacharius and Gediel had beaten them to the gates. The pairs approached one another with cagey steps, beneath the shadow of the grand cathedral.

"Where's Dominic?" Joel asked his elder akha.

"I thought he'd be with you," Zacharius replied.

"He must still be with the alders, or they're prepping him for the mission," Zaajah said.

"Either way, it's obvious you're of the same mind," Gediel said.

"What's your meaning?" Joel asked, scowling.

"Sephr needs to be notified of what's happening. Why are you here?" Gediel asked.

Joel lifted his chin, admonished by the svarg. He nodded.

"Good. Shall we go in?" Gediel asked.

The great carved doors of the armory swung inward, revealing a long, red granite hall. Passing through the archway, they also passed under the watchful gaze of two heavily armed cherubim and their war hounds, trained by Praefect Fenrir himself. The black eyes of the four-legged sentinels followed them until they were well inside. A matched set of Powers stood to either side of the entrance interior. In the far-off apse, a seraph floated before the great seal of Walhall, a downward-pointed, open-palm hand with an eye. Another set of Powers guarded the base of the steps that led to the chancel. The seraph took note of them but seemed uninterested, and rearranged the plates of armor that partially covered his wings. He had no worries of intruders, because the apse floor was the resting place of a long, red lung with a hoary gold beard and suspicious eye. Its great head rose. Like a dog, it stood up, circled, and lay back down.

Four thrones stood guard as well, two for each towering colonnade that lined the length of the hall. At each heel stood what looked like small sculptures of the lung in the apse. However, clear lenses washed over the eyes, putting the notion of them being mere effigies to rest. The click of nails on stone announced the presence of other guardian souls in the room. The guardians of this armory noted everyone who came and went, and made sure that only those who belonged passed the inner doors. They had nothing to fear, since Alex went to the High Council and the news would circulate. Still, no one could be sure how they reported what they saw or heard.

"Zacharius!" A voice bellowed from somewhere beyond the pillars, statues, and armaments. "Welcome to Walhall! What brings an alder to my rock?"

"Dux Sephr, we come to warn you of an impending battle," Zacharius answered, as a giant warrior emerged from his hiding spot near the chancel.

"A stroke of serendipity." The giant grinned. "I have just been standing here, horribly bored."

Sephr appeared as a svarg, but was a seraph, just like General Mikhael and the others boasting such high rank. He wore a circlet of gold in his black curls, denoting his special charge, and had a coarse, dark beard. His teeth flashed a brilliant white against his warm golden skin. The news put a twinkle in his black eyes and a flush in his cheeks. The great sable wings rose in anticipation. Joel knew he'd like what they had to say. The Dux was always eager to open his armory against the hordes of shadowalkers. He was girded in heavy cloth and mail armor, with a spiny mace tucked into his belt. The shirt of rectangular scales, with button centers—a mark of the armory battalions—was in ready condition. These guardians did not just like to battle; they were made for it. When they were not fighting, they were preparing to. Sephr was ready to fly out that instant.

As part of their duties, the Walhall guardians also fitted the legion young-lings with their second skins, a very proud moment among warriors. The skins were stored until the time came to move on to other duties. Joel remembered the day he'd reported there for a fitting, barely a graduate of the Ordo Priori. Sephr presided over the ceremony, wearing a very different mien, one much graver than what he wore at present. The elder officio still kept a curved blade at his side, and it was still just as intimidating these many years later. After all, he was the master of arms, a giant who had earned his title and orders.

"Perhaps so, but we've yet to see. My khata has run to the Samsara in fear of punishment from the High Council. They plan to retrieve her as we speak," Zach clarified.

"Captain Maiel? What has she done? Is there another temple in her honor?" Sephr suddenly looked ill.

"No, Dux, nothing so simple as that. She fears she fell from favor and seeks to fix her mistakes so she may return to us, reputation intact," Zacharius replied.

Sephr scowled deeply. He chewed his tongue, ruminating on the news.

"Is this about the little human child?" Sephr asked. Zacharius nodded and he was stunned. "I suited Maiel myself. I never sensed a single thread bent in that direction. Her atman was clear," Sephr said.

Sephr gave a sheepish grin in response to their questioning gazes, embarrassed at the suggestion he might have been mistaken in his forecasts of their bend toward ascendance or destruction.

"For years my Order fitted the others. You get a sense of these things," Sephr explained. "What has caused this rift?" he asked as they fell uncomfortably silent.

"Time with the humans—dark intrusions by ill-intending imps."

"You think there'll be a fight to take her over?" Sephr asked.

Zacharius nodded.

"Why have they not sent Mikhael or one of the other svargs to retrieve her? Uriel or Gabriel would surely give them what for. Even Raphael would turn his cheek from his art for a chance to best those who threaten that erela. Not even Bade?" Sephr asked, glancing at Gediel.

"A good question. They didn't even ask the outposts to help in the girl's transition. That's why we believe she's being tested, unless more occurs than we understand," Zacharius replied.

"It's always more than we understand. I'll spread the word through Walhall." Sephr smiled.

"Thank you. In the meantime, you should know, they plan to send her husband after her. This may avert a confrontation in the end, if he can succeed," Zacharius replied.

"That gives me great pause." Sephr frowned.

Joel and his akha exchanged glances.

"Dominic, isn't it? I remember him well—very eager to achieve greatness and very willing to take it without earning. Quite confusing, their ketu. I had her pegged for someone more like—"

Sephr cut himself off. His eyes flicked to Gediel again, but just as quickly returned to Zacharius.

"Well, quite frankly, more like you and me," he laughed.

"Yes, well. What we think is of little consequence in that matter," Zacharius replied, guarding his curiosity about Gediel. "They are to bring Dominic here for a fitting. He left the legions to become a painter and put his efforts into rising. He'll not be prepared properly for facing the people of Jahannam unless they're toddlers or gallery owners. I fear we have no time to correct that," Zacharius continued.

Sephr nodded with a grin. "I'll fit him myself. I'd like to know if anything's changed."

"As one who's not clouded by years of watching, I can tell you he hasn't," Gediel replied.

Joel and the others were stunned by Gediel's declaration. Gediel raised an eyebrow at them and was about to speak again when the doors to the hall opened. A much sought after guardian entered and cast the thought out of their minds.

Evocati Luthias was much like Sephr, though a younger version. He wore leather and steel armor, accented by a pattern of green-crossed squares. He strode toward them, his round leather shield on his back and his long sword slung loose at his side. His brown hair was drawn back into a braid, and a short beard of the same hue upon his chin came to a point. He looked devilish, right down to his pale eyes.

"Did you start the party without me, akha? Where's my boy?" Luthias grinned.

"He's not arrived yet," Joel informed him.

Luthias put his arm about Joel.

"I could go for the girl myself if you'd told me sooner. I'd bring that hellcat back here kicking and screaming, one way or another. You'd think you were afraid of her. Get me that sweet Cal to help, and I'll show you boys how things are done. How are you, Dux Sephr?" he asked.

"Good to see you, Evocati. How's the life of a guardian treating you?"

"It's better than wandering the wastes, but the lad is stubborn," Luthias said.

Alexandrael strode through the open gate, silencing their banter. She held her habited-head high and her hands clasped before her breast. Her face was blank, telling nothing of how the interview had gone. Behind her, Dominic strode with his head low, eyes shaded by his brow. He looked exhausted, if not completely spent. Humans were much less careful with their feelings and made an easy read, especially when fatigued as he was. It appeared things were quite thorny, but their presence assured that they had a mission. Then Dominic caught sight of his guardian and his dark expression eased. Luthias grasped Dominic's arm and patted his shoulder, assuring the man that all would be well.

Sephr left them to greet the elder alder. He grasped her arm and smiled warmly before guiding her to the rest of them. She carefully avoided the eyes of her sons. Something troubled her and it made the hard lines of her features deepen. Joel folded his arms and sought the answer from his friend. Distracted by the hall, a place he hadn't been for an aeon, Dominic had no idea Joel leapt into his thoughts. Outwardly, the soul appeared a curious child, but inwardly he was confused and scared. There was nothing there to cause great concern, except that he believed the High Council meant to execute them both. The assumption was quite reasonable from the human's perspective, and it made Joel gloomy to see him like this.

"The High Council allowed us a brief window to retrieve Maiel back to Zion," Alex explained. She reluctantly added, "Dominic is selected for the mission."

Joel's form clenched at the idea, a rather odd reaction to have when they all guessed Dominic would be sent. Digging deeper into the human's mind, Joel sought answers to what he lately noticed. Dominic rubbed his throat and fidgeted as if something was annoying him, similar to how incarnated humans behaved when they became ill with some virus. Joel puzzled for a time and recalled the throat housed two of the strongest points of their energy. If denied expression, the block would often manifest itself in discomfort or even pain. Joel prodded for more, but Dominic's mind slammed closed. The human shifted on his feet, gritting his teeth and refusing to meet their gazes. His reaction toward a friendly examination was rather violent. Joel raised a brow, returning his attention to his mother's continued speech. Joel bided his time for when he and Zacharius could candidly speak on the matter. Something quite peculiar had transpired. Dominic was suspicious of what he faced and whom to trust.

"Sephr, I've come to have him prepared for his journey. If there's any advantage you can give our fight, please do. I'm afraid we'll need all we can get. It's been some time since he's fought with the legions and he may have forgotten the training—"

"The vote of confidence is reassuring," Dominic growled, clearing his throat.

Sephr chuckled. "It's like riding a bicycle. Do not worry."

Alex gave him a reproachful glance, then held her hand out indicating he should go to the back of the hall, ahead of them. Dominic looked the others over before begrudgingly complying. Sephr gently assured him, guiding the way to the sepulchre and the narrow hall beyond, where they would undertake his fitting. Dominic said nothing, but peered back to be sure Luthias also followed.

Joel lingered in the nave, taking the moment to pull Zacharius aside. With a touch to his akha's arm, he gestured him toward a secluded corner. Joel kept his eye on the others until they disappeared. His akha waited with a questioning stare.

"Did you notice?" Joel asked.

Zacharius frowned.

"He kept rubbing his throat," Joel explained.

Zacharius remained unimpressed.

"The energy's blocked. There's something he hides—perhaps our golden boy isn't doing as well as we think. They say that's how the fall begins," Joel said.

"Harsh allegations," Zacharius warned him.

"I know what I saw," Joel said.

"Our khata wanders Earth and you're worried Dominic has a secret? She's your twin and my little khata. At some point, one of us would have felt a change in him through her," Zacharius said, then stepped toward the sepulchre.

"You never liked him, neither has Argus. I dare not mention Matula Magiel's sentiments," Joel said, grasping his akha's robe.

Zacharius nodded, folding his hands.

"Yes, well, it explains the imp in their house."

"An imp? Why didn't you say anything sooner? We need to watch him carefully. I have loved him as an akha and my feelings easily veil the truth to save me hurt," Joel said.

"Your work with humans clouds your judgment, indeed. I thought it might make you overreact," Zacharius said.

Joel opened his mouth to verbally lay his akha flat.

"Joel! Zach! Where are those sons of mine?" their amba called, silencing him.

Alex wandered back to the hall to find the akha whispering. They shut their mouths and she motioned them forward, offering an admonishing stare they knew too well.

"Keep this between us. There's no need to alarm the others," Joel said. "Likely they already know."

Sephr led the way through the inner maze of Wallhal's armory. He stopped outside a red leather door, crisscrossed with gold straps and dotted with gold buttons. A signal of his hand asked the other duta to wait outside while he took Dominic inside. The fitting was a sacred rite always presided over by the armory guard, rarely by their leader and never by outsiders. Each youngling who came to Walhall would be taken to the sepulchre to meet with a single legiona who remained the youngling's arms keeper for the duration of his or her duties. When Sephr opened the door, Joel saw his regiment's keeper. She nodded to him and then the door closed.

"I'm going to Otzar; prepare them for his arrival," Zacharius said.

Alex nodded, though she appeared troubled and distant. Her eyes shifted with her thoughts. Joel didn't dare to delve into her mind. He was in no mood to be taken to task, though he needed to know.

"I'll go with you," Gediel volunteered.

"A good idea for both of you. Perhaps you can sway them to send Luthias with him," Alex said, practically pushing them out the door.

"It'd be suicide to send a human alone, but they might have another in mind for this task. It shouldn't take much convincing. The Evocati is the obvious choice," Gediel said, then turned to the engel. "Don't you agree?"

"If they don't send me, then you have to ask yourself what they're really about."

Alex looked bothered by the guardian's words.

"What troubles you, amba?" Joel asked.

"You mean aside from my daughter being hunted by the Baron of Acheron—and possibly our own hunted too?" she asked, a touch sarcastic. Pacing the room, she tried to calm herself and gather her words. "I fear we're to lose at least one of them."

"Adonai wouldn't send him if he weren't sure of success," Zacharius countered.

"Unless he's got something else in mind," Gediel said, seeing a possibility they didn't dare speak.

The Watcher had the upper hand in this game. They were lucky to have him on their side.

"If the king does, then he's not sharing his plans with us, though we do his work," Zaajah chimed in.

"For good reason," Alex said. She sighed. "Our Dominic—must yet make his choice."

"Yet? I thought he made that choice when he accepted the ketu to our khata," Joel questioned, quite concerned in light of his suspicions.

"Dominic has chosen," Luthias insisted.

"Indeed, so we all thought," Alex replied. She pursed her lips. After a brief pause, she added, "Alas, being human, I fear he has a tendency to change his mind. He's not capable of seeing fully until much of his path has played out before him. It may be that he's decided not to return to the legions, or any post for that matter. His thoughts are quite erratic—sharp—all very shaded."

"To be expected after what he's suffered," Luthias said, defending his friend.

Alex bowed her head in reluctant agreement.

"When he's sorted out with Sephr, we'll have the path ready and a guardian secured," Zacharius said.

The younger alder took his leave, with Gediel and Luthias filing behind. Luthias scowled, sickened by the conversation. It was best he went, before it ended in heated words that couldn't be taken back.

"When you were raised a svarg, we were yet younglings," Joel said, when they had gone. His amba stopped pacing to give him her attention and he continued, "My khata had just been wed. You left us for a time to see this through ourselves. Likewise, you raised us alone, because janya had been raised shortly after we'd been born to you. Risings don't take three thousand years for all, it is true, but you took longer. Have you forgotten you were there when the Conflict of Hosts occurred? Janya fought in that war beside Mikhael. Dominic has been given no such trial by which to prove himself. He's only had lives to decay his heart. Lives in which he's been made blind as a newborn. Yet we expect him to excel. My khata's anger isn't from becoming more human. It's from watching her husband misused by her own kind, like a hated pet."

"There're others of his kind and they've successfully made the journey," Alex reminded him.

"Engels like Luthias are rare, and he took his time as did the others," Zaajah said sadly.

"Not so rare that we don't all know at least one," Alex countered.

"That's unfair to compare him with the prince," Joel said.

"Not the prince. There are others of less renown," Alex said. She paced again. Gesturing, she gathered her words carefully and continued, "My experience tells me something isn't right, is all. It's a wisdom I learned in the years before the Conflict. Gediel could tell you the same. Not that I believe Dominic is lost, but there are just—just things that remind me of those we fought."

Zaajah looked worried. They both knew Dominic showed the same darkening that the false ones showed in the days before they were cast out. Joel had sensed it himself before he'd shut him out of his mind. Joel froze at the suspicion affirmed by another. If he burned down, they couldn't send Dominic to save Maiel. He'd only find temptation and dark paths. Maiel would never get home.

"There's still hope, no matter how small," Alex said, reading Joel's thoughts.

"Then we have faith," Zaajah demanded.

"And not question his loyalty? Or the danger it poses to Mai?" Joel added.

They fell silent, each looking troubled with the knowledge they shared.

The discussion ended, as they sensed a turbulent future in it. Time passed quickly while they waited for Dominic to return; they were so steeped in preoccupation over the coming events. The human reemerged in the familiar gold armor of his old regiment. His penannular gleamed brightly after its long rest; it set the chest piece ablaze. The nostalgia of the image made Joel grin, even though he wore his armor daily. He grasped the breastplate by the openings of the arms and tugged. The piece was a little loose, as his sattva had shrunk a bit with disuse. However, the plate still held a remnant of his old energy. Dominic's features looked brighter, if not wholly warmed. The armor did its job, amplifying his resonance and wrapping him in a protective cocoon. Perhaps they never should have let him take it off.

"Where's Luthias?" Dominic asked.

"Gone to secure the best possible guide for your mission," Alex answered.

Dominic was confused.

"It—looks strange." Zaajah quickly changed the subject, nearing him and eyeing the plate.

"It's his bare back." Joel smiled.

"I'd appreciate you not talking about my bare backside. I'm a married man."

"You'll earn your wings with this. I'd make a wager on it. If I cared to be rich," Joel said, stepping back to look at him.

"Not if he fails, my friend. You bring Maiel back, whatever the cost. We leave none behind," Zaajah said, a bit sternly.

"She's my wife. If she doesn't come back, neither do I," Dominic replied in kind.

"You'll need to track her, like we do." Joel refocused them, not wishing to have any more of his suspicions confirmed. "We don't have much time, but I should be able to teach you quickly."

"I'll try, but my energy is low and fails me already," Dominic said. He grabbed at his throat again.

"Is there something you wish to tell me?" Joel asked, not letting the gesture pass this time.

Dominic froze at the question, but then he shook his head and dropped his hand to his side.

"It's just fear. Set it aside. Deny it. She's your mate. The love you have for her can't fail you. And you need to stop blaming yourself. This is written or it wouldn't be happening. Learn what you can and move forward," Joel reassured him.

"I can't imagine eternity without her," Dominic said.

A green light pulsed in his friend's eyes. Joel's mouth curled in a slow, astonished smile. The light showed that for which they'd hoped. He could now be assured an energy block caused the problem, likely from Dominic holding his tongue too long, a common problem of muses, and that an increase in his resonance was at last acclimating his sattva to higher resonances. Joel patted Dominic's shoulder.

"Hold that in your heart. She belongs here with us," Joel said.

"How do I find her?"

"Close your eyes. Picture her in your mind. Reach with your heart. Your need is your guide," Joel instructed.

"What does that mean?" Dominic scoffed at the mystical instructions.

Joel waited for him to comply.

Dominic shut his eyes, still smiling. He did as he thought Joel instructed, but there was nothing but his wishful thinking. He stood a moment, staring into the nothing behind his lids. Bouncing on the balls of his feet, he raised his brows and admitted to them that he felt no connection.

Joel approached him and placed his palm on Dominic's forehead. Dominic's eyes popped open, startled by the move.

"You're blocked for some reason and the tether is weak," Joel said. He grit his teeth and added, "I'll open your ways and show you the path."

"Why'd you never mention this before?" Dominic asked.

"Shut your eyes," Joel ordered.

Dominic closed his eyes. After a pause, Joel explained.

"We perhaps took for granted your bond. It comes as nothing to us, but your lower energies need to be worked on—trained."

"Thousands of years and you just thought of this now," Dominic said.

"You never seemed to have trouble finding each other before," Joel replied. They traded frowns. Joel nodded and added, "You gave us no cause to question it. Perhaps that's why your throat troubles you. The pain reminds you that you need to speak up. In hindsight, either a guardian or one of the alders should have taught you our arts, starting the day you were announced."

"You think?"

"Concentrate. Now isn't the time to let anger over the past take precedence," Joel said.

"Yes, Captain," Dominic replied.

"How'd you find her in Acheron if you can't find her now?" Joel teased.

"You took me. Remember? Astral is much easier besides."

Joel couldn't help but smile as well. A long time had passed since the man called him captain. Returning to the matter at hand, he traversed the knots tying up his friend's mind. There were many of them and many shadows hidden along the way. Such scars were normal for a soul his age, but they must be cleared before he ever hoped to rise. These were the memories and things that held him back. A sad revelation. Joel grit his teeth. It wasn't yet Dominic's time. He was far from reaching the resonance that would initiate his rising, despite his effort. Then how was it he displayed symptoms?

"Your paths are open, but shadows and blocks will stay until they're addressed," Joel said. He stepped back and watched him for a moment. There was still time to turn this around. "You'll need to meditate while you're gone to keep them clear, at least once per revolution of the Earth. Open your eyes," Joel added.

Dominic opened his eyes. They glowed a dull shade of jade. Joel tried to hide his fears, as he didn't want to alert the man to the signs of the darkness inside him. A nest of blackness was building in his core, choking the light of his atman. Taking a slow circle around his friend, Joel considered the strange conflict. The darkness alone could have veiled her atman from his heart, but that would have meant it was contained within him since before they met. Maiel's decay made a great deal more sense. If Dominic was harboring a flawed atman, he put a dangerous curse on his khata. Humans, when taken by the darker forces of their worlds, became insatiable for energy. Jiangshi. Vampires. Maiel's atman would reject him no matter how strong the bond, until he succeeded in causing her to burn, or she succeeded in eliminating the dark. He might have been feeding on her without knowing it this entire time.

Joel continued the lesson, showing Dominic how to track her—a remotely dangerous trick that could backfire later. However, it wasn't anything they couldn't handle, if needed. Joel raised his arm and pointed to the wall. A painting hung in a framed alcove.

"Stare at nothing—there."

Dominic stared.

"Picture her and reach again," Joel insisted.

Dominic stared until his eyes widened and his vision blurred. He drew in a deep breath, exhaling it in a heavy sigh. Still nothing. Joel stepped in front of him again and laid his palm on his forehead.

"Hard-headed—I'll walk you through it then," Joel said, intending to form the bond himself; it would show Dominic's mind the way.

"Stubborn human thought. Think like us if you want to be one of us," Zaajah whispered, not understanding the entire issue.

"Follow my energy. You feel my hand on your head, follow it back to my wrist, elbow, the shoulder, my atman. Now picture your wife. Follow the image back to her. The string is long; keep following. Follow it back. Follow it," Joel said.

Dominic suddenly sucked in a breath and stumbled backward. His back struck the wall and his eyes popped open. Clutching at his armored chest, he sucked in air as if he were suffocating and struggled to stay on his feet as his consciousness faltered. The women rushed to his aid, together keeping him upright. It was as if something had kicked him. Joel waited, hoping the connection stuck.

"I felt her. I felt her pain," Dominic panted.

"Good, I sense the same," Joel said.

"Good?" Dominic asked, skeptical.

"We must hurry to Otzar. I don't know about you, but I don't wish to feel that for the rest of eternity."

Dominic caught his breath, still clutching at his chest. He nodded, looking more afraid than ever.

CHAPTER 9

"DAD," A VOICE CALLED TO DOMINIC from the passage behind him as he and the others walked the bluish corridor toward the entrance of Otzar and the White Gate.

There were at least a dozen among them who could claim the title, but Dominic faced the owner of the voice knowing it was meant for him. His companions, Alex, Joel, and Zaajah, patiently waited, also knowing the source of that call. His eldest child, a reflection of his bygone youth, brought his twin khata and Samuel with him to see their father off. Gragrafel stood near, protective escort of the brood. The four younglings looked as mournful as their grandsire. It reminded him of days long lost and his mind filled with the anxieties of what failing them would bring.

"Dad, we've come to bid you fair journey," Ian spoke again. His features softened and he smiled.

Dominic went to him and put his arms around his son in a firm embrace.

"I'll bring her back," Dominic promised.

"We know," Ian said, trying not to sound forced.

"Listen to your granpitarau. They're truly wise."

Ian nodded.

Samuel frowned at his father, but Dominic gave him a hug anyway. The younger boy melted against him, needing the affection more than the others. He could feel the fear running through him, along with his constant emptiness. His daughters eyed him reluctantly and he laid a kiss on both their foreheads, squeezing them to each of his sides. Much like their mother, they were selfless free spirits who never seemed too jarred by any happening until now. They bore a smile almost always, but today their faces were grim. Surrounded by his children, he felt weak in his resolve to go, but his desire to succeed grew keen. It wouldn't be enough to just bring her back. There was a change to be made once that happened. He shut his eyes a moment and swore to his heart he would only endeavor to repair the damage he'd done.

"I'll be back soon. Take good care of the little ones and don't leave it to your khata. One day you'll have children and you'll need to know how to care for them," Dominic told them. He paused, holding the girls and trying to imprint them on his mind, a charm to gird his resolve. "Listen to your granpitarau and matula Corabael while I'm away. They know a thing or two."

"Uncle Zacharius was going to have a svarg give us instruction," Chaiel whispered.

"Don't learn too fast. I want to be here when you're raised," Dominic told her.

"Dominic, we haven't much time," Joel called to him.

"We'll be vigilant with the twins," Amaiel promised him.

"Us as well," Ian said, putting his arm around his younger brother.

Samuel didn't look so convinced and Dominic smiled.

"Be good," Dominic said, tousling Samuel's hair.

They whispered I love yous; letting go tore a hole in Dominic's center. He pushed himself to continue. Even if he didn't see rest for another three thousand years in the Pits of Acheron, he had to go right now. He turned toward the White Gate with all the strength he was capable of mustering. The others preceded him and he spared his children a brief glance over his shoulder.

"The ways are confusing and a guide is necessary to find where you're to report. None but the muses and dominion alders charged with this duty know the passages and halls of Otzar. Please be patient in this sacred place. As you know already, it is full of travelers, but Otzar also contains the doors to direct interface," Alex said, a tremble in her voice hinting at the unrest within her. "For this journey you'll be sent into the Samsara as you are. We can't spare the time to grow a vessel. There'll be no cords to hold you here. You must be very careful and listen to your guardian."

"Very few are allowed the privilege of just walking in. You should feel honored," Joel told him with a proud curl of the lips.

"I don't care about honors. I want my wife," Dominic said, quite moody as they entered an empty antechamber.

Dominic swallowed the fiery dryness in his throat. They moved along the deep spaces toward the White Gate. In the distance of the high-vaulted hall was a frieze depicting Trailokya. It was the only ornamentation in sight, aside from a seemingly endless repetition of perfectly spaced narrow pillars. The architecture was clean. The pillars holding up the ceiling were smooth-edged, as if the room had been polished out of the rock. It reminded him of the lift chamber to the High Council room. He walked this path more than a few times, but never without Maiel—he remembered being distracted by her lustrous beauty.

Alex approached the marble relief and pressed her hand on a starry globe being fought over by carvings of danava and duta. Dominic looked up the wall to see where there was a supposed likeness of Adonai in the beginning days. With several hollow knocks, the great bolt and gears slid apart. It roused his attention. He could never quite see that high anyway.

A light illumined a crack in the thick marble and peaked in a point at the center of the globe. The ribbon of light widened until the sculpture was revealed as two halves of the famed gate. The next room, the Red Corridor, was of the same smooth white stone, but there it was the same tone as milk warmed by the Perpetual Light, instead of blue snow in the light's vacancy. A warm glow came from a ceiling of leaded panes. The glass, alternately frosted and clear, obscured the side of the citadel mountain above. This passage was much shorter and the ceiling not quite so high as the others. The adornments of this room were of gold and red fabrics, in the shapes of carpets and tapestries, giving the space its name.

"Alder Alexandrael," a dominion guard called from the other end of the Red Corridor.

Alex led the way, along a gold and red carpet stretching the length to another much smaller door. The dominion guard was clad in the brown robes of his order, and leaned on a menacing halberd. He watched them from a pair of milk-white eyes sunken into a dark-skinned face. His elongated skull was bald but for a circlet of long white hair growing from just above the oval ears. This stunning crown was adorned by a ring of silver. He lifted his four white wings, in warning and to bar the way. His defensive demeanor was a hallmark of his kind.

Dominic only saw Otzar guardians when he came there to fulfill his dharma. Very few alders reached the status of dominion and all served inside the cloister of Otzar, which they never left. They were a rare breed who could be trusted to guard such a place with unerring loyalty and no rest.

"King Adonai ordered this soul to retrieve Captain Maiel," Alex explained.

"We've been informed. Your guide of the ways waits beyond this door. Take care that you stay on your path and don't stray in thought or step. If any of the souls are disturbed, there'll be dire consequences," the dominion said, a tad threatening.

They took their job exasperatingly seriously.

"Yes, we understand the rules. He's been incarnating for many years and has been on this path each time," Alex curtly replied.

"Things change," the dominion bit back, peering hard at Dominic.

Dominic met his stare. The flame in his throat grew. He swallowed, finding his mouth even drier. Though he wanted to grasp at the discomfort, he held his hands tight to his side. His body pulsed with anxiety. His duty was clear and none would stand in his way. Whoever was responsible for taking Maiel guaranteed their own undoing.

Joel took a step nearer to the guard.

"Whatever it is you sense, alder, if we don't proceed and make quick work of this, you'll have helped to make it permanent. Open your doors," Joel demanded.

The dominion regarded him for several tense moments, mulling over the possibilities. Dominic cleared his throat. They wanted to hear from him.

"It's okay. Joel—it's okay," he rasped. He cleared his throat.

All eyes turned to him. Though he felt oddly self-conscious, he formed a response that was sure to get them past this blockade. It was a matter of hitting their formalities, which was the key to many interactions, he discovered.

"Guardian of Otzar, I'm here to use your ways and bring my wife back. I was assigned this duty by King Adonai Elohim himself. If he trusts me, then none should have quarrel with our passing."

The knot in Dominic's throat spread like fire down his neck and over his shoulders. The dominion tried to break the barrier on his mind. Dominic thrust back with his thoughts, producing a glare that elicited a suspicious expression from his sparring partner. He knew then that the effort had given away the fire inside him. The dominion opened his mouth to reply, but then bit down and held his silence. Dominic refused to utter another word and reveal his weakness. The standoff came to end as the dominion drew up stiffly and stepped aside. The white eyes remained on him as they entered the narrow corridor of sullen blue. The passage was lit by an unseen source. It was like a tunnel bored through ice. The guard sniffed the air and scowled as if something foul touched his senses. Then the door closed and they stood alone, awaiting their guide.

Alex turned to him. "Are you feeling well?"

"Exhausted. I just want to get on my way. We've waited too long already," Dominic rasped.

"If we need to go to Acheron, we'll go. We have your back," Zaajah said.

Dominic nodded but the anger didn't subside from his features. Joel clamped a reassuring hand on his friend's shoulder. There would be time to rest when Dominic got back. He only hoped that his family and friends would let Dominic and Maiel be for a good while. There were wounds to heal and they couldn't do that with an audience hovering. But, he would make the argument once they returned and proved all of Zion wrong.

"Dominic," a soft voice called.

A featureless virtue stood in the opening of the east-facing corridor. They claimed no mark of identity except a shroud of thin robes and four opalescent wings. Dominic stared, completely stunned. It appeared to stare back despite having no eyes. Somehow, he understood its intentions and attitude. His eyes slipped over the undulating colors, wondering just how it spoke with no mouth. The figure reminded him of a luminescent sea worm. This might be his future if he chose the path of a muse, a glorified sea worm. He wasn't sure he could rise to a place where he would be unrecognizable to everyone except when he filled them with feeling. Virtues were a secretive sect that spent their existence in the higher reaches of Zion or within the walls of Otzar. He would be separated from Maiel until she rose to one of the races housed there as well. The eyes he loved so much would be hidden behind red lenses, and her form would be encased in a heavy suit of gleaming silver armor. Their children would have to fend for themselves; Dominic would never see them again. He wasn't sure he liked the idea, but there was so much time before then.

"Please follow me," the virtue spoke again.

Their guide floated just above the floor, moving up the corridor. Each motion it made left a thin dust of light in its wake. The manifestation was fascinating to him, now that he toyed with the idea of becoming one. He reached to catch the glitter. The fire in his throat grew more intense, spreading further in his chest and down his arms as soon as it touched his skin.

"Samsara will slow the spread. The flesh will insulate you and give you more time," the virtue spoke again.

"Give me more time for what?" Dominic asked, his voice quite rough.

"The change," the virtue said in return, not entirely answering the question.

"Change?"

"This way. Your friends will arrive close behind you." The virtue waved them forward.

"Good. Zacharius was successful then. I wonder who they were able to command on such short notice. Cal would be a wise selection—Bade wiser still," Alex said.

The virtue remained silent. Dominic thought it obvious that Luthias would go with him. It was a foolish question with which to waste their time, unless Alex knew something to the contrary.

A pulse of anguish tore through his chest. Dominic gripped his heart, falling against the wall. It was Maiel and something was terribly wrong. As the feeling progressed and he regained his feet, abnormal strength took over. The others quickly came to his aid. He choked down a hoarse growl, afraid of the wrathful sensation that made him desperate to strike something. They backed off. He gestured and thanked them, straightening his breastplate with a sharp tug, convincing himself that he was merely overwrought. The growl was no more than frustration, but his apology didn't have the desired effect. The others saw what had just happened differently.

The virtue took the moment to study him, head slightly cocked in a quizzical fashion. Then, without a word, it turned up the passage. Dominic's thoughts stilled, stunned by the action. He'd never seen such control and balance. The glance, though blind, was telling. Something had happened inside him and the blind duta had seen it without judgment. Behind him, his companions' whispers stirred him awake from his thoughts. They believed he wasn't aware that their hissing was as loud as if they were standing close to his ear. Dominic followed the virtue, inspired to duck the cloying fingers of damnation simply to prove for himself that he could.

The blue corridor ended at the base of what was called the well. The view reminded Dominic of a pit prison. Otzar rose into the height of the mountain, a tall wending cone in which the Perpetual Light radiated from the top and blotted out the highest levels of the hive. Crystallized atman fell to a pool of velvet in the center of the room, blue, green, red, yellow, and all shades in between. Others floated, which made it difficult to secure them. Openings like the niches of a crypt, tall enough and wide enough to stand in, coiled along the walls one after another, up and beyond the light. Several brown-robed dominions busily walked in and around the vast area, while others stood on guard. The sexless virtues floated in the open expanse, inspecting the cords of light reaching into the brilliance, while others collected the crystals. The dim tunnel muted their eyes so that the colors of gold and red encountered were quite bold. The light was blinding.

The virtue urged them past the entrance to another corridor and onward through the hive. They soon emerged on a higher vantage point overlooking the niches. Each time it seemed they had risen several stories, but they had gone no further into the mountain. The openings into each hive revealed new colors and sights. It also revealed the presence of dominions and virtues working with the souls entrusted to their care while interfacing in the old way of entering Samsara. Among them, muses flitted near, casting their grace on the sleeping masses. Dominic eyed them, forgetting his mission for a brief moment. Their guide allowed him the observation, perhaps sensing his connection to them.

Dominic was increasingly inspired. Some were like children, both duta and human, others like animals, and some known to no other world as anything more than fantasy, much like the souls from worlds beyond Earth. It was the nature of their being to extend their forms into shapes of all kind. So creative were their minds that they could not house themselves inside expectations, while some found comfort in embracing who they had been.

The calling pulled upon him once more, but the fire spreading within also offered quite a convincing case for giving into it. He weighed both, wondering if he were deluding himself. Whichever he chose, was this meeting expectation or destiny?

Passing yet more cells to enter another corridor that wound still higher, Dominic took another pause. This alcove housed a soul weeping over the fading form of another until the other's dim light was gone and she sat mourning alone. Her pleas for her mate to return and the tang of her misery brought more fear in his heart than the burning in his core. The woman's guardian and a pair of the Otzar guardians tried to console her, but there was no consolation for such a loss. Her mate had fallen to Jahannam. Dominic stared in rapt attention, half sure he witnessed his fate. Tears should have stung his eyes and the anxiety should have burned in his throat, but instead, he felt stronger and drawn closer to the suffering. Then the woman screamed and all that was left was smoke.

Joel touched his shoulder. The captain gave him a censuring look, signaling him not to ogle the demise of the wayward. He scanned the others' faces. They must be aware of his change. Why did they trust him to rescue Maiel? The scales in their eyes measured the risk. Did he go just to burn down in Samsara and save them the horror of seeing it? Turning away, Dominic followed their patient guide. Again, they whispered. Gritting his teeth, Dominic forced his thoughts to focus on the journey. Soon, he would prove them wrong.

Dominic thought his legs would give out before they reached their destination. He wondered why they had no lift constructed into the well, but then he guessed that someone somewhere was keeping a close eye on their progress as an assessment. Yet there was no trace of intrusion upon his mind. Dominic stretched the muscles in his neck and swallowed to ease his throat. Perhaps the point was to clean him up a bit before he joined the extraction.

The passage led to a small room the tone and texture of bleached bones. It was actually half passageway and half niche. Here the arches were also filled with reposing travelers, but these slept in the blinding light. Dominic noticed the shining circlets on their heads and he stared in astonishment. He wondered what the svargs were doing incarnated into Samsara. They were capable of walking there in their own forms. They could manifest a seemingly mortal sattva if needed. Time had changed Earth a great deal, he guessed. It had grown dangerous for their kind to cross the khajala and make themselves known in the face of vast historical sources and burgeoning technologies. Religions and research, both built on what humans scarcely remembered of the home they'd left behind, made for an intolerant landscape. The belief in and leveraging of such incomplete information, often twisted by the shadowy forces of the enemy, caused great conflict and evil. These institutions would try to murder them in the name of science or in the name of preservation, and the enemy would be inclined to help. Thus, the need for anonymity had grown great. It was a balance they had forged to fulfill the souls' need to grow.

Dominic blinked. The blank, blue face of their guide was turned toward him. He frowned, drawing in a deep breath. Of course that understanding was not his own. At least, she—yes, she—was a well-meaning teacher. He allowed the virtue to float about the surface of his mind, careful to not allow her any deeper.

Stranger than the presence of incarnated svargaduta, or even the guide's telepathic communications, were the multiple tethers leading from the reposed travelers to somewhere inside the light. While Dominic marveled at these phenomena, a svarg rose from his bed. The half-closed eyes eerily lolled. He faced them, as if he saw Dominic, and a snarl curled the corner of his lips. A woman shared her alcove with this svarg alder, and whispered to the wall, tapping it and swaying. Suddenly, Otzar resembled a Samsaran asylum, or perhaps the labyrinths of the shadow lands. He swallowed, sensing the threat these figures posed.

A virtue appeared from the reaches of the niche and urged the travelers back to their biers. The engel was laid back down and lulled into a deeper trance, while another came to assist in the care of the woman. Their lines were checked and strengthened.

"Sometimes,when they sleep or their vessel is injured, they wake," their guide explained.

Dominic nodded. "I remember."

Indeed, he did. During the course of an early incarnation, a long illness took him, but not before he woke several times in Otzar, barely aware or capable of understanding what had happened. He remembered how disconcerting it was for his clouded mind before the lines released and he came back to who he really was. Maiel had had similar experiences, dreaming of her true self, sometimes afraid of the visions, sometimes inspired. The travels had always been most difficult on her. He remembered her mentioning the light behind her lids whenever she shut her eyes, day or night. It glimmered just beyond reach, something that caused longing and melancholy.

"The duta never lose connection with their true selves. They are constantly reminded because of the resonance of their atman. They're difficult to keep connected in the physical realm. Here, we can keep them closer to the perpetual light, to ease the longing. They can see it when they shut their eyes or cross into the astrals during the appliance's resting sequence. That is why some have two cords. You may remember it as dreams," the virtue explained.

Holding her arm out to indicate their route, the guide ended their lesson. Dominic followed her into a low antechamber that ended before a door bearing the seal of Otzar, a loop-headed cross. The virtue placed her lucent hand on the symbol, turning it like a key. The mark lit with a pale blue light. She pressed the symbol to complete unlocking it and the surface dissolved before their eyes, like a ripple through the water.

Their guide urged them to enter the dim chamber beyond. This was the gate from which direct interfaces were made. His kind weren't skilled at unlocking quantum wormholes; their resonance was too weak or unfocused to manage the extensive energy. Instead they relied on the duta who manipulated them as easily as a child with a wind-up toy.

Their footsteps echoed against the smooth walls and polished floor. The space was round with a low-vaulted ceiling and recurring arches along the walls. The seal of Samsara was recreated in the stone below their feet. In the center rested a rather ornate and large font, a piece quite out of place against the smooth construction. The seal also appeared in the gothic arches circling the walls. From the waters of the vessel, an azure glow cast undulating lines on the ceiling. The vessel contained much more than water. The liquid was a viscous substance in which wisps of white hot sparks twirled, much like the filmy, silver fluid suspended in the arches. The font was a kapalanum, an ancient tool duta used to observe incarnated assigns from a distance. The main function of the kapalanum was to aid a guardian in the proper timing and placement of assigns inside of bio-interface appliances according to their dharma agreement and karmic debts. Dominic hoped they meant to use it to land him close to his wife and save them all a lot of time.

The door shimmered closed, entombing them. A distant whisper floated in the air, answered by another and another. Dominic looked for the source, but none of his companions spoke and there was no one else present. Their eyes switched about; they heard the sound as well. Stepping around the perimeter of the circular vault, he studied the arches filling the walls, one after another. Four greater arches, each crowned by a keystone stamped with a letter, and twelve slighter arches, three after each larger, were all framed with various scrollwork and details. Dominic touched the stone. It felt like ice. He looked at the keystones and spun in a circle. The room was a giant compass of the other universe. Dominic reached his hand to touch the viscous barrier. The swirls of lights and sparks gravitated to his skin. The force pulled at him. Joel grabbed him by the shoulders and pulled him back to the others.

The virtue faced them, patiently standing beside the smaller arch between the north and east gate. They waited for the guide to speak, but instead she held her silence. The portal seal activated, awaiting its moment to be opened again.

At that moment, Zach strode through the entrance, his black robes flying. Behind the tall engel followed a small youngling and then Gediel. Dominic stared at them, wondering who the child was and where they had left Luthias. He eyed the youngling, certain Luthias wasn't going with him.

"Lena," Zaajah gasped.

"Captain Zaajah." The girl smiled, sounding mature for a child of her apparent years.

"They have granted you a guardian to guide and protect you on your journey," Zach told him.

"Just don't tell me this is the guardian," Dominic said, scoffing.

Zach stared at him, as did Gediel. The hard stare of their luminescent eyes could not tell him what he wanted to hear. Drawing up his shoulders, he drew a deep, despairing breath.

"Lena? The child my wife was guarding? But she's only a soul. They can't be serious. Where's Luthias?" Dominic asked, outraged.

Lena raised an eyebrow and displayed her small set of jet wings. She met his consternation with a smirk.

"The king has temporarily granted her all she'll need for this mission, making her an erela as much as Zaajah or my khata. She'll return without you if necessary, but will serve you in your quest as well as Evocati Luthias could, if not better. Besides, dear akha, she has a vested interest in your success. The mission stands between her and her rising," Zach told him.

"I owe Maiel for the comfort she brought to my transition. Her love and guidance kept me and my family safe, while risking her own safety in the effort. I accepted the duty as repayment."

"A youngling," Dominic breathed, still skeptical.

If they were going to send a child, they could have sent his eldest and given him the assistance of someone who was at least partially trained.

"Their faith knows no bounds," he derisively added.

"We harbor no doubt as to your abilities, after three thousand years, despite everything," Joel said.

Dominic's eyes narrowed.

"Everyone who goes to Samsara has a guardian. She's been prepared by Adonai himself. You can take heart that she's ready to face even Lucifer," Joel insisted.

"The High Council selected a proficient guide to aid you on your task. One you can trust," Zach assured him.

Dominic still questioned the motives for sticking him with this child. Lena watched him, resolute, and the others were unlikely to budge either. He hoped Luthias would come through the door and demand he be allowed to uphold his duty. Dominic nodded, acquiescing to their wishes. They needed to move forward with or without his guardian.

"I am glad to have your faith. I'm not sure it's well placed," Dominic told Joel. "Thank you for your gift of assistance," he said, turning to Lena.

The child smiled, reminding Dominic of his daughters. He managed a weak smile in return, troubled by what he knew and the danger it posed in Samsara. The devils and imps would hunt them fiercely. His instincts would drive him to protect her, only until the burning claimed him, but the distraction could very well cripple their efforts from the beginning. Moreover, could she survive if he turned on her?

Gediel approached, carrying a black robe over his arm. He looked at Dominic with his too deep seeing eyes. By the watcher's expression, they were about to have a confrontation. Likely, Gediel sensed the fire and his natural reaction was to put it out. Dominic braced, which provoked a wry twist on the engel's lips. Dominic welcomed having it out with him at last, even if the engel bested him.

"I've brought you one of my coats. It'll hide you better than any garment can. Your atman is muted by the material, but not completely hidden. So don't stay in one spot too long. The moment you stop, the shades will sense a weak signal giving away your location. They won't hesitate to converge on you to feed," Gediel said, holding up the long, leather trench coat.

Dominic gave a sour expression, provoked by what the watcher treated him to instead. He took the garment, daydreaming of a challenge of fists. The trench was constructed of ordinary leather, similar to the heavy wool one he wore in his last incarnation. He had died in it, shot to death on the front lines of a war. And it wasn't nearly as fine as the one the owner wore. Still annoyed and suspicious, his eyes went to Gediel's. He guessed it came from a time long ago, when the svarg was younger and slighter. A neatly disguised insult. After all, Gediel had the most to gain from his loss. To offer help was perplexing, but when help was a thinly-disguised weapon it made much more sense. In fact, he wouldn't be surprised if the coat suffocated him, or swallowed him the moment he put it on.

"Thank you," Dominic said, with a telling tone.

"I do it for her. She'll never recover from your loss and I don't wish to watch my friend fade. It would be one more tool in my jyoti's arsenal to win me. Don't mistake that I have very selfish reasons," Gediel replied.

"Don't mistake that I forget it," Dominic replied.

Dominic scowled, surprised the primus was honest. Joel took the coat from his hands and helped him put it on before he could insult the watcher further. The fire that burned from his throat to his core suddenly quenched. Gediel folded his arms. A satisfied expression crossed his features. Dominic regarded him suspiciously.

"Behave yourselves. We don't have time for these childish antagonisms," Alex said heatedly.

Dominic checked the fit of the coat, choosing to listen to Alex. His armor was gone, replaced by a pair of simple slacks and a heavy fisherman's sweater. Lifting each foot, he checked the fit of the boots and frowned deeply. Without his armor he was helpless against the shades.

"The coat has a cloaking device, like I said," Gediel responded to his obvious worry.

Luthias still hadn't arrived. Yet they continued to prepare for his insertion into Samsara. He should have been excited for the opportunity to prove himself. His wife and her comrades were always bursting with enthusiasm before a mission. Instead, he was torn, but mostly afraid. So many years had passed since he'd last seen that world. Technology was quick to change, he wasn't sure he would fit in so easily, or adapt well enough to complete the mission successfully. Lena had just left Earth, however. The selection made a tiny bit more sense.

"Do you still feel her?" Zaajah asked.

Dominic nodded. Maiel danced like a buzzing bee inside his head, stinging his heart. He would be glad to get her back and stop the horrible sensations she caused him.

"Don't fear their soldiers; it's their only strength. You've faced them before. This journey won't be different."

"We'll be here for you when you have need of us. But be sparing in your requests. We can only answer once without raising the attention of the council. They didn't say we could save her. They sent you," Alex added.

"Better than nothing," Dominic said, a little gloomy.

Alex folded him in her arms with a tight squeeze. Her warm energy filled him. Dominic hugged her back, surprised that she so willingly helped him against customary methods—something an alder never did. Though Maiel was her daughter, he thought they would be glad to be rid of him. Her actions remained suspect, as he had seen the alders go about such things in similarly meandering ways.

"Know that we love you both. Bring Maiel back to us," Alex said.

Tears stood in the mother's eyes. She kissed his forehead. Dominic nodded, unable to speak. She was the only mother he knew, since his parents had left him to grow up in the legions alone. Try as she might, she had never been very warm toward him until that moment.

Dominic felt hardy and focused with the addition of her affection, the coat, and the girl. It was quite an array of reinforcing strength. The task ahead stood in his mind with no thought of what he would gain in completing it. No hint of fear or suspicion cracked the veneer. But guilt stilled his tongue. Guilt over his doubt in them.

Pocketing his hands, Dominic waited for what came next. The others watched him, sad to send him on this mission alone, though such reluctance was foolish. There was no one else who could bring her back. Just like in the Pits of Acheron, his voice would wake reason.

"Are we ready then?" Dominic asked as the silence lengthened.

Lena moved to his side and took his hand. She smiled at him.

"You can succeed if you want to," she said.

Dominic doubted that simply wanting to succeed would win the battle he faced. They weren't facing a schoolroom test. These were full danava, a baron, and his prince. Not to mention the flame hiding within his core, sure to take over the moment he took off the coat. No soul on Earth would get it back on his shoulders then. If he succumbed, could Lena save Maiel? He supposed the girl was capable. Of course that depended on the girl surviving while entrusted to his care. He shut his eyes and squeezed Lena's hand. Maiel would never forgive him if any harm came to the girl. The assignment made still further sense. A deep breath, then he opened his eyes to speak. Zach advanced from the portal.

The young alder looked serious as always, considering Dominic from a set of eyes disturbingly similar to his sister's. Dominic felt like a corpse on a dissecting table, a subject uncomfortably exposed.

Something stung Dominic behind his ear. He covered the wound with his hand, sucking in his breath.

"What was that?" Dominic asked, his face pinched.

Joel stepped from behind him, holding a tuft of gold hair. The engel stepped to the kapalanum and dropped the hair in the fluid. The light brightened from the atman as they surrounded the offering.

"To follow you from here," Joel explained.

Dominic scowled, but was thankful they intended to keep an eye on him.

"If you have need of us…" Zach said, abruptly shoving him through an arch. The last Dominic heard was Zach's distant, "Call."

Dominic fell through an expansive emptiness. A sudden impact against his side elicited a grunt. He rolled, unable to stop and unable to see. It was dark and the smell was unpleasant. He came to a stop and he found himself lying on his stomach in a field. He tried to see in the dark, wondering if he was just thrown into Asfodel Fields. The stench filling his nose was close to the undertone of sulfur that plagued the atmosphere of Jahannam. He blinked in order to focus. A pile of manure was inches from his nose. He shook his head and pushed onto his knees away from it.

"Dominic," Lena called.

Lena rushed to his side, placing a small hand on his shoulder. She looked dazed, but not harmed.

"You're not very good at that, are you?" Lena smiled.

"Some of us don't have wings to help. I'm fine, thank you for asking," Dominic replied, regaining his feet.

Lena tried not to laugh, sputtering into her hand. Dominic half-smiled, infected by her joy. Bearings gained, he brushed the dirt off his legs.

The moon shone down from a clear night sky and outlined the tops of the trees surrounding the field. Dominic knew that it was autumn by the crispness in the air. The field had been harvested some time ago and lay fallow with sparse dead weeds. Giant round bales dotted the chilly distance, moldering in their abandonment. He swatted his sleeves and scowled at the dark.

A tug on his sleeve brought Dominic's attention back to Lena. She stared worriedly behind them. Dominic followed her troubled gaze. Their landing place was near to the road. A barbed fence obstructed the path across the ditch, but the concern Lena had was for the rusty truck that had stopped and the driver who stared anxiously at them from behind his wheel.

"They forgot to mention we'd be seen," Dominic mumbled, trying not to move his mouth.

"You there! Are you all right?" the old man asked, with a distinctly British accent. The tones quickly determined a clearer picture of where they were, not only a vague when. "You took quite a fall just then," the man went on.

Dominic waved.

"We're fine. Just fine. Thank you," Dominic replied. "If you'd go away," Dominic added under his breath.

"Is there someone with you, lad?" the old man asked, trying to see around him.

Lena hid behind Dominic's leg. She covered her mouth to stop her warm breath from puffing in the cold night air.

"I don't think he can see me. I'm not sure though," Lena told him.

"Just wonderful." Dominic exhaled and raised his palms to the sky. Muttering a curse under his breath, he slapped his hands back against his sides.

"What's that, boy?" the old man called to him.

Dominic scratched the back of his neck and struggled for something to say. Lena blinked at him, unable to help. This was exactly why he needed Luthias. The engel would have warned him before he made a fool of himself. This child couldn't even tell if she was visible or not. Callidora, even with her ineptitude, would have been an improvement.

"Nothing—I think I hit my head harder than I thought," Dominic said, gesturing dismissively.

"Ah, American—what the devil are you doing in a corn field at night? Do you have a place to stay, boy?" the old man persisted.

Dominic stared. Of course he was American. They put him there wearing the flesh of his last incarnation to save time. How had this happened? And more importantly, how was Maiel going to react? He'd hoped to leave that life behind, convinced it had caused this outcome.

"You better come with me. My wife'll feed you and we'll give you a safe place to rest. The doctor'll be in bed this hour. Best you see him in the morning for that lump," the old man said, getting out of the rickety vehicle.

Dominic offered a blithe, but small, twist of the lips. Taking his first step, his feet were immediately tripped by a lump lying there. Avoiding another fall, he danced aside and saw that an army green pack lay there with the hilt of his gladius poking from the flap. The old man was certain not to take kindly to the sight of the weapon. Grabbing the bag, he shoved the weapon down and found a change of clothes in which to wrap it. The pocket concealed his weapon more than he thought it would. The pommel didn't even show. Swinging the pack onto his back, he walked to the fence.

"That's a good lad." The old man held his hands out.

Dominic reluctantly handed his pack over.

"It's okay. He's okay," Lena said.

Lena crawled through the wires, careful not to touch them and alarm the human to her presence. Dominic carefully made his way over the barbs, leaning on an old post. When he made it to the other side, the old man handed back his pack with a grin that was all gums.

"Come along then," The old man waved him toward the car. He paused to look him over and continued, "You aren't on that stuff are you? Fall in any shit? My wife'll mend your clothes if you did. Blasted sheep shit everywhere in the corn fields after harvest. Can't keep them out of the stuff, but it's worse when the farmers don't care like that one there. Guess he thinks it makes for better soil next planting."

"Stuff?" Dominic asked.

"Stuff. Dope. All the kids are doing it, no offense. I hope," the man said, laughing.

"Oh, no—no. I tripped over a rut in the field. Shouldn't have tried to cross it. Thought I was making a good short cut—just missed the shit," Dominic said.

They wandered up the ditch and the old man went to his truck door. Dominic stepped around the other side. He examined the road, expecting a crew of shadows or watchers to sprint toward them. The darkness filled the spaces, but no horde. He grabbed the handle of the truck door and tried it. The door held fast.

"You have to wiggle it and give it a tug." The old man smiled, struggling with it from the inside.

Lena snuck into the bed of the truck, where the farmer had built up the side walls with wood panels to carry larger loads. Having wings had its advantages—she lifted in the air past the barrier and set back down without any trouble. Her little voice expressed surprise. Dominic finally got the door open and saw through the broken back window that a guardian was in the bed with her. He climbed in next to the old man. The truck was from the forties and in a sad state of affairs. Dominic frowned, nostalgic.

"Fancy bit of luck." Lena smiled at the guardian in the truck bed beside her. They shook hands.

The old man shut his door and cranked the shift lever into gear. He smiled at Dominic.

"On our way," the man said.

The truck lurched from the shoulder quickly, pinning Dominic to the seat. He was surprised by the pickup of the old heap. The old man gave a little chuckle.

"Worked on the engine a bit. She's got pickup, yeah? You sure you're feeling all right, lad?"

Dominic smiled reassuringly and nodded. He would be just fine, as soon as he determined their direction and they got on their way. At least the run-in provided him with the presence of a full-fledged guardian and transportation. His mind eased with the security it gave, even if for the briefest of time.

CHAPTER 10

Máriabesnyő, Hungary

MAIEL CONTINUED EAST into the darkening evening. It took a good measure of her remaining energy before she found the atman nestled in a village in northeastern Hungary. She recognized the architecture and some of the landmarks as she carved through the distance. It had been a long time since she was last there, but she was sure. Her sense of direction never failed her. Picking along a tree-lined field, she kept her eye on the light of a buttercup building in the distance. A breeze blew and it carried the soft scent of autumn and a deep-reaching chill.

The baron crept back into the dark far behind and would have quite the time tracking her, unless the hapless watchers decided to also follow and clue him in. Nonetheless, moving to a sanctuary where she could at last rest was imperative. Her energy waned dangerously. She couldn't hope to battle Morgentus successfully without all of her strength. Maiel lifted her arm. Her form was becoming flesh-bound. Soon, her wings would wither and she would be trapped there. Death would be the only way to open the gate home again—if she could ever find death. The fallen who didn't descend to Jahannam were cursed to linger in Samsara with unnaturally long lives, in order to prove their virtue to Zion.

Mist crept along the forest floor. Maiel half-expected a deadly shade to jump out at her. Much of the time the shades would use their cunning to keep hidden from her senses. A rattle echoed among the tree trunks, affirming her mistrust. The long shadows of the trunks and branches hid whatever was out there. It sounded like a serpent, possibly a Bhogin. Probably just a rodent with a nut. Daring another step forward, she was met with another round of the rattling. A shadow dashed before her, quickly rounding behind.

Then it was gone. Maiel's nostrils became more sensitive; they caught the foul stench. Frowning, she flexed her fists to feel the articulated armor covering her fingers and to prepare herself for a fight. Whatever that was, it was more annoying than dangerous. A remarkably old hobgoblin.

Maiel stepped forward, hoping to bait the little blighter. Imps weren't imaginative creatures. Repetition was their creed. They had an entirely twisted sense of humor and an utter lack of skill. As she hoped, the rattling came again. She closed her eyes, immersing herself in her higher senses. The air parted as it moved close. Striking like a cat, she grabbed the imp by the throat and held it in a crushing grip. The imp struggled, unable to break free and quite regretful that it had bothered her. Maiel sneered, watching the coil of shadows that made its form. The imp was nearly a smoker, nearly a serpent. Very old indeed. Imps often became gremlin soldiers, completely unrelated to the races of Trailokya; they were their own aberration.

"Not your day," Maiel said.

The imp rattled again. The sound came from three bony slits in each side of its throat. Maiel eyed the creature, making note of every detail. The face was flat, round, and featureless. It stared at her from large, glassy black eyes. The skin was chameleon, shifting from greens to browns, to blues to black. Hair patched its body making it look somewhat like a fallen faun, but it had no horns and no hooves. Instead, it bore a pair of leathery wings and set of sharp fangs. A rather large pair of pointed ears framed its round head and a rat-like tail whipped the high grass. Of course, like all shades, it emitted smoke from its pores. It seemed to be mimicking every known shade in Jahannam, but that was the brilliance of its kind. They were formed of emotional energy and bore the print of every donor.

The imp pulled at her fingers, desperate to be free and hardly caring that it cut itself on the sharp claws of her gauntlets. The flesh bled dark blue on the shining metal. Maiel squeezed harder. One quick twist of her wrist and it would be dead.

"Relinquish," it hissed at her, demanding its release instead of pleading. "Relinquish."

"No," Maiel said.

Drawing her long knife from her belt, she prepared to finish the imp. The shade called out, tears spilling from its eyes. Maiel hesitated. The blustering raised doubt. This confused creature might be a wayward soul and not just an imp created by the acid of angry hearts. Her hand released and the imp fell backward. Pushing through the bed of leaves, the creature looked stunned. Abruptly, the eyes and mouth took on a very distinct turn of evil.

"Stultus." The imp snapped its teeth.

The gills rattled and it darted behind the trees. Maiel took her bow from the quiver and readied an arrow. She should have known better. Stepping forward, she carefully watched the field and wood. The angry blight wouldn't allow her to cross the wood without a nuisance tax, and leaving him there would only give him the means to terrorize the town worse than before. Besides, the imp would betray her location, if it hadn't already.

Ducking beneath a branch and stepping over a rough rock wall in the way, Maiel picked closer to the road beyond the wood, always keeping the light of the buttercup building in view. The imp dashed past her, turning her around. She cursed under her breath and faced the road again. He'd tried to confuse her so she would lose her way. She wondered how many travelers this thing had consumed over the years.

The wood grew denser, but Maiel pressed on. Relaxing the string of her bow, she drew her knife again. The shade repeated its tactics. In a few more steps, it ran at her again, brushing against her back. Maiel responded quickly, tucking the knife behind her. She felt the imp strike the blade after rounding once more. It howled and stumbled, having impaled itself. Facing the beast, she quickly readied an arrow and took the shot without hesitation. The arrow pinned him to a broken stump through the wide eye socket. He twitched with the last throes of existence. Maiel fixed her bow on her back and drew her sword.

"Stultus." She frowned at it.

"He'll find you—take you to Acheron. The fire builds in your heart. You'll be his bride. You're one of us," the imp taunted.

"Let him come and he'll taste truth. I'll send him to Oblivion right behind you," Maiel said.

"Morgentus's whore is what you'll be. He's already claimed you. No way back now."

The imp pitifully laughed and the gills clacked before it stilled forever. The sattva melted, turning to smoke and sinking into the ground. She picked up the arrow, wiped it clean, and tucked it away. Retrieving her blade from a pile of leaves, she eyed the farm field she had just crossed and the shadows of the forest surrounding her. Cleaning the black blood from the knife, she hoped she had not given the baron a means to find her. Maiel sheathed the dagger in her calf holster and returned to gaining the buttercup building. Still able to send an imp to Oblivion should have cheered her, but it just made her more cross.

Maiel hurried across the road and through a gate in front of a quaint country church. The buttercup building belonged to the Catholic faith, complete with an onion-topped tower and crosses. Churches repelled her very being. As far as she was concerned, they were marked by the vile darkness of usury and other abuses. However, the last places of safety for her kind in Samsara were often connected to them. The humans built their dwellings and temples on energy points, making them inaccessible to but a few. Though the atman of well-intending humans created a circle of protection that kept the demons at bay, eventually those barriers weakened and the sacred turned profane. She hesitated, but there was little choice.

The drive and nearby road were crowded by vehicles and old horse carts, a mixture of tradition, the yoke that held humanity back, and progress. Organ music mixed with ill-tuned voices. As it passed through the walls, the sound was muffled and incoherent. A service was underway with a hymn to some half-concocted deity. Maiel shook her head ruefully and dared to move closer.

Despite the danger incarnated humans posed to her—for they never quite understood—Maiel required the sanctuary the atman promised. They were a dangerous race, hardly ever controlling their desires or their hearty tempers. When they inhabited their appliance, intent on implementing carefully planned dharma, humans forgot their real home. Thus, memories turned into mystical oddities or fantasies. It was a wonder they accomplished anything. Yet, humans were all she had to rely on. If she could find a selfless one among them, she might have a chance against Morgentus. Somehow, despite the poison that permeated such structures and those who frequented them, they were often the bastion of hope. This one housed that striking atman. She detected it over great distances, and it was what had drawn her there.

Maiel crept along the building until she found a window she could look through. Each light was high up on the exterior with no footing to reach it, except one. A niche in the stone provided the perfect step up. Climbing, she soon peered through a crack in the opaque glass. Inside the church, humans sat in pews listening to a vratin deliver his sermon. She smelled the evil and lies, mixed with sweet innocence and truth. Maiel grimaced at the abomination.

She scanned several faces. The clarity of her sight, still intact despite the loss of energy, provided a vision that would disturb anyone of lesser resolve. Several of the human faces twisted into garish miens, while a few others glowed with the light of her kind. Mudeaters and lightwalkers alike shared the room. Some were unaware, but those completely aware were the problem. Guardians of both worlds, circling each other and ready to strike, also shared the space. Shadowborn plotted against lightborn and the fray pulsed with angst. The statues looked on, frightened and unable to retreat, their atman too small and slow to carry them. A marditavya climbed backwards up the plaster, hissing and whining in protest.

Maiel found the much sought-after resonance. It was cloistered inside a rather tall, thin man hiding in the pulpit behind an enormous old book. The human's sattva was ensconced in a bio-vessel, and did not freely roam. His kindly face was swaddled in a beard going gray. Hair of the same hue was tied at the nape of his neck, not shorn like the other members of his order. He wore heavy white robes, but no glinting finery like other vratin. Every finger was bare. An honest human vratin—let alone a soul—was a strange thing to find in Samsara. But as she already suspected, a church was the place to find it.

The vratin continued on in the language of the people he served, barely audible through the glass and stone. The words were impure, but still annoyed the shadows, as they were spoken from a pure heart. Mudeaters lined the chancel steps, barred from his perch by some force. They snapped their teeth and hissed to badger him. She marveled at his patent resilience. Determination kept him on task, as he faced these tormentors like one of her own. It was possible the radiance of his extraordinary atman alone held them back, but the addition of three lightwalkers behind him made the efforts of the mudeaters pitiable. None of this was visible to the humans watching on.

Maiel counted four humans presiding at the service as vratin. Her eyes swept their faces, wondering which was unguarded. Reaching with her mind, she was able pair them off. Her eyes widened when it became obvious the atman she sought was defenseless, but for the gracious assistance of his companions' guardians. Maiel puzzled over this, wondering if one of the mudeaters had gotten lucky and stole his guide. Soldiers often attempted to usurp guardianship in an effort to break a soul, pushing it toward the dark with constant manipulations. This man resonated far too high to make such a case. The light he emitted, like a star on the surface of the planet, should have drawn every shade in the hemisphere, but only the guardians of the shadowborn dared to present themselves.

The danava would be quite piqued if she sought aid from this man. Her presence, even if brief, was certain to land him on an arduous path. She frowned. Her need didn't warrant the cost, but where else was she to go?

The vratin continued, still unaware of her surveillance. His energy lured her with a familiarity that flickered in his thread. There was no choice, and he appeared quite capable of handling the dark advance. The last question that remained was how to go to him with this many witnesses.

Maiel's eyes shifted over the congregation again. A high mountaintop or clear ocean would have been better, but this was the highest and farthest she could hope to reach; she was too exhausted to slide away again so soon. The only mountains nearby were soaked in generations of blood and made a better sanctuary for the enemy than it did for her. The only seas close enough were just as tormented. Doorways to the Domdaniel provided another way to capture her, and would sink her into the waters and torture her in the caverns below, where none would think to look.

Spreading her great red wings, Maiel stepped back and floated gently to the ground. The dragon on her arm prickled and the hair stood on the back of her neck. She faced the buildings and yard. Monuments dotted the space inside the fence and a narrow path led to other buildings at the back of the church. The prickling warnings ran along every mark in her skin, pooling into her core with foreboding. This was no reaction to the small nuisances that filled the church. Morgentus either followed on her heels, refusing to give her up, or was led there by the damned imp in the wood.

Maiel hurried to the entrance, no longer having the time to debate where she would shelter. Either the congregation would see her and be ter-ror-stricken or she would pass among them unseen. Either way, she must hide within the compass of this man's resonance until Morgentus had left. She needed to find the right moment to address the man.

"You can't hide, not even here," Morgentus said.

Halting mid-stride, Maiel watched Morgentus step through the church-yard gate. His boots smoked each time they touched the ground, but he was little bothered. The vratin had managed to guard the grounds, but the barrier was weak.

Maiel backed up to the church door, keeping her eyes on her pursuer. Morgentus's pace quickened and she ran. Falling against the heavy wood panels, she pushed hard, but they stubbornly resisted. Giving the rest of her strength to the effort, the panels gave way just as Morgentus stomped up the steps. The force of her push thrust her beyond the threshold and her enemy's reach. Maiel rolled onto her backside and slid along the stone floor further into the interior, until her back pressed against a pew. Her strength was nearly gone and he saw it. A smile split the baron's lips as he watched her, the smoke billowing around him. She was mistaken in her hope. The candle flames lengthened, tall and reedy. The heat of their blaze stressed the glass votives until they cracked with machine gun pops. He taunted her, standing beyond the door. The door was no barrier, just like the grounds. Morgentus was relishing the moment, for he would have her soon.

*   *   *

The nave door thrust inward and an ill wind passed into the church. A flutter of dry leaves skittered along the aisle amid the startled gasps of the flock. The priest saying Mass had just descended to prepare communion. He looked into the darkness outside his church with a wary eye, seeing a black shadow standing there, glowering at something from a ghostly face. Something familiar in the form raised his interest, but the distance prevented immediate recognition. The prayer candle flames blazed high. Continuing with the service, he nodded to one of his fellow clergymen. The man hurried up the aisle to shut the doors, quite lucky not to see what he stepped toward. The glass holding the votive exploded, halting him in his tracks, but a nod from the priest urged him on.

Crossing the chancel, determined to carry on despite the intrusion, the priest caught sight of a woman reclining on the floor. Her pale skin emanated an azure glow, boasting the luster of pearls. Her flame hair spilled down her back in a great cascade and he paused with surprise at such a vision. Eyeing the thick cords of her hair, he slowly realized that he wasn't looking at a mere woman. The glossy red fluttered and he saw she had wings. The glint of her armor blinded his eyes as she shifted to hide in the back corner near an altar of candles. The priest turned back to the great altar, not wishing to bring attention to the female or the force harassing her. Focusing on the communion was taxing after what he saw. His mind raced with thoughts he dare not think in present company.

The other clergyman shut the doors and a murmur rushed around the gathered parishioners like an ocean wave. The priest's voice rang over them as he performed the ceremony, trying to keep them focused on only him. The messenger that burst through his doors required he keep his tongue and finish his duties quickly. To his left, the glow of a duta guardian crossed into his sight. Then the glow showed on his right. They were curious about the newcomer, but he couldn't let them go to her and draw the attention of the evil ones to that spot. With a guarded glance, he sent them back to their duties.

The shadows, guardians, and souls appeared surprisingly unaware. The female's energy must have been low, masked by the threat and the others in the room. The priest's eyes betrayed his concern, but his mouth calmly spoke the words of the service. The cadence kept the guardians of both factions focused on him and one another, forgetting the newcomer. If they became aware, certain members of the congregation were capable of causing great harm to her. In truth, most of the congregation were trustworthy. They were a superstitious lot and believed in ghosts; however that belief didn't extend to the holy ghost or any such spirit that represented the church. The majority experienced apparitions or the like, which made them suspicious of some other world. These incarnated beings would tell you they did if asked, but when pressed, they dithered and revealed uncertainties. The church service was merely a device to satisfy the desire for ritual, perhaps conformity or constancy, as well. The church's importance waned with humanity's progress. There simply was no proof and everyone knew that. But, then, that is why they called it faith and not science. The presence of the host would change that. Some would panic. Some would plot. Others would observe with quiet joy and reluctance. It was the plotters that would make use of the event to restore the reach of the church, but mostly they would use it just to amplify their tenuous powers. These were the people who concerned him.

An assistant carried the paten and wine goblet as the presentation continued. The female was out of the aisle and safe from detection for the moment. Keeping the concern from his features, he managed to present the body and blood to those seeking it, even the half-bred shadowborn who dreamed of a day they would chew his bones. The symbolic ritual had no capacity to heal or save them. All it did was become a sinister act with which to torment him. Careful not to get nipped, his eyes trailed back and forth between the souls and the back of the church.

Once the congregation departed, the head priest was at last alone with only the other clerics to dismiss. He mumbled to them in a deep Hungarian accent, instructing them to put the ritual items away. One of the brothers took his heavy vestments. The men did as they were asked. still unaware of what hid in the back of the church. The guardians eyed him, but he gestured for them to stand back, exhibiting a wariness that spoke of tricks in the past.

Wandering the pews, the priest pretended to look for lost belongings his flock may have left behind. Bibles were left on the seats, earrings had fallen from ears, and a coin or two was left behind for the coffers. He put the books on their shelves, one eye on the back of the church. When the other men parted, he remained in the nave, deciding on how to approach the envoy. The priest rounded·the last pew, slow but intent, half-expecting her to be gone. To his surprise, she was not.

The messenger lay facing the wall beneath the iron rack of ruined candles. The votives that survived the dark intrusion cast gleaming points of light on her armor. The lustrous red wings were wrapped protectively around her body. Her pale skin was so ghost-like it gave him chills. When she didn't move, he grew concerned that she was dead. Then she breathed. The motion was a source of some relief, though she was unaware of him and therefore dangerous. He struggled to figure out a way to approach her and ascertain the nature of this visit.

Pressing the tips of his fingers together, the priest tread carefully forward, avoiding the long red cords spread over the floor. The details of her form came into sharper focus: a quiver of arrows, the shine of her shield, the glow of her blade. Where patches of skin showed, he now clearly saw she was marked by tattoos. Words failed him. This was one of the guardians and a battle-hardened one, at that. He cleared his throat, hoping that startling her would spur his brain. Duta soldiers were a rash lot and she'd demand an answer of him.

The winged emissary stirred at the sound. Spotting his shadow from the corner of her eye, she spun around in a whirl of red. He stumbled backward, just avoiding being struck. She held a curved knife a small breadth away from his Adam's apple. He held his hands up to calm her.

"Come no closer, vratin," she warned, lurid eyes pinning him from inside her prickly helmet.

"Welcome to my humble shelter, messenger. You're safe. No need for knives and warnings," the priest said, forced to spit out something before he was struck down.

"In a church? I still hear his call. Your walls are no barrier," she said, sneering.

"The demon won't enter here," the priest assured her.

"And yet there are danava and shadowborn mixing with ardhodita and duta," she countered, pressing the blade to his throat.

"Yes, the shades come to stop my work, but as you can see, I don't give up easily, and neither do your kin."

The envoy eyed him. He offered a smile. She put the knife back in its sheath on her leg. Folding her arms, she stood over him, expecting more words. The priest rubbed his throat instead and took several steadying breaths. She was rather tall and quite strong-looking, yet he could tell she was exhausted by her trial. He was exceptionally tall himself, but she stood above him. Perhaps it was just the height of her helmet. The priest was glad she didn't panic and make use of her strength. He wasn't quite ready to be martyred.

"You look exhausted. Please, trust me. I can offer sanctuary. You may stay as long as you need," the priest said.

"I followed an atman to this place," she said, ignoring his invitation.

"Atman?" He stared, struck by the utterance.

"Your life and light—that which you are," she replied, a little confused and a little annoyed at having to explain.

"Yes. Yes, I know."

Then she asked, still further puzzled, "What are you? Vratin?"

"I'm a priest, yes. Father Gregely Orius," he answered, a little amused.

Her eyes narrowed. "You're more than a priest, Gregely Orius. But, you already know that, don't you?"

Father Orius shook his head and laughed through his nose.

"Let us hold that for another day," he said.

Her shoulders relaxed, but she regarded him with little trust.

"I'll yield the question for now, vratin."

Orius was relieved. She had a very long, difficult tale to tell him. And this was not the place to tell it. The demon hunting her would soon return with reinforcements. The church wasn't strong enough to hold them back. They needed to move to higher ground, safe from danava reach. Besides, he couldn't protect her if he divulged his secrets before their time, and he didn't dare tell the secrets when he suspected a secret order had sent her to his door, once again attempting to cajole him into their ranks.

"Where is this sanctuary you speak of? I grow weak and need a place to meditate."

"Follow me," Orius said, indicating the aisle.

The messenger stared intensely, waiting for Orius to lead the way. He took stock of her full height and the nature of her dress again. Did she really think he could deceive her? He nodded, understanding. She didn't know him and had no reason to believe he led her to sanctuary. His eyes scanned her tattoos, noticing part of a dragon that decorated her arm. His brows knitted together as he puzzled out the meaning. She battled a strong demon and belonged to an old and proud family. Orius turned and made his way up the aisle. She followed him. Her stride was surprisingly quiet, given the weight of her armor.

"What brings you to Hungary?" Orius said.

"That thing you saw in the door," she answered.

"Yes, he looked rather troublesome. Has he been bothering you long?" He smiled, a little relieved it wasn't what he suspected.

"Just since I destroyed his pet a few days ago," she answered, looking over the gaudy interior of the church.

"Where are your friends to help you?"

"Would that they could be with me, but they remain in Zion."

"He gave you the dragon?"

The girl eyed him without answering. He nodded and let the question go. The look was answer enough and he was thankful to let her be, so long as her markings didn't include a triangle and eye.

Orius led her toward the chancel. She easily crossed and took the steps. He paused to peer behind him, in case any shade or imp lingered. The messenger stared at the crucifix hung in the apse. His eyes trailed to the violent carving and back.

"It is a reminder of what they can hope to achieve with perseverance. It's not meant to offend," Orius said to her.

"Of rising or fading? It's not simply an icon of what he did here, but of what his fellow souls did to him," she returned.

Orius pursed his lips and shook his leg, unsure of how to respond to such a statement. He decided to remain silent on the matter, as she was most correct. Her kind didn't lie. The kind he lived among did, and they were skilled at twisting out some bizarre interpretations.

"Sometimes, I wonder what humans mean by making these temples," she said, as he led her through a door at the back.

"It's funny you should mention it; I find myself wondering the same thing." Orius gave her a small smile.

"Why do you do it?"

"Because I have this memory," he said. He scanned his church. Wistful, he added, "A face not belonging to any man or any being of the known universe—a facet of light, barely perceptible, fluttering behind closed lids. It is fantasy, or madness to most nowadays."

The messenger said nothing, impassively listening.

The strange pair emerged in a courtyard at the back of the church. The envoy studied her surroundings, concerned to be out in the open, but he urged her forward. Another building sat just down a little path. It was as safe as could be. The warded ground there would hold strong against dark intrusion. The wind picked up and dangerously swayed trees. Orius turned to her. She frowned at the dark sky.

"Your friend is persistent."

"I warned you."

"Hurry. It's just this way," Orius said.

Orius grasped her arm. He thought for certain she was only an apparition, but his hand clamped down on an appendage as solid as his own. He hesitated a moment as she peered down at him, displeased. Her blue eyes blazed with an inexplicable light. In that pause, he was sure he was about to receive a blow for taking such liberty, but she moved forward and allowed him to guide her to the rectory.

"You will fall to me! They cannot hide you for long," a voice called out to her as they entered the front door of the house.

Orius turned to shut the door. The demon stood in the yard glaring at them. The churning smoke that rose from the ground smelled of sulfur. Orius's breath stopped, realizing why this figure was so familiar. He hesitated and the demon grinned at him. Shocked, he slammed the door closed and tucked away his feelings. He dare not acknowledge this and allow the demon a way inside. It wasn't possible that this one could find him there. His heart raced as he leaned against the door.

The messenger also saw the demon through the small squares of glass at the top of the entrance. Behind her, his assistant stood agape. He held a tray in his hands, rattling dishes and spilling tea. Orius flicked the lock with his thumb and quickly went to him. Wresting the tray from the man's hand, he set it on the sideboard.

"Thank you, Father Gallo. That'll be all," Orius said gently.

Orius rubbed his hands together to dry them. The younger priest stammered and stared. His arm rose and he pointed to their guest. She turned to the newcomer, perplexed by the other human's anxiety, and informed them that the demon had gone. Orius excused the man once more. He offered the envoy an apologetic smile.

"Are you hungry? Thirsty? Or, would you like just a room to rest?" he asked.

"The sanctuary, if you please," she flatly replied.

Orius did as asked and led her up the stairs to a small interior room. With no windows and only one door, the shade had no entry. A cross hung on the far wall. It also contained a cot and a small table on which a lamp rested. Against the bare wall opposite the bed sat a little wooden chair, and beside the door a broken old dresser. He gestured toward the plaster cubicle. Once settled, he left her to rest. She would be safe there for some time, even if the demon lingered outside the house. With no portal to enter the room from the outside, the demon would be busy figuring a way to wend his filth into their midst, but the rectory was well protected and contained several seasoned guardians. Orius sighed, knowing that unless she moved on, the shade would eventually make his way inward and they would be hard tested to be rid of him without relinquishing the female. Such a conflict would gain the attention of those he wished to keep out: a meddling congregation of dangerous spies and travelers.

Habitually making the sign of the cross over the closed door, Orius wrapped his rosary about the knob and staggered toward the steps. Father Gallo would be in his room saying as many prayers as he knew. He was a sensitive young man who was easily upset and certainly didn't do well with the greater mysteries. The guardians promised not to appear to the other priests and upset the nature of their reality. There was only so much he could tell them before knowledge became dangerous. Her presence was sure to strain the secrets he kept.

Orius chuckled to himself, as if blessing a door made any difference. She would be safe there because of the guardians' wards, not because of his silly rituals.

"What trouble brought you to us? Why does he follow you here? What does he want with you, erela?" Orius wondered aloud.

Orius prayed to the powers that be that she would not turn out to be an operative from the band of Samsaran travelers. He scowled, wondering if his pride was going to endanger the girl and whether he had best contact the travelers instead of hiding from them. Orius stepped back from the door with a deep frown. Fate had a funny way of coming for you even when you thought you hid well from it.

Returning downstairs, Orius sought his assistant to explain as best he could without causing more unease to the nervous man.

CHAPTER 11

DOMINIC RELUCTANTLY FOLLOWED his host into the dim little kitchen of an old farmhouse. Inside, a woman hovered over a kettle and a large steaming pot of something that smelled amazing. She stirred the ingredients, not noticing them. At her elbow was the gentle glow of her guardian. Dominic tried not to notice, but the duta nodded with a curious look in his eye. The farmer's wife turned her ample body and gave a smile to her husband as he bid her a kindly hello. Her smile wavered as she noticed Dominic, but her eyes remained kind.

"How's your day, Birdie?"

"Just fine—who's your friend, dear?"

The old man gave her a smile and stuck his thumb toward Dominic. He stuttered a moment, appearing to have forgotten, then laughed at himself for realizing he hadn't asked.

"I never asked," the man said.

"Proper host you are," the woman said, setting out a pair of bowls. She winked at Dominic and he felt more at ease.

"Found the lad on the way home. He was crossing Thomas's field and bumped his head," Birdie's husband explained.

Dominic watched Lena approach the woman's guardian. The pair whispered together, their telling eyes on him. Waiting patiently in the entryway was the man's guardian. She managed to enter the kitchen and stepped out of the way into a corner, suspiciously eyeing the guests but keeping silent.

"You're a tourist? Are you hurt?"

"Yes and no, ma'am," Dominic answered both questions, looking embarrassed.

The guardians were sure to bother him later, so there was no sense in staring and causing the couple to think he suffered from more than clumsiness.

The old man sat down and indicated the other chair in the cramped room. Dominic reluctantly lifted his pack off his shoulder. Birdie took it from him, setting it in the entryway on a rickety bench littered with muddy work boots.

"You have a seat—rest yourself," Birdie said, waving at the table.

Dominic did as he was told. The kettle whistled shrilly. She took it off the heat, abandoning him to her husband.

"Was chatting up no one in particular, so I said to me-self, I better take the boy home and see he gets to the doctor in the morning," the old man went on.

Birdie filled a pot for tea, giving a little laugh at the story he told.

"Are you hungry? We've plenty of stew—made it fresh today from our own lambs." She smiled at her guest. "You were probably just cursing your luck as any sane man'd do."

Dominic nodded. She set the teapot between them and he looked over the room, trying to see his guide. Lena managed to tuck herself against the wall beside him. Rubbing his hands together, he tried not to look too strange. He gave a smile to his hostess and thanked her.

"That'd be lovely," he said. She set down a pair of cups and poured. "Indeed, I was cursing, ma'am." He tried to laugh; he was oddly uncomfortable in the cozy kitchen.

Birdie smiled, pleased to feed him. While she served, she asked his name. She set the bowls on the table. In them the food was piled high and steaming.

"Dominic—uh—Dominic Newlyn," he answered.

The eyes of the guardians were still tight on him.

"Pleasure to meet you, Dominic Newlyn. This is my husband Guillian and I'm Fionna, but everyone just calls me Birdie."

"The pleasure's mine. If Guillian didn't see me, I'd probably be lying in the field still," Dominic said.

Birdie stared through him. It was a strange glance in which he felt sure she weighed the truth of his story and even his worth. She turned away to gather a board and knife from the cupboard. She settled the piece on her baker's rack and sliced them some bread.

"Where do you come from? Newlyn? That's a Cornish name, maybe? You sound American. Are you looking for some ancestors?" Birdie put out the bread and a crock of butter, rattling off the list of questions faster than a machine gun.

"This is delicious," he said, chewing a bit of lamb.

The flavors were highly pronounced and made his palette recoil. Dominic heard the guardians tittering at his discomfort. He was a gifted actor, however, and so the couple believed his words despite his nausea.

"Take it easy, Dominic Newlyn. Your senses are very keen here," Birdie's guardian told him, placing a hand on his shoulder.

"Ooo, careful, it's a bit hot," Birdie said, thinking he scalded his tongue.

"Sorry," he said, forcing the bite down. "Uh... no. I've come from my art college—uh... west of here. I haven't been back to the States in a few years. Been busy following a graduate program so I can teach in New York," he said.

"An artist, huh? And you sure you're not on that stuff?" Guillian asked, eating the stew as if it were his last meal. He paused, peering at him from squinty eyes. "Are you a Communist?"

Dominic denied drug use again, laughing at the man's insistence. He thought he cut a rather benign figure, though maybe a little too Aryan to appear harmless to these Brits.

Birdie prepared herself a cup of tea and then sat in the chair between them. She shook her head and laughed, gesturing her husband off the track of the present conversation.

"Don't be silly, Guillian. He thinks all the young people are on drugs or spying for the Communists. Watches too much telly. Oh, the kids these days and their fashions. What school do you attend?" Birdie asked.

Dominic smiled. "Well, most of them probably are on that stuff, but not me. I'm a married man and can't dabble in things that don't put food on the table. Spying certainly wouldn't help. I'm attending—Oxford."

"A clever lad." Birdie shook his arm. She leaned toward her husband and added, "See that, Guillian. Not all of them are on heroin and working for the Russians. Such nonsense and you know it. Now, you wouldn't have stopped if you really thought so."

Guillian made a noise of complaint and shooed her off. He returned to his stew and tea. Birdie looked at Dominic with a warm smile.

"Do you have a place to stay?" Birdie asked him.

"No, ma'am, I don't. I thought I'd find a stop on my way."

"It's after seven o'clock now. Most places will be closed up for the night," she said, doubtful.

"He can stay here the night," Guillian said, slurping the last of the gravy from his bowl.

Birdie rolled her eyes at his rudeness and smiled at their guest. "Of course he can."

"I really can't—I have to keep moving. I'm due in Essex tomorrow—supposed to meet my wife for a small getaway."

"Oh, that's just lovely! Guillian, isn't that lovely?"

Guillian playfully scrunched his face at her.

"Did you walk all this way? From Oxford?"

Dominic nodded. He had no idea where the university was or if it even had a program for art. Worse, he had no idea where Essex was in relation to his present location, something a student with his claims would know. He held his breath as Guillian eyed him. The man was shrewd, a bit of a comedian, but he couldn't tell which role he was playing at the moment.

"You're barmy or on drugs—or she's a fine bit of stuff, I'd wager. Is she your contact? Selling secrets to the Communists?" Guillian laughed into his tea cup.

"I'm sorry—yes, yes, she's a beautiful girl. At least she was the last time I saw her." Dominic smiled, feeling the heat rise in his face. The panic eased some, as he realized the man was joking with him.

"Don't let a woman make a fool of you, lad. You should've made her come and get you," Guillian told him.

"She doesn't know her way around, she just flew over to visit. She lives in—New York. I haven't seen her in months," Dominic explained.

"Romantic," Birdie sighed wistfully. Her eyes sparkled as he blushed. "Well, you're welcome to stay the night and we'll bring you over to Essex in the morning. Walking won't get you there on time and the poor thing'll be worried sick. Why, you've only made it a third of the way." Birdie grinned.

"That far? If I may ask, where exactly am I?" Dominic said, pushing his spoon around his bowl.

"Little Missenden," Birdie said. She laughed, feeling sorry for him. "None of your friends have a car? Why didn't you take the rail?"

"No money. Everything I make goes to New York or for school. And, I have very few friends, being married. But, still, I couldn't impose—"

"Nonsense. You'll stay here. I'll ring the doctor early and then we can get started," Guillian insisted.

Dominic sighed. He couldn't refuse them.

"Eat up and I'll show you the room."

Thanking them again, Dominic returned to eating. His palate was still sensitive and each bite was more difficult than the last. He persevered, answering Guillian's questions as his wife disappeared into other parts of the house. His stomach was about to turn when he finished the last bit.

"There now." Birdie stroked his arm, returning as he put away the last bit of bread and drank the remains of his tea in an effort to rinse out his mouth.

The woman cleaned up the table around him. Once he swallowed, she dragged away his cup and bowl. Her soft voice murmured a little song. Birdie looked at him with a mix of nostalgia and delight. His presence probably evoked a memory from the past, but that was a tale he had no time to hear.

Birdie made sure he was full, offering him a slice of pie and more tea. He thanked her, but refused, hoping she wouldn't insist. His stomach couldn't handle another bite of Samsaran food. Guillian saved him, suggesting they show him where he'd sleep. The hour was hardly late, but he imagined this couple turned in and rose early.

Guillian led the way, climbing a set of narrow stairs to a narrow hall. His guardian followed behind Dominic and Lena, causing him to feel quite sandwiched in. The farmer opened the first door by the landing and switched on a lamp. He was surprised to find a decent-sized room beyond the door. Two twin beds were placed along the walls, with a wide dormer window in the middle. Guillian explained the space once belonged to his sons, but they grew up some time ago and left it empty. It wasn't so empty as he suggested. A pair of matching beds, two dressers and a bureau filled the space. Some discarded sacks of clothes lay at the foot of a large armoire that may have been an antique and was in slight disrepair. Here and there, the relics of boyhood still occupied the space.

"It's used if they come by for a visit. The both of them work in the big city now and don't have much time for us. Do you have children?"

"Not yet," Dominic lied. "But I hope to have a bunch if she's willing."

"Can be a bitter disappointment, Mr. Newlyn. They grow up and they leave."

Dominic smiled at him and the man smiled back, regretting the tender comment.

"Knock if you need anything. Well, you've had a long day. I'll leave you to it," Guillian said.

Guillian was about to exit when his wife, carrying Dominic's pack, blockaded him. She smiled knowingly and handed his things over. Dominic thanked her and waited for them to leave, unsure of what to do with himself while they remained. The guardians stared and Lena explored.

"The loo is down the hall at the end. The door is always open if it's not occupied. Feel free to shower when you get up. Fresh towels are in the cupboard under the basin. I'll have breakfast waiting when you come down. Guillian will wake you at five." Birdie smiled at him, filling the pause.

"The earlier the better. I want to be to Essex as soon as I can," Dominic said.

"Very good, chap. We'll see you at dawn and have the doctor come round. Did you need an aspirin or anything?" Dominic shook his head and she inclined hers. "Sleep well, Mr. Newlyn."

Guillian and Birdie made their exit, closing the door behind them. Dominic blew out his breath and threw himself down on the bed nearest the door. He stared at the dingy ceiling. The lamp cast an odd set of circles that his eyes followed around and around. Guillian's words had grabbed his attention. He felt bad for the old man. If his children left him, he would be devastated, but that was the eventuality all parents faced, unlike his, who were the ones who did the leaving. They were both too busy with their own incarnations and had had nothing to do with him since he joined the legion. Dominic sighed. Being a child could be a bitter disappointment too.

"Sleep light, Dominic. I sense shadows wandering our way," Lena said, ending his brooding. "Their guardians said imps wander the woods about here. They're old and very nasty. They've even seen shadowalkers pass through," she added.

Lena stood on the bureau to peer through the window. Her small wings were spread for balance as the rickety desk rocked under her weight. A deep frown darkened her brightness and her eyes scanned the horizon helplessly. It sounded more like the guardian had told her a bedtime story to give her nightmares.

"What do you see?"

"I see a dark cloud rolling overhead. It cloaks the farmhouse from our friends. They'll try to attack come nighttide," Lena replied. She sniffed. "Do you smell that?"

The wind gusted and thrust a branch across the roof above the window. The diamond panes rattled ominously. Dominic was startled, but Lena was unaffected as she watched out the window. She cast a deep sigh, disappointed and bored. The sudden gust just happened to take the smell away.

"Keep your pack close and your defenses at hand," she added, not believing in chance.

"Perhaps we should just leave. Gediel said we need to keep moving so they can't track us. These people could be harmed," Dominic said.

"You look tired. You should rest. I'll watch over you," Lena said, ignoring his concern.

Dominic snorted and lay back down. She was as stubborn as his wife. He wondered how much of Maiel had rubbed off on her while babysitting. His thoughts slipped over memories of his erela in a number of examples, like when she gave birth to Mikey entirely alone and insisted on carrying on with her duties as if nothing had happened. She scared him to death sometimes. The memories turned toward softer moments.

Joel had taught him to reach out to her and so he did. She was east, southeast to be exact. The pain now mixed with frustration and an undercurrent of dread. He wished he could wrap his wife up in his arms, smell her hair and just hold her to know she was his. He'd let her pound him to a pulp until every wave of anger disappeared. Her strange notions would be laid to rest, if given the chance.

Dominic reached deeper along the line that tied them, wondering if he could send her some kind of message, since he received something like that from her in the way of her emotions. As he embraced the control to accomplish the transmission, the burning in his throat returned, drying and stinging until he let go. He shoved back and the line broke. Afraid of what he had just encountered, he examined the room for the bogeymen of which Lena spoke.

"You feel her pain," Lena said, looking out the window.

Dominic blinked. He still sat on the bed and the room was safe and sound. He nodded and then sighed into his hand. Lies were easier than explaining what happened inside him. Perhaps they would understand and not judge him unfit to carry forward. He wondered how hard it would be to cut himself free of the path and let her go before he dragged her down with him. His heart thumped in his chest, pounding with the hope and rage that engulfed his being. Either way, he was certain he would lose her. Draping his arm over his eyes, he hid his face. Lena watched him, though she stared out the window. She was tracking his thoughts. He hated the idea of her witnessing his decline. She was a spy watching him descend into weakness.

"Have faith—we'll find her before he succeeds."

Dominic sat up, unable to lie there and fall into a meditation that would lock his mind on his wife. He stared at the distant wall, feeling Lena's eyes carefully measuring him in return. Pressing the knuckles of his hand into his lips, he fought the urge to reach to her again, but it was too strong and she was there. Scowling at the blank plaster, he fought the tears filling his eyes until they overwhelmed him. Maiel was reaching him.

"Damn it, Doll Face. We could have handled this together," he rasped, feeling quite certain that his thoughts would be carried to her, and that somehow what he said would decide their future.

"Is it Maiel? Where are you sensing her?" Lena asked. She jumped down and placed her hands on his knees. "Does she call? Show me."

Dominic sniffed and covered his face with a hand. Maiel was gone. He forced his emotions back; he refused to cry in front of the girl. He had a job to do and it didn't include blathering like an infant. Determined to set his gut reactions and knee-jerk desires aside, Dominic pointed out the direction for the girl. Once Lena was amply distracted with seeking her wayward hero, he slumped back onto the bed, wriggling around to get comfortable on the thin mattress. He stared at the wall and then his lids slowly closed as the trance took over; the glow of the lamp was dark red behind his eyelids. The room disappeared around him and he felt like he was falling, endlessly falling.

"That's our direction, then. We start in the morning," Lena said, with renewed hope.

The girl sat on the desk, making the old furniture rock noisily.

Dominic's eyes popped open, dismayed by the falling sensation and sounds. He stared at the grain of the wood paneling until his lids were too heavy to hold open. Drifting away, he asked himself why Lena couldn't sense his wife. If she were given the same abilities as the duta she impersonated, that should have been easy. Success wasn't what they had in mind.

The falling sensation drew him down into thoughts that would have frightened him in days gone by, but tonight it felt as though he was finally on the right path. The dark was merely the unknown, not a horrific fantasy of a fate worse than death.

*   *   *

Three shadows scurried along the hedgerow of a grazing field. The moon shone from above, making it hard to maneuver in the unusually bright and open areas. Even with the insistence of the light, the trio crossed the road and came up to a farmhouse fence. The first, a corpse, peered over the stone boundary. His face was deformed, as though a sculptor frustrated by his David flung upon it handfuls of coarse concrete to spite the perfect lines. He was still fresh in his decay and hoped to become the ideal of his dark breed, with all the flesh and organs gone from his skeleton. For now, he dragged his dead flesh around. His sightless eyes roved the lawn between the house and where he hid. Sniffing the air, he caught the scent of something near. He ran his thick white tongue over his twisted lips.

This second shade, also a corpse, boasted a scar running from the remaining flesh above his ear to below his shoulder. The wound healed badly, exposing horn-like bones along the clavicle. The ear, severed in half, spread with scar tissue that resembled melted flesh. Staring from eyeless sockets, it clutched the stones of the fence. The dried-flesh fingers flexed, practicing the act he longed to perform upon the soul they'd come to torment. The rock scraped under his touch, all the flesh nearly dried from his skeleton. The corpse sneered at the house, drooling black saliva in anticipation of feeding.

The third, an incubus, crouched along the road. It resembled a monkey with a long, drawn face and long, sharp fangs. Its hooves clacked on the ground as it moved. Whipping a long tail, it crawled up to the fence and over. From a set of black eyes, it peered into the window high up on the roof. It tipped its head further back and howled, sounding like a tortured hound. Sheep bleated in panic and the wind howled back.

"This is where Morgentus said he'd be," the incubus said.

All three menaces were of small stature, no more than half as tall as their known nemeses, the lightwalkers. It was by no means a measurement of how much terror they could cause, as these soldiers successfully tormented a flock of humans each. They were once two young Cetians and an ikyls, fallen and then tortured in the dark of Jahannam to resemble monsters and serve the danava. Tonight they meant to show the enemy they were not to be trifled with and earn their place in the dark legions. Their assignment was simple: to delay the soul sent to rescue a fallen do-gooder. Meanwhile, Morgentus would hunt his quarry, an erela he fancied since she'd wandered his labyrinth.

The monkey-faced incubus checked the stars and moon. Time to be about their business and secure their lord's gratefulness. A sweet morsel would be thrown to them once the baron grew tired of her. To gnaw at her pretty bones one day was worth every hardship.

The first led the way, keeping within the shadows lest someone watched. Finding a lit window on the side of the structure, the scarred corpse climbed the aged roofs of the house's additions and peered inside, taking care not to be seen by the small guardian that was present. Adonai's pets made too much trouble, even one this small. If she caught their scent it would spoil the surprise and lessen the reward.

"He got pigeon with 'em. Stay down," the fresher corpse said, its mouth broken by decomposition.

The trio ducked back into the shadows and listened to the sheep call. It was tempting to feast on the herd and leave the farm without completing the task. Morgentus would eventually find out, but they would be sated and he would have his trophy by that time. There was no telling the ability of the tiny erela, or if other guardians lurked within. The confrontation might end in a shade or three lost instead.

The promise of a pair of strong atman on which to feed tempered their scheming. The trio hunkered down in the shadows and waited. The best time to strike was when the human slept. The humans were always vulnerable when they slept, and they gave up the sweetest buffet ever to be tasted. The humans' fear would be unbridled.

"We wait the sleep in old-dark. We eat the flesh of the more scared from the sleep."

"You're welcome to it. I'll have the pigeon and then feast on her battered bones," the incubus said.

CHAPTER 12

DOMINIC STARED AT THE BACK OF HIS EYELIDS. The falling sensation subsided and he lay there aware of everything around him. Unable to meditate, he couldn't escape his anxiety and improve his outlook or energy. Lena hummed softly to herself, still sitting on the top of the desk. The song was one his wife sang to their children when they refused to settle down and were unmanageable, especially when they'd spent their last bit of energy. He smiled with the warmth of the memory. Dominic would give anything to be back there, when they were just small and new. Longing brought back the memory of his firstborn as if it had happened a moment ago. Ian's infant face gave surprising comfort.

Rhythmic thuds startled Dominic upright. Just he and Lena were in the room. She stared past him to the wall, her eyes growing wider. The wood creaked. Rhythmic pounding followed. Dominic knew without seeing that he must move and he jumped to his feet. Facing the wall, he continued backward as the plaster and wood stretched like rubber. Dust cascaded to the floor with each recoil. The motion continued. Faces and hands he wasn't eager to see rolled against the barrier, seeking a way through the ward. The guardians had protected the farmer's house, but wards were weak and the demons would break it in a few minutes. That was its purpose, to hold while they prepared.

"We're here," a voice said, none too soon.

"You should keep to your assigns," Dominic told the guardian.

"We are. They break our house's ward. This is our fight," the farmer's guardian said.

"They're here for me. I'm tracking a legiona that came down without orders," Dominic said.

The guardians stared warily. They probably doubted him, but they had little reason to believe he was lying either. Their eyes went back to the shade, forcing its sattva through the warding.

"We know. Ready your blade, soul," Birdie's guardian said, wielding his own.

They faced the wall, ready for whatever threatened their home. The barrier rolled and pressed. Three shades pushed their faces against the ward. One finally slipped through, emerging from under the bed. Its gnarled features froze Dominic to the floor boards. Corpses, he thought. He stared as it crept closer.

"Dominic!" Lena hollered, rising onto her tiptoes, trying to get higher than she was on top of the desk.

"I see it," Dominic called back.

The second and third broke the barrier, hissing and snapping their teeth. Their clawed hands wielded ruined weapons. The guardians smirked, hardly intimidated by these three.

"Lightwalkers, stand down. We take this soul, not your assigns," the second corpse growled.

"All souls are our assigns, mudeater," Birdie's guardian replied.

"Shut your lying mouths and try me if you think you can," Dominic said, drawing the sword from his pack.

Not listening to his guide, he left the blade on the opposite wall, an interior wall they were certain not to penetrate. He smirked. Still further proof Lena was too inexperienced to fulfill her calling.

One of the maggots laughed, drawing his attention to the bed Dominic had occupied a moment earlier. The monkey-faced incubus laughed at him and the others looked pleased with the challenge. He wasn't sure which breed he disliked more. Then the shades dashed forward. He and the guardians were faster. They crossed their swords, catching all three of the black weapons aimed at Dominic. Shrieks of anger filled the room. The trio disappeared in a puff of smoke, which dispersed across the room in quick circles to confuse their prey. Windows rattled and the lamp fell over. Frames on the wall jumped off their pins or clattered against the plaster.

"Get rid of them quick. This noise'll wake the farmer," Dominic said.

Lena screamed as she was thrown to a bed. The incubus pressed her into the corner.

"How's your stay in paradise, pigeon? Don't get used to it, it's gonna be a short one," he said. His lascivious eyes studied her. "You're a pretty one. I'll enjoy chewing your meat. But first I'll gut you with my bone and pluck your wings while you scream," he said, as Lena struggled to break free of him.

Dominic kept one eye on Lena. The incubus meant to harm her in ways he dare not think of. However, the corpses were doing their part to hold him and the others back. Suddenly, he stabbed his sword in the whirl of smoke that came too close. The corpse stilled and slipped to the floor. The incubus's head came round and he hissed. Dominic lunged, shutting his eyes in anticipation of a strike. A miss and he'd lose his only link to Zion, putting his small guardian out of the game until her guts were back together, but that was far better than letting the incubus have his way. Dominic's blade struck something gristly and then stopped. Opening his eyes, he saw Lena lying on the bed, her feet in the belly of their adversary and her hands pressed to its chest. The end of the incubus's sword gleamed less than an inch from her. The claws of the incubus were sunk in her arm. Grabbing hold of the menace, Dominic flipped the corpse off her and yanked his blade free. She clung to his side, watching the other guardians finish the battle.

The room was quiet once more. The guardians stood over the evaporating carcasses, expecting another round. Dominic set his wide-eyed guide on the desk and inspected her wound. Her arm bled from filthy punctures. Dominic's anger flared. Anger for sending him with a defenseless child and anger that his enemies were so dishonorable. This was no place for Lena, untrained and so small. Only Adonai knew what they would do to her in the reaches of the abyss if the weak ones succeeded in getting this close.

The farmer's guardian attended the wound and tears. Dominic assessed the rest of the damage. Clothes and blankets were tossed everywhere. He picked up the lamp and set it on the bureau. The bulb was broken. He sighed, wondering how he would explain this.

"Mr. Newlyn? Are you all right?" Birdie's voice called through the door and then gave a hurried rap.

The knob twisted, but the door was locked.

"Son? What's going on?" He heard the farmer.

Dominic looked to the guardians. If the farmers saw the state of the room, he had no ready explanation. He went to the door and unlocked it. The ashen faces of his hosts looked back at him from the lit hall.

"I'm so sorry. I got up to go to the bathroom and knocked the lamp over. I tried to find my way to the door and tripped on my bag, pulled a drawer out of the dresser here."

"You all right?" Guillian asked, looking puzzled. Dominic nodded. "Accident prone, aren't you?" he laughed.

Dominic grinned sheepishly and ran a hand through his hair, stalling. That explanation would not answer why the picture frames fell from the wall, or the armoire had been emptied.

"Painfully so," he answered.

"Let me help you get things straight," Birdie said, trying to insert herself in the room.

"No, I'll pick up—and pay you for anything that's damaged. I'm sorry I woke you."

"You'll need a new bulb for that lamp," Guillian said, pushing past.

The farmer was strong and easily leveraged him back. Dominic fell against the dresser, stammering more excuses. His voice trailed off when he saw the room straight as a pin except the lamp, which lay on its side. His pack sat in the middle of the floor and a drawer from the dresser was tipped out. He looked for Lena, who sat in the far corner with her legs drawn up tight to her chest. She watched the farmer over her skinny knees. The punctures were gone from her shoulder and her tears dried. The other guardians had gone.

Guillian opened a drawer in the bureau and pulled out a fresh bulb. He made the change, set the lamp back on the table and switched it on. Birdie excused Dominic to the bathroom with a whisper and wave of her arm. She insisted on picking up the overturned drawer. Dominic wandered down the hall, escaping their questioning glances. The guardians stood in the opening of opposing doors, staring confidently at him.

"You fight well, son of Newlyn, but you're no watcher," Birdie's guardian said.

"You're welcome," the other said.

Dominic blew out his breath, irritated by their jibes. He wasn't about to answer them or engage in a conversation in the hallway and add a few more questions to the farmers' long list. He was frustrated at their arrogance in assuming he was incapable of handling the situation. And the sheer audacity of mentioning watchers, the usual sect sent to retrieve anything and anyone the council sought. Watchers had caused all the problems since the beginning.

Dominic shut the bathroom door a little harder than he intended. He waited to hear from the farmers, but he only heard silence. He drew in a breath. His anger was getting the best of him. Spinning the spigots on the sink, he ran the cool water from the faucet over his hands. The bath did little to bring his temperature back down. His energy pulsed hard through the temporary vessel, but steadied as he thought over his success. His eyes flashed in the mirror. The image of himself flickered as if he were under a thin flow of water. Green mixed with blood in his iris. He blinked but the image remained. Splashing his face with cold water, he looked again and his reflection returned to normal. Quite unexpectedly, the spigots turned on by themselves and the water rushed, threatening to cleave the tap. The mirror now reflected the image of another in his place. Draped in a silver suit tied by a sash of crimson, the platinum-haired ghost watched him from a blood-riddled yellow gaze. A smile turned the blood-red mouth to one side; the ghost was amused by his terror. This is what basking in a surly mood won him.

"Belial," Dominic breathed.

The image disappeared as suddenly as it had come. The water filled the sink, steaming and roiling. Dominic stared for several moments at his reflection. He wasn't sure he looked back at himself, but was certain he disliked having the sight this close to Jahannam. Hot water lapped his waist and startled him back to the moment. The basin overflowed in a steaming deluge. Dominic struggled to turn off the faucet, but the spigots burned his hands. Recoiling, his wide eyes roamed over the tiny bathroom for something to throw over them. He grabbed a towel and wrestled the taps until the water stopped. The boiling liquid receded slowly down the drain. He tossed the towel on the floor and sopped up the water. Then, all was dry and the steam gone. Dominic hovered over the floor, stunned.

Hardly wishing to remain in the haunted bathroom, Dominic hurried out and back to the bedroom. The farmer and his wife had retired without another word. He closed the door and wandered to the center of the room. Lena tensely watched him.

"They shouldn't have sent you down here. They treat us like cattle, disregarding consequences. Half of us don't even know what for," Dominic said.

"I'm capable. I was wondering if you were," Lena whispered.

Dominic scratched the back of his head. Was she not the one who just took an incubi blade to her limb? Lena was shaken and angry. She regarded him, eyes filled with questions. Dominic dropped his gaze and went to the narrow bed, warily eyeing the walls. He rested his head in his hands, dueling forces vying within.

"You did well against them," Lena told him from behind her knees. He sat silent. The silence continued and then she asked, "Why are you seeing the dark prince?"

"Just another trophy for his wall," Dominic mumbled.

Lena saw his mind as clearly as her own. She should know that there was no point in remaining there a moment longer. He gathered his things with a dejected sigh. Holding Gediel's coat, he considered throwing it in the bag, but slung it on his shoulders before his thoughts talked him out of it. He slung his pack on his back and faced his guide.

Lena was very much his wife's assign. In fact, she resembled Callidora in training. The obstinate caginess, the rude callousness. Her personality was perfect for the Moon Order. Next he expected a protest against leaving. He spoke before she could.

"I told you they were in danger. We leave now."

Lena silently passed him. Dominic followed and they quietly made their way out of the farmhouse. Crossing the lawn, he cast a glance over his shoulder. The guardians watched from the room they had vacated, dour expressions on both. Dominic waved, then pressed on. He hoped the couple wouldn't search for him come morning, suspecting there was more to their stray than he let on.

CHAPTER 13

MAIEL SAT CROSS-LEGGED on the narrow cot. After inspecting the room, she found it to be as safe as any sanctuary could be in Samsara. Meaning there were no windows and one entrance. None of the walls touched the exterior and vents were nonexistent. Either way, this was where the resonance was and she was resigned to her situation.

Maiel settled down to meditate and regain her strength shortly after the vratin left. Her sword lay at the ready across her lap. The shield usually on her back sat against the rickety side table and her helmet was placed on top. She'd even discarded her bow and arrow, propping them in the corner. At the base of the quiver rested her gauntlets and greaves. Her sandals lay on the floor below her perch.

Relaxed into the exercise of meditation for some time, Maiel didn't expect the soft knock on the door. She opened her eyes. The vratin with the oddly strong atman stood on the other side awaiting her invitation. She bid him enter and returned to her focus.

"I hope you don't mind, but I brought you some soup. It's a bit cold tonight," he said, entering with a clamor.

The vratin stood dumb, with a tray awkwardly held in his hands, noticing her pose and discarded armaments. The bowl steamed beside a squat teapot. He quietly closed the door with his foot and set the tray aside.

"Thank you, but I'll not need to eat," she said, returning to her meditation.

"You'll find that you do," he said with a smile, sitting in a chair that faced her. "Eat. Eat and you'll take form and have time to amend your mistakes. Starve and you'll fade, fall to the shadows and suffer."

Maiel opened her eyes. The light of them made her gaze quite intense, while she paused a moment to consider what the soul had to say. She felt stronger and much calmer with the little rest she had already taken. What he said wasn't possibly true. Still, the vratin's words offered some insight about himself. He knew of the necessity of food in preventing an atman from descending too far. It was a strange bit of knowledge for a simple soul. Other details also left her suspicious, like his resonance and sight.

Maiel scanned the man's face for a clue to his character. He regarded her in similar fashion, predicting her concerns. His face was kind but stern, a familiar expression among duta when their advice was ignored. However, luck didn't provide her with a duta. His pale blue eyes, like polished agate, confirmed that he was just a man.

"Try to eat. You'll feel much better," the vratin pleaded.

Orius had unbound his graying dark hair and traded his robes for a simple black frock and white collar. He looked simpler, but no less determined. He folded his arm over his middle and placed the opposite hand over his mouth. Maiel's eyes narrowed. Something about him was familiar; perhaps he was a friend from home.

Maiel held out her hand, keeping her eye on him to discern exactly what was so familiar. The bowl of soup he brought lifted from the tray into the air. When it settled on her palm, she lifted her other hand and the spoon shot with violent force into her grasp. The vratin rubbed his bottom lip with a finger, unimpressed or careful. She sniffed the steam and a delicate scent tingled her nostrils. She raised her spoon reluctantly, knowing that food in Samsara could be strong.

"I made it as bland as possible."

Maiel's eyes shot to his. He knew that as well.

Orius shrugged.

The atman in this vratin's core must be a key to his puzzle. No doubt he had insight due to his relationship with the other guardians. Perhaps they simply provided answers to his questions moments before he'd rejoined her. Of course, it was highly likely he was a leader from one of the outposts. She eyed him, searching for the mark of the group.

Spooning the soup in her mouth, Maiel found the man was good to his word. She set the spoon down and drank the contents of the bowl, not spilling a drop. The warmth spread through her. She tried to focus and clarify her thoughts. She blinked at the empty bowl, uncomfortable with the effect, as though her atman had thrust roots into the ground, or she had just woken to a bright early morning after a long splendid sleep.

"I'm sure you have many questions—but for now, you need to rest. I'll return in the morning with breakfast. You're safe here. You may sleep. He can't enter the rectory, not yet," Orius said. He took the empty bowl and spoon.

"I am sure you have many questions," Maiel said, watching him set the bowl and spoon on the tray.

Orius paused and she smiled to herself. He quietly returned to the chair. His pale eyes dissected her, the familiarity of them putting her on edge. Why could she not place him?

"How is it that you and your vratin can see me?" Maiel asked.

"That is a long story better left for when you are rested."

"As a fallen, I can't stay here forever," Maiel said.

Vratin Orius's brows knitted. "You? Fallen?"

Maiel nodded. "Are you frightened?"

"Hardly," Orius scoffed. He chuckled, shifting in the rickety chair. "What happened?"

"Three days ago while defending my assign's passage home, I allowed a mudeater to distract me. I took his life and then secured the assign for transport."

"And what is the problem in this? It sounds as though you did your duty properly."

"I didn't take his life to secure the assign. I took it because I wanted to."

Orius's brows knitted. The humor left his face.

"You're natural enemies. It'd be a surprise if you didn't feel this way."

"I hated him for being near me and all I thought of was casting him into Oblivion and the soul be damned if it were lost in the middle of the battle. My foolishness saw two more innocent souls stung with his venom and now their paths are broken."

Orius tapped his fingers on his leg and chewed his lip, carefully processing what she'd said. When his silence continued, she felt a need to explain further. Revenge had brought her so low. He should be able to comprehend the emotion. That thought fixed the source of familiarity at last. He looked like her pursuer, the Baron Morgentus, though older and kinder. Was it possible that Morgentus had at last tricked her? Her eyes slipped to his hands, to look for the putrid ends. If the vratin was Morgentus, he would have had to repent every evil he'd ever committed in a matter of moments and been restored to Zion, and instantly returned to this spot in the matter of a few Earth hours. That was simply impossible and his atman radiated far differently. So, then, who was this Orius? The name was right on the tip of her tongue; it was a taste of something in the past. She ran through the names of every being she knew who had fallen or was recently incarnated into Samsara.

"I ran from my alders—my king. I came here—to Earth to make things right again. I could barely focus and I only made things worse. Now—now that fiend follows me everywhere. Had I not gone to his labyrinth, he would never have known me."

"King? From your king you can't hide, not anywhere," Orius said, distracted and mumbling.

"The alders foresee everything—why wouldn't they tell me this shade waited here to ensnare me?"

"Oh—well, perhaps they did and perhaps you didn't listen," Orius said, folding his arms and sitting back. "You said you went to his labyrinth?"

"You're not speaking with a member of your congregation, Vratin," Maiel petulantly reminded him.

Their gazes remained locked. She puzzled over his identity, confounded at the meaning he held for her. If he was Morgentus in some elaborate disguise, then it was best she stop speaking. Likewise, if he reported to the outpost, he'd be dangerous for other reasons.

"Acheron's beast is best left to another time," Maiel said.

"There's always a reason, but we're not always ready to hear it. While you rest, think on that. Think on the possibilities you haven't exhausted," Orius said.

"You haven't asked me what an alder is, Vratin Orius," Maiel said. He turned back and she added, "Or what Acheron is."

"I assume an alder is a bureaucrat, like anywhere. As for Acheron, I'm versed in all the lore that tries to define hell. In the morning—if you promise to share your stories of Acheron and alders with me, I'll share my story with you," he replied.

Maiel was almost certain he was an outpost leader.

Orius left, removing the tray except for the teapot and cup. She smelled the leaves steeping in the hot water. The gleam on the bow of the porcelain caught her eye while she puzzled on what had just passed. Folding back into meditation, she took the vratin's advice. The riddle of his existence might be found there too. Her mind soon wandered the narrows of her questions, looking for paths she failed to discern before. The best way was to examine everything, so she turned to the very beginning. Her thoughts travelled back through time to her last incarnation. Under the protection of her dearest friend, she put all focus on her husband's growth, but even with such committed support, Dominic egregiously failed his dharma, and left her to wonder if her husband really wanted to rise.

The teapot lifted from the tray and poured its contents into the cup beside it. The cup then floated toward her and she lifted her hand to accept it. She breathed the steam from the comforting brew, then sipped. The liquid warmed and comforted, but it didn't warm the cold feeling in her core. Maiel sent the cup back to the dresser.

With her head resting on her fist, Maiel stared at the empty chair. All the ruminating in the world couldn't answer her questions, or so it seemed.

Her head lifted, as she perceived Orius's suggestion in a different manner. Starting with the return from her previous incarnation, Maiel examined each time she stood before her alders. She recalled their words and examined their speech for twists of meaning. If they weren't forthcoming, then they didn't trust her. If they didn't trust her—most likely because of her stint in the Pits of Acheron—why would they send her to guard such an important soul? With Morgentus chasing her across the planet, it looked like they had good reason not to trust her, but risking Lena was pure madness. It made no sense. Her failures might be long-lived, but this was by far more grievous. To bind her with an immature soul, even under Adonai's blessing, was enough to condemn them. Such actions added up to a dire agenda. They sought to flush a shade from the ranks. But who?

The question numbed her from her fingers to her toes. The shade could be her own self, though she fancied herself quite loyal to the king, and was scared to even think of disappointing Mikhael and losing his favor. More likely it was a council member. They knew how to connive and they held many fates in their hands. Her lack of faith in their work was dangerous, but their failure to alert her to their efforts was worse. Alas, the possibility was insane, since they frequented the White City right under the noses of those who ferreted out such heretics. She poured another cup of tea, drank it and returned to her deliberations. The thoughts bubbling from her small shift in perspective opened monstrous possibilities she hardly wanted to confront. Most likely of all, Dominic could be the shade. Her shoulders sank as she went over their history in a panic of defense upon his behalf. That history did little to defend him. If any of them fell from Zion, things were sure to get worse very soon.

Her thoughts turned to the alder Dominic shared with her. Maxiel, of course, had a hand in this dharma. She stared into space, staggered to have come up with such a notion. That connection was quite convenient, and even if Maxiel was gruff and seemingly unfeeling, he was a highly regarded official.

The maddening thoughts filling her head exhausted the little energy Maiel regained. She shook her head to clear the cobwebs. It was time to rest and worry over the details later. She collapsed on the narrow cot. Something reached toward her just as she shut her eyes. The feeling was like a caress that roused her for a night of tender embraces. Maiel drew the energy closer to discern the source. Then, suddenly, the affection shifted to a scalding pressure. The intensity deepened until it felt like a fist wrapped tightly around her throat. Another pressure squeezed her side as if it gripped her to rend her sattva in two. The hands burned like hellfire. She struggled to free her mind, violently slamming closed the connection. Gulping air, Maiel sat up, expecting Morgentus to be standing before her. No shade or shadow was out of place. She sat safe and alone.

Maiel's frantic thoughts coalesced back into a focused calm. The caress first reminded her of Dominic's touch, but the pressure held a foreign signature. She whispered his name, settling her head in her hands. She refused to believe he would handle her in such a manner. Her sattva still stung with the remnants. There was no doubt they were his. Tears filled her eyes. Collapsing back on the cot, Maiel wept, afraid and confused. She was unable to imagine why he would treat her so. Unless, as she feared, he faded.

Despite exhaustion and terror, Maiel reached across the distances until she could almost smell him. She took the last bit of energy to spare and wrapped it around him like a protective cocoon. Whatever was written, Dominic was still her husband. Once she returned home, despite Morgentus's efforts, she faced greater obstacles than being reprimanded for insubordination.

Maiel released the line. Lying on the cot, she stared at the empty wall, still reeling from the hatred in his touch. Her side ached and her throat burned. In all their time together, he never raised a hand. There was more to this attack, just like there was more to find in the memories of the near past. Her energy waned until her eyes closed and her thoughts ceased to hurry. The fluttering thought of needing to run Callidora through command exercises repeated in a loop. The erela smiled at her from beyond the Avernus. She stood in the practice room. A dim blue filtered the vision.

"I know a way to mend it. Let go," Callidora whispered, then smiled.

Hours later, Maiel woke to a soft patter on the door. She scowled at the plaster wall opposite the tiny bed and wondered how she fell into so deep a trance. Callidora's words repeated in her brain. Lifting herself, she felt how heavy her limbs had become, as if tied down by lead anchors. She still wore her armor, but the gear had never weighed her down before. Blinking, she wiped the sleep from her eyes and noticed that her hand was full and flush. The tone of her skin was almost blue elsewhere. She worriedly eyed the appendage. A cold shiver ran through her. The penannular was weak and unable to hide her from view. She touched the cuirass, afraid the metal would crumble at the slightest pressure. It felt solid, for now.

The patter came again. Maiel glared at the door, and then bid entry. The vratin's young attendant scuffled inside. He set a tray on the dresser. His small voice muttered repeated excuses. He bowed his head, clutching his hands tight around a rosary.

"Thank you," Maiel managed.

The vratin stared. He was brought to silence by the sound of her voice. He wore a pair of thick-framed glasses over his dark eyes. Removing the accessory, he wiped them clean and looked at her again. Shuffling closer, he placed his fingers on her neck. Maiel raised an eyebrow, waiting for his explanation. She would have crushed his wrist in her fist and demanded he speak his intentions, if she couldn't already read them. He was a very worried young man, both wiry and frail. Her arrival shook his resolve immensely, but reinforced his sense of the universe.

"A pulse," he muttered, popping back.

The vratin looked startled by this and his reaction made Maiel frown. She forgot her dreams, and focused on the vibrations of her resonance.

"Thank you, Father Gallo." Orius appeared in the door.

"She has a pulse," the younger vratin repeated, startled by the revelation. He pointed at her. "She's—she's alive."

"I can see," Orius replied with a lift of the brows.

Gallo's hand slipped back to his side. He looked between them, confused.

"That'll be all. You may go about your work," Orius instructed.

"Yes, Father Orius," he said nervously, then skirted around him, shutting the door behind him.

Maiel stared at the closed panel. Orius sat in the rickety chair opposite her.

"Nervous little fellow," Maiel said.

"Quite," Orius agreed, chewing his thumb.

Maiel watched him lost in a thought.

"He's very brave, also," Maiel said, recapturing his attention. She continued, "No one lays a hand on me without answering for it."

Orius smiled a little, still distracted by his struggle to think of the right place to start their conversation. Maiel shrugged and went to the tray the younger man brought. Orius's eyes followed her. She kept her back to him, confident he was no threat. He was far too handsome and clear-minded to be the danava, and too patient and kindly to be an outpost man. She looked over the tray filled with a surprising array of food. A small bowl of oatmeal, another bowl of sliced fruit, some bread and a plate of eggs was presented before her. He'd even brought fried bacon and sausages, her favorite when travelling Earth. The meal smelled wonderful.

"Father Gallo insisted you would be disgusted by the pig meat, though he's seen me eat it a thousand times," Orius said. He chuckled, saying, "Some notions die hard."

"Is he vegetarian?" Maiel asked, taking up the tray and returning to sit on the bed.

"The scripture," Orius reminded her.

"The Bible, you call it," Maiel said, chewing a slice of melon.

"Talmud and the like," Orius said.

Maiel placed the egg and bacon on the bread and made a sandwich.

She spoke rapidly between bites and chews. "We don't eat much where I come from. It's mostly unnecessary, but we do have food. It's a shame that animals must give their lives to sustain your bodies, but so is the way of this flesh-world. It's equally puzzling to me though, why some believe that certain lives are better than others for nourishment, as if it will hurt their standing in Zion. To vilify one for being unclean—that is the worst part of it. Pigs are wonderful souls. Very smart and loving. Then some of you say that a plant has no feelings and to eat them is kinder. Is it because they have no faces with which you identify? I feel most sorry for these souls. The wretched things can't even call out, even beg for their lives. It's all so puzzling."

Orius listened to her, growing steadily amused as she rambled on. Placing his hands on his knees, he sat up, ready to begin their conversation. Yes, he was a kindly man despite his similarity to the baron, and seemed quite wise. Maiel wondered how he came to be with the church and not with a mate and house full of children.

"How do you feel this morning?" he asked her.

"I feel hunger," Maiel said, stuffing spoonfuls of oatmeal in her mouth as fast as she was able, between her breath and words.

"It's not too strong?"

"No," Maiel said around a mouthful.

"Because you're forming a mortal shell. You need the elements in the food to complete it," Orius said. He folded his arms and tapped a finger on his lip thoughtfully. "You do look better than last night. I was sure you would fade before the dawn came."

Maiel stopped eating. She stared at the nearly empty crockery with regret. Starving herself would have been a ticket straight to Acheron for certain. However, the vratin was insistent on that not happening. She wiped her fingers and mouth. Morgentus might have done the same, to work his poison into her more slowly and permanently. The outposts would likely do the same to win her service. Her sattva nervously thrummed with worry. She was certain he wasn't who he claimed.

"How do you know so much?" Maiel asked, unable to hold back the question any longer.

Orius smiled. He sat back and struggled to find the right words.

"I have experience with your kind, those who guard my fellow priests. You asked me last night how I see them? I'm gifted with that sight."

That sounded like an outpost man.

"Why don't you have a guardian? All souls must have guardians."

"You noticed." Orius sighed, and his demeanor became guarded. "You've many questions. Finish your breakfast and I'll take you for a walk in the garden. I can answer you more comfortably in the open air. I have so much to tell you. I hardly know where to begin."

Maiel swallowed her food and noticed how taxed he suddenly looked. His eyes filled with despair. If this was an illusion perpetrated by the labyrinth master, it was a very good one. He might have been able to fool her once, but he shouldn't be able to do it again so easily. The dragon on her arm was silent and an inspection of his features bore no more fruit. Did he have her already? She scanned the memory of each moment since the hunt began. It increasingly stunk of the outposts.

"I understand more than you know, vratin. As the damage progresses, my penannular will die—I'll lose my erelan attributes, the feathers of my wings and then the wings themselves will wither. My height will diminish with my strength. A bio-interface appliance will form around my resonance and I'll become more and more human—until I'm as weak and mortal as you. I'll be vulnerable to the devices of my dark enemy," she told him.

Maiel watched him eye her. The regret on his face couldn't change a thing.

"I only fear how my existence shall be without the light of King Adonai. I'll welcome them to kill me then. A terrible prison I'll occupy," Maiel said sadly.

"I can't describe how it feels to no longer bask in the light," Orius said, leaning forward with his arms resting on his legs and his hands pressed tight together. His eyes were honest. "I can tell you this: once the light has left you, only then are you lost. But—it hasn't left you. Don't give up hope."

Orius had nothing to offer her that she didn't already know. She returned to the remaining food on her tray.

Once finished with her meal, Maiel walked beside her host in the portico leading to the gardens of the rectory. A danava would have skulked in the shadows, despising the sunlight. Instead, he listened empathetically as she spoke on the matter of her arrival in his parish. His arms were tucked benignly behind his back, comfortable in the pleasant weather.

"If he foresaw this trouble, why didn't he warn me?" she asked, more relaxed.

"It's not for him to discover. It's for you to discover and show how you'll handle the tasks set before you. Is it the job of your teacher to take your tests? To study for you? Do you expect your boss to do the work and supervise you? No. We must do our work ourselves, detestable as it may be at times," the vratin replied.

I know the way to right this. Callidora's words came back to her.

"I'm a respected officio. I've served without fail for millennia. Why don't I deserve their candor?" Maiel asked.

"Do you? Why didn't you ask before you stormed out?"

Maiel stared ahead without answer. The vratin was clever, but then again, he wasn't enmeshed in the alders' games. However, he was no danava, either. Maiel frowned, looking to him without a word to say. An odd mix of emotions had sent her packing, all of which made no sense once her feelings calmed, but it was too late to mend her actions.

The priest chuckled at her speechlessness and held his arm out to indicate a narrow gravel path. In the full of the sun, the warm light on her skin gave her such radiance it made her companion pause. She turned to him, wondering where he would lead her next. He regarded her with a peculiar expression and she wondered why his conversation reminded her of her second in command. Perhaps the erela reached out to her, having gotten word of her absence. She would be anxious, to say the least. Perhaps the pale blue of his eyes reminded her of Callidora's nearly white ones.

"What name shall I give you, brave one?" Orius asked in uncertain awe.

"They call me—" Maiel replied.

"No," Orius threw up his hand to stop her from speaking. "To have your real name would be to have great power. I'll not risk it."

Orius stepped past her. He looked over the garden, deep in thought. Maiel was quite curious as to what he would say and do next. He was different than the vratin she recalled from her history, leaving her amused and uncertain. He turned back and pointed.

"Bethiah—daughter of God—or—Adonai as you call him."

Maiel raised an eyebrow. It was no worse than any other label she wore. The fact that he didn't know her, and wasn't even interested in her real name, suggested that the outpost wasn't involved here at all.

"Yes. Bethiah," he murmured to himself.

"Adonai isn't my janya," she told him, confused by his reasoning for the label.

"It's under his watchful presence and light that we grow and become greater. It's to him that each soul owes its substance," Orius said.

Maiel held her tongue; they had quite different impressions. A breeze ran through the garden bobbing the limbs of trees and the petals of flowers. She watched the grass ripple like water and was reminded of her field. Adonai's essence was there, though fleeting. She shut her eyes and turned her face to the warm sun. Her mind stretched out to the light, but a khajala held them apart.

"I feel pain," Maiel said, eyes brimming with tears at her separation from Adonai.

The agony of being denied the light underscored her growing weakness. The mixture of longing and regret stifled her breath. The emotion was not foreign to her. Indeed it was one of the most familiar emotions she experienced since Dominic came in her life; desire being the other. The lack of control over her cares was a source of greater stress.

"You need more rest, Bethiah. This change can be overwhelming, but I swear to you all is not lost. Come sit down." Orius said, taking hold of her arm.

The vratin brought her to a table set on a border of shade inside the walled garden. His presence was strangely comforting, like the wing of a dear friend, a favorite uncle. Indeed, Orius was fast in becoming the only friend she had during this trial. The tiny monastery indeed housed hope and refreshed her outlook on humanity. This was a startling revelation, considering with whom Orius shared his features. Sitting on the cracked wood bench, Maiel turned her face to the sun. Soaking in the warm radiance, she breathed deeply to settle the storm inside. Her head throbbed as she strained closer to the light. She rubbed her neck and returned to the moment. If she didn't get stronger, the gateway home would be inaccessible and then it was a matter of time before Morgentus got his wish. She stroked the surface of the ridge of the penannular on her cuirass. The atman was slumbering, dangerously drained without her atman to augment it. She frowned. Morgentus must have targeted the device, hoping to strip her armor.

"The brothers are curious about you. I promised you would meet with them," Vratin Orius said, drawing her back to the present.

Maiel opened her mouth to decline the invitation, but was silenced by the approach of the man he called Gallo. A reedy thin erela with ochre hair kept to the younger man's side. Maiel quickly recognized the Mukuru Order symbol on her breast. Her dark face framed a kind smile that immediately eased her uncertainty. Her assign carried a pitcher and some glasses. His nervous smile eased to awkwardness as he sat at the table. The guardian placed her long-fingered hands upon Maiel's shoulders and the warmth of the energy greatly improved that of Maiel's, but it wouldn't last without the light to nourish her.

"They have much to ask you. I promise they won't pester you long," Orius said.

Gallo's guardian went to her assign. Maiel felt strong again and her mood improved along with it. She frowned but accepted. Orius patted her hand understanding, and then gestured the waiting vratin to join them.

"Timor, bring the others. Come," he called them.

Maiel watched the brown-frocked men come from behind a hedge in the garden, each accompanied by their constant ethereal companions. She recognized the orders, two from Star, one from Fire and a Phoenix, a Mercury, another two from Avia and Aeris, and the last from the mysterious Order of Odin. The one he called Timor was the youngest to the brotherhood and claimed the mysterious Odin. The majority of them hadn't been present at the Mass last night and she wasn't sure they resided in the monastery or were called upon by her friend during the night. Distracting her from this assessment, Gallo poured water into the glasses he brought and set one before her. He drew a small pad and writing utensil from his pocket.

"You haven't answered my questions," Maiel said before the others began their interview.

The monks circled the table, studying her from every angle as their commander eyed her. Their guardians drifted through the garden, keeping their distance in a telling manner. If it weren't for them, she would have been concerned, although their behavior suggested that she was in greater trouble than first surmised. At least their presence kept Morgentus away.

"I'll answer your questions once you answer mine," Maiel added.

"Of course, as I promised."

"How did you know I fell? You said the guardians told you, but you're too familiar with the symptoms and I don't see them flocking to my side to lend aid," Maiel quickly started.

"They'll keep you safe, though they can't offer the answer or the doorway back. You see, Bethiah, it wasn't long ago—the same thing happened to another winged messenger, and he found his way here to their care," Orius said.

Maiel searched his eyes and then the eyes of the younger vratin. Gallo looked uneasy again. She switched her gaze back to the elder. Her kind continued to fall from time to time, as their path often took them close to darkness. Sometimes, the lessons did nothing to stop an atman which arced toward the negative half. Other times, events propelled a clear atman through a rigorous gauntlet that made it murky. The long way around was no less honorable than a direct route. Either way, duta may find themselves trapped in Samsara with no way back but through a lengthy trial. Recalling the strength of Orius's resonance, she realized his meaning. The fallen one wasn't the young man beside him or one of the other vratin. It was Orius. The puzzle came into greater focus and she tried to imagine him with wings and a form less aged.

"Oriael, guardian of the light. You've aged, but how? Why didn't you say so sooner?" Maiel asked in disbelief.

Maiel's eyes shifted over his features. This explained his similarity to Morgentus. Oriael had fallen within a short period after his younger akha was taken by the Conflict. All the younglings knew the tale. It was taught in the Ordo Priori as a lesson in control and loyalty. He was a fallen one, and at one time the most exemplary character. Not only did this eradicate the possibility of him being Morgentus, but it also negated any involvement by the outposts. Oriael had not just become recidia, but rather a rogue.

Oriael's mistake was his love for his akha, despite Morgentus's flaws. A forgiving engel, he had hoped to quell his appetites through focused duty, but Morgentus defied his akha, council, and king. He stole to Samsara, and stole the woman that turned his head. Sabereh, a simple farmwife, was never heard from again. The tale varied from there. Some said Morgentus raped her and when she became pregnant with his ardhodita, her husband cast her to the wastes, where Morgentus made her loyal to him. Others said Sabereh abandoned her husband for the promise of influence and riches, smitten by the dark engel, and broke her oaths. Those days were so long ago, the story was treated as fantasy. This meeting made it quite real.

"As you know, the dark ones never give in," Orius said. He sheepishly smiled and inclined his head, as if to apologize for not speaking sooner. "I needed to be sure you were who you said you were."

"You said the shades can't enter here."

"It's true—to a point. But they find ways eventually. They always do. That room is the only haven I've kept these many years. They will break it eventually," he explained.

Maiel swallowed. He gave his room to keep her safe. Morgentus was sure to take advantage of that. He would snatch him the moment he let his guard down and force her hand, knowing she wouldn't allow someone to suffer in her place.

"And what of your atrin?" she dared to ask aloud.

Orius clamped his mouth closed, despite her use of the word which meant demon brother in human languages. His chin lifted, almost indignant that she'd mentioned him. Orius hadn't expected her to make the connection. How could he know the story of his fall was well discussed in the duta schools? Or that it became of special interest to her when her friend revealed the fate of his jyoti? Gediel hadn't fallen despite his relation, but that didn't mean his fear and guilt might not eventually break him. Her mind slipped toward her old friend and his wolfish stare, which filled her with a calming sensation of encouragement. If he could survive such a trial, then this should be no problem for her. She softly smiled, remembering how he felt in her arms when they hugged. Her atman pulsed with a burst of high resonance, putting her off balance. She shook her head to clear the spinning.

Orius's voice drew her back to the present, but he didn't notice the change in her.

"The brothers protect me from the shades that come and go—outstandingly so. They're wise for humans and have much to offer their kind. Yet the church silences them because it teaches that these gifts come from darkness. They're sent to the farthest reaches with the smallest congregations or shuffled into monasteries with no contact. Teachings of faith often lead to fear and the result is violence. I managed to convince our leaders to send them to me, promising that I could keep them quiet and safe. My intention was to keep them safe from the forces that might seek to use them, either the outposts or the shadowalkers."

Orius checked to see if his meaning was clear. He drew a deep breath and answered her other question with some reluctance.

"This is the first time I've seen my atrin since—"

Orius cut himself off. He didn't want the others to know. The link might cause him to lose their trust.

Maiel digested everything Orius had said; her eyebrows pinched together. Morgentus wouldn't stay away for long. He'd seen his atrin last night and was likely plotting to knock two birds from the limb with a single stone. Maiel muttered a curse under her breath. Once again she was putting people in danger. She was foolish not to reach out to the outposts for help. She thought they would harm her or make her work for them with no hope of going back again.

"The priesthood is riddled with shadowborn and shadowalker. I don't want you running off thinking you're putting us in any more danger than we already know," he continued, quite tellingly, when the silence between them lengthened.

"We see such from beyond the Avernus. Is there any way back from this, Vratin Orius? A way that isn't known?" Maiel asked.

"Just call me Orius. Titles are so very unnecessary between friends. At least, I hope that we can be friends, despite an unfortunate relation."

"Orius," Maiel repeated.

Orius smiled and squeezed her hand. He gave a nod, truly thankful.

"There are only the three ways back," Orius held up three fingers. Maiel listened intently as he continued, "If you return to unquestioned fealty before your flesh is complete, you'll be able to access the way gate back to Zion. If your flesh is complete, you must die, but it isn't just any death you must die. You must be martyred—a death for a cause or life with no thought to your own salvation. You must give your life for what you believe in. Once you're flesh, you can't die any other way, except to fade. By giving way to the darkness and descending. I don't advise this last route, as it ends in Oblivion."

"If I eat, you said I'd be mortal. Why'd you curse me to this?" Maiel said.

"I fed you only enough to deny your enemies. You'll not fade and deliver yourself to the baron. Make no mistake, Bethiah. You were fading. Your penannular isn't functioning, is it? It's better you become flesh and pay your penance in this world. Though your enemies may torment you, their power is much weaker here."

Maiel looked at her hands. She wondered how fading wasn't the wiser choice. She may have gone back to Acheron, but she would've fought them—and her family would have come to help. She might even be back home that very moment. She closed the fingers of her hands, making fists. Then again, Morgentus might have trapped her there as he did before, when she had been foolish enough to let her fears overcome her.

"Did you dream last night?" Orius asked her.

"I don't remember," Maiel lied.

"If you sleep again, remember that the astral plane is a place of communication. You may reach your friends there and they might be able to help, but be wary. The astral plane is open to any."

"I hadn't thought of it. I was distracted with—I'll try to remember during my meditations," Maiel said, not knowing why she lied, but her gut reaction was to share only necessary details.

Callidora flashed in her mind. The image of her shorn braid clasped in the leader's hand followed. She decided not to disclose such images quite yet. Her evocati tried to contact her. There must be a way back, one of which he wasn't aware.

"Now that we have answered your questions, Bethiah, the brothers wish to ask some of you. Is that fair?"

Maiel nodded. She welcomed the interview.

"Good. Let us carry on then."

The other men circled close. Vratin Gallo readied his notebook and pen. Righting his glasses, he cleared his throat. With a bob of his head and a kindly smile, he spoke.

"Welcome to our humble parish, Bethiah, messenger of Adonai true—"

Maiel stared, astonished by the sea of words spilling from his lips. It was as if he was paying homage to a queen. Orius clapped a hand on Gallo's shoulder to cut him off. If left to speak, the man would have continued until the sun set.

"My apologies, sacred messenger. I'm Father Salvatore Gallo and I've been selected by the brothers to ask you some questions." Gallo blushed.

"Salvatore, I think she understands why you're here." Orius's voice rumbled with laughter.

Maiel patiently waited. She could very nearly smell the fear.

"I remain unsure on how to welcome you to our church. I've dreamed of this nearly all my life. Please forgive my formalities and ramblings," Gallo said. She stared. He swallowed and added, "We'll stop whenever you've had enough."

Maiel's mien put him off and he looked to Orius to be sure he should continue. The elder vratin smiled warmly and lifted his brows to encourage him to continue. Maiel nearly sighed from boredom, when he finally stammered out the first question.

"Father Orius answered these same questions when he arrived at the rectory. The first—where are you from?"

"Eden," Maiel replied.

Gallo's eyes widened inside the thick frames of his glasses. After a moment, he remembered himself and hurriedly scribbled in his notebook. If these men were operatives for the orders of Samsara, they wouldn't be asking such questions. All the answers they'd seek would be delivered from a watcher in Zion, transported via council documents. Maiel relaxed a little, certain at last that they had no ties with those who could make her stay difficult.

"What is your function?"

"Function?"

"What is your purpose, the work you do?"

"I'm a legiona; I serve as captain in King Adonai's armies, first legion under General Mikhael."

"A legion-uh?"

"An officio—soldier," Maiel replied.

"How old are you?"

"Five thousand four hundred and sixty Earth years," Maiel rattled off the number.

Gallo peered at her from behind his glasses, astonished.

"My God. You don't look a day over twenty-five," Gallo said.

Maiel was confused by this statement.

Beside him stood the eldest of the clan. He breathed an odd sound and fell to dreaming, adding more years to those he'd already claimed. She raised an eyebrow and allowed the corners of her mouth to curl into a slight smile, amused by the old man's reaction to her age. He was far older than his bio-vessel allowed him to recall, but she left that to other days. Gallo muttered an excuse for him, calling him Thomas. Maiel eyed Thomas, reading through his energy that his years were ending. The appliance was breaking down, but she didn't mention this, as it had a way of alarming souls, and Thomas was already quite aware of his mortality.

"Why are you here?"

"I came to set two souls back on their paths, but my efforts failed when I was forced to abandon them to draw off my pursuer," Maiel replied.

Gallo persisted for some time, rooting out the reasons of her manifestation in his world. He pondered the similarity to his own form and the decidedly inexplicable skill of invisibility of her kind. Maiel did her best to explain to him, but it was difficult to explain in terms he would understand. Duta technology was like wizardry to them. She was far from a scientist or doctor, but recalled the basics taught to her in school. Those were subjects better left to alders who worried over them. She was able to explain that their forms weren't as similar as they appeared.

Gallo drew their conversation away from anatomy to questions about Zion and its differences from Samsara. They briefly spoke on the Samsaran creation of religion and the lack of it in Zion. Gallo was intrigued by the revelation, but he seemed most interested in her family and her ketu. The occurrence of such pair bonding somewhat confused him, in light of what he thought he knew as taught by his faith. Gallo didn't push any subject for too long; Orius hinted he switch topics by coughing or clearing his throat. He then questioned her on her present experience.

"What are the symptoms you experience in this—well, what you term 'a fall?'"

"Mortal form. Demonic pestilence," Maiel replied flatly, grown tired of the weighty conversation.

Orius reminded them of his presence again, chuckling at her response. Gallo nervously peered between them. Orius's eyes sparkled with delight. The younger vratin made himself laugh; their visitor meant to be amusing. Maiel smiled, revealing that she did indeed jest. He stared at her, his laughter turning to awe.

"Fear," Maiel said. She cleared her throat, hating to admit it. "I feel fear and mistrust. These aren't emotions we experience easily."

Orius stared at her, suddenly lost in deep thought. That wasn't surprising. After all, he understood better than anyone what was happening. Realizing his caustic little atrin was at the heart of it, concern was the least of the former Power's reactions. She sensed that his thoughts pieced her story together. He struggled to make sense of why his atrin focused on her, and how it was possible that he managed to manipulate a legiona into such a situation. It would be good to have a second mind on the task. Maiel grasped his forearm, and saw the wistful longing for home in his expression. His fingers closed on her forearm.

"You stare at me like my elder akha. What do you see?"

Gallo stopped scribbling. He noticed Orius's thoughtful mien. His eyes flicked between them hoping he wouldn't miss what came next. It must have been most interesting to him to see his beliefs proven, even if the reality of the situation was vastly different from what he thought.

"I can't help but wonder," he said then paused. He scowled, hesitating to continue. "What if—what if this is some kind of test," Orius replied.

"Like a rite of passage? Trial by fire," Gallo dramatically said.

Maiel doubted it was so simple a matter. She folded her arms. Morgentus would hardly cooperate with her kind to help her rise. She shook her head and frowned. No, this was Morgentus taking advantage of her momentary weakness. She was far too young and still had much to learn before she would be given a silver crown to top her head.

"It would explain a great deal, yes?" Gallo said, now losing himself in thought.

"I have a friend near Budapest who might be able to help us. Once we present your case to him, he may see a way to get you home again. He's been working with me for the greater portion of his career," said Orius.

Maiel ran a hand over the surface of the table, feeling the rough texture. Her eyes followed her fingers and the grain of the wood, not wishing to show them her reluctance. This friend of Orius sounded like someone seeking to impress him or lead him astray. After all, Orius was dealing with incarnated humans and they could be treacherous animals. Unfortunately, he became too much like them. He'd lost his discernment right along with his wings and retained his blind forgiveness. His atrin was capable of tormenting him in ways that didn't require his presence, as there were other danava in his employ.

"I promise you, he means well. He's a man of the cloth, yes, but versed in ancient lore. They say he has the ear of General Mikhael himself. You said you serve his legion, I trust that's the ear you wish to reach."

"If you're so willing to reach out to the general, why not the outposts?"

"The outposts are troublesome. They have their own agenda and I get the distinct impression they might cause you more trouble. It's best that you reach someone sympathetic to you. Mikhael would be far better than some officio who's never met you," Orius explained.

Maiel's attention was captured. The corners of her mouth pulled down with doubt. Mikhael wouldn't have anything to do with a Samsaran vratin. He hadn't played guardian in eons and only fools thought they called him to their side to care for some banal task. Then again, there were certain souls who were unique and kept honest contact with duta while incarnated. If this man truly spoke with a duta he mistook for Mikhael, then he could get her home. They just needed to remind the brazen one of the misstep he'd made against the general. Mikhael was as unlikely to leave her there, test or not, than he was to be a soul's guide, and any duta impersonating him would be quick to amend, lest they suffer his wrath. Besides, if they could free the man—who she suspected was a danava—they would both secure their paths back to Zion. On the other side of the coin, it seemed much more likely the outpost would have such ability to contact one of the highest generals in Zion. Their mission was to protect Earth and if she surrendered to them, they would be forced to treat her with decency. But, the thought of that became distorted with anxious worries about aggressive tactics.

"I don't mean to get your hopes up. It's mere myth—and I've yet to see it, despite my many years at this church. We both know Mikhael has better things to do."

"You trust him anyway?" Maiel asked, quite skeptical.

"All I have is time, Bethiah. It can't hurt and if he's beset by danava. Then we'll be doing him a favor," Orius said, shrugging.

"Has he helped you at all?"

Orius nodded. His eyes held conviction, but Maiel was only assured a danava fooled him.

"We'll need to leave our sanctuary," Maiel said to remind him, both hoping he was right and hoping he would reconsider.

Exposing themselves meant each of the factions they hoped to avoid or engage would chase them down, making it impossible to discern one from the other.

"I sense it'll be worth the danger for both of us. Of course, we'll need to disguise you; the basilica is very popular with pilgrims and they're not used to seeing women with wings who stand over seven feet tall and wield a gladius," he added, noticing one of the brothers studying the crimson feathers of her wing.

Maiel looked over her shoulder at the man. It was Thomas. The elderly monk took his hand back and muttered an apology in Latin. Maiel frowned at him, drawing her feathers close and smoothing the mussed barbs. She would miss them when they were gone. If she had any vanity at all, it was her pride in her strong ruby wings. She sniffed, feeling each vane and rachis slide between her fingers.

"I can't stay here. When should we go?" Maiel asked, acquiescing.

"I'll make a call this evening, after supper. Hopefully he'll be available to speak," Orius replied.

Maiel nodded.

"Gentlemen—thank you for your patience, but I think our guest would like to enjoy the sun for a bit. She's been through a great deal," Orius said to the vratin.

The vratin bowed and thanked her, taking their leave without complaint or delay. Their guardians went with them, casting reluctant glances in her direction. Even Gallo and his Mukuru guardian left them with no further questions or long stares. She listened to their retreat, feeling alone and censured. Orius remained, watching her waiver on the edge of bittersweet reflections. Maiel liked the vratin, despite their aloofness. After all, they saw a fallen one who possibly threatened the safety of their assigns. The vratin, also, were not like other humans. Their energy was surprisingly clean. Smiling softly about their innocent inspections, her energy slowly rose as her sattva absorbed the light of the sun. She longed for the moon; it could fill her quickly and return her focus.

"You'll survive this. When you're ready to speak again, I'd like to hear more of your story. I think we have much to share and may find something that can help us gain closure," he told her.

"Stay."

Orius looked at her, surprised.

"Tell me why you avoided the outposts," Maiel said, needing to know before she agreed to go to the man he had suggested.

Orius drew a deep breath through his nose. He nodded and took her hand.

"When I came to Earth, my direction was uncertain. Morgentus's betrayal tore me up like nothing else could. I trusted no one. When the Illuminati approached me, they wanted to engage me in their service, protecting Earth from danava and shadowalkers. I was no longer certain who or what needed protecting. The outpost didn't like my refusal and pursued me for decades, dogging every step I took through every nation I wandered. They are every-where, watching, like in the old days. They're the remains of what caused my brother to fall. I finally made them understand that there was no way I would become a turncoat and serve them. To this day, I have no contact with them. I'm certain, that if it is what you truly want, it would take little to uncover one watching this very church," Orius replied.

Maiel held his gaze. His reasoning made sense. The watchers of the orig-inal outposts were among those who defied the king during The Conflict. A burning atman would be more likely to hide among the rogues' gallery than in any other circle. She quietly agreed to see his friend instead.

CHAPTER 14

GEDIEL RUSHED FROM THE GATE OF OTZAR. He parted from the others in pursuit of Evocati Luthias, whom he sent at Mikhael's request to prepare for a small reconnaissance. Uriel easily gave his release, seeming to know more than she let on, and with that came Voil's acceptance. With Dominic out of the way and the girl set to intercept their wayward erela, he felt more at ease to find the answers to his questions. Whether they wanted to reveal the truths they kept locked away or not, he would eventually dig them up. In the meantime, he was confident Maiel could hold her own until more help was available. A slight indication of trouble and he'd break the barrier himself. He knew she didn't take the track of a rogue, working alone to defy the king. He knew her too well, despite what others thought. She was the same girl he entrusted with the care of his beloved Argus. The dedicated officio sought to reweave a tapestry that unraveled around them all. If she failed, it would wreck her family and those too close.

"Gediel," a voice called his name.

Turning back, he sighted Joel trotting after him.

"Where are you off to so quickly? We should stick together in case we're needed."

"I have an assignment to attend—Voil has a task. If you need me, call. I'll be in Elysion preparing for a short time. After that, I'm not sure you'll be able to find me easily until after the moon rises."

Joel's eyes narrowed. The sun-soldier knew he was on more than a simple assignment from the watcher leader. Gediel excused himself, hoping Joel would accept his request with no further explanation. Halfway through the room, Joel called him again. Gediel slowed to a halt. He turned, gripping the hilt of his sword and grinding his teeth. Joel approached him with that narrow gaze.

"Does this assignment have anything to do with my khata?"

"Indirectly," Gediel replied, unable to lie.

Joel set his hands on his hips and puffed out his chest. Gediel eyed him, thinking he'd gone mad believing he needed to defend her against him.

"I'm going to find a duta who went missing not too long ago. It seems the council's team was unable to retrieve him yet," Gediel continued.

"Gamael," Joel said the name.

Gediel stared, careful not to betray his emotions.

"If you'll excuse me, I don't wish to waste another moment. He's been lost too long and there are too many answers to be had from him."

"Yes, of course," Joel said stepping back.

Gediel saw many unspoken questions cross Joel's face. Taking the silence for his chance to retreat, Gediel turned from him and continued into the outer halls of the citadel. Luthias would be waiting at the kennels and he couldn't delay this mission any longer.

Reaching the front gates of Zion, Gediel looked over his shoulder to be sure none of Maiel's family and friends, or anyone else followed him. Both seeing and sensing he was alone, he took a step out of the gate's entrance, disappearing into the next opening. His foot fell on the grass outside of a sprawling earthen compound. The sculpted structures were merged to the hillside and around a stream, all curves and bends that created a surreal smooth-lined cob dwelling. Among the trees, a white wolf rested, watching the moon hung high in the blue sky and the sun's descent. The wolf took no notice of Gediel's approach until he stood at his front door. Then the animal stood on his four legs and joined him.

"Captain Chiron, has Evocati Luthias come?" Gediel said to him.

The wolf's thoughts told him the guardian had arrived. He waited by the kennels as they arranged themselves. Chiron's mate, Imnek, looked after him. Gediel patted Chiron's head and went inside his home. In the dim interior, he wandered through the maze of rooms seeking his bedroom. He entered the space, an amorphous room fashioned by his own hands from clay when he was just a youngling. It encompassed the hill and the streams. The water made an island on which his bed stood, a large and rustic piece of furniture made of twined branches and carved panels. He wouldn't use that anytime soon. Rest was a distant dream. He sighed.

The stream trickled beneath a rock arch that served as a bridge to the other side of the room. Suddenly, he was surrounded by the essence of the erela he sought. She reached to him from beyond the barriers, but why him? Surely one of the others would have been preferred. They had not spoken in ages. Her eyes stared at him from the confines of his mind and he was transported to a time long ago. Floating in the sacred pool, foreheads gently touching, it was a moment lost forever. Gediel steadied himself and returned the distant embrace with one of reassurance. They were on their way. She just needed to hold out a bit longer. The connection broke as his eyes opened. If he held on, he'd go crazy. Gediel stared at his empty room. Her scent was a delicate strain in the air.

Gediel blinked and tried to recall why he came home. The water rushed and he watched it for several moments, losing himself in thought. His eyes followed the path of water that streamed out of the room. A hillside crested just beyond an arched door, flanked by two windows in the opposite wall. Path stones wound to the top. He stared at the grassy knoll and the two oddly placed palms that stood there. It never looked quite right, but he could never think of a thing he wanted to put there. The bare hillside made him sad.

Gediel frowned. The erela had scattered his thoughts too easily. He recalled his purpose. His face pinched in a deep scowl as he crossed the small bridge to the other part of the chamber. His boots clicked on the higher flat stone that skirted the stream and led to another cavity. This room was smaller and more distinct in shape, nearly a square. He used it for a meditation space and kept his weapons in a cabinet there. The floor was a slab of polished, variegated agate. The old wooden relic he used to house his armaments took up nearly one wall. Keeping his back to the hillside, he opened the worn doors and looked over his stock. The most important piece sat on a small shelf alone. He clipped the penannular to his jacket first, then flipped several knives into his many pockets. Removing the sword he carried, he took up another, a much heavier one with a wolf's head pommel. Gediel strapped the belt around his waist, checking his remaining stock for anything he missed. Satisfied that he had all the equipment he would need, he exited through the opening overlooking the hill.

Gediel walked along the rolling hills, some of which made up the roof of his compound, and came down the other side where the stream disappeared into the forest. Several caves were dug into the high cliff. Wolves and dogs alike made their homes in them. The sound of puppies yipping accompanied the sound of the stream. Any other day, the pups would have filled him with joy by their mere presence, but today he carried too much for it to bring him happiness. They danced around his feet, hoping for a petting, but he disappointed them.

Gediel approached Luthias, where the engel stood on the edge of the wood. The young soldier smoked a pipe, his arms tensely crossed, as he stared into the trees. The fog suspended between the trunks signaled the edge of Elysion, the Khajala. Beyond the forest they would find the snows of the southern pole mountains that rested in darkness most of the year. Though his sorrel wings were relaxed, Luthias was ready to fight should an imp decide to manifest from the shadows.

"Are you sure you want to do this?" Luthias asked him.

"Gamael's been in Acheron too long," Gediel said. "I don't like that they're dragging their feet. He may know something, like what alder wanted him lost."

"You think Maxiel had something to do with all this?"

"I wouldn't put it past that cranky old bastard," Gediel said, sneering.

Gediel had never thought much of the alder, especially since he doled out orders to a certain erela and her mate, orders that would see the latter delayed in his evolution for centuries more, and assure his descent into darkness.

"Something's off about him. He'd think nothing of throwing a duta in Jahannam to cover his mistakes," Gediel added.

Luthias grimaced. "It's no secret that some duta aren't keen on mixing with the humans, but would he bring them harm?"

"Truthfully? Not unless he's lost the path," Gediel said.

"Be careful who you say that to. You may outrank Maxiel, but he has the favor of those who may make your situation difficult. He'll bring up your jyoti faster than a vratin would point to his holy book," Luthias warned.

"I live on the snow border. How much more difficult can they make it?" Gediel smiled.

"I hope you fancy travelling the astrals." Luthias grinned, with a heavy strike to Gediel's arm.

"Let's go. I have others I need to find as well," Gediel said.

"In Acheron?"

"No, in Zion," Gediel answered. It was his turn to jest. "That'll be much harder," he added.

Gediel whistled and a trio of wolves emerged from the caves, Chiron leading them.

Luthias cleaned out his pipe and tucked it away. He gave a nod and they disappeared from the banks of the stream along with the wolves. When they reappeared, the party stood before a long pier jutting into a snow-banked river. Khajala clouded the view all around. A cog ship was moored about halfway down the planks, facing the icy desert. Gediel motioned Luthias forward. They were the only life for miles. Their boots clomped against the boards, the only sound in the endless nothingness.. The wolves confidently sauntered along with them. The mists came alive with whispers. The guard-ian and watcher ignored them and made their way on board the cog. While Gediel loosed the moorings, Luthias unstrapped the sail and the wolves settled mid-ship. The sail's fabric billowed and filled. Then the vessel moved forward. Gediel stood in the bow, watching their approach to an enormous way gate. Luthias joined him.

"I remember the day we brought her back from Acheron," Luthias said.

Gediel activated the gate to Jahannam from a small console at the wheel, a round seal bearing two pyramids and a line, one atop the other, the symbol of air and fire. Five black pearls circled round and a cross capped the fore with an eye in its brace. Lastly, two cross pins locked the lower pyramid in place, along with three onyx nail heads in the corners. The seal glowed with pale light. The eye of the King watched the field. An azure laser beamed from the bow sprit. The gate opened onto darkness.

Luthias bared his teeth, still hurt by the memories this crossing brought.

"A pale slight thing she was, barely a recollection of who or what she'd been. I thought certain Dominic would've turned over all of Jahannam to get her back. Something in him must have snapped when they took her. He wasn't the same man. Joel and I actually had to convince him to go."

"They didn't take her. She put herself there because of him. I am afraid that Dominic isn't who you think," Gediel admitted.

"What do you mean, Primus?" Luthias gruffly asked, taking offense.

"It's like you said, he should have sacked Acheron to get her back. You or I would've violently done so, but he didn't. Why?"

"First you call out Maxiel for being a shade and now Dom?" Luthias sneered.

"I call what I see. He didn't exactly chase after her this time either," Gediel replied stoically.

"You watchers are all alike, suspicious of everyone. You'll make a right Power someday."

"I've no intention of moving on from what I do. At least I can admit it," Gediel said.

"You're still hunting your jyoti?"

"We both know my destiny."

They stared at one another to see who would flinch first. Luthias gripped the rail and sneered at the khajala as they passed through the gate. The structure resembled a bridge, and reflected in the water, making a complete circle. A number of such gates dotted Zion and the out-worlds, but only a few could access them. Gediel left him there, retreating to the wheel in order to keep their course straight. He was in no mood to cross swords with a guardian. The young duta would have fought and lost over nothing. Luthias was loyal to a fault, much like his friend's wife. But they weren't the only ones loyal to an idea that couldn't be had. His eyes shifted over the timbers of the cog as it was swallowed by the portal. Chiron looked back at him. It was a very direct look that assumed much. Gediel grit his teeth and narrowed his eyes. He didn't need reminding. Chiron turned his attention back to the fog, upset with his commander's response.

The ship slowly sailed on, and their trip felt like ages had passed. The vessel at last crossed into still, dead waters and the sail fell flat. It was a darker than normal night, without a moon. They were at the nothing between the worlds: Avernus. Jumping from the stern, Gediel took up one of the starboard oars. His companion joined him at port. Hard rowing was ahead of them, but they couldn't risk floating idly through space. Once they crossed this darkness, and the strange Astral ways, the Domdaniel would take them to the mouth of the Lethe and Sheol beyond. They hoped they would find their ship docked there when they returned from the heart of the shadow lands. Acheron was in the heart of the prison and not easily reached undetected. They would lose much energy in this mission and the vessel was their only hope back.

The light disappeared behind them. Gediel touched the red and yellow star, pinching together the triangles. He put down his oar and went back to the rudder wheel at the stern. Heavy black plates now accented his dark clothes. The triangles shifted to the center of his chest. A wolfish black and silver helmet crowned his head. Luthias followed the cue, clicking the sword of his penannular. He nervously eyed the distance. Silver spilled like mercury over his sattva, forming a well-articulated suit of armor. The plate resembled the armaments of the Powers, but without the distinctive insect-like helmet or tree heraldry of the Astrals on the breast. Gediel smiled at the fancy showpiece, wondering how well the guardian could fight in such a binding costume. Though he too wore armor, the plates did not cover every inch. They protected the necessary areas, but did not limit his movement.

"Don't you worry your pretty little head. I'll show them a thing or two if they come for us." Luthias grinned madly.

The tone of his voice and the expression on his face led Gediel to cast off all doubt Luthias was the right engel for the job. The guardian was eager to throw himself into the midst of the shadow hordes, and plenty were to be had where they were going. He was probably more eager to fight than anyone he knew, except maybe Mikhael. Gediel lowered his gaze, saddened that Dominic failed to realize how lucky he was to have him, and chose instead to shame the guardian with his failures.

An object thumped the boat, clomping along the underside and pulling Gediel's attention back to the moment. Gediel held the cog steady on course, peering ahead into the darkness. They were past the other layers, and float-ing on the Domdaniel. Here their course took them through a vast sea of drowned souls floating upon the black water's surface. The air carried whispers of suffering as the boat carved a path through the bodies, edging closer to Sheol, the dead beaches of Erebus. The Old Man of Crete, or Yahweh's statue, would soon be discernible in the dark against the vast khajala between Jahannam and Astral. Yahweh, a watcher, had given up his existence to help seal the path to Jahannam and drown the dark world, a seraph atman imprisoned upon a cliff face that sunk deep in the waters. His now stone figure stood as a mutilated testament to the evil he guarded against. No one even knew anymore if he was still on Zion's side. The bodies of lost souls continued to thump against the boat, returning Gediel to the present. Their thrashing would turn fierce before they entered the Lethe, hoping to find salvation on the cog or drown those who dared pass over them.

The thrashing began as expected, raising a deafening cadence in the limitless dark that could warn Jahannam's soldiers of their intrusion. The souls struggled to snap the ship planks with their bare hands, in hope of sinking the vessel and feeding on the passengers. The boards, however, held tight. The rotting hands recoiled when pressed too long to the wood, burned by the vessel from Zion. They thrashed the water angrily, wanting the sattva and atman. Bold marditavya climbed despite the burning. A flaxen aghartian slipped over the rail, bloated with the water of her damnation. Barnacles stuck to her skin and her hair was streaked with green algae. She was nearly a doll, hauntingly like the object that gave them their name. Luthias drew his sword and without hesitation drove his blade through her middle. With a shove of his boot for leverage, he cast her back to the watery prison. The impact cleared the path before their bow as the other souls scurried to feed upon the remains.

"They're only going to get uglier," Gediel sneered.

"You've come this way before? Alone?" Luthias asked.

Gediel gave a slow nod.

"This is a good day," Gediel replied, keeping his eye on the black horizon.

Luthias stared, sickened by the frenzy.

The small vessel cleared the deep of the Domdaniel. A soft fog rose from the water where the boards touched the surface. Hissing, like that of a heavy rain, replaced the whispers and moans of the damned. A bleak mist formed a barrier between them and the land. The bow pressed through and they sailed up a glassy black river in the wake of the Old Man's falls.

The distant shores of Sheol looked abandoned, dusty, and hot. However, they were not as empty as they appeared. Souls languished here, desperate and therefore dangerous. It was a land of imps too: manifestations of torment. Where there were souls and imps, soldiers and worse could also be found.

The cog slipped up to a derelict dock and stopped. This was where Kharon docked his skiff when making his deliveries or accepting the fare of some shade. They moored the boat and made their way toward land, cautiously watching and careful not to touch the water of the river, lest they forget why they came and went wandering until a prince took them prisoner.

"Do you know your direction, Pritanni?" Gediel asked Luthias, calling the guardian by his order.

Luthias nodded.

"We've no time to waste. I'll meet you at the gate of the pit," Gediel said.

The pair stepped forward, mounting speed until they disappeared into the storm at the edge of Sheol. Sliding in that plane would call attention to their presence, but they had little choice. Walking there would take days, even with their clear sight. Gediel needed to find Gamael immediately to bring him back for healing and pump him for information. The wolves followed, barking and yipping excitedly.

Gediel arrived at the gate first, faster because of his resonance and practice. He stood on a narrow stone path jutting from the entrance of the maze into a narrow black stream that wound around Acheron like a useless moat. Beyond the entrance lay what many called the pits, a vast labyrinth with the baron's manor at the center. Acheron was the deepest duta dared to go on solo missions. The labyrinth made a prison for atman, both stolen or earned, and kept them by the confusing network of passages. However, Acheron was more than a maddening prison. The miles of passages worked like a farm from which they cultivated sustenance out of the energy from the atman they kept. This is what made the baron so important to the princes and why they had put up with his bumbling so long. He was adept in the cultivation of soul atman for food.

Gediel's gaze lifted to the keystone of the slender archway. The passage it framed appeared to go on forever. A series of lanterns disappeared into infinity. At his knees his four-legged companions crouched and growled. He patted Chiron on the head, easing him. They each knew the moment they were inside the halls would change. The motion was imperceptible, triggered by the presence of an unknown atman. The Lord of the Labyrinth wasn't loathe to feeding on one of his own, unless that danava could cause him discomfort. Thus, a duta was prized game; an eternal banquet if it could be had.

"We must wait for the guardian," Gediel said to his furry companions.

A peculiar disturbance swirled the reedy stream behind him. Gediel faced the perpetrator. A serpent drank from the poisonous water on the opposite bank, only feet from where Gediel and the wolves stood. The sightless shade crept low to the ground and boasted smooth scales instead of skin. The sleek head raised and it turned its nose in his direction. Water dripped from the sharp mouth. The serpent snuffled the air and then stared at him. It hissed from its pointed mouth. The snake's long tongue slipped over its muzzle. Its hunger was its end.

Gediel grabbed the hilt of his sword the second the beast leapt toward him. A great growl sounded in the dark and Luthias emerged in time to grab the tail and yank the shadow back. It fell to the ground with a bounce and shook its head in surprise. Possessing a small brain, by the time he registered the gravity of the situation, Luthias had struck, pinning it to the rancid ground from which it drank. He kicked it into the stream and watched the form slowly dissolve.

"Just in time, mate." Luthias smiled.

The guardian hopped across the narrow stream and joined Gediel at the door of the labyrinth.

"By my calculations, Gamael's held in the western corridors," Gediel told him.

"You're welcome." Luthias smiled. After a pause, he added, "How do we know which is which when we're inside?" It was an obvious question with an obvious answer.

"We don't go inside." Gediel smiled, with a glint in his golden eyes.

Luthias watched him, puzzled by his answer and warned by his heightened resonance. Gediel approached the gate and leapt to the top of the wall, grabbing the crest and swinging up. He bent down and the wolves leapt into his waiting arms one at a time. Luthias shook his head, unsure this was a good idea.

"This isn't very secretive," Luthias said.

Gediel smiled down at him, hands on his hips. He'd been going this way for nearly all his missions, and they still didn't expect it. The senile shades waited on the lower floors of the labyrinth for the strays to come by. They didn't think of looking above, mostly because there was so much to eat below. Worrying if they learned their lesson was of no concern to him. The shades served themselves, and weren't likely to share information that would take food from their mouths.

Luthias struggled to climb the smooth walls like the watcher before him, eventually crawling to the top. Gediel used the delay to pick out their route. Once Luthias sat on the wall catching his breath, the watcher returned his attention to him.

"Perhaps you should quit that pipe, guardian," Gediel suggested.

"I'd rather die." Luthias smirked.

"You just might."

"Some hope, but it'll be a cold day in hell when the King has dispossessed me."

That was the cause of their confidence. To die, for a duta, was a permanent end to a long process of suffering, utter destruction in Oblivion. There was no other way to die but suffer. Suffer they could and greatly so. Gediel thought of his friend. His chest tightened with anxiety. They needed to get moving. He wouldn't let them cast her into Oblivion without a fight. Chiron whimpered and licked his hand, assuring that Gediel wouldn't be alone in that effort.

Luthias took another gulp of air and stood.

"Right—then. Let's get Gamael and get out of here," Luthias said.

The guardian faced the labyrinth and the grandeur of their mission. The corridors and walls spread before them in an endless network of channels, an abyss of geometric shapes. It was said to have no end, though it was ensconced at the heart of Acheron, the northernmost reaches lying under the shadow of the princes' vast dwelling. The crown of the baron's manor stood in the dark distance, overseeing the lair from a crumbling hill.

"It's bigger than when I last saw it," Luthias said, staring off in the distance.

The guardian's face revealed his fear. Gediel thumped his back, offering him a confident grin. If he stayed near and did as he was ordered, there would be little trouble.

"It's exactly the same. You just never saw it from up here before." Gediel lied.

The shades continually built the labyrinth out, hence the narrow slab of stone at the current entrance. It wasn't necessary to tell the guardian that, or how it increased by acres each cycle of a Jahannam year, just like the stretches of their world. The evocati needed to remain focused on his task if they were to get to Gamael and rescue him quickly.

"Thank Adonai for that." Luthias marveled.

Gediel strode west along the wall. The wolves lumbered after him, unafraid of falling off the narrow path. Gediel called to Luthias over his shoulder. The other engel broke his stare with the labyrinth and hurried to catch up. They walked for some time, chatting quietly about past adventures. The young guardian saw quite a bit more than Gediel expected. By his descriptions, there was evidence someone was working toward this goal all along. Of course, that was another reason for taking the guardian with him. Tongues loosened among friends and Luthias needed to be made a friend.

Maiel's fall would be quite rewarding for the danava. It would take away one of the greatest assets Zion claimed. Morgentus was a fool to think that she was going to be his alone. Gediel listened intently to Luthias's stories, cataloging the ominous points of proof, despite his thoughts constantly returning to the reason for being there. Though he actively hunted here, he never heard of her name on their list of targeted soldiers. That in itself was odd, as she and Zaajah ran frequent rescue missions. Though their duties were usually to retrieve a comrade or dig out a soul that was stolen from the keepers, they also led a few missions to steal back souls being kept against their will. This should have made their names common. The High Council too easily dismissed her as a mere captain, not high enough in the ranks to attract the attention of the baron. They were wrong. Maiel had crossed the shade and he had taken notice. Through him, the princes took notice as well.

Gediel halted. Black mist rose along the walls. He never should have felt so secure in his assessment of the mudeaters. They were obviously capable of adapting from time to time. A trio formed from a cloud of smoke. Then, three more and so on, until the small annoyances became a small army intent on feeding or at least leaving a nasty mark. Smokers. Gediel sneered at their stink and drew a pair of short blades from his belt. The narrow ground would make fighting hard and a full swing of his sword could topple him and his comrade into the warren.

"I thought you said they didn't come up here," Luthias said as more filled in behind him.

"They've learned their lessons." Gediel sneered, as the smokers charged toward them.

The enemy wielded only malicious claws and fangs as weapons, more than enough to sate their hatred and tear a hole or two. Luthias put his back to Gediel's, wondering aloud how many more there were. The black mist that birthed them eagerly wound all over the tops of the passages. Gediel struck the first blow, carving into the flank of the nearest adversary. It fell to the labyrinth floor screeching. The others hesitated and the black smoke retreated for the time being.

"Keep moving. They may've been expecting us. We fight as we go or risk waking a prince in delaying to engage the mass. We have to do this fast. We can't turn back," Gediel said.

Gediel lifted his foot and kicked a shade and a few of the others off the walls. Another leapt at him from where it crouched, several passages to the east. It then pushed off footholds between, gaining height and speed. Gediel called out a warning just before he was knocked backward. He skidded along the top of a passage, coming to a stop with his head dangling off the end like bait. A few of its mouthy friends jumped and snapped, trying to reach him from below. The danava crouched on top of him, dripping its black venom on his armor.

"Impudent lightwalker," the thing growled.

An acrid tongue snaked down to his face. Gediel's skin burned where it touched him and he screamed, pushing back on the monster. Chiron and the other four-legged companions leapt across the walls to their leader, leaving Luthias to face the horde alone. Gediel struggled to break the danava's hold. For a lowly soldier, it was rather strong, perhaps amplified by the dark and the steady food supply. His blade glinted and he stabbed the shade into its bony chest. Chiron clamped down on the tail, yanking it back and freeing his knife. Gediel quickly got to his feet using his wings to keep balance. He pushed the wounded smoker over the edge. The stinking hulk would keep the cannibals busy for a time.

Gediel raced back. His companion swung a blade wildly. It failed to harm a single shade, but it kept them back.

Landing solidly, Gediel ducked just under Luthias's blade. The engel turned round. Gediel held up his hands to stop him from striking blindly. The guardian smiled.

"I thought you'd run off without me," he said.

"Change in plans. We go into the labyrinth," Gediel said.

"And somehow that's going to be better?"

Gediel stepped over the edge. He disappeared in the darkness. Then the wolves followed, leaving Luthias alone again. The guardian cursed. Their enemy drew closer and though he was cautious of the watcher's leadership, he was sure he didn't wish to stay and battle the horde without him. He followed his companions and found Gediel crouching in the dark with his pets.

"What now?"

"We run," Gediel said, as the shadows came down from above.

"Yes. I see how that's better," Luthias replied.

Gediel hurried up the passage, almost disappearing in the bleakness before his friend gave pursuit in his heavy armor. They rounded corners and dashed through doorways until the howls and calls of the shades were a distant groan. Gediel stepped carefully, observing the passage ahead. He could hear the walls shifting around them. He closed his eyes, lifting his face up to the dark, seeking the faint glimmer that would lead them to their comrade.

"Angels. Angels! True angels! My salvation," a voice trembled in the dusk.

Gediel skidded to a halt. A woman ran to them from the dark distance. She was no shade nor apparition, but smelled of a nasty wickedness. A soul marked by the darkness. He took a step back, sure she meant to run them down or continue to block their route.

"Please help me. I beg you," she pleaded, dropping to her knees before them. She wore a rag that barely covered her flesh.

Chiron bared his teeth in a hearty growl. Gediel touched the crown of the wolf's head and he ceased.

"What manner of hellhound is this you keep, my angels?" she asked, scurrying back.

Luthias looked around Gediel's shoulder.

"A danava's whore," Luthias said.

"Not yet, but she's marked by Morgentus," Gediel said, grasping her hair in his heavily armored hand and turning her forehead to the dim light.

"He burned me and stole me to these dark ways. I didn't want to come."

"You put yourself here," Gediel said, releasing her

"So says your dark friend, but I committed no sin. I'm innocent," she declared, half mad from the Lethe's waters.

She got to her feet, using the wall for support. Walking with her hands along the stone, she inched closer.

"The ferryman betrayed me. He took my coins and didn't carry me across as promised. He said I was too pretty to release and then he imprisoned me in his boat," the woman continued.

"Only the most privileged of dark souls get that honor. A jiangshi, I'd wager," Luthias said.

The woman's eyes filled with tears. Gediel's expression was filled with uncertainty. Her thoughts revealed her misdeeds, though she claimed to have forgotten them in the Lethe. He also saw what she planned and what she might yet do. This female wasn't to be trusted, but there was no way around her. He couldn't strike her down until she became one of them. Her soul might yet turn from its grievous journey and seek the light.

"What do we do?" Luthias asked, seeing the dilemma.

Gediel shook his head. The woman neared them. Her pleading eyes were a front. She would strike at them the moment they turned their backs.

"What do they call you?"

"The water washed away my memories," she answered, somewhat honestly. Her eyes switched between them. Then she added, "He called me Cursia, for I am now cursed."

"Cursia," Gediel said, surprised she spoke the truth.

Cursia neared, getting a closer look at her audience. A seductive look filled her eyes.

"Have you heard of one they call Gamael?" Gediel asked, halting her.

"The old broken man?" she replied, trying to get a better look at him from her tiptoes.

Gediel held her back with his outstretched arm and scowled.

"So powerful," she rasped, sniffing his arm.

Gediel sensed the nature of her evil, as flashes of her future darted through his mind. He took his hand back, disgusted by the display. She chewed her bottom lip, interpreting it differently. She thought she weakened him; she thought he was displaying disgust to throw off his friend. Cursia was obviously not familiar with duta or honesty.

"He's on the other side of that passage," she answered, pointing with her chin in the direction of a passage that crossed the maze some distance ahead.

They would be lucky to make that straight path before a changing wall altered their route. The scarlet light glowing from the arch promised even more horror. This was where the labyrinth turned into caves and buried spaces.

"Take me with you. I'll show you the way," Cursia pleaded.

Gediel thought over her request. She could be trusted if it served her needs, as she had proved by answering their questions honestly. Of course, they couldn't take her beyond the khajala. However, he could leave her at the outer edges of this cursed world. He pushed her toward the red light, deciding to do what he could. After all, kindness might change her fate.

Chiron growled again, reminding her to keep her distance this time. She frowned back at him, disappointed that her charms failed to gain her desire.

"If you show us where they're keeping him, we can take you to Asfodel Fields. Morgentus can't track you there." Gediel offered her the bait.

Cursia eyed him, twirling her hair around her fingers. A slow smile curled her lips.

"I can do that. He won't be home for a long while yet," she said.

Cursia turned up the passage, talking to herself. Gediel followed, with Luthias reluctantly joining him. The guardian held his weapon at the ready, quite nervous about the marditavya. Gediel smirked, allowing him the comfort of his impotent blade.

Entering the caverns, the duta found a place where there was no escape. Traversing a gauntlet of muggy halls, Cursia brought them to a small room. It was suffocating inside the cell, with a fire burning beneath the stones. The glow came from grates in the floor and a ceiling that overlooked ovens. In a pile of moldy hay, Gamael lay chained to the prison. His wings were broken and his limbs weakened from constant beatings. The rags dressing his sattva were marked with filth and blood. His armor was gone and his sword was all he had with which to defend himself. The blade was coated with dried black blood and his fingers were worn, cracked, and bruised. Bite wounds scarred his wrists. He still fought their attempts at feeding from him.

"Gamael," Gediel said.

The old guardian lifted his head. He had been close to rising in the days before his disappearance. The light in his eyes shone dim from lack of rest.

He opened his mouth to speak, but he couldn't form the words. It was so dry and hot that the air stole his breath.

"Tell them Cursia found you and brought you help," the woman pleaded, crouching down and touching his wounded foot.

Gamael held his sword toward her and the seal Morgentus wrought on her forehead glowed once again. The veins beneath her skin darkened and lifted to the surface, as each sinew strained. Her eyes changed to black orbs, reflecting a single point of light. She bared her teeth, irritated that he threatened her.

"We'll take you out of here as we promised," Gediel said, urging her back.

Gamael coughed, trying to get to his feet. In his other hand, he clutched tight the lion penannular of Leo, from the Order he served.

"I'm sorry," he wheezed. A cough overtook him. "I'm not in my proper attire to greet you, great Fenrir and noble Pritanni."

"No worries about that, lad," Luthias told him, using his sword to move Cursia back.

Gediel worked the lock on the guardian's shackles with a crude key he had hidden in his pocket.

"Is Lena safe?" he asked.

"Indeed she is. Brought back by one of the finest who took up your post when these blighters stole you away," Luthias replied.

The lock fell open and the chains looped through them could be removed with little effort. Gediel helped Gamael to stand on his spindly legs. He put his arm around the old duta's shoulder.

"Show us the way back," Gediel demanded of Cursia with a frown. When she opened her mouth to refuse, he silenced her with, "Or no deal."

"You promised," she cried.

"If you want me to keep it, you'll show us the way out," Gediel replied.

Cursia scrambled out the door ahead of them, muttering about the master returning. She looked afraid and this left Gediel uneasy. The seal she bore linked her to the infernal beast that made these passages his home. There had been more treacherous acts, but he was prepared for whatever Morgentus planned. It wouldn't be the first time they met.

The rescuers crossed a passage in the outer reaches and rediscovered where they left the horde of smoking beasts looking for them. One of the soldiers stood in a shaft of desolate light, sniffing toward them. It caught their scent and a call rose up that was echoed by hundreds more. They pawed and clawed one another to be the first to attack.

"Leave me. They'll pursue and I'll only slow your escape," Gamael said, as they rushed into another corridor.

"You've information I need. Besides, we leave none behind, Gamael. You know that," Gediel replied with an anxious smile. The old duta returned the sentiment.

The demons piled up against the wall as they failed to make the turn in the passage, too eager to beat the others to the food. Ahead of them, Cursia hurried around a corner and abruptly stopped. She backed into them, watching something beyond. Gediel peered around the corner to see a hulking figure in ratty cloth blocking their passage. He nudged Gamael over to Luthias and drew his sword.

"A wraith. Nothing to worry about," Gediel told him.

"Nothing to worry about? They haven't been chasing you around this godforsaken place for days," Cursia scoffed.

"Not recently, no," Gediel said, stepping into the passage.

"I have to agree with the girl, mate. They're not anything to sneeze at," Luthias said, the concern showing in his eyes.

"No worries. You won't have to rely on your charm to get you home," Gediel replied.

The apparition took no notice of the watcher as he carefully drew nearer. The howls of the horde grew louder behind them. They must have sorted their ranks and caught the trail. Gediel halted. The call might wake the wraith. A breeze stirred the tattered robes of the frightful shade. The passages fell silent.

"Hurry up. We don't have much time," Luthias pressed him.

Likely the walls had shifted to close them out, but that would hardly hold the smoking horde back. Now that they knew his secret, they would use it and scale the walls to find them. Besides, the walls would eventually open again. If anything, the shadowwalkers had patience. Right now, they were not his concern. The thing floating before him was of greater danger. Wraiths were a touchy breed of shade, fallen naiades with nasty attitudes and endless hunger. They stood as still as death, waiting for a victim to come close enough for their bony hands to grab. That wasn't the end of it, however. Being captured by a wraith was the most unpleasant thing any being could suffer. They pulled and tore while battering you against the walls. And that was before they used their long teeth. It was as though they tried to viciously squeeze the essence from the fruit they plucked from the maze. Gediel took another step and it slowly turned. The skeletal fingers, unusually long, peeked out from the end of the robe sleeves. Wraiths had no legs, instead getting about by levitating through the passages. It was an advantage, he supposed, but it gave him a means to get past without their notice. He was able to do so when he came alone. He could not guarantee the others would be successful with his solution.

Gediel knelt down to see if the passage beyond was clear. If there was more than one, he would need to rethink his plan. The passage was marked by vaporous shafts of light, but no other shade than the empty darkness. Gediel sighed with relief. Edging carefully beneath the wraith, he attempted to crawl past the creature. Then the black descended. Gediel cursed, knowing what came next. He heard Chiron call to the other wolves. Their nails tapped on the stone as they ran toward him. The wraith took hold of its wide-eyed victim, battering him against the walls and tearing at his limbs. The wolves leapt into the fight. The monster screeched like a vulture defending her nest. Gediel felt the sharp fingers close on his wing. He struggled to pull free, but the shade wrenched the appendage and drew its first feeding from his cry. Dangling from the wraith's claw, he watched in horror as the face came free of the black rags. The wolves had no effect on it. It tossed him and them around as it screeched horribly. The teeth bit down on his leg, pinching his armor tight. Gediel screamed again, trying to find a hold on the monster. He broke apart several fingers, but this only made the creature angrier.

"Quit playing with it, Primus!" Luthias said.

The wolves tore at the rags of the shade's garments and crushed what bone they could find with their teeth. The wraith thrashed and tossed Gediel into the air in order to deal with the wolves first. Chiron was smarter and called a retreat. Gediel floated high above the walls of the labyrinth, arms pinwheeling. The throw afforded him a glance at the distance to the exit. He needed to get them out before Morgentus returned, or worse. Gritting his teeth, he rolled and drew his great sword. He flapped his injured wings, buying himself another moment. Then, he dropped back toward the waiting wraith, blade aimed. He landed like a creature much greater in size, kneeling on top of the collapsed bones. His sword had struck through the skull and buried inches into the stone beneath. The wolves tugged on the rags of the cloak to be sure it was destroyed. With a sharp tug, Gediel freed his weapon and the wraith exploded into a dust cloud. Black mist hovered above the stone floor until the cursed stone eagerly drank it up. The wolves sneezed and trotted up the passage away from the acrid smoke.

"Come on. We're almost out," Gediel ordered the others, straining to stretch his back so he could walk.

The wolves led the way with Cursia following after. Gediel waited for the guardian and their new friend. His head spun with the pain of his injuries and the loss of energy from the fight with the wraith.

"It's not far now," Gediel told the old duta, helping to support him.

"You better be right about her," Luthias said, noticing the change in the svargaduta.

"I will be until we get to the fields. Then I fear we've made a new enemy," Gediel said.

Gediel knew Cursia would plead for them to rescue her, but she was sentenced by her history and the mark she bore. Her path would be hard, but if she meant to escape, she would need to do so without them. If she remembered who she was, then that became the least likely path.

They emerged from the passages onto the narrow stone platform. Morgentus stood on the opposite bank of the stream, arriving home just in time. He flashed his teeth at them and cursed.

"You don't come into my house and steal my things," he said, pointing at them.

"This one is ours and we take the woman to fulfill a promise," Gediel said.

"Gediel! Thorn in my side! Your aryika will deal with you. First my exalted atrin and now you!" Morgentus sneered.

"Take him to the boat," Gediel said releasing Gamael to Luthias. He grabbed the woman, saying to her, "I am fulfilling my promise, nothing more. The rest is up to you."

Cursia's eyes were full of fear. She trembled, afraid of Morgentus. There was a slim chance she would choose right. He had to give it to her.

"Stay where you are! I wouldn't want you to miss out on a family reunion," Morgentus ordered.

The evocati disappeared, followed by each wolf. Gediel faced the baron alone. He hoisted Cursia into his arms, meaning to carry her to safety despite her master's wishes.

"She doesn't deserve redemption and neither do you," Morgentus said.

"Every soul does," Gediel replied.

"I'll feed her your liver, after I let your grand aryika whip your insolent hide," Morgentus rasped.

"You have to find us first." Gediel smiled.

In a blink, Gediel landed in a field of asphodel flowers. Souls wandered about, lost in the reverie of a pale sun and its delicate warmth. This outer ring of Jahannam was the dark mirror of Elysion, shaded from the true brilliance of the perpetual light. Here there were only whispers of salvation, a prison with no walls. A madhouse without doctors. The red and white flowers grew for miles in every direction; they were the only guards. Their scent hid the souls from the dregs of Jahannam, allowing them to heal if they ever could. Because of this, the fields were a place of hope to the fallen.

Gediel set Cursia on her feet and walked away.

"Wait! Please," she called to him.

Gediel reluctantly faced her.

"Please take me with you," Cursia wept, pulling at the armor on his shoulder. He winced in pain as she continued, "He'll find me here and I can't go back to that place. I can't."

"Then don't. What you do is up to you. You'll need to face your true history to be free. He can't find you here unless you allow him. That's all I can do for you," Gediel replied.

Gediel stepped closer, whispering the truth of what she faced in her ear. The mark burned into her forehead disappeared in a hissing puff of smoke. Cursia's eyes flooded with tears as she listened. Her lips trembled, unable to speak the words of denial burning her throat. Gediel stepped back and watched her for a moment. The words settled on her mind, but it would be up to her to decide what to do with them. Her tearful gaze looked upon the distance. She collapsed to the ground.

Gediel turned away. He disappeared and slid from that place to join his friends. He could hear the woman screaming after him. Her pleas turned to curses. In the fields, she would be made to reflect upon the truth, straying over the vast spaces without a single danava to torment her. She would torment herself enough. If she wanted, she could let the Labyrinth Lord find her and be dragged back to the nightmare they'd freed her from. She could also choose to reach to the light. He just could not bring her past the Avernus with so heavy a weight pulling her down. If her bitterness passed, there was hope she wouldn't become the monster he saw in her future.

*   *   *

The Baron of Acheron gnashed his teeth. A throng of soldiers piled up in the entrance. They whined and slunk away, too late to do what he kept them for. Lightwalkers had burglarized his hold and not a soul in all of Acheron had lifted a finger to prevent them. The duta came there too often and each time they stole from him. Shouting the names of his two devotees, he stalked across the black stream and mounted the steps to his front door. This was far too much to take, after discovering his recidia akha in possession of his erela. The bastard thought to hide from him once he learned of his fall, as if becoming a sacerdos would protect him. Well, he would find out what these things won him very soon.

Grag and Segrius appeared in swirls of smoke where Morgentus once stood.

"Bring Cursia back here. Put your best soldiers on that damn church and then get back to work making the red erela fall," Morgentus growled.

The baron paused at the door of his labyrinth. His mind wound around his encounters on Earth and the presence of the lightwalkers in his refuge.

They made their moves to retrieve her before he could. He wondered if coming for Gamael had been a ruse to distract him while they rescued her. He turned back to his soldiers. He never should have marked that stupid whore. What did it matter to him if someone stole her? She wasn't what he sought anyhow, but now he would be sure to give her a place in his plans. While his poison worked on an unholy trinity, he would become the prince's favorite, but only if the prince remained patient enough to reap the harvest.

"Bring me her husband. The human they call Dominic," Morgentus said.

Grag nodded. A grin split his face, revealing his rotten teeth. The anger of his master inspired his wrath.

Morgentus stepped inside his labyrinth. The walls turned aside, making a straight tunnel for him to follow to his manor. He had hoped to return and find his new treasure waiting. His appetites had grown commanding and couldn't wait to be sated by the female he really wanted. Morgentus's features sharpened the more he thought of it. He hated spilling his seed in the barren wombs of the dried-up harem he was left with. Heirs were needed if he was to hold his kingdom. The thought turned his mind back to his dear atrin. If it weren't for him, he would have one. Maiel's armor was nearly drained. Once the penannular died, he could finally have her. He disappeared in a cloud of smoke.

Distracted by the anger filling his head, Morgentus ignored a pair of shades who let themselves into his hive. He walked the streets of his labyrinthine city, just in sight of the gates of Acheron's palace. Strange scents tickled his nostrils. He carefully continued, looking in the shadows. The city appeared empty, but he knew that a thousand eyes watched him pass. The shadows always watched. Then the favorite nephilim of the prince stood in his path, turned aside as if he little cared if Morgentus walked right past him. Ezrodial's massive figure was lit by an icy lantern which he held up with a thick arm. The trespasser wore no shirt, exposing his bulky muscles. Morgentus was drawn to the flash of bare flesh. He toyed with the idea of having the prince's son, relishing how sick it would make Belial.

Ezrodial faced Morgentus and the baron halted. The stringy black hair still blocked the giant's features; he was handsome despite resembling a freshly dead corpse. The nephilim quickly closed the distance on heavily booted feet and thick black-clad legs. Morgentus considered retreating, but it would mean his title. Instead, he threw his shoulders back, spread his wings and drew up to his full height. He still stood far shorter than the grunt. A glimpse of movement turned his attention behind him. The filmy robes of a Jiangshi asuri billowed along the passage. The pet of Ezrodial. Her black hair was tied into a loose bun away from her pale dead face. The vampire's features turned his stomach. As the pink and white silk settled, the flash of her red sash distracted him again. In one quick breath, she stood a pace away, peering with a peculiar stare. Morgentus eyed her blood-red lips, knowing that fangs hid behind them. Her eyes followed Morgentus as he stepped aside to keep both her and her companion in his sight. These two were not to be trusted by anyone.

"Belial summons you," the Jiangshi said.

Morgentus smiled and moved to step past her companion. The giant clamped his hand on his neck and the three disappeared in a tornado of black dust. When the whirl stopped, Morgentus was dropped at the gate of his master. He stumbled forward, smugly thinking the messengers had run back to the shadows to hide from his retribution. If he crossed their paths again, he would be sure to thank them with his boot heel, pets of his master or not. Then he saw the nephilim kneeling before the prince. Belial stroked the black hair and placed a loving kiss on the beast's forehead. The prince dismissed him with an indulgent and hushed word.

The gate opened and Morgentus passed into Belial's courtyard. The prince paced across a tattered red rug that extended from his door through the dust. The palace looked like a twisted fairy tale and the prince looked twisted and charming, appearing as he once was when he basked in the glory of the light. This was before the duta threw him out over false accusations from a lying soul. Morgentus always thought the illusion made him look feminine; he was so slightly built and pale. His golden hair was long and reached to his waist. The prince wore robes that reminded him of the messenger he sent moments ago. It didn't suit him as well as his true form: tall and broad-shouldered, with great horns. It was a masterful form that commanded great obedience. His now dainty hands were not half as remarkable as when they were the size of three men's hands.

From his pacing, the baron could tell Belial was little pleased.

"Great master," Morgentus said approaching him. "The red erela weakens," he added with a bow.

"You let Gediel steal from you. He comes to your labyrinth and mocks you constantly." Belial changed the subject, towering over Morgentus despite the latter's belief that this form was unimpressive.

"I'll call on his aryika to sit in ambush," Morgentus said.

"Prince Gediel has better things to do than reunite with his unfortunate relations," Belial said. "Yet the boy's powerful and walks the precipice between dark and light with too much ease. The next time he comes, plant the seed to make him fall. Then you may bother the prince and tell him his heir has come to reign beside him," Belial continued, seeing the worth of yoking the other prince to him by the favor.

"As you wish, my lord." Morgentus bowed with a hidden sneer.

"The red erela, as you so fondly call her, you're mistaken about her, blinded by your lust," Belial said.

"No, my liege. I saw her. She's fallen to Earth. Most of the work is done. She's in the care of my atrin, a sacerdos. The seeds I planted are growing. I ask for patience to let it bloom."

"It's not enough. Adonai still holds her to him. Remember, she's the key. If they discover this, our war will fail," Belial said.

"It's not long now. She becomes mortal," Morgentus said.

"What of her companions? Do you think they came to the rescue of their friend without thought to what he knows? And as for your sacerdos akha, Oriael will die a saint. Not even I can change that."

"They'll send her mate, a mere ape, to rescue her. I feel it in my bones, your highness. They think he'll prove himself, but they have no eyes to see what we started."

"Mere ape? Mere apes have caused me more misery than your simple mind can fathom. Break him or I'll crush you and command another in your place. And they will have the pleasure of your mistress," Belial growled.

The baron grew angry, much to Belial's delight. A smile parted the prince's lips, his yellow teeth layered in blood.

"Perhaps Ezrodial would like to taste her," Belial said, lifting his hand and summoning the nephilim who'd dragged Morgentus there. Belial took his son's face in his hands and added, "Would you like the red female, Ezrodial?"

"Master, if I may," Morgentus said, pushing his anger down. He toyed with the idea of telling him what he had done to ensure their success. "We may use the human still."

Ezrodial sneered, most unhappy with being blocked.

Belial stared at him. The flame of anger flashed in the prince's eyes. Morgentus bobbed his head and backed away, quite censured. The baron exited before his master changed his mind and split his skull on the stone courtyard. However, Morgentus merely made a show of leaving, letting the black smoke lie to the prince. Within a breath, Morgentus returned behind the cover of the wall. From this vantage, he listened to Belial pace. Other footsteps scraped the stone, joining him.

"Follow him. If he fails me again, extinguish him. Then you both bring me this red erela so that I can learn what makes these fools slaves to her," his master said.

Morgentus seethed, grinding his teeth hard. He disappeared in a flurry of smoke. There were other masters in Jahannam who would listen to what he had to say, and they would reap the glory he would win from their alliance.

CHAPTER 15

SEPHR HUNCHED OVER a swiftly spinning grinding wheel. Sparks sprayed in every direction. A pair of dark round goggles protected his eyes from any stray metal flakes. Straightening from the wheel, he flipped a lever and the goggles became clear. He marveled at the smooth finish of a long silver blade. The alloy was burning hot to the touch and sharp enough to cleave steel. He turned and passed the weapon back to its owner, Mikhael.

"There, now. Promise you won't break it this time. That is some of my best work. I would hate to scrap it."

Mikhael grinned, taking his sword in hand. He eyed the blade, pleased with the work. Giving it a try, he swung it through the air. The blade sang with each pass. Then he checked the carved chalcopyrite pommel to be sure the ore hadn't been harmed in the mending. The peacock tones of the stone glinted at him.

"That depends on what the dark princes make me do. It'll be a cold day in hell when I let them take Captain Maiel without a fight," Mikhael said.

Sephr looked across the space, filled with all the tools and equipment a smith could need. Two of his arms men hammered a new sword on the other side of the room. A proud youngling was soon to be made. The pounding hammers couldn't pound the thoughts out of Mikhael's head, and the warmth of the company couldn't take away the cold he felt. He looked through the great window on the western wall. The sun had set and the moon rose in its place.

"If they don't return soon, it'll be known throughout Zion," Sephr said.

Mikhael sheathed his sword and looked as stoic as ever.

"They'll be here soon," Mikhael assured him.

Sephr nodded, and his friend put an arm about his shoulder. They walked out of the smithy into the cool air. The night was silent as it blanketed Zion in a dark cobalt hue. The early stars twinkled and the moon peeked above the skyline of the citadel like an enormous ghost. A sudden scraping sound roused them from their watch. They turned back to the doors.

Gediel and Luthias came along the west mall, a causeway that fenced the base of the armory. Between them, they carried the broken guardian they believed lost to them. Mikhael rushed to help. He easily assisted Gamael, allowing his rescuers to catch their breath. The old engel smiled, looking as though he would faint into a trance at any moment.

"You've looked better, old friend," Mikhael said to him. To the others, he added, "Let's get him inside where he can rest."

"I have to question him before we take him for healing," Gediel said, concerned he was about to lose his information inside Zion.

The others turned to the svarg, noticing the damage to his armor and wings and couldn't help but see the pained tilt of his trunk.

"I'm not going to betray you. Make the questions quick. They expect him before the moon has fully risen. Perhaps you should go with him," Mikhael said.

Gediel nodded, running a hand through his hair.

"There's no time for that."

Sephr retreated inside to gather a stool and pitcher of water from the armory shop. He brought the items to where they could set Gamael against the outer ring wall. The guardian barely held himself up. His head lolled sleepily. Gediel knelt at his side, taking the bruised arm in greeting.

"You're safe now, Gamael."

The old engel opened his eyes and stared at him. He placed his broken hand on Gediel's head with thanks. A small smile curled his mouth and tears filled his eyes.

"I owe you my life, boy," Gamael croaked.

Sephr offered the old guardian a clay mug of water. He took it in his broken hands and stared inside the cup.

"Rest a moment before we take you to the alders for healing," Gediel told him.

Gamael nodded and dryly muttered something unintelligible. He drank from the pitcher, nearly exhausting himself in the effort. Water seeped through his damaged tunic. The extent of his injuries told them they had little time before he fell into a coma.

"Do you have enough strength to answer a few questions?"

"For you, boy, I'll do anything."

Gediel's eyes lit up with hope.

"Do you know why they took you?"

"They wanted the child. They said she would bring them the red erela. I didn't know who that was until they called her name in their infernal halls. I refused to help them, so they chained me. Each time I refused further, they beat me. The visions they tortured me with—I told myself it was their trickery. I did not relent."

"Did they say why they wanted her?"

"They said she would rule the labyrinth when they had done with me and she would see to my end if I didn't help them. I didn't believe them. They lie," Gamael answered.

"Rightly so. Maiel would sooner eat Argus than turn," Sephr growled.

"Did they say anything else that you remember?" Gediel pressed.

"They want war, but so it is always. They said this time they would win and they would take back Zion. The princes had found a way," Gamael said, growing more faint. "Mikhael would be too weak with grief to stop them—losing—his friends," Gamael forced out.

"So it is always," Gediel breathed, putting a steadying hand on the old man's shoulder. "We'll take you to rest now, Gamael. Don't tell anyone we spoke to you of this."

"Something's wrong," Gamael said. "One shouldn't reside inside Zion if he's fallen so low," he added, hardly knowing what he said.

"That's why it's best that you rest and speak to no one," Gediel said, suspecting Gamael had heard more, but was too weak to concentrate. "You'll be safe, noble guardian."

Gamael looked at him, assured of that.

"He's poisoned. Nails pin him down," the Leo guardian said, his eyes glazed with pain.

Gediel frowned.

"Evocati, take him to the alders," Gediel said, rising to his full height with some difficulty.

Luthias did as asked, accompanied by one of the wolves. Gediel played with the straps of his bracers and stared into the darkness, not watching him go. Lost deep in thought, he didn't see Chiron take a seat in front of him and stare expectantly, waiting for orders. Gediel was too distracted with planning his next move and putting together what Gamael said with the rest of what they knew.

"Morgentus might have convinced Belial to do this, but he's not just doing it to open the gates of Jahannam. If causing her to fall starts a war, then he'll be raised in his master's esteem, certainly. It's more than that. I'd wager that Morgentus has been manipulated by his dear prince," Gediel said.

Silence fell.

"Why have they chosen Maiel? Are there no whores in all of Jahannam to satisfy them?" Sephr asked, disgusted.

"Because she crossed swords with the baron and left her mark. She escaped, but not without leaving them with something. Morgentus wants revenge, for as long as he can stand her. And he thought telling Belial it would hurt Mikhael was simply a clever manipulation. However, Belial manipulated him. He wants her to hurt you. He knows what she is to you, General," Gediel replied, gesturing toward the general with his last words.

"Her loss would hurt us all, but I'm not willing to fall to my knees over this. I love her as a daughter, yes, but I will not fall for it. It must be more than you see yet," Mikhael said.

"The more hurt, the greater the revenge. Morgentus and his master both get what they want. If only she had never set foot in Acheron. They would not know what we do," Sephr said, looking out over the city to hide the despair in his eyes.

Gediel shook his head. He wasn't satisfied with the explanation that Morgentus worked this out alone, nor that his ruler double-played him.

"There must be more than just causing a captain of your legion to fall. I agree, General. It doesn't explain the flame inside Dominic or his involvement. They would just take her if they wanted to rape her," Gediel mumbled. He turned. "I have to find Jushur. You'll need to tell the others my assignment is going to take longer than I suspected and I'll be delayed until the next moonrise, at least."

Sephr nodded and the wolf leader took off, running east. His form was a streak of light quickly followed by two others. Sephr looked to Mikhael.

"Not a word," Mikhael said, gritting his teeth. "Ready the battalions. Belial won't be easily put off. He'll want his war and, by Adonai, we'll give it to him. Weak with grief—he'll see. He'll not take my soldiers without me taking his hide," Mikhael promised, with a grave mien.

*   *   *

Joel crossed his arms and sat back against the stone frame of the western Earth gate. Across from him, Zaajah stared into the vessel that occupied the center of the ways. The bit of gold hair they had taken from him allowed them to follow Dominic's every move. This was meant to keep them less tempted to aid him, and allow the man to prove himself. Such sights, as those in the farmhouse, pinched Zaajah's brows together. She sighed, seeing their assign leave the safety of the farm and the help of the guardians who lived there. Zaajah stepped back, drained by the stress of the visions. Her

eyes went to the silent virtue who still stood beside the north arch. The senti-
nel had kept her silence since their travelers went through the Samsara gate;
she was put there to observe and report to the council.

Zaajah wandered to the arch through which Zacharius pushed Dominic.
He saw that she contemplated joining him. His muscles tensed, ready to
join her if she did. At his side, Zacharius stirred from a deep meditation. The
elder engel rose and took notice of Zaajah, too. A frown pulled down the
corners of his mouth as he suspected the same.

"Lena and Dominic still struggle in the land of the lion," Zacharius
said. His voice brought Zaajah out of her deliberation. She looked to them,
masking her emotions perfectly, but was too late for her to deny if she was
accused. "Morgentus sends his rabble to stop them. He haunts our khata
himself, thinking he can woo her to his side. His efforts are relentless."

"She'll not give in to him," Zaajah said.

"Maiel's atman forms a bio-vessel. Her presence weakens in my heart. I'm
afraid they may succeed," Zacharius said going to the font. He stared at the
vision. "There's still some hope."

"What have you seen?" Joel asked.

"She's found refuge in a monastery. There's a man there who was once
one of us," Zacharius said.

"A fallen one?" Zaajah asked worriedly.

"One who has devoted his time to returning to Zion."

"Who?" Joel asked.

"That I can't see. I need to go to Akash and seek that record," Zacharius
said, touching the fluid inside the bowl.

The image rippled, going out of focus, just like the vision had. The focus
was now on a man none of them were familiar with.

"We can't afford to involve anyone else. Think of another way," Alex said
entering the room.

Zacharius continued to watch the image in the kapalanum. He said nothing in opposition to his amba's order. She joined him at the vessel and he
quickly returned to his observation of Dominic. Alex cast him a suspicious
glance, but then settled her eyes on what developed.

Their amba returned from a visit with Matula Magiel to measure the
temperature of the council and let them know the mission was underway.
The worn look of her features attested to the strain the visit put her under.
Matula Magiel shared something that didn't bode well for the mission. Joel
was sure the council would rescind their permission, leaving his khata to
her own devices. Even if they did, he was sure Dominic would refuse to
return. Whatever overcame him would take root, devastating the years of

work they had done, and ensure Morgentus's success. Were they so blind to that outcome?

"What did Matula Magiel say?" Joel asked, unable to wait for his amba to share.

Alex's features were dressed in gloom.

"Mikhael prepares the battalions for war. You'll be summoned to your regiments when they are ready."

"Ibajah will command the regiment in my absence. I'll not leave here until she returns," Zaajah said.

"As will my leader, Rathiel," Joel told her.

"You risk angering the council by your words. But, I'm thankful for your devotion," Alex warned.

"She's our khata. I'd cut off my own arm and eat it before I let them leave her there so they can fight their war," Joel said.

"The council has looked toward war with the princes of Jahannam for some time. This is just an excuse to let them wage it," Zaajah spat.

"If Dux Horus hears you say that," Alex smiled a little. She touched Zaajah's face to console her. "I suspect something is happening within the ranks of the alders that hasn't happened for some time. Whatever passes from this moment forward, we focus on returning Maiel to her rightful place. There may still be losses we have to accept," she said, returning to the kapalanum and watching Dominic walk an old road in the dark of night.

Joel understood her meaning and it struck him a mortal blow. His khata was less likely to leave her husband behind than they were to leave her on Earth. To work toward that would only cripple their chances. He neared the kapalanum and placed his hands on the rim. Someone needed to take action. Dominic needed their help, regardless of what they wanted for him. Having decided to go against orders already, there was no reason not to continue and win this small battle for the greater good.

"We work with Earth time then. What are Dominic's obstacles, Zacharius?" Joel asked, assuming command from Alex.

Zacharius raised an eyebrow, noting the shift in who had the upper hand. Joel was very brave for going against their amba, but she was in no way prepared to fight this battle. Her son had practice in tactics on the field of fire. One of them had to command and he was the wiser choice. As a guardian and as a soldier, he had been to Samsara a time or two. His skills to handle the next steps were far superior to that of any alder. More than that, he was Dominic's friend and could predict the man's moves with better accuracy than anyone except maybe his guardian.

Zaajah stepped to Joel's side in a show of support. Two guardians faced a pair of alders. Zacharius clasped his hands and stepped to a neutral position beside the kapalanum. His move didn't declare a side, but he wasn't favoring their amba either.

Alex's gaze lowered in acceptance.

"He must make his way from the lion cliffs to the nest of the great turul in the east—without currency. It'll make his voyage nearly impossible in mortal flesh," Zacharius said, sharing the rest of his vision.

The entrance of the ways opened and Mikhael appeared. They stared as he joined him; they were rather surprised he stepped from his lofty seat to watch this. He was the supreme commander of the first legion and should have been busy fielding orders as they prepared to go into battle. Instead, he joined Joel beside the font. Joel blinked, not sure what to say, suspecting he was about to take both him and Zaajah to their orders, or worse. He swallowed in anticipation of bad news. Had they decided to leave his khata to fend for herself?

"Take him this, but offer him no further assistance. I expect to see you both when the time comes and your leaders can apprise you quickly of the battle strategies," Mikhael said, unlooping the strings of a small purse tied to his belt. It rattled with coins.

Joel took the bag, confused. The timing was uncanny. He opened his mouth to question the gift, but decided otherwise.

"Don't defy me," Mikhael warned.

"As you wish it, commander," Joel stammered, examining the general's face for the answer to his unspoken question.

"Gamael has been retrieved. We learned nothing, as he's badly wounded," Mikhael said.

Joel and the others were saddened by the information. Mikhael smiled consolingly and then stepped near the virtue, saying no more. He regarded the guide of the ways, making it known by a simple glance that none of this was to pass beyond the door he came through. Joel went to the gate that would take him to his friend. He stared at the surface. He could only pass through once and worried this was a poor use of his turn. The seconds ticked by.

"Go to him, but remain cloaked until he has need of you. Give him the money as I said, but only when you're sure he'll use it wisely. This will tell us how much time he has left," the general said.

Joel nodded and cast an unsure glance over his shoulder. Touching the gold circle pinned to the shoulder of his uniform, he prepared for the worst that Samsara had to offer. Protected by the armor of his order, he crossed through the shimmering way to complete the task.

Joel stepped from a brilliant vertical shaft of blue light. It faded, as if the worlds slid back together, a scar healing instantly in the firmament. The faint odor of accursed fire tickled his nostrils. With a sickened frown, he looked for the man he came for. An automobile hurried up the road past him, flashing its lights. The dark shadows of Dominic and Lena were revealed only for a moment by the light.

Joel slid nearer, passing him unseen. The smell of sulfur grew stronger. He ducked into the trees and waited. From his vantage in a steep ditch, the shadow of his friend was contoured by moonlight. At Dominic's side, the soft glimmer of his guardian was a shining apparition. Joel's heart warmed with the girl's bravery. She smiled despite the recent attack by a devious incubus. It seemed little dogged her spirit.

Joel leaned against the tree to wait until they passed. The rhythmic cadence of Dominic's boots against the hardened earth drew closer. Joel's radiant gaze followed. The flash of his eyes attracted Lena's attention. Joel stepped from the shadows, a finger before his lips. Lena grinned, overjoyed to see him.

The pair continued. Joel used the opportunity to reconnoiter the road behind them. He suspected there would be followers drawn to the strange energy of the odd couple. In no time, shades and imps scooted along the ditch and road. Joel quickly dispatched the nuisances and proceeded after his friends. Straggling, he kept a watchful eye, as Zach suggested. If Dominic realized he had come, then the man would not only beg for help, but would make it impossible to assess his progress. Dominic needed this journey to help himself realize he was capable and to secure the safety of his wife. If they gave him more than was necessary, then that lesson would be delayed until the next catastrophe. There was one thing he was right about: they'd neglected his real need, coddling him like a delicate bit of porcelain instead of teaching him what he needed to reinforce an upward path.

Hours passed before they walked through a real village. Joel wandered closer, keeping his companions in sight, lest unwitting shades thought to pester them. Lena peered over her shoulder, chewing the fingernails of one hand. She sensed trouble. Joel gestured her to remain calm, but her glances attracted Dominic's attention.

"What is it?"

"Nothing," Lena lied.

Dominic frowned, knowing better.

Joel joined them, allowing himself to be seen before his friend exploded, goaded by annoyance and mistrust. The gold armor at first startled Dominic. He jumped back, ready to fight, then realized his friend had come and relaxed, shamefaced. Joel laughed.

"You're not moving fast enough," Joel said.

"It's good to see you," Dominic breathed.

"I just came to give you this."

Joel handed him the purse. Dominic took the delivery, just as confused as his friend when he received it from Mikhael. From the pouch, he pulled a wad of paper bills. He looked to his friend, his brow deeply furrowed.

"Money? Where did you get this?"

"You'll need it to continue further. We landed you as close as the last signal allowed, but she's moved since then, and rapidly. Mikhael sends the bag with the express order not to help you further. Let's just say I didn't exactly obey. The path behind is clear, but there are enemies ahead. Find transportation and go east. Zacharius said she's in the nest of the great turul. I hope that makes some sense to you."

"What the hell is a turul?" Dominic scowled.

"I don't pretend to understand an alder's visions. I apologize, but he had no other answer than that. I must go," Joel replied. Dominic looked disappointed. "Hurry, akha. Her time grows short. Guide him well. Guide him quickly. Morgentus's minions come for you both," he added, to encourage them.

Joel faded from their view. Dominic stared for a moment longer, wise enough to know his brother hadn't gone. Lena looked to her assign, chewing her finger again.

"Maybe it's an animal? Like England. England has a lion. If it has a nest it might be a dragon or a bird," Lena said.

"Maybe. Let's see if we can get a ride south. Joel's right. We're taking too long this way."

Dominic gave up on his friend and led the girl deeper into the village as dawn drew near. She looked back several times, quite able to see Joel standing there. A plea was clear on her face, but he could give them no further assistance. Joel frowned apologetically.

"We should ask someone about the two-rule," Lena said, taking Dominic's hand.

"The only bird I remember in Europe is an eagle that flew over Germany. It's better than nothing and I know where it is." Dominic sighed, still feeling slighted.

Joel followed them and they soon discovered a lonely rail station.

"Amersham. Now we know where we are again. If only we had maps," Dominic said, reading the rail sign.

A train whistle split the peace and they moved to inquire about passage at the ticket counter. Dominic was reasoning out that he had to get to the continent. Good.

Joel took his leave, assured the pair would make wise use of Mikhael's gift. Drawing his sword, he then raised his free hand. The Zion Seal illumined in the air, glowing with bluish electricity through the lettering and symbols. He pressed a sequence of squares and the way opened to him. He looked toward Lena and her assign; he was uneasy that he could not stay. Stepping into the light, he left them to their duty and returned to the others, waiting for news.

Joel passed back into the room with the kapalanum. Mikhael had gone. Zaajah watched the water in the font, keeping close watch of their delegate. He sensed the urgent pulse in her energy. Joel joined her, holding his tongue. No one spoke. Despite their silence, it was clear that from this point forward Dominic and Lena worked alone. If they succeeded, they would be heralded as heroes. If they failed, they would be shunned as outcasts.

CHAPTER 16

ORIUS HUNCHED OVER HIS DESK, preparing the sermon for the fast-approaching Sunday. His thoughts rolled about, his mind full of distractions. He set his pen down, giving in to them. Staring at nothing in particular, he allowed his thoughts to wander and they went to the subject of his latest trouble. Bethiah had spent most of the day inside the safe room. She meditated more than a Buddhist monk. A smile brightened his features at the image. He remembered his own first days on Earth. They too had been haunted by shadows and blissful moments when he thought he could still feel, if not see, the light of Adonai shining down on him. Those days had gone. He felt lost in the space between being human and inhuman. Unable to die, he passed from place to place starting over, but never finding the way back. He didn't want that to be her future if he could help it by the use of his hard-won wisdom.

Rubbing his hands together, Orius tried to concentrate on his work. This life had given him responsibilities he took very seriously. The paper on his desk was half filled with scribbles he barely recognized. His eyes grew tired and his back stiff. Rubbing the bridge of his nose, he picked up the pen again, determined to get his work done. Despite his resolve to the contrary, focusing on the task was simply not to happen that day, or at least right then. A different immediacy took hold of him. He rasped a delicate curse, throwing the pen down. His eyes settled on the phone and he lost all thought of the sermon. There was someone he needed to contact. It was a call he'd been putting off since the day before. Complacency took over with as he wondered why his brother decided not to bless them with a visit since the night she had arrived. If he continued to put it off, he might be risking a serious consequence. Morgentus wouldn't remain absent for long. Still, he hoped one of her own would come for her. It was a hope he still had for himself, but now that his brother had found him, it was quite unlikely to happen before the spoiled bastard destroyed them both. He grimaced, thinking of another group who might help, though he had refused their hand generations ago. Orius shook his head. No. He couldn't reach out to them now. That bridge was burned.

Orius reluctantly picked up the handset, then set it back fumbling for his address book. His mind was so full that he couldn't recall the number. Thumbing through the pages, he found the number and quickly dialed before he lost his nerve. Clasping his forehead in his hands, he turned his face down and shut his eyes. He could only hope this was the right thing to do. He was never very sure of the archbishop or his staff. They had their ideas about things, usually twisted by the dogma of men owned by some shade who dared walk the Earth to spite Adonai. The line clicked and some-one greeted him on the other end. Orius lost both his thoughts and worry, so startled was he by the sudden voice.

"Yes, yes. This is Father Gregely Orius in Máriabesnyő. Might I be able to speak with Archbishop Geitz?"

The voice on the other end explained that the archbishop was quite busy that day, but he would check if Father Orius could hold one moment. Orius agreed. He eyed the rotary dial, rethinking the call once more. He wasn't sure he wanted to know if the man was a charlatan or not. The father had lived under the illusion of a supposed bond with another world for some time and it had done little harm. Who was he to question such things? After all, there he stood, a matter beyond the comprehension of the clergy, although they pretended to have the knowledge that qualified them to such authority. Even if they did lie to him, that was nothing compared to his mistake. He too once knew Mikhael, so it wasn't strange to him that someone among the multitude of souls in this world would also. After his fall, any human had better standing than he.

The voice on the other end returned to ask him to hold once more while he sent the call through. The phone clicked, went silent, and then rang. Orius thought to hang up. It was the last chance not to start down this path, before he saw the entire monastery embroiled in scandal. Was the bridge burned between him and the outpost? He muttered to himself, unable to decide.

"Gregely!" A voice called over the line.

"Archbishop Geitz," Orius called back.

"How are you, man? How are the brothers? They treating you well?"

"I'm well. I'm well. The brothers are wonderful as always. Very busy with harvesting the late crops these days. Look, Archbishop. I apologize for inter-rupting you."

"Nonsense, Gregely. I always have time for you. What's on your mind?"

"It's rather difficult to explain, sir," Orius hesitated. He lost his nerve.

"Start at the beginning, man. It can't be that bad." Geitz laughed.

"I'm afraid it is, sir. In a way." Orius smiled.

Geitz held his silence.

"It's happened again. I wasn't sure I should trouble you with this, but I thought you might be the best person to help—considering your connections," Orius said.

"Recidia or Grigori?" Geitz said.

"Neither," Orius said. "Well, she's fast becoming like me   recidia," Orius stammered. "But—"

"She?" Geitz asked, sounding surprised.

"Yes, a female. They're known as erela among my kind," Orius replied.

Orius rolled his eyes. He probably should not have mentioned that fact. It would blow the doors off the teachings Rome had dictated to the churches for centuries. Even the legends insisted the host was made of sexless beings, conspicuously male if not boyish in aspect. It didn't matter what he told them otherwise. He rubbed his eyes again, not wanting to think about the implications of their fetish for boyish waifs and what was kept behind the walls of most churches.

"She came the night before last. I was in the middle of my sermon when the doors of the church blew open. I thought it was just the wind, but when I stepped down to prepare communion... there she was," Orius continued.

"Fascinating. Did anyone see her?" Geitz replied.

"No. There's more," Orius said, but he wouldn't tell him everything. How could he ever explain a demonic brother to these men? They needed an out, in case Geitz proved to be a danger and there was no choice but to reach out to the outpost and humble himself.

"Go on," Geitz encouraged him.

"She's being persecuted by a dark presence."

Orius absently doodled on the half-written page.

"Where there's one, you'll find the other not too far. I'd expect no less. After all, we have the long experience of your fall," Geitz replied.

"What's your advice? She's becoming mortal and I'm afraid we don't have much time before she meets the same fate as mine," Orius asked, after a pause.

"Let me think on it. I'll call you this evening after supper. That'll be enough time to come up with an idea or two. Keep your head, Gregely. Perhaps she was sent to rescue you."

Orius laughed, unconvinced. He told Geitz he looked forward to speaking with him again. Hanging up the receiver, he looked at the sermon and prayed he had not just placed a call that would alert Rome and send them both into an earthly Jahannam.

Upon the page, his doodle took the distinct shape of a triangle and eye. Orius stared at the scribble, then hurriedly balled up the paper and threw it in the trash. No. He wouldn't be made to reach there. Bethiah needed to be returned, not recruited. Orius sighed, lowering his head to his hand.

Geitz was only an acquaintance, not a friend he could trust without question. If only one of the brothers was an archbishop instead. Orius sat back, closing his eyes. A moment of meditation might do him some good as well. He drew that scribble for a reason. His own mind was telling him the way, but he couldn't risk involving them and hurting her further.

A soft knock disrupted Orius's concentration. He called and the door of the office opened. Father Gallo entered and called him to dinner. Orius looked through the window behind his desk. The sun was still rather bright. He wondered at the earliness of the meal. Gallo smiled at him, cheered by some secret.

"I thought the brothers were busy in the fields," Orius said, getting to his feet.

"They finished the harvest early this afternoon and wanted to surprise you and our guest with a special meal." Gallo beamed proudly.

Orius nodded, eased by the warm invitation. These men were the best the church had to offer and it hid them away. Orius gathered them in the hope that they could win leverage someday. No such luck yet. Suddenly, his desire to return to Zion felt like betrayal. His place was in that world, though, guarding assigns and battling their demons. Staying on Earth was merely a dodge from duty that held little purpose beyond learning from a long-ago punishment.

"Have you called our guest down?"

"She's waiting in the dining room. We've been going over some things the better part of the day. I hope you weren't looking for me," Gallo replied.

"Oh—no, of course. I hope it's been enlightening."

Father Gallo was reluctant to be in her presence on his own, as were the other priests, so this news surprised Orius. They'd warmed to her quite well.

"Not in the least, Father Orius. Every answer raises many more questions. I'm simply exhausted."

In the dining room, the brothers laid out a feast that stunned Orius. They would eat for days. Their guest sat at the table with her back to him, chewing a roll she took from one of the overflowing trays. Yegor, one of the younger brothers, inspected her armor, quite fascinated by the perfection of it. He looked as small as a child beside her, and just as curious. She was a patient teacher, telling him all she knew of the armor's maker.

"Bethiah."

Orius took a seat opposite her at the table. Their guest looked at him. Her flat stare was no longer as startling as it once was. It was just her manner. If you spoke, you would have something to say, and she was simply paying the best attention. Moreover, duta soldiers were not known for their emotiveness. Orius smiled at her. He had much to tell her too, when the time came.

"You look well," he told her.

"I feel much better for the rest," she replied. "Thank you," she added with a slight smile.

The brothers gathered about the table and her friend left her for a seat and his supper. She watched them pray over the food and then sit. Their rituals and activities intrigued her. Likewise, her wonder at them intrigued the monks. They lived under the illusion that they acted perfectly in the way of the Lord, as they would say. Her mirth at their confusion was at first unsettling, but quickly whet their appetite to know how better they could serve. Unfortunately for them, the girl had no answers beyond telling them to follow their path, or their dharma, as she called it. It was a contract agreed upon before entering into life. They still didn't know what that meant, and struggled with what sounded like heresy and the teachings of other practices.

"Brothers," Orius said to them, grasping firm hold of their attention. "You've outdone yourselves. I thank you."

Father Gallo served their guest first, setting a heaping plate before her. He made his way around the table, starting with Orius and finally seating himself when the brothers had all been given a meal. The girl was focused on her food, especially enjoying the mashed potatoes and gravy. He smiled, tasting the food himself, but finding he wasn't all that hungry after his phone call. His worry filled his belly enough.

"If I may," Father Gallo said, finishing a bite. "You mentioned in our last interview that you have a husband. Was I correct in hearing he's human?"

"Yes, that's right," she replied, continuing eating. "But he'll rise soon and earn his wings."

"Rise?" Gallo said, taking out his notebook. The man should have been a reporter.

"Yes—rise," she replied. "It means to—evolve, to put it in your terms. He'll pass from one existence and become another, reborn."

"Reborn in Christ?"

"No." She laughed. "The prince is a man. He can't birth children. He'll be reborn to pitarau, who are duta, whoever they may be. The soul chooses with guidance from its atman."

"What is an atman?" a brother asked.

"That which is you. The crystal that was shed from Nirvana," she replied, as Gallo quivered like a child, knowing the answer.

"Brilliant," Gallo said excited.

The girl continued her meal, seeing he was lost to his thoughts. Gallo ignored his plate, pushing it aside to make room for his notebook. He scribbled for several minutes before he hit a mental wall. His brow furrowed and he tapped his pencil on his lips.

"You have more questions," she said, noticing his struggle.

"You're most kind to tolerate me," Gallo said to her.

"Not in the least. It's both a pleasure and my duty to answer," she replied.

"I've so many more questions now. Where do I begin? How does a soul go about rising? You say you have children? Are they like you or are they like him?"

"Souls go to Samsara, the universe that Earth is part of, to learn, or they remain in Zion, taking another path of learning. That's what I referred to earlier, the dharma—your path. Either path helps them to grow and eventually their atman becomes so full and so strong, it must be housed within a new sattva, or form," she answered. He smiled, still unclear. "My children are like us—ardhodita, half-duta."

"Fascinating. So a soul that doesn't grow, the light would fade?"

At this, she stared at him. Something troubling flickered in her eyes.

"No—no. Not necessarily. There are souls who wish to remain as they are, content in their current resonance. Still, eventually, we all must grow. It's up to you if you grow fast or slow," she replied, stuffing her mouth with a forkful of carrots.

"But you must come to a certain understanding, which helps you to move away from where you think you want to be, something that makes you desire more?"

"Yes—something like that," she replied distantly.

"Can you describe ardhodita in greater detail?"

"You should eat your supper, Father Gallo," Orius said, deciding she had had enough of his questions for the moment. Orius gave her an apologetic glance. "I remember my wife still. It's been the greatest pain that I suffer, not being able to see her and knowing I left her with no children to occupy her time."

The girl stopped eating. She stared at her plate and he knew he'd caused her more pain. He rubbed his thumb against his palm, trying to think of a way to make it less painful and give her hope as he intended.

"You'll see your husband soon. Sooner than you know," Orius said.

"How have you survived?" she asked.

"Day to day. I keep my eye on the goal and tell myself that each day that passes, I get closer to returning home. It becomes duty and the pain lessens with the distraction of work," Orius replied.

"Is that what ties us here? The pain?"

"It may be," Orius said with a shrug. She eyed him and he continued. "But becoming recidia—it's more than the pain of being separated from loved ones. It's the pain of your doubt, recanting what you know—Adonai, yourself."

"I don't doubt Adonai, only my own service to him. If we come to answers that make no sense—reasons that only come from our desire, how can they be worthy of what he tries to create?"

"You mentioned that you were here trying to fix a wrong you did," Orius said. "You say slaughtering a demon out of want and hate is wrong. What if you were manipulated to feel that way? What if they played on your natural hatred for the dark and made you think they could bring you down by it?"

"There's nothing more just than a fight against the fallen one," Father Gallo said.

Her eyes switched between them. The thought planted a seed and the light of her eyes brightened a little.

"When I came here, I had no one to tell me such things. I was angry and refused anyone's help. I can at last be the person I needed to be and save someone from the mistakes I have made. You're willing, it seems. All I ask in return is that you let my wife know that I'll return and that my love for her is as strong as the day of our ketu."

Bethiah smiled and her wings lifted at his request. Orius smiled back. She was idealistic, much like himself. So long as she focused on those things, her heart would remain full of what she needed to make her journey home. He felt better for having been tactless.

"That reminds me," Father Gallo said. "Recidia and Grigori. Perhaps you can shed some light on the Hebrew scripture that speaks of the Nephilim. You are married to a human, but you weren't cast from grace for this. What is the difference?"

She laughed and Orius chuckled. The other brothers listened intently while they enjoyed their supper, hoping to learn more about the world they thought they served. Orius at last felt hungry, having unburdened his heart from the worry that could do her more harm than good. Calling Geitz was the right thing to do. They needed to use this opportunity to enlighten men, but also to return her home. They could accomplish both with little effort. The other possibility would mute her and the opportunity would slip by mankind.

"Grigori—are the shadowwalkers who broke their oaths. They raped human females, some only committed adultery to be with a woman, but their children were born of darkness for their betrayal and were deformed by it. One doesn't idly choose to commit such acts. It's out of want, without reason, and disregards the hurt it will cause others. They wanted to cause pain, to feed their selfish desire."

"What if you become unhappy with your husband or wife?"

"You wouldn't be bound," she replied simply. "Ketot are made by the atman. Pairs are hewn from the same material and seek one another until they become one again. Ketot are simply announced by our king."

"Because he knows all."

"King Adonai sees much and is very wise, but he doesn't abuse his seat to decide the futures of any. They are responsible for themselves," she replied.

Bethiah ate some more, the plate of food nearly devoured.

"You attribute some odd faculty to him, as if he's a puppet master. Yet you talk about free will," she scoffed.

"The Earth is his creation and he moves it to his desire. Such as terrible storms and disease, or flourishing crops and famine, sickness and healing," Father Gallo said. "Is that not right?" he asked, remembering that he was no longer certain of anything.

"The Earth is one of many worlds, but the king doesn't move them to his desire unless necessary to affect the lives of those who come here to learn. That would be entered in the dharma agreed to for the lives present in that time. You forget that there are others who exist to devour the light of the atman within any sattva. Your failure is his success."

"Lucifer?" Gallo said.

"Among others," she said.

"Like the one who followed her here," Orius said.

"A Grigori," she replied. "Yes. His name is Morgentus, Baron of the Labyrinth of Acheron. The Baron, as he is called, traps souls and feeds on them."

"How did he come by such a title—and knowing you?" Gallo asked.

Orius clamped his mouth shut, waiting for her to tell the tale. He had not admitted to anyone but her that the demon was his brother. Though he knew the story better than anyone, he would not be moved to mention it, but Bethiah told them what she'd learned.

"Morgentus raped a woman and his seed was wiped from the Earth in a flood. Not all Nephilim were destroyed and cast into Oblivion, however. Some dhatri pleaded out of love for the children they created with stolen mates and they were granted amnesty. Their descendants walk among you to this day. Some even redeemed themselves and became souls. Morgentus was enraged when his child wasn't spared and he has hated the lightwalkers ever since. He murdered the woman he raped, blaming her above all others for not praying to spare his son. Some say she's in his maze, in the farthest depths, still tortured by his anger. None have ever been able to find her, try as we might to end her torment. Because of this, he has made it his duty to trap souls and uses the labyrinth to befuddle any who wander his way. But we leave none behind, Father Gallo." She smiled at him. "So long as you hold the light in your heart. We'll come for you. We'll track you until the end, as we still seek her."

"You go into hell?"

"Jahannam. Regularly," she answered with a delighted grin.

"You seem to enjoy the idea. It makes me shudder to think of what torments you would see there. Absolutely frightening to be touched by devils."

"Torments we inflict by stealing those who aren't theirs. Morgentus loses his revenge."

"Wondrous," Gallo said, jotting the information down. "You said his child was cast into Oblivion. What does that mean? Did you meet Morgentus on your journeys to free trapped souls?"

"Utter destruction. He was completely destroyed and I met the Grigori when I became trapped in his lair," she replied.

The admission stopped the meal and the brothers regarded her with surprise.

"They can trap angels?" Gallo said surprised.

"Duta. Please. There is no such thing as the angels. Not as you've envisioned them. They're a fantasy of your memory of duta," she corrected him, terrified of being labeled that name and worshipped as a god. "They can, they have, and they do. They succeed in keeping only those who really wish to be there. We view it only as a test of our will. It's something to be proud of. We're tested and proven. My friends said I had passed, though doubt fills me at this time."

"If you don't mind," Orius said, "I would most like to hear what happened. It may shed some light on our situation."

Bethiah nodded and imparted her tale. She spoke of a lifetime that ended a few years prior. It began in the 1930s in the United States. She spoke of the flourishing lives of her parents, the love she'd found and their life together, how he had been her teacher and how they had hidden their affair. They were only a few years apart in age and it was a chemistry that wouldn't be denied. Still, the stigma caused them great suffering. When the superintendent of her school discovered the incident, her then-husband was forced to leave his appointment. Her life had been easy up until then and she attributed that easiness to her downfall.

"I was terrible at math, you see. I had no interest until I realized that without passing I would have to stay in school another year. My janya would've been furious at such an embarrassment. So I stayed after class to get tutoring. Dominic was very handsome, very charming—I enjoyed his company too much. I used every advantage I'd been born with to gain his attentions. We must have succumbed to our bond, because there was nothing to stop us from coming together. Very quickly, staying after school became a regular appointment and I learned a great deal more than just arithmetic.

Another teacher took notice—my English instructor. He wasn't pleased at all. You see, he flirted with all the girls, and there were rumors he'd had relationships with a few. Unlike Dominic, this man was nearly our pitarau's age and had no business chasing anyone, not with a wife and children at home. One girl that he had his way with moved and we whispered about what happened to her. I was just another he wanted to add to the list; I was far too pretty to escape unscathed from such a lecher. But anyway, I soon graduated and Dominic and I were married in six months. My janya was very angry. He hoped I would make a better ketu. You see, he moved up in Atlanta society and he wanted to keep moving up. He intended me for some banker friend of his, triple my age, but rich as a king. For my father, marrying a teacher was beneath our standing. I tried to remind him it was I who'd be marrying and not he. Having a beautiful daughter was just a bartering chip. He disliked my attitude and lack of ambition, so he cut me off from the family when I refused to get divorced and let him pass me on to his friends. My amba—my mother— was beside herself. So when my husband died in the war, never having seen his firstborn, she saw it as her opportunity to bring me back home. My janya saw it as a way to show me he was right, and gave me an offer: I could return on the condition that I give up my child for adoption and pretend nothing had ever happened. I decided to stay with my in-laws instead. My baby was all I had left of the man I loved. There was no way I'd give him up.

Dominic and I had moved out west to Oklahoma to live with his parents and start a family before the war. The house was just an endless reminder of him. His pictures everywhere. When war broke out, all the men were swept up in the calculated nationalism. We had an argument the night before he left for the army. Somehow, I knew he wouldn't return and I couldn't stand the idea. Something told me to delay him for as long as possible, but it was hopeless and he ran off to play hero, leaving me a month pregnant and wondering how I would get through. I had no heart to deny him, not really, not when the war sought men to fight in honor of freedom. I just wanted to hold him close a bit longer, as if that was all that it would take to protect him from dying. Yet, there I was, a widow with a baby. I tried to move on; I went to California. I was a chorus girl, living the life and thinking things might get better. I met movie stars and artists. I even tried dating. It was fabulous and I started to know what happiness was once more.

Then my boy became sick—polio. I held out hope he'd live, even if he had to walk with braces or be in a wheelchair for the rest of his life. I loved him so very much, it didn't matter, so long as he stayed. He was my only link to the one I had loved and the star that saw me through the darkness. I couldn't stand it when my son died. I became inconsolable.

After his funeral, my amba brought me back to Atlanta at last, but nothing fixed the hole I had been left with. I just sat for hours watching the days go by, biding my time and praying to die. I wouldn't even cry anymore. I just begged a God I thought I knew to have mercy and end my suffering. It never happened and I soon felt lost and forgotten.

Around that time, my amba heard of a hospital in Massachusetts, one that dealt with depression in women. She thought surely that was all I needed, someone to listen and a place to rest far away from all the reminders. Once they admitted me, though, the doctors had no intention of me getting better. They liked to test things on the patients, new pills and tonics—electric shock and all kinds of unimaginable tortures. It was a horrifying place and my family left me there, their dirty secret. They insisted that the doctors would cure me, but we all knew it was a lie to hide the embarrassing truth. What else could they do, with me slowly going insane in their house? That's when things got worse. The doctors and staff knew they wouldn't be checking in on me. The orderlies were brutal, the nurses cruel, and the doctors cared only for their experiments. When one of the orderlies raped me, they ignored my claims as delusions resulting from my depression. They said I was hysterical. They increased my doses and upped the duration of the shock treatment. He did it again and again. No one would listen. But they knew. It panicked them when my family showed up for another visit. They knew I would tell them. If my family listened—they couldn't have such things getting out. They'd be shut down. So they scheduled me for surgery and drugged me up until they got their approval. They were going to stick a needle, here, past my eye—twirl it around a little. It wrecks the brain and makes you complacent. They called it a lobotomy, the surest treatment for curing depression. It supposedly made the patient incapable of being sad anymore. It made them incapable of doing anything anymore. I saw the results of it all around me.

Despite my garbled warnings and tearful pleas, my pitarau approved the surgery and I was scheduled to be their living experiment and the orderly's willing victim for the rest of my days. I saved every pill they gave me inside a hole in my mattress. Then I took every single one the night before the surgery was scheduled. All of it happened because Dominic failed to follow his path. He left me wallowing in purgatory."

Father Gallo stared at her with his mouth agape. Orius continued eating. He had seen enough suffering that such tales no longer affected him. He remembered the war well and the attitudes of which she spoke. His heart had nearly turned to stone in the middle of it all, just to save himself from the torment of witnessing hell on Earth. So, instead of commenting, he listened and pieced together a great deal more than the girl probably even knew. It sounded to him as if the shades had worked for her fall longer than just a few days. He'd wager all the chalices in the church on it.

"What happened after that?" Father Gallo said with awe.

"Being what I am, I couldn't accept what I'd done. The act created a prison for me and I cast myself into Acheron for punishment."

"Suicide is a sin," Father Gallo said, crossing himself.

"No," she said to him, "suicide is having enough. It's trying to save your atman from further damage. Giving up was an unbearable thing to my heart, though. I was ashamed. How could I call myself a brave warrior and not face my dharma?"

"I would have done the same," Orius assured her.

"It was a terrible fate and, as I said, one that I found out wasn't meant to be. Happily, my true family found me and remained at my prison door until the voice of my husband finally breached the walls and broke me free."

"Wondrous is this bond of marriage between husband and wife," Father Gallo said.

Maiel laughed. Her joy at his statement made him question it.

"Marriage—you've mentioned it before, but I must correct your idea on what that means. Humans are one of the most interesting species in Samsara. In ketu, there is no ceremony. No papers. Just the bond and agreements accompanied by the karmic and dharmic laws. It's not like your Earthly understanding. Two souls... they just match—ketu. Any two—somehow the pair just find each other and that is all."

"Any two?"

"Any two souls can be ketu," she said.

"Two men?" one of the brothers piped up.

"If they match," she said, serving herself more of the potatoes. She poured gravy on top until it pooled on her plate. "You seem confused."

"This can't be," Father Gallo said. "The scripture says—what do you mean no ceremony? How does one know you are ketu?"

The brothers laughed at his reluctance to listen, reminding him of whom he spoke with.

"How does one know you're married if they didn't attend your wedding? What difference does it make? A moment ago you thought there was no mating at all and that females didn't exist in Zion." She ate some of her potatoes. "How would all the risen souls be born again? You may call it marriage if you like, but it is far more than your concept of such a bond. In our tongue, it is ketu—the match," she said with her mouth full.

"Forgive me, messenger, but it clearly states that marriage is defined—"

"As between a man and woman? A woman and her deceased husband's brother? Her kidnapper, rapist, et cetera. Foolishness. That would have me wed to my demonic captor, if it were so. A ketu is more like the pair bonding in birds, Father Gallo. When two atman choose each other, there is an unbreakable bond. Whatever they evolve into is their own business. There is nothing more celebrated in Zion than the bond of love, for it is the blessing of higher resonance; the way to Nirvana. Your book was written by frighteningly controlling men who rewrote historical documents and compiled them as a means of control over those they ruled."

Orius smiled to himself. Any more from her and she would turn the church on its ear. She was more likely to have Geitz try to execute her than anything. If she did become recidia, he would need to counsel her on holding her tongue and allow time to reveal the human lies.

"That changes a great deal," Father Gallo said in shock.

"Not really. You'll see the truth eventually. The book is filled with half-truths and lies. Use it wisely if you can use it at all. It is from imperfect memory, meant to seat power in the hands of few," she said.

"Half-truths—the word of God? It makes me fear we speak with a grigori and not a messenger." Father Gallo shook his head.

"Word of God? He who you call a god is a watcher over the path to Jahannam, not the king. Surely, you're aware of the books origins in the ninth century? That its creation was overseen by shadowborn."

When he did not agree, she offered her hand. He eyed it, unsure of what she wanted.

"Let me show you the truth. If I still have the strength to," she said.

Father Gallo reluctantly took her hand.

"Promise what you see won't be shared outside this monastery or the witnesses who are here today without close care. It may be treated as heresy and endanger your life and the good you can do with it. There are many who will violently protect what they think they know to keep the control it gives them," she warned.

"I promise," the father agreed.

The girl closed her hand around the priest's. A bluish light filled her and spread to his flesh, winding up his arm and about his head. His eyes popped open and he stared into nothing, as if seeing a great spectacle. With his mouth wide, he gulped air into his lungs, unable to catch his breath. Then it was over; a spark died in his eye. Bethiah returned to her potatoes. Gallo sat silent, reflecting on what she had imparted to him.

"I suppose that'll make you a saint now," she said, with a mouthful of mashed potatoes. "They'll cut you up and distribute you around Hungary. A holy relic."

Gallo's eyes came back to hers and he, surprisingly, laughed.

"Saint Gallo," Orius said and shook his head.

"Canonized? Not damn likely," the man said, still laughing. He stopped, realizing there were now things in his head he couldn't have possibly been privy to. The brothers stared at him startled. "My apologies, brothers," he said for their sake, unable to stifle the joy of using curse words, something he hadn't indulged since boyhood.

"I can show each of you something you wish to know, if you're willing. I feel strong enough, but I must warn you that it will change everything," she said.

The brothers looked to one another, then to Orius. He nodded, knowing they trusted him and waited for his approval in all things. They quietly agreed.

"Then I'll oversee your meditation this evening, and teach you more than you'd learn from that book in a hundred years of studying it. I trust you'll be wise in the use of such knowledge," she said.

"Though it may be our downfall. We'll carry your message and share what we can with those who'll listen," one of the brothers declared.

Orius finished his meal and excused himself to his duties once more. He sat in the office well after dark, putting the finishing touches on his sermon for the time being. Reviewing his notes, he spoke the words aloud in a murmur. The phone suddenly rang, startling him. He stared at it, as if he forgot what a phone was or what he should do with it. It rang again, more insistent. Orius jumped and picked up the receiver. He stammered, trying to remember his words.

"Father Gregely Orius," he said.

"Bring her to the basilica in Esztergom," a voice said on the other end. It was Geitz, returning his call as promised. "Does anyone other than the brothers know of her?"

"Just us," Orius replied. How could he get her there safely? The fear returned. "By what means should we come to you?"

"I'll send a car in the morning. Share this with no one. Do you understand? She'll be in grave danger. There are those who would keep her here to satisfy their own desire. I'll pray to Michael this eve and when you come to me, mark my words, he'll have heard our prayer. Perhaps we may even see him," Geitz said.

"That may be more than we can hope. But I'll have her ready by morning," Orius said. If it were possible, then why had his friends not shown themselves to him? Why did he call the general by his anglicized name?

"That's a good man. I'll see you then. Keep up your prayers," Geitz said.

Geitz hung up the phone. Orius sat with the receiver to his ear, increasingly unsure of help at the basilica. Taking her by car was just what his brother would expect. The moment she set foot beyond their sanctuary, he would be at their heels. He wasn't sure he could protect her, or she him.

Orius rose from his desk as he put the receiver back in its cradle. Passing from the rectory into the monastery that housed the brothers, he found Bethiah sitting with the men and amusing them with tales of home. She spoke fondly of her friends and a wolf that had allied with her Order to fight the shades. He listened to her stories for a moment, not wishing to spoil the fun for them. She wouldn't be with them for much longer and he couldn't deny the brothers the truth they had spent their lives devoted to. They had come to him too late, and though they made no declaration, it was likely they no more believed him than the liars who came before. Like them, he was unable to perform miracles to prove himself. All he had was his sight, doomed for eternity to see the devils that hunted him and the friends he would never stand by again. She had proved his story true the moment they'd met her.

Bethiah looked over her shoulder, sensing his presence. She smiled at him and the brothers welcomed him to their circle. Now that the news was imparted, she surprised him by being delighted. Not wishing to cast doubt upon her heart more than it already had been, he smiled back and encouraged the telling of more tales.

"Tell them about the Orders," Orius said. "What Order are you?"

"Order of the Moon," she replied. "My brother is in the Order of the Sun. Our armor, as you can see by mine, is made to honor our division. My brother is always in gold."

"Diana and Apollo," one of the brothers said.

She reluctantly smiled, not answering.

"Is that a sapphire on your sword? The one in your room? How come you by such finery?" one of the brothers asked.

"Yes, it houses the atman of the sword," she replied. "We receive our weapons in a ceremony when we are placed in our Order. They have no monetary worth, but their value is nothing money can buy."

"Objects have life?"

"I'm unsure of what you mean by life. Most have a resonance. The sword is given an atman, because it is the hand of Adonai. I can only slay those he declares lost forever, sending their existence into Oblivion to be unmade. Without it, the danava heal and return to fight us again."

"Does he ever deny his permission?"

"Very often. He holds out hope they'll right their wrongs and come back home. They too are his children," she said.

Her eyes went to Orius and they regarded each other, thinking of what that meant to them.

"You must tell me more about the Orders," Father Gallo said, breaking the silence.

"This," Bethiah said, indicating her penannular, "is called a penannular. It houses the armor we wear. It also indicates rank. Mine is a small full moon, the mark of a captain. My leader wears a waxing three-quarter moon, and so down to our younglings who bear the empty circle or new moon. Above my rank, the moon eventually fills the entire circle."

Father Gallo scribbled hastily in his notebook.

*   *   *

Gediel and Luthias walked the north halls toward the Ordo Prioria, a place neither had been since before they were assigned to duty. With their armor put away, their pace was quicker, except for the lag because of Gediel's wound. Neither engel spoke. Finding the truth was all Gediel concentrated on. He nearly forgot his companion and his pain.

A shrill whistle split the air. Gediel faced the path behind. The tree-lined road was empty. He exchanged curious glances with Luthias.

"Shouldn't you have reported this to me?" A voice startled them from behind.

Both duta spun around. A black-robed watcher stared down his nose at them. A crown of silver sat on the top of his head. Long, straight tresses of ebony hair spilled over his shoulders. His black eyes switched between them, nested in a strong, bronzed face. Voil.

"Commander," Gediel rasped.

Luthias saluted.

"Primus," Voil said, clearly not pleased.

"I was asked by Mikhael to check into a matter. It won't take long," Gediel explained.

"I have need of you elsewhere," Voil countered.

"Magnus, by chance?"

"No. What do you know of that?"

"That's the matter I'm checking for Mikhael," Gediel replied.

"Did he even bother to clear you with General Uriel?"

"Moments ago."

Voil assessed Gediel, the former as stoic as the young alder called Zacharius. Gediel pondered his chances of continuing his mission, while images of the epic staring contest between the aforementioned duta skipped through his mind. He struggled not to laugh.

"Your insolence isn't amusing, Primus," Voil said.

"Of course not, Commander."

"You're injured." Voil noticed.

Gediel gestured in agreement.

"You should have that looked at. It will slow you down."

Voil eyed him again.

"Yes, Commander," Gediel said.

"This slides this time, because I suspect your orders come from higher than General Mikhael. Brief me when you've finished and then I have work for you."

Gediel inclined his head.

Voil looked at Luthias in disfavor, then blinked out of sight as he went elsewhere.

"Perhaps you should have reported to him first," Luthias said.

"He's always like that."

"Zach and he'd get along rather well then," Luthias jested, echoing Gediel's thoughts.

Gediel snickered, refusing to say more.

Soon, the pair was surrounded by younglings and those entrusted to their schooling. The students stared at them and whispered as they passed. It seemed the wolf leader or his secretive Order had a certain celebrity status among the younglings. Luthias looked uncomfortable with the attention, but Gediel was not shaken. Indeed, he was used to it, attracting eyes everywhere he went in Zion by his unique appearance. It was a wonder he was able to spy at all.

Gediel spotted the headmaster and grinned broadly, excited to see the Principality. The headmaster had emerged from the order's halls to walk among his assigns, who were filling the courtyard with a great deal of noise. His presence always assured they'd behave themselves. The principality loomed above the children, like a giant mobile statue. Gediel pushed through the crowd of children to join him.

"Gediel!" the statue spoke with delighted surprise. "What brings a member of Fenrir to our doors? Have you come to collect the new younglings? It's quite early yet."

"No, Jushur. I'm here about someone else. A human called Dominic. May we speak in private?" Gediel asked.

The Principality cautiously considered him. He gave a slow nod, then turned and led the way back inside the Ordo halls. Gediel and Luthias followed him through several passages before they entered the headmaster's chambers in one of the spiny spires. When the door shut, their host urged them to sit. He placed his ivory form on a softly cushioned couch and waited for an explanation regarding their intrusion into his cloister.

"Perhaps one of our mentors can see to your injuries, Primus," Jushur said when Gediel winced.

"Thank you, no. We don't have time," Gediel said.

"Did you fall from a cliff, forget you could fly?"

"Playing with a wraith. It'll mend," Gediel explained.

Jushur nodded solemnly.

"Jushur, it's been a long time since you've heard the name 'Dominic' uttered. Tell us what you remember of him." Gediel went straight to the topic.

An erela Principality set a tray on the table between them, then excused herself in a soft voice. None of the engels seemed interested in what she brought, not with Dominic's name hanging in the air between them.

"Why do you not ask your friend? He knows as much as I, if not more. I haven't seen the boy since I rose," Jushur said, once she had gone.

"You seem angry," Gediel said.

"Not anger." Jushur dismissed the idea with a laugh. "I've been forgotten and this one—he has undone my work. I'm frustrated," Jushur said, gesturing to the evocati, then leaning forward to whisper.

Luthias moved to leave. His hot head could end this interview quickly, but Gediel clamped a hand on his arm and kept him still. With a single shake of his head, he censured the young guardian. The guardian sneered, but kept his seat.

"I've come to determine just that. Dominic was doing well under your instruction. What changed?" Gediel asked, releasing Luthias.

Jushur eyed him warily again.

"You trained me, Jushur. Don't you forget that," Luthias snapped.

Gediel sighed. He should have left him standing in the schoolyard.

"I haven't forgotten, but the memories from my time as a guardian are indistinct. It was so very long ago."

Jushur held a secret. The stress made the fresh lines in his face deeper and the shadows about his eyes darken. Without the Principality's cooperation, the information he received from Gamael and everything else would hang too loosely together. He sensed the schoolmaster desired to speak, but something held his tongue. The secret must be damning. Gediel only feared it may condemn the friend he was working to save.

"Was there nothing that gave you pause about Dominic? Nothing that made you think you worked in vain?"

"He was a striking youth. Very bright and very driven. He wasn't unique among the humans, but he wasn't just like them either. His atman was in between. It should've been born as a duta, but somehow decided to become clay instead. Always undecided and indolent."

Jushur sighed. He peered past them, recalling the old memories. His aspect took on the appearance of a disappointed janya.

"You said things changed when Luthias took over your duties as guardian. Was it sudden or did things turn after the course of time?"

"Dominic wasn't happy to see me go. He felt betrayed by the alders who told him I was to rise. I did my best to let him know that I was still available to him, but he never came to see me after that day. You must understand that his pitarau had moved on from him when he entered the legion. He had no family to speak of and he saw me as his surrogate janya. He was hurt to be abandoned again," Jushur said.

"Hence your anger with Luthias," Gediel said.

"My disappointment—not with Evocati Luthias. Dominic's ambition was greater than his strength to control it. Under proper guidance, he would have learned to control it. I was so sure he was bound for the highest of muses, so I worked as diligently as I was able. I found him difficult to instruct, but not impossible. He was unfocused and lazy, daydreaming all the time. Nothing that isn't part of a young muse. They're all fidgety. You must learn how to handle them. Quite frankly, Luthias was too young to be given such an assign."

Luthias shook his head and muttered under his breath.

"Luthias has been a proficient guide, though his vigilance hasn't been able to contain that ambition, but not for lack of trying," Gediel told Jushur.

"I've been informed of what passes. You can be assured that Dominic wouldn't be in such straits if he were still under my care. He needs a firm hand, not an indulgent one," Jushur said.

Pensive, the headmaster stared at the floor.

Gediel placed his hand on the evocati's arm before the soldier countered the statement. The tension tightened the guardian's muscles, but Luthias proudly held his tongue. It was true. He was too young to be trusted with such a delicate task. However, he wasn't as slothful as implied and deserved more praise than would be given for his work. Befriending Dominic was simply his style, and in reflection it likely delayed the burning, which was the greater point.

"Something else troubles you," Gediel said, hoping to hear the inner thoughts of the headmaster.

"I witnessed her through many years. Maiel never needed a guardian for more than protection against the forces invisible to her, blinded so by the flesh of Samsara. Zaajah's job was easy and she was sometimes called upon to help me in mine. Dominic enjoyed being mortal, very much so—indulging in vices that often poisoned the mind as well as the flesh. He could be so cruel. They're ill-matched. It never made any sense to me."

"I'm not to blame for his ways since you left him, if you suggest he was bent toward the shadow to begin with. Your presence only prolonged this," Luthias growled.

Gediel gripped his shoulder tight, quickly silencing the young guardian.

"That's why they gave him Captain Maiel, so she could save him," Gediel breathed, astonished at the thought.

"Perhaps we're all to blame for his ways—but not her. She should've been his guardian, not his wife. He loved her more than even Adonai—or did when I watched over him last. I don't mean to say otherwise. It's just that his actions sometimes erred on the side of harshness." Jushur fell silent, reflecting in sadness over the past. He continued with a distracted sigh, "He wasn't bent toward the shadow, just curious about it."

Jushur fell silent, allowing Gediel time to contemplate what he revealed to them.

"Of course, that's why they bound them," Gediel whispered to himself, not listening. His chin popped up and his eyes narrowed. "Did he ever come into contact with a danava? Was he left with them for any length of time?"

Jushur shook his head and stammered as he spoke. Dominic hadn't been exposed to a shade's influence, at least not for long. Gediel rubbed his chin.

"What of Acheron? Had he been there?"

"Never. He was at least obedient in that while I protected him," Jushur said.

"That's true. He only came into contact with Acheron when Mai was stolen. He reached her from the Astral Ways. Her akha and I took him," Luthias said.

"The Astral Ways," Gediel repeated, growing distant.

A light winked on in the back of his mind. He had almost forgotten about them. Any number of parasites could have found their way into his mind. If they examined him, they were sure to find the binding nails left behind. Gediel flexed his fist. Unfortunately, he was out of their hands and that couldn't be done until he returned. By then, it might be too late.

"Thank you, Jushur. I know that we've taken you away from your students, so we won't detain you any longer. If any alders come to ask, tell them that we came to seek a youngling to aid in our quest, one we could use as bait for the shadowalkers. Tell them you refused and we went to seek someone else from our orders."

Jushur nodded, confused by the instructions. Gediel excused them from Jushur's chambers and they made their way out of the Ordo Prioria alone. Holding his tongue, Gediel quietly obsessed over the implications of the information gained. They needed the help of others, those who could peer backward through time. If he was right, their journey would take them into the places between worlds, where they would uncover the answers that yet remained. This catastrophe was bigger than a danava's lust or a human faltering on his path.

CHAPTER 17

DOMINIC STEPPED FROM THE TRAIN, looking for his connection to Dover. He shook his head, tired and bewildered. The passengers meandering the platform were a cacophony of color and styles that hurt the eye. Lena trotted along behind him, hurrying to catch up. Her face was peaceful but focused. Guessing by her expression, the train station was safe for now. Unable to locate his changeover, he approached a uniformed woman he assumed worked there. Her cheap makeup and silly hairstyle reminded him of clowns he saw the last time he came to Earth.

"Just missed it, sir. Another'll be along in an hour. You could take a train to London and then over if you wanted. Wouldn't be any longer," the woman said in a high-pitched voice.

"Thank you. Is there a men's room around here?" Dominic asked, disappointed.

The woman lazily pointed over her shoulder. Dominic thanked her again and stepped into the terminal. He found the restroom, a filthy, cold space of gross tiles that was occupied by one brown sport-coated traveler. He wore brown trousers with brown shoes and combed his brown hair. The brown man eyed him with brown eyes, then returned to rinsing his comb. His brown moustache twitched. Dominic put his head down and made his way to the last stall, the wider cubicle intended for guests with wheelchairs. He couldn't expect Lena to stand outside with people coming and going, or with the strange character who was there, and he needed the space. She followed him without question, taking his hand and sticking close. Her expression changed to apprehension. Something was wrong. Her black eyes remained on the brown man.

"Shadowborn," she whispered.

Dominic squeezed her hand reassuringly. He closed them in the stall and dropped his pack in her hands. He sat on the edge of the toilet and ran his fingers through his hair. Now wasn't the time to engage trouble. He took a deep breath, hoping she was wrong. He felt so tired. The brown man was just another weirdo in a train station, never mind that he was suspiciously made of too much brown.

"We need to keep moving," Lena said.

Dominic nodded.

"Check the bag; see if there's more money," she instructed.

Lena peered through the crack in the door and watched the man at the sink.

"I think he knows I'm here. Wait—use the toilet. If you pretend you're peeing he might think twice," she said.

"What?"

"Just do it," Lena hissed. She covered her eyes and pressed her face to the door.

Dominic did as he was instructed. He didn't even know if he could go. He stood there, waiting, but nothing. The idea of her behind him locked down his bladder. Technically, he understood that he might need to go, as he had eaten and drunk the night before. However, he wasn't accustomed to what happened while travelling with temporary flesh in Samsara. His head tipped back and he stared at the greenish lights. An odd sensation followed. Dominic was delighted to find that everything worked just as it did when he was incarnated.

Zipping up, he kicked the lever to flush. Dominic sat back down. Lena jumped back, gasping as though she saw something beyond the door. She pressed herself to the tiled wall, slinking back, afraid.

"We've gotta keep moving. Check the money," she instructed.

Dominic pulled the purse from his pocket and sat on the toilet. Inside was a wad of paper notes wound into a neat roll. They had plenty. He just wasn't sure what they faced from there on out and if that roll was all they needed.

"There's enough cash," Dominic said to satisfy her.

"Count it," she urged, attaching to his leg.

Dominic did so and found the bills parted and parted. There seemed no end and the count continued higher.

"There's more than enough," he said.

That satisfied his guide. She lay against his arm silently.

"They said the nest of the turul. You mentioned an eagle in Germany. What if the nest is the home? A home would be the capital. We may need to go to the capital," Lena spoke, watching the gaps in the cubicle with worry.

"Berlin, yeah. When we get over the channel, we'll find a train to take us there. Right now, we have to get to Dover, even if we're walking. If we stay here, they'll corner us in," Dominic said.

"I can try to cloak you, but my energy might bring them to me and they'll know I don't belong here," Lena said, hugging his arm.

"Never mind that. I need to meditate and this is as good a place as any," Dominic replied.

"That man out there. I think he's shadowborn. He's trying to listen. If you meditate now, he'll know what you are," Lena said.

"Probably pissed I used the handicap toilet." Dominic smiled, pulling his arm free and setting her on her own feet a step away from him. He shut his eyes and tried to concentrate. "I suppose he has a right," he added.

Lena leaned against his shoulder, refusing to be separated from him. This show of fear didn't sit well in his gut. She was less concerned with the mudeaters who'd found them at the farm house. Dominic released a long exhale in an attempt to relax. All he needed was to pass a quiet hour in this cubicle. Joel told him he must rest often if he meant to keep his strength up and the burning at bay. The opportunity had yet to come. Whatever started the fire in his throat concerned the others, though they'd refused to mention it. He was going to do as he was told. He wasn't about to allow some brown rube who might be a shade interrupt.

Dominic fell into a trance quickly and it swept the weariness of the night away. His legs felt strong again and his feet no longer ached. The hunger pressing his gut disappeared. Floating in a cloud, like a warm blanket wrapped about him, he found a strange sense of peace. At first he thought Lena shielded him, but then he recognized the markers. The resonance faded, indicating that Maiel had reached out to him some time ago; it was unmistakable. He drew a deep breath, trying to smell her. She was warm and welcoming, unlike the burning inferno raging in his core. The image of a late morning entered his mind: he and Maiel basking beside the water in the gold shimmer of sunlight. Her face smiled back and then all went dark and she was gone.

"Hey! Ya gonna spend all day in that cubicle, mate? What if a cripple comes and needs it? Nice of ya to take it up on 'em? What? He supposed to piss himself?" A voice called from the other side of the toilet door. The man banged on it, shaking the whole unit.

"I'll be out in a minute. I'm not feeling well."

"Having a bender doesn't excuse ya to take up that cubicle," the man insisted.

Lena's grip tightened on Dominic's arm. He gestured for her to stay behind him. Looping the pack straps on his hand, he swung it onto his shoulder. They could sit in the waiting area with others, where it would be safe in the presence of their guardians and too many witnesses for shades to cause trouble. He could easily meditate, pretending to sleep.

Dominic exited the cubicle.

"Yar kind makes me want to puke. Bloody Americans! Ya think ya own the place. It's us who owns you."

"I don't want a fight. I'm out of there. Just go about your business. Nothing to lose your head over. No one was put out," Dominic said, trying to step away.

"I should pop ya one. My uncle's a cripple from the war," the brown man said, sticking his finger in Dominic's face.

The blood in Dominic's veins rushed. The damn vagrant had to go there. Narrowing his eyes, he stiffened his back and stood his ground. Subtle hints of sulfur floated off the brown coat, confirming Lena's suspicion. The brown man was a shadowborn, possibly a shadowalker, somehow hiding its true form.

"Yeah, that so?" Dominic replied.

"That's so," the brown man countered.

"That's a great disguise," Dominic said, straightening the man's lapels.

The brown man eyed him.

"But—uh—I know what you are. So, keep your ass fucking nose out of my face before I cut it off. I died in the war. You can't get more crippled than that," Dominic said with a sneer.

"Ya just try it mate. Ya fucking nutter. You died in the war, eh?" the brown man challenged, making himself appear larger.

"Wouldn't be a challenge at all," Dominic replied.

"Ya think, so mate? You're barmy ain't ya?"

"Why don't you go back to the shadow that shit you out and ask them if I'm crazy," Dominic said.

The blade of his sword glinted in the shade's eye as he pulled it from the pack.

"What ya gonna do with that, love? I's only doing the right thing. It's not right taking up that cubicle. Yar mad," the brown man said, backing off and throwing his hands up.

Dominic grit his teeth. The jackass was no more than a troublemaker. He turned away and left the restroom, tucking his weapon back in his bag and hoping the brown man didn't decide to go to security about it. They'd drag him away to the madhouse for sure.

With Lena close to his side, Dominic found the waiting area, and there they made do until the next train to Dover. Dominic scanned the room and the other passengers. Their guardians stared along with them. Dominic continued into the room and most lost interest in them. A girl in a pink sleeveless sweater continued to track his movements. Her eyes were ringed with heavy black liner and her bleached hair went to her shoulders, where it curled up. She reminded him for a moment of a girl from home. Her paleness anyway. Grabbing her boyfriend's arm, she hid her face. The muscles of Dominic's face relaxed and he realized that he still wore a terrible scowl. With a regretful frown, he slipped his bag off his shoulder and set it on a chair by the windows.

Dominic stared at his blurry reflection in the glass panes. He stared a long moment, appearing to study the odd little garden beyond. The day grew long and they still had no idea where they were meant to go. In his mind, Dominic reached for the remnants of Maiel that he had encountered, but the markers of her essence were all gone. He drew the energy tighter anyway, until he felt stronger, then sat.

The spot by the window allowed a view of the whole room and its occupants. Lena took the seat on his other side. She clung tight to his arm, pulling her feet beneath her. Dominic wished he could hug her, or do something to assure her she was safe again. Even the smallest gesture of caring worked to relax his children when they were tired or afraid.

Exhaling his frustration, Dominic roughly pawed through his pack. Her head rested against his back and he felt the tension leave her. This would be over soon and she would be safe in the womb of her new amba, growing a real set of wings; then she would never be afraid again. A pair of erelas drew in close and cooed over her, saving him the worry.

In his pack, Dominic found a passport. The green cover bore the seal of the United States. He flipped it open and saw his picture inside. It looked familiar, like a forgotten possession of an earlier time. Reading the name filled him with sadness. Brian McAllister. It was the name he'd used during the war, before he died. He dropped the passport back in the bag and wished he had looked sooner. If Birdie or Guillian saw, they'd turn him in for a spy. Beneath a change of clothes and some socks, he found a gun. He didn't need to check to know it was loaded. The last item was a paperback atlas. The maps looked old and they held the names of places that hadn't existed for eons. He flipped the pages until he found Europe under the dates of the war. There were other pages that followed, ranging into the future. Going backward, the years regressed to ancient times. It was a handy piece of technology. Whatever map he needed would be at his fingertips in moments, but the gadget would never raise eyebrows, bound as it was as an old book.

Dominic looked around to see if anyone watched. The people were too busy inside their own heads to care. He dug the tickets from his coat pocket and read them over. The dates would be on there and he could then find the corresponding map. It was late October, 1960. It had been about fifteen years since he was last there. He scanned the room again. Though things had changed, the ghosts of the past always remained. At least the difference in time explained the odd fashion and hideous decor of the train stop.

Thumbing through the atlas, he found the map he needed. Once they crossed to France, the trip was nearly over. Berlin was no more than a couple hours away. If only the trains ran over the water, he thought, shutting the book and putting it back in the bag. He folded his arms, then rested an ankle on his knee. Finding a clock on the wall, he watched the seconds tick by. Time slowed.

"Ten o'clock to Dover, platform two," a voice called over a speaker.

Several people got to their feet and started out of the room. Dominic drew a deep breath. He hadn't realized he had fallen into a trance. Lena leaned on his arm, picking at the skirt covering her legs. He placed a hand on the side of her face and gave her a squeeze while no one was looking.

"Do you feel better?" Lena asked as they walked to the train.

Dominic cleared his throat, unable to speak without appearing completely crazy. He smiled a little, hoping she would understand.

"That man's getting on our train. He's looking at you," Lena said.

The brown man stood yards ahead on the platform. His sports coat stood out against the navy and black ones. He looked at them and got on board.

"We'll just stay back here and hope he doesn't bother us," Dominic said.

"I have a feeling he will."

"Don't be so optimistic," Dominic replied.

A woman stood in the door of the train staring at him.

"Sorry, just having a bit of trouble with a gentleman I met in the bathroom. Think he wants to rob me or something. Gives you the creeps. You start talking to yourself," he explained.

"Whatever floats your boat, honey. But take my advice. You should lay off the stuff," the woman said, forcing back a smile.

Dominic snorted and pushed past her. He found his seat and threw his bag next to him to keep a place for Lena if the train filled. He doubted she wanted to ride on someone's lap or stand all the way to Dover, however far it was. The door to the passenger car opened and the brown man entered. He scrutinized the interior until he spotted Dominic. A broad grin contorted his face in a horrific expression. Then, he walked toward them, placing himself in a seat diagonally behind theirs.

"I told you," Lena said uneasily.

"We'll be away from him soon."

"He's staring," Lena whined.

"Don't look at him."

Lena sat back and squeezed Dominic's backpack closer. She looked more worried than his introverted son Samuel on his birthday. He patted her hand and she inched closer to him.

The car didn't fill as he feared. They were virtually alone with the man stalking them. The only occupants were a few lone travelers and an elderly couple. Their presence would make it tough for the man to bother them, but he suspected the guy was about intimidation rather than action. He'd nearly pissed himself in the bathroom at the sight of the sword. Now he just pursued them to push a few buttons and see what they would do. He was just another jackass. Dominic remembered the gun in his bag. He knew how to use it, if needed. For him, witnesses were not a problem.

The brown man stood once the train was underway. He pushed into the empty seats behind them.

Peering over the head rest, he asked, "Yar one of those nouveau riche come here on tour? Backpacking or something?"

The brown man tried to grab the pack, but Lena held it tight. He sneered.

"I wouldn't do that," Dominic said.

"Why not?" The brown man threw himself down in the open seat beside them.

"You don't want to upset her. She's stronger than she looks," Dominic replied, watching out the window.

"Yeah—you're a nut, eh. She who?"

"I know you can see her. We both know I wasn't holding the bag, so why couldn't you take it?" Dominic said, continuing to look out the window. He sighed heavily. When the brown man didn't answer, he added, "If you were just some prick, you'd have run off by now. But you're not, are you?" Dominic said.

"Thas right, ducky. I'm big trouble." The brown man laughed.

"You'd like to think so, but you're just another lowlife jackass with a chip on your shoulder. Did your daddy spank you too much? Or did he touch you in other ways?" Dominic taunted.

The brown man's face turned red with rage.

"Which kind are you? Imp? Smoker? Mudeater? Let me guess, snake—no those ugly barbarian guys."

The man's eyes narrowed.

"Ah, yeah. I thought so. You need to get out of that seat before I let her show you her ugly side," Dominic pressed.

"I ain't moving, mate."

"You are—and you can go back to whoever holds your leash and tell them you never saw me," Dominic said.

"My boss'd make quick work of you," the brown man laughed, getting nice and comfortable.

"Which one? Belial—Morgentus?"

The brown man eyed him. He cleared his throat, pretending to laugh and get comfortable in the seat again.

"What'd they promise you? Probably a room full of money. So petty—so small. You could have at least asked for a kingdom. That's what I would've asked for."

"What're ya talking about, yar crazy."

"You know what I'm talking about. How much are you getting for your soul? Do you even have one—shadowborn?"

Dominic eyed the brown man.

"Don't ya call me that. Ya think you're special moving about with them lightwalkers. Ya think you have it all," he growled, betraying himself.

"I do and you have nothing—no matter what they pay you, you still have nothing."

"I'll have your red erela—like sweet strawberries in my mouth. I'll eat her and then I'll cut up that sweet flesh and really eat it."

"Romantic, but I have to let you know that she'd waste you to Oblivion before you laid a cell of skin on her," Dominic replied calmly and smoothly, despite the raging inferno inside him.

The brown man reached for Dominic's throat, but something stopped him. His angry features relaxed and he stared at Dominic without seeing. Lena pressed him back.

"You'll go to the front of the train and get off at the next stop. You've never heard of Dover and you've never heard of us," she told him.

The brown man's eyes blackened over. He looked frozen or dead under Lena's hand. Suddenly he stood and left the passenger car.

Dominic took a breath, relieved that they'd escaped the shade with no attention drawn. Lena stared at her hand, amazed by her triumph. A smile slowly blossomed on her tiny lips. Her fear left in the wake of learning of what she was capable. Dominic folded his arms and shut his eyes, boiling with anger as the shade's words repeated in his head. Despite his touchy mood, Lena placed her head on his arm. The warmth built in his throat. He pulled the coat tighter around him and it subsided. His attention slipped to the passing countryside beyond the window. Time was running out, and not just for Maiel.

* * *

Alex watched the lights of the city dwellings blink on, one by one, as the dark came. The long shadows and icy glow cast by the Perpetual Light made her feel cold. Her habit dangled at her side as her white hair waved in the breeze. Her dark eyes glistened with pain, but no other sign of her emotions touched her aged face. The sun set and her daughter was not home for another passing of the light. She just stared at the carvings, ribs, capitals, finials, and crockets. Her eyes traced the spires and buttresses, the mullion, piers and spandrels. Maiel could be found in none. All echoes. No breath.

Zach joined her at the rail of the balcony. He carried the same plain expression and bearing as his janya. Like him, there was no emotion that would cripple him into showing his concern to anyone. Grasping the rail, he leaned over the side and stared down at Zion. Far below he saw the inhabitants going about their duties and diversions. They seemed so insignificant; it was as if he could crush them with a stroke of his thumb.

"We won't see Gediel tonight," his amba said.

Zach shifted his attention to her. She stared at the distant skyline.

"The moon is just rising," Zach said.

"I'm afraid the task he's on will detain him longer than Mikhael said." Alex turned away from the White City and went back inside.

Zacharius followed his amba and they returned to the room of ways. Joel and Zaajah kept their vigil at the kapalanum, watching Dominic's every move. They looked troubled, but said nothing when he entered the room. He stepped around them, watching and waiting.

Joel looked to Zaajah, then to him. He hesitated to speak, but his features didn't hide his emotions. Something had happened while they were away. Whatever it was, it wasn't good.

"A soldier has found him. It must be working with Morgentus," Joel finally spoke.

"We knew he would show his face at some point," Alex said.

"He may need us again." Joel looked back into the kapalanum. "He's not even found where she is yet. At this rate he'll have each of us drop by to clean up his mess before he leaves England," Joel continued.

"Then we trust Lena can do her job without us," Alex said frankly.

"She's just a youngling," Zaajah reminded her.

"Lena is very special."

"Special isn't a weapon strong enough to fight the Lord of the Labyrinth," Joel said.

"Dominic can't rely on us to help him every time he runs into a delay. Not anymore. Lena will be fine and has her instructions. I trust she'll be wise and follow them."

"This isn't about getting Maiel back, is it?" Joel asked.

Their amba folded her hands and avoided his gaze. As an alder she was privy to certain information deemed unnecessary for the legions to know. Joel stepped around the font and stood before her, waiting for an explanation.

He made an imposing figure, but she was still as tall as he and his amba. She looked to him with surprise that he would try to bully her.

"Of course it's about getting her back. It just isn't the only thing we're concerned with," Alex said.

"Amba," Joel growled.

"One thing you must always know, my boy. Nothing's ever written in stone until it is finished."

"You led her to believe she's fallen," Joel said.

"She wasn't going to play hide-and-seek with him for us, not with the reasons we could give. Your khata's a stubborn girl."

"You think Dominic has turned against us?" Zaajah asked, hardly able to believe such a thing.

Maiel would have known long ago if that were the case, and spoken up to them.

"No. It isn't Dominic we're after either. Although he shows curious changes that don't come with rising," Alex said.

"Well, it's no wonder, with what you've done to him. He thinks his family is about to fall apart. Zaajah could've told you herself that he loves her more than anything," Joel said.

Alex regarded him tellingly. He had just answered his own question.

"If he can't learn that his loyalty is a love greater than anything he now feels for her — and where that loyalty should lie, then, well —"

"Why do we even bother to find a ketu if this is true," Joel muttered, going back to the waters. He stared at the vision and shook his head. "It makes no sense to put him through this. He's been through enough. So has she."

"A divorce is unprecedented," Zach said.

"I know that you don't understand, because your loyalty is already proven and given. One half of a whole belonging to the light."

"My wife doesn't confuse me. Nor does Dominic's family confuse him," Joel said.

"If you labored with his experiences, you'd not be confused? If Cora turned on us and decided the other path was the way she was meant to go, you wouldn't follow her."

"Don't be so sure, amba. If Cora made such an insane decision — I wager I'd follow her to whatever fool's end."

"Very noble, but very untrue. We both know it."

"And if janya left you for the darkness?"

"I would expect any one of us to end his existence," Alex replied.

Joel was stunned. He stammered, trying to find the words to express his disgust.

"I'm not saying I wouldn't be sad or very nearly broken. I'm just sure that ultimately my response would be the same response I'd have to any other shadowalker, if not worse."

"Then they're both being tested," Zaajah said hopeful.

"You're going to side with her?" Joel asked betrayed.

"I would hunt Ibajah if he became a danava. I understand what she means. We stand for what is right. Could you just become one of them? Could you hold onto something that would never again be as it was? A cruel specter of your past? She would no longer be Cora." She paused, watching his anger soften. "There'd be no love. Whatever you had would be utterly betrayed. Cora would be gone."

Joel stared into the kapalanum, hearing the sense of what she said, but unable to reconcile it inside his heart. Perhaps Joel was just too close to both their khata and Dominic. He knew him for so long and saw his unquestionable devotion to his family. It was simply not possible he would betray them. When Joel thought of Corabael, he knew it wasn't possible either. Even if his heart was clouded by his affection for his own wife, he was sure he knew his khata and her husband had the very same bond. But perhaps they wouldn't be at this impasse if Dominic had faith in his path.

Zach turned his attention back to his amba. He strode past her, pausing to place a consoling hand on her shoulder. It must have been very difficult to use her family to flush out the shadow. Her dark eyes went to her eldest's and he saw the glimmer of indecision that caused her pain. It wasn't Maiel, however, that they truly worried about. Not directly anyway. Her husband had the council concerned. Since Joel had mentioned his suspicions in Walhall, he'd found himself doubting the man's ability to finish the mission. And, just like his akha, he worried that Dominic relied too heavily upon their hand to clear his path. He never tried to think his way through on his own, and at this point, taking the time to do so was a detriment. Joel didn't truly speak for loyalty to Dominic. He feared the loss of his khata. As her twin, that would be devastating.

Zach paced the room, looking to each arch, their symbols lighting up under the track of his gaze. He wondered if he should leave them and go to Gediel. He was sure the watcher didn't need his help, but it might make him feel better to understand where he was on the mission. His amba's admission made it obvious why Gediel was involved. Someone other than Dominic was burning down and he suspected exactly who. Gediel was a brilliant choice to sniff him out. An alder who burned down wouldn't look to Uriel's units for a spy. His eye would be on Maiel's legion. However, something else needled him. Dominic had stagnated for too long and experienced the symptoms of another path, all while a shade haunted their home. Dominic had failed to learn the skills he needed to rise. The mission could very well damn him and his khata. Zach suspected this moment would have been his rising, if things played out different, and that was what confused them.

Zach lowered his head and drew a deep breath.

"Akha," Joel said.

Joel and Zaajah eyed him.

"What troubles you?" Joel asked.

Zach stalled, carefully forming his words. This was nothing they didn't already know. He didn't wish to cause them more concern by not using the best explanation he could find. Stepping to the font, he set his hands on the rim and looked at the image they monitored so closely. Dominic was at least moving again and the adventure could still go entirely in their favor.

"You remember when I brought one of my assigns back? Jeremiah, the boy. I wasn't approachable for some time. I had trouble allowing them to follow through with his difficult path, until I knew exactly what the intentions were," Zach said.

"Yes, I remember." Joel folded his arms on the rim of the kapalanum. The azure liquid turned his golden features green.

"I still did what was asked of me. That's what we do, because we know we can't know everything. Our loyalty to the king—our trust and love for him is what holds us together. The day you let that go is the day you'll become a shadow. I care very much for the souls I guard, like you care for Dominic, and would let no one cause them undue pains," Zach said.

Not being family, Jeremiah may have been a poor example, but it was a time they all knew it was very difficult for him. A time that was similar in terms of the potential losses. He hoped the example would make things clearer to his akha.

"I understand that," Joel said irritably.

"Then trust our amba. There's a shadow that threatens our kingdom from the inside. It has come before and it will again. Let us do our work to be rid of it, so she may heal," Zach said.

"Your surety will see you rise quickly," Joel said, still raw.

"You came to me, suspicious of him first," Zach reminded him.

Zach and his akha locked gazes. He understood Joel's anger. Their khata and her husband were caught in the middle of it, with no knowledge of what really happened. Either of them, or both, could be lost to the darkness if things didn't go as planned. Joel would suffer profoundly and thus the dominos would fall.

"Should I find Gediel?" Zach asked their amba, still holding his akha's gaze.

"He'll come when he's found something. Let us just hope he's quicker than I've a mind to believe," Alex said.

Their amba set herself on the stonework between the gates, crossing her legs and adjusting her robes. There was no more to be said until he did return.

CHAPTER 18

THE BROWN MAN WALKED to the front of the train with an indescribable focus. Inside of the first car before the engine, he stopped mid-track, slowly turned, and went back to the entry he had just left. He followed each step as instructed, literally. Morgentus stood in the stairwell, the scenery flashing behind him in a blur of colors. The man faced him, bleary-eyed from his run-in with the little duta guardian.

"Grag—you simple-minded fool," Morgentus rasped.

Grag's eyes cleared and the form he held shifted to once more emulate an el. He looked around, as though confused about where he was.

"You let a child command you away from your duty. I'll send Segrius in your place, something I should've done to begin with. Go back to Belial and tell him how you've failed him," Morgentus said, coming to the top step. He leaned close to the other atrin.

"Morgentus—"

"Don't speak my name. I'll not suffer for your mistakes. Not this close to having what I want," Morgentus hissed.

Grag stood still, watching his commander's eyes blaze. His lips parted, but his voice failed. Clacking bones behind his ear startled him. Over his shoulder, Segrius chattered his cruel teeth again. Grag frowned, knowing he had no friends so long as he was Morgentus's soldier. They would thoughtlessly betray him to get one step ahead. His mind raced as he formulated a plan to preserve his life for a while longer.

"Take him to Belial and report that I've found the human. I move to set the trap," Morgentus ordered.

Segrius cocked his head in acknowledgement. Then the serpent latched onto Grag's thick form. He hissed in his ear, telling him his time had come to an end. Segrius had sought the seat for years. Now he at last obtained it.

Morgentus smiled and said, "You're not going to get a taste of the pigeon, Grag. I would have enjoyed watching you do your worst. Why can none of you just do as I ask?"

Morgentus turned and clawed a hole in the fabric of space. A smoking tear appeared before the train exit.

"Return to me quickly—bring me back a company of your servants. We end this by tonight," Morgentus instructed his new chief.

Segrius bared his teeth and jumped through the tear. The opening knitted together behind them. Watching the blurred scenery, Morgentus plotted his next steps. Subtlety was required. He could not claim the human for his plan if he didn't take care to ensnare him. The soul was too aware of their efforts to do so. However, the nails he drove into his sattva, when he dared to take Maiel back, were already working. With a little patience from his prince, Dominic would fall into their hands without raising another finger. Unfortunately, the prince wasn't known for patience. He wanted his war now.

Morgentus entered the second passenger car and made his way through the rest until he reached the back of the train. The passengers' guards watched him pass, their eyes full of suspicion, if not fear. Standing outside the last car, he watched his quarry enjoying their last moments of peace. Dominic was busy taking in the scenery, unaware of the threat that lurked so near. His small guardian was turned around, watching a pair of old people converse and cuddle. It was a normal scene.

The demon's eyes swept the compartment, wondering if he could strike at that moment. There were only humans inside and each was protected by one pathetic guardian. He turned away, wishing at least one shadowborn had been in there. If he made a move without another of his kind to even the odds, he might find himself overpowered by the lightwalkers inside.

Morgentus stepped down the stairwell and disappeared in a whirl of smoke. While he waited for a better time to acquire the king piece from the chessboard, he would need to set the board to make everything fall into place more quickly. There was one who owed him a favor and could assure his success. He smiled, stepping out of the smoke onto the banks of the River Styx. The water steamed with icy fog. He stepped along the edge, waiting. The water stirred and he looked just in time to see something move beneath the surface.

"Leviathan," Morgentus called. "I have need of a favor—you owe me."

Morgentus knelt on the bank and touched the water. It burned his skin and he grimaced, sucking in a breath. The suddenness of the pain turned his eyes the tell-tale black. He wiped his frozen fingers on his jacket. A section of fabric sizzled, crinkled up, and disintegrated. He scanned the surface of the river. The banks were quiet and the waters moved swiftly toward the heart of Jahannam. His friend was being reclusive that day.

"Leviathan!" Morgentus called again, veins throbbing.

A tentacle shot across the water, knocking him backward. Morgentus scrambled back, hissing a threat at the prince. He must have caught him in a bad mood. The tentacle waved in front of him, swelled like an onion, until a face peered down at him. Morgentus caught his breath, rethinking his demanding tones.

"Why do you come to Styx, Baron?" Leviathan asked in a gasping voice.

"I need your help," Morgentus admitted.

"You need help? Why don't you seek help from Belial?" Leviathan said, drawing higher out of the river.

Morgentus got to his feet and brushed the dust off his coat.

"I've found the husband of the erela I seek. If I can subdue him, drag him down to us, she will be mine," Morgentus replied, finding himself unable to look away from the eyes of the face.

"Petty desire. Why would I concern myself so you can satisfy your lust of some duta," Leviathan replied.

"There will be much suffering if she falls. It will fill your waters with enough fare to keep you full for generations," Morgentus replied.

The face looked interested.

"What need you of me?"

"I need you to help my soldiers. They'll push him over the edge. You'll bring him through the Domdaniel and trap him there. If they know I've taken him, they'll know where to look. They won't think of you."

"Is he to be returned once you have the duta?"

"Do what you will with him once you take him. I don't want anyone left who can turn her back to the light. He tricked me before. Not again," Morgentus said.

"Belial has told all of the princes you aren't to be trusted, baron," Leviathan said.

"Are any of us trustworthy, atrin?"

A smile slowly twisted the corners of Leviathan's mouth.

"He'll be on the last channel ferry from Dover to Calais. I hope to see you there," Morgentus said.

Morgentus stepped back and was enveloped in a black cloud. When he appeared again, it was at the iron gate of the church in Hungary. Night had descended over the Earth, making his abilities greater. He could almost smell her; she was barely protected by the walls of the structure. The thing called faith of these humans and his atrin amused him. What good was plaster and wood against his strength? He grinned. They almost had it right, but their constant bickering kept them easy to manipulate and spoiled their efforts. Nothing and nowhere was sacred, except the perpetual light, a place his kind could never get near without great suffering. It was all that protected Zion from them, but not for long. He rubbed his hands together and stalked toward the church. There were a few hours to spend before his soldiers were in place. While he waited, he hoped to thank his esteemed atrin for taking such good care of his property.

A familiar hiss called his name. Morgentus turned to Segrius, who waited at the gate beyond the weak human ward.

"Our forces are in place. I'll delay him until the last run of the ferry, when Leviathan'll be ready to take him. If anything goes wrong, I'll send a shadowborn to follow him. The girl may be some trouble, but I've something in mind that'll make it easier," Segrius said.

"Very good, Segrius. Remind me to make it worth your while for not making use of you sooner. Fail me and I'll have a new coat from your hide," Morgentus said, facing the church where Oriael hid.

Segrius inclined his head and bared his teeth. He snapped his jaws sharply. The danava disappeared in the next moment, a spiral of black. The earth was scorched where he once stood. Smoke dissipated into the air, leaving the scent of sulfur.

Morgentus opened the church's front door with a thrust of energy from his outstretched hand. The barrier collapsed inward and banged against the inner wall of the building. Morgentus stepped into the nave unbarred by symbols or holy relics. He looked about the expanse, calculating his next move. The church was dimly lit, as there was no service that evening. Not a soul could be detected. He stepped up the aisle and the prayer candles burst forth with rabid flame. He grinned, chuckling to himself. Their trinkets were so much fun to play with.

"Your majesty," he said, bowing toward the crucifix.

Straightening, he laughed and watched his existence distress the interior. Tremors rippled through the building as if it wanted to shake him out. So, his atrin had the guardians ward their little palace. What a weak-minded little fool, he mused.

"Where to begin?" he exclaimed.

Morgentus raised his hands and cast the bibles from the shelves, rending leaves from their bindings. The volumes exploded overhead and fell like confetti, a shower of useless nothing, an homage to the marditavya Charlemagne who created them. Throwing his arms forward, he sent the pews sliding toward the entrance. They made an impossibly stacked pile to either side of the doors, pinning them open. Turning round and round, he lost himself in the ecstasy of trashing something precious to his long-lost sibling; he was hardly able to choose what next to spoil. His eyes settled on the pretty glass. Placing his hands over his heart, he danced in the now clear space. The glass of the windows melted, running like molten rainbow sugar.

"Shadowalker!" a voice called from the door.

Morgentus turned, hoping to find Oriael. Instead, four guardians stood inside the door with their swords drawn. He laughed and continued his dance, spinning round and round until he neared them. Then he took his leave, disappearing in a black cloud. His laugh mocked them, filling the church with contempt. Skulking imps joined the chorus, mocking the light-walkers who once threatened them. The pews fell and the candles went out. His akha was a coward, but they would meet whether he wanted to or not.

* * *

The train rolled to a stop at Dover station. Dominic rubbed his eyes and stood, slinging his pack onto his back. Once the danava left them, he was able to focus on some rest. Strength had fully returned to his limbs and his mind was clear. He stepped out of the train car and wandered around the station, stopping to inquire about the ferry. A surly old man behind a dirty counter pointed and went back to his work beneath the information sign. Dominic stood outside, guessing which way the old man had meant. The sun was bright and the sky clear. With such fine weather, the ferry should be running on time.

Spotting a café across the street, Dominic decided to ask for directions again. A horn blew, startling him mid-run. A taxi stood a few feet from him. The driver leaned out his window to yell. Dominic apologized and waved back before continuing across. He shook his head, wondering why he hadn't seen it. As he muttered a curse, he looked for Lena. She stood on the sidewalk outside the café watching him.

"Why didn't you say something?" he asked.

"Is it my job to make sure you cross a street safely too? I thought you could handle it on your own. I was wrong." Lena replied, sounding more and more like Callidora.

"I'm just distracted." Dominic frowned.

"You're clumsy and forgetful, too," Lena said.

"Let's just focus on finding the ferry," Dominic said. "I want to get on board as soon as possible. No more delays."

Lena smiled. "Why don't you just flag a cab?"

Dominic stopped moving. He shut his eyes. Releasing his breath in irritation, he turned and walked back toward the station.

"Hail a cab. It's hail a cab," he snottily remarked, sounding like one of his sons.

A black cab pulled up as soon as he raised his hand. He and Lena climbed in and he asked for the ferry. The driver turned his ratty head and explained it might not be running. There was fog on the channel. He said the sea was strange that way, could be perfectly calm one minute and a gale force the next. There was most likely a storm coming off the sea. Dominic nodded and said that he had to go to the ferry regardless. The man shrugged and drove the car as directed by his passenger, keeping watch of him in the rearview mirror. Dominic remained quiet and held his gaze on the town passing by. The sight of shadow and light competing for atman depressed him. He was tired of the battling and muttered to himself about it. He licked his lips to shut off the whispers but it was too late.

The driver continued to inspect him from a pair of strange eyes. Like the brown man in the bathroom a few hours ago, this guy wasn't right. The cabby made him uncomfortable for good reason: there was no guardian accompanying him.

Dominic rubbed his leg. Drumming his fingers on his knee, he tried not to look panicked. He hoped his demeanor would just come across as rushed, but if this was another shade or shadowborn, then it mattered little. The burning in his throat returned. It was slight, barely detectable, as if he had a sore throat from pollen. He cleared his voice and tightened his coat around him. The moment he took the jacket off, he knew it would be worse than ever, possibly spread to every part of him. How long had this been happening, held at bay by his wife's resonance? No wonder he'd failed her. He was a marditavya and could only seek to destroy the lightwalker he professed to love. Tears stung his eyes, but he refused to cry. Now wasn't the time to lose himself in self-pity. The clock ticked. If he found Maiel, that would prove whose side he was on and that would be the end of it. After all, it was his choice and the shades couldn't take that from him.

Balling his fist, Dominic pressed the knuckles of one hand to his mouth. A memory, decades old, floated above the surface of his mind. He tried to choke it down, but it refused to relent. His hand slid over the seat and he grabbed his bag. Holding the pack close, he fought the emotions. Then he wondered if there might be a purpose to it, so he let his mind wander to find out.

"I'll never leave you," he heard himself tell her.

The view of a hospital prison was less frightening than the reality that had been hers. The memory was just a faded image of the nightmare.

Maiel was locked behind a door with a small window on top. It resembled a door from a hospital, including a number painted on the surface. Between the wire squares in the glass, he could see her sitting on her bed, staring into nothingness. She was just a phantom of the erela he knew. The fire of her hair was dulled, a copper in desperate need of polishing. She looked barely older than when he left her at the station to go with his unit; he had been a young officer ready to beat back Jerry. Ten years had passed, but he clearly recalled going off to Europe, just in time to train for some big offensive, where most would die before a full day in France was through. There were rumors they'd be crossing the channel to give the Germans a taste of their own medicine. The thought filled him with the arrogance of his gender and age. He told her not to worry, they'd be there to cheerlead the Brits. He had been so wrong. It took a while, but they did make the crossing. He didn't remember much more than that. A couple days, maybe weeks, passed after the beach fight. Something about a field and too tired to keep marching. A bombed-out town. His chest hurt.

"Annie-belle," his voice came again. "I'll never leave you. If this is where you're going to stay. Then I'm here too."

"You're dead," her voice returned, echoing off his skull. "You can't be here. I can't see you anymore. If the doctor finds out I've been talking to you again—what do I do if the doctor finds out? I can't. Please go away." Her voice stung his ears, it was shrill with fear.

"He's not a doctor, Annie. You're not in the hospital anymore. They can't hurt you, but he can. I need you to hear me. I need you to open this door. I promised you I would love you forever and I'm sorry I didn't listen, but I'm here now, Doll Face. I didn't leave you. I've been right here. Please see me. You just have to wake up and open your door. You didn't do anything wrong. I promise. It was my fault, Angel. No one's gonna be mad at you, Annie. Please."

Maiel shivered several times then crossed the room to hide in the corner. He couldn't reach her. Every time was the same. She would shake like that, in revulsion, like her skin was crawling, or she lost control because of the shocks, and hide in the corner. First the tears would come, and suddenly she would explode, tearing the room apart until she fainted and left the Astral. The process would start again, still trapped in her nightmare, but this time trapped far from help in Acheron as a prisoner of her own guilt. That guilt was fed by the demon, who developed a rather strong infatuation for her.

Dominic saw the pale face, grinning mockingly at him. Joel stood at his shoulder watching one end of the passage. Zaajah watched the other. Callidora was supposed to be there, but he couldn't see her. Perhaps his memory was fading. Perhaps she went to report to Annie's alder, Maxiel. It was just an old dream now anyway. She was Maiel, not Annie.

Panic rose up from Dominic's stomach. They had to leave before Morgentus got to them. The baron's touch would leave a permanent mark. They weren't travelling there in dreams. They used the paths of the astral world, which was much like the Avernus, woven in and through everything, providing access to her thoughts when they escaped the labyrinth, where her tormentor threatened them with the multitude of his servants if they dared to trespass.

The mission was risky, with real consequences, and he had a questionable recollection of the time. The goal was to plant the seed in hopes that Maiel would remember herself. Then they could no longer hold her in either place. Sleeping or waking, the hospital was her prison. Morgentus and her guilt made sure of that. Dominic's heart ached at the thought.

Morgentus's laughter mocked him. A hand cupped the back of his head and he stood alone at the door of her prison. His mind slipped between worlds, between realities. Whispers lulled him to a deeper space. Sharp barbs penetrated the soft flesh of his throat. Opening his mouth to call out, he found his voice was gone. His eyes popped open and he stood at the mouth of the astrals, blinking at the stone pavers of the Gyuto garden. The pain faded.

Dominic returned to the present. His declaration to her at the door of her prison vibrated in his head. Indeed, he wouldn't leave her, not for anything. Whatever happened, she would be at his side through it all. She was his wife and everything to him. The twin to his atman. If she fell, he fell too. No being in all existence would rend that bond.

"Right. We're here, mate," the driver said, interrupting his thoughts.

The port terminal was now before him. A clear sky stretched out as far as he could see in any direction. His eyes flicked to the driver. He passed him a few notes and climbed out of the cab, refusing the change. The man thanked him and drove off. Dominic scowled at the scene. Sattva without vessels wandered in search of a way across the water. Duta mingled among them with the occasional shade. Out in the open of daylight, danava avoided being too troublesome, sneaking a taste here and there. The duta responded with force, slamming down a red ash staff. His blue hair waved in the breeze. He stared hard at Dominic and Lena for doubting his authority, but he said nothing, and returned to his post. Aeris Order guardians were a touchy lot. Dominic grimaced. There wasn't an Order that wasn't full of haughty duta.

"A ferry's coming in." Lena pointed. She took his hand. "Hurry. It'll probably be going back out."

They found the ticket desk and the girl behind the counter reiterated what the taxi driver said. There was fog on the water a few miles out. It hadn't rolled inland yet, but was forcing the boats to stay in port. She apologized for the inconvenience. Attempting not to notice the gremlin gnawing on the counter or reveal his displeasure at its presence, Dominic thanked her. He wandered away, figuring out what to do next.

Lena backed away from the desk, watching the woman from narrowed eyes. She also seemed doubtful of the explanation. In fact, she looked angry. Dominic walked toward the fence and watched the people unloading from the ferry. They looked happy, busy, or indifferent. To enjoy any of those moods apart from his current circumstances would have been like a vacation. Instead, he was stuck there on a mission that seemed impossible to even start. There was no evidence of fog, unless it was what looked like a slip of land on the horizon.

"Something's not right," Lena said.

"Let's find a place to stay until the ferry runs again," Dominic whispered.

Lena followed behind him and they walked along the docks until he found a place they could rest. It was a quiet pub, looking much like any other in England, except for its lack of shades. It afforded a view of the port and that was all he needed. Dominic seated himself at the window and waited for someone to come over. His attention was on a boat slipping back out to sea, loaded with passengers and vehicles. He frowned and turned back in time to see a rough-looking woman stepping toward him. She smiled and smacked her chewing gum.

"What'll I get for you, love?" she asked in a husky voice.

Dominic ordered a beer and said he needed a minute with the menu. The woman grabbed it from his hands and walked away telling him she'd bring him the pot roast and potatoes. She told him he looked right starved. Dominic gave a small smile and turned his attention back to the sea. Ships came and went with no apparent delay and the sky still looked clear. He sighed, sensing he'd been lied to, but Lena said nothing of an enemy being near. Perhaps the ticket girl just hated Americans and gave him a hard time. Gremlins were imps, just annoyances. They didn't watch over shadowborn.

"Taking the ferry over?" the woman asked. She returned with a large glass of beer and his lunch. She set it in front of him. He thought she would have thrown it at him with his luck of late.

"I was going to, but the girl at the ticket counter told me a fog is rolling in," Dominic replied.

"Did she? I bet I know which one. Always being a troublemaker. Well, I'll tell you this, there's clear weather for three days straight. Not a drop of rain. That's not normal, but that's what there is."

"I had a feeling by the lay of the sky," Dominic replied.

Dominic sipped his beer and took a forkful of meat. While he chewed, the woman stood by his table watching outside. The pub was almost empty. A cat languished high up on the back of the bar shelf. A couple sat in the back booth, huddled up and whispering. Their guardians danced in the middle of the room to no music. The bartender wiped down his bar for the tenth time since Dominic entered. His swarthy unseen companion stood with his arms folded, watching everyone carefully. Only one man sat at the bar. Arms folded, he stared at nothing while his guardian tried to convince him to leave. At Dominic's back, he heard a couple guys chatting about fishing. He guessed the auburn-haired guardian sitting at the end of the bar facing him was the waitress's. She looked like an alder. It was rare for them to guard a human. What was not rare was her stare of dislike in his direction.

"Well, would you look at that," the woman said.

The waitress's eyes widened as she watched out the window. Dominic turned his head to see what had her so awestruck. The channel disappeared behind a blanket of white mist creeping into the port. At least he hadn't been lied to. After watching the other ferry take off, he thought he had screwed things up again. Still, he was anxious to get his journey underway, but by the look of the sudden stormy sky, that wouldn't be for some time.

"I guess the girl was right," the waitress said, slapping his arm.

"That makes me feel a bit better," Dominic said.

"Got somewhere to be, huh?" the woman asked intuitively.

"Meeting up with my wife — at the turul, in uh —"

"You going to Budapest? I spent my honeymoon in Budapest. Course, my wonderful husband had some work while we were there. Cheeky boy, but I miss him, cheap as he was."

The waitress was just about the age Annie would have been if she had lived. He watched her stare at the fog and smiled. She must have lost her husband in the war too. His gaze shifted to Lena and she grinned at him. A sparkle lit up her eyes and her wings perked up. This was a bit of luck, as she would say, regardless of the delay. Just maybe the whole thing was orchestrated to help him find his bearings. He felt his hope swell. Now, they just had to cross the channel to be on their way.

"It's a great city. I love the architecture," Dominic said, making things up to keep her talking.

"The royal palace is just lovely. They have those birds all over the country, you know. Ugly things, but they seem to like them."

Dominic nodded. It was the most beautiful bird in the world to him right then. He shoveled the pot roast in his mouth and drank, renewed by this chance encounter. He felt ravenous for the first time since being there. At this rate, in another few days, he'd have to experience a mortal death to get back home. So long as he completed the mission successfully, he didn't care and would feed his body to ensure it.

"You stick around as long as you need," the waitress told him, going back to work. She sat at the bar and talked with the man sitting there.

Dominic looked around the room again. No one seemed interested in him for once. He decided to fish out the atlas again and see if he could map their route. The rain poured down in sheets, blinding their view from the window. Lena watched it with longing growing on her face. He had seen the expression before. Whenever it rained, Maiel moped about the house, missing the light that nourished her.

"Getting bored yet?" Dominic whispered to her.

Lena shook her head, watching the water come down on the panes. Dominic stared, wondering why they had chosen the child. He thought about her display of skill on the train. She was smart and kind of strong, but Luthias and he would have been in Budapest by now. The guardian would have been strong enough to carry him if he had to. Of course, Luthias might have needed reminding to slow down so Dominic could keep up. Luthias felt a kinship with Maiel; he was like another brother. That sentiment almost guaranteed the guardian would've abandoned him to run off to her.

"Do you need anything?" Dominic asked, regretting his outburst earlier.

Lena looked at him surprised. It was the first time he had considered her needs. She looked at the wet panes and back to him. She ran her hand over the surface of the table and shook her head no again. Dominic waited a moment before returning to his atlas. He flipped through the pages, figuring out a decent route, in case they couldn't find better transportation than their feet. Dominic felt eyes on him. He looked to Lena, but she watched the rain. He scanned the room and found the alder staring at him still. He gave a slight nod of his head and went back to his book. The alder had other ideas, joining them at their table.

"You don't even recognize me," the alder said, peering through him with gray eyes.

Dominic looked up from his maps, a bit put off by the intrusion. She smiled at him, sparkling gray eyes full of amusement. Trying to focus better on the somewhat familiar face, he squinted. Realizing that someone might be watching their exchange, he scanned the room again and then returned to her. She now sat beside Lena.

"Oh, don't worry. They can't see me or hear you. They're perfectly distracted by their own troubles. You seriously don't recognize me?" the alder continued.

Dominic shook his head. He almost recognized the voice and demeanor, but he was sure he didn't know her. She laughed.

"I'm your dear wife's amba. It's Alex, silly boy," she said.

Dominic stared. For his whole life Alex had been the mature gray-haired and dark-eyed svarg alder, always on the cusp of rising, who never quite made the leap. Dominic thought she stalled her evolution for her children, in order to care for them while they were still small, despite being able to return to them once she had grown again. In that she was unlike his own progenitors, who abandoned him for their own progress. Alex's husband, however, had left his family to rise alone. Gragrafel rose to become a svarg just after the birth of his twins, Joel and Maiel, and rose again to principality before Maiel's ketu. Both lived through a rising each, refusing to abandon the children they had in their previous resonance, or have any more. Duta could be odd like that. Their attachments to their younglings were strong and held for many generations.

"Alex," Dominic said astonished. Regaining himself he asked, "Why are you here?"

"To warn you," she replied.

Dominic put the atlas back in his bag.

"You're being followed by Morgentus. He'll be on the ferry this evening. I can't clear your path and get you across any sooner. There are just too many and Mikhael is nowhere to be found. I'm sorry," she said hurriedly, ending with a tone that sounded like empathy.

"Perhaps he's located Maiel."

"No. It's not that."

"Is anyone else looking for her?"

"Just you, Dominic. You must succeed."

"Then why don't you help me? We could blink there. I've found the city she's in."

"You must do this on your own. You know why," she replied, as she stood and walked away, sounding tired. Alex looked over her shoulder at him, standing before the symbol that opened her way home. "The armies are on the move. Secure my daughter before the battle begins. Take care with your next call. Our numbers grow thin."

Dominic watched her leave, half thinking of giving chase as the hole closed like mercury drops flowing back together. He slammed a fist on the table and cursed. The loud sounds captured the attention of the others in the pub. He frowned and apologized for startling them, lying that he nearly dropped his fork. They went back to their conversations. His gaze swept the room.

The divisions in the room became a little clearer with Alex's leaving. The waitress's guardian was the man sitting at the bar and the one whispering to him was her dead husband. She had been talking to the stoic bartender, whose guardian was hidden on a high shelf: a young muse who fancied the shape of a cat.

Dominic rubbed his head. It was all getting to be too much. He could see why they didn't have the sight while incarnated. Everything was too busy and distracting this way. He returned to his meal, worrying that he was weakening without enough meditation. Food was the only other way he could sustain himself, despite the risks. Scowling, he sensed Lena's attention on him.

"She meant well," Lena whispered.

"Maybe so, but we wouldn't be here if they started doing as they should have a long time ago."

"You'd blame them for this? They've only ever helped you. You know that's true," Lena said.

"No, Lena. You're just as fooled as the rest. They don't let us get wings. Why do you think they sent you with me? There's always one more test, one more mission." Dominic paused, making sure no one looked in his direction.

Lena's shoulders sagged. She folded her hands and watched him, unsure of what to say, but showing that her heart was saddened by his words.

Dominic continued to eat. The hot food soothed the fire in his throat as it slid down. He drank the pint of beer, hoping to numb the pain by other means. From here out, he would run this mission his way. He grabbed his pack and went to the waitress.

"Do you know a place I could get a room until the ferries are running again?"

The waitress smiled. She pointed her two fingers, pinching a cigarette.

"I'll ring you when I hear." She winked.

Dominic nodded and flashed a smile. "That would be lovely."

The waitress took a drag on her cigarette and watched him go, smiling and shaking her head. He stepped out the door and walked in the direction she pointed. The rain still came down hard. Lightning flashed. A distant rumble of thunder rolled across the port. A sign for an inn swung in the wind a few doors away. He quickly made his way toward it. Stepping through the door, he shook off the water in his hair and looked at the dark sky. He hoped the storm would burn itself out in a couple hours but frowned, doubtful of any such luck.

CHAPTER 19

ORIUS SPOKE TO A CURIOUS DETECTIVE in the broken doorway of his church. The police tried to make sense of the extensive vandalism, but he had few answers to their probing questions. In the early hours of the morning, he and the brothers had been woken by the guardians to be told the demon had returned. The time since did little to wake slumbering minds to the reality of what had happened. Exhausted and confused, they went to the church to find that a townsperson had summoned the police. The sirens pierced the night sky as they careened up the street to rescue the parish priest.

Despite their groggy uselessness, the police interviewed each brother, jotting down notes on all that was said. Others busily snapped photographs of the damage and discussed the damage in whispers of astonishment. Their demeanor was slow and stern at all times, despite the awe the scene should have inspired.

A few patrol cars carelessly parked on the street with flashing lights. The commotion of their arrival had woken whoever managed to sleep through the attack. It was just as well. Orius didn't relish the idea of having to explain his brother to the authorities. They would have him quickly committed.

Fresh from their comfortable beds, the locals stood in the open gate, inspecting the scene for themselves. Most hoped for a bit of scandal to brighten their dull lives. In response to their curiosity, a police line had been drawn to keep them back and to prevent spoiling of any evidence. To their dismay, the scandal they'd hoped for turned out to be spiteful devastation.

The state of the church was simply heartbreaking. Orius had spent two decades there, speaking from the pulpit and from his heart. He'd survived the war and the recent upheaval in their country. The church had also survived these events. Through it all, he'd helped the people of his congregation survive; he'd told them of a place he once knew and barely remembered, he'd assisted them in major life events, and bid them farewell when their lives came to an end. He'd served them regardless of the shadow they harbored or the light they fostered. Each was an atman who required respect. He merely hoped to reinforce that choice with the best chance of being right. Tonight, he saw the fruits of that labor smashed and spoiled on the ground. These were the things that aged him. His hair grew in grayer in recent years. He looked little more than fifty years of age to them, but he saw himself as a recidia closer to death with each day's passing. At least he assumed so, recidia aged through their experiences like normal duta with each proof of their lessening resonance, only then drawing closer to the death that would release them.

Though the books might not be salvageable, and the stained glass certainly not, the space was still well intact. Candles could be replaced. Someone would manage to get them more books and the village was likely to do what they could to make sure their pews were whole once more. Vandalism such as this was pointless in accomplishing the perpetrator's cause because it always served to bring the victims together in response. Indeed, this was a message and not an action to put them out. Morgentus told them he could touch them whenever he wanted and that he wasn't pleased with them barring access to Bethiah.

Orius crossed his arms and nodded in response to another question. The detective was all business, as if he suspected the brothers capable of such an atrocity. He was so very naive for a human, with a very old and strict guardian. Orius rubbed the tips of his fingers together, thankful for the increased number of guardians. If they sent a shadowborn, it could make things very difficult for them. The man stared at him, waiting for a response, but Orius's attention was on the broken church. Orius's eyes, glowering with anger, swept over the room again.

"Thank you, Father, for your time. We'd like to have another day before you begin cleaning up. I understand your reluctance, but if we're to catch the men who did this, it'd be most helpful," the detective said.

"Yes, yes. Of course," Orius agreed, just to be rid of him.

The detective held out his hand to usher Orius from his nave. Orius reluctantly complied. He emerged from the church and immediately received the voices of the townspeople. He hesitated as police tape was put up across the door. The lights of the patrol cars flashed on his face. The people watched from the gate to see if he would answer them. He wished he could have sent Bethiah in his stead. She would have offered them more comfort. He went to them, hoping he offered something, even if it was slight. To his surprise, the resilient parishioners gave comfort to him. They expressed their concern for him and the brothers, and wanted to be sure they were all right. He assured them their church would return to pristine condition soon, and that service would be given in other buildings until the reconstruction was finished.

Their smiles filled him with hope. He returned the expression, sweeping his gaze over them. There was a man there, shadowborn by no choice of his own. He removed the cap from his head and offered his carpentry skills to the brothers for no cost. Orius gratefully accepted, much to the chagrin of the man's dark overseer.

The brothers congregated on the lawn behind him. Their usually pleasant faces were contorted with tattered emotions. He left the congregation to join them, noting that Father Gallo was absent. When he inquired, he was told the father had gone to guard their guest. Gallo had rightly surmised the vandalism was caused by their friend, not a random hoodlum. Orius hurried to the rectory, fearing he'd left his friends at the hands of evil. Bethiah would compromise herself to protect Father Gallo, despite the presence of his guardian, but the erela who shadowed the young priest was in danger as well. She wasn't strong enough to thwart Morgentus.

Orius raced up the stairs and found the door to her room closed. The rosary was still strung about the knob. Voices whispered. He knocked on the door and entered, fearing he would find his brother within. Instead, he found Father Gallo sitting beside Bethiah on her cot, marking up his well-worn bible. They looked engrossed in their work, not bothered in the least by the recent events. The dark guardian leaned against the dresser, turning her ochre head in his direction with a lazy glance.

"Father Gallo," Orius interrupted.

The younger priest looked up from making notes in the margin of his book. He closed the cover and gave a soft smile.

"How bad is it?"

"Bad," Orius replied.

"I apologize for this," Bethiah said.

"It's not your fault," Orius reminded her.

"I should've stayed home and met with the alders, accepting my censure. It was my duty. This wouldn't have happened if I didn't run," she said.

"But it did happen. We'll heal, Bethiah. Don't hang your head in shame. That gives too much power to your enemy," Orius said. He made her look at him, cupping her pretty face in his hands. He smiled reassuringly. "There, now. Only one person deserves blame for the desecration and that's the danava who hunts you. Someday, soon, you'll make him pay his debts."

"What've the police said?" Father Gallo asked.

"They insist it was vandals with flame torches. Ridiculous idea—I let them believe it. The case will go unsolved."

"Torches couldn't melt the glass without setting the wood on fire," Father Gallo said, looking distracted by his thoughts.

"They found a scorch mark beside the gate as proof. Said that was where they lit it." Orius folded his arms and crossed his legs.

"Are we still to go to Esztergom?" Bethiah asked.

"Most certainly. Our little parish can't handle much more attention from our friend. Hopefully the seat of our church will intimidate him enough to keep him away," Orius said.

The erela looked concerned. He knew she had no faith in their trinkets and baubles. He didn't either, not really, but he did have faith that the presence of statues and images of her kind would reignite the flame of her atman. This trip would do her good, regardless of the risk. In the meantime, they needed to prepare. He stood, hesitant to leave.

"Perhaps, for now, we should stick together," he said.

"You think he'll return?" Father Gallo asked.

"I know he will," Orius said ominously. "Come. We've much to do to prepare for our journey."

Orius went to the dresser and gathered some clothing. When he turned back, Bethiah had fitted her armaments on her person, her helmet under her arm. He gave her a nod and then led the way to his office downstairs. Entering the room, he tossed the garments on the couch. The erela explored, enjoying the globe and other odd objects he kept there. He let her occupy herself while he went to his desk and opened the top drawer. In the back, he kept a relic of his past. He pulled the penannular out of hiding. The circular device, a silver tree with a ruby knothole, glinted in the lamplight. It was the symbol of the Powers and Seal of the Astral.

"You still have it," she said.

"Yes—it's dead. The atman died shortly after I fell," Orius said sadly.

"It's just asleep. It'll wake when you're restored," she assured him, picking it up.

Bethiah studied it for a moment, curious about the piece. The tree seal slipped aside and beneath was a decurio moon shield. She replaced the tree and passed it back, quite surprised. He gathered they never mentioned his order in the lesson. Orius took the useless bit of jewelry in hand. An ever so slight vibration tingled his fingers. His eyes went to hers and she offered him the slightest of smiles. While they were occupied with the penannular, Father Gallo pulled a suitcase from the closet and packed it with the clothes Orius brought. He then joined them, unaware of the exchange.

"Will you bring that with you?" Father Gallo asked, holding the satchel open.

Orius nodded and gave it to him to drop in his bag. Father Gallo did so and zipped the bag closed. The elder priest stared for a long time, making his friends wonder. He suddenly sucked in a breath and spoke.

"On second thought, Father Gallo, I wish you and the brothers to keep it for me," Orius said.

"You will be returning?" Father Gallo questioned, disquieted by the suggestion.

"I will return when Bethiah is safe again," Orius said, smiling. He laughed a little. "It does me no good and I don't want Geitz to claim it because of that. It is our relic and I know it will be in safe hands if left here," he explained.

Father Gallo nodded and took the small shield back out of the case. He tucked it in his pocket. His eyes sparkled with pride at being given the duty.

"Gather the brothers in the flower garden. Tell them I wish us to pray for the church," Orius instructed his assistant.

Father Gallo nodded and set the case down. He left quickly to carry out his orders, leaving Bethiah alone with Orius. She wandered along the bookcase reading the spines. Orius went to her side and looked the volumes over. He had a strange feeling he wouldn't look on them ever again. Her arrival had him thinking of moving on again. Perhaps they were meant to go together and find their way back to the light. Her atman still burned brightly. Though her form became mortal, he still sensed who she really was.

"I didn't want to say so in front of Father Gallo, but—we may not return," Orius told her. "To protect the brothers from the danava, I think it wiser for us to stay away."

"Orius," she said.

Her expression shifted. The idea caused her pain, but she must know he was right. She had nothing to say in rebuttal other than his name. The protest would have stayed him any other time, but his primary duty was to protect the men who had housed him safely for all these years. If they stayed at the monastery, his brother would wait and reach out against more than just the priests. Morgentus was strong enough to best them on his own, but the baron liked to be thorough. He'd bring others. The risk to his friends and the town was too great. He owed them the forethought to realize this.

"I won't argue the matter with you," Orius said.

"I won't argue the matter with you. The baron will hurt them if he wants. If we're not here to threaten him, then that makes it easier," she replied.

"He'll follow after you," Orius said.

Bethiah frowned, believing she knew better. As she saw the matter, Morgentus desecrated the church to exhibit both his supremacy and displeasure with them. The damage was a warning that he planned to return to thank the priests for keeping her from him. His little brother was dangerously obsessed. Not only would he return to this parish, Morgentus would follow them to Esztergom. There simply was no escape from his reach, not in Samsara. Orius offered a small smile to console these fears. Leaving was the best chance the brothers had.

"The brothers are waiting," Orius said, not wishing to fuel her fears or fan the flames of an argument.

Bethiah inclined her head and preceded him from the room. He took up his bag and set it at the rectory door. Following her to the garden, he found the brothers still gathering under Father Gallo's instruction. Once the men had arranged themselves, he found himself hard-pressed for words. He cleared his throat to buy a second more. The messenger's fears were rubbing off on him, awakening long memories.

"Tomorrow—or rather, later this morning, we'll leave to meet with Archbishop Geitz. Of course, as you know, I don't need to beg you to be vigilant while I'm absent. This display, this abuse that was done to you, I fear it won't be his last efforts on our behalf. We crossed a vulgar thing by harboring our friend behind these walls. The shadow will have you know the grave wound it suffered for our kindness to her."

Orius looked at each face. They listened to him stoic as statue warriors. He was speechless from his fear of what they faced and his love of each of them. Bethiah wasn't the only light they harbored in their walls that threatened their peace, if not their lives. Morgentus saw him in the garden the first night and the baron was sure to be overflowing with plans of revenge. The brothers faced costs they couldn't afford.

"Let us pray for the safety of our home," Orius said, pulling Bethiah to her knees at his side.

The erela eyed him, confused. He patted her shoulder, knowing this was a strange practice to her. Orius led them in a prayer, though his heart knew that it would do nothing to protect them. He simply meant to ease their fear. Bethiah's words of warning played in his mind until the words he meant to say became impossible to speak. Bowing his head, he turned silent instead.

When the priests and monks stood from the prayer, Orius called Father Gallo to his side. He put his arm about the young man's shoulders and walked him back to the rectory. He checked that their precious cargo followed. Reluctantly, she did, after bidding farewell to her new friends, a touch of the hand here, a hug and even a kiss to a bare head.

"I fear the entity will return and take revenge on those who sheltered her," Orius said.

"We'll keep careful watch," Gallo tried to assure him.

Orius shook his head. He didn't want them to keep watch. He wanted them safe from his brother.

"If he comes, be sure you escape. Don't stand and fight. Get as far away as you can; take the relic and your notes. Share what you've learned with a flock worthy of such gifts, if they'll hear it."

Father Gallo was struck by Orius's insistence. He peered at the elder priest with no answer. His thoughts pushed his eyebrows together. Orius gestured for the younger man's notebook, which was always on his person along with a stub of a pencil. The objects were reluctantly given to him. Gallo watched with curiosity as he scribbled a symbol on one of the empty pages. The triangle framing an eye once stood for great risk as Orius strove toward returning home. For Gallo, it might mean the only chance of survival.

"Trust no one outside our brothers, unless they bear this mark. Any stranger that comes to you. It will be here, on the chest. You won't find them by searching, but they'll find you. Make them prove who they are. If they come, go with them. It means you're in great danger," Orius explained.

Gallo was confused. He stammered, not knowing what to say.

"Promise me. Whatever happens—you must escape."

Father Gallo stammered excuses.

"Am I the one he pursues?" he finally asked.

"He won't know to whom she gave the gift."

"I can't leave them to be destroyed by this darkness."

"Salvatore," Orius pleaded.

"I'll do my best, if my heart allows."

"It will allow. What you carry is more precious than any relic kept by the church. We both know that if he kills them, they'll return to Zion. He can't destroy them. He can only destroy the vessels that allow their journey on Earth. Their guardians will keep their real bodies safe."

Gallo nodded in anguished agreement.

"It's just a suit," Orius insisted as if the younger man were merely being childish.

Gallo hung his head. The suit was all he knew to be real even after the opening of his mind. Orius patted his shoulder again.

Orius returned to the rectory, followed by Bethiah. She paused only a moment to look upon Father Gallo and determine what they were saying. Her deep perceptiveness couldn't interpret the meaning of his expression, beyond his fear of being examined by her. Taking hold of her braids, she cut the bottom few inches from the length of one. She then plucked a long feather from her wing and pressed the trophies into his hand.

"If you need me, hold these and call out," Bethiah said, whispering her name in his ear.

Gallo nodded with tears in his eyes. He trembled, afraid. After kissing his cheek, she left him on the lawn with his brothers, seeking the safety of the office.

The hours passed in slow silence. Then a rap on the door roused them from their meditations. Orius listened as his second answered. Father Gallo entered the office. His eyes were ringed with red circles. With a frown and nod, Orius understood without the need for speech. The car from the archbishop had arrived. The ride to Esztergom would begin in moments. His eyes went to his assign. Without ceremony, they wrapped her in a long, deep-hooded cover, quickly sewn together from the brothers' old frocks, and made their exit.

*   *   *

Gediel stalked along the tree-lined path leading to a bright glow deep in the dark woods of Eden. His wings stiffened where they lay resting on his back and side. The appendages at last stopped trickling blood. As for his leg, it begged for rest, but he ignored it along with all the other scrapes and bruises. He would have gone back to Acheron to pull her out with worse wounds, if need be.

The library of Eden was the surest place to find the answers he sought. This was the place they kept sensitive records meant to be less accessible than those inside the White City, but keeping with the pretense of availability. It made them seem less interesting. However, that didn't mean the information was less protected. The guardians of the library bore a title that had become taboo in Samsara: the three witches. Once inside the library, they would need to convince the Sisters to allow them access to their resources.

"Do you know these Sisters well?" Luthias asked.

"Other than they are witches? No, Evocati. I don't spend much time reviewing these records. My requests have always gone through channels that have only brought me in the path of the cherubim who roam here," Gediel replied, only half paying attention.

"Okay, watcher. How do you propose we get them to use the kapalanum for us—especially when you bleed all over their pristine marble floors?"

"Well, first, we get passed the cherubim guards. And, then, ask them—say please." Gediel smiled.

"Great plan," Luthias said, sneering.

Together, the guardian and watcher approached the entrance of the library. As Gediel mentioned, it was guarded by a pair of armored cherubim:

one engel and one erela. They lay on their podiums and watched Gediel and his friend pass, half interested. Gediel imagined quite a few of his profession came there and his presence wasn't alarming or even terribly impressive. Cherubim were at the height of all resonance possible in Zion. However, Gediel remained uneasy. The four-legged duta were known to violently protect their assign if it were deemed necessary.

Beyond the cherubim, the doors opened and they entered into an open courtyard with a well-groomed garden and fountain. The space was closed inside of a wrought iron cage. The only sound heard was trickling water. Gediel peered behind him. The guards still watched. The gates closed, fencing them in.

"Welcome to Akash," a gentle voice interrupted his observation of the garden.

A young alder stood before another set of doors at the opposite end. The garden was located at the center of a cross-shaped complex that sprawled in four directions like a small enclosed city. The large black iron gates to each wing stood closed. The atmosphere was forbidding.

The witch's head wasn't dressed in the accustomed alder habit. Instead, she wore her long raven tresses loose to the waist. Her black wings hung on her back, resembling a feathery cloak. Upon her sattva, she wore a green gown the tone of the forest, a fine jeweled girdle about her waist with a matching pendant upon her throat, and a circlet upon her crown that came to a point above the center of her forehead, from which draped a polished stone. A warm smile welcomed them and her diamond eyes glinted brightly. Her appearance matched every stereotype of a witch on Earth. Yet the alders of the library were far gentler than those who worked in the councils. Though the Sisters and their librarians celebrated silence, they were grateful to speak with any atman interested in their records. The written word was their passion. However, they fiercely guarded this vast treasure from those whose motives ran against the grain of their sensibilities. Gediel only hoped this Sister would be as welcoming as she appeared, once he told her the reason for their visit.

"Thank you, Sister."

"Suriel," she said, giving her name.

"Thank you, Sister Suriel," Gediel corrected himself.

"Why have you come to the library, Fenrir?"

"My travels have me understand you keep certain records within these walls—records not accessible to everyone," Gediel said, as Suriel strode closer.

"All knowledge is accessible to the one who seeks it, watcher," Suriel replied, clasping her long-fingered hands at her waist. The well-groomed nails were polished and pointed.

Gediel opened his mouth, not sure what to say next. Suriel's white eyes peered through him, cataloging his heart. This is what made the witches so dangerous, they were dominions posing as seraphs posing as svargs. No one knew how old they were, or to which incarnation they belonged. But the treasure they guarded suggested they were uppermost of incarnations in Zion. When Suriel's focus switched to Luthias, Gediel's mind broke free of the ice and he was able to form thoughts into words. They were dominions, he guessed by the interlude, and by her eyes and the bend of her crown. He eyed her dark olive skin.

"I'm on a mission to determine if — if a certain individual has been lost to the shadow. It's very important we use your kapalanum, to understand this soul's history. They've been exhibiting symptoms of a burning."

"A soul's past is between him and Adonai," Suriel replied.

Gediel clamped his mouth shut. He wasn't sure what to say that would convince the sister to open the kapalanum to them. Her mind pressed against his, seeking his true purpose. He slammed back her intrusion and she cocked her head to the side, surprised by the energy of his refusal.

"Please," Luthias suddenly blurted.

Gediel looked to him, shocked he would try something so foolish. Luthias shrugged.

"Saving a soul from the dark is also our goal," Suriel said. Her eyes scanned both of them again. After a pause, she indicated the western hall, and added, "This way. The librarian will show you the path, while I gather my khata."

Gediel nodded. He didn't think simply saying please would actually work. He supposed it was more than that, but the guardian's plea may have been what was needed. After all, he was Dominic's guardian and his interest in his past was warranted. Taking hold of his friend's arm, he pulled the awestruck soldier toward the hall the erela had indicated. A cherubim waited at the door. Silently, it turned and led them along the corridor.

Just past the gate, the library began. Books snugly filled the shelf walls. They passed into a wider space with tables and still more shelves that spanned from floor to ceiling. This space led to a two-story room, with shelves on both floors. Great windows allowed the moonlight in between the stacks. The ceiling was painted like the night sky and dotted by silver stars. Lamps hung from the ribs of the vaulting. The library stretched into a dim distance, with no apparent end, all filled with books and relics. Between tables in glass cases, vehicles of Samsara were displayed. Luthias longingly stared at a silver Porsche painted with the number 130. Gediel raised an eyebrow at him, signaling him to focus on the mission.

The quiet cherubim turned and they found an archway where they entered a low-ceilinged passage filled with still more books and relics from the worlds beyond their borders. This wing held Earth items. The records and museum pieces became older, more worn, and more dusty with each step. They sidled around a chariot and through a narrow door. At the end of this passage they came to a marble niche. Their guide uttered a breathy word. Scraping stones slid apart until it revealed a spiral staircase leading downward. The guide stepped aside and waited for them to descend.

Gediel led the way, even though the librarians could lock them in the library as their prisoners. It was a risk they had to take, hoping no order or idea to do so had been given. By the time anyone missed them, the mission would have ended, most likely in a bad way. Gediel knew that not every alder in the White City tried to hide the truth. The longer the threat remained, the more souls it would affect. As the Sister said, they too were interested in saving souls from the shadow. He hoped that was still true.

The door closed as they wound to the bottom, left to their own devices by the librarian. Gediel looked to Luthias. His companion appeared suspicious, but Gediel gave a soft smile and jutted his chin at the dim passage before them. Going back wasn't an option. They came there for information that meant a great deal to the success of his assign's mission. Luthias followed him along the narrow corridor, until they found themselves in an arched room opening on the outdoors. The guardian muttered a curse, thinking they'd been tricked into a prison cell.

Gediel exited into a garden caged like the other in ornate wrought iron. However, it was no prison cell. In the center stood the kapalanum. Its waters glowed a pale yellow and cast a golden light on the overhanging trees. Gediel stalked toward it, wondering where the Sisters hid themselves.

The pair had reached the desired kapalanum, but there was no one to aid in their viewing. Gediel peeked into the font. The gold waters were already primed with a vision. An image of Maiel lay before their eyes. She sat among human vratin in the Samsara, eating their food and answering their questions. Gediel wished he could reach into the water and pull her back to them, but it was a view of the past. This kapalanum only showed history, never the present and never the future. The third and final kapalanum that had the power of prediction would never be viewed by him or any of his kind. It was kept in the White City and guarded by the light guardians, its violet waters only for the use of Adonai and Metatron. His kind could only access the Otzar relic and the kapalanum before them if their keepers allowed. Between the two, they would have to piece together what they could only guess the third would say.

"Welcome, Gediel," a voice startled him from his viewing.

Suriel had gathered her khata. The three witches emerged from the dark spaces of the garden, converging on the kapalanum. Luthias stepped closer to him, hand on the hilt of his sword. Gediel touched his arm to remind him they were on their side. The Sisters looked into the vision. They were triplets; each identical to the next. Their clear-eyed stares returned to him.

"The kapalanum reads your heart and shows you the answer to your questions," Suriel said.

"She's safe in their care, but this may not last," the second Sister said, passing her hand over the water. It changed to show Morgentus at the same church.

"She can be saved from the shadow, if they send the right engel to complete the job," the third sister replied.

Images of the past which he preferred kept in the dark flickered before his eyes. The pool glistened in the late day sun. Foreheads touched.

"She's not the one we question," Gediel growled. "Her husband—"

"The kapalanum reads the heart," Suriel repeated.

Gediel felt Luthias's questioning eyes upon him.

"Right now, it needs to read my lips," Gediel said insistently.

The third Sister passed her hand over the surface of the water, just as Joel flew through the air, bent on destroying young Gediel's last chance at happiness. The image shifted. They saw a young boy who looked a great deal like Ian. It was Dominic as a toddler.

"Watch and it will answer all of your questions," the third sister said.

Gediel lost himself in the images. His mind asked a question and the water responded with the answer. Time slipped away as he learned every detail of Dominic's life. His body relaxed. The stiffness slowly seeped away. By the time he looked up again, the sky had begun to lighten. Luthias lay at the foot of a tree, meditating soundly in the arms of the witches. The erelas lay about him, their limbs twined. Gediel shook his head, not sure what had passed while he was distracted. Whatever the guardian had done to distract them, he was grateful.

Stepping back, he realized the soreness of his leg was gone. He looked to find the pant leg mended, as well as the limb beneath. He flapped his wings and they were unbroken. The librarians had healed him. He scowled darkly. No doubt they'd stolen into his thoughts while he was distracted as well.

"Luthias," Gediel said. He looked up to the sky as it grew purple with the coming sunrise. Then he said, "We must go."

Luthias held his breath and carefully unwound himself from the exhausted erelas. He sheepishly smiled and joined Gediel on the path back to the library. Gediel frowned at him, then turned and walked toward the opening. In silence, they made their way through the west wing and out the front door before the witches woke.

"Why are we in such a rush? I think I was getting to like the library. Ah—look at that! See? You're all better," Luthias said, noticing Gediel's healed wounds.

"Don't think that you got more from them than you gave," Gediel said. Luthias raised a brow, fighting a grin. Gediel added, "They read you like their books."

"Well, they can read my pages a little more if they feel like. I feel like a new engel," Luthias replied.

"Three wives? All khata? You're a greedy and strange engel," Gediel said, humoring the guardian's fantasy, though no such thing would happen.

The guardians of Akash had kept both of them distracted in a trance that opened their minds wide to them. Gediel still felt the remnants of their energy picking through his mind.

Luthias laughed richly. A side effect of such interrogations was a clearing of the thought process, compensation that could never repay the violation.

"Where are we off to now?"

"The astrals before they shut the ways for the duration of the sun," Gediel said. He shook off the haunting remnants in his mind. He continued, "The gate is in the east, in the Order of Gyuto's haven at the farthest edge of Arcadia. I have a question that must be answered there before we return."

They stepped down the tree-lined path, disappearing from sight as they slid to their next destination: Arcadia's edge. Gediel put his foot on the road to the Gyuto sanctuary first. The entrance and wall were only yards ahead, watched over by two younglings in red and gold robes. Their shaven heads lolled with fatigue. Their masters would be displeased.

Gediel whistled, a long shrill sound. The boys lifted their heads, startled by the sudden noise. It wasn't meant for them. It was meant for the four-legged soldiers that appeared behind him from nowhere, one white wolf and two gray ones, all in heavy plate armor. The younglings pointed and smiled, chattering about the Order of Fenrir's legendary watcher and Captain Chiron.

Frowning in disgust, Gediel came to tower over the boys. Behind him, Luthias stomped to a halt. The boys looked between them, worried about the meaning of their arrival.

"Where's your praefect?" Gediel asked.

"Praefect Shen is in meditation until the ways are to be closed," one of the boys answered.

"Wake him. Tell him Gediel has come to use the ways. I have an important question that needs answering," Gediel said.

The boy regarded him a moment. He was hesitant to wake his commander, and for good reason. Their teachings demanded complete compliance and order. To break that practice could bring more difficult lessons to assure the younglings didn't stray again. It sounded cruel, but their specialty was utilizing the Astral and that realm was unforgiving to minds that didn't practice rigid control and focus. The slightest lack of discipline could lead to torments worse than Jahannam had to offer. So the boy would be punished, regardless of the reason for interrupting meditation.

Chiron barked, making the youngling jump. Gediel watched him hold up his hand to beg the wolf to be quiet. Chiron's bark could wake every single Gyuto and make his day the worst he'd ever have. The youngling nodded at Gediel, agreeing to disturb his commander. He turned to his friend and ordered him back to guarding the entrance to their shrine. He gestured for the visitors to follow him. Gediel didn't hesitate. It wasn't as though Shen would beat the boy. He'd simply be given hard tasks to teach better compliance.

Gediel followed closely. Beyond the white wall of the Gyuto city was a network of homes and gardens on meandering paths. White screens and wood beams, cherry trees and tall ferns. The scooped roofs with their terracotta tiles were some of the most ornate in all of Arcadia. The architecture was both unique and pleasing to the eye. The commander's compound was toward the center. There they found a cherry tree in full blossom. On a bench beneath the pink flowers sat the praefect. Shen's eyes were shut, but Gediel knew he saw more than he let on. He waited for the commander to acknowledge him, his eyes drawn to a pair of doves cuddling in the crook of a branch in the cherry tree. Their coos were the only sound in the entire compound.

Shen sat quietly as the sun rose behind them. His long black hair lifted in a delicate breeze. A cascade of flowers fell from the branches, tousling the feathers of the doves and making them twitch.

"Why have you come?" Shen asked, still in meditation.

"To use your gate," Gediel replied, his eyes slipping from the birds to the praefect.

"You're late," Shen said, opening his black eyes.

The engel stared blankly at Gediel, but then smiled. Fine whiskers framed his mouth. He smoothed his beard, tugging on the long part at his chin.

"I was just about to close the gate," Shen said.

"How long can we have?"

"Time is relative, Gediel. You could wander for many passings of the sun and moon before the Astral tells you what you wish to know," Shen told him.

"I don't have that much time," Gediel replied.

"Then you'll need a guide."

Shen stroked his beard, thinking of who among his legion would be best. "Dao-Ming!" the praefect shouted.

A slim erela dashed from the house with a tea tray. She carried the offering to her commander, bowing at his feet. She set the tray down on his table, then bowed again. Gediel noticed Luthias step forward and raised his hand to stop him. Luthias halted, but his eyes didn't leave the fifth erela of the Shen clan. Gediel smirked. The guardian was still very connected to his Samsaran appetites. He believed he had already tried three that night and now he looked for a fourth.

"Dao-Ming, you will guide my friends in the Astral. They seek answers to their questions and a path back," Shen said sternly.

Dao-Ming sat back on her feet and bowed her head, silently accepting the assignment. Her black eyes flicked between them, lingering longer on the evocati. A slight blush blossomed on her cheeks. Luthias smiled, his eyes sparkling. For a moment, Gediel thought he saw a light pulse in both sets of irises.

"Draco Dao-Ming is my fifth daughter and among us the most skilled master in the Astral. I look forward to calling her evocati soon. She will guide you safely—if the nature of your questions allows." Shen drew Gediel's attention back to the mission.

"Thank you," Gediel said with a nod.

Shen nodded in return and his daughter served him his first cup of tea. He sipped, savoring the brew. He smiled at Dao-Ming, pleased and proud. He released her to her duty.

Dao-Ming got to her feet and greeted Gediel and the eager Luthias. She then guided them to the eastern end of the garden, activating her penannular. Two heavily armored guards stood next to an arch in the wall. Beyond the opening, they saw a field and distant trees, as if it just led to the field borders of Gyuto. Dao-Ming whispered a few words into the opening and the image became a shimmering sheet of silver, then a mirror. The tree symbol blazed in ethereal blue, awaiting her command. She faced them.

"Have you travelled in Astral before, Primus?" she asked.

Gediel nodded.

"Evocati?"

Luthias nodded. "A fair few times, draco."

"Remember that our enemies may access this world. Focus on only the questions you must have answers to. The ways beyond this door are fickle and will follow the flow of your mind. Whatever you think may manifest itself. You must control your thoughts, for they can do you the greatest harm. Be wary that the Astral still holds the thoughts of those who came before you. This world can be treacherous for the inexperienced. I will do my best to tether our vessels to the path, but you must cooperate with me."

"Maybe I should stay here," Luthias said.

"I need you to tell me the truth of what we see, evocati. You've faced worse if you've seen Morgentus," Gediel replied.

"That's what I'm worried about. I don't want to see that bloke again. A nasty troll that one," Luthias said.

"He won't come near us, if he knows what's best for him," Gediel assured his companion, grabbing hold of his arm.

"What about the girl?" Luthias asked, indicating Dao-Ming.

"I may only be a draco, but be assured I can handle myself," Dao-Ming said, insulted.

Dao-Ming grasped the hilts of the swords on her hips. Carrying the insult with her, she walked up the steps to the gateway. The tree pulsed as she pressed the corresponding sequence. She stepped through the arch with her nose raised.

Luthias watched her disappear and become like a reflection in the entrance. A dim-witted grin screwed up his face.

"I hope that's true. It'd be a shame to see such a pretty girl extinguished," Luthias said.

"She can hear you. Hope that Shen can't. His daughters are his treasures and he and his sons guard them like dragons," Gediel said, nodding toward a guard that walked one of the Lungs, of which he spoke, being raised there.

Luthias cringed. Gediel took hold of him and stepped through the gate. The wolves joined them last. On the other side, they stood on a gray flat stone surrounded by the milky mist of khajala. The wolves paced, whining at the veil. Dao-Ming faced them on the edge of it. Something permeated the air, as if what they saw wasn't quite right. Luthias peered about him, alarmed by the lack of sights.

"You're in the entrance of the Astral. You can remain here and view the manifestations that will come, or dare to step farther in and be part of them," Dao-Ming told them.

Gediel strode forward, disappearing into the mist. Dao-Ming followed after him, leaving Luthias to decide if he would remain behind, or get lost trying to find them again. Gediel heard his footsteps and was glad that he would be joining them. He needed him to be sure that what he saw was the truth or his own mind making up what he wanted to know.

The rock changed to grass, but the mist persisted. Through it, they saw the ruins left by voyagers in the past. Dao-Ming instructed him to ask his question before they wandered too far. Gediel paused. His wolves stood to either side of him scrutinizing the fog. Gediel carefully focused, fixing his thoughts on the single task. The nothingness rolled back and they stood in the middle of the council chambers. Ebony stone replaced the unseen. Alders brushed past them in and out of the rooms. Luthias turned round and round, waiting for the visions to attack.

"They can't see you. They're just dreams," Dao-Ming assured Luthias. "What do you seek from here?" she asked the Wolf Leader.

Gediel turned around slowly, looking about the chambers for something. His eyes settled on a message runner. He strode after him and the others followed suit. The messenger navigated the maze-like halls until he entered a room where a council was in session. They discussed something in a cryptic half-language. Gediel eyed them, then walked around the room. The space they stood in was the viewing nave. It was where the soul or duta under question stood before his or her council. A low wall of ebony stone separated the nave from the council dais, erected at varying heights. Several sat there, one spaced at the far left end, while four others crowded together toward the right of the bottom table. The messenger dropped a scroll before them and took to a chair along the wall of the nave. Other runners and servants sat in chairs against the walls. A door stood at the left end, in view of the farthest councilor. It opened and Maxiel entered the room. He strode to the other end where he mounted the step to the council dais. He pushed past the others and took another step to the highest seat. The others stopped talking and then the entrance opened again. Maiel entered. She stood before them in the yellow gown of her order, which she wore when the armor was tucked away. Her red ringlets cascaded down her red-winged back. Gediel felt his breath still as he looked at her. He remembered this. She was just a youngling only a few millennia old and already stunning. By this time, they had been friends for a long while, his heart already lost to her. He reached toward her face.

"Councilor Maxiel. The Order of the Moon has sent me to report to you." Her young voice filled the chamber, self-assured as always.

Gediel drew his hand back, remembering where he was before he caused them to fly off track.

"Ah, Draco Maiel, is it? Glad you could join us. Congratulations upon your ketu, youngling. You must be excited to begin your lives," Maxiel said.

Maiel was there to receive her orders for Dominic's first incarnation with her.

Maiel nodded to her councilor. She licked her lips and folded her hands to stop them from fidgeting. Gediel walked a circle around her, a smile curling the corners of his lips. He stepped up to the place Maxiel occupied, as quick as if blinking. He stared at the side of the councilor's face and then the image shifted and they sat in a red velvet room: the councilor's chambers.

Maxiel was at his bureau staring into nothing.

"We shouldn't be here," Dao-Ming said, now standing beside Gediel, stunned at what he had done.

"I've come to find an answer to my question. I won't leave until I have it and this is the place where we find it," Gediel told her.

"Walking into another's dream is dangerous. It's even worse when the dreamer is a higher being than yourself," Dao-Ming warned him.

"He's no higher than I," Gediel said, stepping back, the motion taking her with him.

Maxiel stood from his table and neared a fireplace. He was dreaming and couldn't hear them, but if they continued, they would enter his sphere of consciousness. Luthias and the wolves remained still on the other side of the room. They waited for him to continue or assure them that he hadn't in fact become aware of their presence.

"He's a council member," Dao-Ming whispered, noticing the many feathers on the floor.

"Let us hope he is," Gediel said, watching the subject turn around.

Gediel looked back to the desk. The Seal of Jahannam was etched in the surface. The clue sent an icy shiver down Gediel's back. He then spotted the amputated wings dangling from the seat. Gediel turned toward the engel, stunned by what he had done.

Maxiel grasped at his neck with a bloody hand. The end of a black probe stuck from the flesh, bleeding under his collar. He sawed his wings off, and tossed the weapon on the fire. Gediel's brow furrowed, remembering this was simply a dream, a reflection of reality. The literal images just made it easier to discern exactly how the conditions of the mission had changed. The councilor burned, the nails a claim of his handlers. Cutting off his wings was a sign of Maxiel's complicity.

Dao-Ming pointed behind Gediel. A dark figure entered the room, cloaked in a black robe and hood. Chiron growled in response. The wolf was quite adept in Astral. This was no apparition perpetrated by their thoughts. The figure was as real as they. The hood lowered and the figure looked at them.

"What you seek isn't in this realm," the golden-haired danava said.

Gediel grimaced. The pale skin and gold hair were the wasted remnants of the danava's features. Drawing his sword, Gediel pushed their guide behind him.

"Belial," Gediel said.

"Son of the Forsaken. How soon before you join me?" Belial replied with a wide smile.

"What are you doing here?"

"I could ask you the same." His eyes drifted to Luthias and the wolves, then to the cowering erela.

"This place is no more yours than mine. I've come to find out who bent Maxiel's path and I see that answer before me, don't I?"

Belial confirmed with a proud expression that actually admitted his pleasure.

"He doesn't even know he does a prince's work. Astonishingly, he's more simple-minded than the human with whom your erela mated. But—I suspect our nails don't defile the human so quickly because of your meddling. Why in all creation would you help him?" Belial laughed.

The prince placed a hand on Maxiel's shoulder. The councilor lowered his head onto the mantle and wept, gripping the edges of the marble with bleeding hands.

"Oh, have I said something I shouldn't? One never knows when he's in mixed company." Belial grinned.

The prince watched Maxiel slump to the floor before his fire.

"Dominic's atman was always weak and craved power to make him greater. He should've been born less than human. I think a beetle would have done fine," Belial said, sneering.

Gediel looked to Maxiel and then back to the danava.

"He falls to me this night and will wake in Jahannam where my children will feed on his flesh. Then, for his cooperation, he'll be made one of my chiefs," Belial informed them.

"To what purpose? You'll never pass the gates of Zion. You threw that away when you took Lucifer's side," Gediel said.

Belial laughed. "You think so, so—linearly. You don't see the minutiae behind what you've been told."

"I could say the same of you." Gediel grinned.

Belial smiled back at him, peering for a long moment. He stepped away from the councilor, who was lost in the throes of his guilt. Dao-Ming ducked behind Gediel's wings before the prince could pay her any heed.

"You belong with us, with your aryika. Your lustful heart betrays you. You long for a mated erela. Now you understand us. Now you can come home," he said, suddenly standing very close.

Belial held a nail at the ready. If he planted it in Gediel's flesh, he would know soon enough if his path was as the danava said.

"My heart's with the light and my aryika can rot in the pits of Acheron for eternity without me."

"He won't have to if you carry this through," Belial said smiling into his face, flipping the nail between his fingers.

The prince probed Gediel's emotions just by looking at him. A curious expression took over his features.

"Do you even know what's so special about this erela? Why does my slave Morgentus pursue her? Why do the humans want her? Why do you want her?"

"I know nothing of what you speak," Gediel said.

"Dao-Ming, get us out of here," Luthias ordered.

"Of course you know. Tell me," Belial said, pressing the nail against the underside of Gediel's jaw.

"I came to know Maxiel's mind, not your sick musings," Gediel replied, pressing a blade against Belial's abdomen. "Why do you want her?"

"Draco!" Luthias called.

"Jealousy, Primus? The great Wolf Leader is a Grigori," Belial hissed.

The wolves howled and barked. Gediel held his sword tight, the wolf head cutting into his flesh. He flicked his wrist and the blade sliced a gash in Belial's middle. The prince staggered back, eyes turned to white flame. He growled from a blood-red mouth, lunging to grasp the blade of Gediel's sword. Gediel swung his free arm behind him and grabbed hold of Dao-Ming, pushing them back the way they came. Belial released the weapon used against him as it cut and burned his skin. They stood in the nave of the council room, but before they could back away, Belial was there. His form became that of a hulking horned beast. He shattered the walls, wildly swinging his head and arms.

"Dao-Ming, take us back now!" Luthias barked.

The girl, frightened nearly to tears, shook her head and then shut her eyes. She whispered a few words and they stood on the rock at the mouth of the gate.

"Back through the gates, now!" Gediel grabbed her hand.

The wolves jumped through the open portal first, followed by Luthias. Gediel ran toward the opening. He could smell sulfur as the fog turned dark. Belial wasn't far behind. Gediel pushed the erela through the opening and leapt after her. Rolling down the steps and onto the stones of the dim garden, he looked back to see a horned head push the barrier of the Astral gate. A red symbol became black coal dust. It roared, then burst into white flame.

The way gate barrier struck the intruder back and the guards closed the wooden doors, barring the entrance to the Astrals. They looked down at Gediel with grim frowns.

"You nearly killed my daughter. Foolish watcher, why did you take such chances?" Shen asked, his temper roused.

Dao-Ming lay on top of the guardian who caught her as she was thrown from the gate. Her father roughly picked her up, glaring at Luthias. Blood stained her robes, but it wasn't hers. The awful smears hissed, then lifted in a smoke that left the nose burned.

Gediel caught his breath and slowly got to his feet, struck by the late hour. He looked himself over to see if Belial had managed to wound him. The blood wasn't his, nor was it Luthias's. Grasping the hilt of his sword he picked it up from the paving stones, where it dripped putrid black ooze. The stains disappeared the same as the others.

Chiron inspected him, sniffing for nails.

"Maxiel is lost to the shadow. He'll take others with him if we don't move quickly," Gediel said to him, remembering the disturbing images.

Belial nearly stole their guide too, but he decided not to share that. Chiron finished and he gave the wolf a pat.

Shen blinked, not knowing what to say. He flipped his long sleeves aside, leaving his daughter to the care of her khata. The other erelas surrounded her, wiping her brow with their silken robes. She watched the door with frightened eyes.

"He can't cross into Zion without the key. I wouldn't use your entrance for a while though. He'll be waiting for someone to return, so he can have a taste of the revenge he's sought since his fall," Gediel assured her.

"Prince Belial," the girl whispered.

"Our gate is poisoned," Shen growled.

"It'll be clean in a few passings of the sun and moon. A small price to pay for saving one of our own."

Shen set his fists on his hips and raised a reproachful brow at this. Gediel stepped away. He had promised to return sooner than this with answers. He hadn't thought it would take so long. Thankfully, Belial had willingly revealed the information he needed. His arrogance served them well.

Luthias hesitated behind him, wanting to ease Dao-Ming's fear.

"My assign thanks you. He and his wife are both in danger. Neither would survive the other's fall. Thank you. I'm sorry it took such a price." The guardian tried to smooth things with the fifth master.

Shen stared at him darkly. His frown didn't ease up as Gediel passed out of sight, either. Luthias decided what he said would have to be enough, and a retreat was in order. He ran after his friend, catching up to his quick stride in the outer garden.

Gediel was determined to continue forward without another word. Luthias clapped a hand on his shoulder and drew him back.

"You're walking like he's on your heels, Primus." Luthias smiled.

"He just might be," Gediel said, coming to a halt.

They faced each other.

"You saw what I saw?" Gediel asked. Luthias nodded. "Then we have what we need. We return to Alexandrael with this," Gediel continued, walking on.

"I also heard what he said about Maiel. What did he mean by it?"

"He was just taunting us," Gediel lied, frowning hard.

"That was no taunt, Wolf Leader. It's rumored that you exiled yourself upon their ketu because of a treacherous heart. And I saw the waters in Akash. I would know if this rumor is true."

"Like all rumors it has some truth, evocati."

Gediel turned from him and started walking.

"I did in fact exile myself when my friend was bound. A coincidence that I was also given my assignment as watcher."

Luthias grit his teeth. Gediel evaded the question, as the very skilled watcher he was.

"I'll meet you outside of Sephr's smithy by the time the moon rises," Gediel said, leaving him as he slid far to the west.

"Where are you off to now?" the guardian hollered after him, as he disappeared.

A gray mist passed through the marble arch of the moon. The silver bars were open to those who sought the pearl road and its reward. Members of the order, visiting souls, and others came and went freely. Others tracked through the vast courtyard and its statues and topiaries. The main building, in which their praefect was housed, rested a hundred yards from the gate overlooking the stretch with a great yawning mouth, and was lined by pillars that stood higher than ten duta stacked foot to shoulder. The entire space was walled in with marble.

Gediel peered around an ancient olive tree making its home in the shadow of the arch. He didn't want anyone, especially a member of the order, to lay eyes on him. His presence would raise too many questions. There would be enough speculation without him adding to it. Sliding from shadow to shadow, Gediel made his way along the south wall toward the great hall of battalion three and into the gardens beyond.

An ikyls watcher played his flute, surrounded by a herd of sheep and goats. His gold eyes, the same make as the animals which he herded, followed Gediel's track and he nodded to the soul in response. The faun wore a blue cuirass and a numeri penannular, the new moon. His presence was sure to be reported to praefect Hecate. Nothing missed a watcher, no matter his rank. Coincidence hadn't placed him there either. League, as the others called him, was a young gate watcher for the order. He was meant to intercept him.

Gediel found the barracks—fenced in by a thick wall of fir trees—that housed the garrison under the authority of the renowned flame-haired duta. The primus hesitated outside the marble entrance. Strawberry trees lined the walk and several of her soldiers lay about with no command. Edging toward the walk, he stopped and backed away. An imposing erela stomped down the white steps, wearing the uniform of her order, a pale-hued toga with the moon penannular securing it over her shoulder. Upon her hip was a blade. Her eyes flashed with silver lightning. She whipped her platinum head to and fro, disgusted by the display.

"Get about your duties!" the leader Callidora ordered. She grasped the thick mane of her hair, worked into a flawless tail at the back of her head.

The erela was Maiel's second and as hard a taskmaster as her literally more colorful mistress. Callidora muttered under her breath about their laziness, cursing them and her commander. She loved Maiel, but the captain's absence tried her patience. She smacked one of the engels with the flat of her sword to soothe her irritation.

Gediel held his breath as the soldiers disappeared inside. Callidora stepped down the walk, spying out any that might think to defy her. Her silver sandals sparkled, but made no sound. Her teeth were bared in a snarl. She sensed someone near, but looked uncertain as to who it was. She paused, sniffing the air. She was much like her commander in tactics. Gediel shut his eyes and cursed.

"You can come out, Wolf Leader," Callidora muttered.

Gediel stepped from the shadows. The erela nodded and walked back toward the marble house. He followed, not speaking a word. She would ask him soon enough why he came, or perhaps she already knew.

Gediel's eyes nervously shifted around the garden. He hadn't been there in eons and it felt strange to pass that way once more, though not a thing had changed. Blue flowers dipped and swayed in the breeze. The lawn was manicured and the shrubs sculpted. They scuffed up the steps and came to the door, both panels bearing the watchful moon symbol of their order; some souls called it an eye. The moment he felt his fight or flight instinct, he began to question the necessity of this interview.

"So what brings you to our halls?" Callidora asked.

Gediel smirked. Callidora was direct. She faced him just inside the door. Her stern gaze pierced through him, though she already knew what he wanted. Thus, Gediel held his tongue and considered the marble floor and ring of arches. Beyond, the surface dropped off into a circle of steps that ringed a blue marble floor several feet below. He slowly made his way into the amphitheater. It was eerily silent now. The stillness contrasted with the usual revelry which he had been party to in years past—the same explosive festivities that gained them the endearing nickname of Lunatics. A smile curled the corner of his lips as he remembered long ago. His eyes slipped up the high dome and back down. He could almost hear the beats thumping off the interior, the lights spinning round, and the sea of limbs undulating as they danced away worries and frustrations. It would be called "rave" in the Samsara sometime in the late twentieth century. Regardless of titles, very good times were had here and though it resembled the hedonistic parties of Rome and Greece, and those yet to come, they didn't carry the same shades of intent. They just liked to dance and be close, sharing their secrets and displaying talents useless on a battlefield. This was how they survived the ugliness, the hardships, and the losses.

A niche on the western side accommodated a stage about a head taller than he. Gediel slowly stepped down the stairs with his eyes on it. He recalled the nights he'd watched members of the units break their vocal chords as they belted out their hearts to music that wouldn't be heard by a soul for thousands of years. He pictured their expressive faces and heard the words filled with real feeling. The lights flashed around them. Their outlandish costumes were a part of the show they lived for. This is what the Order fought to protect. Home and each other. They were family.

Through the figures of his memory, he saw Zaajah and Maiel dancing together. Callidora had tried out a song she just wrote for the first time, still a youngling. She had one of the best voices among them. The duta lost themselves in the music, jumping and strutting as if the sounds pulled them like marionettes. It was the night he realized what he felt for their leader. He was younger then, though he looked not a single day older now. It showed in how he carried himself and what he would and wouldn't say. He saw himself, arm around her waist as they danced, lost in the music as much as in each other. Stepping toward the image, it faded. If only he had known how to speak up then.

Gediel stood still, feeling the rhythm beat through his sattva. His throat burned with regret. Drawing a deep breath, he steadied himself. Callidora joined him on the floor.

"We've missed having you at our celebrations," Callidora said.

"Youthful games. I've grown too old," Gediel replied.

Callidora snorted doubtfully.

Gediel's eyes locked on the stage. He remembered Maiel performing for her troops. Frivolous, he told himself. Gritting his teeth, he blinked away the memories. The room was charged up with so much energy it felt like he would drown in it. One residual string that threatened to drag him down forever.

"You used to have fun here," Callidora rasped. "Whatever happened?" she dared to ask.

Gediel eyed her. She gave a wry smile and shook her head. Her duck-white wings fluttered. Gediel cleared his throat.

"I see," Callidora said, guarding her satisfaction. "You've come for something?"

Gediel remained silent. She walked up the steps on the other side of the amphitheater, hesitating when he didn't follow. Gediel cast a last glance at his memories and followed her. It would be best that he left the room and its traces of the past behind.

Exiting into the garden through the north hall, they walked until they came to the indoor practice rooms. Callidora opened the door. This was where the captain and other officios usually trained. The hall was lined with silver mirrors on three sides and great glass arches on the outer wall. If he recalled correctly, there was a pool in the next room and one beyond the windows. He could see the water reflecting on the painted ceiling. Silver and blue marked every crevice that was not marble or ivory or alabaster white. A depiction of the full moon lay at the center of the floor and above.

Gediel paced halfway across the room. The walking poles were still engaged. Someone had been practicing their balance before suddenly leaving and forgetting them. The cherrywood staffs suddenly disappeared. He heard Callidora muttering under her breath again about lazy inebriates. She definitely had her hands full while her commander was away. The Order of the Moon was full of highly intelligent duta who needed to keep busy with routine. Those duteous ranks were laboring under a great despair that made them listless and sullen. He felt the blight whispering through the passages, making the air stale. Even Callidora seemed exhausted.

"She'll be back soon, Cal," Gediel assured her.

"You can't guarantee that," Callidora growled.

"You need to be ready," he said, turning.

Their eyes locked and he saw hopelessness had eroded her resolve.

"What'll you all do if she's raised?" Gediel challenged her.

Callidora frowned at the floor and picked at her fingertips.

"You're expected to lead them in her absence. This is how you thank her hard work? This isn't what she trained you to do. You should be more than ready to face this by now," Gediel said, snapping into the role of a commander.

Callidora continued to ignore him.

"Lunatics—that title was hard earned, but here you are, crying yourselves to sleep every night because your mistress has left you," Gediel mocked her.

Callidora's eyes rose, flashing with moonlight.

"Don't tell me my place, Primus. I've earned it and I know it very well," Callidora hissed.

"You're a puppy if you think this is how you lead," Gediel rasped. He stalked toward her. "You'll be expected to lead her units against the danava horde. They won't take pity on you because you are leaderless. It's what they wanted. She trained you to lead them with or without her."

Callidora glared at him.

"Find what you've come for quickly. You don't belong here. You may order the younglings of Fenrir as you please, but I'm no youngling and you're in my house," Callidora said.

The Moon leader spun out of the room, leaving him alone to inspect their quarters. The door shut him in and he fell against the wall, crushed by the energy he found there without the leader to hold it back. The buckles and findings of his coat scratched the glassy surface of the mirror. Gediel focused on why he had come and pushed back the impressions its inhabitants left. This was no time to lose his resolve like a schoolboy breaking into his teacher's office. Besides, Callidora had brought him there. She knew what he was after and gave him the key. He chased her out to save her being reprimanded by the praefect for doing so.

Gediel faced the room. It felt like midnight in the vast stillness of space. He strode toward the middle, eyeing the equipment scattered throughout the room. The balance poles leapt up. He eyed them warily. Something was wrong. He remembered when Maiel walked like a nimble gazelle along the poles, then returned on her hands. He used to watch her train, as she and Zaajah shared fighting techniques. He shook his head to clear the images. They were distracting, but so much of her energy was imprinted there that he could hardly escape it.

Crossing the room, Gediel looked through the arch to the indoor pool. It was dark inside the hall; the windows were covered with flowing drapery. Turning toward the tall windows that opened onto the courtyard in the center of the barracks and practice halls, he gazed upon another glistening pool stretched out along the middle of the space. Some of the younglings were enjoying a swim. Callidora appeared to shoo them off their duties. He gave a slight smile and returned to his examination.

Gediel wandered through the halls, passing under the curious gazes of younglings and soldiers alike. He nodded to some, ignored others. Eventually, he sat in the garden, staring at the glowing blue water. The halls were clean, as he expected. There were just ages of memories to be found there. It wouldn't be nearly so draining if he could have savored them. However, he very much had to forget. The more time he spent there, the harder it would become to let go. A deep scowl darkened his features. What he wanted, in the depths of his being, needed to be forgotten. Drawing a deep breath, he pushed his feelings back.

"Guilty conscience? I wouldn't expect that from you," a gruff voice called from behind.

Gediel peered over his shoulder. A black-skinned duta joined him at the edge of the pool. His eyes matched his blue armor. A silver circlet glistened upon his brow. He was the Optio of the third battalion, Bade. Maiel was in line to replace him upon his rising. League reported to him as expected, but Gediel was surprised to see Bade instead of the order's leader, Hecate, or Decurio Artemis, her khata. The dealings of the Moon were vast and likely kept the erelas busy and unable to attend him.

"You've come to tell me my captain is still lost. I already know this. Tell me what I don't know."

Bade stared into the water. The reflection of the pool gave him a bluish glow. He waited for Gediel to speak.

"Why?" Gediel asked.

"Why not?" Bade replied.

Gediel looked to him, confused.

"Why must there be an answer that suits you? Or anyone? Ask what. It's a greater vantage," Bade replied. After a pause, he added, "And stop sulking. This is no way for a watcher to act, especially one of your caliber. I want my captain back. You're the one who will do it, Primus."

Gediel's mouth popped open, but he quickly thought better of speaking.

"Get out of my house, Wolf Leader," Bade ordered.

Gediel jumped down and complied with the order. As he turned, he saw the corner of Bade's mouth turn up. The surly man watched him until he was well out of sight.

Stalking through the garden at the back of the main building, Gediel saw something white glisten behind the trees. Dismissing the disturbance as a youngling hiding from work, he continued to the steps. Callidora called him back. He halted midstride and slowly faced her.

"I apologize for earlier," she said, embarrassed.

Callidora took his hand and pressed something into the palm.

"I have meditated over this with no success. My khata won't come as she promised."

Callidora held his gaze to be sure he would help, and then backed away, tears filling her eyes.

"Bring that back to me. Bring my khata back to me," Callidora said, a tremor in her voice.

Gediel was puzzled by this. He turned his hand over and looked at what she had given him. A flame-tinged braid fitted with a moon-shaped metal bit snaked through his fingers. He felt a tremble in his chest. Maiel gave a braided lock of her hair to those who made her unit. With it, they could call her to them whenever needed. The fire in the strands glinted at him. So long as the crimson glared so boldly, she was all right. The moment the flame ebbed, he would know they had lost her. Callidora knew that too, and refused to spare him this knowledge. It was the one thing that would make him follow through.

Turning his gaze to the darkened sky, he wondered how many of them knew. Had it been so obvious to all but her? His gaze returned to the braid and he tucked it inside his jacket, as aware of its presence as if she stood beside him. Clamping his teeth down, he warned himself away from being so sentimental. Pointless emotions had no place in any of the work he had yet to do.

CHAPTER 20

THE SHRILL RING OF A TELEPHONE woke Dominic from a long black fall. He rolled over and rubbed his eyes. A television babbled on the other side of the room. The late evening light streamed through the window, and though it was pale and weak, it made his eyes squint. He hadn't pulled the curtains over his window and from beyond the panes he could see that the sky was still platinum with rain clouds. The telephone rang again. He fumbled across the nightstand to pick it up. Dragging the receiver to his ear, the television remote fell to the floor. The cord was short and dragged the telephone toward him. It bumped the lamp, nearly toppling it. He quickly sat up and caught the objects before they fell and broke. With a heavy sigh he drawled a tired hello into the mouthpiece.

"Hello there, handsome." The waitress's voice sounded hollow across the line. "Ferries are running. Better hurry up, they said they may shut down again."

"Thank you," Dominic said, trying to sit up.

As he set the receiver back in the cradle, he pushed the blankets the rest of the way off his legs and rose from the bed. He grabbed his pack and looked around the room. Lena was nowhere to be seen. The waitress's words echoed in his ears. He had no time to look for her. Slinging his pack on his shoulder, he left.

Once he'd checked out of the small inn, Dominic made his way toward the ferry docks again. The same woman stared along the cliffs. He asked for a ticket, casting his gaze about for his guardian. She was still absent. The young woman gave him his ticket and returned to her staring contest with the cliffs. Dominic made his way to the docked boat that would carry him to France. He soon stood in line, smashed up with other passengers ready to board. Suddenly he saw the girl standing at his hip, a faint and translucent ghost. With a grimace, he looked over the heads of the other passengers. He wished they were alone so he could warn her.

At last, the passengers boarded. Wandering along the wet deck, he made his way toward the back. Few people appeared interested in the seats still facing the port; they were probably more interested in where they were going than where they'd been. Either way, it made for a chance to explain that he was losing his sight.

"Where have you been?" Dominic asked the girl.

"Right beside you," Lena replied.

"I fell asleep," Dominic said, worried. He looked at the docks and gray-green water.

"I know." Lena sat down.

Lena sounded dismayed. Dominic cast a sidelong glance to see if she looked concerned. He hadn't slept much since his last lifetime. He usually didn't need sleep. Having sent him there in mortal form had had dire consequences, some still yet to manifest themselves. What if he collapsed from exhaustion when Maiel needed him most?

"Your form is becoming stronger—mortal. It's making it harder to reveal myself to you. The sight'll leave you, the more flesh you take on," Lena added.

"So you're saying I'm either getting fat or our time grows thin," Dominic said, turning and sitting down.

Passengers wandered closer. He didn't have much time to clearly understand the consequences.

"You should stay at the front, where the most people are," Lena advised.

"I'd rather stay away from them," Dominic said, taking the atlas back out and looking over the many faces of the Earth over the years.

"I sense a shadow," Lena said, staring at him.

"Even more reason. I want to see the knife coming at me. Can't do that in a crowd."

Lena stared at him hard.

Dominic sighed and put the book back in his bag. She wasn't about to let him ignore her. Her eyes bored into him like hot augers. Dragging his bag after him, he made his way toward the bow of the ferry. The horn blew and the crew made the last preparations for the crossing. He paused a moment, noticing their strange traits: long sallow faces with ragged teeth. One smiled at him and he nodded in return, continuing on. It was a passing thought, paranoia.

The front of the boat wasn't nearly as packed as the line had let on. He supposed that the passengers were spread about different levels. Finding a seat, he put down his bag and tried to relax. Lena joined him, taking the empty seat between him and a mother of four. He felt the girl's stare. Crossing his arms, he shut his eyes, and decided to meditate until they reached the opposite shore. He didn't want to talk, even if it didn't really matter what the other passengers thought of him. The fact that his sight was leaving him worried him a great deal more. A little focus might help keep what was left.

Dominic watched the light play on the inside of his lids. Lena pressed against his arm, her small hand resting on his elbow. Reaching deeper into his own mind, he stretched toward the energy-renewing nothingness. The effort felt slow, inhibited, like swimming in a muddy bog. Slogging through the barrier, he drew on the strength to fill the void growing inside him. The light behind his eyes went dim and slowly faded to black. The next sight he saw was a long corridor. The plaster walls glowed with pale blue light from an open door too many strides away. He pushed toward it, but the door slammed shut. He stood watching it, the light streaming from the cracks. His heart pounded in his ears. A face flashed before his eyes and Dominic jumped back, startled. The hall was empty, but his eyes hunted for it. The air buzzed like electricity. A crackling sound shattered the silence and the face appeared again, this time attached to a full form. It flickered in and out, but he was able to make out most of the features. The long white hair and hollow eyes reminded him of something he was unable to put a name to. The silence returned and the figure glowered at him. The deathly expression shifted. Whoever it was made it clear that he was aware. The figure smiled, then threateningly laughed.

Dominic's body propelled backward, as if he ran from the nightmare. He wondered if he had accidentally fallen asleep again. He tried to open his eyes, but was afraid to turn his gaze from the figure before him. Then he realized he was locked in. His mind and body were paralyzed by sleep or fear.

Finally forcing his eyes open, Dominic drew a long gasping breath. He blinked, trying to focus on his surroundings. Night had fallen and the boat was lit with cold green-white lamps. The other passengers were gone. Coming quickly to his senses he scanned the area, turning this way and that. Suddenly he caught sight of Lena beside the rail. Her black wings were spread wide as she watched the sea. She slowly turned and her gaze went past him.

"I should've gone another way," Dominic said, wiping his face.

Dominic blinked and Lena's gaze was normal once more, but she stood at his knee, having moved rather quickly from the rail to him.

"There was no other way—no safe way," Lena told him.

Dominic watched her, waiting for her eyes to roll over gray. He wiped his mouth, trying to gather his senses. She looked solid again. At least his meditation worked as he had hoped. He wondered how long it would take, though. Lena sat beside him.

"Where'd everyone go?"

"Who?"

Dominic twisted around in his seat to see the empty deck. It should've been obvious who he meant. He laughed a little and returned to his small guardian. She stared ahead at nothing in particular. Her short legs swung back and forth. She reminded him of someone, and not Callidora.

"I can see you better now."

"Oh. What do you see?"

Dominic watched her profile. Something wasn't right, and it was more than just the missing passengers. A light smell wafted across his nose on the breeze, a smell like a blown-out match. The nerves along his spine pulsed. Sitting quite still, he tried to think through his next move.

"In this light?" Dominic said, trying to make a joke to distract whoever it was who sat beside him.

Lena's face slowly turned toward him again, but the wrong way, twisting up her neck like a screw. The flicker of a shadow crossed her features. Her black eyes blinked and the gray washed over them again. Dominic held himself as still as possible. A thousand panicked thoughts scrambled his senses. He swallowed as the flame responded. He clamped it down and stilled his mind, pretending he didn't notice.

"Did you think you could just walk to her?" Lena's voice blasted at him, sounding like three or four very angry people.

Dominic held his position. The sword was in the pack behind him, unreachable. A slow smile spread on the lips of the shadowalker. It was in his head, at least the part that took on flesh, picking at his brain. He shut it out, showing his teeth in a disgusted snarl.

"We can't let that happen. Boats sink. Planes crash," the shadowalker continued.

"I didn't figure you would," Dominic found his voice.

The shadowalker laughed, turning away. Dominic took the chance, snatching up his pack and putting distance between them. When he turned back, no one was in the seats. He stood alone, listening to the sound of the engines. Finding the hilt of his sword, he pulled it free and swung the pack on his back. Tightening the straps, he knew he was about to face a fight. Without the few things they had afforded him, this battle would be too easily won by their enemies.

Dominic examined the space, not so sure he was alone. Carefully stepping toward the center aisle, he felt the air cool and grow heavy. The night sky beyond the windows was clear, with twinkling stars and a slice of moon. The water stretched for miles in any direction. They should have been docked in France by then. Dominic made his way to the last place he had seen Lena. The seats were empty there too. He turned and a crewmember walked by, eyeing him coldly. A twisted grin opened the man's mouth, displaying his gray teeth. A pinpoint of light shone in his dead, black eyes.

"Dominic!" he heard his name cried. It echoed off the metal and fiber boat.

Startled by the sudden sound, he turned back. A leather-clad man with pale skin held the little girl to him. The danava's pasty hand clamped across her mouth so she couldn't speak. Terror rose in his heart. This man was familiar to him. Flashes of his memory bubbled up. The pain in his throat burned like an inferno. He looked to where he'd left the double. A mudeater sat in her place; a mangled torso with chattering teeth.

"Take your time, ape," the man hissed.

"Morgentus," Dominic breathed.

"There now. See. You're not as slow as they think." Morgentus smiled.

"Let her go," Dominic said.

"And have her call her friends?" He shook his head.

"What do you want?"

"What does anyone want? Help accomplishing their ends. I've come for you, because you can help me accomplish my ends."

"I won't help you do anything," Dominic said.

"Accomplish," he repeated the word, disliking Dominic's choice. It didn't emphasize Dominic's failures enough. "You already have. Why stop now?" He grinned, when the human stood dumbfounded.

Dominic's eyes switched from Morgentus's to Lena and back. The girl trembled with terror, tears streaming from her eyes. He felt her plea in his heart.

"Stop that now, pigeon. I can snap your neck and make things very painful for you," Morgentus warned Lena.

Lena's small hands grasped his arms, trying to pry herself free. She cried, fighting for each breath.

Dominic saw his daughters in the child guide. Her struggle fed the flame in his gut and he embraced it. The flicker ran down his limbs and he grasped his sword at the ready.

"You're nearly there," Morgentus said to him.

The baron's sattva responded in kind, eyes blackening over and dark veins swelling.

Dominic hesitated as red dots formed on his skin. Blood.

"Tricks won't save you from me," Morgentus continued.

The shade cocked his head toward the sea. In the moonlight, a great hulk arched its back just above the waves. Dominic hoped it was a whale trailing the ferry, but something told him that was a foolish idea. How the baron was able to convince the prince of the Domdaniel to serve him was the real trick.

"Poor little monkey. You never should have crawled out of your tree to play with the big kids," Morgentus said, laughing.

"Humans didn't cause your pain, Morgentus. You did this to yourself. You broke laws and you did it to my people."

"Because of you. Had I been given the crimson bride I deserved, none of this would have happened. We each should have been given the mates we deserved. Don't you agree?" Morgentus said, dangerously close to losing his composure.

"I have the only mate I was ever destined for, and you had yours until you betrayed her," Dominic said.

"Really? You think you were destined for her. Don't you ever wonder why she never raised a finger to help you in all the years you tried to rise?"

Dominic raised an eyebrow, fighting the acid fire filling his mouth. Maiel had always struggled to help him. His mind flickered. Or had she struggled for a reason to bother?

"Because she belonged to another," Morgentus said, regaining his attention.

Morgentus gave a slow smile, seeing the tears that glistened in Dominic's eyes. Speaking his suspicions aloud made quick work of the defenses he'd built. It wasn't Morgentus she was destined for. Dominic raised his sword, refusing to think more of it. The baron only meant to weaken him.

"You'll regret saying that. She doesn't belong to him. He doesn't deserve her," Dominic warned.

"Gediel? No, not Gediel, you buffoon. Maiel is my bride," Morgentus said.

They stared at one another and Dominic felt his senses return to him. Morgentus's poison lost its hold. He lied from delusions. Dominic grit his teeth, disgusted he'd dared believe Maiel was hewn from the same stone as the abomination that rested in his decaying core. But it was too late now. He had embraced the fire to defend her and the child. His gut twisted, threatening to empty on the ferry deck.

"She's mine. Her destiny is to fall and reign as the mistress of my labyrinth," Morgentus said.

"And what do you plan for the other mistress?" a voice challenged.

Morgentus's eyes switched from Dominic to the passage behind him.

"Let the child go," Dominic heard as he turned.

Magiel stepped from the shadows, hands twined at her waist. She looked more serious than when he told a joke and she refused to laugh at the punchline. Dominic was never so grateful to see her.

"Lightwalker!" Morgentus hissed.

The shade shoved Lena aside and lunged for the elder erela. She may have been at the height of her incarnation, but she was not easy to wrestle down. Magiel was a svarg and barons were like puppies to her.

Certain the aunt could manage on her own, Dominic lowered his sword and ran to Lena. The child lay on the deck, gasping for breath. Her face was burned where the baron had touched her. Dominic picked her up and backed away from the deadly rivals.

Magiel flapped her great white wings and toppled the danava onto the deck of the ship. Morgentus scrambled backward, hissing and cursing her. Dominic made his way out of the room, hoping to protect Lena from the sight. It wasn't something a child of any kind should witness. In spite of his care, Dominic's back hit a barrier. He darted around to face it. The crew and passengers filled the passage and deck. Their hollow eyes peered at him. Each orb held the telltale point of light which revealed their damnation. Their expressionless faces looked forward, awaiting orders. Dominic held his breath, hoping they were simply possessed by the demon Magiel thrashed. Then the front crewman's expression shifted to a sneer. Corpses.

"Dominic," Lena whispered, clasping his shoulders tight.

"No worries, youngling," a familiar voice spoke from behind them.

Lena was grabbed out of his hands, but before Dominic could react, the horde called out their anger in a deafening chorus. To either side of him, he saw the gold armor of his former regiment. He looked to the leader, Rathiel, and to one of the squad sergeants, Athiel. Their faces had never held such appeal in all the days they'd served. A third from the Order of the Sun protected Lena between his armor and wing. She peered around his leg, unsure their numbers could match those of the corpses.

"Your commander's lost. Unless you want to find yourselves permanently dealt with, you will back down," Rathiel growled at them.

"Look at the canaries—how they sing, but can they sing underwater?" the crewman hissed.

"Have it your way," Athiel said.

The crewman eyed them. Dominic raised his sword. They were not likely to back off and the assault would be fast and wild. The crewman smirked. Then the horde disappeared in a heavy cloud of black smoke—a move he hadn't expected. The glass in the windows burst, cascading across the floor like glitter.

"Stand your ground," Rathiel ordered.

The ferry rocked, nearly jostling him off his feet. The others looked concerned with the sudden motion. Dissipating like fog under sunlight, the smoke took its exit and they each knew whatever struck the vessel was no frail foe. The horde merely provided a distraction until the prince got in place.

"Leviathan," the leader said, surprised.

"That vile shade ran away like a wounded deer," Magiel said, entering the space.

Dominic watched her stoic expression scan each of them.

"Why are you just standing there? Leviathan won't take pity on those who stand down," she said impatiently.

"He'll sink the boat," Lena said.

"Of course he will. I suggest you make your moves quickly. Regroup at the Sun Fortress," Magiel replied. She stood before them.

"You can't take me back. I'll find her," Dominic cried.

"I hadn't planned on it. I was speaking to them," Magiel said with a nod to his friends.

Magiel watched him for a silent moment, then disappeared in a wink of light as tentacles snaked in through the open windows. Rathiel grabbed hold of him. Before he could ask what they were doing, Athiel took his arm and quickly ran his dagger blade across Dominic's exposed forearm, making a deep gash.

"What the hell is wrong with you?" Dominic demanded as he struggled against them.

"He'll follow us if he senses you've gone. Your blood will keep him here."

Athiel smiled. Dominic doubted he dealt with his friends any longer. His blood pooled on the deck. The tactic made sense, but what about the rest of the mission? A wound like this could lay him up for days. Rathiel clasped his fist over the wound.

"Let's get out of here before he realizes the trick."

Dominic opened his mouth to ask what they had planned, but was stunned to silence when he saw his wound healed to a mere welt. In the next moment, he gasped for air as he bobbed in the icy, rough water. Land formed a black barrier against the sky behind him, as he splashed about to get his bearings.

"Swim, Dominic," he heard Lena say. She was in the water, wiping her hair from her eyes.

Dominic grabbed her arm and pulled her to him. He told her to hang on and swam toward the lights in the distance. The water sapped the warmth from his body and the current took all his strength to fight. He hoped his blood on the deck of the ship would be enough to distract the greatest terror of Jahannam. Lena whispered in his ear, encouraging him forward. His limbs trembled as he fought against the black water. His eyes stung from the salt water. Memories of a similar beach landing haunted him.

In truth, the beach was too far to reach before Leviathan realized he'd been tricked. The water sloshed in Dominic's face, blotting out the lights that provided direction. He sputtered and blinked, but it made his eyes sting worse. He worked his arms, trying to swim faster. The choppy sea was unforgiving. Waves grew taller and more frequent, slapping him back and forth and making it hard to breathe. Dominic tried to look back to see if the danava found them. Lena whispered for him to keep going and not to look back.

The sound of the surf filled his ears. The beach was close. A flash lit the world before them, coming from where they left the boat. Leviathan held the boat high in the air. Massive tentacles twisted the ferry, trying to tear it apart. He saw three brilliant dots against the sky. The Sun duta still fought the hulking monster, distracting him while they escaped. Dominic turned back and swam harder. His arms burned, but his fear gave him the stamina to keep pushing. From behind, he heard the metal of the ferry's frame break. The ship was torn asunder and Leviathan pitched the two halves back and forth; he was angry at being cheated. Dominic watched the twisted wreck, black against the sky, shaken in all directions. Lights flickered on and off.

"Lena! Slide us now!"

"I can't."

"Do it now!"

"I can't," she cried, watching the beast tear the boat like foil.

"If you don't want to find out what drowning is like, do it now."

"I'm not strong enough to move us both," Lena told him.

"Are you strong enough not to be torn in two?"

A tentacle wavered in the air, then shot toward them.

Lena shut her eyes, squeezing the coat collar at the back of Dominic's neck.

"Do it now. I know you can!" Dominic said, just as he felt himself suddenly thrust forward.

A shrill cry rang in his ears and he felt the ground beneath his feet. He stood in a field just past the sand dunes of the beach. Lena clung to his back, slowly slipping down as she lost her grip. She wept quietly, afraid they had failed in their mission and become prisoners of the Domdaniel for eternity.

Dominic stared into the dark, catching his breath. He grabbed her small hands and helped her to her feet. She blinked up at him and he smiled. Her eyes shown with a hot white ring. Kneeling down, he pulled her to him and kissed her head. Crushed against him, he felt her fill him with hope.

"Thank you," he said.

Lena buried her face in his shoulder and wept.

Dominic watched the beast struggle in the channel, unable to get close enough to reach them without beaching himself in the shallows. Angry he'd lost his quarry, Leviathan pitched the pieces of the ferry toward the beach. They crashed on the land with a terrible sound.

The dots disappeared, arching across the sky like shooting stars. They were alone again. Dominic grabbed her hand. They couldn't wait around for more shadowalkers to find them. Cresting the dunes, he encouraged Lena with praise for her effort and searched for a road and their way.

* * *

Gediel approached the entrance of Walhall's smith shop. The wolves circled him in streams of light, falling in behind. Luthias stepped from the shadows, giving him a questioning gaze, but the primus was intent on the door. The door opened and Sephr filled the space, hands on hips. His dark gaze reflected the expressions of his visitors, as if he already knew what they were there for. Gediel whispered a few words close to the arms keeper's ear. Sephr's black mien grew even darker. He gave a sharp nod and stepped aside.

"Evocati," Gediel said, facing his new friend.

Luthias looked over his nose.

"Take a squad and be sure that Maxiel no longer haunts his halls. Belial promised he would fall this night. I want to know that he has. Report to me at the kapalanum in Otzar at sunrise."

Luthias looked between the svargs. His blue eyes were cold as stone. He gave a sharp nod and slid off to do as asked. Gediel was sure he would enjoy the assignment; time to avenge a friend's pain. In the meantime, Gediel would speak with Sephr alone.

"Do you need to make a report to Voil?" Sephr asked.

"Not yet. I'm not quite finished," Gediel said.

"If your commander doesn't miss you—come inside and rest for a while," Sephr said.

"I was hoping you would ask." Gediel grinned.

Gediel followed the broad-shouldered dux through the smithy and into the halls of Walhall, trailed by Chiron and his seconds. The larger svarg led the way to the kitchens. A few younglings busily straightened the pantry, with the help of an infant Lung whose blue scales had yet to harden and turn red. The infant was delighted by the wolves and wound about them, rubbing her lengthy body against their fur and nuzzling their muzzles. The pack gently tolerated the caresses, though she was already substantially strong.

Sephr dismissed the younglings to other duties, leaving him and Gediel with a warm fire and the dark room. They complied once they set down bowls of water for the wolves. Gediel sat at the heavy worktable, staring into the shadows. Sephr quietly pulled out two mugs of ale and set the giant cups on the table. Gediel opened and closed his fist, not indicating that he felt Sephr's stare. The other svarg raised his cup and drank. Gediel laughed weakly, coming back to the moment, and emptied the cup set before him.

"What else did you find in the ways?" Sephr asked.

"You said earlier that when you fit the younglings you get a sense of them, their destiny," Gediel said, setting the cup down.

Sephr looked at the empty cups, regretful. This matter would take a little more liquid courage than they were both accustomed to. Taking the cups back to the cask, he refilled them and returned.

"You also said you thought Captain Maiel was destined for a very different ketu," Gediel added, holding onto his cup.

"I did. I said both those things." Sephr smiled.

The watcher drank, but more slowly this time.

Sephr drew a deep breath and spoke again, "I thought she was destined for one ahead of her incarnation. It's an easy mistake to make."

"What if you weren't mistaken?"

"The ketu is made. I could hardly be mistaken." Sephr laughed into his cup.

"Have you ever been wrong before?"

Sephr shook his head.

"Naturally," Gediel said, baring his teeth. Chiron nudged his arm and whined, placing his head in Gediel's lap for comfort.

"The Astral can mess with your head; so can the shadow princes. Don't think on it, watcher. Belial simply read a passing thought and used it against you," Sephr said.

Gediel drank from his cup, then realized he would need the rest to speak again. He emptied the ale and rose to fill his cup. Sephr's gaze stuck to his back, seeing more than Gediel was comfortable with. His mind spun with a thousand questions and they all made him angrier. Chiron barked and cocked his head. He didn't think the drink necessary and Gediel just felt foolish for getting caught idealizing an old friend. If only the alpha leader understood, but he gathered that he did and refused to condemn him any more than his other friends would have.

"He knows your aryika's disgrace haunts you and thinks it a means to bring you to their level. They've wanted you since your birth. I don't blame them. If I had to choose anyone to fight beside, it would be you," Sephr said, trying to soothe him.

That wasn't what bothered him. He hadn't thought of his aryika for some time. It was others who brought him up. It was too dangerous to give that shade a thought. Walking back to the table, he exhaled and sat. He opened his mouth but found words still eluded him. Crossing his ankles under the table, he hunched up and returned to his cup. Between the astrals and Callidora, he forgot how to speak all over again. Chiron placed his paw on his lap. Gediel gave a scratch to his ears and tried to find cheer in the happy expression he got in return.

"This really bothers you. Take your time, lad," Sephr said.

"Belial called me—Grigori," Gediel began, but immediately stopped.

With that, Sephr poured another cup from the cask. When he returned to the table, Gediel finished his third cup. The effects reached his mind. His tongue finally loosened. He looked at Sephr, somewhat reluctant still. What he was about to say could damn him to his aryika's house in moments.

"I've been in love with her since she was a youngling," Gediel blurted. "I thought it would fade with her ketu, but it remained—as strong as the day I brought her Argus to the last time I saw her in the White City."

Sephr stared at him, his expression unchanged.

"That shouldn't be, but I can't right my mind or heart. I'm as treacherous as my aryika," Gediel said gnashing his teeth.

"It's only ever been obvious to those who watch you, watcher. But we're not to judge." Sephr said gently.

"Then why does Adonai not cast me out and get it over with?"

"There are things in the works that even I can't understand. Perhaps your test is to deny your love for her. The attraction will fade when you find the atman that's meant for you," Sephr said.

"I'm svargaduta and my destiny is to face my aryika in the final battle. All of the other svargs my age have found their ketu. I'm the only one."

"Not the only one. One of the few, maybe," Sephr replied with a grin.

"This is no time to make light of the situation. I can't go before the High Council and accuse Maxiel of betraying us when I myself betray Adonai."

"Why didn't you speak up to her sooner?" Sephr asked after a brief pause.

Gediel stared into his empty cup. That was the question that had bothered him since the day he'd left her Argus. A grimace twisted his features. Chiron rejoined his soldiers, sensing the conversation get tense and he would best serve at a distance.

"Who would dare walk up to Maiel and profess their undying devotion? She's known for being quite—protective."

"You were afraid of her? She was just a girl," Sephr asked laughing. He drank the rest of his ale. "A grown svarg afraid of a girl!" Sephr roared.

"Have you ever stood against her in battle? You forget, we were friends. I sparred with that red cat more than once. I feared for my very being if I spoke one wrong word. She'd think I was making fun of her."

"The females are all like that—especially in the Moon Order—but only against those they despise. I thought you were friends? You were scared of her, Gediel! Scared she would laugh at you—foolish boy," Sephr said.

"I can't help but think all this could have been avoided if I'd stayed and let her catch me spying on her that day."

"It was too late even then. They had given her to him the evening before. Rest assured you're not the only one who struggled with that determination. It was wise of you to go to the wilds. Zion would have been torn asunder once more for breaking the sacred on behalf of the humans," Sephr told him.

"You knew?"

"I had my suspicions, but I was never made privy to the secret until Mikhael briefed me," Sephr said.

"What of Mikhael?"

"Let us say it was the first time he disagreed with the king. He loves that girl as his own child and fought hard to save her this fate—but Maxiel and his council spoke too convincingly and swayed the decision. I think Adonai knew, even then, what we faced, but he doesn't spare us the trials of our incarnations. If it were up to him and Mikhael, this would never have come to pass. Instead, he hoped Maxiel and Dominic could both overcome their shadows," Sephr replied.

"I sometimes wonder if he should allow us to be the arbiters of fate," Gediel said, staring at the table surface.

"It's the only way to find Nirvana. Are you hungry, my friend? You've been working hard and not taken any rest."

"That may be a good idea. I've a feeling this isn't over with Maxiel's exile. I won't leave her in Samsara. Dominic will have his chance, but I'll be there to make sure she does come home."

Sephr offered him a small smile. Gediel feared he had confessed too much. His head swam with the effects of the ale. He was already an outcast among them, due to a grave blemish in his family history. It wouldn't take much for them to banish him to Acheron and make the circle complete. He only hoped it was in fact his destiny to avenge his family line and take down his aryika, the traitor. Sephr set a steak before him with a board of bread. Gediel soon forgot his troubles in the comfort of food.

Gediel made his way back to the White City once he'd finished his meal. The food would keep him going without rest. The time to give his report had come, but it wouldn't be presented to his commander, Voil, or even Alex. Metatron awaited him for their prearranged appointment. A detour to Otzar was in order now that he had new information. He couldn't keep this from Alex any more than he could bar Metatron from examining his thoughts. Both might be dissuaded, but both would be made suspicious. Metatron would likely call off the mission once briefed, and then send Mikhael to fetch the captain, and Luthias to fetch her husband. His future conversation with Callidora and the others would need to be arranged much more carefully.

At least this information would end any bid to convict Maiel of burning. After all, their efforts put her in this situation and his knowing tied their hands. They faced a great embarrassment, in fact. Regardless, once back in Zion, Maiel faced great hardship, a worse trial than that of the labyrinth or its master. Dominic's soul continued to decline, and at a pace decided by how far Morgentus's poison reached. If they could heal him, the effort would only serve to prolong the inevitable. His atman was created with an inclination to decline. How could they tell her that she was given to him to halt that decline, while her true ketu was thrown aside?

Gediel planned on returning to the borders to hide his shame until the time came to face his aryika. He would not tell Maiel a thing, but he imagined that Magiel or Alex eventually would. Even then, he was certain she wouldn't abandon the man. Despite everything, she somehow still loved him and her eye never strayed.

The walk through Otzar led Gediel not only to the heights where Alex held her vigil near the kapalanum, but closer to an inevitable destiny. The door opened and he entered into the dimness. Their eyes went to him. They looked worn and discouraged, if not accusing. Alex called his name and joined him. She took both his hands in hers and tried to smile.

"What did you find?"

The question dried his mouth and made his tongue stick. He struggled to form a single word. Then her expression shifted. Fear flickered across her eyes. He couldn't leave her wondering.

"Maxiel is burning, as you suspected," Gediel replied.

He ignored Alex's stare and went to the others who kept watch over Dominic's progress in the kapalanum.

"How does he fare?" Gediel asked. He looked in the kapalanum and saw Dominic walking along a dark country road. It was just as they had left him. "Not much progress, I see."

"He's in France. Morgentus sent Leviathan to stop him, but our efforts are getting the better of them." Joel grinned.

Gediel nodded. The human still had one champion.

"You report to Metatron soon? My khata is about to return. You can go with her. While you wait, perhaps I could have a word," Alex said, recapturing his attention.

Gediel considered the meaning of her features. He wondered how much Alex knew. She'd been work in the background before this even came to pass. Her khata's constant criticism of the human drove her to prove Dominic worthy of her daughter. He read the lines in her face. What she ended up proving wasn't as intended. Dominic was the wrong man, but they were unable to question the king in such a decision. So many lies wove their ketu tighter, all to protect Dominic and delay his fated fall. Though Gediel saw he was caught in the middle of this terrible debacle, and though he wanted to fight those who convinced the king it was wise, something in his heart told him all would be well in the end. Fighting would only serve to exhaust him and waste everyone's time. Somehow inside him there was peace despite his cares. Gediel never witnessed the king and his cohorts acting without reason and he never saw anything turn out so badly, except for the Conflict — and even that was only half played out. Things would be righted, one way or another. He simply needed patience.

"Certainly," Gediel said, going to her.

Alex escorted him through the entrance and out a door that opened on a balcony overlooking the White City. The sky was brightening with the sunrise, a soft gold burning away the cobalt. He watched a Victorian balloon carry a pair of lovers over the city. A biplane disrupted the peace, sputtering into the rosy dawn. Some humans were so inspiring, he thought watching it go. His eyes trailed to the dark blue remaining. The moon was small, but large enough to remind him of what he couldn't get his hands on and why. He tapped the triangles on his left shoulder, finally able to relax for the moment. His armor returned to the penannular until it was needed.

"Was that all you learned? I assume you spoke with Cal," Alex said, stepping to the balustrade and peering over the city.

Gediel carefully approached her, suddenly feeling very boxed in. He wasn't sure how he wanted to answer her.

"You know what else I found, Alex," Gediel finally said.

Alex drew herself up, acknowledging the chastisement. Her hands gripped the balustrade tightly. She looked for her composure on the horizon, having failed to expect this reaction. Gediel hadn't expected to reply in such a manner either. The sight of the moon put him in a bitter temper.

"Why did you stand by and allow this to happen to your own daughter?"

"I accept you being angry with me. You should know this is why Mikhael and I sent you — but you forget our oath," Alex replied.

"Oath?"

Alex shut her eyes and gestured dismissively. That was no excuse and she knew it.

"I'm sorry, Gediel. This decision was made without me. You know I would never agree to such things," Alex said.

"You should've told her the moment you learned of this. You didn't need to mention me, but you should've told her the truth of her role," Gediel said.

"I didn't know until the incident of Acheron. Believe me, I confronted Mikhael on this heresy. He managed to silence my tongue until now," Alex admitted.

"Then you and Gragrafel sent for me?"

Alex shook her head.

"Mikhael would do anything for my daughter. This has haunted him since the feast and he sought a way to help her escape the fate, but nothing ever manifested. When Dominic stood in his hall demanding to be heard, he knew then the time had come," Alex explained.

They hid their plans from her as well. Gediel saw in her eyes that this was the truth. He ground his teeth and turned away. She was in pain after learning the truth and keeping the secret just a few short years. What good would it have done? Thousands of years had passed and Maiel adored her family. It would've only made her miserable and driven her deeper into Morgentus's clutches for having been betrayed by her king and commanders.

"Maiel will never turn her back on Adonai," Gediel breathed, closing his eyes.

"I forbid such thoughts. My daughter is pure," Alex crossly rasped.

A fire raged in his belly. Emotions that had been tamped down for too long now vied for attention all at once. Gediel flexed his fist, gathering his thoughts. He could feel the braid in his pocket, uncomfortably warm. Settling his hand over it, he tried to focus on the moment and not his desire. He was not angry with Alex, but he was angry with himself for waiting too long to speak his mind.

"My apologies, Alex. In the end this is as much my fault as anyone's. I should've made my feelings known to her before they could do this." Gediel hung his head.

Leaning on the rail of the balcony, he kept his eyes shut and reordered his senses. He only hoped he could be so controlled in the presence of the High Council. He didn't have much time to gather himself before he would have to reveal the details of his journeys. Alex's hand was suddenly on his shoulder. Her soothing touch meant a great deal to him at the moment.

"I only pray I'm not lost for hatred of what they've done," Gediel murmured.

"Things will be put right from this. I only wish they had done something else and didn't create so much wrong in trying to help one wayward assign," Alex said.

"What of the children, Alex?" Gediel asked. Had anyone thought of the younglings in the outcome?

"They'll mend, as we all will."

Gediel straightened and opened his eyes to see the skyline. He held back the tears that he nearly cried for the children. He could feel a thrumming throughout his resonance. It was a sensation he was familiar with in battle, but he never felt it outside the field.

"Don't speak a word of this to them or my daughter. There's still hope and we must work to make that blossom. I'm so sorry, Gediel," Alex said.

Gediel shook his head. He grasped Alex's hand and gave it a squeeze.

"It'll be my honor to protect her family and in that my love will be expressed. I've wanted nothing more than to avenge my aryika's wrong. I'll be fulfilled when that has come to pass. This is all I ask for. Once he's gone from creation, everything else is nothing to me, but the happiness of my friends. May I be raised swiftly."

Alex raised his hand to her lips and kissed his glove. Tears stood in her eyes, for him and his fate. He smiled weakly and pressed her hand to his chest. He had existed this long without a mate and besides, could not envision one. He knew he would rise once he took down his aryika and all of this would be a distant memory. He only hoped it would remain in the past, of little matter to the Power he would eventually become.

The door of the balcony opened and Magiel appeared before them. Her severe expression was a welcome release from the emotions silencing them. Gediel nodded to Magiel. She looked well for one who had just faced the prince of the deep.

"If that'll be all, Alex," Gediel said in a rough voice.

The Wolf leader half bowed. Alex inclined her head and Gediel swiftly turned away. He followed Magiel and together they left the view of the city at dawn. Gediel tucked away his knowledge and the feelings it caused. It would do him no good and was thus useless. His hand slipped into his pocket. He held tightly onto the braid Callidora had lent him.

CHAPTER 21

MAIEL PEERED FROM UNDER the cowl of the bulky cloak that covered her. She noticed the driver watching them in the rearview mirror. She held his stare, challenging him to continue his spying. Her eyes flashed and that was the last glance he dared. She smiled softly to herself, thinking of everything that brought her to this moment as the countryside slid past her window. If she had half her strength back, she would have been able to carry both Orius and herself to their destination in the blink of an eye. Instead, they were trapped inside the stuffy car slowly rolling over cramped streets. To make matters worse, Orius wasn't talkative. She assumed it was due to the nosy driver. Anything they said would be repeated to the man they visited and he would interpret the information according to his bias. Yet Orius planned to share their greatest secret at the end of the drive. The vratin's mistrust of his elder was increasingly obvious since the first phone call.

Maiel sighed, wondering if she would see her family again. An image of Dominic coming to her rescue played in the back of her mind. The last impression she had had of her husband told her that he'd be unable to make such a rescue again. He had failed to strengthen his skills, and because of this, the others would certainly not allow a rescue either. She was lost there and had to find her way back alone if she could. The rest of the family would follow the rules, ensuring that if no one reached them, she faced her test alone to prove herself and keep the clan name untainted.

Orius touched her arm in consolation, as if he could read her thoughts. Maiel relaxed against the seat. His eyes looked as worried as she imagined her own were. In another time, they could have spoken without the human hearing them. Now they could only gaze at each other and hope their expressions imparted some meaning the other could understand. He gave a weak smile and returned to looking out the window, giving her armored forearm a pat.

The car continued on after a brief halt at an intersection. People dashed across the lane ahead. It was the same thing every minute or so. She wondered how she'd ever withstood the daily debacle humans called life. The mind wipe caused by the bio-vessel sometimes seemed like a blessing. Maiel shut her eyes and decided to focus on regaining some strength in the event Orius's fears were justified. Shrouded in meditation, she wouldn't have to witness the monotonous voyage.

Nearly an hour passed before they arrived at their destination. Maiel opened her eyes, refreshed but not cheered. The car drove up a broad drive, passing tourists and vratin alike. An old wall was littered with rubble and construction signs in which the remains of an old arch in severe disrepair overlooked the lawn. The day was still young and the sun shone brightly in the sky. Maiel wondered why they didn't move her during the night undercover of darkness. At least it would have been more exciting with the promise of shades to combat. In the daylight, there were many humans to hide from, but no immediate threat due to their visibility. Even the shadowborn were wary. Neither world wished themselves disclosed to Samsara. In Zion, it was the law; no interference was allowed that wasn't first adjudicated and approved.

Maiel never felt self-conscious about her appearance, but when the height of most humans barely made it to her shoulder, she stood out. At more than seven feet, she cut an unusual figure among them, sure to be remembered. Thankfully, Orius was quite tall for his adoptive kind, which only heightened the spectacle of their entrance.

The car parked before the front stairs. A young vratin ran down the steps and greeted them, opening the door to the car. The vehicle had gained the attention of several bystanders. Orius climbed out first, then helped her to exit without revealing a glint of armor or crimson locks. She imagined she was quite the sight, as several others stopped to gape at their passage. Orius regarded her nervously. The driver pulled Orius's bag from the trunk and gave it to him. After he accepted the luggage, he gave her a warm, encouraging smile and urged her forward.

The massive buildings were a grotesque display of confused human knowledge. Maiel frowned at it. She supposed it could be considered impressive or even beautiful, but there were too many shadows lurking. The darkness muted the grandeur. The friezes and statues turned to watch her. She lowered her chin, reminding herself to go easy on the humans. After all, flesh disrupted consciousness. They nearly forget everything they had come from and even their purpose. It was not worth casting blame.

"Come along, Bethiah," Orius said, starting up the weathered stairs to the stained edifice.

Maiel followed him, noticing her sandals glinting rather brilliantly in the sunlight. She wondered if anyone had noticed. Reluctant to let a single soul see any part of her, she hurried her pace. They entered the basilica, passing through a tall green door, a narrow entrance, and under one of three arches into the nave. The ancient structure smelled faintly of sulfur and roses. She felt the presence of many strange energies, all disguised by other layers, masks, and costumes. The air grew thicker the farther they trekked. She noticed the few souls and other beings bent in prayer as they sat in dark wooden pews. The vast room was deathly quiet but for their passing. The tapping of her sandals against the marble floor, the creak of her armor's joints, the tremor of the sword strapped to her hip, echoed through the giant room. Orius faced her with a concerned mien, bringing their guide to a stop as well.

"I nearly forgot," Orius said, eyeing her.

The vratin looked around sheepishly. Those sitting in the pews praying looked quite annoyed by their noisy passing. He nodded, mumbling something. An old woman crossed herself and muttered under her breath. There was naught they could do and both their arrival and passing had already made an impression. He shook his head and they continued on their way.

"Nothing for it now," he muttered.

Maiel stepped forward, trying very hard to stay quiet. She drew the cloak tighter about her form. All she could do was silence the sword and try to walk more delicately. She watched the intricate star design of the floor under her feet. This drew her gaze to the marble walls, to the statuary, and the multitude of altars. The gray walls were decorated with enormous frescos, depicting images from the life of the prince's incarnation, at least as humans recalled them. A frown drew her mouth down, but the images took her eyes up. The inside of the dome was ringed by windows, with ornate vaulting above. At the center was a round eye peering back at her. The structure resembled the Seal of Samsara. A pang tore through her core, pulling her chin back down. The statues wept for her. The appliance binding to her atman prevented her from using the ways.

The vratin hurried them into a narrow hall to the right of the altar. They passed a room filled with gold crosses and other treasures of religious antiquity that made her pause. That treasure could feed hundreds. The vratin guiding them urged them forward before she could question their hoarding. Down the passage, he led them into a room that smelled like old books. He continued to the back, explaining the direct route was blocked by the tourists in the crypt at that hour. Without any ceremony, he popped open a secret door behind a niche and gestured. Spiral stairs twisted down through the dark. A thick blanket of dust covered the old stones with no prints. Maiel hesitated, but Orius placed a hand on her shoulder and gave his reassuring smile. The expression failed to inspire hope. She preferred staying with Orius's order, where there was safety despite Morgentus. The other guardians weren't about to let him harm anyone, though. Here there was only suspicion and doubt and rooms filled with shades and a possible marditavya that was sure to betray them to his master. Under such circumstances, Morgentus could walk through the front doors to wherever they hid her to finish his work. This place wasn't the haven it seemed, no matter what hidden route they wandered.

Disregarding her better judgment, Maiel followed the passage down. At the bottom of the steps an old wooden door opened on a dimly lit passage. The tunnel appeared even older, dug from the rock and earth beneath the cathedral centuries ago. Relics, brick, and dust rested against the walls. Maiel was reminded of a labyrinth, and an unsettling feeling crept into her bones. The vratin explained to Orius that this was a very old crypt from a previous church that had been built there. A place that they didn't share with the public. That was convenient. She was about to warn Orius, but his confident gait and expression shut her up.

Their guide next brought them to a dead end and another old door. He produced an old iron key, unlocked the door and pressed the barrier back. The hinges groaned from disuse. A dark alcove appeared before them, an old burial chamber. Lingering shadows immediately retreated beneath the dim light he flipped on. He urged them inside, but Maiel hesitated. Besides feeling like they were in a prison, the wiring was ancient and the smell of electricity warned her not to go in any farther. Orius looked to her knowingly. The vratin flicked another switch, turning on more electric bulbs strung in the center of the long, low room. Orius placed a hand on her back and mumbled some encouragement. The door closed and the locked clicked.

Maiel faced the earthy cell, pacing to the far end. The walls felt close and dense, even though the space was nearly as large as a modest farmhouse basement. There was a long, old table with benches and enough dust on the stone floor to cover a grave. The smell of corpses lingered in the air. Niches covered in dried mud and concrete attested to the function of this space.

Orius set his bag on the table and sat himself on one of the benches.

"You don't find this strange, Orius?" Maiel asked him.

"I'm sure it's just a precaution, Bethiah. After all, they can't be sure you're a lightwalker." Orius smiled.

Maiel found a sturdy stool and dragged it to the far wall. From there, she could see the entire room. Slumping onto the rickety seat, she reached for anyone who might be near. Orius shouldn't have called for help, at least not from this place. They could have relied on themselves to fight Morgentus instead of risking an addition to the evil one's pool of resources. If she could just have reached back into Zion and made contact with her akha. All they needed was to tell them Morgentus hunted her. They would have come. There wasn't an order or commander in all the armies that could stay Joel. As for Zach, no council could rein him in. A tear slipped from her eye.

"I shouldn't have come. We should have asked one of the guardians to help," Maiel said woefully.

Orius looked to her, his arms crossed and his brows knitted.

"The shadow reaches into places that we don't perceive. With a little patience, my friends would've come to me before your akha succeeded in dragging me off. My discernment isn't what it used to be. If it were, I would've realized I had all I needed at your church. Instead, I've condemned us both."

Orius chuckled.

"Don't be so dark. Geitz is just taking care. He trusts my judgment, but one can never be too careful. He's very aware of how imps and shades work."

"I'm not so sure. I may be losing my abilities, but the darkness and light still contrast," Maiel said. She paused, pulling the hood back from her helmet. She adjusted it, uncomfortable. "Have you ever told him of your akha?" she asked.

Before Orius could answer, a knock on the door stopped their dialogue. She flipped the hood back up and Orius called their visitor inside. A vratin entered, carrying a tray. He set it on the table and exited, again locking the door. Maiel looked at the pitcher and loaf of bread. She pulled back her hood and raised an eyebrow at him.

Orius poured a cup of water and drank. With a grin, he informed her it wasn't poisoned. He then pulled a piece of bread from the loaf and ate it. Again, it wasn't poisoned. He then folded his arms and faced the door. He didn't answer the question she'd asked. Maiel took his silence for a no.

Maiel folded her arms and then her legs at the ankles, stretching her length out while resting her back against the cold wall. Her ears filled with a gentle whisper. The room tried to tell its story, but she wasn't strong enough to hear. She shut her eyes and listened, hoping to catch even one word. The voices became more insistent. A strange buzz radiated through her. The voices grew louder; the noise was like a thousand voices all shouting at once behind thick glass.

Another knock sounded at the door. The voices instantly ceased. Maiel opened her eyes and looked in the direction of the door. Orius motioned for her to replace her hood. She sat up, drawing her legs back to the stool. She shifted the cloak to conceal every inch. Orius called to whoever had come. The vratin who brought them water and bread returned, along with a spotted old man in the same raiment of the clergy.

"Archbishop Geitz, it's so good to see you, my old friend." Orius grinned, towering over the human.

"Gregely," Geitz greeted him eagerly.

Maiel sat still, waiting for them to acknowledge her. Geitz wasn't what she'd expected. He was quite a bit older and smaller. His thin white hair and piercing dark gaze reminded her of the elders back home. She sat up taller, regaining her hope.

"How was the drive?" Geitz asked in a raspy tone.

"Lovely, as always, but the traffic was horrendous."

"Good. Good. Yes, it can be this time of morning."

Geitz turned toward her. His smile slowly faded; he was uneasy with finally seeing her. His bow-legged step brought him closer.

"Is this our new friend?"

"Yes," Orius said, unsure if he should allow Geitz to approach further or to slow the introduction.

Maiel peered at them from beneath her cloak. Geitz watched her in return. He lifted his hand and dismissed his companion. The man switched his gaze between Orius and the archbishop. He reluctantly backed out of the room and closed the door. Maiel heard the lock set.

"I am Archbishop Luca Geitz. Welcome to the Basilica of Esztergom, messenger," Geitz said.

Maiel didn't stir. She watched Orius come closer. He placed his hand on her shoulder and whispered reassuringly. Maiel stood, pulling her hood back. She glared down at him, clearly offended at his touch. Geitz stared up at her with his mouth agape.

"My God," Geitz rasped.

"Let me take that," Orius said, helping her take off the cloak, wanting to redirect her temper.

Geitz stumbled backward as she flexed her wings. Maiel held her tongue, waiting for Orius to take the lead. Geitz regained his composure, whispering about saints and holy relics. He took a handkerchief from his pocket and wiped his brow. Orius fetched him a glass of water. The archbishop sipped and stared at her. Feeling a bit parched herself, Maiel poured her own drink and brought the cup to her hand like the night she had first met Orius. Geitz stumbled back, spilling his drink. With a twinkle in her eye, she sipped from the vessel. Orius gave her a reproachful glance. Geitz carefully went to the table and sat on the bench. Maiel sat back on her stool and Orius joined his friend.

"Did you not believe me?" Orius asked him.

Geitz regarded him, reluctant to answer that question. If he admitted to not believing him, then he admitted that he didn't believe that Orius was what he claimed either. He folded his hands together before his face and looked sidelong in Maiel's direction. She returned the gaze and he quickly focused on Orius.

"It is difficult to explain. I believed you or wanted to believe you. It's one of those things, until you see it, it's never quite so grand as it should be," Geitz tried to reply delicately.

"Nothing's quite right in Samsara, a twisted reflection of home," Maiel told him.

Geitz looked toward her, surprised that she spoke and then nodded to acknowledge her speech. He watched her a moment too long and Maiel found herself wondering about her safety again. Geitz lowered his eyes. He bent his head in prayer, then crossed himself. Orius copied him. Maiel shifted on her stool, hearing the voices in the stones again. The whispers had calmed, but they held an edge, like they were desperate to speak but prevented by some threatening force.

"Let us begin," Geitz said, getting to his feet.

Maiel turned her attention from the walls of the basilica to its master. He pressed his hands together before him and smiled at her. She sat up straight and watched him warily. She supposed he was about to interview her to determine if she was as Orius claimed. If she didn't align herself with what they believed, how could she prove her origins? Humans had their rituals and books. They clung tightly to them. The truth that countered their faith could easily condemn her.

"Holy messenger, you'll forgive your humble servants, but it's necessary that we—evaluate your claims. I just wish to ask you some questions." Geitz bowed slightly.

Maiel eyed him, deciding not to correct everything that was wrong with his statement.

"What I answer may not fall in line with your belief of what's truth. How can you test my claims if you don't have the truth?"

Geitz's smile faded. He straightened, not answering her question.

"We'll do our best, Bethiah," Orius assured her.

Orius drew two stools from near the table and set them before her. The men sat facing her. She looked to Orius with doubt. He gave a slight smile, holding that gaze, assuring her that he understood her reluctance to continue. Too bad they were already locked inside a room deep beneath one of their sanctuaries. Maiel's mind flashed with unpleasant memories.

"Your patience is greatly appreciated," Geitz said.

Maiel set her full attention on him, just as she had with Father Gallo, but this time she didn't feel so amused. Geitz's forehead glistened with sweat again and he wiped his brow more than once during the inquiry. She frowned, replying to each of his questions with curt answers. Beside him, Orius's posture was tight; he was vexed and worried by her behavior.

"Why do you think God would do this to you?" Geitz suddenly asked.

Maiel stared at him. She supposed from her experience with Orius's order that by God, he meant King Adonai or some other Jñanasattva of Nirvana. However, Adonai had nothing to do with her being on Earth. She scowled in response, with no words to explain her darkened expression. Geitz drew back, obviously concerned that his wording had provoked her.

"The king has nothing to do with my presence here. I came to correct a mistake I made during my mission, a mistake brought on by the interference of a shadowwalker," Maiel decided to reply.

"She shows greater strength than I. As you remember—I awoke whole, without my armor and wings. She was just forming when I discovered her, and as you can see her wings are still very much attached," Orius chimed in.

"Then how have you determined she's fallen," Geitz murmured.

"We don't take on flesh, though we appear solid to you when we wish to. I have taken on flesh, and it isn't my choice to be visible," Maiel replied, not divulging that the spent penannular had caused her visibility.

Geitz didn't respond. He licked his lips and wiped his brow again. The answers befuddled him more than clarifying the reason for her presence. He drew a deep breath and sighed. Maiel held his gaze. She dug into his eyes, hoping that the remains of her power would help discern his true character. The walls whispered the answer, but their tangled messages remained indecipherable. His atman would tell her, if she could reach it.

"Tell me the whole story of how you came to be on Earth," Geitz asked, crossing his arms.

Maiel relayed the tale to him in a short, undetailed narrative. When she finished, the archbishop stared in stunned silence. His gaze held steady, in contrast to moments ago.

"Your—king, you say he gave you no warning of his intention," Geitz prompted.

"No, as I told you, it was my negligence." Maiel refused to be prompted.

"This is what made you angry? Why you took matters into your own hands? To make amends or to defy the king?" Geitz pressed.

Maiel stared, unblinking. He tried to make her say something that would condemn her.

"You'll never find your way back if you intend to defy the rules and embrace the emotion of anger," Geitz told her, resembling a rather austere professor.

Maiel held his gaze, not answering. He thought to teach her. Laughable.

"Perhaps your true mistake was in attempting to know his intentions. They aren't to be known by any but himself—the truth is beyond our capacity for understanding. Therefore, it's our duty to obey to the letter, or hardship befalls us." Geitz smiled.

"Archbishop, I'm afraid it's more difficult than that. Bethiah—as I've come to call her—is being hunted by a demon. This contest hasn't allowed her rest or to consult her brethren," Orius told him.

"You mentioned on the phone, but I must keep with what I said. Had she obeyed her orders, she wouldn't be in this position," Geitz said distractedly. He eyed her, meeting her gaze. "Bethiah," he breathed.

"Can you help her?" Orius asked.

Maiel's gaze went to her friend. He looked desperate and full of doubt.

"Perhaps, you're right. If I'd gone to my council—" Maiel finally spoke.

"Council?" Geitz cut her off.

"Angels are organized similar to our church, suffice it to say. They take orders like we do, from above," Orius said, a touch impatient, as if he'd already explained this before.

"Well, then. It would be a grave mistake to ignore your betters—but—but, I thought angels did everything as they should. What you tell me brings into question the long held notions of your kind. Is it something else, maybe, that clouds your judgment? It just isn't yours to have free will."

"We are autonomous. Lucifer's story is one of free will. What you speak of is an aberration of man. What appears to be a lack of free will to your kind is simply our acting on ancient wisdom."

Geitz paused, smiling at her. She supposed he meant to look friendly, but the expression reminded her of an imp she'd once stumbled upon. She held her silence again.

"I'm corrected, sacred one," he chuckled. "You mentioned your husband's a human who hopes to elevate to your status. That's blasphemous, as you must know," Geitz said, after a pause.

Maiel bit her tongue, her mouth forming into a flat line. He baited her. However, she wouldn't destroy all of his illusions just yet. In time her moment would come. Right then, she needed to keep her temper, in case Orius was right and he could offer her help.

"Is it a usual practice—making clay into diamonds?" Geitz asked, seeing that his words were affecting her.

"Clay must be tested by fire. We are made from fire, purified at our creation. Through many trials the clay is processed the same. Though they are originally created of different material, they may become duta," Maiel said, going with his analogy. Matters were really more complicated.

Geitz frowned deeply. He didn't like her answer, but she didn't fool herself into believing that he would. Humans such as Geitz seldom reveled in truth, chafing at it instead. It stole their claim to supremacy—the things they actually worshiped.

"I believe you," Geitz said stonily, then nodded with an unsure smile.

The archbishop grit his teeth. He tore his eyes away from her and looked to his friend. His expression softened and he nodded, affirming that he would try. Maiel didn't like his reaction, suspecting he felt her scrutiny. His dark eyes turned back to her, piercing and angry. He gave another smile, but the warmth was still absent.

"I'll try. I believe you," he repeated.

* * *

Magiel paced the entrance to the grand council chamber. Gediel wondered if she knew what he had discovered. Her khata kept the secret from everyone, but did she spare her closest relation the knowledge? Magiel didn't let on, but she was one of the best he knew at guarding against any show of emotion. Even Zacharius was second to her. Gediel smiled, reminded of the young alder. Zach's stoicism was in harmony with his wicked wit. And he was loyal.

The High Council's chamber door opened and Gediel followed Magiel onto the balcony. He could see a pale blue sky beyond the opening. Lemitus wasn't to be seen in her usual place. Corpheus and Denius had switched seats and were engaged in some sort of staring contest. The two councilors passed the time exploring each other's minds on some contested issue. Metatron joined them from the kapalanum chamber at the high end of the room. His dark eyes landed on Gediel and stuck. A violet light faded from his eyes.

"What progress have you made?" he asked.

"You were just watching, I presume," Gediel replied.

Magiel looked at him, surprised. Metatron eyed him, annoyed by his boldness. However, Gediel wasn't the only one among his rank who gave him trouble. His friend had taught him not to fear the council and to challenge them from time to time. They often forgot with whom they dealt and needed reminding.

"In fact, I've been watching you, Primus Gediel—watcher—or what will become of you," Metatron replied. He stepped around them and joined his companions. Lemitus appeared in the opening, offering Gediel an imperceptible smile. "If you're wondering, not much has changed."

"I'll prove my line and avenge my family name, but that isn't why we come before you," Gediel said.

"Dominic's closer in his search for his wife," Magiel said, interrupting them.

"Belial gains dominion in Samsara. He reaches out to take the erela Maiel. He also reaches for six others. They may already be lost to us," Metatron replied.

"One more Earth day and Dominic will have reached her," Magiel replied.

"Who are the other four?" Gediel asked, noting the more important information that Metatron had shared with them.

"After all that work, you don't know?"

Metatron faced him, as both Corpheus and Denius came out of their meditation. Gediel saw that he hadn't gathered all the intelligence he could have. He was obviously distracted by the damning tidbit of information he'd received.

"Lena and Dominic surely, but who else?" Magiel breathed.

"This night, he laid claim to Maxiel," Gediel added.

"A long time ago, just after the Conflict of Hosts, a guardian of the light saw the destruction and waste that was laid by the dissenters. He lost his younger akha, whom he loved dearly, and struggled hard to preserve this young duta by regimenting his every move. His loyalty to the king faltered when he watched his sibling committed grievous sins. He believed they weren't that different, being hewn from the same rock, and that he also wasn't worthy of his rank and station. Worse, he saw Adonai's reaction to the crimes as weakness. The king should've known that Lucifer and his companions turned their backs on their posts and prevented it from coming to pass, as he had controlled his akha. What he didn't realize is that the Conflict served to remind us that choices have consequences and some choices require great deliberation. If we interfere with an atman's autonomy, we will never know who is loyal and who is to betray us," Metatron said, revealing the reason behind his reluctance to intervene.

"Decurio Oriael?" Magiel said, confused.

Magiel's complexion paled. She stepped away from them and wandered along the balcony. Gediel patiently waited for her to speak. She was a youngling during the Conflict, as was her khata. Oriael was already a legend among the higher incarnations and a model for what they each could achieve. It was strange that he fell, but so was the fall of his aryika.

"Oriael was one of the finest guardians the light claimed. A soldier of the Moon Order. He reached the rank of Power quickly, well on his way to his final rising. No one saw his fall coming. It shouldn't have been possible— just like my niece," Magiel said.

"It's always possible, if they ignore the path," Corpheus said.

"Comforting. Who are the others?" Gediel frowned.

"A human that has been connected to Oriael during his service as vratin," Metatron said.

"We can save him easily enough," Magiel said.

"Not this one. He's been in service to Belial for the majority of his entire incarnation. He fades as we speak. Nor can you save Dominic. He burns with the fire and will betray us all to preserve his ketu."

"Any of us would," Magiel defended him.

"No. We wouldn't," Gediel mumbled.

"Adonai has given his command," Metatron said gravely.

"Then we bring four back—but you said seven, atman," Gediel said.

Metatron eyed him, but didn't reply.

"To return to us, Dominic will need to sacrifice himself for the others," Denius said, whipping his tail insistently.

"Maiel and Lena are the only important souls. They must return, but the others can be sacrificed," Metatron added.

"Who is the last?" Gediel posed the question again.

Metatron assessed him with a stern glance.

"You."

Magiel gasped.

Gediel felt the response reverberate through his sattva. This was to be expected.

"Your duty is to secure Oriael, Lena, and Captain Maiel. No more," Metatron said.

"We leave none behind," Gediel said.

"You don't have a choice," Metatron told him.

Gediel and the seraph stared at one another in a test of wills.

"What is it that you wish of us?" Magiel asked, breaking the spell.

"Make sure Dominic goes to the basilica in Hungary, then stand down and let him be taken by Morgentus. It's the only way for him to return to us, if he will, and it will shake Maiel out of her doubt. She'll face the labyrinth lord, but she'll not cast him into Oblivion. Not yet. Adonai has need of him still. His ambition is the key to ending this conflict once and for all. As for Oriael, Belial will see to him and the burning vratin. You won't intervene and prevent his return. He's far too important to you."

Magiel inclined her head, accepting the order without question. Gediel found himself hesitant. He offered a reluctant nod and a wary glance to the councilors instead.

"That will be all, alder Magiel," Metatron said to her.

"Thank you for your graciousness," Magiel said, turning from them in a sweeping bow.

Gediel's back stiffened and his chin raised. He heard the entrance door open and shut behind the alder. He was now alone with the council. For a moment, he thought they had no interest in what it was he'd uncovered. Metatron's dark gaze said otherwise.

"Give your report, and then you may see Commander Voil," Metatron demanded.

"Maxiel has been the cause of the fall and dark efforts that poisoned the soul. There may be no way of turning Dominic back, if there ever was. Morgentus staked his claim with a nail many years ago. He's been burning down ever since. I suggest an investigation into anyone he's had contact with in that time," Gediel said.

"The future has always declared their burning. The nail only made that process faster for Maxiel," Metatron admitted.

"Then why waste her on the human?" Gediel asked.

"Why are you concerned, Primus Gediel?"

"I think you know the answer to that," Gediel said, eyes flashing silver.

"Keep to your wolves and dogs, watcher. That is a matter of council business."

"Stealing a mate for another isn't council business. You walk a thin line that could see you wed to Belial for betraying the light, Metatron. Their ketu is a dishonor to the king."

"It's obvious that you've far to go before you understand the complexities of our plans," Metatron replied.

"You just mentioned a moment ago that they're targeting me. Didn't you think that would be the way?"

Gediel cast his eyes over the others. Their stoic expressions asserted their compliance with the decision that had been made long ago. This new development meant little to them. Only Lemitus showed a glimmer of remorse, for she loved her warrior children. Gediel returned his gaze to the head councilor. Metatron studied him. He gathered by his interest in his future that they thought this news would send him over the edge.

"It's not I who walks a thin line," Metatron growled.

"The result of this trial will prove our loyalty, I hope, once and for all. How you could question Captain Maiel eludes me, but I've seen you put Mikhael through his paces from time to time. Perhaps it amuses you. Let me ask you this, though—what if the others have been implanted with the same poison? Each encountered Morgentus in the Astrals."

"You really don't understand why?"

Gediel had no answer to that question that he hadn't already alluded to. His jaw squeezed tight, and he ground his teeth together.

"This doesn't really have anything to do with her does it, because she's been tested and proven her unfailing will. Once free of these bonds, she'll rise quickly. Dominic, however, has proven he's irrational and selfish. He loves her though and is loyal to her ideals," Gediel replied.

"Not him," Metatron said. He waited a beat, to watch Gediel take in his words. Then he added, "He's all but lost to us. One last trial will prove how tenuous his loyalty is. The poison you speak of—has already done its work. He's not strong enough to survive it."

"Why not cast him out now?"

"We both know we would lose her. His loss is asking too much in her present state of mind. She'll have to be shown what he is. It'll not be an easy task. It never has been. In the meantime, it has shown us the mettle of your atman and we continue with the plan as is," Metatron replied.

"Oriael would be proud to see that you've gone to such lengths, though they are late," Gediel challenged.

"Oriael understood that in some cases rigid control is the only answer. We weighed our options and this gave Dominic the greatest chance. I hope you will come to see that, and that more than your dharma matters in the equation, Primus," Metatron warned.

Gediel clamped his teeth together, refusing to speak another word. He wasn't being selfish in questioning their tactics. The price was simply too high.

"For now, watcher. Hold back Evocati Luthias. Take him so that you can both make amends to Shen for polluting his door to the Astrals. You're dismissed."

Gediel swallowed the terrible taste in his mouth. They took her to give her to a lesser threat. He inclined his head stiffly and turned to leave under their watchful gaze before the tears spilled from his eyes.

Magiel awaited him in the antechamber. Her dark eyes betrayed the emotions overcoming her.

"Their abilities have grown too great to lose them to darkness," she said.

"Don't believe for one moment that such will come to pass," Gediel said, placing his hands on her arms.

"What can we possibly do to make this right?"

"I have a plan. Follow your khata and be sure that she does as they have requested. Leave the rest to me," Gediel said, walking down the hall, away from the reach of the councilors.

Magiel hurried to keep up with him. She looked little eased by his confidence. "Have you no faith in me?" he asked.

"I can only hope your plan works, whatever it is," Magiel replied, tormented by her thoughts.

Gediel grinned. He harbored no doubts in the plan he formulated, nor his ability to carry it out. However, the many variables suggested he should examine his ideas again, to be sure he could account for each possibility and return with their four threatened atman. They didn't leave any behind, but he was willing to sacrifice any of them if it made the difference between losing Maiel and securing her. That fact bothered him, but now he understood from what this reluctance stemmed and he could manage the instinct.

"Don't do anything rash," Magiel said.

Gediel paused and looked askance at her. Did she really think him capable?

"I almost grew fond of him. Yet something always bothered me. It's no secret I don't care much for any of them, but him—in particular—a shade and flame stirred inside that heart. Deceitful, lazy, flippant, and horribly clumsy. How he deserved my niece before you, I'll never be able to understand. They have wronged you both in this, and I can't help thinking he may have been saved if they were honest with us," Magiel said, taking his arm.

"Perhaps, but it's our duty to do what we can for souls in their journeys. None of those attributes should condemn them. They're children compared to us. See Maiel's sacrifice as honorable and mine as well," Gediel said, also struggling with their reasons to test their trust.

"Pity—that's what the others will feel for you."

"They already do, but when I have slain my aryika and sent that stain on my family's name into Oblivion, then they'll have respect. Our allegiance to the king will never be questioned again."

CHAPTER 22

DOMINIC WATCHED THE ROAD in both directions, a long straight tract with a few dips, running generally north to south. He thought for certain the shades would be pursued after Athiel and Rathiel left them in the ocean. At least his clothes had dried out. He felt only a little damp and chill in the crisp night air.

Shifting his bag on his back, Dominic concentrated on the path ahead. By his very damp atlas, he could see they had quite a long walk before the next town. The hair on the back of his neck rose as he made the assessment. He patted it back down and came to a halt. Lena turned to see why, opening her mouth to speak. Her eyes glinted with a reflection of light. She stared with apprehension at something gaining on them. Dominic turned back around. Headlamps flashed along the road in their direction.

"Just a car," Dominic said, walking past the girl.

Lena didn't move. She watched it come and for a moment Dominic wondered if Morgentus's henchman had figured out another way to run them down. The car moved unusually fast. The engine growled as the driver mashed the gas pedal. The lights flashed as it struck ruts in the road. The tinny sound of the radio disrupted the peace. It was too late to run. The car passed, kicking up leaves and dust. The red taillights lit up and it squealed to a halt. Dominic cursed.

"Don't get in that car," Lena advised with alarm.

Dominic gestured. It was a convertible sports car. Candy red. A woman with a scarf over her head was in the driver's seat. She smiled over her shoulder at him. The curl of her red lips put him quite at ease. He couldn't make out the melodic voice over the purr of the engine. He excused himself, shrugging.

"American?" she said with a laugh. "Do you need a ride?"

"Is it that obvious? Where are you headed?" Dominic asked, slowly approaching the car.

"The way you're dressed. I hope to reach Paris, but who knows by morning." She smiled with brilliant white teeth.

"That's where I was headed. My ferry got in late and there were no taxis," Dominic said.

"Just like an American. Too busy to stop. Get in. You can't walk there." She eyed him, appearing pleased with what she saw.

Dominic threw his bag behind the seat and opened the door. This was a nice bit of luck. He climbed in, as Lena ran and jumped into the tiny jump seat, reiterating her warning. The woman took off, pressing down hard on the gas before he could even close the door. He managed to pry it shut without catching a limb, finger, or toe. They passed along the road at a higher speed than advisable at night on such curved routes.

"You running from something?" Dominic asked.

The woman smiled. Her dark hair peeked out from under the scarf, curling in the wind. She was pretty, as far as human women went. The soft lines around her mouth and eyes spoke of a few years of wisdom. She was in her late thirties, maybe forty. What could she have to run from? By that age, most women were married and taking care of their children. She was thin as a rail, narrow-hipped and small breasted. He doubted she had even one child.

"My husband—a brutal oaf. Are you scared?" she finally answered.

Dominic frowned. He took for granted that others enjoyed a happy life. Then, he was reminded why he was there. His wife had run from him, and though he was no brute, he might be an oaf. He wiped his face with his hand, sorry he'd asked.

"Got rough with me one too many times. I decided no more. I put my life on hold. I was just a foolish child when I married him. Now, I'm taking my time back," she continued.

Dominic rubbed his lip with his pointer finger and watched the road.

"Too much information," she said, laughing.

Dominic gave her a sidelong glance. Her warm demeanor and smile tugged at his heart. He found himself smiling back.

"No—no," Dominic replied. "Just hope he's not following."

"Not tonight. I gave him a sleeping pill. By the time he wakes, I'll be in Paris and he won't find me there until I'm a famous painter."

The woman laughed. Dominic felt intoxicated by her. She piqued his curiosity and other interests. Her pretty face turned to him and her eyes glinted with mischief. They were green or brown or something in between.

"What do they call you?" she asked.

"Dominic," he answered, turning toward her in the seat, running his arm along the door and the other along the back of the seat.

"I'm Madeleine." She offered her hand.

They shook hands. Lena entered his vision from the corner of his eye. Her little face was pinched up with distaste. She gained his attention for a brief glance, shaking her head to warn him about something she felt. Dominic turned away so he couldn't see her anymore. Lena's advice, rarely given, wasn't always the best. Her mistrust of the woman came of the residual panic she'd felt after being nearly drown by Leviathan. Madeleine was a godsend. They'd reach Paris in a couple hours instead of a couple of days. There was nothing to be concerned about.

"Pleasure to meet you, Madeleine," Dominic said.

"You have no idea. Are you hungry, Dominic? We should stop for something to eat when the sun rises. French food is a treat for Americans."

"Not yet, but I'm sure I will be starved by the time we get there."

"Good. Then we can stop for both of us. I need to sell this thing, so no one finds me. I think I will get a little yellow car."

Madeleine filled the time with talk about her dreams. She'd wanted to go to school for art, but her parents couldn't afford it. When she'd met her husband, Jules, he'd promised her the world. He was a good boy and she loved him dearly. That was all to change. When their marriage produced no children, he stopped paying for art lessons and stayed at work longer hours. She suspected he succumbed to having an affair, which was devastating to her at first, but soon it became the least of her worries. After a few years of the cold shoulder and a deepening rift, he turned to the bottle for comfort and used his fists and words to pound her down.

Sitting in the gold light of the sunrise, they enjoyed a cup of coffee and lighter conversation. The deeper she delved, the more he realized that he had said too much. Falling more in line with the disguise he used with the sheep farmers, he started talking about his term as an art student to throw her off the scent should she be a friend of his enemy. Madeleine was enthralled, perhaps seeing more there than he intended. Still, it put a smile on her face. Though she was mature, she was still quite lovely and her exuberance drew him in.

Madeleine then begged him to sell her car for her. Her reasoning was sound. They'd be looking for a woman of her description and if she traded the car, then they would have her trail. Dominic obliged, adding to Lena's distress. He offered her no consolation either. They parted for a good portion of the morning while he hunted down the perfect car. He returned to the café in a butter-toned Sprite.

A gasp escaped Dominic's pleased host. Madeleine giggled like a girl on Christmas, tears coming to her eyes. He felt proud for the first time in ages, strutting to the curb. She folded him in her arms and the hug lingered a beat too long. Lena glowered from her position on the rag roof. So what if he needed his ego stroked a little? It wasn't as though he was abandoning the mission.

"Let's continue our drive, beautiful boy," Madeleine said, glowing in the noon sun. "I hope this new car will be as enjoyable as the last."

The pale yellow scarf covering her dark hair reminded him of home. He nodded and they climbed into her new dream car. It wasn't much of a change from the other one, but the police wouldn't be looking for a buttercream car if her husband turned her in. Lena sat with her arms crossed, glowering at the wind. He supposed she pouted because the woman hadn't shown the snakes beneath her wig or proven to be a banshee or vampire. Madeleine was just a woman, and wouldn't prove the girl's jealousies right. She was merely a stroke of luck, a wayward traveler en route to her destiny like him.

Dominic waved good-bye to Madeleine as he stood on the sidewalk, steps from the train station in Paris. She waved back to him, smiling with a brilliant grin. Her dream was to live in Paris and do something, anything of worth, but mostly to find respect for just being who she was. Dominic empathized deeply with her and watched her little Sprite disappear in the congested traffic. Horns, engines, and human chatter made the morning buzz with an energy he hadn't felt since he'd last seen Zion. This was Paris. He looked around, a little disappointed that it had changed so much. He preferred the turn of the twentieth century, its grandiose style and art. Lena stood by a remnant of the past: a doorway of a dress shop. She stared at a long, red gown and imagined herself in it. He cleared his throat and she smiled, returning reluctantly to his side. She reminded him of his little girls again. Glancing at the beautiful gown, he knew someone who could make the simple satin design a stunning work of art. He put his hand on Lena's head and tousled her hair, feeling his mood lightened. She giggled, pushing his hand away.

In a few short strides, they entered the train station to face the only means available to them in thwarting Morgentus before he captured Maiel. Purchasing the tickets and boarding the train went smoothly. Travelers milled through the station. Some noticed him, some ignored him. Their faces were plain, ordinary, and forgettable. Just the same, any one of them could have been a shade or shadowborn. He could no longer tell. A brown sports coat startled him, but he soon eased up when it belonged to a stranger he knew nothing about. To be safe from spying eyes and ears he knew would be near, he rented a private berth on each train. This way he would also be free to communicate with his guardian, and only link to Zion. Even if there were no shades, being overheard could complicate things when a concerned citizen summoned the authorities to cart him off to a hospital.

Facing each other on the seats of their cabin, both Lena and Dominic found they had nothing to say. He gathered the girl disapproved of him ignoring her advice about Madeleine. It mattered little, as she had brought them safely to Paris despite what Lena thought would happen. The girl closed her eyes and folded her legs, deciding to meditate. It was more like she chose to shun him for her mistake. A small apology would have cleared the air.

Dominic looked at the tickets and went through the steps between here and their destination. It mattered because each stop was a marker of progress. They would change trains in Munich, and pass through several stops in large cities before ending their journey in Budapest. That might be dangerous, given the probability of a run-in. He looked out the window, seeing the French countryside pass quickly, and wondered if this counted for moving. If the shades couldn't track them while they were moving, could they track them while they were stationary on a vehicle? It was an odd question to ask, but his experience told him that such nuances could make for interesting exceptions. Those exceptions might have influenced a different choice in transportation. The route seemed pretty straightforward, until variables such as that came into play. Watchers were known to leave such details out, especially the watcher who gave him the advice. They all had secret agendas, but especially that one. Thankfully, Dominic knew Gediel's plot and could plan around him.

Dominic's mind returned to Madeleine and her little car. It was a lucky coincidence that brought him into contact with such a lovely creature. He thought of her hair curling in the wind. The bright smile flickered in his memory. Then a cold chill ran down his back. Madeleine's guardian wasn't to be seen. Dominic looked toward Lena. Her face was blank as she rested. He settled back, recalling that he hadn't seen a single guardian since waking in the Dover hotel. Whether it was a shade who told him or not, he was in fact running out of time, as the sight declined and his body became mortal.

Dominic removed the warped atlas from the bag and thumbed through it again, trying not to think on it anymore. Lena would claim he wasted their time. Madeleine had been completely alone, and the taxi driver was also alone; both had had a perfect opportunity to stab him, but he still had made it past unscathed. Dominic bit the inside of his cheek, forcing his mind to focus. This wasn't the time to compare who was smarter, especially when she was just a child.

Flipping through the atlas, Dominic searched for the location that offered the ideal hiding place for his missing wife. Time ticked away quickly in Samsara and his attention slipped to the other woman. Had Madeleine been abandoned like him? Whatever her story, he was thankful it included him when it did. A similar stroke of luck could lead them right to Maiel. His eyes went to Lena again. Fearful that she could read his thoughts, he also wondered at her real purpose. The child was still unable to track his wife. Suspiciously, she left out the absence of Madeleine's guardian, or that of the taxi driver still further back. The girl drew further inward, holding her secret.

"Shades, shadows, and fallen—the closer we get, the harder they'll look for us—the more they'll try to trap you. Be aware of that as we go. Listen to what advice I have to give you next time. Certainly they'll start with your thoughts," Lena said without opening her eyes.

"It'd be nice if you shared that you were going to be in my head," Dominic said, airing his suspicion at last. He sighed, annoyed that he was so harsh. "Never mind. If we make it all the way to Budapest on these trains, that'll be a miracle," he added.

Lena opened her eyes.

"You must feel the same," Dominic said.

"You share your thoughts with Luthias willingly, as your guardian. It was assumed you would do the same with me," Lena said. Her mature eyes bored into him. "We'll succeed and I'll be of more help to you once we reach Budapest. Until then, I can only protect you from the shades that cross our paths. We agreed this is your destiny, Dominic. Didn't we? That you were to find and rescue Captain Maiel? If you wish me to help, then say the word and we can end this quickly, or you can make her proud," Lena said, just needling him further.

Lena stared at him a moment longer, then shut her eyes and continued to recharge her energy. She was too much like Callidora and it made him wonder what was their intention with the child. Dominic watched her sit there as still as a statue. Bringing up Luthias only returned him to idealizing the mission in a fantasy that was never going to be. Together they'd have already made it to Budapest and would already be closing in on Maiel, if not already returning her home. As for Luthias being allowed inside his head, he was used to it and learned there was nothing to fear from the duta. He had no such grace period with Lena.

Silence proved the wiser course of action. She offhandedly called him lazy, but that wasn't going to get the better of him. Dominic bit his lip before more choice words damaged the mission. Turning his eye back to the book in his hand, he examined a map of Budapest, seeing dozens of churches, state buildings, and other important seats. Such high-profile places made sense to his idea of a grand rescue, but didn't make sense for Maiel. His wife avoided prominent places, hating the attention they brought. The question was, would she function the same in this situation? To hide or be exposed would be determined by her assessment of the danger. From whom had she sought aid, if anyone? Where would they go? He had no answers and Lena wasn't even helping him to uncover the questions that could get the answers. He shoved the atlas back in his pack and folded his arms.

Dominic shifted on his seat several times, unable to find a comfortable position. His body ached from the ferry debacle and his full stomach lulled him to laziness. He looked to see if his agitated motions woke Lena, but she sat still, eyes closed and expressionless. Dominic threw his arms wide, drowning in despair and a weakened resolve. His gaze turned to the window and his thoughts went to Paris.

The rapidly passing scenery hypnotized him. He faced hours of monotony with only an atlas, a bag of money, and not one clue of what to do with them. Of course his mind might entertain itself with thoughts of the intriguing Madeleine. Such musings might also annoy his guard, doubly satisfying. He smiled softly, enjoying the idea.

The fire in Dominic's throat dried his mouth. He swallowed to wash it away. The flame resisted and stung him. Dominic blinked slowly, exhausted by the constant battle to hold the burning at bay. After all his time and practice, Dominic never developed the skills needed to protect himself in such moments. There were a great many things he took for granted and lazed around about. For instance, he took for granted Maiel's constancy. His wife was the last duta he imagined turning against the king; she was loyal to a fault. But then, she didn't turn against Adonai, as he saw it. She only hid from the king, worried he'd be angry with the outcome of her mission, the hard strike against Lena. She was right—he didn't understand. If he hadn't been so pathetic on that night, if he'd exercised the authority of being the man in his home, she'd still be there. Instead, he let her tantrum escalate and now he was in hot water for her actions.

Dominic's gaze returned to his guide. He should meditate like her, according to Joel's advice. Yet every time he made an attempt, it seemed to bring in their enemies. Still, the focus might help him to reach out to Maiel and find out where she was. Now that he knew Lena could slide, that information might leverage her to do it again and bring an end to their journey. She told him to just ask.

"You should get some sleep," Lena said, echoing his thoughts.

The girl still meditated and Dominic didn't feel her poking through his thoughts. His brow furrowed at the coincidence. Despite the creeping feeling her interjections now gave him, Dominic pulled down the overhead bunk. As she said, he shared all his thoughts with Luthias, whether he realized it or not. There was nothing in his mind to hide from her. Lying down comfortably, he shut his eyes and let sleep take him, falling ever down into the dark.

When Dominic awoke, they'd just crossed into the city limits of Munich. Lena stood on her tiptoes, using the bench below as a stool. She peered at him, her eyes a ring of warm amber, starkly contrasting with the gray early morning. While he slept, she cloaked him from their enemy. He knew because the falling stopped and he dreamed something. Rested but starved, he hoped aloud that the next train would have a dining car. She frowned at him and he smiled. Jumping down, he quickly put his bag together and set the bed back in the wall. She wanted his thanks, but he wasn't feeling keen on thanking her for doing what was expected. If she was to be raised a guardian, she had better get used to that.

Mistrust of one another took greater hold as they boarded the next train. Dominic settled his things in their berth and then went to find food, without a word to Lena. Her doleful mien stuck in his mind as he passed through the cars. The dining area was some distance from the safety of his cabin. He looked around, hoping that the few people there didn't take notice of him. He approached the waiter and made his request. He saw the eyes of the other passengers turn to him. Some lingered longer than he liked. As the waiter made the call to the kitchen, he asked if it could be delivered to his berth. The man assented reluctantly, but Dominic coaxed him into it with several bank notes.

"Can I get you anything else, sir?"

"Bourbon," Dominic replied.

"How do you take it?" the man asked, not the least alarmed by such a request at such an early hour.

"Water," Dominic replied, watching the rain on the windows.

The other occupants of the dining car tried hard to ignore him, except one. A woman sat in the corner facing a male companion. He could only make out the back of his shiny black head. Her eyes returned to Dominic again and again. Her platinum hair was wound up in a large mound, accented with a skinny black bow. She smoked a cigarette like a silver screen femme fatale. Her companion looked over his shoulder in Dominic's direction. The waiter set down his glass, giving him good reason to look away. The black eyes of the woman's companion reminded him of Morgentus. Dominic raised the drink to his mouth and sipped.

"Cheers," he said to the waiter and turned out of the car to return to his berth.

Partway through the other car, he noticed the couple enter the passage. They chatted and pretended not to notice him, but something about them raised the hair on the back of his neck. Crossing into the next car, he drank his bourbon in one swallow and set the glass outside someone's door to throw them off. He quickened his pace, getting out of sight. Reaching his car, he leaned into a run but was halted by a man exiting. Dominic drew up short and gave a meek apology, passing the man in an awkward sidestep. Opening the door of his berth, he jumped inside and locked the door.

"What is it?" Lena asked.

"I think they've found us. I may have lost them long enough for us to get out of here," Dominic said.

Lena looked uncertain. She probably smelled the alcohol on his breath.

"What did they look like?"

Dominic shushed her, seeing shadows beneath the door. Lena got to her feet and stood between him and the door. Dominic pulled her closer, always the protective father. Despite what he felt about her duty, he couldn't allow her to face danava alone. Someone tried the knob, rattling the door. The shadow stood still, as if it stared through the door straight at them. Then the shadow left.

"You could at least say hello," a voice spoke from behind them.

"When was the last time you found locks kept us out?" another familiar voice spoke.

Dominic turned. His heart raced and he stopped breathing. The blond woman sat there, smoking her cigarette. Across from her was the man. She smiled at him and took another puff. Lena laughed, peeking around his side. Dominic thought the girl had lost her mind, until the intruders faded into a somewhat less threatening couple. Zach sat across from Callidora.

"You were expecting someone else?" Zach asked, looking gray.

"I was," Dominic admitted, remembering the cloaking of the penannular could be gauged creatively to manifest an illusion.

Lena went to Zach, folding herself into his lap. The alder gave her a loving embrace and kissed her forehead. Dominic would never understand why his girls, or any girl, seemed to love him so much. Regardless of the affection he showed then, Zach was cold, a bureaucrat, and his sense of humor bordered on evil. So why was he still glad to see him?

"We've come because Zach foresees trouble as you get nearer to your journey's end. They may attack your train," Callidora told him.

"Several may attack your train," Zach corrected.

Dominic nodded and took a seat beside the erela. He wished they could stay to fight off that threat, but he knew they could only offer this warning. Magiel already went far beyond their rules by facing the prince of the Domdaniel to save them. Another show like that would bring too much attention to their quest from all sides. He imagined that Belial wasn't pleased at all and it would be more than Leviathan they faced next time.

Zach studied him, Lena clinging to his side, looking much happier than he had ever seen her. Dominic's mood soured. Was this her importance? Was she going to be his bride? The way she cozied up to his brother was too unusual not to take notice. That meant Zach had found his ketu, news to the entire family. Dominic sat back and tried to piece together the odd attachment. It just looked perverse in its current state.

"Morgentus is regrouping after the fight we gave him. He'll want revenge and that makes him more dangerous. He already hates you for claiming our khata for your wife. Now you've shamed him," Callidora said.

"Magiel shamed him and the prince. Athiel and Rathiel threw us in the ocean," Dominic corrected him.

"You got away. That's enough to shame him. You don't need to fight to cause him pain with Belial and the other princes," Zach said.

"Hopefully Belial will finish him and Morgentus won't return," Dominic said.

"He'll only be replaced, most likely by something much worse," Callidora said, sneering.

"We need Morgentus to stay where he is," Zach said.

"I'd say that's madness, but there must be good reason," Dominic said, not convinced.

Dominic wanted to tear Lena from Zach's side before the sight caused him to vomit.

"Morgentus is a nuisance but he'll help us in the end," Callidora said, barely reassuring him.

"It's madness," Dominic replied.

"Metatron has given his order. We'll cut him down by the end of this, but he'll return to cause more trouble in your future. This journey will teach you much about him. Consider it a training exercise for the final battle," Zach said.

"Final battle?" Dominic repeated.

"Not that final battle," Callidora said.

"Thank God," Dominic sighed.

They fell silent and the sound of the train filled the gap.

"How long can you stay?" Dominic finally asked.

"We only came to warn you. Keep to yourselves as much as possible. We'll be watching," Callidora said.

A knock on the cabin door stole Dominic's attention. He looked back to see Lena alone on her seat. He swallowed his disappointment. Another knock sounded. Dominic begrudgingly answered. A member of the train's staff stood there with a covered plate. Not waiting for a greeting or word, he instructed Dominic to leave it outside the door when he finished. Dominic gave him one of the bank notes and took the plate. The ceramic was almost too warm to the touch, but he took comfort in knowing his hunger would be satisfied with a fresh meal.

Predictably, the food tasted terrible, but Dominic ate every bite, too hungry to really care. Following the waiter's directions, he set the plate outside the door and took the opportunity to spy on the passageway. Someone had shut off the overhead lights, though the sun wasn't to be seen that day. The dim floor lamps cast an eerie blue glow. Rain fell hard, pinging off the glass, making the morning more like late evening. Gray countryside stretched beyond the windows below a platinum and smoke sky. Twinkling lights of towns and cities looked like a smeared painting.

Dominic noticed that the lights were on in other parts of the train as it snaked a curve along the track and the other cars came into view beyond the glass. His apprehension increased. Thankfully the hall was empty. His neck prickled in warning. The door to the passage opened and an elderly woman shuffled toward him, barely seeing past the end of her nose. He quickly shut his door and latched it. This was not a good sign: now he was startled at the sight of an old lady. Lena smiled at him, stifling a laugh as her eyes sparkled with enjoyment.

"What did they tell you?" Dominic asked, knowing his brother could tell her things that he would not hear.

"The same he told you," Lena replied, still grinning at his fright.

"And Callidora? Can I trust you?" Dominic eyed her.

"Why not?"

"What is Zach to you?" Dominic asked.

Lena eyed him, her expression twisting up with disgust.

"Sick little man," Lena replied angrily.

Dominic waved her off. He hadn't meant to sound so blunt. Trust wasn't the issue between them. The issue was with himself and the shadows lurking beyond their door. He lay back and watched the clouds. The gloom filled him with a sense of safety, but he gathered the lights being turned off was a signal to either Morgentus or his soldiers. Despite the timing of the warning and the pending attack, he felt better knowing they were watched closely. Just as meditation brought in their enemies, their enemy's arrival brought his friends. He could relax and trust in them.

Lena lost her sparkle, watching the base of the door. Dominic followed her gaze, but it was dark in the passage and he saw nothing. Her attention returned to him. He held his breath, waiting for her to speak. Her expression was chilling. The fire in his throat spread down his chest. He wondered in earnest if he could trust her. Lena shut her eyes and sat back, returning to her meditations. Dominic lay back, using his bag as a pillow. Deep suspicion of how she might betray him returned. They'd stolen her from him once; what if they came in the disguise of his friends only to replace her with a shade again? The visit from his friends hadn't comforted him after all. He mistrusted the chance, afraid of what would come next. His experiences since the farmhouse were weighing on his psyche.

"Remember what I said. You should rest. I'll watch over you," Lena told him.

Dominic filled his mind with horrible ideas, but the girl didn't stir. He made his thoughts more shocking. No reaction. Dominic shrugged, baffled at how she echoed his thoughts. Perhaps she was strong enough to exercise that bizarre intelligence of her species. Whatever it was, the advice she'd just given sounded solid to him.

Between bouts of sleep, the rain came and went. The train stopped in Salzburg, Linz, and a few smaller villages along the way, dragging the voyage out painfully. In a few more short hours, they would pass through Vienna and turn southeast for Budapest. That was the leg of the journey Zach was concerned about. He was certain Morgentus and his minions would show their faces soon. That was true. Shades would lick their wounds only so long and return in force to try again until Belial had enough of their ineptitude and came himself.

Dominic grew restless at the approach to Vienna. His dreams were masked by shadows. In them he saw the baron and his wife. He dreamed he lost the battle above a sprawling city. The images bothered him, but despite how strong he was rumored to be, the baron continually failed to win Maiel. Did he lack real desire, or was Maiel charmed? Her image danced through his memories. Morgentus was a fool if he didn't really desire her. Maiel was a treasure.

If he were in Morgentus's shoes, Dominic mused, he wouldn't have so easily been turned away. Instead of descending in a mad storm, he would have plotted and carefully picked away her walls with the patience of the king. After a delicate campaign of undermining her every mission, he'd make his ultimate move to kidnap her. Toying and gloating to torment her, as Morgentus did, only served to make her emotions stronger against him. Once safe in his lair, he would lock her in the deepest depths, where the others didn't dare to tread. That would give him all the time he needed to turn her. It was a simple task. Maiel wanted to be loved and appreciated, just like Madeleine. Swooping in to help her, softening her with niceties to contrast with the hardened shades who waited to vex her, would prove he was her loving protector. At last curious about him, Maiel's guard would fall. Thus her memories would be exposed. Morgentus would blacken the cherished history of her husband using every half-truth available. Feeling betrayed, she'd turn against her king, realizing he ensured her husband remained a clumsy human. For a finishing touch to assure the dark transition, he'd sate her anger, setting her loose on the shadows of the labyrinth, letting her build a craving for cruelty. When the last feather dropped from her untidy wings, the deed would be done and no one would come from Zion to reclaim her.

The task was really too easy, even though the shadowwalkers bungled it every time. Perhaps there was some anomaly he missed. Maiel was stubborn, but when faced with the loss of her family she could be worked around a bit. After all, family was her foundation. More likely, Morgentus's need to be desired by her was the source of these glitches.

Dominic had a solid plan to turn his wife over to the danava by the time the train left Vienna. His guardian was ignoring him, likely cross at such thoughts. Dominic blamed the sullen mood of the day, which encouraged putrid ideas. However, his mood lightened as they escaped another stop without incident. Until then, Dominic sought the supposed assassins in every face and shadow they came across, an exhausting task. The train chugged up to speed and he decided Morgentus was ignoring them, sensing no threat. While they idled along, the baron had plenty of time to corner Maiel.

Lena said nothing on the matter, remaining in her meditation. Dominic looked to her, hoping for a word outside his brain to help him piece together the reason for the calm. He suspected her silence was born from the knowledge that Maiel wasn't in Budapest, and had either moved on or been taken prisoner. Either way, Lena played dumb, probably afraid to accept blame in failing the mission. Luthias would have nobly apologized and then helped him to plot a solid plan forward. Though gruff, he was a sincere engel. The hours would have been filled with tales of exploits past, keeping him distracted until the next battle raged. Instead, he sat opposite a silent china doll with no past to speak of and no quality of character, a mere child who'd died from some illness of the brain. An illness that probably crept into her sattva mind and crippled her even now. In such a state, what could she possibly offer the effort? They needed to plan as they closed in on their destination, not meditate.

"I thought we'd do better by taking a car," Lena suddenly spoke. Her eyes were sad and the corners of her mouth were turned down. "You were right. The train is slow, but we've made it further than I believed possible without seeing a shadow. Maybe Zach was mistaken," she continued.

"Zach's never mistaken," Dominic replied, guilty about his accusatory thoughts, seeing he had hurt her.

"He's wrong about you," Lena said, opening her eyes.

Dominic smiled, almost laughing. Zach always thought his little human brother would fail and remain a human, if not utterly fall to shadow. So far, the alder was right.

"Tell me, Lena. How long've you been incarnating?" Dominic asked, changing the subject.

"In Earth years? Over two thousand," Lena answered.

"I thought you were just a girl; I'm sorry."

"I am to you. You're a bit older than I am. This form you see—it will fade as I remember who I truly am, a young woman—maybe an old woman. I have many memories, but they seem like dreams. I still hardly know," Lena said.

Dominic folded his hands over his stomach and looked out the window. Dusky clouds passed over his features as he despaired again. She was so much younger than he, yet she was more progressed. It shouldn't have bothered him. Atman came to their destiny in their own time. If he'd concerned himself with the task, he'd be at home playing with his youngest after a nice lunch. Maiel would be near, entertaining the other children as they prepared for their next incarnation. He drew a deep breath, anxious that she'd slipped away, that he'd slipped away. Now they faced less time to cover every detail of their next life together and it would be so important—the only thing standing between him and imprisonment in Jahannam.

"I always hated the transition back," Dominic said, understanding of what she spoke.

"Me too," Lena mumbled.

Lena had died only a few short days ago. She closed her eyes, still saddened, and returned to her meditation. The process would have been undergone in Otzar with the help of a muse, but the assignment had taken her away. Remembering who she was would help them in their quest. The sooner she knew, the sooner she'd have the wisdom to face the task.

A soft patter on the door disrupted his thoughts. Dominic answered. A young lady with a cart smiled up at him. She offered him several things, tittering them off in a heavily accented voice. She was probably a student or a young wife, working her way through school or fighting to make ends meet for a layabout husband. She was far too young to be anything else, except maybe a husband hunter. Some women preferred to set up with a man that allowed them to skip work. By the batting of her false lashes, he gathered she fell in the latter column. Dominic took a cup of coffee and sweet roll, passing flirtatious looks back. Then he abruptly shut himself away again, amused by the encounter. Lena watched him resume his seat. He offered her the roll, but she shook her head. The girl wasn't amused by the same diversions. With a shrug he bit into the roll and forgot about it.

The train came to a sudden jerky stop. The hot coffee spilled on his lap and he erupted with a curse. He set the cup down and pushed the roll aside. Looking out the window, the train snaked up a bend in the tracks, but there was no apparent reason for stopping. Something black slammed against the window. Dominic jumped. A gloved hand slid from the glass. He looked out again. A pair of young policemen laughed as they ran up the tracks toward the engine. His heart slowed to normal pace, but his anger throbbed hard in his temples. He grit his teeth and threw the coffee cup against the door.

"Dominic!" Lena admonished.

The prank cracked the last bit of his mask, a carefully rendered façade of calm and gentleness. Dominic rounded on her, ready to let loose every angry word he had in his brain at that moment. His hands ached to grip her throat. Another patter on the door stalled him. He swung it open and the bright-faced girl that served him coffee moments ago stepped back, startled. Her flirtatious polish came off instantly. In a self-conscious stammer she told him that some loose cows were blocking the tracks ahead. She tried not to notice the coffee spilled on his pants and told him to please excuse the train staff, as they would be a few minutes clearing the animals before they continued on. Dominic coldly thanked her and shut the door in her face as she offered him another cup of coffee.

"We need to go," Lena said.

"It's just a coincidence," Dominic said, taking a bite of the roll.

"Not this time. Can't you smell that?" Lena asked standing. She peered out the window.

Dominic chewed the roll and stared at her with no answer. He wasn't about to leave the train. They would get to Budapest in a short time. If they jumped off and ran through the fields, it might be days before they found a ride or a way there. Lena was just jumpy because the others warned them Morgentus might come.

"Dominic, you must listen."

Dominic sat back and finished the roll. The panic in her eyes grew stronger. She trembled from head to foot.

"All right," Dominic said, taking up his bag.

"Hurry." Lena grabbed his hand as they left the cabin.

Passengers wandered out of their berths, looking to see the cattle and those working to move them. Dominic wove through them, then pushed through the door between the cars and down the narrow steps toward the side the policemen were on. Pushing the lever, he unlocked the door and jumped down. In the distance, the young officers who startled him chatted and scanned the fields. There was no one else nearby. A knot of trees stood a few yards from the edge of the tracks and he could see a town beyond that. He watched them a moment longer, afraid to move or stay lest they saw him. Their faces twisted, revealing their true nature. Shadowalkers.

Bolting toward the trees, Dominic slid down the embankment. Lifting his head, he saw the police run toward him. Dominic cursed and jumped into the trees, hoping he could lose them fast. Zach's warning had saved their mission.

Dominic ran until he found a pub open at that hour. He quickly ducked inside. The inhabitants took little notice of him, though the bartender seemed curious. Dominic approached carefully and sat on a stool, tossing his bag to the floor. The man spoke in a deep Austrian accent. Dominic shook his head. He did not speak their language, but he did see guardians poking around the place and he was relieved.

"English," Dominic said to him and apologized.

The bartender nodded. "I speak a little."

"Do you know where I can get a cab to Budapest, or rent a car—get a car?"

"Best to go to Vienna, cab can take you there," the man replied.

Dominic grimaced. That was no good. He'd just come from there.

"How close to the border are we? Border?"

"Drive an hour, you reach Hungary, Budapest—another two hours," the man stammered.

Dominic sighed, hanging his head.

"I know someone who's selling a car, if you have cash," an older man a few stools down said.

The old man tipped the rest of his drink into his mouth and swallowed. The bartender stepped away with a guarded aspect. Dominic nodded to the old man, interested despite the bartender's distinct indication that he should ignore him.

"I have cash."

"It's not much, but should get you there," the man continued.

"Cheap?"

"I can get you a good deal. Cheaper than a taxi that far," he added, smiling.

A police car passed on the street with lights spinning and the siren screaming. Dominic followed it with a nervous gaze.

"That'd save my life," Dominic told the old man.

"You in some kind of trouble?"

"No—no trouble. Just running out of time to get where I'm going," Dominic replied, noting the young duta behind the man.

"It's no matter to me, boy. Come along then. We'll see about that car," the old man said.

Dominic followed the man out to the street. They walked two blocks, then crossed and walked a few more. The area grew seamier and the people looked sore-eyed. The old man led them to a rundown garage. Trash and parts blocked the façade and filled the windows of the old stone house, hemmed in on all sides by rundown townhouses and shops. A skinny man in need of a shave exited the door. His sharp eyes pinned Dominic. He and the old man had a brief exchange.

"A hundred quid as your kind say, no questions. Leave it in the parking area for Buda Castle," the old man translated.

Dominic looked at the skinny man. They thought he was English. He gathered by then that they were just Austrian crooks, and not of the organized kind. What luck to fall in with these two, he thought. They could be shadowborn, unknowingly calling stronger minions from every street and door straight to him. Dominic smiled, casting his eyes to spot the duta again. At least, their assumptions about him assured him they were idiots. The skinny man laughed. He held out his hand, muttering on about something. The duta was still there and Dominic spied a youngling in the window watching him.

"He asked, what choice do you have? The only place to rent is back in Vienna and you've no way there."

"Let's see the car." Dominic said, pinning the younger criminal with a hard stare.

The old man interpreted and the skinny man laughed. He said something and Dominic was sure it was a jab. The skinny man directed them inside. They passed through what he assumed was an auto parts store into a back hall. The youngling and other guardian followed. They emerged on the other side of the block where the garage was located. This side of the shop looked in much better order. The skinny man brought them to a once beautiful gray Mercedes coupe. The paint was lusterless, the body a little beaten, but the tires had tread and the interior was intact.

"1956, Mercedes 2-20 coupe. She runs great, but doesn't look like much. It's the closest you'll ever get to owning one of these in your lifetime," the old man said proudly.

"Four years old and beat to shit? What are you trafficking?" Dominic asked, clamping his mouth, sourly unimpressed.

The old man obliged by interpreting again. The skinny man smiled at him. His dark eyes told him not to press the subject. He lit a cigarette and puffed away. Tattoos snaked from under the leather jacket cuff.

"Drugs, money? I can get it there, but I've gotta know what I'm hauling." Dominic did press.

There was good reason they'd beat the piss out of a very expensive car in just four years. He guessed the vehicle made the trip quite frequently in the hands of strangers.

The old man hesitated, but did his duty. Now the skinny man looked like the criminal he was. He eyed Dominic, not responding.

"So let me get this straight. I'm paying you for the privilege of hauling your shit. How about I take the car to the drop for free. Do you have papers? Can you make me some? I'll cross borders and I'm sure the officers'll be interested in what you have. I'll take it for free, if you get me some papers and tell me what I'm hauling. I'll even leave you my identification so you can come find me if I don't show up. I need to know, so I can play it smart," Dominic said.

Dominic gave him the identification from his wallet. The man took it, uncertain of what was being said. The old man filled him in and he looked delighted by the prospect. He looked at Dominic again, studying his face.

"I have a wife and son who'll be at that address," Dominic tempted them.

"All right, Brian MacAllister."

"We've got a deal." The old man shook his hand, grinning.

The skinny man pocketed the identification and also shook his hand.

"I'll send it on to you once the job is done. How long are you staying in Budapest?"

The skinny man spoke decent English after all.

"A week, then I go back home."

"Maybe I'll expand in America. I'll call on you, eh?"

"Anytime. I could use some extra cash," Dominic said.

"I like you MacAllister—come inside. I'll get you the papers. What name do you prefer?"

"Dominic. Dominic Newson will do."

Dominic followed the men back into the shop. It was over an hour before the skinny man produced the papers. During that time, his new contact made several phone calls, some kid entered and snapped his picture, and then they sat in guarded silence. Customers came and went. Dominic tried to keep his eyes on the window, but they wandered and he spotted another tattoo peeking from the skinny man's shirt, which he wore half open. Dominic could have sworn it was the outpost symbol. The man was an Earth Watcher. Very strange.

They watched Dominic closely in return. They had questions for him as well, but they didn't dare to speak. When he thought his wait was for nothing and the day would end there, the boy returned to the shop with a big yellow envelope. He threw it down and held out his hand to the skinny man behind the counter. The skinny man gestured toward Dominic, telling him to pay the kid a quid. The kid went to him holding out his hand as a demand for compensation. Irritated that he'd still ended up paying something, Dominic dug in his pack for the wad of bills. He worked some free, carefully looked to see what he had and then passed the bills to the boy. The kid grinned at him and said something Dominic assumed was a thank you.

"There's your papers," the skinny man said, throwing him the envelope.

Dominic opened the envelope and thumbed through the contents. They had done a decent job with such short notice. This was no fly-by-night operation. Though he couldn't read a single word, it appeared like the real documentation he expected. Dominic was certain they were outpost men, the only ones capable of such clean work so fast. Dominic nodded to the skinny man, then thanked the old man and took his leave of them.

Dominic climbed behind the driver's wheel of the car and started it up. He adjusted his mirrors as he navigated the circuitous roads of the town. They had just over a quarter tank of gas to get them where they were headed. Dominic frowned, knowing it wouldn't be enough. Still, they were on their way again. Glancing in the rearview mirror, Dominic saw Lena in the back seat, looking pale. He smiled at her and she just shook her head in disbelief. He shrugged and then laughed, rolling through the stations on the radio for some distraction. Dealing with such characters was not what she would have done, but it got them what they needed.

"What's the worst that could have happened?" he asked, not receiving a response.

"Illuminati aren't to be trifled with," Lena said.

"You think we just happened to find them?"

Lena stared.

"They find you," Dominic replied.

Approaching the border checkpoint, Dominic's heart pounded, concerned that his fake documents wouldn't make the cut. He dumped the contents of the envelope on the front seat and tried to make sense of the papers. He knew the soldiers would ask and he had no idea what piece was what. He should have just left everything in the envelope and pulled it out of the glove box when they asked. Muttering under his breath, he realized he wouldn't understand a word they said. He drove the car up behind the last in line and put it in neutral. Gathering up his papers, he shoved them back in the envelope and stuffed it in the glove box. Nervously, he watched the other drivers and the things they gave through the window. His eyes shifted and he wondered how he would ever do this without detection. Whatever he hauled for those two miscreants, he'd be left to explain on his own from a prison cell. When they discovered his one identity was a fraud and the other belonged to a dead American veteran, it'd be too late for Maiel. No explanation would free him in time.

One by one, they neared the checkpoint. Guards paced in long coats, bored and irritated. He chewed his thumbnail, trying to think of some way that didn't involve him having to talk. They were sure to look for trouble, just to break up the monotony. A guard walked from their checkpoint barracks, a German shepherd on a leash at his side. Dominic's stomach dropped.

"Pretend you're deaf," Lena's small voice came from the back.

Dominic looked in the rearview mirror at her. That might just work. He thought it through, switching his gaze forward again. He was next. Pulling up, he parked where the guard pointed. One of the others came to his window and he lowered the glass. The dog sauntered past. Fishing out the envelope from the glove box, he handed it over without being asked. The man eyed him suspiciously. He motioned to his ear and muttered. The guard looked confused, then nodded when he finally caught the meaning.

After rifling through the contents of the envelope, they returned to the car and handed his things back. The first guard signaled him forward and the barrier rose. The shepherd strode by again, sniffing the air. Dominic set the envelope down. He smiled and nodded to the guards, continuing on. They crossed into Hungary without ceremony. Dominic's stomach churned. He watched the guards in the rearview mirror. The first still watched him as they disappeared along the road.

"I can't believe that worked," Lena said, watching out the back.

Dominic turned pale. He could use a drink after all these brushes with danger.

They passed a large city on the north horizon. Dominic guessed that it was Győr, by the copious studying he'd done of the atlas. That meant the next big cityscape they saw was their destination. Budapest was just an hour or so away.

The highway brought them into the fields of Nowhere, Hungary. The gas gauge slipped to just above empty, smashing his hope. Miles back they had passed a service station, possibly their last chance to fill the tank before it dried out. The car wouldn't make the return either. He shook his head, imagining them stranded in the Hungarian countryside with no means to their goal.

Dominic shook his head. He reminded himself the drop was just a cover story. He didn't care where the car was left. The identification they'd left with the outpost men belonged to a man who had died in the war. There was no wife and child for drug-traffickers or Illuminati to threaten. Blinking slowly, he gathered his senses. The meat sack forming around his sattva started to cloud his mind.

"You all right?" Lena asked, appearing at his shoulder.

"Yeah—yeah. I was just thinking we wouldn't make it to the drop point. At least, I convinced myself of the story," Dominic said irritated.

Lena giggled.

"We're almost there. Don't lose your focus now," Lena said, more serious.

"Lost it a long time ago," Dominic breathed ruefully.

Lena patted his arm and sat back still grinning.

"You'll find a gas station ahead."

Dominic cast a few questioning glances over his shoulder.

"How—"

"There was a sign," she replied.

Dominic rolled his eyes. Of course there was a sign and of course he didn't see it. He adjusted uncomfortably in his seat and watched carefully. The station appeared around a bend in the road, just on the outskirts of a small village. He pulled in and parked. A bell rang and a middle-aged man came out. A sudden familiar urge nagged him. His eyes drifted over the dashboard, surprised he needed to use a bathroom, but then all he ingested during the past few days flashed in a vulgar memory. Flexing his hands before his eyes, he noticed how solid his form had become. The station attendant knocked on his window, startling him. The man smiled and raised his palm apologetically.

Dominic got out of the car. "Restroom?" he asked.

The man pointed to the station and handed him a key. Dominic closed himself into the cramped little room. It was cleaner than he expected. The walls were scratched with graffiti. The mirror was old, the silver corroding on the back, and he could barely see his face in it. Shuffling to the toilet, he sighed and did what he'd come to do. The relief was exquisite, in that odd mix of the repulsive and the pleasant. Exhaling deeply, he finished. Two cracked porcelain spigots sat atop the sink. Hesitantly, he turned them. Groaning came from the walls, then water sputtered out, splashing him. He quickly tightened the spigots down, too late to save his pants.

"Clumsy shit," he growled.

He wiped his face with his hands, and after several deep breaths, Dominic calmed himself. The tips of his fingers slipped from his eyes and he glanced at himself in the mirror. Bronze stubble flanked his jaw, looking thick in the icy ultraviolet light. His eyes jerked aside, spotting a figure behind him. He looked again and nothing was there. Turning in a circle, he made sure.

"Crap," he muttered, suspecting an imp had just discovered him, or the mirror was playing a nasty trick, like in England.

Fumbling his way out of the toilet, the attendant returned inside. Dominic quickly composed himself. The man said something to him, laughing and offering a handkerchief from his back pocket. Dominic waved him away and made his way around the narrow aisles. He grabbed a few bottles and snacks. His stomach growled as the attendant rang him up.

Exiting the store, a shadow dashed past him. A glimmer of gold caught Dominic's eye and he nearly dropped the groceries. Screeching tires tore his attention in the other direction. A black car came to a fast stop. Smoke rose from the pavement. The tires squealed again as the vehicle spun around, nearly pushing other cars off the road. It leapt toward the gas station exit, jumping as it lost traction.

"Dominic," his name was shouted.

Dominic looked in the direction of the voice, the same direction the shadow had gone. Zaajah stood there waving him toward her. She ducked behind the side of the station. The car engine roared. Dominic turned just in time to see the car steering toward him. Throwing the groceries, he jumped and rolled behind the station. The car smashed into the cinderblock wall. Dominic stared with wide eyes. The tires spun wildly, smoke billowing from the rubber as it heated. The car was stuck and the driver was still trying to move forward to mow him down.

"Dominic!" Zaajah called him again.

Dominic scrambled to his feet. Zaajah pulled him to safety at the back of the building. The car engine revved and the tires squealed. From the opposite side, the attendant ran into the woods. Whoever drove the car was dangerous and not intimidated by injury or death. The driver spoke to his companion, guttural voices snarling. Dominic dared to peek around the corner. Argus and Shee stood guard, the hair high on their backs.

"Good timing," Dominic said, leaning back against the building.

"You won't think so in a moment," Zaajah said flatly.

"It's always good to see you."

"More are coming. I brought you Argus and Shee. They'll find Maiel for you and offer far more protection than Lena alone. You're going to need it. You should be flattered; they're rolling out their forces in great numbers just to stop you," Zaajah continued.

"Consider me flattered," Dominic rasped, not quite flattered.

"You better get back to Lena," Zaajah said.

"Shit—Lena," Dominic gasped.

The girl was still in the car waiting for him, perfect bait for the danava. He peered around the edge of the building again. One of the shades got out, an unfamiliar figure to him, but not surprising as they went through soldier and marditavya so fast. Thankfully, it wasn't Morgentus, but he wagered the thing was dangerous just the same: a tough barrier to his way out of there. The head came round, boasting tattoos and piercings and skin like that of a toad. Two horns arched from its head.

"Get to the car," Zaajah said. "Don't stop until you've found her. I'll take care of the Shedu."

Zaajah dashed around him before he could argue. Her favorite short blade glinted in the late day sun. The shadowalker turned just as she came up behind him. With a battle cry, Zaajah struck at his throat, slicing it, and planted her foot in his middle to push him back to the car he'd climbed from. Surprise was her advantage, but Shedu were poor fighters, the cursed form of fallen Hyadeans, slow and thick-headed. But they did make excellent bounty hunters for souls, for they were relentless and callous.

Zaajah's attack succeeded in shutting down pursuit from this hunter, perhaps permanently if Morgentus had gauged their abilities wrong. The Shedu turned to ash, giving Dominic his chance. The wolves followed him to the car. He struggled to open the door as he buzzed with adrenaline. The door at last swung open and the wolves leapt inside. He jumped in the driver's seat, locking them in.

"Hurry!" Lena cried, as he fumbled with the keys.

Dominic's hands shook uncontrollably. He shoved the key into the ignition and turned it. Looking out the windshield, he saw Zaajah step behind the Shedu car. The engine revved and the wheels spun. There was more than one. The new driver attempted to dislodge the car from the wall. Its wheels gained traction. Dominic turned the key again. The car choked and then came alive. Shifting it into drive, he stepped on the gas and steered out of the station lot, raising a trail of dust and stones, and forcing several cars off the road.

In the rearview, Dominic saw their pursuers break free of the station wall. Zaajah darted to the road in the other direction. Dominic stepped on the gas harder. The old girl had a little pickup left in her. The last he saw, the black car drove onto the road at top speed. In his head, Dominic heard Zaajah say not today, as the car sped toward her. The blazing white filled her. A smile curled the corners of his lips. Then the car struck Zaajah, the back end rising in the air as it crumpled against her, jolting the enjoyment of her bravery right out of him. The wrecked vehicle dropped back to the ground, the front end twisted beyond repair and the axle bowed. The Shedu wouldn't follow now. Zaajah shook off the hit and pulled the grunt from the window. The erela was injured, but she had saved them.

"We have a long way to go. Don't celebrate yet," Lena told him.

The wolves whimpered and Dominic's smile became a frown. He didn't need to be reminded, especially after his wife's best friend had nearly destroyed herself to help them get away. At some point, Morgentus would find them. No doubt the baron was well aware of the few arteries into the city. The fight with his nemesis was just beginning. Gripping the steering wheel tight, he promised himself that he would end the baron's existence slowly, so he could savor the revenge and make it clear that endangering his family was a grave mistake.

The day lengthened and the highway led to a set of tollbooths. Adrenaline soared easily after the gas station and his heart pumped as they approached the barrier. A frustrated exhalation escaped Dominic's lips. These booths were just one more delay. Traffic bottlenecked, creeping forward at a turtle's pace. Any one of them could contain a minion. Pulling into line, he surveyed the area for signs of the baron's soldiers. To either side were police vehicles. Police had already pulled over a handful of cars. Dominic feared they'd be next, as if the contraband he hauled, whatever it was, waved a giant flag.

Dominic pinned his gaze on the trunk of the car in front of him. When it pulled away from the booth, he took his turn, his limbs trembling with the expectation of danger. An older woman smiled down at him from a sundried face; graying brown hair was tied up under a scarf. A couple of her teeth were missing, but her eyes were bright with the remnants of youth. She passed him a ticket with her arthritic hand. Dominic nodded his thanks and reached for the paper. A sudden gust blew it to the ground.

"Oh, I'm so sorry. Let me pick that up," the woman rasped in a strangely deep voice.

"No—I've got it," Dominic replied, popping the door open.

"Stay in your car. Let me help you," she said.

Dominic reached for the ticket as she opened the panel to her cubicle. He froze, realizing she was speaking English to him. The door of the car suddenly closed on his arm. A shout tore from his lips. The horns of the cars behind sounded.

"Belial wants your head! Your head he'll have!" the rough voice growled.

Lena cried out, pushing back on the door. Argus trampled over him, snarling and snapping his great teeth. Dominic pushed with his shoulder as the metal door crushed sinew and bone. The wolf must have reached the woman because the door gave way and he was able to pull his arm back into the car. Argus leapt to the back where Shee kept the woman at bay with flashes of her fangs. Dominic planted his foot on the gas and peeled out. Through the rearview mirror, he saw the attendant raise her arm. Shots fired and he ducked down as they made holes in the back window before shattering it. Another glance and the police opened fire on the woman. She dropped to the ground and it all became panicked flight. Cars and trucks weaved in and out to avoid the gunfire. Then someone made the wrong choice. A truck merging back onto the highway met with a passenger car. Dominic looked away. At least the accident would keep the police from pursuing him. He pressed down on the gas, determined to put as much space between them and the police, who would be quite interested in why a grandmother had suddenly shot at his car.

"Everybody all right?" Dominic asked, after several minutes of silence.

The wolves whimpered and Lena sat back down from staring out the back. She brushed the broken glass aside.

"I need warning," Dominic snapped, nursing his wrist.

"I'm sorry. I didn't know," Lena said.

"If you're here to guard me, do it, damn it. One of these times they'll make their mark and our mission ends. Pay attention—have you learned nothing? They'll never stop until we're dead," Dominic hollered.

"I'm doing the best I can on my own. This is my first time guarding anyone," Lena reminded him.

Dominic scrubbed a hand over his face, angry with himself for losing his temper with her. Shee sniffed his ear reassuringly, then lay down with her mate and Lena. The girl hung her head, guiltily. His tongue stuck to the roof of his mouth. Even if he wanted to apologize, he didn't know how, because he was right. Balling his good fist, he squeezed until his anger subsided.

"Check the bag for bandages. I need to wrap this arm," Dominic said, his voice surprisingly gentle.

CHAPTER 23

ORIUS LOUNGED IN A CHAIR facing an ornate bedstead. Maiel slept on the mattress above the blankets, still dressed in her armor. She told him that she didn't trust Geitz and refused to remove one link of her protection until they were safe again. He doubted that she truly slept, either. She probably meditated, rebuilding her strength for what she believed was to come. Rising to his feet, he let her have her way. The moment of peace allowed him to have a conversation with Geitz alone, where he might get a sense of her suspicions.

Exiting their apartments in Esztergom's residence, Orius made his way down the hall toward the stairs. A fellow clergyman appeared ahead of him from another room. He stopped the man and asked where he might find the archbishop's office. The man eyed him, then responded with a deep frown and vague directions. The priest turned his back and left Orius standing there alone. Orius watched him go, confused by the man's reluctance to offer help. He folded his hands behind his back and pursed his lips, assuming he was just spoiled by the cordial and humble brothers of his small parish. Finding a set of stairs, he searched for the office with the directions he was given.

Orius emerged in a garden. Surprise turned to delight when he discovered he had no farther to go. Geitz walked with his head tilted down, deep in worried thoughts. Orius rushed to him, smiling pleasantly. The other man lifted his chin and peered at him hard, as if Orius were an intruder. Orius drew up short. He didn't expect such a severe reception. After all, he'd just brought proof of his origins and proof of the whole meaning of their existence. Likely Geitz had already thought of the trouble it would stir up in Rome, but once things were smoothed out, it would only strengthen them.

"Bethiah is sleeping. I wanted to take the opportunity to thank you for your help, Archbishop," Orius said.

The archbishop nodded, appearing not the least moved by the appreciation.
"This changes everything," Geitz finally said.

"Not really," Orius countered.

Geitz laughed derisively.

"God turns his back to test your kind in a moment of doubt—I won't, though it may rend the Vatican. That's where we should turn, you know. They'll want to know why you didn't go to them first. Father Orius, do you have any idea what this means?"

Orius chose not to speak. Geitz wandered into the garden away from Orius in hopes of finding an answer to tie this up. Orius felt sorry for the man. What he knew was twisted-up rubbish. He followed the archbishop until the man faced him again.

"You should rest yourself. When she wakes, she'll need both of us clear-headed, to see a way around all this," Geitz said, not quite meeting his gaze.

Orius nodded and gave a soft smile.

"What?" Geitz asked.

"You're a true friend, Archbishop. I couldn't have done this without you," Orius said.

Something black passed over Geitz's face. Orius had chosen the words hoping to elicit a response. He watched the older man a moment, seeing through him for the first time. He sensed the heart of the archbishop, as it reached toward power.

"You flatter me—but I'm only doing what's expected. You'd do the same and have," Geitz told him, obscuring the hate in his voice.

Orius kept smiling, though it ceased to touch his eyes. He groped toward an explanation that would uphold the integrity of the church and the man. Perhaps he simply felt the lingering despair and the gnaw of hunger that set Bethiah on edge. Both were shadowy emotions, sure to unsettle any duta, but that explanation didn't satisfy. Bethiah had better sight than he and her warning had been right.

Orius left the archbishop to the garden, planning to wander the grounds on his own. A sense of what troubled the archbishop may linger in some crevice uncorrupted and awaiting his discovery. Imps and shades couldn't touch Samsara without leaving signs everywhere, and he feared he'd just caught sight of one. If Geitz wasn't to be trusted, there would be more shades to prove it.

Orius cast a glimpse over his shoulder, only to see a shadow pass between him and the archbishop. The signs would be hard to find, even if they were numerous, as most of those dabbling in the darker side hid their tendencies well. Guarding his fears from his features, he moved on to locate more. One shadow imp was not enough to convict anyone, but he still suspected he'd dragged his friend right into the heart of peril.

Reentering the seminary residence, Orius would explore there first.

*   *   *

Geitz stared at the gravel path until he was sure Orius had moved on. The archbishop slightly lifted his chin, glowering at the other priest. When the tall man disappeared inside, Geitz drew a heavy breath and wandered down the lawn. No one took interest in his passing. Almost always, every priest would hail him or the visitors would hound him for a prayer. He'd nearly reached the other end and the road before he realized how far he'd gone. Turning about, a shadow passed along the trees, like a cloud passing over a hillside on a bright sunny day. His attention lifted to the sky. He shifted his face in the other direction, pretending not to see. It was perhaps better to deliberate the matter in his office, behind closed doors, where certain parties might interject a thought or two without causing a scene. Geitz spat a curse under his breath and strode back toward the seminary buildings.

Above the trees and beyond a wall that grew in height the deeper it reached into the hill, Geitz spied the dome of his palace, the basilica. The shadow crept along the wall. His mouth pulled into a rueful grimace. Muttering under his breath again, he hurried his pace. A sound, like a burst of air escaping a leaky hose, breathed in his ear. Though his attention snapped to it immediately, the voice rambled away on a rushing breeze. His heart was struck by the fear of its meaning.

"I'm coming. I'm coming," Geitz muttered, frustrated that he could move along no faster.

Geitz dismissed his staff from his chambers and cloistered himself in his bedroom. Despite his many years, he moved with agility and quickly drew the curtains closed. The voice returned, far more urgent. Wiping his brow, he skirted an antique armoire at the far end of the chamber, the only furniture on that wall. He glanced at the door, worried. The voice hissed again and he inched closer. Opening the panels, he took a step back. An ancient relic sat in the bottom, housed inside a glass casket with lacy adornments.

The panels of the armoire shuddered, groaning as the grain swelled. The pulsing was slow, like the rise and fall of the breast with each breath. Then the motion grew more intense. The wood creaked and the gold-crowned head of a pale apparition pushed through the seemingly solid surface, as though it were rendered from sticky mud. The apparition continued forward, crushing the casket of bones beneath its feet. Belial grinned with sharp teeth and piercing yellow eyes. He towered over the archbishop and the man fell to his knees before him. Belial chuckled, revealing his blood-red tongue, spreading his cadaverous wings.

"Orius brought the female to us. He calls her Bethiah, but I believe she's the one you look for. The red erela," Geitz rambled.

"Where is the kesarini now, sacerdos?" Belial asked.

"Below us on the east end. She rests—her energy is weak. A mortal shell forms around her. Now is the time, my prince, if you're to ever strike," Geitz replied. He dared to look at the prince and received a cautionary eye in return.

"She's not fallen, clown. It's the trickery of the liar king. Wake her before her strength returns. It will only make things more difficult for you, when you try to sacrifice the priest to me." Belial sneered. He stepped cautiously to the center of the room, then stopped and turned back to the archbishop.

"As you wish it, my prince." Geitz bowed his head.

"Turn her by the next moon. Prove to me that you're wiser than the Labyrinth Lord and you'll have what is his. She must become one of us, sacerdos, or Adonai won't be provoked to war. She must fall, to secure the heir."

Geitz smiled, grateful for the faith and gifts of his leader. He pressed his palms together and nodded in agreement. Belial frowned, displeased by the groveling. The old man got to his feet, assuming a more dignified pose. The prince watched him closely, unhappy with what he saw. He hated humans as much as he hated the day of his sentence.

"It shall easily be done, your grace," Geitz assured him.

Belial folded his arms, appearing to lose himself in thought. Geitz patiently waited, but the grand Acherite prince said nothing. In truth, he probed the weak mind of his marditavya. He wanted to know what Geitz forgot to share.

"Orius may yet try to stop us before we can prepare him for the altar. I fear he already suspects my treachery," Geitz asked.

Belial's eyes turned to him.

"Oriael is mortal, no less set in his ways, but much weaker of limb. I'm sure you'll determine the best way in which to deal with the recidia," Belial said, as though it were obvious.

Geitz looked through the room, troubled that his prince left such a delicate choice to his care. Orius was unlikely to fall for any ploy he could lay at his feet. However, he had been wandering the Earth for thousands of years and his sight was dim. Regardless, not one hardship had caused him to waver, as though he still had the discernment of his former station. Frankly, the matter was a thorny one. His mind ran through scenarios, seeking the perfect trap.

"One more thing, Archbishop—a human was dispatched to intercept our prize. He travels by car from the east and will be in your village by this evening. If he's allowed inside your church, you will fail. Morgentus and his soldiers failed to stop him. You will stop him. His only protection is a child made to look like an erela, but she is no duta. I saw to that. I trust they won't be a problem for you, Geitz," Belial said, stepping closer to him.

Geitz froze at this news. If the baron had been incapable of the task, what made the prince think a simple marditavya could win out? Afraid to refuse the prince, Geitz nodded his acceptance of the task.

"With great pleasure," Geitz reluctantly said.

Belial grinned, clapping his sharp-fingered hand on Geitz's shoulder. Geitz shook, startled by the touch. The prince's skin felt like a hot iron. He trembled, stifling a cry.

"Good man," Belial hissed.

Geitz slipped to his knees, burned through his clothes. The garment smoked and he bit back a plea of mercy. Belial grinned at the agony he'd wrought. The touch was a warning of what was sure to come if this man failed.

In a whirl of smoke, the prince left the way he came. The armoire trembled violently until the doors slammed closed. Geitz stumbled to a chair, fighting to catch his breath. His shoulder pained him greatly, but he knew the burn was nothing compared to the pain he would feel if he was unsuccessful. He placed a hand on the injured shoulder. The smoldering jacket was hot to the touch but he found the shoulder of the jacket perfectly intact. Drawing the garment aside, he checked the shirt to find the same, but his skin still prickled beneath. He stumbled to his bathroom, undoing the shirt to look at his flesh. As suspected, a claw mark burn raged red on his flesh. He winced and set to dressing the wound.

The chambers he enjoyed in his station at Esztergom became eerily silent. With the wound dressed, Geitz put himself back together. The dark energy of his visitor still hung in the air. He examined the spaces. Dallying to dress a burn would irritate the prince when he'd given an urgent task. Geitz vacillated, equally afraid to provide the demon with a means to break free of the room through his absence.

Eyeing the armoire, Geitz had the distinct impression he was being watched. He carefully made his way to the antique and even more carefully opened the panels. The casket of bones was intact, but in the back of the armoire the finish was ruined as though exposed to a great heat. The boards trembled and smoke blasted from the space, scalding his face and choking his lungs.

Geitz cried out, backing away. He stopped trembling several moments later, kneeling on the floor and cupping his burned face in his hands. The cool air returned to the room and his burns no longer stung. Geitz drew a handkerchief and wiped his face. Shaking off the fright, he opened the curtain on one of his windows and pushed the pane open. A gust of icy fall air spilled into the room. Before he dared to enter the messenger's presence, he needed to erase the scent of the prince from his clothes. Looking over the garden, he saw the sky darken in the distant east. He didn't have much time to prepare his sacrifice or turn the erela. The longer he delayed, the more strength she gained. He must waste that strength to win his prize and he finally had a good idea how.

* * *

Gediel scowled, impatient. He and Luthias had an assignment, and the time had not quite come for the watcher to enter Samsara and join the others, who possibly needed to intervene. All their efforts would be spoiled if he moved before then. His stomach twisted anxiously. Pushing himself toward the Gyuto Order walls, he tried to remind himself that he had orders and he was stronger than his emotions, no matter their reason.

Shen stood at the entrance of his order, observing their approach with a severe aspect. That look went a long way to squash Gediel's desires. Gediel chewed his tongue. He wasn't used to apologizing for his actions, especially when they were necessary. He was no youngling learning his lessons, but Voil agreed with the orders and would be sure to check that he fulfilled them. Shen should have understood that the cost of the damage to his gate was worth the information they had gained. Regardless, Gediel was thankful the praefect appeared not to know his mission; that ignorance offered a means to refocus his energy while he waited to continue the mission.

At the Wolf Leader's side a very sheepish Luthias walked with less certainty than he was known for. Under hunched shoulders, the guardian stared over his nose at the opening, as if the guarded mien could ward off punishments. A deep frown marred his face, as the walls stood firm. Gediel thought he would be delighted to return, considering the sudden infatuation the engel had had with Shen's fifth daughter. Luthias wasn't one to remain silent about a pretty face. He spoke about the witches freely, but not a word about the raven-haired girl they had found in Gyuto.

"You should apologize to the Draco. Indebt yourself to her service for putting her in danger," Gediel suggested.

"I wasn't the one who brought Belial to their doorstep. If you recall, I spoke against it," Luthias growled.

"Even more reason," Gediel said, trying not to smile.

Luthias exhaled, quite displeased. The engel refused to talk about the girl, displaying his surliness. Gediel snickered at how upset this made his new friend. He shook his head to get rid of the foolish feeling before they wound up matching fists. By the glare Luthias offered, it was quite a serious matter.

Returning his gaze to the entrance, Gediel watched Dao-Ming take to her janya's side. Irrepressible joy twisted the Wolf Leader's mouth into a grin. Luthias's pace slowed and Gediel slowed with him. The guardian looked as though someone had struck him with a lance. His color paled, but his eyes glowed with a determined light. Gediel cleared his throat, knowing that look well. Dao-Ming's eyes also glowed. He could see the amber fire from there. She lowered her gaze self-consciously.

"Interesting—most interesting," Gediel said, slapping his hand on his new friend's shoulder to urge him forward.

"What?" Luthias asked, trying not to sound concerned as they stumbled closer.

"Nothing," Gediel said, not wishing to embarrass him. He knew exactly how that felt.

"Nothing? I'll never understand you watchers," Luthias hissed.

Gediel smiled. They took the last strides to Shen's door. The commander inflated his chest, looking down his nose at them. His hands were folded inside his robes, but Gediel knew there was no blade at the ready.

"We've come to make amends for poisoning your entrance to the Astral Ways. A report is expected by my commander, Voil, at the conclusion," Gediel said, bowing stiffly.

"And for endangering your daughter, a report is due to the praefect of the Order of Prittani when I've done my penance," Luthias added.

Shen eyed them, still quite cross with their actions.

"We're at your service until you see fit to dismiss us. However, there's a duty yet to be performed in our quest to retrieve a Captain of the Moon Order from Samsara. I can't say when I must go, but swear to return once my obligation to the king is fulfilled in the matter," Gediel added.

Shen looked to Luthias.

"My soul will need fetching as well," the evocati said less dramatically.

Dao-Ming stifled a laugh, pressing her hand to her small bow mouth. This made Luthias grin.

Shen cast his eyes aside and cleared his throat. Luthias and Dao-Ming quickly became serious.

"You'll teach my men the ways of your stealth, Wolf Leader," Shen said to Gediel, turning his shoulder toward the black-leathered guard behind him. He then turned to Luthias and added, "You'll learn manners from my daughters."

Gediel pulled his lips in to keep from laughing. Luthias was indeed a bit rough around the edges. Even now he stammered, struggling to find the proper words while glowering at his hosts, ungraciously accepting the opportunity to spend time with Dao-Ming and her khata. The Gyuto males smiled at his inelegance. Shen left them to the devices of his guards, turning his back in a whirl of robes. He disappeared beyond the wall. He had much meditation to undertake in fixing the astral gate and no time to spare in observing their penance.

Dao-Ming approached Luthias with a smile. "Come with me, guardian."

Gediel watched him go. The guardian cast a fearful gaze over his shoulder as he and his taskmaster were joined by her khata. Gediel waved him away and accompanied the heavily armored guards to their sparring grounds.

The Gyuto soldiers were eager students, helping a great deal to distract him with their ceaseless energy. They ran through their exercises under his watchful guidance, dressed in full armor to prove they had the stamina to keep up. Not one complained. Only the younglings struggled. He shouted orders until he was hoarse, pacing between them with his hands tucked behind his back. A well-placed toe or poke of his blade corrected them. A casual nod of approval strengthened the sapped limbs of the younger warriors.

Sitting on the edge of the sparring square, Gediel wrapped his hands in tape, preparation for individual combat lessons. He needed to measure each of them on his own now that they were warmed up. First in line was Shen's son. A worthy opponent.

Above Gediel's head the sky darkened, twinkling with the first stars and a few silver-bodied airplanes. The red distance turned his thoughts in other directions. Cobalt and crimson. A pang in his chest, both anxiety and excitement, lowered his chin.

The moment was lost with the sound of porcelain shattering on the stone path. Luthias crouched down to pick up broken bits of cups and a teapot. Shen's daughters stood above him, wagging their fingers and tittering all at once. Gediel laughed, seeing the frustration in Luthias's face. They had dressed him in their plainclothes and an apron to control his surliness. Dao-Ming, not bent on breaking his will, went to him. She knelt at his side to help, causing her khata to gasp in shock. Gediel returned to wrapping his hands, a bitter smile fading on his lips.

"I wish I'd said something," Gediel heard a feminine voice.

Zaajah took a seat beside him. Her dark almond eyes stared as if seeing him for the first time. She grasped his forearm with her long-fingered hand and he felt the warmth of her care. Gediel spied a bruise spread over the length of her arm. She must have just returned from playing with their enemies.

"No one blames you," Gediel said.

"I blame me. I'm her khata. I saw and didn't speak," Zaajah said.

"You were younglings, in love with every warrior and each other. You hardly knew. Cal never said a word either, and she was just a child, not quite fettered by modesty."

"Why didn't you say something?"

Gediel sighed. His eyes went to where Luthias held a tray full of a broken tea service. The remnants dripped on the ground. Dao-Ming smiled at him, taking it as one of her khata gave him another lecture. They directed him back to the house, laughing at his clumsiness. He would need to start over, and quickly. Shen was waiting for his evening tea.

"She wouldn't have hurt you," Zaajah said.

"It's more than that. My aryika—the whole of what I had to offer—I wasn't worthy of her," Gediel said.

"Not worthy?"

Gediel snorted, hearing the ridiculousness of what he'd said. A human who was on the path of destruction was far from a better choice.

"Do you know how many would give their wings to claim you? Never so blind a watcher."

Wrapping his hands again, Gediel found he had nothing to say.

"There's no need to think on the past. I'm sorry for bringing it up," Zaajah said, getting back on her feet.

Gediel nodded and also stood. Motioning the leader of one Gyuto squad to the square, the Wolf Leader tried to concentrate on his task. Despite the need to honor his duty, his mind would not cease to worry over other obligations. Looking to Zaajah, he flexed his fists, adjusting the wraps.

"Will you stay until it's time?"

Zaajah nodded. She needed to hide somewhere so the commanders didn't call her to her squads. Their efforts were still concealed, though many worked to avoid the war that Belial incited. The other generals and their commanders wouldn't understand their reluctance to grant the prince his desire and settle their rivalry once and for all. Their small band of compatriots were quite clear that now was not the time, and innumerable souls relied on their success as much as Maiel.

"Only if I can help you train these neophytes." Zaajah grinned.

"Don't let the Gyuto hear you say that. They won't go easy on you. They're more than simple clerics," Gediel replied.

"We'll see," Zaajah said facing the square.

The Gyuto leader waited patiently for Gediel to join him. He obliged, mounting the sparring stage.

"Xia-wu!" Shen shouted to his son.

Gediel turned. The sky was full of lights, all streaking toward the White City.

"Get your squads together. We've been summoned by Gabriel," Shen continued.

Gediel looked to Zaajah and they exchanged knowing glances. The war was about to begin.

CHAPTER 24

MAIEL SAT UP, NOT QUITE AS RESTED as she hoped. Her room grew dark while her eyes were closed and the smell of sulfur spoiled the air. A deep frown turned her expression severe in the dim light. Swinging her legs around, she got up and went to open the curtains. The sun set on the other side of the building, casting long shadows on the ground below. The light would soon be gone and the shadows would close in even more. Vratin and humans continued to wander the streets, innocent, naive, and oblivious of their reality. Opening the rest of the curtains, she hoped not to be caught so unaware by the imps this building housed. If the moon's reflection was strong enough, it would adequately amplify her dwindled strength. Turning back, she eyed the room in search of enemies where the light didn't reach. The whispers were quieter here, less intense than in the basement of the basilica. This building wasn't quite so old with quite as many memories. Maiel realized she'd heard the voices of the imprisoned, those who refused to know they passed on, but who knew the secrets of Esztergom. A gray dashed behind her. She turned quickly and watched the apparition pass through a door, unaware she even stood there.

A crimson glow lit a small spot on the bed, distracting her before she could ward the room. She stepped toward the mattress. To her dismay, several feathers lay on the blanket. Maiel picked up the lost pinion. Tears blurred her eyesight. Quickly gathering them up, she searched for a place to hide them. There was no way she would leave them to the humans, and have them traded as relics and used to anchor authority for their church.

A fireplace sat cold on the wall between her bedroom and the bathroom. She tossed the feathers on the pile of wood. Wiping her eyes, she looked for matches. Her heart pounded in her chest, attesting to the progress of the human-like form she took. Soon, all the feathers would be gone. Her wings would shrivel and fall off, like limbs of a dead tree. Then she would slowly shrink, becoming shorter and thinner, critically weaker than when she arrived. Last, the light of her eyes and the little life of the penannular would be gone. Her atman would be trapped until the lesson was hard-learned. Maiel slammed her fist on the mantel and cried out angrily. Resting her head against the shelf, she wept over the feathers.

An iron wheel on the outer bricks of the fireplace caught her eye. She spun it and heard the gas come on. She spun it back, and looked around for the means to light the fuel. A tiny brass box sat on the edge of the mantel. Lifting the lid, she found the matches inside. With a flick of her thumbnail, she lit the first and watched it burn out. Her tears stopped, as she stared at the small light of the bright flame. She blinked, releasing herself from the allure of the fire. Drawing another matchstick, she turned the wheel again and lit the fire.

The feathers turned black, smoking, then finally burned. Their smell filled the room, disguising the scent of her enemy. She hoped the smell of her burning feathers wouldn't draw them to her. Maiel settled on the floor in front of the fire, watching her feathers disappear in the flames. The heat warmed her cold skin, but not her miserable mood. She found another feather on the floor and tossed it onto the fire.

"Oh, Dominic, what've I done?" Maiel growled into her knee.

"Indeed, what have you done?" a familiar voice asked from behind.

Maiel jumped to her feet, facing the intruder. Morgentus sat on her bed, twirling a ruby feather in his fingers. He gave a slow smile, running the plume under his nose.

"You missed one," he said.

Maiel drew her sword. It felt heavier than she remembered. The atman inside the sapphire hilt grew dim along with her hope for any aid from the world that had created it. Morgentus chuckled, knowing it. He sauntered toward the fire and threw the feather on the charred logs.

"They smell much better when they're not burned," Morgentus said, ignoring the blade aimed at him.

Maiel stepped back, unsure she was strong enough to defend herself against him, despite her prolonged meditation. The shadowalker watched the flames dance, just as assured of her weakness.

"It's really too bad you won't bear them as my wife," Morgentus said, mournful. "A negligible price to pay for the power you'll wield."

"Why do you persist with that impossible desire? I can't stand you and won't be made to," Maiel said, disgusted and angry.

"Because you are mated to me. I'll have what is mine," Morgentus replied. His icy eyes rose from the fire to her blade. He waved a hand. "Can't you feel the pull to me? I can feel you," he added, grinning madly.

A pair of mudeaters emerged from the far shadowed corner of her room. Segrius and his soldier snapped their sharp teeth, taking their time to cross the space toward her. Masking her fear, Maiel recalled the room's layout, hoping to retreat and regroup. She couldn't fight all three, but picking them off as they searched for her was feasible. If she was able to get to the hall, she could retrace her steps from below the basilica to the seminary buildings. The shades wouldn't know their way around and the presence of the relics and other items would cloak her atman, if they were in fact left behind by those who had wielded the light of Zion on Earth. They'd be easy hunting.

Maiel darted to the door. The serpents cried out as their handler shouted orders. The knob twisted slowly. They came at her. Maiel steadied herself, taking a measured breath. Time slowed. She wasn't new to this game. She just needed to stay centered. Retreating gave her the ground from which to fight. Pulling the door open, Maiel shot outside and it slammed closed behind her. Bounding down the hall, she didn't wait to see if they followed. She heard them break through the door, slam against the opposite wall, and scramble to right themselves.

A vratin emerged from one of the many rooms lining the hall, and at his side was a squat little guardian. Their gazes followed Maiel as she ran toward them. The human had to look twice to be sure he saw correctly. His voice broke in raspy Latin as he fell back against the door. She would have warned him what was coming behind her, but she was already descending the stairs. The vratin would need to rely on his guardian's wits to realize that a legiona didn't idly retreat.

Flights below, the sound of another door being torn asunder spurred her on, followed by a primal howl of hunger echoing through the stairwell. Maiel looked up and spotted the serpent leaning over the banister. Segrius's trademark shriek followed, jarring her to quicker action. They descended the stairwell, scrambling over banisters, walls, and steps. Segrius's second dropped on the steps before her. Maiel kicked hard, slamming him back against a wall. She exited the stairs. They were quick and she needed another way to escape them. She took a moment to eye the hall she'd found. Turning the seminary into her own labyrinth, Maiel sought to lead them on a chase sure to exhaust them. While they hunted through every room for her, she would snake her way to safety. She hoped in that journey to stumble upon Orius. This fight was going to take more than just her sword.

Maiel hurdled up the hall into a group of vratin chatting about their lessons. With her wings spread to keep her balance, she made a fantastic sight. They fell silent, staring. Dashing through another door, she found cover in an empty meeting room. The vratin pursued her, but she didn't pause to warn them away. A door at the back led into an office where a lone vratin sorted through some papers. He started to holler, thinking she was a student, but quickly stopped when he saw her leaving through the next door.

In this hasty fashion, Maiel made a circuit until she found another set of stairs. Behind her, the reaction to her pursuers shattered the usually calm atmosphere. There would be much for them to mull over once this was finished, perhaps just what they needed to set them straight.

Maiel made her way through classrooms and offices, exiting at the end into the hall in pursuit of more stairs. Segrius's minion waited. Running at him, she shouted angrily until her throat was sore. The mudeater crouched, wielding his claws at her threateningly. Maiel ran upon him, swatting his face, as she used his knee for a step. Somersaulting over his head, she spun round, planting her foot in his back. Landing in a kneeling crouch, she saw Morgentus exit the last classroom. She jumped up as the serpent regained his senses and took the steps two at a time to evade him. At the bottom of the stairs, Maiel broke through the exit and emerged on the first floor hall. Overhead, the danava trampled down after her, toppling over each other to get to her first. Morgentus shouted at them, frustrated by their absurdity.

Maiel darted toward the first door, hoping she wasn't about to trap herself. Instead, she found another set of stairs. Leaping down them, she found the tunnels Geitz had brought her through from the church. Racing for a hiding place, she didn't hear them coming after her. Somehow they'd lost her trail. However, that was no reason to stop running now.

Continuing deeper into the basement, Maiel opened a door to throw them off her track. Hurrying back, she ran along a cross tunnel and chose a random door. Inside, a pitch-black cavern stretched into forever, like the caves of Abaddon. Tilting her sword forward, the sapphire cast a dull glow over the recess. Statues and relics filled the vast room. A sigh of relief escaped her. She felt for and threw the lock on the door. Afraid her scent would be detectable that close to the opening, Maiel worked her way into the back of the room. Ducking behind a large marble pedestal, she crouched down and watched the crack of light under the door.

Silence encircled her. Clamping her hand on the hilt of her sword, Maiel shone the light upon her surroundings, getting a second look. Atop the pedestal was a statue of a duta. It was meant to be Mikhael, she guessed from a few of the details, but it looked more like a youngling erela. Covering the sapphire, she doused the only light there was. When the silence persisted, she sat down and drew her knees up, resting her arms on them. Her head lowered but her eyes kept watch in the direction of the door.

*   *   *

Orius exited a small study. Closing the door behind him, he heard the rattling of heavy metal plates. At the end of the hall, Maiel ducked through a door in quite a hurry. He opened his mouth to call to her, but was quickly silenced by the arrival of his Grigori brother. Two others joined him. Skin like mud, he knew them for the Baron's nasty little helpers. Morgentus had made his move to take her before anyone could help. Orius jumped back into the room before they saw him. He needed to help her, to distract them before they figured out her route. As his pale-faced brother stepped toward the tunnel door, he remembered the rosary hanging at his waist. He quickly pulled it free, cautiously crossing the hall into a room opposite. He pitched the beads behind him, softly shutting the door and locking it.

"Sneaky, kesarini," Morgentus said, taking the bait.

Orius listened to the footsteps draw nearer. He looked around the room for an escape. Stacks of books lined the walls. The only exit was through the door he had just entered or a pair of windows. Orius moved to the closest window and opened it. After the briefest of hesitations, he climbed out. His brother wasn't as stupid as he thought. The door to his hiding place was forced open. Dashing around the corner of the building, he caught sight of the basilica in the distance. Bethiah would head there in search of help, hoping to find a guardian present.

Hurrying around the other side of the building, he found the residents of the seminary emptying from the front door. The young clergy and their tutors looked startled. Their guardians cast worried glances and whispers about what was happening inside. Some clerics prayed, making the sign of the cross, while others fell to their knees. Some wept, pleading for aid from their long absent prince. Above their heads, the late afternoon clouds gathered. Orius grimaced. None of their incantations would save them. The prince wasn't coming out of Zion for this.

Hoping to go unnoticed, Orius skirted the crowd. Taking the blocked road toward the basilica, he cast a glance over his shoulder several times to be sure that no one followed. Ahead of him, priests retreated to what they thought was safety. He blended in with them, thinking of a way to secure an escape from his brother for both Bethiah and himself. Drawing a ragged breath, he hoped she'd managed to find her way out from underground.

In the dark recesses of Earth, the demons would wield greater strength than she.

Navigating through the rubble and equipment littering the tunnel, Orius picked his way to the basilica. The other priests were filing in around him, panicked and confused by the events. Orius grit his teeth at the foolishness sure to hurt everyone's chance at escape. Most probably they had no idea the buildings were connected, like they didn't admit the evil there was connected to them. His eyes went from face to face, knowing some of them were Geitz's allies.

Despite their futile effort to find shelter in the church, the small group climbed to the portico and found the doors of their house wide open. Through the arches, Orius saw the evil already inside. He cursed under his breath and quickly urged his fellow priests back. At the top of the steps, he called out to them, waving his arms. The priests gathered to him, reluctant, because they didn't know his face.

"I'm Father Gregely Orius from Máriabesnyő. I know you don't know me. I just arrived at the basilica today, but I beg you to listen to me. The church won't offer you sanctuary. The beast can stand anywhere but within the gates of heaven. You must leave this place. Get as far away as you can until daybreak. Trust me. He seeks a—"

"How do you know so much, Father Orius?" one of the nearer clergy asked. "How do we know this isn't your fault? It has come here with you!"

"I understand your concern, but I assure you I'm your friend," Orius said, drawing them back down the steps. "I've been—that is, I'm a demonologist. I was summoned to help the archbishop in his fight against this demon. I beg you to do as I say," Orius lied, hoping they would listen.

The men stared at him. Some whispered and wondered. He couldn't let them into the church, no matter what they decided. Beyond this threshold waited a battle their guardians couldn't save them from. His eyes swept the invisible multitude. One among them gave him a nod. They would do their best to convince the priests to flee.

"Beasts such as this have come before. I've faced them," Orius said.

The men gasped. He saw their guardians clutching at them, whispering in their ears.

"You must trust me. Last night, one, perhaps this one, severely damaged my church. The authorities believe it was vandals, but when you find news of it you'll see the signs of what I speak. I've come to help, to at last vanquish this demon, but not at the price of your lives. You must flee. Run! Run to the edges of the city," Orius told them.

"Father Orius speaks the truth. You should seek safety beyond the city. We'll face this foe alone, as we planned. I won't have you harmed, no matter how much I appreciate your support," Archbishop Geitz said, as he joined them from his evil altar.

Orius tensed as the archbishop stepped to his side. Geitz directed the priests standing near to return to the others and guide them off to the city. They reluctantly complied. He promised them that by morning the evil would be cast out of their home and they could return. Turning to Orius, Geitz gave a devious smile and urged him into the church. Three of his dark brothers emerged on the portico, others joined from the lawn.

"Come with me, Gregely. I'm sure we can settle this together," Geitz said.

"Bethiah doesn't trust you," Orius told him, allowing the clergyman to lead him.

They entered the church and found a few more of his brood inside. They wore their black cassocks, but red sashes crossed their waists. The crosses that usually hung from a beaded chain were absent. Their dark gazes pursued him as he walked to the aisle. The altar was shrouded with black cloth. They had hung a pentagram high above it from several medieval chains, a terrible misuse of the Zion symbol that meant nothing to the princes of Jahannam. Candles burned ferociously, casting light upon their ignorance.

"What is all this?" Orius asked, though he knew.

Bethiah had been right. He should have trusted her judgment and his instincts. After all, she wasn't yet recidia and had her good sense left.

"You know very well," Geitz replied, exasperated by the question.

Orius walked toward the altar, astounded that they had been able to hide this within the basilica. The priests who fell to Geitz's teachings prepared the altar for a dark sermon. Orius guessed that they were going to offer Bethiah to their demon.

"Where's the girl?" Geitz asked him.

"The last I saw—in the seminary, perhaps gone. You won't find her, at least not before dawn. By then, the others will have returned and help will have reached her."

"We'll find her." Geitz gestured toward the relic room.

"I won't let you harm her," Orius said, watching the priests shuffle toward the other entrance to the tunnels.

"You don't have a choice—unless you're stronger than Belial himself," Geitz said, revealing the source of his power.

Orius guarded his features, but the admission clearly dismayed him. The archbishop continued a few steps before turning and facing him. He raised his brows at Orius and then smiled. An arrogant chuckle escaped his throat.

"It's not too late to secure your kingdom, Orius. The prince can still use some men. They would love to count you among them," Geitz said, indicating the altar.

Orius gaped, realizing this ceremony was meant for him. A sacrifice to declare Bethia's allegiance, leading the way for Belial and his minions to overflow Earth.

The archbishop turned and continued to the altar. Orius looked away. Geitz had no idea what he asked of him. Casting his gaze over the desecrated church, he struggled for a single plan that didn't involve someone being sacrificed in the outcome, but there wasn't one. Gathering his courage, he joined Geitz at the darkened altar. If Belial had come, the archbishop was in for a surprise when the prince exposed his real plan. His brother, Morgentus, wouldn't be far behind either. Morgentus would savor his quandary, until he realized that murdering him sent him back to Zion and that he would return with a legion of Powers to undo their plans.

"This way, Father Orius. You must be consecrated before your bloodletting." Geitz stepped aside, holding his arm out to indicate the way.

Orius eyed him. What could he do if he didn't follow?

"Don't hesitate, Father. I can't assure you we'll be kind when we find her if you make this difficult. Cooperate and you can plead with her—cry the virtues of the light."

Geitz's voice changed, carrying the distinct flavor of venom. They already knew where she was. The dark priests needed him to draw her out, because Morgentus had sent her underground. A bead of icy sweat slipped down Orius's back. If he betrayed her, he would never go home again, and the sacrifice they made of him would make him danava. Geitz faced him, smiling arrogantly. One of the priests shuffled up behind Orius, then another. The choice wasn't his any longer.

"We can make you hurt for eternity, lightwalker," Geitz said from a mouth bright with blood.

Orius's eyes flashed with a dazzle of lights. Images formed, flickering like old movies. He lifted his chin, gazing at the archbishop with disgust. What he saw was not memory, but possibility. These were the final steps in his path. The flashes were a message. Instructions.

*　*　*

The sky deepened in bold tones declaring the fleeting moments of the late afternoon. Dominic's eyes shifted to the dashboard clock. No. It was early afternoon yet by the time. He leaned over the wheel for a better look at the sky. Either the glass was dirty or a storm formed along the north horizon. Blue-black clouds rolled in. His senses, however, told him that something more sinister than a nasty a storm was on the horizon.

Flipping the dial on the radio, Dominic tried to find a station that played music. He was worn out by the constant chatter that had taken over the previous channel. He couldn't understand a syllable and it was only feeding his melancholy. A road sign appeared; they were approaching Budapest. His heart lifted. Once they covered a few more kilometers, they would see the cityscape and, in minutes, they would begin their hunt.

The static of the radio cleared and the sound of trumpets blared through the speakers. Coming back down from the startling overture, Dominic felt a nostalgic wave pass through his core. He hadn't heard swing music in quite a while. He listened to the band beat out its rhythm while his mind played images of a young woman in a tight sweater. She looked just enough like his wife and just enough unlike her to be her own person, but they were one and the same. She lay back across his desk at the front of the empty classroom as he undid his pants. He wondered: if Anne knew who she really was, would her fate have come to pass? There was no use in deliberating those possibilities. He shifted the radio knob again before his thoughts carried him further. It still hurt too much to go there. He imagined her lips parting with a soft moan at his touch. He was dragged off to dreamscapes despite the company he kept.

"Argus said you're going the wrong way," Lena said, pushing her face between the seats, and chasing Anne's kiss from his memory.

"They said Budapest," Dominic replied, annoyed by another lie.

Argus pushed his head into the front and barked. He gave a whimper and then showed his teeth.

"All right, all right. Where then?" Dominic asked.

"Another capital?" Lena said. She made a face and added, "The old one."

"Christ," Dominic cursed.

Pulling the car to the side of the road, he dug out his atlas. If he was to find his wife, he would have to rely on himself.

"Hungary is liable to have had twenty capitals since it existed," he grumbled, opening the maps.

Scanning page after page of his atlas, Dominic felt each car and truck that passed on the highway shake the Mercedes. Shee whimpered and he lifted his hand to beg for a moment longer. Argus pushed his way into the passenger seat. Dominic felt the heavy hammer of the wolf's gold eyes on him. He looked at him sidelong. The alpha was quite serious. His gaze shifted from the book to Dominic's eyes. Dominic returned to his study, clearing his throat.

"Did you find anything?" Lena asked, tucking her head between the seat and the window, so she could see the atlas too.

A truck passed, dangerously close, blaring its horn. A gust of air buffeted the car.

"I think so," Dominic said.

Flipping more pages, several maps illustrated a relatively consistent history. However, the incarnations of the Hungarian state were varied over time. If he guessed wrong, or if Argus was mistaken, they would be delayed that much longer. From what he determined, the country had changed its capital only once. The former seat of political influence was now a seat of ecclesiastical domination. Ironically, that made sense.

"Well?" Lena asked impatiently.

"Esztergom—in the north," Dominic replied, thinking of the storm that brewed in the north.

Argus lowered his head with relief. Lena regarded him, looking just as uncertain. Behind her, Shee pranced on the back seat, growing anxious. Dominic yanked the transmission lever back to drive and slowly pulled forward, careful not to end their trip by colliding with a shipping truck or speeding car. Releasing an exasperated breath, he stuck his fingers in his hair, combing it back roughly and stepped on the gas.

"Where are you going?" Lena asked. "Argus said you were right."

"I can't turn around here. We'll have to find a route after we reach Budapest," Dominic explained, irritated by the news.

Lena sat back, looking glum. She folded her arms and watched out the window. Argus climbed back with her, lying on the seat with his head in her lap. They had no reason to trust his judgment.

The travelers continued east in silence. The cities surrounding Budapest rose slowly on the horizon, swallowing the farm-swaddled road. The new sights were a welcome change after the leagues of green fields. Dominic's body revived from the drudgery-induced numbness. His eager eyes sought out road signs, hoping he could manage to translate them. Dominic's energy quickly grew dark again as he steered the car around the main hub of Budapest. At least he was headed generally north. Then Argus made a sound from the back seat.

"He wants you to keep left ahead," Lena said. The wolf groused and she added, "Toward a triangle."

Dominic blinked his eyes. Lena expected him to take directions from a wolf. He regarded the three guides sitting on the back seat through the mirror, skeptical that the animal could navigate at all. His mouth tightened, preventing him from voicing his doubt and falling into a fit of rage at her incompetence. He simply wasn't sure about any of them. Argus didn't particularly care for him. The family of duta he'd married into didn't either. They sent him with a child who struggled to guide him and wolves who spoke in another language unable to guide him. Naturally he suspected this was all meant to delay him.

Passing another road sign, Dominic recognized the city name of their destination. He sighed, guilty once more. Argus might not like him, but his best friend still needed his help. The wolf wouldn't fail Maiel. His loyalty was hers for eternity. Dominic continued as he was directed, setting his skepticism aside. They soon passed merging traffic in the shape of a triangle. He adjusted in his seat, flexing his fingers around the steering wheel. It tweaked his conscience that they were right.

Argus made another sound. His great white head appeared between the seats. The eerie gold eyes stared at the roadway. Dominic waited to learn what he was saying now.

"Follow this road to the end and make a left," Lena said, crawling up beside her new friend.

Dominic gestured, still biting his tongue. Lena's dark eyes were on him. When she at last sat back, Argus went with her and he was left with some much-needed space. The burning in his throat tickled until he coughed it clear. He knew the coat no longer worked to hide his symptoms. Turning the rearview mirror toward his face, he looked to see if his eyes revealed the glow he had seen days ago. Indeed, they did. A ring of green fire circled each iris. Yet the whites of his eyes looked irritated. He blinked a few times. The light remained and so did the redness. Flipping the mirror back, he tried to clear them by opening and closing them. He told himself he was just tired, then convinced himself it wouldn't be much longer.

"Something follows us," Lena said, cautiously watching out the back.

The wolves growled, low and rough.

"What?" Dominic exhaled, annoyed.

Dominic looked in his mirrors. The view wasn't promising from any of them. Another long black car followed at a distance, but it was impossible to determine whether they were being tracked by it. He could not escape either. The car in front of them kept a slow pace and the opposing traffic was too thick. Dominic weaved to see if anyone was ahead. Watching the suspect vehicle in the rearview mirror, he decided he would pass the car in front and see if they gave chase. When the chance presented itself, he pressed the gas and swung into the other lane. Pushing the broken old car to its limit, he passed the obstruction and turned back into his lane, eyes switching between mirrors and windows. He kept his foot on the gas. The other car shrunk in the distance. He smiled, feeling assured they weren't followed, but merely stuck in traffic with everyone else on the road. Then the car he passed appeared to lose control. It bobbled left then right and finally jerked aside into a ditch. The car Lena spotted sped up to gain on them.

"Shit," Dominic growled.

The wolves agreed.

At the next side street, Dominic cranked the wheel and took them off their route.

"Hang on!" he shouted to his passengers.

The car handled remarkably well, taking the sudden turn wide but solidly. A small smile curled the corners of Dominic's mouth. He pressed on the gas and the old Mercedes roared forward. Their pursuer made the turn as well without such graceful execution. Dominic nodded and repeated the turn in another direction. Lena gripped the back of his seat, trying not to slide with each turn.

"Shedu won't be stopped that easily," Lena said.

The pursuing car appeared in a cross street ahead of them. Dominic stared, puzzled by their pursuer's speed and luck as the black car parked in the street to block their passage.

"I told you!" Lena said.

Dominic stomped on the brakes, bringing the car to an abrupt stop. Grabbing the lever, he quickly stuck the transmission in reverse. Another car pulled in behind, explaining the impossible arrival of the first car. There were two hemming them in. Dominic waited, slowly returning the transmission to drive. His mind raced as he thought of a way out.

"Dominic! What're you doing?" Lena asked, trying to caution him.

The other car pulled up to his bumper, pushing the little coupe toward the second car. Pressing hard on the brake, he gave them a surprising fight. His eyes scanned ahead, trying to figure out which way the other car would go if he jumped.

"Getting us out of here. Hold on," Dominic finally replied.

Planting his foot firmly on the gas, Dominic headed the little coupe toward the other car. Their pursuer raced behind them, while the other backed up to prevent them slipping around. With surprising dexterity, he managed to turn the car around without being struck by the other cars or flipping over. The first car struck the other at full speed, turning them both in the wrong direction and possibly flattening their tires. Not waiting for a wave good-bye, he mashed the gas pedal down again and drove them through side streets until no one was in sight.

"That should keep them away for a bit, don't you think?" Dominic grinned.

"You needlessly risked your life," Lena said, folding her arms as she sat at attention in the middle of the backseat.

Dominic laughed. "We'd best get moving again. Which way, Argus?"

Argus panted, wagging his tail. He gave a sharp yip, which Dominic took for approval. His mate cleaned Lena's face, not offering her opinion.

CHAPTER 25

GRAGRAFEL STOOD PACES behind one of the grand generals of the four armies of Zion. Mikhael assessed his assembled soldiers and patiently waited to give the order to deploy, his pair of griffins standing attentively to either side of him. In each direction, the other officios stood above their legions doing the same. Uriel gazed over her scarlet shoulders toward him, as Dux Horus whispered in her ear from behind his great, golden falcon helm. Gragrafel's chin shifted to the other side and he saw the dusky Gabriel in his emerald armor, in command of wondrous troops that stretched their influence into the deepest reaches of Samsara. Beyond Gabriel stood the gold- and ivory-clad Raphael. The sky was dotted by the souls of the air, fowl, and far more fantastical creatures, as well as air skiffs and transports for those who couldn't blink, slide, or fly. Folding his great arms, the general in front of Gragrafel scowled, impatient at having to wait for word from the supreme commander, Metatron. Mikhael's stony features expressed other emotions as well. His eyes swept the hundreds of wings, plates, and limbs, the varied faces of soul and duta. The armaments glinted in the setting sun and he frowned deeper, missing the red and blue he wanted to see there. Gragrafel decided to wait.

"That's the last of them, General," Sephr said, approaching from behind.

Sephr's leaders went to the other corps commanders. The Moon Order squads, once commanded by Maiel, were among them, leaderless.

"Not every last one," Mikhael replied.

Sephr shrugged, amused by the absences.

The general's eagle gaze could pinpoint each soldier. In his head, he kept a record of each, from family to friends. The newest youngling could approach him and be delighted to find that he knew their name, who was in their family, the skills at which they excelled, and something that interested them the most. The other commanders were quite capable of the same, but didn't use the knowledge to much effect. Though he was infallible in his faith and wisdom, he led with his heart. The others led from duty and tradition.

Gragrafel decided to make his presence known, now that Sephr had safely disturbed the general. The Principality maneuvered his marble-like form to stand at the general's side. Again, he waited patiently for his time to speak. Mikhael most likely knew Gragrafel was to blame for the absence of three key fighters from his divisions and the one from his sister general's elite units. The old engel said nothing. He wasn't about to claim the honor, when they were both working to retrieve Maiel.

"We'll stand at the gates and strike as soon as they rear their heads. Your man better have our erela in hand by then or his mission ends in failure," Mikhael said.

Gragrafel nodded. The blustering didn't bother him.

"No worries, alder. I'll not come back without both," Mikhael said, softening.

"You best not. We may still save him," Gragrafel said dryly.

Turning to Sephr, Mikhael unfolded his thick arms. His features drew into a terrible scowl. Like Gragrafel, he wasn't sure saving the human was the best thing for his captain, but he would sooner regret failing her than leave her to fall before she realized Dominic's threat. The attachment she and Dominic had was as good as real. Perhaps, in time, she would turn naturally toward the ketu they'd betrayed. Regardless, it wasn't her general who would be blamed, for he fought hard against creating this terrible secret. He only hoped she came to understand the purpose of the act and chose not to follow her husband should he decide to side with the princes of Abaddon. Because of the advanced stage of his burning, Dominic blamed the entire duta race, though blame deserved to be placed with just a few of the hierarchy. The king may have decreed it, but matters were far more complicated than just the king passing orders. The match was made to give the boy another chance to save himself from the abyss. This wasn't a truth that would remain hidden. Both would find out. Unfortunately, how they perceived such actions was up to them. Sadly, Gragrafel knew the human would never acknowledge his guilt. That attitude might serve to make his daughter angry with her friends. One hope they had was in Gediel's discovery of the truth and that his atman now pulled on Maiel. The magnetism of their attraction would grow and skew the odds of the mission's success.

"We can't wait any longer," Mikhael said, waking the principality from his reflection.

Sephr gave a sharp nod. He waved his arm above his head. Several runners made their way to the other generals. Mikhael returned to observing his army. The horns blew and the energy rushed through the throngs of soldiers; even he was moved despite having stood here many times through the ages. Many danava would be destroyed that night. If Mikhael had his way, Abaddon would be no more and every soul would be avenged their wrongs.

Gragrafel's brows knitted together, wishing it were so.

"Now it is my turn to oblige their request for war," Mikhael said.

Gragrafel's black eyes followed him. The noise deafened as they moved all at once. The sky was set ablaze with the light of their passing. The prep fields now stood empty, sandy shores. In their hasty exit, the air snapped and a great breeze blew, nearly toppling trees and those who remained behind. Gragrafel stood strong in the gust, his robes, hair, and wings fluttering. It was a sight he had not seen since the Conflict, back when he was a warrior like his twins. He hoped he would not see it again. He hoped this was the last and that his grandchildren wouldn't be forced to fight such battles in the coming millennia.

Stirring from his vigil, Gragrafel walked back along the vacant platform. Other alders who came to watch the spectacle retreated back to their duties. He couldn't, as yet. His mind was overfull, missing his daughter and not quite finding solace in her children while she was gone. He walked slower than the rest and was soon left behind, a mournful, aged figure on the mall.

Reaching the end of the platform, a black figure flickered at the base of the Walhall causeway. Gragrafel lifted his heavy chin. He'd nearly forgot he had called upon his eldest. The stoic features of the young engel's face comforted him, though they were hard like stone.

"Janya—you called," Zacharius said, stepping up a small flight of stairs.

Gragrafel tried to smile at him, but it felt weak and brought tears to his eyes. He grasped his eldest son's arm.

"Yes—just in time."

Gragrafel led him back toward the mountain. His gaze went up the slopes to the pillar of light blazing at the tip. There was no tremor from on high. Gragrafel sighed. Sometimes he wished he were still a warrior. He would have pulled his fiery daughter back by her sharp little braids, then given her a sound spanking for being such a fool. Gritting his teeth, he took a seat on one of the benches that overlooked the fields. He was silent and his son patiently waited for him to say why he was summoned. He lost himself in memories of his little girl when she was only as high as his knee. He was an old svarg then, passing on to higher resonance. Had he been patient, and waited for her to grow, none of this would have happened, because he wouldn't have allowed it. An infant, even one that was a principality, had little sway.

Zacharius tucked his hands behind his back to show he was eager to continue.

"Go to him—tell him there's no time left. He must hurry if he wants to save himself. Adonai has sent his legions to wage battle with the danava."

Gragrafel came to a stop. He soaked in every detail of his eldest child. The red hair was his wife's, though hers was now long faded. A smile managed to change his expression, though Zacharius still looked quite serious. He cupped the side of Zacharius's head and ruefully smiled. The patriarch's eyes glimmered with torment. Taking his hand back, he steadied his emotions.

"Don't tell him that Mikhael will bring them back either way. None are to know that."

Zacharius regarded him a moment, then nodded. He disappeared in a few steps, carrying out the duty given him.

Gragrafel turned back to the fields. His black eyes stared at the vast vacancy. Perhaps he'd wait there until she returned. If he kept vigil, if he kept his mind on her survival, then she was sure to conquer her obstinance and fears. He decided to do so, listening to the soft song of the birds and remembering when his children were just children and didn't require the rescuing of shadowy svarg.

*   *   *

Maiel lifted her head from her arm. Hours passed since she had hidden in the underground treasure room. The smell of sulfur grew fainter, but wasn't entirely gone. Biting her lip, she wondered if she could finally move. She needed distance between her and the danava. The bold atrin would exhaust himself hunting every inch of the church grounds if he believed she was still there. His capability was great, perhaps greater than her own even at full capacity. How else was he able to wall her up inside his labyrinth? The memory of it made her tremble. She had to escape without him knowing or she was done.

Coaxing herself onto her feet, Maiel went to reconnoiter the passageway. She couldn't very well sit there until she faded. Sooner or later, a vratin or shade would find her. Gritting her teeth, she used the fading light of her sword to find her way back to the door. Pushing the heavy timbers back just enough, she peered through the crack. The passage beyond was clear. The dim orange light of bare bulbs made the rock look like aged ivory. She opened the door a little more and took another look, repeating the process until she was able to exit the room with something resembling confidence.

A sudden scuffing sound behind her drew her attention. The end of the passage stood empty, but panic overtook reason. She forgot the rest of the passage extending behind the door. A rat pushed along the wall, dragging a snarled knot of grass. Feeling foolish, Maiel drew her sword and pulled her shield from her back. She turned toward the archway to the main passage. With a deep and wary breath, she steadied the quaver of fear winding through her limbs. The feeling slid down her spine, threatening to send her back to the room to hide a while longer. She swore unseen eyes watched each step. Pushing the fear down, she moved forward.

At the entrance of the passage, a shadowy figure darted past her. Maiel jumped back and fell into a defensive stance. The figure reappeared; a man retracing his steps. It was Orius. He looked as startled as she.

"Thank God I found you," Orius said quietly, folding her in his arms.

Maiel lowered her sword.

"I was right," Maiel said.

Orius stepped back to see no harm had come to her. He nodded regretfully.

"My pride wouldn't let me admit I lost all ability of discernment. I'd apologize as you deserve, but that would take time and staying here is too dangerous."

"Morgentus is here," Maiel said.

"He's seen you?"

Maiel nodded.

"We must get you away from here," Orius said, distracted by his thoughts.

Taking hold of her arm, Orius led her toward the door of the labyrinth through which she'd entered. She pulled back and shook her head. The danava were up there.

"You're trembling," Orius said, surprised.

"The demon was in the seminary. He's probably waiting for me to return that way," Maiel said to him.

"We have to try." Orius assured her with a smile. She allowed him to move her toward the stairs.

"There she is. Well done, Orius," a voice called down the passage.

The pair halted. Geitz stood in the distant unlit reaches of the main passage. He sauntered toward them, wearing a twisted grin. The archbishop's entire aspect had changed. An indescribable darkness muted his eyes. Deep angry lines troubled his mouth. He looked aged beyond his already numerous years: his white hair shocked into disarray and his skin marked like a battle-scarred jinn.

Maiel, feeling betrayed, looked to Orius. He apologized, explaining he was trying to lead her out. Maiel wasn't sure she could trust him.

"I'll deliver you to him, no matter the cost. Don't fight me, messenger. Things'll go much easier if you just come along," Geitz said to Maiel.

Orius pushed her behind him protectively.

"I can stand against him," Maiel insisted.

Orius picked up a discarded metal cross from the floor.

"Run to the basilica when I tell you, there are marditavya there, but not the demon—keep going, don't stop for anything. I will find you wherever you get to," Orius instructed her.

"Let me put him down," Maiel said, grabbing hold of his sleeve.

Orius looked through her and she knew his time had come. She felt the words frozen in her throat. Then Geitz chuckled, continuing toward them.

"How touching," Geitz prodded them.

"You've nearly returned to us. Come away with me. Don't do this now," Maiel said.

"Do let him try, my little bird. I'll enjoy bashing his head to dust with the very object he threatens me with. Where's your Christ now, sacerdos!" Geitz continued to taunt.

"Maiel, I must do this. I must save you from them," Orius said, prying her fingers from his arm.

Orius touched her face and smiled. Maiel shook her head, trying to keep the tears from falling.

"It's my time, captain. You'll see me again. I swear to it," Orius said.

"Touching." Geitz grinned.

Maiel reluctantly released him. She couldn't deny him his destiny. Stepping back, she watched him stalk toward the archbishop. A tear slipped from her eye.

Orius lifted the cross and ran at the archbishop. The men fell together, the fallen duta dwarfing the fallen human. Maiel picked along the wall, holding her sword defensively. The men wrestled, fighting for the cross. Though he looked old, the archbishop fought off Orius with inhuman strength. She hesitated. If she helped him, they could escape together.

"Run, Bethiah!" Orius growled.

Orius used all his strength to shove his adversary against the stone wall. Geitz's head bounced off the rock. The archbishop laughed, mocking his efforts to hurt him.

"We're the last of those you'll wrong in the name of your blasphemous master," Orius said, raising the cross above his head.

Geitz stared at the object with surprise. He fell to laughter.

"You think you can protect her from me—from Belial? You can't protect yourself, sacerdos," Geitz said, revealing a knife.

"Go!" Orius ordered Maiel. "I can—I will," Orius said to the archbishop.

Geitz laughed more. He moved suddenly, slicing at Orius with the blade. The fallen angel may have lost his wings, but he moved quickly and lightly, as if he still bore them. Maiel turned away, running into the shadows of the passage.

"That's right, my dove. Right into our hands." Geitz sneered.

"You've picked a fight you can't win, marditavya," Orius growled.

"I suppose you would know, fallen—miserable pretender," Geitz said, lunging at him with his last words.

Orius deflected the blade with the heavy cross. Geitz lost his hold on the weapon, reeling along the floor to snatch it back up. Orius took advantage of the man's prone position. Hoisting the iron cross above his head, he swung it toward his adversary. Geitz rolled over, brandishing the knife, and ducked to avoid the cross. He then leapt to his feet with the nimbleness of a man half his age. Grasping Orius about the neck, he pushed the man's arms down and sunk the blade into his chest. Orius dropped the heavy cross, instantly weakened by the surprise blow.

"She's not fallen. Her friends will come and you'll burn in hell for laying a hand on her," Orius growled.

"We shall see about that, eh," Geitz said, picking up the cross.

Orius froze, limbs unable to move. His eyes stared into the distance of the passage. Collapsing to his knees, he tried to pull the knife from his chest. The pain made him wince. The weapon was dug in quite deeply. Yanking hard, he freed himself of the barb and fell forward. The knife clattered on the dusty ground. Geitz stood over him, and with a wide swing, hammered his skull with the iron cross.

"No!" Maiel cried, watching him fall.

"Half's done, and so my task shall be complete in moments. Come back here, you impudent slattern," Geitz hollered.

Geitz stepped over Orius's corpse. He found Maiel in the dark of the passage. He cast the bloodied cross aside. She turned and finally ran.

"Where were we?" Geitz called out to her, his haunting voice carrying through the passage.

In the dark, it was impossible to find the exit. Every door looked like the next. At the end of the passage, she turned and faced her pursuer. He stalked toward her, half mad with the success of taking down her guardian. She looked past him to Orius laid out on the ground. This was no time to mourn his passing. He'd finally sacrificed himself and regained his passage home. He knew bringing Geitz there would result in this, but he did it with the intention of setting her free.

"I won't give in to this," Maiel whispered to herself.

"What's that, chicken? Stay right there. I'll soon end your torment, just like I did your friend," Geitz said, laughing.

Maiel spied the door they'd come through upon their arrival. Looking back at Geitz, she saw him notice the shift in her mien. She scowled hard at him, the light in her eyes pulsing brightly. The hilt of her sword even glowed stronger. Geitz bared his teeth in a slow, devious grin. The rumble of his evil laughter echoed off the walls. Drawing a deep breath, Maiel centered herself. Dashing as fast as she was able, she reached the door. Geitz screamed, displeased he had lost her. He jumped forward, running along the passage like an animal on all fours. He ran over the wall and along the ceiling, moving faster with each wheel of his arms and legs. Maiel pulled the door open and hurried into the stairwell beyond.

"You have no choice! It already owns you!" she heard Geitz call after her in an eerie voice.

Flipping the bolt, she wedged the device with the head of an arrow. The door jolted against its stone mountings. Maiel crept up the steps, holding her eyes on the lock. He'd work his way through the old bolt in short order. She didn't need to stick around to find out exactly how long that would take.

CHAPTER 26

DOMINIC CLIMBED OUT OF THE CAR, where he'd parked on a quiet street in the middle of the quaint old city of Esztergom. The day was ending, filled with long shadows between buildings and under trees. Despite the late hour and a clear understanding of what he faced, arriving in Esztergom gave him a strange sense of relief. By then, Maiel would be surrounded by all kinds of shades and mudeaters. He would be lucky to get within a mile of wherever she hid. The challenge was welcome. He looked around, half expecting a dark mob and half wondering where to begin. The city was much larger than he expected for old Europe. He sighed with despair.

"Where to now?" Dominic asked his guide.

Lena looked to the wolves. Her small mouth twisted.

"He can't tell," Lena said.

"What do you mean, he can't tell?" Dominic responded.

Looking to be certain they were still alone, Dominic stepped closer to where the girl stood on the sidewalk with her four-legged friends. Lena shook her head. Dominic set his fists on his hips and leaned over her as if he could intimidate an answer out of her.

"He can't find her anymore. He said there's too much darkness," Lena told him.

Argus growled low. Shee went to her mate's side, her head low and her eyes on Dominic. Neither animal appeared intimidated. Rather, they looked ready to pounce on him.

"Argus—"

"Akha," a voice called from behind.

Dominic spun around. A red and black apparition stood there.

"Damn it," Dominic cursed at being startled.

The foggy image belonged to only one being.

"Damn what?" Zach asked as his form cleared and Dominic's heart slowed.

"Why are you here?" Dominic demanded.

"I thought you'd be glad to see me. Instead you demand I send some unknown thing into the chasm of Jahannam?" Zach answered.

Zach assessed him, but his face didn't reveal what he saw. Dominic narrowed his eyes, holding his ground. The expression was odd, considering it was a little late for him to try and act authoritatively, after failing to do so when needed centuries ago. Dominic drew a deep breath through his nose and his temper cooled some. Zach wasn't there to poke fun.

"Our janya sent me. He wanted me to let you know that you've run out of time. King Adonai has sent his legions to the gates. They wait to engage Belial should he make his move."

"I need more time. This is the city. I can't just conjure her from the stones, but I'm getting closer," Dominic replied.

Zach pursed his lips, doubtful. Dominic looked to Lena, gesturing toward the alder for her to confirm their progress. She stared back at him stonily. Of course she took Zach's side. Their weird little connection guaranteed it.

"Obviously not enough," Dominic said.

"Obviously," Lena muttered.

Stepping toward him, Zach gave a slight curl of his lip. He straightened Dominic's collar and dusted his shoulders roughly. His eyes looked him over again, displeased with his state of disarray.

"My sister's wellbeing hangs in the balance. I need you to stop fighting us and listen," Zach advised.

The fire in Dominic's throat flared at Zach's touch and flared even higher at his words. A desire to pummel his brother-in-law's face, to watch him bleed, overtook his senses. Gripping his fists at his sides, he imagined the pleasure it would give him to tear the flesh straight from the alder's hide. He nearly felt the wings in his hands as he bent and broke them. Zach grasped his shoulders, jarring him out of his musings. Dominic stared back at him, almost confused by the touch, almost confused as to who he was.

"Speed and stealth are your only allies. Leave your pursuers to us. We'll do our best to keep the dark at bay. Don't doubt our ability to make their hunt a painful one. Trust in your guides. They know the way. Argus hasn't lost her. She's in the dark and that spreads her signal to all shadows."

Dominic scowled at him. He must have overheard Lena say Argus had lost all sense of her. He doubted Zach knew any more than the rest of them. After all, if they knew so much, why did they let him struggle to reach her? Instead, he stood there offering him riddles.

"There," Zach said, pointing his finger behind him. "You'll find her there."

Dominic turned to where he pointed. A green dome poked above the trees in the distance. Argus trotted forward, his ears pricked and his nose working. Behind him, Shee howled.

"How do I—" Dominic said, stopping when he saw Zach had gone. "Get her back across..." Dominic mumbled his thought anyway.

Dominic faced his guide. Lena propped herself against a building with one foot on the wall. She crossed her arms and smiled at him, delighted with what had transpired. Of course she was. Dominic sneered, shaking his head.

"C'mon. We can get there on foot easier. It's not that far," Dominic said.

"It may be farther than you think and we don't have much time," Lena said.

"Yes, well, we don't know the roads around here and frankly I don't want to be pulled over with that car. I have no idea what we've been hauling all over, if anything."

"You have a point," Lena said, pushing off the wall.

"Glad you can agree with me," Dominic said.

"I haven't argued with you yet," Lena said frankly.

Dominic retrieved his pack from the car. Slinging the bag on his shoulder, he crossed the street and then headed in the direction of the dome. Lena fell into step beside him, taking his hand. She hadn't done that since they began the journey, and it was strange she did so after how he had spoken to her. He swallowed, regretting his misjudgment of the small guardian.

Several times, the dome disappeared behind buildings and trees. Dominic held the direction in his mind, hoping that eventually he would see his way clear to a road that led up to it. Being this close to their destination, he didn't dare hail a cab or ask for assistance. There was no telling who stood in the crowd waiting to delay them. Then, as Argus trotted ahead of him, he realized that he had the best guide for the task. With the building pointed out to them, Argus could surely figure out a way to get to it. By his stride, he was eager to be moving and the limitations of Dominic's human legs were the only thing holding him back.

"Lead the way, boy," Dominic said.

Argus trotted faster. Dominic ran to keep up. The effort soon rewarded them. The dome was the centerpiece of a vast gothic structure overlooking the Danube. Set between two bell towers, it boasted a tall crucifix, marking it as a very specific kind of building. They stood far below the grand church with no evident way to climb the hill and reach it. Argus barked and Dominic realized he had stopped to ogle. The wolf was pointed toward another street that bent in an opposing direction. Dominic bit his lip, deciding that he should not argue with a guide that had proven his ability to lead. Dominic loped after him. The wolf continued, leading at a fast pace.

Amid stares and curious gazes, Dominic jogged through the city, always moving in sight of the basilica but never seeming closer. Dodging pedestrians and traffic, his stamina ran low, but his need to get to her pushed him near his limit. On a dark empty street, that push gave way and he came to a hard stop, fighting for each breath. Argus barked, encouraging him to continue, while Shee nudged him with her nose. Lena took to his side.

"Just let me catch my breath," Dominic said, between gasps.

"We're almost there." Lena patted his back.

Dominic breathed hard. He nodded, crouched over his knees and unable to respond. Argus trotted back to him. Staring Dominic in the eyes, the wolf made the most compelling argument for continuing. This was only the beginning, the wolf told him through his thoughts. He had a much larger battle once Maiel was safe at home. Trying to smile, Dominic again nodded. The first thing on his list was to whip back into shape. There was no way he could rejoin the legions in such condition. He only had his lack of vision, perhaps what he should call selfishness, to blame for every minute of suffering he now experienced. Straightening, he drew a very deep breath.

"Let's go," Dominic said in a raspy voice.

The fire burned through every limb. On the hill in the distance, the great dome stood against the blue sky, an apparition in the waning light. They needed to run a lot farther to reach it. Argus started again first, darting along the street with ease. Lena kept to his side as they hurried on. Shee protected the rear, knowing how imps and shades crawled out of every crevice for the opportunity of stopping them. Glory would be high in Abaddon for the one who ruined duta plans now.

Closing the distance, they were overtaken by men and guardians retreating in the opposite direction. Only the guardians took notice of the wolves or child. The men tried to stop him, demanding he turn back with them. By their priestly raiment, he knew they belonged to the church on the hill. Their fearful warnings and countenances affirmed Zach's announcement. Morgentus had found her. In that same thought, Dominic knew the baron brought reinforcements. Belial had also crossed the foul gates.

Despite the danger and the beseeching caution of the exiled priests, Dominic pushed through the mob. The entrance of the great dome stood open to him. The inspiring sight filled him with dread. The sun set the rim of sky surrounding the storm on fire. Raising their muzzles, the wolves called. They must have regained a sense of her presence.

"We have to hurry," Lena said, her features strained with apprehension.

"We're here. Now we just have to pull her from that stone prison and be done," Dominic said, stalking up the road.

At the top of the hill, Dominic stood in awe of the enormous structure. The façade of pillars, the twin bell towers, and the statuary all spoke of a place the soul remembered in fragments. Such grandeur was a relic of the past, when men more clearly recalled their roots. Now they built a reflection of the loss they harbored inside. The clean lines, smooth surfaces, and empty spaces they called brilliant and modern were simply the manifestation of a vapid blankness of mind. Even Abaddon and the other lands of Jahannam built more inspiring structures than present humans. Yet there was hope that such starkness of detail would result in their concentrating on what truly mattered, given no distraction in vaulting, pane or carving. The plainness would give them room where they could then think only of themselves or the brittle and fleeting things they treasured, one miniscule bit at a time.

Dominic walked to the steps, baring his teeth in a sneer for his kind, the ones who squandered their abilities in self-abusive languor. While his thoughts filled with hatred for his race, a figure came around the base of a broad pillar before the door of the church. Dominic looked into the face of his nemesis. Morgentus smiled down at him.

"How have you been, Dominic? Have my soldiers treated you well?" Morgentus smiled.

"Morgentus," Dominic hissed.

Dominic pulled the sack from his shoulder and drew the sword from inside before dropping the bag on the stones. Morgentus waved his hand. Segrius and his soldier emerged from the shadows. Dominic hesitated, then recalled Zach's words. He was accompanied by guardians that could defend him and still more who waited to run to his defense should the enemy overwhelm him still.

"Maiel will soon be mine and I'll revel in your fall, as you watch me enjoy your place at her side," Morgentus needled him.

"You couldn't keep her the first time. What makes you think she'll follow you now?" Dominic countered.

"Well, you've helped with that," Morgentus said, stepping down the stairs.

The shadowalker grinned at him, touching the end of the sword and pushing the blade aside as if it were no more than a low branch in his path. The serpent slithered closer. Dominic wasn't sure he could wait for the others to back him up, as his desire to bury the baron once and for all became stronger than his desire to rescue his wife. Gritting his teeth, Dominic embraced the fire, letting it burn through him. With this new power, he'd hold his own until they came.

Low growls drew near. The mudeaters halted, quite familiar with the dogs of Zion.

"Is that all you have?" Morgentus mocked him.

"Find out," Dominic replied.

The human and the shade circled each other. Morgentus backed away, spreading his leathery wings. He lifted his chin and defiantly stared at Dominic and his sword. The baron's sattva grew taller and broader; short horns emerged from the skull in a backward curl. His black eyes returned and his claws grew into thick talons.

"When the sun is set, what will you do then against all the shades that linger just beneath the surface of this accursed hill?" Morgentus laughed in a rough chorus of evil.

"The question is, how will you defend your prince when the armies of Zion are loosed to claim his head? You hardly amount to the force required to meet us in battle—no matter how ugly you get," Dominic replied.

Dominic's counter had the desired effect. Morgentus's eyes grew blacker and his features more severe. Dominic smiled. Strength surged through him, a white hot flame. Verdant light flashed in his eyes. Blood ran over the orbs and seeped from his skin.

"You won't keep her either. The fire claims you. Jahannam is where you belong, marditavya. Not with her," Morgentus growled.

Dominic lunged after him, striking with the sword. The mudeaters jumped at his back, but the wolves moved faster. Grabbing hold of the serpents, they pushed and pulled them back. Morgentus drew a long sword from his hip to meet Dominic in battle. Tracking across the stairs and onto the portico, dodging swipes and stabs, Dominic saw Lena dash toward the doors to get inside, away from the fray. She struggled to open the heavy barriers. Distracted by the girl, Dominic found himself spun around and pushed into one of the pillars. Morgentus darted after him, moving like a ragged black sheet of cloth in a whipping wind. Dominic threw himself across the portico stones to avoid the advance, and Morgentus fell hard against the pillar. The baron growled, quite displeased he had missed. Dominic struggled to his feet, ready for the next attack.

"Get that door open," Dominic called to Lena.

They must get inside. He needed to reach Maiel. Morgentus fell on him, striking with the flat of his blade. Dominic deflected more strikes, but his stamina was at its end. The sweat dripped down his temples and his limbs struggled to raise the weapon. Determination wavered as he waited for those who'd promised help. From the corner of his eye, he saw Lena push open the heavy panels. Her small frame disappeared inside. Dominic called out to her, as he pushed Morgentus back.

* * *

Maiel shoved her weight against the door at the top of the spiral stairs leading out of the old crypt. She stumbled into the dark, odd-smelling meeting room with the long table. Given more time, she would have propped the heavy table against the niche and put a stop to Geitz's pursuit. The piece of furniture was heavy and would take some effort to move. The sounds below forced her to abandon the idea. Instead, she piled all the chairs before it. With the door barricaded, Maiel passed into the hall beyond and shut the door, flipping the lock to slow him further. She looked in both directions, unsure of which way led to an exit. Low chanting suggested a possibility, though it held the timbre of malevolence. Likely the voices were Geitz's followers and likely they stood at the altar staining the church with their poisoned desires.

Hurrying down the hall, Maiel entered the candlelit nave. The dark vratin who prayed at the altar ceased his chants and the others trailed off with him. They regained their feet, faces shaded by their hoods. Their shadowy guards—daeva—lounged about the wide space, spoiling the meaning of all they touched. One clung to a winged statue, stroking it suggestively. Another lay on the altar, drinking from a bottle of wine and eating wafers from a gold box. Eyes peered from the dark pews and the high balcony of the organ. Her eyes turned up, where she saw a broad-winged succubus clinging to the scales of the dome. All eyes watched her approach. Then, she spotted a misshapen jiangshi lift its face from the torn abdomen of its dark vratin. The vampire's lips dripped with blood as it chewed a piece of intestine. The candles flickered and hissed; that was the only sound.

Spreading her wings, Maiel raised her sword. Her features hardened. The stink of their betrayal nauseated. They muttered, backing away from the altar.

"Traitors!" Maiel hoarsely declared.

The vratin muttered back at her. Their curses were impotent, but they were too stupid to realize it. Maiel stalked toward them. They scattered, taking their shadows with them. The foul guardians didn't dare abandon their assigns and have them stolen by a duta. They preferred the shame of retreat to the pain of a shameful rout. Maiel moved quickly and grasped the wing of the succubus when she made the mistake of wheeling too close. Pulling it back, she threw the danava across the star-marked floor. The asuri slid, striking her head against the stairs. The alabaster devil rose onto her backward legs and screamed, cradling her damaged head. Maiel smirked, walking back to where he crouched.

"Blasted duta. Always sticking their noses where they don't belong," the succubus hissed.

"Perhaps the slime of Jahannam should stay where they belonged, then we would as well."

"One day, Zion will be ours again and the souls will serve us, as it should be," the shade told her, backing away.

Maiel strode toward the former ikyls. She skulked around the marble floor, keeping a cautious eye on the captain. Catching the asuri's forgotten tail beneath her sandal, she anchored the beast, causing the succubus great anguish. The monster jumped, both sets of claws brandished as knives. With a strike of her gauntlet, she set the shadow back.

"Not so rough, kesarini. I'm beginning to think you like me," the succubus said suggestively.

"Tell me why you're here," Maiel demanded.

The shade rubbed her sore jaw, rolling onto her knobby haunches. Before the devil could respond, Maiel heard the chairs in the other room crashing to the floor. Geitz had made his way through. The groan of metal hinges echoed through the nave, tearing her attention in the other direction. The outdoor lights glimmered beyond. A raven-haired child ran between the arches, halting part way.

"Lena," Maiel gasped, forgetting the asuri at her feet.

Lena's eyes sparkled like ebony. Her small black wings flapped with the joy of seeing her guardian again. Maiel was surprised to see the girl, even more shocked that she boasted the full wings of a duta, a youngling barely old enough to be out of the Ordo Priori.

The succubus pulled her tail back, setting Maiel and her thoughts off balance. Running along the walls, she retreated, escaping into the open air. Lena's cheery features became alarmed. Maiel peered over her shoulder. Geitz joined them. His reddened face resembled a madman's mask. The tips of his fingers bled from the effort of digging his way through the mess to get to her.

"What's this? You've already brought us a pigeon for the supper table," Geitz said, gleeful at the prospect of Maiel surrendering Lena to him.

Geitz laughed. The sound was deep and rich, echoing through the basilica. His eyes stared hard, as though they would roll out of their sockets. Then the orbs turned up and rolled to whiteness. The white cleared to show an iris of pale yellow. The laughter continued, but the sound shifted. Something in the maddening chortle turned her cold. The vratin's mouth became a bloody gash. Maiel stepped back, sensing that a far greater menace had descended on the dome.

A shadow passed through the open door of the basilica and then the heavy panel slammed shut. Lena jumped. The dark figure crouched before the door; there was the sound of metal dragging as it moved. Whoever it was had just barred their exit. Gold eyes flashed in the dark arches. The maniacal laughter of the archbishop stopped. A low rumble echoed around the floor. From the dark arches, a pair of wolves emerged. Between them strode a man, his shape and golden head unmistakable. The doors of the basilica jolted, pounded on the outside by a formidable force. The building trembled as the man sought another entry.

"You'll have to do without. I've come to take her home and no priest, not even one possessed by Belial, will stop me," Dominic said.

"Dominic," Maiel breathed.

"Try it," Geitz challenged him.

"You haven't been able to stop me yet and I just left your backup outside. You tell me who's going to win this." Dominic pointed behind with his sword.

Dominic stepped to the priest with a confident stride. His green eyes flashed with an emerald glow, each orb wrapped in blood. Maiel's legs disappeared beneath her. Tears filled her eyes. He smelled of sulfur. She trembled as he placed himself between her and the archbishop. His gaze went through her, despite the slanted grin she came to love as a sign of his good nature. He faced the archbishop, drawing a gun from his pocket.

"What have I done to you?" Maiel asked, barely able to speak.

"Without a bio-vessel—what can you do?" Dominic mocked his adversary.

"Why don't we find out?" the archbishop grinned.

"Why don't we?" Dominic smiled.

A gunshot echoed through the building like a thunder clap. Lena clapped her hands over her ears, squeezing her eyes tightly shut. Unable to watch, Maiel ran from her husband through the doors on the opposite side of the altar. Dominic's burning eyes were sealed to her memory. There was no path home now. She must remain in Samsara, forever running from the shadowwalkers who hunted her. Her failure in the face of centuries of effort was beyond excuse.

CHAPTER 27

DOMINIC STARED AT THE CORPSE lying on the marble floor. His arm slowly lowered back to his side. After a couple twitches the priest went still. Blood pooled beneath the dead man's arm, leaking from the hole in his chest and back. Dominic stepped across the room to stand over him and make sure he was dead. He didn't recall putting the gun in his trench pocket. The idea popped into his head suddenly, like a random memory triggered by a smell or color. When he reached for it, it was there. Staring at the shocked expression frozen on the dead face, he retraced his steps. Unless Lena put it there, it should have been in the bag he'd left outside on the portico. He looked at the gun. Then he looked at the sword clutched in his other hand.

A shuffling sound roused Dominic's attention to the pews behind him. He looked, hoisting the gun in the direction of the noise. His eyes settled on Lena. She approached, wearing her oddly mature expression. He settled the gun in the trench coat pocket.

"Gediel," Lena said.

"But I had one in the bag," Dominic replied.

"He's a clever spy—thinks things through. That's why he gave you the coat. He knew you'd keep it on to save yourself, but the bag could be lost or dropped," Lena said, coming to the last pew.

The girl's eyes watched him closely. He nodded. She made sense.

Dominic turned. He'd nearly forgot about his wife, so immersed in the pleasure of shooting the priest. She was no longer there. He looked over the altar, pews, and balcony. She wasn't in any of those places. Panic seized him as he came full circle. Maiel had run from them again. Lena pointed toward a set of doors on the left. Dominic took a step toward them.

"Where are you going?" a gnashing voice spoke from the other direction.

Dominic faced the utterance. A disturbing sight stood there. Long gold hair framed a face of gray marble in which rested two gold eyes. He wore a crown of gold and robes of silver tied with a crimson sash. A blood red mouth curled into a scornful grin. Dominic opened his mouth to utter a curse, but found himself silenced. The figure was no man, but a danava and one of the mightiest he had ever crossed paths with in all his centuries. The Prince of Acheron, he whom they feared, set his sights on Maiel in a tired effort to bait Mikhael into war. The gun would be of no use against Belial, and the sword would only prolong a painful death at the ends of the danava's claws.

Belial disappeared in a roiling cloud of smoke. Lena gasped and retreated to the arches near the entrance. The demon reappeared, perching on the wall. He speedily jumped to the altar and then climbed the hanging pentacle. He looked like a giant horned bat, except for his pale marbled skin. Dominic watched him closely, feeling his senses heightened. His eyes saw faster, his nose smelled finer, and his ears heard louder. The energy pulsing through him, the fire that began in his throat, was an inferno of ecstasy. His heart ached to lay claim to Belial's destruction, but his gut hungered for the power the flame gave him.

"You belong to me, marditavya. You'll do as I command," Belial hissed, backing up the chains that held the pentagram in place.

Belial grinned down at him, working his way slowly up the chains.

"I belong to myself," Dominic replied.

"Adonai will be most displeased with that answer," Belial called down from the ceiling. The prince laughed at his own jest.

The prince's claws chipped the frescos, sending a shower of plaster onto Dominic's head. He squinted, raising his arms protectively. His heart pumped harder at the declaration. Under the high roof of the portico, he became a lost soul. The fire took him, burning furiously. No longer was clay being fired into a diamond. The clay was just burning down.

"Always moving backward—too foolish to know what's light and what's dark," Belial said, watching him from the dome.

"You can't have her. No matter what happens to me, she doesn't belong with you," Dominic replied.

"Nor does she belong to you, thief—liar—defiler," Belial accused.

Dominic bared his teeth. Drawing the gun, he fired three shots at the demon's chest. The weapon was useless. The bullets struck him, and blood dripped from the wounds, which sealed up in the next moment. With enough shots, he could cause him to fall from his perch, but no more.

Belial screeched with displeasure, pitching himself from the dome. His wings were incapable of sustaining flight. Instead, he threw himself from place to place, a smoking cloud of anguish. Finally landing before Dominic, he let out a yell that shook the foundations of the basilica. The joints groaned and a fine dust fell from above. Statues rattled on their pedestals and the glass reliquaries shattered.

"Embrace the gift I give you or there'll be no place to call home!" Belial demanded, growing larger and darker.

Dominic replied with a derisive huff. The display was pathetic, compared with all the stories he had been told. Dominic threw the gun across the floor.

"Your begging is weak, but I'm flattered by your attention," Dominic mocked.

"I'll gnaw your soul in Acheron while my minions fuck your wife," Belial declared.

"You'll have to catch her first, and so far, you're not doing a very good job." Dominic shrugged.

Perhaps the prince's taunt was meant to have more of an effect than it did, but Dominic knew danava would say these things. He also knew that in order to carry out their desires, he'd have to abandon her, and that was the one thing he wouldn't do. His mere presence made Belial a fool. If he burned as they wanted, he would have fallen. Once there, he'd have taken Acheron's pit and kept his wife there. Then he'd spend all eternity slicing their throats for condemning them.

Belial threw his head back and roared with anger. The building shook from rafter to footing with the prince's rage. A statue of a saint fell from its niche, breaking to bits on the hard floor. Dominic raised his sword and ran toward the horned beast. Drawing the blade back, he thrust it at Belial's chest. The blow was halted by a thick fist larger than his head. Belial crumpled the sword like tinfoil. His hand dripped black blood as he tossed it aside like a useless trinket, causing Dominic to fall on his back. Dominic stared at the beast, awaiting his next strike, from which he was defenseless. The danava's blood hissed as it boiled off the marble floor. The prince licked his hand clean, savoring the moment, eyes burning with the promise of pain. A sick grin twisted up the gnarled face. With his good hand, he reached toward Dominic, who closed his eyes, accepting the trust left in his heart.

Lightning flashed. The stones of the basilica vibrated with a clap of thunder. Belial howled, crossing his arms before his face. Dominic scrambled back, avoiding the claws. Struggling to right himself, Dominic saw Joel free his sword from the demon's tail. The appendage whipped, spraying the walls and surroundings with blood. The sudden appearance of the golden duta surprised him, leaving him to stand frozen as Joel stepped wide, but confidently, to avoid the enemy. From the shadows of the prince's other side, a black-robed engel joined them. Zach moved to Dominic's defense, placing himself between man and beast.

"You thought no one had his back?" Joel asked.

"The marditavya is mine to deal with!" Belial growled.

Zach helped Dominic to his feet. The red-haired brother offered his best consoling expression, one that wasn't much different than his usual dour mien. It was quite welcome.

"Some rules are made to be broken. Go get our erela. We'll handle this one," Zach said.

Lena rushed to his side, briefly hugging the alder, before leading Dominic in the direction of Maiel's retreat.

"Thank you," she whispered against Zach's robes.

The embrace ended and Dominic dashed through the doors, followed by his small guardian. Belial was little pleased. He straightened his back, towering above them. The beast's glittering eyes pursued them until they departed. The panels slammed shut, barring the way back. Dominic paused, looking over his shoulder to be sure the prince didn't follow. The doors rattled, then stopped. On the other side, the prince's hooves drummed the marble floor. Then came another roar.

"Dominic, hurry!" Lena called to him.

Turning back, the hall was pitch black, but for a fiery glow at the end of the long corridor. Setting his jaw, Dominic stepped forward. A whispered voice carried through the air. It distracted his thoughts like a nattering fly, calling him to stand down. Finding an unlit candelabra, Dominic grabbed hold of the piece and unscrewed the footing. Popping the candles from the top, he eyed the new, trident-like weapon.

"Hurry," Lena hissed, waving him forward.

Dominic swung the pointy staff a couple times, then grinned. They might have destroyed his sword, but he was resourceful enough to find other means to cause pain. By his guardian's expression, his mien became increasingly alarming. She said nothing, waving him toward her again. Her eyes betrayed her worry. He followed after her, holding onto the staff tightly. The point of being there slipped from his mind. Now his thoughts filled with flashes of bashing Lena's skull in with the wrought iron, feasting on her flesh and blood as she slowly died. His stomach clenched with pain, hollow and in desperate need of sustenance. She moved ahead of him, not taking her eyes away. She came up against the distant door at the back of the church. Trapped. Wide-eyed, she watched him near. Then doors slammed closed. Dominic stood in the dark, alone and surprised. Lena's muffled calls were a distant, eerie cadence. A smell, like honeysuckle on a late spring breeze, floated around him. Grasping the candelabra with both hands, he set his feet wide, expecting an imp to attack any moment. The fire in his throat eased. His sore eyes closed, finding momentary solace behind the moist lids. For a moment, peace eased his hunger, as if he drifted into sleep. Snapping his eyes open again, he rejected the urge to give up. Maiel. He remembered. They were there to save his wife.

Lena was silent, but Dominic sensed her presence just out of reach in the next section of the passage. Slowly, he worked his way forward until he found the doors that blocked his path. Pressing on them, they felt like rock, neither budging nor bending. They were both trapped.

Dominic growled, thrusting the iron bar at the door to break the barrier down.

"Lena! Back away, as far as you can get," Dominic said.

There was no reply. He struck again. The doors thrummed with the blows, unyielding and wrapped in an impassible ward. Dominic's hands ached. He dropped the weapon and instead threw his shoulder at the door. The hinges creaked. The wood splintered, but they wouldn't open. Exhausted, he slid to the cold stone floor. His eyes wandered the dark, barely able to make out details. This was how it ended, alone, trapped between light and dark. The honeysuckle surrounded him again and peace washed away the fire and consciousness.

* * *

Joel circled the hulking beast to which the once great Seraphim Belial had declined into. Tales of Belial's glory before the Conflict of Hosts had been taught to all the younglings at school. The stinking monster before them hardly resembled the former leader. His sattva was so bent and twisted by betrayal that all his beauty had vanished. His eyes, though they sparkled with the light of gold, cast only a reflection. The light had entirely left him ages ago. It was folly to believe that one day he would return to their ranks as a tempered and wise being. Belial despised Zion for holding him responsible for his choices, for punishing the children he created, for blaming them for their own violence. The children of Jahannam were inmates of a madhouse, too blind to see their faults and regression, or the consequences that must come of failing one's dharma. Consequences came of all decisions. Their perception prevented them from seeing truth.

"Where were we?" Joel said, not particularly caring.

Zach carefully circled the prince several paces behind. Belial's eyes watched them closely. Now that he had lost the prizes he'd bothered to cross the gates for, the prince thought better of risking his atman. It took great energy to remain in Samsara, and the wounds Joel planned for him would make the trip back quick and lasting. Belial would skulk inside his broken-down prison. There, he'd hide from the usurpers who waited for his weakness by which to unseat him, hoping for pity or passing shade that could provide energy on which to re-form. Abaddon would be cast into its own war. The danava would devour one another to gain his crown.

The giant drew a blade strapped on his back, a cruel crescent of steel he gripped with both hands. It took a skilled soldier to wield such a weapon. The Order of Horus was the most skilled in Zion, able to remove a head without the enemy realizing it until the victim stared up at their own trunk. Belial had been one of those warriors.

Preparing his gladius, Joel smiled at the forsaken beast.

"You've arrived too late, again. The war has already begun." Belial spun his web.

"Too late, Belial? Perhaps for you. I doubt any ointment could mend that skin," Joel replied.

"The only war is the one that will be fought in Jahannam for your crown, when we send you back without a head," Zach added.

Belial frowned at this jest and snorted. He swung the crescent blade, baring his teeth. Joel leaned back, as the weapon swung at his throat. The danava was too slow. His akha stuck the prince in the back with his narrow blade. Zach darted out of the way as Belial swung toward him. The prince roared as the blade once again missed its mark.

"Fools! Fools—Adonai will abandon you. As he does with all who realize they know better than he," Belial growled, stalking toward Joel.

Joel darted from his reach. Spreading his wings wide, he leapt into the air and came down on the hairy head of their foe, planting his foot between the horns. With a twisting vault, he landed at his akha's side. A grin brightened his already sunny features. The horned demon had enormous strength, but was a ponderous fighter, for his massive form stole the atrin's energy. In other words, he was a slothful heap.

Belial turned around. The beast shrank, regaining the mangled remnant of his former glory. He wavered, off-balance, but quickly regained his bearings. This change made things more interesting. The smile on his face faded, leaving a stony expression similar to Zach's. Now the prince would move like a mad crow, only leaving them time to merely react.

"Gloating doves—I'll pluck your feathers and roast your limbs on my fire," Belial hissed.

Belial stared through them. The akha readied their weapons, knowing what would come next. Belial became a flurry of smoke, flying around the enormous chapel, peeling plaster, pushing over sconces, and toppling statues. Joel and Zach stood with their backs to one another, waiting for the moment to make their strike. They listened and sensed his place. When the cloud descended above them, screaming so loud that the glass in the panes of the dome shattered into a sparking cascade, the akha grasped each other's shield arm. Joel nodded, receiving a nod in return from Zach. Their expressions and bodies revealed the poise of their training. In a whirl of wings and white flame, they gave Belial the fight he begged for.

How much time passed before the battle ended was unknowable. Joel knelt on the floor, resting his sore limbs. Lifting his chin, he looked to his akha, leaning on the skinny alder blade he loved. Joel got to his feet with some difficulty. His limbs felt heavy, as though he carried the weight of another. A cut was sore and red across his bicep, and bled to his elbow. His knuckles stung, scraped of their skin. Bruises marked his bronze skin. He winced at a sting above his eye. He wiped his brow and found another cut. Limping toward the alder, he spotted a trickle of blood on Zach's lip. The engel didn't speak. He just met Joel with a slight curl of the corners of his bloodied mouth.

Looking toward the altar of the basilica, the akha viewed their work. Belial's head sat on the shrouded marble table, the yellow eyes closed. The bloody mouth was partway open, baring sharp teeth. Above that, wound in the chains and pentagram of the dark vratin, hung the rest of his broken sattva. The featherless wings were broken and torn.

They'd spent so much of the dark prince's energy that the danava was unable to repair himself or fade to his cursed home. They were exhausted themselves, hoping this was the last time they would strike him down that night. The sattva twitched, causing the chains to clink and jingle. Joel stepped toward the head. Grasping a knife from his belt, he drove that blade deep into the skull and moved it around to be sure the deed was done. The head crumbled like ash. Raising his eyes, he watched the sattva deteriorate in the same manner. Sighing in relief, he retrieved his blade from the altar, where a cloud of smoke hovered. The fog gathered and left through the broken dome. It was exasperating to be denied the honor of ending the prince's reign, but for now he was no longer a concern. Joel descended the steps and looked around the damaged building.

"Zaajah said Oriael would be in the tunnels below," Joel said.

Zach opened his mouth to speak, but turned his face toward the door through which Dominic had escaped the prince. He scowled deeply.

"What is it?"

"Amba—matula—they've trapped Dominic in the hall," Zach said, walking toward the door.

"He's grown dangerous then," Joel replied.

"The flame is weak, but the stink of jiangshi hovers," Zach turned back to say.

"Perhaps they wait for us," Joel said, going to the doors.

Joel pushed open one of the panels and stepped inside. Before him stretched a tall but narrow passage. Another set of doors, closed at the other end, created a cell. Before the second panels, two tall and thin black-robed figures guarded the way. They turned their faces toward him, one after the other. His amba's eyes glistened with unshed tears. Matula Magiel's features were hard as an anvil. He didn't ask why they barricaded Dominic; Zach's warning stunk through the halls. The failure was just as stinging and flagrant.

"He must die to shed this. He must make a sacrifice of himself to reset a balance," his amba said.

Joel approached the elder erela, wanting to counter her, but he knew she was right.

"You're hurt," she noticed, touching his jaw and elbow.

"What of the child?" Zach asked, referring to the small guardian they'd sent with him.

Joel scowled at her. She stammered, trying to find the right words to speak.

"Lena keeps watch of your sister," Alex finally managed.

Alex winced at such a ridiculous thing to say. She shook her head and looked back to the doors. Placing her hand on the panel, she looked regretful, if not apologetic.

"Let him out. Let him finish this," Joel said.

"You don't understand," Alex said.

The weight of each eye saw through his speech to whatever madness gave birth to such ideas. Joel didn't waver. The matter was clear, but he wasn't about to let them do this. He set his jaw harder and made his stance broader. The request may have been madness, but it was the only way to end this as they planned, giving Dominic a chance. The silence continued. Then Zach stepped closer, adding his weight to the argument. Surprisingly, their matula backed down first. Alex stammered again, unable to find a thing to say in defense of the orders she carried out. She nodded.

"Very well, then," Alex said.

Alex faced the doors, her head hung low. The groan of hinges echoed far from where they stood. They eyed one another, waiting to see if Alex would in fact free him. Doors closed and then the sound came again, but closer. Shuffling feet and the scrape of something heavy as it dragged across the marble followed. Joel was satisfied, but he wished he could go with him. He wanted to see how far Dominic had fallen, to measure the moment he defied his destiny. In their rush to defend him against Belial, they'd failed to take account of his status. If he overcame, then Dominic's triumph would be great.

CHAPTER 28

CROUCHING IN THE SHADOW of an old stone table, Lena watched Morgentus arrogantly strut before Maiel's readied sword. In full form, he broke his way into the church through the unused back door. One of the green panels swung open and closed in a violent breeze. The captain who'd watched over her during her illness, without a glimmer of weakness, stood before the exit, disillusioned. A feather slipped to the floor, joining several others. The red feathers scattered as the door opened again. Lena made herself as small as possible, afraid of the change overcoming her friend. Her brilliance had faded and, with it, her comforting serenity. Tears slipped from Lena's enlarged eyes. Then her attention slipped to the wolves holding Morgentus's henchman at bay, snapping their jaws and drawing their black blood if challenged.

"At last she puts down her claws." Morgentus smiled.

The dark atrin paced, suggestively eyeing his prisoner. His mere presence blocked Maiel from escape. Lena sensed that a hesitance to abandon a friend also held her to that building; she needed to take his atman from the hands of their enemy.

Lena shut her eyes, calling to the others from her heart. Dominic was trapped in the hall behind. The brothers, who could have swept in and done away with the refuse, dealt with a frighteningly larger problem. As for anyone else, there simply was no one beyond the room who could help. When the doors had closed her in there, an unsettling fear overtook her. She knew. She knew the others weren't coming. Not for Maiel. Not for her. Maiel would face her fate alone, and she would be witness to the captain's fall. Desperate to help her friend, she defied her orders to leave the moment she'd gotten the church door open for Dominic. She'd found her very being wouldn't allow such cowardice. However, if the demons found her crouching beside the table, it would mean her end as well. Maiel couldn't save her this time.

Wrapping her arms around the table leg, Lena drew on the strength of the stone. Her large eyes glistened in the candle glow as she watched Maiel hold the baron at bay with no more than a threat. She wondered why Maiel didn't jump through the broken door and try to find freedom. This was unlike any soldier she knew. What did she plan?

"They're not coming for you," Morgentus said, when Maiel refused to acknowledge him.

Maiel watched him. Her face flickered with understanding. She never thought they would, until he said it. Her shoulders drew up and she lifted her chin. Peering down her nose at her tormentor, her eyes narrowed with loathing. Lena blinked, clearing the tears. She saw the change flicker in the erela's eyes.

"Think on it, Maiel! What's he given you? This human—countless, thankless brats. Weak ardhodita," Morgentus shouted, losing his composure.

The danava spun around, throwing his hands up. Maiel used his distracted flamboyance to see her escape. She sheathed her blade and ran to the doors at the opposite end of the room. The panels were bolted tight. She desperately struggled to open them. They shivered in the jam, but wouldn't relent. Morgentus recovered from his diatribe. His expression turned black and he hastily joined her. Pressing his twisted form against her, he brought her efforts to a stop, displaying a small, lucent, violet crystal.

"Such games you play. I could chase you for eons in the labyrinth. There are rooms there—where I could take my time, no one would find us for years. Come with me and I'll let my atrin go," Morgentus breathed in her ear.

Maiel grimaced, refusing to speak and give him further words to warp for his amusement, especially to betray her affection for his akha. The monster managed enough without her prompting. Maiel turned, grasping him by his collar. The Labyrinth Lord's guard fell, thinking she actually warmed to him. Maiel's mouth curled in anticipated delight. That, too, was taken the wrong way. Forcing Morgentus to the floor with her foot on his stomach, she flipped him, throwing his rancid sattva like a toy. He lost his grasp of the atman, which slid across the floor, stopping at the door to the outside. He went in the opposite direction.

Maiel regained her feet, glancing at the purple spark. Morgentus sneered, surprised by her actions. Lena held her breath, waiting for what would come next. The expression Maiel wore reminded her of a nightmare she'd once had, but the object of the captain's hate wasn't to be taken lightly either. These two enemies would tear each other apart, along with anyone who got between them.

"Get her!" Morgentus ordered, slamming his fist on the floor.

Segrius and his companion tried to leave the guardianship of the wolves, but they were well-tempered by the four-legged warriors. Maiel rushed back to the doors, giving them a hard kick. They swung back with a snap and hung crookedly on their broken hinges. The wolves charged after her, leaving Lena alone with the demons.

Lena held her breath, waiting for one of them to find her hiding there. Morgentus got to his feet, pausing as though he sensed her presence. Instead, he ordered his inept minions to give chase. The demon sauntered after his quarry. His steps stopped at the door. He turned his head and looked in her direction. Lena pressed herself back behind the table. The stone shuddered, then pushed against her, and slid across the floor to the wall beyond the door she entered through. The stone pressed against her until it could go no further. She held her tongue, though she was painfully entombed by the mammoth slab.

"Sit tight, akha. I'll be back," Morgentus said, leaving the atman where it fell.

Morgentus retreated.

Counting to five, Lena waited to be sure the baron had abandoned the room. She pried herself free and crawled across the marble floor. Looking around, she saw that the table had been moved to block the door. The panel suddenly pulled back and Dominic stared down at her. His eyes glowed, but the red was nearly gone from them. He looked more himself.

"Where are they?" Dominic asked, as he jumped over the table, holding the candelabra for a weapon.

Lena hesitated to answer the question or to follow. The others must have been just behind, because no one else could have warded those doors with such force. She'd be safer to wait for them. The change in Dominic scared her and she had her instructions to abandon him if this came to pass. Her focus now was Maiel. They'd made it clear that when he gave into the flame, he would try to feed from her. She stepped back, keeping her distance. Her eyes slipped to the doors through which Maiel escaped when she was pursued by the shadowwalkers.

Dominic ran in the direction Lena indicated by her glance. The green door slammed and rattled as it swung closed behind the girl. The force startled Lena, doing so again as it was instantly torn open once more, granting a wide view of the city and river below. The wind whipped around her. Thick clouds rolled with flashes of light. Lena shivered. The door closed with a slam. She looked around, still alone in the flickering light. The flashes in the windows overhead reminded her of a promise she made to someone very important. Lena scurried across the room and snatched up the atman

Morgentus had tried to steal. She stared at the light within and gave a soft smile and nod. A kind voice assured her that she would be safe, and that her friends needed her. Pocketing the crystal, she chased after her assign. No one was safe with Dominic, but she had a mission to complete. Maiel would have done no less. She couldn't fail her now, not when her friend faced destruction.

Lena ran through the passage, emerging back in the nave. She looked to either side, but saw no one. Carefully picking her way to the aisle, she observed the wreckage scattered throughout the vast room, making the trek difficult. A sulfurous odor lingered. Lena quickened her pace, searching the pews as she passed. Her path led to the arches and the arcade beyond. The sound of metal dropping on the stone floor pulled her attention aside. She saw a shadow pass in the doorway. She chased after it, finding a small chamber with a spiral staircase and a door that opened to the outside. Through the open door, the base of the bell tower, a small garden and a wood blocked the view of the city. Lights twinkled between the branches and leaves as the wind wildly swayed the trees. Wolves howled behind her. Shee and Argus dashed out, disappearing in a streak of light. Lena called to them, but they were gone.

The sky clouded over and the night grew black and restless. The distant sound of thunder rolled above the blanket that hid the moon and stars. Lena swallowed, wondering if the others had also retreated, leaving her there on her own. Did she chase a scurrilous imp or Dominic to the towers? Backing inside, her resonance pulsed in cold dread. Through a narrow door, she found a set of red granite stairs, a spiral to the roof. The weapon Dominic had made lay discarded at the bottom.

Circling up the first few steps, Lena hesitated to follow where they led. The rust-colored stones twisted quite high, disappearing into a consuming darkness. Peering into the dark, a flicker of something passed at the top. Boots scraped the stone, piquing her curiosity.

Lena gripped the fixed rod set through the center meant as a railing. With both hands on the old pipe, she set her foot on the next step. She stared up the spiral, trying to make herself move. Her sattva refused. The railing shook in her hands, as if someone had struck it. Slowly, she raised her other foot to take another step. The dark appeared to flap again, like the beating wings of a danava. She paused. Swallowing her fear, she forced another step. The top was sackcloth black, blacker than her hair. It was the perfect place for an imp or daeva to hide. Thunder rolled, halting her again. Lena blinked and drew a deep breath. With a miserable frown, she forced herself to climb to the top. The staircase narrowed.

Emerging from the stairs, Lena stepped out onto the dome. A catwalk of wood planks circled the base. A flimsy fence was the only thing standing between her and a dreadful fall. She peered over the edge, losing her breath. Lightning flashed in the sky and the thunder reminded her of why she was there. The darkness made it hard to see around the broad dome. She peered to the left and then the right. The tails of Dominic's coat waved in the storm winds. Lena measured her steps, so as not to startle him.

"Dominic," Lena called, but her words were swallowed by the storm.

Rain poured down suddenly and hard, stinging like nettles. Lena held her hands out. The rain did not touch her, it was as if some barrier protected her skin. She reached to grab hold of his coat sleeve, but a large shadow slipped between her and Dominic. Knocked back, she slid beneath the rail. At the edge of the copper slope, her feet hit another fence and she stopped abruptly. Lena clung to the wet roof, eyes large with fright. Pulling herself back up, she saw the sky roil as Maiel stood at the roof's edge. Lena called to her, but the wind swallowed her voice.

The clouds spun into a shaft, like a tornado reaching hopelessly to the ground. The wind blew harder, the lightning flashed bolder, and the thunder rolled louder. Lena stared in awe as the clouds opened like a great gate in the sky. Holding tight to the fence, she looked to the base of the cloud pillar. The ground burned; there was a gaping hole filled with infernal sights. It looked like a volcano vent had opened beneath the hill. The openings, above and below, widened and threatened to swallow the Earth. Lena shut her eyes. They were too late.

*   *   *

Maiel stood on the farthest edge of the dome. The Danube wended by and the clouds rolled in. Esztergom lay nestled in shadow, windows shining with light. Deep dread embedded itself in her core. Knowledge that this was the end. Morgentus had found her and wasn't about to let her escape this time. She was tired, too weak to slide from his influence and seek refuge in yet another place. This perch would have to do. It was the highest point accessible. If only the clouds would part and let the moonlight in. The radiance would give some strength, would tip the scales in her favor. She just needed to strike one fatal blow, then he and his damned gang would run back to Acheron, the pathetic despoilers they were, and she could begin her lonely journey, a recidia imprisoned upon Earth, to watch the rise and fall of lives, to lose friends and be tormented by their passing.

Yet there was another choice. If she jumped, the deadly gate would send her straight to Jahannam. Once there, the weariness in her limbs would give way to strength of another kind. Determination would never carry her back home from there, but Morgentus would never lay a hand on her. Tears filled her eyes, knowing such a choice was too dangerous a thing to attempt. Just as likely the fall would render her helpless: she'd be placed right into his hands and no one would ever come to her rescue. The princes, after all, declared all her kind the enemy of Jahannam. With their help, Morgentus had hidden his stolen bride for thousands of years in the deepest parts of his labyrinth. Not once had any mission discovered the woman. There were also the other missing, like the guardian Gamael, for whom the alders claimed active missions. He had yet to return to Zion. Of course, none of them had given themselves to the dark and yet had hope.

Raising her arm before her eyes, Maiel saw that her sattva was nearly mortal, so pale and fragile. If she jumped now, the gate might refuse her. Thus, she would not fade, but remain trapped in a sattva irreparably broken. Her hand slid down the smooth surface of the metal covering her abdomen. The brilliant sheen of the cobalt armor faded to blackish midnight. The shine was muted, like the glow of the atman in her sword and in her eyes. Rusty feathers blew out before her on a gusty wind. The penannular would be dead in no time, and her armor gone with it. The dangers facing her then were far worse than anything she'd faced yet.

Lighting flashed in the sky above. The clouds rolled violently with the thunder. The delicate scent of home mixed with the sulfur of the shades. How could she consider giving into her enemies, even as a means of defeating them? Hissing rain fell from the black clouds in torrents. The drops touched her skin, chilling and soaking her. Unable to bear the judgment of her failure and the weight of her hopeless thoughts, she embraced the storm, letting her tears at last fall in a silent farewell to what was lost.

Boot steps on the planks behind roused her from her acceptance of fate. She turned her chin. A dark figure stood on the dome catwalk. It wasn't Morgentus, as she'd expected. Instead, the golden-haired soul responsible for all this stood there. Turning her face from him, she frowned. Below them, the ground lit on fire. The danava came to collect a prize. The pits of Jahannam opened, promising she would fall. The last thing she wanted to see before her fall was him. Her stomach twisted at that thought. Never in the ages of their ketu had she ever felt so. Setting her eyes on the far horizon, she knew it was the loss of favor that twisted her feelings. As her atman grew dim, so would her love. In the dark, affection would be a sentiment to be met with the utmost derision. Incapable of ending such attachment, she would delight in denying her husband, who would be incapable of parting from her.

"Maiel," he called to her.

Maiel turned her head, but wouldn't look at him. Loathing tugged at her sinews.

"Maiel, no."

Maiel rolled her eyes back to the distance. He climbed over the rail and carefully moved down the slope to where she stood. Even a fall to the next roof would kill his human form. She looked past the edge, thinking of helping that along. His movements distracted her as he knelt down to pick something up. It was one of her feathers, pasted to the roof by the rain. He spun the sodden plume between his fingers, frowning at it. She recalled how much he had enjoyed the red feathers of her wings. The emotion turned over and over, until she considered smashing his face into the back of his skull. Her fists squeezed tightly. With a tremor, she pushed back the thought. In a moment of vacillation, happy memories crept in and begged her to fight to preserve them instead.

Dominic dropped the feather and came to stand behind her. He didn't touch her, but she felt the heat of his dark presence at her back. She blinked the tears from her eyes, hating him for following her there, hating him for so much more. The emotion opened the way for the dark to take deeper roots.

"I've come to take you home," Dominic said.

"I can't go home—I failed my post and so have you," Maiel replied.

The threads of flame split the ground apart across the entire hillside. They stretched up the basilica walls, seeking prey. The mouth of the opening, a black pit, ringed downward into Jahannam. Forms wriggled and writhed in its midst. Above, the threads of bale shuddered through the clouds in webbing vines. The gate in the sky, the innards of an ivory mountain, ringed upward into Zion. A pillar of brilliant light reached to hold the dark at bay. The opposing legions came not for a simple atman, but for a war. Oh, the foolish of fools, Maiel thought, weeping at the sight.

"Come down from here and let me prove you wrong," Dominic pleaded.

"It's too late," Maiel replied, feeling the emotions subside into a strange peace as she accepted this end.

The intensity of the storm grew with the intensity of her emotions. Then a twinkling of the light she longed for manifested itself at the apex of the vortex. The legions marched. Guilt and hope wrestled inside her breast. There would be much to answer for.

"Come now, or you will fail," Dominic said, stretching his hand out to her.

Maiel held her gaze on the horizon. There was another set of footsteps on the roof and a low growl. Turning, she saw that Morgentus had finally shown his face, flanked by his mud-eating serpents. He moved fast, empowered by the night and the coming hell fires. His malefic hands grabbed Dominic, pressing a claw to his throat. Dominic struggled, unable to gain leverage enough to escape. Maiel turned to watch them, thinking how typical this was for the soul, how much she felt this was necessary and just.

"You've been a thorn in my side too long, boy!" Morgentus growled.

The shadowalker's black eyes held Maiel where she stood. He pressed his claw through the flesh of Dominic's throat. The skin split in a ragged gash, and his blood flowed eagerly. It seemed too easy, almost staged. Maiel stood frozen, staring at the scene for several moments. The horror would not settle into her thoughts and then it suddenly struck her. Morgentus grinned, pushing Dominic toward her. Maiel caught her husband as he crumpled against her. He fought to speak, but just sputtered helplessly. Morgentus had cut deep.

"Dominic!" she called out, waking from her nightmare to a very real one.

The anger and hatred Maiel felt for her husband washed away in the realization of her fears. In his desperate gaze, she saw the print of his struggle and his earnest bid to fight destiny. He became what they'd hoped to avoid. This change was the fault of those who withheld information from the ones they expected to help Dominic succeed. Against his nature, Dominic used the embrace of the flame to defeat their enemies. Pressing the collar of his sweater around the wound, she tried to stop the blood. The blood flowed over the links of her armored fingers.

"No—please no. I'm sorry. No. This can't happen. I'm sorry!" Maiel pleaded for his life.

Morgentus paced, laughing at her anguish. Dragging his claw across his tongue, he tasted Dominic's blood. His black eyes flashed with the vigor it gave him.

"Take your time, my angel. We have eternity," Morgentus mocked.

Maiel scowled at the baron. Dominic lay in her lap, choking on his own blood, yet the pig thought only of his desire. Dominic fought for his breath, trembling against death. His jade green eyes found hers, the light and fire gone from them. He tried to smile, though the gasps made it impossible. His mouth moved, trying to speak. She hushed him, touching the lips she had kissed for centuries. Her body ached with the thought that this was the last time. He grasped her arm with surprising strength and tried to speak again.

"This—had—to—happen. Mai—I—I—sorry. I—you," he forced out, trying to call her name and declare his devotion.

"Don't talk," Maiel said. "Luthias'll be here any minute and he'll take you home. You'll be safe. This wasn't your fault. None of this. Please. This wasn't your fault," Maiel told him.

Placing a kiss on his lips, the touch scalded her skin. She recoiled in pain. Weeping for his demise, she cursed herself for forgetting her place. Then her husband's hand and body went limp. Maiel gasped in agony, crying to any who would help.

"Dominic. Dominic!" she called with no response. "No. Please, no! This is my fault. Don't die. Not like this. I can fix you—I can fix him," she cried, as tears slipped from her eyes.

Morgentus laughed, mocking the terrible scene he had created.

Maiel gazed upon her husband's face, jade eyes staring at nothing, his lips parted in their final embrace.

"Dominic!" a small voice called from the railing of the dome.

Maiel lifted her pained gaze. Lena stood in the rain. Her black wings spread wide. She raced to them, kneeling at her assign's feet. She should have been in Otzar. She should be home safe with her new mother. Maiel reached for her before Morgentus decided to wound her even deeper. She'd failed Dominic, but she wouldn't fail another. She must keep the girl safe until help came.

Blood washed from the roof with the rain. The roar of flames reverberated around them as Maiel and Lena huddled close. Once black, the clouds turned white for miles around as something brighter than the sun filled them from above. Maiel watched dismay come over the face of her adversary. Getting to her feet, she left Lena at Dominic's side. Drawing her sword, she felt the strength of Zion fill her, at last meeting her hope. The glow of that force illumined her crown. Blue eyes turned bright.

"King Adonai, give us strength to avenge thee this day. Danava, by the light of my oath, I send you to Oblivion for your wickedness," Maiel declared.

"Not today, pet," Morgentus replied.

Morgentus bared his sharp teeth in a vow to meet with her again. Touching the tip of Maiel's outstretched blade, he set her off balance.

"Soon," he said, with a grin.

Pushing back on the blade, he forced Maiel to pinwheel her arms in an effort to maintain her perch or topple from the edge of the roof. She'd never had the strength to face him. The shade disappeared in a whirl of smoke, laughing as he went. Losing the grip on her sword, she watched it fall backward toward the flame. The sapphire glinted brightly. A smoky figure darted at her from along the lip of the dome. A black-gloved hand, the fingers conspicuously bare, grasped her sword as she toppled backward. Then she felt someone pressed along her back. An arm snaked around her waist and she ceased to fall. The light grew brighter as they passed higher and higher, the speed beyond comprehension. Closing her eyes to the blinding radiance, she heard a familiar voice whisper in her ear.

"I've got you," he said.

Maiel's mind slipped as the pressure grew too great and she disappeared inside of a dream, rising still higher and faster. The force of that speed destroyed thought. Blinding whiteness. Rapture. Then, nothing.

CHAPTER 29

GEDIEL HID AT THE EDGE of the garden behind the cypress trees and shrubbery of Gragrafel's villa. The garden rested in the peaceful warmth of daylight. Just ahead stood the bed laid out for their ailing daughter upon her return. Several passings of the sun and moon and she still hadn't awakened. For two days, the flesh remained thick about her, the poison of Morgentus's barbs anchoring it tight. The pale glow of her true form returned once the clerics of Otzar removed the nails and the flesh faded. Gediel stepped back behind the portico of the house. He still felt her pressed to him, the scent filling his nose, seven days since the recovery.

Sitting on the stairs, Gediel watched the younglings of her unit coming and going from the front entrance. Nearly the whole battalion sat on the other side of the hedge wall, Mikhael, Bade, and Callidora included. League's flute carried on the breeze. They wanted to know the moment she awoke. At least that would give him cover to escape back to Elysion before she saw him.

Beside his feet, Chiron lay stretched out with a small bird in his sights. The flitting wings made his ears stand on end. He sighed and then laid his head on his front paws. The alpha wolf had grown tired of their vigil, longing for home and the packs. Gediel scratched the wolf's head, reassuring the captain it would be worth the wait.

A soft sigh was carried on a delicate breeze, tickling his senses awake. He jumped up and looked between the trees. Maiel stirred beneath the light coverings. Beside her bed, Shee jumped up to her feet. Argus licked his mistress's face and pressed himself against her and fiercely wagged his tail. Gediel's eyes blurred with tears. He knew he should leave, but he just wanted to see her face.

Maiel sat up, rubbing Argus's ears back and placing a kiss on the tip of his black nose. Her eyes glowed powerfully, full of the light that fed her. A beaming grin brightened the once shaded features. Gediel blinked, seeing the image of her on top of the basilica. A laugh bubbled from her throat. He smiled, assured at last she wouldn't fade. She was home for good.

A Sun Order soldier in a gold tunic dashed into the garden. Gediel's eyes flicked in that direction. Dominic rushed to his wife, embracing her. Gediel backed away, as their lips touched. He was no longer needed.

Chiron jumped up and followed him to the front of the house. The alarm would be raised immediately—he had to leave now. Gragrafel's house would buzz with visitors and business. To linger would only make unbearable the ache in his chest. He couldn't see her again, not with what he knew.

"Ah, Gediel!" Alex called, as he turned away from the front door to make his exit.

Gediel paused and faced her with a forced smile. Her bright features were radiantly enlivened at the return of her only daughter.

"I was just looking for you," Alex said, pulling her white robes out of the way of her steps. Her white hair hung loose over her shoulders and her black eyes sparkled like jewels. "Did you need anything dear?" she asked, noticing his troubled features.

Gediel shook his head.

"I was just leaving, as you have no more need of me," Gediel said.

"Of course you—"

The alder was cut off by a youngling who raced from the house shouting that Maiel was awake. The alarm was raised and the house went into immediate turmoil. Alex eyed him. She patted his arm and nodded.

"Thank you, though that will never be enough," she said.

Gediel placed his hand on hers and nodded. Turning his back, he and Chiron moved to take a hushed leave, but he was faced with another obstacle. Mikhael and the Moon Order officios stood paces away, including the Moon Order Praefect, Hecate, and her sister Decurio Artemis. He was suddenly reminded of the trophy in his pocket. His hand jerked toward it, but he corrected the motion and greeted his friends with forced enthusiasm.

"She's just woken," Gediel said.

They smiled soft, bittersweet expressions.

"I must report to Voil on the mission," Gediel excused himself.

"Many thanks to you, watcher, for the return of my captain," Bade said, grasping his forearm.

Mikhael gave him a nod and pat on the shoulder. The officios stepped around him, but Callidora remained. She watched him expectantly. He thought she waited for him to return the braid now that he had retrieved Maiel. Shamefaced, he hoped she would forget it. Drawing the fiery lock from his pocket he offered it to the leader. Callidora closed his fist around the braid.

"I have no more need of that. She's here," she said, gesturing to her heart.

In the small skirmishes that had taken place, Callidora led the unit with distinction and gained her confidence and the respect of her commanders at last. There seemed a great many reasons for all of this to have happened. However, none would satisfy the emptiness he felt. Gediel tucked the token back in his pocket. It wouldn't help him move on, though he suspected Callidora planned it so.

"Don't stray far, Wolf Leader," Callidora said to him.

Gediel opened his mouth to ask the reason.

"We'll speak again soon. Now, I wish to see my sister," she cut him off.

Callidora stepped around him. She hesitated and turned back.

"Thank you," she said.

Callidora continued toward Gragrafel's house. Looking rather puzzled, Gediel stood watch a moment too long. Mikhael and Bade grinned at him from the steps, believing they saw a spark between him and Callidora. His mien darkened and he grit his teeth. Callidora wasn't his and he wouldn't accept such a ketu, even if the king demanded. The engels took note of his scorn and he turned away from them to continue home.

Standing on the outskirts of his grange, Gediel breathed in the fresh air and focused on his duties. The dogs and wolves had been ignored for too long. They needed their training and such excursions into other realms only delayed their development and hurt the armies they would soon join.

Chiron ran ahead, his tongue lolling happily from his mouth. His gait was joyous, though his master was gloomy. In fact, everyone seemed good-humored that day. Gediel shook his head and wiped his brow. Some of the wolves and dogs gathered to greet him, wagging their tails so hard their back ends swayed. He mumbled to them and went inside the house. They piled in after him.

Gediel entered his bedroom. The brook cheerfully chattered as it wound about the bed, under the narrow bridge to the other side of the room and out across the bottom of the hillside. Crossing the little bridge to put away his collection of weapons, he noticed the hill. More trees grew there and a narrow stream of water poured into the brook from its rise. He squinted, trying to see better. Gediel shook his head again and went to discard his armor and weapons. Once the blades and other accoutrements were tucked inside his cabinet, he turned out of the room and followed the path along the stream from his bedroom to see what was causing the waterfall. At the base of the new stream, he set his hands on his hips and scowled. He wondered if the dogs had been busy on the hill, digging holes again and thus rerouting a spring. Trudging to the top, he found that several tiny saplings sprung from the ground in a crescent pattern. At the center, a spring bubbled up from inside the cracked bedrock and through the soil, making a strong spout.

Shifting his attention toward the streams, he saw they were full, but not overflowing. They seemed wider and deeper. The flow emptied into the capable river beyond the wood. Scratching his head he wondered at this odd development. The hill had been barren for centuries. Not a thing would grow there but two palms, and he'd never quite figured out what he wanted to place on it. So, instead, he left the ground naked with its low tufts of grass for company. Now it seemed the hill had other ideas in mind.

Chiron howled as he sauntered into the compound of caves and niches where the dogs and wolves made their homes. Gediel looked in that direction. The sky was bright blue, with a bright sun and a few chubby clouds. Muttering under his breath, he cursed all the cheerfulness again. Stalking down the hill, he went to check on the hounds. There was simply no explanation, but he was sure in time he would understand what had happened to his home while he was gone. The packs could never keep a secret from him.

* * *

Maiel leaned back from the kiss Dominic pressed to her lips. She studied his face, caressing his short gold hair. He looked rested, his eyes a quiet jade once more. Stroking the start of a beard, grown while they were parted, she smiled at him. Her energy quickened, but not like it used to. With sparkling eyes, she concealed her worry. Dismissing the change as no more than a reaction to the previous chaos, she rested her head on his shoulder and put her arms around him. The breeze blew across her face and the garden danced around them. The sunshine warmed her chilled insides. It must have just been the fight that left her cold, or the way she had abandoned him and hope. She shut her eyes to the memory. Gray flashed in her mind's eye.

The tinkling, infectious laughter of children flitted on the breeze. The corners of her mouth curled, as she was warmed to her core by the sound. The children ran to them, circling the bed and piling upon it. She felt nearly whole sitting there in all of their arms. Yet something was missing and it felt more key than any of their pulsing energies. Maiel shut her eyes and pulled Dominic closer. She hoped he wouldn't speak and ruin the moment. Something said that one word from him would start the whole foray over again. Burying her face in his neck she tried to quiet her fears, but something in his scent made her edgy.

Flashes lit up her memory. Standing on the edge of the rooftop, she had nearly fallen to her death, but someone had saved her. The voice echoed in her ears. I've got you. Maiel peered over her husband's shoulder, watching the wolves leap through a flowerbed, chasing a butterfly. The puppies trailed after, trying to keep up on their short legs. A flash of gray wing fluttered in her mind. Black armor. She shut her eyes and heard his voice again. Suddenly it was like he was holding her and the rush of emotion made her tremble.

Dominic lay dead on the roof, unable to catch her. Even if he had, he would have been a flash of gold, as would her akha or Mikhael. Perhaps Zach came to her aid, but no, that didn't match her memory.

"All right. Everyone give your amba some air. She just woke up," Dominic said, his voice vibrating through his chest.

Dominic released her, scooting the children off the bed. The smallest stayed, for he knew that she would want a wordless comfort to coo in her ear. He smiled at her and kissed the top of her head. Maiel lay back with the twins cradled at each side. Light played through the trees on the canopy over her bed. She wondered how long she had slept. She imagined it was for some time, by Dominic's appearance. Spreading her wings beneath her, she checked the feathers. Each crimson plume and pinion had been restored. They felt strong as she flexed them.

The quiet was quickly interrupted by the arrival of her amba and janya. The erela led the engel to her side, beaming with puzzling pride. Maiel stared at them, resembling her elder akha for a brief moment. The matriarch sat on the side of her bed and stole the nearest twin. Bouncing the boy on her knee, she caused spluttering and giggles that made Maiel grimace. Gurgling sounds were the last thing she wanted to hear right then. To comfort herself, she pulled the remaining twin closer and kissed her blushing head.

"That was some scare you gave us," Alex said.

"I gave you? You scared me with all that nonsense about the council and Ganesha," Maiel said.

"Did we?" Alex asked softly.

Her amba gave her a sidelong glance with a doubtful smile. Maiel looked away, breathing in the scent of her child and watching birds flounder in the grass. She felt strangely comfortable as she stared into the west. Her bower was on the crest of the hill, to the other side of a thick knot of trees. She wondered why they didn't let her rest there. The water would have lent more energy to her healing than the bare light. Sighing, she lay back on the pillows and thought of her pool.

"Don't leave quite yet," her amba said.

Maiel rolled her head to look at the erela.

"Are you sure you're ready? You've been sleeping days, my darling. I just want to be sure you're strong enough to go home. I wouldn't dream of keeping you if you were," Alex said.

Maiel grasped her amba's hand.

"Tell me what happened—while I was gone," Maiel said.

Alex's expression was telling. A shadow passed over her eyes. Then she laid the baby back beside his amba. With a loving touch she placed her hand on Maiel's stomach.

"Your akha—your whole family just worked to bring you home," Alex said, avoiding her gaze.

"Anyone else?"

"Your commanders, your best friend, young Lena, Cal, the general," Alex replied, with an expression that warned her from digging too deeply.

Maiel sighed. None of them had gray wings. But, then, she already knew who those wings belonged to. They were too unique to be anonymous.

"Where's Lena?"

"Lena—is in the belly of her new and very excited amba," Alex said, happy to change the subject.

"Who?"

"In fact, you did miss out on a bit," Alex said, laughing.

After a brief pause, she answered the question.

"Evocati Luthias has his ketu. Shen's fifth daughter, the Draco Dao-Ming," Alex said.

"Luthias, a janya," Maiel said, shocked. "Has the king gone mad?"

"Oh, no, my darling girl. But those two have gone completely mad for each other. They cannot be parted. I'm afraid your next incarnation will be accompanied by his wife. At least we know Dominic can use the help," Alex laughed.

"Fantastic," Maiel said, a little dismayed.

"Lena left you this," Alex said, taking folded sheets of paper from the shoulder of her robes.

Maiel took the sheets, still warm with her amba's energy.

"I'll leave you to read it alone," Alex said, patting her daughter's stomach again.

Maiel unfolded the sheets and looked at the elegant scrawl drawn across the pages. It was handwriting well beyond the skill of a child, but then she so easily forgot Lena was no child. The girl's smiling face was a memory of an incarnation from which she had just parted. Lena was a grown woman, and soon she would boast a set of wings to complement her years and skill, though she would otherwise occupy an infantile state.

In her letter, Lena wrote an apology for not being there to see her awaken. However, the majority of the message was to thank Maiel for her service in guarding a common soul with the valor that would make her proud to call herself a duta. The girl excused her guardian's panic and told the story of a gallant being, one who faced danava and shades to restore her mate and family to their due dharma, while saving a few souls along the way. Maiel lowered the paper and wiped her eyes. Was that truly what she had done? It seemed more like a bad tantrum.

Attempting to sit up, she found her youngest sound asleep on each wing, pinning her to the bed. She set the letter aside and folded her arms over her stomach, smiling softly. A silver glint drew her eye toward the house. One of the heavily armored Powers stood there, the red lenses of his helm turned toward the bed. Four great white wings with ribbing of silver rested upon his back. She noticed a red cloth tied to his side atop his sword. The Power was nearly unbearable to look at in the bright midday sun. The figure moved closer, coming under the shade of an olive tree, and removed the helmet.

"Doesn't that make the pretty picture," the Power spoke.

Maiel stared. Until the helmet came away, she couldn't place the voice, though she knew it. Maiel stared.

"I don't expect you to remember—"

"Oriael," Maiel tearfully breathed his name.

"Brilliant she is, then." Oriael smiled.

Maiel took hold of his armored arm and squeezed. They didn't need words after the days they'd spent together. It was merely her duty and that she truly felt. She, at least, meant it when they said they would leave none behind.

"I just came to make sure you woke. Otherwise, I was going straight to Acheron to fish you out with a contingent headed by Mikhael. You disappoint me for not allowing me the pleasure of squaring with my atrin," Oriael said.

"I thought I would never see you again," Maiel said, not wishing to release him just yet.

A tug on the silver spine of his great wing, armor meant to strengthen and protect, Maiel marveled at his return.

"But here I am—oh, I nearly forgot. I brought you something."

Oriael untied the red cloth at his side and placed it carefully in her hands. A small white-and-tan-plumed owlet sneezed at her. Taking a step it bobbled and fell over. Maiel was awestruck by the gift.

"This is youngling Pallus—a new watcher that my wife has been nurturing in the aviary of the cloisters. She wanted your order to conscript him—to watch over you when others cannot, and to thank you for returning her wayward husband," Oriael said, tears in his eyes.

Pallus yawned unceremoniously. Carefully holding her new friend, she gave Oriael a lengthy hug.

"You didn't have to die for me. I would've brought you home another way," Maiel mumbled through tears.

"I explained all that to you. Sometimes there's no other path but suffering to show us the truth. I was proud to give my life to protect you from my atrin and I'll do so again if needed."

Oriael folded his arms about her and smiled softly. Words were useless to express the bond they forged so quickly.

"I hear my captain's awake!" A loud voice burst in on the bittersweet exchange.

Pallus squawked loudly and flew to the top of the canopy for safety. Oriael attempted to get him down as the general joined them, but the youngling was frightened by the outburst and the appearance of a duta so great. He finally coaxed the bird onto his finger to comfort him.

Mikhael joined them, putting his thick arm on Oriael's shoulder and nearly dwarfing the battle-hardened Power. The general smiled down at her. Commander Bade joined them, followed by her reluctant leader. The order's commanders remained on the steps, bowing their heads in respect.

"Such a pretty amba." Mikhael smiled down at her. Gasping as he recalled something, he added, "Have I mentioned my wife's having our fifteenth child? It's a girl, at least I hope for a girl. I want to name her Omaiel. I hope you'll allow it."

"Of course," Maiel agreed to the honor.

"We'll see if you are willing after you spend fifteen weeks playing youngling to your commanders in the battalion, erela. You didn't think you'd slide free of my wrath, did you?" Mikhael pointed his finger and then grinned.

"Of course not," Maiel said guiltily.

Mikhael scooped up the babies, startling them awake. She waited for the children to cry their displeasure, but they only giggled in the arms of her general. His great face dazzled them and they reached for his curly locks.

"Just like your amba. Can't scare the lot of you. You'll make good soldiers," he told them.

Maiel sat up, flexing her wings. She felt cold, thinking of how many children Mikhael had. She wondered if she too would have so many. She and Dominic were halfway there. Her eyes lowered to the blanket and she frowned, not quite keen on the idea. There once was a time such ideas made her ecstatic with joy. Now she wasn't sure she could bear the great years it took to nurture an atman to adulthood. All that time in loneliness.

Feeling Callidora's eyes on her, she reached out to the erela and the leader fell into her arms, squeezing her tightly.

"Where is Zaajah?" Maiel asked, missing her other friend.

"Paying penance for defying Uriel. You'll join her as soon as you're strong enough. Then I'd wager neither of you'll step out of line again," Mikhael answered.

"I wager we won't," Maiel said distracted.

The images of her rescue flashed in her mind again. The touch. The gray wing. The whisper. Her stomach churned. All fell silent as she ruminated on the meaning. Perhaps it was Cal who'd pulled her home. But the voice.

"We best let you rest some more. I'll have the general leave the children to their janya," Callidora said.

Callidora smiled, but Maiel couldn't return the sentiment or her glance. The others walked away and her attention slipped back to the hillside and the pool she knew was beyond it. The clouds that spread a shadow across the ground seemed like an omen, despite the bright sunlight that persisted. None of them would speak on the matter, but she sensed they also knew.

This time, she would not run, but she knew whatever they faced threatened to shred their lives to tatters, never to be mended.

"Take your time, Captain," Callidora said, grasping Maiel's forearm.

Maiel looked to her and she saw that the erela understood more than she realized.

"You've been through a nightmare," Callidora said, her eyes shifting to the dragon tattoo on Maiel's arm.

The mark had become more detailed. Morgentus lived…

GLOSSARY OF TERMS

Abaddon, Abaddonians. The only province to be ruled by more than one prince and not divided. Ruling princes: Asmodeus, Amon, Belphegor, Azazel, brothers when duta, brothers as danava; the inhabitants of Abaddon.

Acheron River. River of Woe.

Acheron, Acherites. A central province ruled by Prince Belial and his nobility; the inhabitants of Acheron.

Adonai Elohim, King. The jñanasattva from Nirvana who oversees the rule of Zion, often called God by Samsaran races. He permits the lower resonating atman to pass into Zion so that they may become jñanasattva and return home.

Aghart. The home planet of the Aghartians.

Aghartians. A race of souls, humanoid in build, but taller-like duta, with pale blue skin and platinum hair.

Akash. The record of all times. A museum and library containing the tomes and treasures of all the worlds which are deemed dangerous to be left loose in just anyone's hands. Artifacts from Samsara are stored here and replaced with duplicate models to remove their dangerous power. Home of the three witches or sisters.

akha. The duta term for brother.

alder. A classification of duta who are assigned to administrative, bureaucratic, and exploratory vocations; councilor.

Alexandrael, Alder. A highly respected member of the council of Zion, mother of Captain Maiel, Captain Joel, and Alder Zacharius.

Amaiel. The ardhodita child of Captain Maiel and Dominic Newlyn; twin sister of Chaiel; muse.

amba. The duta term for mother.

ampa. The duta term for grandmother.

Ananta. The home planet of the naga.

Arcadia. A term encompassing the vast stretch of land that is home to the orders. Arcadia wraps beneath Zion province and is parted by the Gihon River.

ardhodita. A half duta and half human hybrid, not to be confused with nephilim.

Argus. The alpha wolf in Captain Maiel's squad.

Artemis, Decurio, Moon Order. The svargaduta brigade commander of the Moon Order, sister of Hecate.

aryika. The shadowalker term for grandfather.

Asfodel Fields. The forgotten reaches where souls are left to wander at will but never cross back to the higher realms because their resonance anchors them in Jahannam. It is a place of redemption overseen by Prince Mammon, who is too lazy to herd the souls into his wastes.

assign. An atman in incarnation under guardianship by council orders.

Astral. The fourth world, the mental plane, where thought forges reality.

asuri. The shadowalkers' term for female.

Athiel, Sergeant, Sun Order. A squad leader under Captain Joel; guardian.

atman. The resonance that makes a person; the heart of a person that can only be ended by being cast in Oblivion.

atrin. The shadowalkers' term for male.

Aurai. A soul race, an avian race of semi-humanoids capable of flight. This race does not cooperate with the UWOS.

Avernus. The third world, which acts as another barrier between Zion and Astral.

Bachlach. Former Boarwellum; inhabitant of Jahannam.

Bade, Primus, Moon Order. The regiment commander overseeing Maiel's company.

Bale, or Bale Fire. The expression of the perpetual light through a duta in the process of casting a being to Oblivion.

Barachiel, General. A svargaduta field commander of the Order of Illuminati on Earth.

barbarians. Former els; inhabitants of Jahannam.

baron. See ranks section.

Belial, Prince, Acheron. A former seraphim and commander in the Order of Horus; Belial was cast out of Zion during the Conflict Of Hosts.

bhogin. Former nagas; inhabitants of Jahannam.

bio-vessel. The physical body that makes it possible for a soul or any being to inhabit Samsara. Also called skin suit or bio-interface appliance (BIA).

Blue Passages. The tunnels into the Otzar well.

Boarwellum. A soul race of a tree-like people with a gentle, humorous nature. As pacifists, this race does not cooperate with the UWOS.

Brian McCallister. Dominic Newlyn's incarnation during the early 20th century and World War II.

Burning Down. The process by which an atman becomes darker, evil, if you will, and treads the path to destruction. It is often a violent experience, fraught with great agony. The projected body feels like it is on fire (hence the name). Dark thoughts inhabit the mind, and often dark actions are taken.

Caer Wydion Galaxy. The Samsara galaxy in which Earth exists.

Callidora, Evocati, Moon Order. The second in command to Captain Maiel.

Cecitiel, Alder. The dominion protector of the Akash; one of the Three Sisters, also called the Three Witches.

Cetians. A race of souls, tan-skinned, hairless humanoid.

Chaiel. The ardhodita child of Captain Maiel and Dominic Newlyn, twin sister of Amaiel; muse soul.

cherubim. A six-winged race of duta, appearing as a lion-bodied soul, much like a sphinx. This race is predisposed toward inspiration and muse aspects in Zion.

Chiron, Captain, Order of Fenrir. The alpha leader of watcher Gediel's packs; sire of Argus and mate of Imnek. An Arctic wolf soul.

Cocytus. The northernmost province of Jahannam where Lucifer is imprisoned in ice. Is also the name of a river in Jahannam, known as the river of lamentation.

Conflict of Hosts. A war to cleanse Zion of oath breakers. A great number of duta were cast into the prison realm of Jahannam for crimes against their assigns, as well as breaking their dharmic oaths. Also called The Conflict.

Corabael. Captain Joel's wife; muse.

Corpheus. See Throne Corpheus

Cursia. A marditavya soul, a servant of Baron Morgentus, stolen from Kharon's ferry to do the Baron's dirty work.

daeva. Former grails; inhabitant of Jahannam.

danava. A race of beings formerly a part of Zion before the Conflict of Hosts. They defied the will of dharma and harmed souls in the process through violence (rape, murder, etc.).

Dao-Ming, Draco, Order of Gyuto. Astral Master and daughter of Shen, Praefect Order of Gyuto.

Denius, High Councilor, Cherubim. Member of the governing High Council.

dharma. The life contract, or plan for incarnation.

dhatri. The shadowalker term for mother.

dhatros. The shadowalker term for grandmother.

dolls. Former Aghartians; inhabitants of Jahannam.

Domdaniel. The waters and sub-ocean caverns ruled by Prince Leviathan. Waterways have long been perceived as portals to and from the underworld.

Dominic Newlyn. The husband of Captain Maiel, and human muse soul who once served as a milite in the Sun Order.

dominions. A four-winged and statuesque race of duta with olive skin and white hair. Their gaze is pure light, making them excellent alder leaders.

drago. Soul race of reptilian humanoids. This race does not cooperate with the UWOS.

duta. Single-set winged race of duta and human-like race of beings descended from the Jñanasattva creation of Zion. Their height sets them apart from other souls at over seven feet for the shortest of their kind. They're known for their certitude and focus. They have vast knowledge and great strength and often assist souls in reaching their level of incarnation. They are guides and record keepers of all souls. This is the largest race of lightwalkers in Zion. Also, general term for the original race of Zion.

Eden. An island province parted by the Urva Sea from Arcadia.

els. The soul race of giant humanoids with gray skin and bulky musculature, hairless. This race does not cooperate with the UWOS.

Elysion. The southern pole island continent of Zion.

engel. The duta term for male.

Erebus, Erebian. The desert province ruled by Prince Gediel.

erela. The duta term for female.

evocati. See ranks section.

Ezrodial. Belial's nephilim son.

Father Salvatore Galo. Italian Catholic priest serving in Hungary under Orius.

Gabriel, General. The svargaduta commander of Legion 2.

Gamael, Order of Leo. Lena's former guardian. An elder.

Ganesha, Lord Councilor, High Council of Zion. Throne, head of all councils in the councils of Zion; reports to Metatron and The High Council. Ganesha is the final approver on all dharmic paths.

Gediel, Prince of Erebus. Former seraph and patriarch of Fenrir. Gediel's crimes ejected him from Zion, but he harbors hope of a return and believes that his grandson, who bears his name, will be the key.

Gediel, Primus and Wolf Leader, Order of Fenrir. Svargaduta grandson of the fallen prince of Erebus. He trains wolves and other canid souls to fight in the legions against the dark menace of Jahannam. Gediel is a member of the suspect group called watchers, a secretive sect of spies and observers.

Gehenna, Gehennites. The fiery province ruled by Prince Beelzebub; the inhabitants of Gehenna.

Giants. A large construct of intertwined imps, shadowalker and danava. A Jahannam Trojan horse.

Gihon River. The sea inlet and river that separates the provinces of Zion and Arcadia.

Grag. A simple-minded shadowalker in the service of Baron Morgentus. Grag was an el before his crimes against his kind cast him in Jahannam and made him a barbarian.

Gragrafel, Alder. Captain Maiel's father; a principality.

Grail. The taller version of twin species from a twin world, Zeta Reticulan.

granpitarau. The duta term for grandparents.

grays. Disembodied sattva left to roam Samsara; they feed on the energy of unwary incarnated souls, not to be confused with wayward souls who are referred to as simply sattva.

Gregely Orius. Hungarian Catholic priest from the mid-twentieth century.

Gremlin. A well-formed imp, usually very old. They echo the forms of the fallen races. See also Imp.

grey. The shorter version of twin species from a twin world, Zeta Reticulan.

Grigori. Also, oath breakers. The duta who become danava after defying their dharma. In the past, these beings committed heinous crimes against the people of Samsara whom they were charged to protect.

Hecate, Praefect, Moon Order. The svargaduta division (order) commander of the Moon Order; sister of Hecate.

High Council, Council of Zion. As the supreme authority before King Adonai, they enforce the laws and head the bureaucracy which governs Zion, made up of Seraph Metatron, Throne Corpheus, Seraph Lemitus, and Cherub Denius.

Hyadeans. A soul race, humanoid in build, with bullheads like a minotaur.

Hyades. The home planet of the Hyadeans.

Ian. The first born ardhodita child of Captain Maiel and Dominic Newlyn.

Ibajah, Evocati, Order of Horus. Loyal second to Captain Zaajah.

ikyls. A soul race, humanoid in build, with legs like a capra aegagrus hircus (goat), native to the planet Satyr.

Illuminati. An order set with the protection of their planets in Samsara, maligned by Jahannam shadowwalkers on Earth, and a few other outlands. See United Watcher Orders of Samsara and Magnus Castle.

Imnek, Order of Fenrir. Alpha Second of watcher Gediel's pack, mother of Argus, and mate of Chiron; Arctic wolf soul.

Imps. Negative energy that forms a seemingly sentient being. See also Gremlin.

Incubus/Succubus. Former ikyl; inhabitant of Jahannam.

Jahannam. The sixth realm, and the prison world where the lowest resonance beings exist. These beings feed upon one another and struggle to return to Zion. Their violent tendencies are dangerous to other atman.

janya. The duta term for father.

jiangshi. A fallen human; vampire.

Jinn. A soul race, crimson-skinned humanoids with minimal body hair (head and face). Their temperature burns much hotter than other races, causing steam or smoke to rise from their lower bio-vessels. This process gave rise to the myth that their legs are gaseous in nature. This race does not cooperate with the UWOS.

Jñanasattva. A race of beings from Nirvana. They are the highest resonance a being can achieve. This resonance is a state of being unlimited. It is neither evil, nor good. The opposite of this state would be the state of non-existence, a state experienced in Oblivion.

Joel, Captain, Sun Order. Part muse, warrior. Like his twin sister, Maiel, Joel's alternate sattva is a mountain lion.

Jushur, Headmaster, Ordo Priori. Principality and former guardian of Dominic Newlyn.

jyoti. The duta term for grandfather.

kapalanum. A seeing device. There are only three in existence and all are located in Zion, one each for the past, present, and future.

karma. A difficult concept that is most easily defined as an imbalance, positive or negative, from failing or harming, or helping and following dharma. They are events that carry lessons through the continuing dharma.

kesarini. A derogatory shadowalker term for female, usually used against souls and duta.

Keshi. Former orions; inhabitants of Jahannam.

ketu/ketot. The duta term for a bonded pair (single/plural); Also known as The Match or marriage.

khajala. The fog. A barrier between all provinces and places of Zion, especially in Eden and Elysion. It is thought to be created by the churning of the Urva. The fog prevents traveling.

Kharon, Prince. The landless prince, the ferry man, weakest of the seraphim who fell.

khata. The duta term for sister.

Labyrinth Lord, see Morgentus.

League, Numeri, Moon Order. An ikyls soul and watcher.

legiona(e). A military classified duta.

Lemitus. See Seraph Lemitus.

Lena. Captain Maiel's young assign, a highly developed human soul.

Leodes. The home planet of Jinn. A world of fire uninhabitable by the other races.

Lethe. River of Forgetting.

lightwalkers. Slang term to mean all races of duta.

Luca Geitz, Archbishop. Catholic archbishop of Hungary at Esztergom Basilica.

Lucifer, Prince, King of Jahannam. Self-proclaimed king of Jahannam. Lucifer is the seraph who served the king beside Metatron before the Conflict of Hosts. His refusal to obey orders and his cruelty toward souls cast him in Jahannam, where he is to be kept within an icy prison until the end of Trailokya.

Lung. Soul known as dragons in human legends.

Luthias, Evocati, Pritanni Order. The duta guardian of Dominic Newlyn.

Magiel, Alder. A respected member of the council of Zion, Alexandrael's twin sister.

Magnus Castle. The Illuminati base on Earth, in the empty territory of the Grant clan territories, within the Cairngorms National Park. UWOS territory.

Maiel, Captain, Moon Order. Part muse, but strongly geared toward the warrior life, duta guardian. Her alternate sattva is a mountain lion.

Marditavya. A soul slave of a danava.

matula. The duta term for aunt.

Maxiel, Alder. The head councilor of Dominic Newlyn's appointed alders.

Mepheus. Mikhael's principality door guard in the White City.

Metatron, see Seraph Metatron

Metiel. The ardhodita infant of Captain Maiel and Dominic Newlyn; twin brother of Muriel; a muse.

Michael, Mikey. Fourth born ardhodita child of Captain Maiel and Dominic Newlyn.

Mikhael, General. The svargaduta commander of Legion 1.

Morgentus, Baron of Acheron. Baron of the Pits of Acheron;, Lord serving Belial.

Mort. A wily adversary who tries to steal Lena from Captain Maiel during Lena's ejection from her bio-vessel. Mort is a bhogin, and what becomes of wayward naga.

Mount Zion. Northernmost and highest point in Zion, seat of government and house of King Adonai.

mudeater. See serpents.

Muriel. The ardhodita infant of Captain Maiel and Dominic Newlyn, twin sister of Metiel; a muse.

muse. Duta charged with inspiration of other beings. A trademark of this kind of duta is indeterminate sattva, or shape-shifting.

nagas. The soul race, humanoid in build, with double or triple arms with a serpentine lower half.

naiades. A soul race of amphibious humanoids with camouflage pigmentation. They share their planet with the ikyls. As pacifists, this race does not cooperate with the UWOS.

nephilim. Children born from the rape/adultery of souls by duta, often considered monsters/giants; the children of The Conflict.

Oblivion. The seventh realm, the nothing, where atman are sent when they cannot resonate higher and are too dangerous to others to be free. In the nothing, atman are destroyed. It is non-existence. A void.

Old man of Crete. See Yahweh.

Orders. Orders are divisions of Legion Milites and Officios, divided by their talent and resonance to best serve Zion. The following are some examples of orders:

Order of Aeris	Order of Mukuru
Order of Avia	Order of Odin
Order of Fenrir	Order of Pritanni
Order of Fire	Order of Terra
Order of Gyuto	Order of the Moon
Order of Horus	Order of the Phoenix
Order of Illuminati	Order of the Star
Order of Leo	Order of the Sun
Order of Mercury	

Ordo Prioria. The duta and ardhodita training schools.
Oriael, Decurio, The Cloisters. Power and guardian of Light; former Moon Order soldier.

Orion. The home planet of the Orions.

Orions. The soul race of semi-humanoid beings; upper torso is humanoid, lower extremities and second torso is Equine in nature. Orions hale from Orion.

Otzar (Guff). The well of souls, a hollow in Mount Zion where the perpetual light descends and the atman from Nirvana of lower resonance collect; home of higher duta races, from virtues to cherubim.

Pallus, Moon Order. A youngling owl and watcher under command of Captain Maiel as a scout.

Penannular. Nanotechnology used by duta to house their armor, powered by an atman. It also provides a cloaking to their manifestation when in other worlds.

Phlegethon. River of Fire.

Pit of Acheron. A confounding network of mazes that surrounds the seat of Baron Morgentus's power. The pit is a place to forget captured atman and farm them as food for other shadowalkers.

pitarau. The duta term for parents.

pitr. The duta term for uncle.

Powers. The four-winged race of duta, supreme command of the military arts, guardians of light.

Praefect. See ranks section.

Primus. see ranks section.

Principalities. A single-set winged race of duta. They are the final incarnation before an atman is certain of its trajectory through one of the three paths to Nirvana. The principality is a willowy figure with ivory skin and hair, and black eyes. Their form is reminiscent of statuary and they can often be found standing in observation and meditation. Their predisposition is yet varied at this stage.

Raphael, General. The svargaduta commander of Legion 3.

Rathiel, Evocati, Sun Order. Leader of Captain Joel's platoons.

recidia. A duta who break the oath without criminal behavior; often returns upon a great sacrifice.

Red Corridor. The second gate of Otzar.

Sabereh. A marditavya soul; Morgentus's stolen human wife.

sacerdos. The shadowalker term for priest; Latin for priest.

Samsara. The fifth realm and home of Earth and other habitable soul planets; the physical plane.

Samuel. The third born ardhodita child of Captain Maiel and Dominic Newlyn.

Saraqel, Alder. The dominion protector of the Akash; one of the Three Sisters, also called the Three Witches.

sattva. A soul body, not to be confused with a bio-vessel.

Satyr. The home planet of the ikyls and naiades.

Segrius. A calculating serpent in the service of Baron Morgentus. Segrius commands a horde of his fellow serpents, who were once drago.

selkies. A former vetehinen, inhabitant of Jahannam.

Sephr, Dux, Arms Keeper. The commander of Walhall and keeper of the armory of Zion.

Seraph Lemitus, High Councilor. A member of the governing High Council.

Seraph Metatron, The Voice, Supreme Councilor. Head of the High Council; a seraph of high mental faculty, he sees far and deep. He oversees Zion as Regent in service to King Adonai.

seraphim, seraph. A six-winged race of duta, appearing as a wheel of wings and eyes. The form of their sattva is unknown, for it is hidden behind the wings. This race is predisposed to the military aspects in Zion.

serpents. Former drago; inhabitants of Jahannam. Also called mudeaters.

shadowalker. General term for all of the races of Jahannam.

shadowborn. A soul that is incarnated and guarded by shadowalkers.

Shedu. Former Hyadeans; inhabitants of Jahannam.

Shee. Argus's wild born soul mate and second in pack order.

Shen, Praefect, Order of Gyuto. An astral way gatekeeper of Zion; father of Draco Dao-Ming, division commander.

Sheol, Sheolerites. The beach and strip of land between the Domdaniel and the rest of Jahannam, also called The Grave. The province is ruled by Prince Azrael. Also, the inhabitants of this land.

skeletons. Former Cetians; inhabitants of Jahannam. Also called corpses.

smokers. Former Jinn; inhabitants of Jahannam.

souls. Lesser resonant atman who inhabit bio-vessels to improve their resonance to higher levels; plant and animal life of Samsara.

Suriel, Alder. The dominion protector of the Akash; one of the Three Sisters, also called the Three Witches.

Styx. River of Hate.

svargaduta, svarg. A single-set winged race of duta. This variant incarnation of atman is the second largest of the duta race. They appear exactly the same as the lesser incarnation of duta, but their mental and physical abilities are far stronger. It is the preferred manifestation for most of the duta races, up to seraphim. Their predisposition is yet varied at this stage.

Tartarus, Tartarens. A dusty province of giants where Prince Astaroth reigns.

Thomas. A Catholic monk.

Three Sisters. The dominion protectors of the Akash; also called the Three Witches.

throne. A six-winged race of duta, appearing as a giant man with four faces (an eagle, a man, a bull, and a lion). This race is predisposed to the alder aspects of Zion.

Throne Corpheus, High Councilor. A member of the governing High Council.

Timor. A Catholic monk.

Tophet, Tophecians. The dead province of Prince Samael.

Trailokya. The term used to describe the intertwined worlds of Zion, Samsara, and Jahannam.

Union, see United Watcher Orders of Samsara.

United Watcher Orders of Samsara (UWOS). The orders representing all beings stretched through the galaxies of Samsara; see also Illuminati. Also referred to as the union.

Uriel, General. The svargaduta commander of Legion 4; twin sister of Anpiel.

Urva Sea. The ocean in Zion.

vapya. The shadowalker term for father.

vatrin. The shadowalker term for priest.

vetehinen. A soul race, humanoid in upper trunk, lower extremity formed as a fish tail. In Samsara this race does not cooperate with the UWOS. They are also called mermen.

virtue. The four-winged race of duta; supreme muses and guardians of incarnate beings. Their sattva are luminescent energy and have no discernible faces or gender. Their senses are focused through psychic interface. Their focus is on inspiring all around them.

voice, the. See Seraph Metatron.

Voil, Commander. The supreme Commander of all watchers.

Walhall. The armory of Zion.

watchers. A specially trained group of souls or duta who scout, spy, or run special ops missions. They usually work alone and are the best at what they do.

White City, White Citadel. The mountain/castle and fortress of King Adonai, home of high officials Otzar and Walhall.

White Gate. The entrance of Otzar, a bas-relief of the Trailokya creation and war.

wraiths. Former naiads; inhabitants of Jahannam.

Yahushua, The Prince. A human soul raised to duta after his extreme dharma; considered the son of Adonai.

Yahweh. Also known as The Old man of Crete, is a guardian who enclosed himself inside of a statue to keep watch of the Domdaniel gate into Jahannam. The tears that poor from the stone feed the rivers and sea of the dark world. The tears are the torrential negative energies from the misdeeds and suffering of souls in Samsara. Yahweh is consistently mistaken as the one God of several Earth Religions, and goes by several other names.

Yegor. A Catholic monk.

Zaajah, Captain, Order of Horus. The intractable best friend of Captain Maiel; duta guardian.

Zacharius, Alder. The elder brother of Captain Maiel and first son of Gragrafel and Alexandrael.

Zion. The second world, born from Nirvana. It is an endless realm similar to Earth and other habitable planets of Samsara; even-tempered climate in most regions and one vast sea.

Zion Province. The dense city province ringing the mountain and White City.

RANKS, ORDERS, AND FORMATIONS IN TRAILOKYA

Zion's Legionae Ranks:

The ranks of Officios (officer ranks) can only be achieved by duta races and are subject to resonance qualifications:

General. Highest rank in the legions.
Dux. Second commander under General, in command of corps.
Praefect. Third commander under General, in command of divisions (orders).
Decurio. Brigade commander.
Primus. Regiment commander.
Optio. Battalion commander.
Captain. Company commander.
Evocati. Platoon commander.

The ranks of Milites (general ranks, youngest) are achieved by duta and soul, and are also subject to resonance qualifications:

Dracos. Specialists, senior squad leaders.
Sergeants. Squad leaders.
Legio. Squad member.
Numeri. Lowest ranking squad member.
Youngling. Squad trainee.

Legion makeup:

Legion. Four or more army groups.
Corps. Two or more divisions.
Division. Two to four brigades.
Brigade. Two regiments, battalions.
Regiment. Two or more battallions.
Battalion. Two to six companies.
Company. Two to eight platoons.
Platoon. Two or more squads.
Squad. Eight to thirteen milites commanded by draco; included in ranks are one to two sergeants, a number of legio, numeri and younglings.

The Danava Ranks:

Danava are ranked on a racial standard that can rarely be overcome by merit to Lucifer, their prince and ruler. The following ranks are in order from highest to lowest. All but princehood can be achieved through service to the princes by any entity, and is attributed to the level of misdeed inflicted by the bearer of the title, with favoritism paid to the bearer's race. The dark power they wield is directly connected to their resonance which is affected by their psychological outlook and physical actions. Princehood was achieved by seraph who were cast into the prison following The Conflict. If a prince is defeated and cast into Oblivion, this vacancy would lead to civil war in a world already marked by unrest.

King. Jahannam does not have an official king, as the only king is Adonai. Lucifer attempts to claim this title, fashioning himself as the dark mirror of Adonai, but he does not wield the power associated with such a position, as he was never Jñanasattva, and is in fact almost the antithesis of the King of Zion.

Princes. Rulers of Jahannam who were once seraphim. The reigning princes are Lucifer, Asmodeus, Amon, Belphegor, Azazel, Belial, Astaroth, Beelzebub, Samael, Gediel, Mammon, Azrael, Leviathan, and Kharon.

Dukes. Former cherubim cast into Jahannam.

Counts. Former thrones cast into Jahannam.

Earls. Former Powers cast into Jahannam.

Barons. Former virtues cast into Jahannam.

Lords. Former dominions cast into Jahannam.

Knights. Former principalities cast into Jahannam.

Chiefs. Former svargaduta or duta cast into Jahannam.

Soldiers. Danava younglings.

Marditavya. Wayward souls, hell-masses, slaves.

Praise for The Shadow Soul

"The Shadow Soul is a fascinating page turner that brings to the table everything a reader would want: a strong and interesting cast of characters, a twisting and intriguing plot, and an elaborate fantasy world that is both mesmerizing and brutal."

– Kara Storti, author of Indigo in D-Town

*

"The dynamic journey of the soul, as developed by Kelly Williams, opens up a startling possibility for reality. This world is a journey of self-discovery, treacherous and challenging. Thankfully, we've got such powerful guardians watching over us."

– Robert Elliott, alum, University of New England

*

" A so-real-you-can-almost-see-it vivid brushstrokes of setting and surroundings···Themes of mythology, individual courage and spirituality...classic struggle of good versus evil, are but a few of the many strings which firmly pull at one's heart as the reader follows the harrowing ordeals of Captain Maiel."

– Joseph Wilson, marketing professional and freelance artist, Philadelphia

Other Works by K. Williams

Blue Honor (2009)

Blue Honor tracks four tightly twining families during the American Civil War. Each member is asked to sacrifice more than their share to see friends and loved ones through the terrible times. The only certainty they have is that nothing will be the same··· War weary, they all march on to duty.

"This has been my second K. William's read and both have been an absolute delight. Ms. Williams has the ability to transport the reader into her world and befriend the characters she cares so deeply about. Blue Honor is a definite two thumbs up from me!" — Mary Wexler, Actor, *Justice is Mind.*

OP-DEC: Operation Deceit (2011)

A World War II spy thriller in the noir style. An American heiress and her middle aged Aunt are pitted against forces of Nazi Germany in this tale of family betrayal.

"Op-Dec is a riveting read with plenty of twists and turns, highly recommended."
– Logan, Mid-West Book Review

The Trailokya Trilogy, Book Two: Burning Down (2016)

In this exciting sequel to The Shadow Soul, Burning Down returns readers to the world of Trailokya to find Captain Maiel on the cusp of an incarnation. Concern over her husband deepens as secrets unravel and the truth threatens her very existence.

Coming Summer 2016.

33191023R00279

Made in the USA
Middletown, DE
03 July 2016